POLAND
1939

LITHUANIA

SIA

POLESIE

Bug

Pripet

Brzesc

A   N   D

Deblin

yszew
ow
nsk

Lublin

VOLHYNIA

Zamosc

Tomaszow

San

Janow Woods

Jaroslaw

Lwow

EASTERN MALOPOLSKA

PODOLE

S O V I E T   R U S S I A

Stryi

RPATHIAN MTS.

Kolomyia

Dniester

R U M A N I A

GARY

0   50   100   150   200

KILOMETERS

Map drawn by Miklos Pinther

The thousand hour day

The thousand hour day

W. S. Kuniczak

THE DIAL PRESS

NEW YORK

1966

For my father

For my father

About the Author

W. S. Kuniczak was born in Lwow, Poland, in 1930. The son of a professional soldier whose military-diplomatic responsibilities took him throughout the continent, he lived in almost every major country in pre-World War II Europe. After the German invasion of Poland in 1939, he escaped to Great Britain.

Mr. Kuniczak studied at the University of London and came to the United States in 1950 to continue his education. He received degrees from Alliance College and Columbia University and served in Korea with the 7th Infantry Division. He has subsequently worked as a newspaperman and as an advertising executive in Cleveland and Pittsburgh. *The Thousand Hour Day* was completed in Quintana Roo, Mexico, where he lives on the Caribbean coast.

Mr. Kuniczak is presently at work on *The Sempinski Affair,* a novel which The Dial Press will publish in 1967, and he is translating into English the works of the great Polish writer Henryk Sienkiewicz.

Acknowledgments

During the two years it took me to gather and verify the historical material contained in this novel, and in the two years of writing, I drew upon the memories of more than seven hundred Poles, Germans, Englishmen and Frenchmen whose roles in the "September War" ranged from those of fighting soldier to commander-in-chief. I read an enormous number of diaries, manuscripts and memoirs, and I was given access to much government material still considered to be confidential. Though I am deeply obliged to each person who has helped me, I could not possibly thank every one by name. In some instances, such public acknowledgment would do informants a disservice.

But three men offered aid that went far beyond the demands of either duty, friendship or kinship. They are Brigadier General Kazimierz Glabisz, a brilliant military historian and, in September of 1939, emergency assignments officer on the personal staff of Marshal Smigly-Rydz; my father, Colonel S. B. Kuniczak, whose encyclopaedic technical knowledge insured the accuracy of details; and Max Gartenberg, my agent and friend, who assisted in the editing of the final manuscript. I hope that in thanking them I can symbolically discharge my debt of gratitude to all who gave help when it was needed.

W.S.K.

Hang yourself, brave Crillon;
We fought at Arques and you
were not there.

Fall 1939

---

*And soon, my friend, we shall
have no more time for dances. . . .*

Fall 1939

Thursday, August the twenty-fourth

I   THE GENERAL

He woke at first light: up instantly out of sleep and totally awake without effort, the way he woke each morning before day came. It was cool then and quiet in the bluegrey light and he could work undisturbed. He got a lot of work done if he was undisturbed. Work was the answer to a lot of things.

He looked at the woman in his bed. She slept heavily, completely.

He thought: She is like that; that is why she came to me in the first place. There are no halfmeasures for her. When she sleeps she sleeps; that is all. When she is awake she is completely, all-the-way awake, as though even into that simple state she had to pour all of herself.

That is youth. That is being young. Everything is of prime importance. You commit yourself irrevocably and utterly. You charge headlong into everything. You do incredibly foolish things which you would not do, under any circumstance, if you were older. But when you are young what matters is the moment; it is the doing of the thing that is important, not the form of it.

If I were younger I might have seen some other way, he thought, feeling the new regret and old anticipation, thinking that this day would, perhaps, not be an ordinary day, that it would be different from the others. The heat and flatness and unseasonable dryness would be there, of course, and the crushing sameness would continue unrelieved, but somewhere in the red woods the messenger was coming, if this was the day on which he was to come.

He would be coming now through the woods, down from the main road, a soldier or a courierofficer or a mailman or a Posts and Telegraphs deliveryboy, and his message would call General Janusz Prus back into the Army. Out of the house and from the dry fields back into the Army.

I wish there had been something else I could have done, he told her without speaking. Some way that wouldn't hurt you as this will; a more open way. But it was either this way or not at all for me, you see. They wouldn't have called me if I hadn't asked them.

The General listened to the breathing of the woman.

I have waited so long for this message and now it is coming. Perhaps now. In the red woods. In a leatherbag. The messenger is slow and unconcerned and unaware of the importance of the contents of the leatherbag, and he is probably young and he is not the glittering courierofficer who should be carrying a message of this kind, but, by God, he will do. He will do.

Go on sleeping, he thought, looking at the woman: Day will come soon enough.

Looking at her, he thought his luck had not deserted him. His soldier's luck was with him after all. His star had not entirely set. He was still fortunate. Fortunate to have found her or been found by her. He was never sure which

3

of them had done the seeking. He had not supposed that anyone would take him as he was: a general who was not a general, a legend no longer to be believed, a man not quite complete.

There was the matter of the missing arm.

True, he had another.

It was an adequate arm for what it had to do. It could hold a pencil. It could scribble memoirs. It could scratch an armpit and a puckered elbow. And the other, the one made of wood, was a reasonable facsimile. That is all that matters nowadays: to be a reasonable facsimile of what one has been.

The wooden arm looked sufficient in its leather glove. It even looked heroic. It looked distinguished and it was a badge: a professional endorsement like scars and eyepatches and monocles and medals and riding cups and fencing foils and a leathery posterior and muscled calves and a straight back and chapters in history books (no longer printed) and paintings (no longer hung in public places) and laudatory songs (no longer sung) and all the other trappings of a national monument.

The General shrugged. A *former* monument!

You don't last as a national monument. Only pigeons have any lasting use for you. People . . . well, people. They forget. They don't forgive what they don't understand. They offer either love or hate—equally limitless: only the hot extremes with nothing in between. They either worship you or nail you to a cross. They weigh only the visible evidences like a wooden arm. It is a badge they recognize and it is a nuisance. That business with the straps at night and in the morning . . . there is something obscene about that.

But it was this arm or the lack of it that showed her who he was so that she recognized him at once when they met at a reception given (in honor of no one now remembered) by her husband, the distinguished Professor Zbigniew Karolewski, who had been her father's closest friend and whom she married to replace her father, a man given to positive statements and sonorous phrases and dignity and a deplorable digestion. —*This and your look,* she said. *I mean the look you wear: like an eagle. And the newspaper photographs of you and your staff in the Ukraine. You looked like a schoolboy on an outing with his older brothers. So serious . . . so intent . . . but mostly it was the arm. Do you mind talking about it?*

—*No.* It had amused him to see her so intent. Also, he was a little flattered. Also, he thought her beautiful and, judging by her husband, not unavailable. This helps. A cavalryman has an obligation to women both beautiful and available.

—*I knew who you were, you see, as soon as I saw you because of that arm.*

—*Then I shall not regret its loss.*

She bowed a little to the gallantry. It was the usual gallantry. She said, looking away and off the balcony on which they stood with their backs to the room and her husband and her husband's guests: —*I have very much wanted to meet you. There has been so much written and said about you. There have been so many arguments.* And then, because he looked amused: —*My husband admires you very much.*

—*Even now?*

—*Even now. He is a historian. He admires men who defy the inevitable.*

You were the only one to defy Pilsudski. He says that the defiance was magnificent.

—There was no defiance, he said carefully. You had to be careful. You had to make people understand that there was no defiance.

—What?

—I only fought against him. There was no defiance.

—There is a difference?

—Yes.

—I do not understand.

—Pilsudski understood.

—What?

—Duty.

—Duty. Yes. Well. No one else fought against him.

—No one else had the opportunity to fight.

—Well, she said. *Yes. At any rate. Meeting you is almost like meeting a page out of a history book.*

—Or Santa Claus?

—Or Santa Claus, she agreed. *I could never quite believe in you or understand that arm.*

He looked at it, the wooden extension of his elbow and the artfully arranged hand in the leather glove making an obscene shadow on the bedside table.

—How could you do it? How could you order a man to cut off your arm? What kind of man are you to have so much contempt for pain, for your own flesh?

It was just something that had to be done. Like doing your duty. Like defending a corrupt government against a coup. You did not question things like that. You did not try to understand. Things happened. When they happened they were facts. You did not question facts. You did your duty. You were a soldier, not a politician. You did what you had to do, as with the arm. Shrapnel shatters your arm. It is the first day of the siege of Warsaw and you are on the barricade on the Most Kierbedzia and Pilsudski's gunners are the wonderul artillerymen of the First Legionowa Division, who are probably the best gunners in the Army and possibly in the world, and they bracket the bridge to keep you on it and one of their shells shatters your arm. The wound is dressed badly. It rots and swells and stinks and things grate in it. Flecks of black metal and grey bone creep upward through the putrefying flesh. It is corruption. It is filth. It is agony. You take this agony with you from place to place while the siege lasts. It lasts only three days. This is two days longer than you had expected. You measure these days in seconds, not in hours. Sixty seconds times sixty is an hour or 3,960 seconds, which, multiplied by twenty-four, gives you 95,040 distinct moments of agony. These, when multiplied by three, are 285,120 separate eternities of pain. Each second is an eternity of pain and of waiting. You wait for help that doesn't come. Railway workers have struck in favor of the Hero of the Nation. They will not bring the troops from the southern garrisons. Telegraphs have been blocked by the postal workers. The days go on and the agony goes on and shards of pain creep upward and you take this corruption and this agony and you lay it across a barricade. It is the standard barricade of flagstones

5

and an overturned streetcar and an iron bed. A generation of middleclass citizens has been conceived on this iron bed. You lay your pain across this iron frame and you say: —*Cut.* The arm offends you. You will cut it off. Grzes stares. He does not understand. He smiles and shakes his head. You say: —*Dog's blood! Cut!* Grzes takes your saber and straddles the bedframe like a horse. He rises in imaginary stirrups and lifts the saber for the downstroke and you observe the regulation upswing of the saber, and Grzes stares at you and shakes and begins to weep and shakes his head and wetness spreads along his cheeks and the stubble shines and the saber lifts and he stares and blinks and snorts and shakes his head and you say: —*Did you hear me? Cut!* and the saber wheels around in the regulation manner and swings down and you watch it coming and you approve the properly executed downstroke and you hear a distant *thunk* metallic on the bedframe and you faint.

And the arm is gone.

Eventually the pain is also gone. All the pains are gone. You have telescoped an eternity of doubting pain into one bright moment. There is beauty in the simplicity and the justice of it. It is not a thing you have to understand.

—*You say Pilsudski understood,* she said, narrowing her brows, with the young, intent look, the wellremembered eagerness. *Well. If he did. If he truly understood all this about duty . . . where was his sense of it?*

—*The Army's duty is to defend the nation from any enemy, inside or outside the border. Pilsudski was the Army.*

—*And you? What were you?*

—*I was a soldier.*

—*What was your duty then?*

—*A soldier's duty is to his oath.*

—*And that means to the government?*

—*Yes.*

—*Even if you despise it?*

—*Yes.*

—*Even that kind of government?*

—*Especially then.*

—*You have no doubts about anything, have you?*

She was angry. Why was she angry and what was there to doubt?

—*No.*

—*It must be easy for you.*

—*What must?*

—*Everything. It must be wonderful to have no doubts.*

Doubts.

A man can have no doubts about his duty.

About other things, yes, possibly. Although even *that* was a sign of weakness, and weakness, like lack of courage and lack of honor, should be a failing foreign to a soldier.

He had no doubts about the rights and wrongs of 1926. His oath had been to the government. A despicable government, true, but the legal one. The

6

Government of the Commonwealth which held his oath. A mass of querulous politicians (thirty-five independent political parties unable to agree on anything, to consider anything; fistfights in the Sejm and in the Senat; no budget passed for two years, unemployment, the zloty a devaluated joke—*When you see a man with a large crate he is going shopping, when you see one with a little bag he is coming home*—starvation, riots, poverty, despair, cannibalism in the villages and the contempt of foreigners who said that perhaps it had been an error to permit this country's life again and that, perhaps, the Germans, who are so neat, so orderly, so industrious and so wonderfully efficient, were right after all: *Verfluchte Polen,* dirty Poles). What was there to doubt, to question, to consider? The fact that Pilsudski was his friend, that he loved the Old Man as he never loved his father, that he had raised Pilsudski's name in nomination for the marshal's baton and that they had fought together and schemed together and plotted their country's independence in the old days and filled a common page of history, did not lessen the validity of a soldier's oath when the Marshal, Hero of the Nation, brought his divisions into Warsaw. The General (who had awakened in the greying room of morning with the woman sleeping and his dark, wooden arm making shadows) wheeled cannon into Lazienki Park and dug up the Saxon Gardens and barricaded the bridges and surrounded the Belweder with trenches and defended this particularly noxious government and lost; and lost an arm, an army and a career and, later, a family, and knew (in that light-bluegreying room of morning) that in time it would not matter what oaths he had taken or to whom or whom he had defended or what he had refused to compromise.

Because sooner or later the message would come.

Today?

Tomorrow?

It did not matter.

Sometime.

That was what mattered: that it would come sometime. It was inevitable. History assured it: since 900 A.D. Poland had not had twenty consecutive years of peace. Until the message came, work was the answer. Work or sleep, brother of death, first cousin to oblivion. He wished that he had Lala's capacity for sleep.

He looked at her. He thought himself truly fortunate. In her eyes I have never ceased to be.

But now a cold, grey light came through the windows and slid about him. It cast a checkered shadow on the floor. It made the floor a chessboard; his slippers were pawns on it. I won't be one, he thought, getting up.

You could see in him a chapter of Polish history—possibly several chapters. The narrow, sloping eyes showed Tartar blood. Dark skin and naked chin confirmed it; the chin had a particular nakedness, a particular smoothness, as though a beard would not or could not grow there. He moved with a peculiar halting stride, a sort of curious stagger, as if uncomfortable on the ground, not used to it. Leanness and hardness and vitality. Scars and the fact that one long arm was missing at the elbow did not subtract from this.

But it was his face, principally, that gave him definition: nose (thin and hooked), brown scars canceling out a cheekbone, mouth like the dry edge of destruction, and the narrow eyes.

He stretched, yawned. He fingered the hard flesh about his amputated elbow. He stood in front of his writing table, swaying a little.

—*My duty was clear. Although I sympathized with the point of view expressed by the Army and, indeed, welcomed the changes promised by the coup, I could not bring myself to join the conspiracy. It was a matter of deciding between a dear wish and my duty as a soldier. My duty was to the legally elected government. It was despicable and corrupt but it held my oath. And so . . .*

And so.

The table and the paper. The table overflowed with paper: notes, notebooks, maps and battlemaps, sketches and situation reports, yellow slips of communicationspaper, diaries, battleorders, pencils, erasers, photographs, photostats and letters—the equipment of a memoirist, the battlegear of a historian.

He thought: God save me, I am a historian. There was an irony in this that he didn't care to think about: Lala's dull, benign, heroworshiping husband had been a historian armed with a full complement of manuscripts, papers, photostats and a musty smell.

But, he conceded, there was a need for him to write his memoirs. There were things to be said about 1926. And about the coup. Not explained, of course. A soldier does not explain or apologize. But *said*. Without them, or his attempt to say them, there would be no reason to wake in the morning.

—*And so . . .*

And so I didn't join Pilsudski in the coup and was defeated as I knew I would be and that is why I'm here not elsewhere, a historian by God instead of a soldier: a general without command at forty-nine. The bluegrey light of morning is coming through the windows and it is a light that I remember from so many mornings; it is a time for being up and in the saddle and riding and leading and commanding and hearing the drydoor squeak of leather and the jingle of bridlechains and the small clickings and rattlings of fourteen hundred sabers against stirrupirons and the dry rattle of lance pennons in the wind and the stamp of fourteen hundred horses clattering behind me on a country track.

Instead: a memoirist, a flatulent historian. And these are now my days: dead, grey days stretching from breakfast to eternity . . . Breakfast. You have it in the dining room in dressing gown and slippers and the green silk scarf. Under the dressing gown you are dressed for riding. Completely uniformed but for the boots and jacket and the hat. The uniform of the day is corduroy and tweed. That is the uniform of the last thirteen years. It makes you a civilian. You wear it every day except Christmas. On Christmas Eve you put on your gala uniform and you wear your medals and you are, once again, Janusz Prus, General of Brigade, and you smell of mothballs. This, however, is not the birthday of the Christ but an ordinary day, and so you wear corduroy and tweed. Lala wears the silk robe with which you are familiar, and you say, looking at her, that it is becoming, that she looks young and innocent and childlike. You have said this every morning for several years. After breakfast you go to the stable. You pat Basia's neck. She neighs a little. She does a little sidestep and a skip when you put your forehead against her neck. She is like a doe. She reminds you of your wife before she (Irena, your wife) decided not to be a doe and to be a tiger. It is uncomfortable to live with a tiger. You are liable to get eaten up at breakfast. You are liable to fall into little pieces and vanish a piece at a time and eventually cease to be. You mount and you ride through the woods. They are familiar and the gates you have to jump are the gates you have jumped for thirteen years and even the mare is not enthused. She gives you a look which is frankly bored. This, too, reminds you of Irena. You have, however, a sense of humor. You grin and you are patient with the mare and you do not have to explain. Basia sighs and takes the gates. She may be bored but she does not want to eat you. She is good about the gates and about the familiarity of the rustic scene. She does not require you to be a national monument. You dismount and you hand the reins to Grzes and he leads Basia to the stable. While Grzes grooms Basia and feeds her and waters her and combs that difficult burr out of her tail you read the letters in the library. There are several letters. There are several each day: enough to show that you are not forgotten. Not enough to allow you to conclude that you are remembered, but enough to indicate that you are still alive. There is most likely a letter from your brother Michal. Michal is now a colonel on the Marshal's staff. The Marshal is, of course, the new one: Smigly-Rydz, a man whom you have never liked or understood. The thought of Smigly-Rydz reminds you of monks. There is something cold and austere about the new marshal. He has an air of one who communes with God before breakfast and there is a question of who is granting the audience to whom. You are used to a different kind of marshal: the old school of the dead Pilsudski. If there must be marshals let them be of the fullblooded school that doesn't shave and polish its head in the morning. Michal has also shaved his head in imitation of the Marshal. This is the new fashion at the General Staff and you think, laughing, that a full staff meeting must be something like a hall of mirrors. But you like Michal, who has remembered you each week for thirteen years while everybody else forgot. You read Michal's letter and you reply to it. Then it is time for lunch. You have the lunch. You find that you are out of cigarettes. You mention this to Lala. She promises to make some in the afternoon. She has an aptitude for making cigarettes. She has an aptitude for many things, love among them, but she is especially good at making cigarettes. She has a small machine for making them and she blends the *Macedonski Numer 1* with the *Polski-Egipski* the way you like tobaccos blended (black and strong enough to kill a horse) and you think, looking at her, that she even looks a little like Bizet's Carmen: young, violent and intractable. While she works you read the *Dziennik Krakowski,* which is a day old when delivered in the country. You comment on the political situation. Lately the situation has been neither good nor bad. It is merely a political situation. Hitler is making demands and he is making speeches and you comment on the latest speech by Smigly-Rydz, who said (in reply to some Hitler speech) that *we won't give a button; not one button,* and this is a valiant speech and Lala agrees that Smigly makes valiant speeches, and it is clear to you that there will be a war. *War is part of the intercourse of the human race*. Clausewitz has said it. You can recite whole chapters of Clausewitz: any soldier can. *We say, therefore, War belongs not to the province of Arts and Sciences, but to the province of social life. It is a conflict of great interests which is settled by bloodshed and only in that is it different from others. It would be better, instead of comparing it with Art, to liken it to business competition, which is also a conflict of human interest and activities; and is still more like State politics, which again, on its part, may be looked upon as a kind of business competition on a great scale. Besides, State politics* (and this includes the politicians' speeches) *is the womb in which War is developed, in which its outlines are hidden in a rudimentary state, like the qualities of living creatures in their embryos.* You read the *Dziennik* and back issues of *Bellona*, the quarterly published by the General Staff, and you grow restless and get up and pace about the room and stare out of the window and say that the land is dry. You speculate about the rain. War may depend on it. It has been an abnormally hot month coming on the heels of an abnormally hot summer and a spring that was like the summers of other years. The land is tired of the heat. The soil is thirsty. Nowhere in Poland has there been enough rain. Some rain had fallen on the first of August; it was not much. It was, in fact, little more than the forecast of a heavy dew: the kind that comes to soothe the soil in summer. The *Dziennik* did not foresee a change. A hot wind is blowing across Europe, dried by the slanting beams of an August sun, gusting from the River Elbe to the Dnieper. Nowhere between these two unrelated points is there any shade. This worries you not only as a man who has livestock grazing in the fields but also as a soldier. All month, as during all the months from March to July, high clouds of yellow dust have blotted out the sun above the German roads leading into Poland. There were great movements of German armies this summer and spring. There was some movement of the Polish Army, a curiously hesitant and uncertain movement. There will be war, you say, and you worry about rain, because rain is important to the Polish Army. Rain makes the Polish roads impassable for anything heavier than a horse. Tanks are useless, trucks sink in mud. But for three months there has been no rain. Both sides of the enormous Polish-German border wear a sweltering sameness. Crops have wilted on both sides. You comment on the heat and you sit down again and pick up the *Bellona* and read an article by Michal on *The Problems of Logistics and Supply for Cavalry Columns Operating Independently Behind Enemy Lines* (which is something you taught him in 1921) and you read Staniszewski's views on *The Use of Parachute Diversionists as a Tactical Factor* (thinking it far-fetched and futuristic) and you read *An Evaluation of the Use of Tanks in the Second Spanish Campaign* by An Observer and you wonder about that a little and recall that Michal's boy, Pawel, who must be at least thirty-five years old and is therefore only fourteen years your junior, and who is a worry to his father, who will not settle down, who lives wildly, whose name is a byword for licentiousness and, yes, for courage (who is, in other words, all that a young man with spirit ought to be, which is why you love him), had been in Spain and fought on the Ebro during that campaign and you make a note to query Michal about that. The thought of Michal's boy brings you to your own. You think about Adam and wonder where he is. You wonder if your son ever thinks about you and decide that he does not. You wonder if your wife ever thinks about you. You think it unlikely. You talk to Lala while she manufactures her two-hundredth cigarette. Then you have dinner. Then the day is ended. You think that it should never have begun.

Work filled some days, or at least the mornings. Memoirs: He thought the word ridiculous. It was the pompous word of a politician, not a soldier.

The General swore a heavy soldier's oath. It made him smile. A cold wind blew up the tail of his nightshirt. He got to work. They can kiss me where the wind blows, he thought about politicians and historians.

Somewhere inside the house a telephone began to ring. The sound was persistent. It reminded him of something unpleasant, something far removed in distance and years. He could not immediately identify this unpleasant something.

The ringing sounded like the measured tinkling of a glockenspiel. His earliest childhood recollections included it: the sound of martial music, the sight of soldiers, a review of some kind at the Schönbrunn, with the kettle-drums going *thump* and the glockenspiel tinkling and his mother holding tight onto his hand and trembling a little, and the dust upcoming from under the horses' hooves into the reviewing stand on a hot Viennese afternoon. Franz Josef (he was told) patted his head.

His earliest childhood terror had been connected with the name of the peculiar tinkling instrument. The word obsessed him. At night he dreamed about a glockenspiel pursuing him—some hairy monster.

His father thought the fear ridiculous. All terrors were ridiculous. His father was a Royal Imperial brigadier and colonel-in-chief of the Schwarzen-berg Hussars. This was an honored regiment in the armies of the Kaiser-König Franz Josef, Emperor of the Austrians, King of Hungary, Sovereign of the Czechs and Slovaks, Poles, Serbs, Croats, Montenegrins, Ruthenians and Ukrainians, assorted Italians, Albanians and Herzegovinians, a Greek or two, and too many Roumanians. It was the only regiment of hussars which wore no whiskers, which, to its pride and regimental honor, formed ranks with naked upper lips. All other mounted guardsmen of the Emperor threatened the skies with hair, but not the Schwarzenbergers. They won their right to facial nudity in the Austro-Prussian war, where some now dead and moldering Schwarzenbergers had, in fact, painted on their musta-chios with boot blacking. To be commander of this legion was an honor. It was a place of trust. To be commander was a testimonial of a kind, especially for a Pole in the Hapsburg's army.

—*Monsters, indeed. Ridiculous!*

It was, of course.

—*No one has anything to fear if he has his honor and loves his country and rides well and shoots straight and tells the truth.*

—*Yes sir.*

—*A man must do his duty. He need fear nothing. Never show fear. Never have it. Never. Always be brave and always do your duty. Be upright, straight. Ah. Stand straight and look me in the eyes. Always stand straight.*

—*Yes sir.*

—An upright man is an honorable man.

—Yes sir.

—Stand straight! Are you fidgeting? An upright man stands straight. He is erect. He is not an animal. An animal walks on four legs but a man is erect. That is the mark of a man: that he has pride with which to walk erect. Always be upright and honorable and always do your duty. That is the only truth, the only reality. Do you understand?

The Brigadier surrendered his hold on reality in Italy in 1916, being upright and honorable and doing his duty. He had mounted an attack against the Italians who, that day, chose to be tenacious.

This is not a quality generally attributed to Italians. The Brigadier had much contempt for the Italians. He despised the Czechs, who are commercially inclined. Few things, the Brigadier believed, were as ridiculous as a Czech, and most of these lived in Italy. The Brigadier's contempt for Italians surpassed even his contempt for Austrians. (*—The only reason why God created Italians was so that Austrians would have someone to defeat.*) The Brigadier's mother was a Prussian (named von Stelle, formerly Gwiazdowski), and Prussians have much contempt for Austrians. They have contempt for everyone except Russians but especially for Austrians. The Brigadier had his mother's profound contempt for Austrians and Italians and, God yes, the Roumanians, who, as everyone knows, are descended from Roman convicts and never quite got over it. Being a Pole he loved Serbs and Slovaks, spoke of the *wisdom of the Swedes,* liked Russians, disliked Ukrainians, liked Byelorussians, despised Jews, wondered about Americans, approved of the English, hated Germans and wondered why God made them.

The Brigadier's many contempts bypassed the Hungarians. There is a Polish proverb on this subject. *While the world lasts the Pole and Magyar will be brothers.* This may not be entirely true, but the Brigadier always tried to recruit Hungarians, a difficult matter since Hungarians, although they like to be hussars, also like mustaches, and as the Schwarzenberg Hussars they had to shave. Despite these hirsute inclinations most of the 1916 Schwarzenberg Hussars were Hungarians, and it was this largely Hungarian legion which charged the Italians in the Brigadier's attack.

The attack failed. The Hungarians did not defeat the Italians. The Brigadier suspected that Roumanians had infiltrated the regiment. Whatever the reason, the attack was decisively repulsed. The attack was resumed after breakfast with the help of cooks (which was simple justice), telephonists, horsehandlers and orderlies, trumpeters and stretcherbearers (who protested), a Czech battalion which had wandered into the area because it seemed quiet and ran away ten minutes after nine o'clock, some terribly ferocious Steiermarkers and the band of the Deutschmeister Regiment of Vienna, a company of Bavarian bicycle troops who were not supposed to be used in any attacks, staff officers (who died bravely), the colorguards, armorers, supply personnel, wagondrivers, the fieldpolice and the crew of an armored train that had run out of coal. All these were once again repulsed, individually and collectively, by the Bersaglieri.

The Bersaglieri are an honored regiment of the Italian Army. They wear plumes in their hats and trot instead of marching and have much *élan.* They have been sometimes confused with the Austrian Landswehr, who also wear plumed hats, but that, as the Brigadier observed, was the extent of the similarity. The Bersaglieri plumes come from the wings of eagles. The Landswehr pluck theirs out of roosters' tails.

The Bersaglieri repulsed each attack that day. They had not heard about why God created Italians. The day passed and they remained unconquered.

The Brigadier adjourned to his tent. It was a Spartan tent patterned after the canvas of Alexander. In the tent he court-martialed himself for negligence of duty. He proved that he had not pressed his attacks with sufficient vigor. He argued both sides of the case, the defense and the prosecution, and found himself guilty and sentenced himself and attempted to execute the sentence the following dawn, the time prescribed for such events by regulations and the usages of war. He wrote some letters, put a pistol to his head, said: —Honor demands it, and pulled the trigger. The bullet crashed through the skull above his temple, spun inside his skull and came to rest having caused a minimum of damage.

The pistolshot attracted the remaining aides and officers of the Brigadier's staff, who found him with buttons cut away, collar insignia removed and braid unstitched, prone beside the portable field desk patterned after Napoleon Bonaparte's campaign furniture in the Invalides. The Brigadier respected Napoleon, although he despised the French. (—A Pole salutes with two fingers for Honor and Fatherland. Others include God and Manhood, thus using two more fingers. The French use four fingers and the thumb, which undoubtedly stands for their Liberté, Égalité, Fraternité, the Croissant and the Apéritif.) The documents of the court-martial were on the desk. The Brigadier's saber was also there, the point turned against him. The staff was stupefied. The Brigadier lay with eyes closed, splashed with blood, apparently dead, with a cigarette stuck to his lower lip. The cigarette burned down to his lip, the Brigadier sat up, swore, slapped his mouth and fainted. A junior officer of the staff also fainted. Each recovered in due time.

Several times in the ensuing months the Brigadier tried to execute the sentence. Each time doctors restrained him. Finally he only tried to shoot himself when the bullet moved to press on some particularly sensitive portion of his brain. The bullet seemed to live a life of its own: It wandered around inside the Brigadier's skull and eluded all surgical probings. The Brigadier was hastily retired. In time he forgot the reason for his terrible headaches. When they came he howled like a dog. Sometimes he shouted commands in his bedroom and drilled invisible regiments.

His possessions, in 1916, consisted of an old whitetimbered house in western Malopolska, eleven uniforms, thirty-two medals and crosses, and a trunk containing one surprising yellow document: The Landsknechte or The Adventurous Simplicissimus by Grimmelshausen.

His sons found the trunk and opened it and read its contents and the younger of the two uniformed men who were the Brigadier's sons wondered whether he knew his father at all. He was then twenty-six and a captain of artillery and had won the Iron Cross (First Class) the previous year in a surprising action against the Italians. In the first years of the Great War the Italians were full of surprises. Janusz Prus was then a lieutenant attached to a German mountain battery equipped with a new and highly secret American mountain gun which, when in transport, rode aboard mules. The battery was commanded by a Prussian captain (named von Bialy) who had much contempt for Poles and did not speak to the lieutenant and ignored the existence of Italians and who was the first to die when the Italians of the Alpine Regiment came out of nowhere to capture the battery.

The battery was resting along a mountain track. The mules nibbled grass. Men slept, drank water, played cards, relieved themselves, told lies, ate, searched themselves for lice, complained, laughed, dug for potatoes in a nearby field, roasted potatoes, ate them, roasted more, and the Prussian captain and his Polish lieutenant sat on tree stumps (the captain's stump was taller) observing. It was a military vignette out of a sixteenth-century painting of the *condottieri*. Peace in the midst of war. Then the Italians came. One moment there was nothing around the battery except grey mountains. Then there were Italians. The Prussian captain stood up, opened his mouth, said —*Ungh*, and fell over the tree stump with his head removed. The lieutenant, who had been juggling with a hot potato, got up and ran (as honor, military training and instinct dictated) for the guns. Some soldiers tried to get the mules to move. The mules were adamant. The Italians were close and running for the secret guns. The lieutenant forced the hot potato under the tail of the lead mule, the mule roared in shocked surprise and charged up the mountainside, other mules followed and the guns were saved. A colonel named von Reichenau came from Berlin to pin the Kaiser's own cross on the lieutenant's chest. Somehow the lieutenant managed not to laugh during the ceremony. All of this fell into neat perspective as the former lieutenant, now captain (who, as Colonel von Reichenau said, would someday be a general), read *The Landsknechte*.

For gluttony and drunkenness, hunger and thirst, wenching and dicing and playing, riot and roaring, murdering and being murdered, slaying and also being slain, torturing and being tortured, hunting and being hunted, harrying and being harried, robbing and being robbed, frightening and being frightened, causing trouble and suffering it, beating and being beaten: in a word, hurting and harming and, in turn, being hurt and harmed, this was their whole life. And in this career they let nothing hinder them, neither winter nor summer, snow nor ice, heat nor cold, rain nor wind, hill nor dale, wet nor dry; ditches, mountain passes, ramparts and walls, fire and water were all the same to them. Father nor mother, sister nor brother, no, nor the danger to their own bodies, souls and consciences, nor even loss of life and heaven itself, or aught else that can be named, will ever stand in their way; forever they toil and moil at their own strange work till at last, little by little, in battles, sieges, attacks, campaigns, yea, and in their winter quarters too (which are the soldiers' earthly paradise if they can but happen upon fat peasants) they perish, they die, they rot and consume away, save but a few who, in their old age (unless they have been right thrifty reivers and robbers) do furnish us with the best of all beggars and vagabonds.

It occurred to the lieutenant that perhaps his father had hidden *The Landsknechte* in the trunk so that no one would read it. Then it occurred to him that perhaps the Brigadier had, indeed, few illusions about his profession, and he wished that he had known the Brigadier before the charge in 1916.

His mother had died earlier. Her death was due partly to his birth, from which she never quite recovered. She was (he remembered) a small, fragile woman with white hair pressed close to a littlegirl head who, in her lucid moments between bouts of pain and dosages of pain-relieving chemicals, told him about Napoleon and Ney and Murat and Marbot. Her grandfather had come to Poland with Napoleon and on their tragic return from Moscow decided to stay, and eventually married, and the woman never quite forgot these gentle French origins. She had a collection of miniatures which showed the Frenchman (his face was cynical, wry and devilish) and his pretty Polish wife, and once, on a treasure hunt in the attics of their old (seventeenth-century) whitetimbered house, he found the shredded blue coat heavy with bullion and a rusty saber inscribed *Pour l'Empéreur*. There were enormous quantities of sabers in and about the house. A German infantry rapier served as a roasting spit. Each ancestor seemed to have several spare sabers. There were, he supposed, enough to arm a troop of cavalry.

His mother tired easily. She spent her days on a chaise longue and slept there in the afternoons. At night, of course, she could not sleep and walked about the house and sometimes went out to stand on lawns in moonlight—a ghostly figure on officers' row.

The Brigadier talked to her about it. It was unthinkable that she should walk about like that: she was practically naked! —*What is wrong with you? Why do you do this? Sickness is sickness but dignity is dignity, by God! If one is ill and suffers one suffers in silence and with dignity. One remains a man or, I suppose, a woman. One does not advertise infirmity.*

In point of fact she was as naked as a ship's yardarm swathed in sails, but in those days (the General supposed) nakedness was a matter of degree: a matter of a bare head or lack of gloves.

The Brigadier brought a doctor home. The doctor's name was Schmidt and he was a lieutenant and both these factors disarmed him before the Brigadier. He examined the woman. He was terribly embarrassed. He said that there was nothing he could do. He was, after all, he said, only an Army doctor. He said that there were certain limitations in military medicine. Physically the Brigadier's Lady seemed capable of return to normal. Mentally (he used the new word: *emotionally*) there was an obstacle he could not remove. —*Why not?* The mind is a secret world, Herr Schmidt explained. Perhaps the Herr General could send his Lady to the country? Perhaps if she was removed from the military? He did not think the Army did her any good.

—*What does the Army have to do with it?* the Brigadier roared. *Is she sick or not? Are you a doctor or not, Lieutenant?* He ordered his wife to be cured.

The boy saw his mother seldom. He did not know her well. He was a little afraid of her (—*A man is not afraid!*) and wondered about her (—*Soldiers do not question the right or wrong of anything.*) and would have liked to know her, but she tired so easily. Sometimes she did not know who he was. Mostly she slept on her chaise longue and at night drifted through the house with nightgown and peignoir trailing and went out to walk in the moonlight, and there one night a young recruit (who was a Hungarian and who was shaken by her ghostly whiteness) gulped a quick *Wer da?* and chambered a round and fired.

The year was 1898. He was then eight. The year was significant: eight is the age of reason. The boy found little reason in the woman's death. He grieved for her. It was a boy's duty to grieve for his mother. He did not know her well and so he did not weep and everyone said he was a proper little soldier.

Meanwhile, the telephone. It rang and was eventually silent and then there were quiet footsteps and a knock and Grzes said that the Pan General was wanted on the telephone. Who was it? The postmaster. He wouldn't tell Grzes what the message was about.

—Well, maybe he'll tell me.

Grzes grinned and scratched his nose and said it was likely.

—Hullo?

A man's voice said: —Hullo-hullo.

It was a self-effacing voice. —Hullo? Do I have the honor? Am I addressing General Prus? Is it my honor?

The General said it was.

—Ah. (A wealth of meaning in this sound: respect, sudden fear, humble servitude.) Sir! Please pardon the intrusion . . . the early hour . . . my apologies . . . but it's a matter of considerable importance . . . we have a telegram from Warsaw, sir . . . a telegram of state weight, I have the honor to report.

—Please read it then.

—Ah . . . that is the problem . . . I cannot read it, sir.

—You cannot read?

—Sir? Why, of course, I am a postmaster, an educated man. But this, sir, is of state weight!

—And this prevents you from reading it?

—I am not empowered.

—What?

—I regret. My regrets, General. It is of state weight and I am not empowered. It is a matter of regulations, sir.

—Not empowered?

—No.

But what was this? The General was amused. Now there was a note of triumph in the little voice all mixed with diffidence and the embarrassment as though to say, Look, I am a postmaster and this is not much, and you are suddenly a general again and this, in our particular society, is much indeed, but it is in my power to say or not to say. This is a godhead of a kind. I *know* and you do *not* and this is the difference.

General Prus remembered him: The postmaster was fat. He had a monstrous belly and he picked his nose. He had a red, sweating, civil servant's face. He was a petty tyrant in the township. It was said that he liked little girls. He had been something or other in Pilsudski's Legion: most likely a mess sergeant. He had blocked the telegraph to the Podhalan garrisons during the coup.

The General laughed.

—You will not read it?

—Sir . . .

Declining, begging the General's pardon in that triumphant voice, the postmaster offered his regrets.

—I regret this sir, truly I regret this. It is indeed a matter for regrets. But he could not open the envelope. —It is, after all, of state weight: a communication of national importance. And he was not empowered to handle communications of national importance.

—I am only of Class Six and only civil servants of Class Five have access to communications of state weight. It was regrettable. He hoped the General would understand. There were, after all, the regulations. But in his opinion, in view of the situation, in view of the times we live in (and having read the telegram as it came in on the wire), he could risk a guess.

—Guess, Postmaster? Prus was laughing.

—Yes sir. I think that I may hazard a guess based on my estimate of the situation.

—Guess, then, Postmaster.

—Of course, sir, you must understand that I do this only in view of the situation.

—Of course.

—But only in that view.

—Of course.

—I know my responsibility. I know my duties.

It was difficult not to laugh. The General succeeded.

—Otherwise I am not empowered. But in view of the situation and the times, such times, your excellency, such times, and in view of my responsibility as an official of the government and my responsibility in the matter of communications it is my guess . . .

He waited. The General obliged: Yes, Postmaster?

—That sir, your excellency, it is an order of mobilization!

—Of mobilization?

—Yes.

He thought: So it has come. So it has come at last. You wait and you have hopes and few illusions because the thing you want is quite impossible, because those who can make it possible don't want you there. You are the catalyst of resistance and they know it. They don't want you there. And you write letters as the time of war comes closer. You write to your brother (the shavenheaded colonel of the General Staff) and you say, not wanting to say it, thinking that, perhaps, they would remember after all and summon you back without your asking, thinking that they'd remember and at the same time have the goodness to forget: If war comes, and I know it will, I want no part of this enforced oblivion. Whether or not I have one arm or two or sixty-five I can be of use. War is my element as it was never yours. I am a soldier. If you must speak to Smigly-Rydz about me, do so. He has never liked me—nor I him if the truth be told—but he is enough of a soldier to know that I can be of use. You must not let them leave me here to be an old man in a quiet house. It is one thing to accept retirement on the pretext of a missing arm when you know that if you oppose this forced retirement it might bring about a civil war; when you know that, through no will of your own, you have become a magnet for the malcontents and a rallying point for politicians. Damn the politicians. It is then your duty to accept oblivion and, if necessary, a publicized disgrace. It is another thing to sit in a quiet house, growing carrots, and watch war come and see the Nation in it and take no part. I beg you, Michal, if you ever loved me: Get me a part in war. I know that you have never agreed with me about the coup and my role in it and that you never shared my definition of a soldier. But you know what I am capable of doing in war. War is not politics. There are no alternate decisions. It is a matter of winning or of losing, and I, thank God, still know how to win battles—I have won them. I think this is important, Michal. I think that we will need to win as many battles as we can in this coming war, because it will be like no war that we have ever seen. This will be total war and a conclusive war, not just a war of one country against another. It will be one way of life poised against another, a battle *à outrance*. He who wins— survives. He who loses will be lost and wiped off any further page of history. This is too much for me to watch as an observer in a quiet house. I may not think that we are perfect as a people or that everything about us can escape censure, but that is not the question. What counts is this: I am a soldier and this is my country (no matter who rules it or how) and now a time is coming when my country will be threatened with absolute destruction and everything that it or I have ever held in any kind of awe, respect, love (call it what you will) is also threatened with absolute destruction. This is what counts. This is all that matters. I cannot sit as an observer in an old white house. Get me a command. Give me some soldiers. I may not always make the right political decision and I may not always take the most advantageous steps to further my career, but you know this, I am a soldier and I can win battles. So speak on my behalf to anyone you have to. I will do anything at all. I will be commandant of a railroad yard if that is all they trust me with. I will train recruits.

You write and wait and write and you do not tell anything about this to the woman who (you think) would not understand this male need to leave her, who (you think) has hinged her life about you and who would follow you gladly, happily, where you go but who would never understand, not in a million womanyears, this male need.

It is perhaps betrayal of a kind: She trusts (you think). And so you do not tell her.

The General hung the telephone receiver on its hook. Grzes grinned at him. He went in to dress. He dressed. He went into the hall where, among several dozen sabers and pistols and rifles and bayonets and other weapons on the walls, there was one great, curved cavalry saber which was not disusestained, which had been carefully tended and polished and which, long ago, had cut off his arm.

He drew it and read the inscription: *Honor i Ojczyzna.*

The word for Country, *Vaterland, La Patrie* changes with the language. The word for Honor is recognizable in all. This is the constant. This is the catalyst. The General swung the saber. The weight of it was terribly familiar. Suddenly he felt foolish. He felt old: a dinosaur.

Was this still true? Did the old values hold? And if not, what had replaced them?

A man can have no doubts.

Honor is duty.

The General scabbarded the saber and put it back on the wall and went outside where the sun had broken out of darkness and spilled over the peaks of the High Tatras and bloodied their peaks and where it was cool. He watched the day come.

The land was flat and parched. It made no promises. It did not welcome anything. The soil begged for moisture. It was hard and cracked. There were no clouds in the noncommittal sky. The crops were cut and stacked. They were not under cover. There was no reason to suppose that anything would happen to the crops: It did not look, after all, as though it would rain.

But this day would not be an ordinary day because the message had come and would be brought to him. The messenger was coming.

The General felt like laughing, so he laughed. He was fiercely glad. And then again he felt the touch of the unaccountable new feeling: this measure of regret.

Regret?

What was there to regret?

The years of waiting were over. They were done.

He waited, peering into the black shadows under the bluetipped pine.

I THE JEW

The old man stepped from the plane and stood on the portable staircase they had rushed to bring up. He looked immeasurably tired. He smiled the terrible telescopic smile and raised the hand to show the paper in it. The wind tore at his hand and at the paper and at the flapping tails of his coat.

He said: *We have gone to Berlin . . . to obtain . . . assurances . . . bring you assurance . . . there will be no war. Yesterday . . . Herr Hitler and I . . . guarantees . . . mutually acceptable . . . peace . . . in our time.*

The wind tore at his words. It scattered them. It scattered the applause of the waiting crowd.

You could see in the newsreel the faces pressed close behind him and the eyes searching as though words alone were not to be believed, as though some further reassurance, some definite assurance, had to be given. But the old man had no assurance to give to anyone. He was a tired old man. All he had was a paper. He raised the paper and the wind struck it immediately and crumpled it around the old man's fist. The wind mussed his long, white hair and tugged at his furled umbrella and dust came up from underfoot (you could see the small, grey particles pelting his long, wellbred English face) and he scrunched up the sentimental droopy eyes and smiled sadly.

Berg squirmed a little in the theater seat as he watched the newsreel. There was a mild applause. This was an old newsreel but it suggested peace and they were showing the old reassuring newsreels often these days.

The theater was hot and stuffy. It smelled of old plush chairs and dust. Berg sweated in the darkness. He felt ill. I must stink, he thought. Fear has its own particular battery of smells.

He thought he saw a man glance at him and the man's nose twitched and he thought: He can smell it. He can smell my fear. Perhaps the man did not smell anything. Perhaps he only wanted a better seat and moved away because of that.

Morys, be a *Mensch:* an ancient admonition.

But being a *Mensch* had nothing to do with courage. It concerned things like study and work and marriage and raising children and meeting obligations and shouldering responsibilities and staying out of trouble. That was all a young Jew was expected to do. It was sufficient for survival. —*You do what you have to do and you will survive,* his father had said. No one said anything about having courage.

His stomach stirred and he thought he would vomit and the thought of such a demonstration in this place added extra dimensions to his fear.

They must not see. I must not be noticed. I must not give offense. I must draw no attention to myself.

Berg closed his eyes and pulled his round black cap down over his ears and bowed down to control his fear and wished for courage.

Beside him Rosenblatt was giggling.

Rosenblatt giggled like a girl when he was excited. He pushed his face into Berg's so that he could whisper.

—How is it with you, Morys? Are you sick?

—No. Not sick.

—Listen you, Morys (suppressing a giggle, whispering), I can help you. Listen. You have to hide so they can't find you. If they can't find you they can't take you for the Army. If they can't take you you will be all right.

—It's not that.

It is something deeper. His fear had nothing to do with going to the Army.

Fear: A painful emotion marked by alarm; dread, disquiet, fright, dismay and consternation, terror and trepidation. Painful agitation in the presence of, or anticipation of, danger. Yes. Dread and dismay imply a loss of courage. Berg wondered how he could have lost something he didn't think he had. The word for his fear was trepidation. Yes. That was it. Berg knew about words. He loved them and he studied them. He felt and sensed his trepidation. It took his dread and added to it the implication of timidity, trembling and hesitation. Words. Words. They were no good to him now.

Beside him Rosenblatt was whispering.

—Not that? Not that? What do you mean not that? If they take you for the Army, will that be good? If you are killed, will that be profitable? If you are not killed maybe you will lose an arm or a leg or maybe both. What is the use of that? I ask you. And even if you don't lose anything they will beat you. That is why they take us, so that they can beat us.

Berg wondered why Rosenblatt used the first person plural. No one was taking Rosenblatt into the Army. It was he, Berg, who had got the red card that said MOBILIZACJA.

The summons was brought that morning by a postman. The postman knew what was in the envelope and he wrinkled his nose, and grinned, and waved his arm in mock farewell and pulled a finger across his throat and said *eeee-eeek* like the sound a pig makes when its throat is cut. Berg blinked at him and made chuckling sounds and Mama quivered and her jowl shook and fat tears started down her cheeks; no news is good news and therefore the contents of the envelope could be cause for weeping. Berg took the envelope and weighed it in his hand. It was light. He was puzzled. He had never received a letter from anyone in his twenty years. Everyone he knew was right there in the Quater and no self-respecting Jew would waste stamp, ink and paper when he could talk instead. True, there was an uncle in Trembowla and an aunt in Brzesc. Berg didn't think the letter was from them. It was too light. No relative of his would waste the ink and paper and the stamp without making the most of it. Thus Berg was puzzled. Also, he discovered, he was excited. He opened the letter. His hands shook and the red card fluttered to the floor like a bird of ill omen. At once his mother shrieked. The postman was grinning. Papa sighed and blinked. Berg read the black words on the card. At first he did not understand. MOBILIZACJA. To mobilize is to render mobile. Mobility, in turn, is characterized by extreme fluidity as mercury or ether. None of this seemed to have any bearing on Berg or to affect Berg and Berg wondered why he was to be concerned. But the postman was grinning and Mama was wailing and Papa was sighing like a horse at the market in Zelazna Brama, and Berg considered the red card and the black word and all its various meanings and tried *to assemble and make ready for use as resources* and rejected this because he didn't think the Polish Commonwealth needed his resources and tried *to assemble and put in state of readiness for war, as an army or a fleet* and could not see himself as either. He thanked the postman and walked him to the door. The postman was disappointed. True, the old woman was wailing, but lately he had seen a number of old women wailing and there was little amusement to be derived from that.

Berg read the card and shortly everything was clear. He was excited and at first could not make up his mind whether this act of being put in readiness for war was good or bad. He had seldom been out of the Quarter, and never longer than a day, except for his Army service two years before. That had been a strange time: not good, not bad, a time he didn't really believe had existed. He had been ready for a terrible time but it hadn't been bad. He had been given uniforms and the cap with the silver eagle. This must have been some sort of talisman because no one did anything terrible to him while he was wearing them. That had confused him immensely in view of the terrible stories told about the Army. The Army wasn't terrible and the time wasn't terrible and he had even learned to speak adequate Polish. He had not been able to imagine himself as a soldier: Soldiers were coarse and large. He was small. He had a large head and a small body and his legs were bowed and it was hard to imagine all that dressed in uniform. But it had not been bad. Not at all bad. It had been surprising. He had not wanted to go into the Army. He had not thought that this Army of the Poles had anything to do with him. He was a Jew, wasn't he? And no Jew that he knew about had ever done anything as a Pole or thought as a Pole or had been interested in anything Polish. The elders of the Quarter carefully brought up the young Jews to avoid anything Polish. They were to stay apart, a nation within a nation, and what happened outside the various Quarters had nothing to do with the Jews. Berg wondered about that when he came back from the Army. He wondered but he did not disagree. He had not disagreed with anyone in his twenty years. He had not supposed that he would ever again go outside the Quarter. He wondered about that a little and regretted it a little and remembered the Jews he had met in the Army, the few that were in it. Some had been from the Quarter. Others lived outside. These were strange Jews, like no one he knew in the Quarter. His father spoke of them with contempt. (—*They are not Jews. They are* goyim *who pray in synagogues.*) Berg kept away from them because they were strange. He came back from the Army and it was soon as though he had never been away and the Quarter settled about him like a cloak and warmed him and protected him, and this too, he supposed, was a talisman of sorts. When you are a Jew and you live in Warsaw you live in the Quarter. The Quarter is an island surrounded by Warsaw. It is an area of steeproofed manywindowed houses huddled against each other. The streets are cobbled. They are old and narrow. There are labyrinths of alleys, malodorous and dark, littered with pieces of grey newsprint and bits of vegetables and black flecks of coaldust and with horsemanure. They are filled with pushcarts and wagons and people and noise. There are more than a million people living in and around Warsaw and a third of them are Jews. It does not occur to you that you might leave the Quarter. Why should you? This is where a Jew belongs. The Quarter is tight and warm and dark and it is a womb in which you are conceived and born and raised and where you live and marry, breed and raise your children and, eventually, die. It is a world unto itself where only your old languages are spoken. It is a state of mind, even a religion of a kind, and nothing that occurs outside the Quarter can possibly concern you.

Outside, the *goyim* live and there is violence and destruction and human imperfection.

Inside is safety and mutual understanding and sympathy and order. And there are customs which are immemorial and it is a world which you and others like you have invented. Why leave it? There is no reason why you should.

He went to get his head shaved for the Army (going to Schmul's which was outside the Quarter, because somehow he did not want anyone he knew to see his *peysy* clipped) and he was puzzled and, yes, pleased too about the novelty of mobilization but he was not afraid.

The barbershop was full. Berg waited and watched the men come in wearing civilian coats and hats and suddenly the hats and coats would disappear and the men were different. Under their coats they were in uniform. Like himself, they were reservists. None of them were Jews. They took their smiles off with their civilian coats. Berg saw Pan Kublarz, who drove the watercart, and Pan Purpura, who delivered coal. He let several men take his turn in the barberchair. They looked at him sternly. They were conscious of their uniforms. This made them solemn and fiercely military. Berg was enormously impressed. Finally it was his turn again and he felt Schmul's hands on his head fingering the *peysy*. —*Short?* —*Short,* he said. —*What about the locks?* Berg trembled. —*I don't know. Are they permitted in the Army now?* Schmul shook his head. Pan Kublarz looked at Berg. —*Army? You? What do they want YOU for?* Berg smiled, nodded, shrunk. —*I don't know,* he said. —*In my time they were more careful about whom they gave the right to wear a uniform,* Pan Kublarz said. He was a veteran of the Bolshevik War. He had been in the cavalry of General Prus. Now he was going to drive a fieldkitchen for a sapper company and he felt abused. Berg smiled, nodded. He tried to be agreeable. —*Always nod, always smile, always be agreeable,* Papa Berg had said. *Always agree and you will survive.*

Berg watched unbelieving as his thick, matted hair fell to the floor. The face in Schmul's mirror became gaunt and naked and somewhat foolish and the sorrowful eyes behind the thick lenses blinked furiously. When he brought his bald, violated head home in the afternoon Mama shrieked and fainted. There was so much wailing. Such shrieks and yells and swayings from side to side. And then the aunts and uncles and cousins and cousins' cousins and neighbors and neighbors' neighbors came to console and commiserate and to cluck and to shake their heads, and the flat filled with them and their sound and Mama put on an old dress so that she could tear it. The women wept enough to flood the Quarter. It was a wonder the old house did not float down the street into the Vistula.

And then the smell came.

Berg smelled the smell. It was the smell of fear.

He smelled it on his mother and on his father and his aunts and uncles; he smelled it on himself. He wished that he were not afraid. He wished he had a courage.

Courage.

Odwaga in Polish. He had better learn more Polish: there was no way out of *that.*

When you had it you were *odwazny* and a soldier.

When you didn't have it you were what?

Berg felt ashamed. Each new hour of wailing added to his fear. The sound of wailing pressed on him and into him and filled him with fears and premonitions and anxieties and worries and imagined horrors. He saw himself dead. He saw himself about to be impaled on a spear. He saw himself about to be dipped in boiling oil. He smelled the smell and wished that he had courage. He had never thought about having or not having courage. But with the smell of fear like a sheet around him he was conscious of the lack.

The lamentation went on all afternoon and each new mourner who came to the flat robbed him of one more portion of such courage as he might have had. The Untenbaums came from Solna, and Rosenblatt the carpenter came, and Aprikozenkranz the undertaker put his thin head inside the room and Mama gave a great shriek at the sight of him, and old Rabbi Feldman also came. The rabbi was ninety years old and his mind often wandered and when he saw the swayings and heard the lamentations he became confused and began reciting the prayer for the dead. Then, because someone shouted at him, he swung into the *Oonsaneh Toekehf* and Berg trembled at the import of the words.

—*On the first day of the year it is inscribed, and on the Fast Day of Atonement it is sealed and determined, how many shall pass by and how many be born; who shall live and who die, who shall finish his allotted time and who not; who is to perish by fire, who by water; who by the sword, who by the wild beast; who by hunger or who by thirst; who by the earthquake or who by the plague; who by strangulation or who by lapidation; who shall be at rest and who shall be wandering; who to remain tranquil, and who shall be disturbed; who shall reap enjoyment, and who be painfully afflicted; who shall grow rich and who become poor; who shall be cast down and who be exalted.*

Berg trembled.

He had no doubt that he would be cast down and painfully afflicted, that he would perish both by thirst and water, that his destruction would be a combination of the sword and fire and strangulation and the casting of stones and that wild beasts would tear him and that a plague would strike him, and he felt immensely sorry for Berg in the face of imminent destruction. *Ooshoovor, Oosfeelor, Ootsdorkor.*

Berg's fear grew into a panic which, in turn, filled his head with aching which pressed water from his eyes. He left the house blindly and ran outside the Quarter to get away from the wailing and the prayers for the dead (keeping his shorn scalp covered), and suddenly, in the sunlit, different, harsh *goy* world outside the Quarter, terror smote him in the stomach and made him ill. He looked for darkness and dankness—the safe, dusty womb of the Quarter—and ran into the theater and buried himself in the hot dry dark.

But he was not to be left alone. No Jew is ever left alone, he supposed. Rosenblatt followed him. Rosenblatt sat beside him and whispered to him and giggled and made him ill.

—I can do this for you. I can get Mendeltort to hide you. Yes. *That* Mendeltort. Do you know another? There is only the one Mendeltort. He will hide you. He will know what to do. He will do this for me. We are like this, Mendeltort and me. (Rosenblatt pushed two fingers under Berg's nose to show how he was with Mendeltort.) Mendeltort will not let them take you. He is a terrible man, *oy,* terrible. I will take you to him.

Rosenblatt told how terrible Mendeltort was. Berg agreed that he was, indeed, terrible.

—But they will find me, he said. You can't hide from them.

Rosenblatt giggled.

—So what happens then? Do you know what happens? They find you with Mendeltort and you know what happens? They say: Good morning Mister Mendeltort, sorry to disturb you. Did we disturb you, Mister Mendeltort? We were looking for somebody, but isn't it funny? Suddenly we can't remember who it was. Please don't get angry, Mister Mendeltort. My, isn't it a hot day?

Berg nodded.

Yes.

That is what would happen. If anyone could save him it was Mendeltort.

But that was not the problem, was it? No. This wasn't what the fear was about.

—Why should I hide? he whispered.

—Why? Why? Rosenblatt giggled. Do you want to live?

—Not everybody is killed in the Army.

—And not everybody is born, either. But how many of those are there? Maybe one, maybe two.

—I don't know, Berg said. He truly did not. He had a headache and he was confused. He was afraid and he wished he had courage. He wished he had never been born. He wished Rosenblatt would stop giggling.

—Listen, Morys, I am telling you. If there is no war why go for the Army? And if there is a war what is it to do with you? It is a war for *them,* not for *us.* Let them kill each other. What is their war to do with us? You tell me that.

—I don't know, Berg said. I really don't know.

Too much was happening all at once: Berg's head ached and his stomach hurt and he was conscious of the sticky moisture running down his sides and he pressed his arms tight against his body but still the sweat came.

He thought: If Rosenblatt had not come I would have found courage. I would know what to do if he went away. He wanted to tell Rosenblatt to leave him alone but he could not do that. It would be impolite. It would give offense. You did not disagree with anyone or offend anyone and you worked hard and saved and studied and then, if God was kind, you survived.

—I don't know, he said. He bowed his head and closed his eyes tight and tried to will courage to come to him.

Instead the unctuous voice of the announcer came. It introduced the Foreign Minister and there was the Pan Minister with lacquered hair and thin patrician nose speaking about courage. Pan Minister spoke about peace and about honor. He said that one could not live without the other. He spoke about the need for patience and for courage. Berg heartily agreed to such a need. Pan Minister said that peace would be maintained but not at the expense of honor.

To this there were some cheers in the theater. Then the screen filled with ranks of stamping infantry and lancers trotted by on spotted horses and the *whoomph-whoomph-whoomph-whoomph* of kettledrums introduced the Marshal.

Our Marshal Smigly-Rydz
He is our chief
We will follow him . . .

Someone stood up in the dry darkness of the theater among the blue spirals of cigarette smoke to sing, then others stood up, and Berg wondered if he should stand up. He did not wish to offend anyone.

Most of the people who stood up were women. They would not go to any war, Berg thought. They could still sing. He watched the soldiers on the screen and his head ached. His stomach turned and nausea made him dizzy.

He did not want to offend anyone and was afraid that he would vomit and did not want to draw attention to himself (being outside the Quarter) and he felt sorry for himself and it was all unfair.

He got up and pushed his way past Rosenblatt. Rosenblatt watched him go. Rosenblatt's mouth was open and he made bleating sounds. Berg ran outside. Outside the sun no longer burned the asphalt. The streets retained the white heat of the day. Berg staggered. His head was filled with pain; hammers rang there. His nose filled with the heat and dryness and with the thick smell, and sweat welled up on his naked, violated head and soon the sweatband of his round black cap stuck to him like an iron ring.

Friday, August the twenty-fifth

I THE HUNTER

The sun cut through the canopy of the tallest tree: It flecked the clearing with indefinite light.

The trees were huge; vertical monoliths dripping chill. Moss formed beards on them. They were hoary trees. The air was still that morning on the forest floor. There was a resonance of his breathing in the place.

It was all greens and blues in the clearing and yellow light laced the grass floor and there was silence which was beautiful and dreadful and overwhelming. The clearing had a freshness and a prettiness; the forest was not pretty. The forest was blackness and menace and mankilling bear. It was trunks and opaque shadows; a darkness that drew all color and life into itself. It was a place for things to die by violence. It was the slaughterhouse of God, Pawel thought on the edge of it.

He faced northeast across the clearing, looking through the forest and across to mountains. The forest was thick at this point. But there were thunderbolt-blasted patches where jasmine was yellow and through these openings he saw the flat, cultivated land southeast of him and the Gory Swietokrzyskie north and northwest of him and he could almost hear Moussorgsky's wild music looking at Lysagora.

Bald Mountain.

This was the forest of it. The sun peered down on it. There was enough light to see tracks: little branches snipped in passing, tufts of hair caught innocently on the thorns. . . . He searched the far end of the clearing but he found no tracks.

He was alone in the clearing; dwarfed by the trees, and they, in turn, by mountains, and so on, up to the naked battlement of superstition. Some cloud hung there at two thousand meters.

Rain? he hoped for it. It was time for rain. The soil was dry, combustible. It showed no tracks. Tracks would be better after rain.

He skirted boulders and the tufted clumps that covered quagmire and soon the naked slope of Lysagora rose before him. The massive flanks were bare. Nothing grew on the sandy yellow nakedness. It was a place of witches and of legends; a corrupt mass like a putrid boil in the greenery of the forest. Clearly, no bear had come that way during the night. Farther along he found that deer and some other inoffensive creatures had been down to the river but had not stayed long. Something had driven them away before drinking.

I could set wires here, he thought. There was a conveniently fallen tree with a rotten fork not too high, not too low. A rifle could be wedged in there, aimed and triggertripped. He could set up a tripwire in a minute, but, of course, he wouldn't.

Not this time. Not for this antagonist.

He made his way back along the track to the southern end. He found a comfortable rock to sit on. Trees and their damp morning smell were around him and the sun was not yet high enough to dazzle him and he felt all right.

A little winded but all right.

You're in fine shape, *Pawelku,* considering.

Considering what?

Everything. Considering everything. We have a great deal to consider. There is the fact of youth not quite there anymore and the fact of your licentiousness. Dear Papa and his rage against *licentiousness.* As Papa has it: you're a sybarite, *Pawelku.* A libertine. You contribute nothing.

Nothing?

Pawel laughed. (But softly because of the forest and the bear in it.)

He waited, watching the mouth of the clearing.

It would come from there.

It came in secret ways: sometimes softly as a breath of wind with tufted tail whipping angry flanks, sometimes with a roar and a leap like a projectile from a catapult, sometimes like a black thunderbolt with upswept tusks or from a tree in a blur of claw and spotted fur. In many places. Many times before. And always It was nothing afterwards.

Always It was defeated and the man erect and It resolved itself into a broken shape: animal, dead, small and therefore pitiful. This time their eyes would meet.

Leaves fell.

They touched in spiral flight.

Treetrunks lay in the clearing.

They rotted damply.

They were taller when fallen than a man was standing.

They were of a size to dwarf all living things. All dead things in the forest dwarfed all living things. The forest gave no sign of ever having welcomed anything alive; and yet it was alive.

Mostly, he thought, with menace.

Wind moved in the tall crowns. Down on the forest floor the air was still. He heard the beating of his heart.

Somewhere in this choice anteroom of death the enemy was waiting. Mine Own Old Enemy by any name. Now in the guise of a bear.

He thought about the bear and about the men the bear had killed.

How many had there been?

There was the old man cutting wood who was found gutted as for stuffing. He was the first. They did not know, then, what had done the killing and

27

talked about *czort,* the demon of the forest. There were goats, sheep, a cow, calves. Then the old man. Then two woodcutters in another clearing. One ran. Death overtook him. One climbed a tree. They found him later in the tree—well, partially. His hands were clasped in it. By that time they knew the sign of the clubfoot where some summer sportsman had shot and then had been afraid to follow, magnanimously letting the bear live.

What made a bear like that?

The wound that slowed him down. Age or some other unforgivable crime. The forest had no mercy for infirmity.

The slow died first. The fleet of foot survived. That was the rule. The bear had been mad with hunger when the old man came. The old man was less fleet and died. And the bear learned that man, unarmored, lacking tooth and claw and this necessary swiftness, could be killed. And was.

Repeatedly.

Time passed.

Time, I have eternities of you.

A fly came down, fat from some secret carcass.

Small things moved.

An ant proceeded up the rotten trunk. The ant was dragging something: some creature, dead, conquered, now to be devoured. That also was the rule: You fall, you are devoured. A beetle staggered drunkenly on the fallen trunk. Brother Beetle. Drunken Brother Beetle. It moved in stupid circles with no legs on one side, only on the other. It trod its absurd *ronde* while death watched confident. Death was a gathering of ants. They watched the beetle on its ridiculous course and from time to time one of them came forward carelessly, as though unwilling to hurry the game along to its inevitable end, and pressed its pointed head softly, caressingly against the thrashing columns of the beetle's legs and took one gently off and carried it away. Soon the beetle stopped. It had no legs. Only small stumps remained where all those galloping columns had been, and for a while the beetle swayed itself from side to side to reach the trunk with the desperate stumps but then gave up. It waited quietly to be butchered. The ants came, swift, efficient. They mounted the sides of the beetle like a battlement and cut away the beetle's armorplate on the T-joint of the wings and lowered the wings, and soon the meat was there, naked and exposed. The armored head moved sadly from side to side and finally it too was severed and taken off, and the wings and the legs and the meat were taken off, and there were no more ants and no more beetle as though the little drama had not taken place, as though they had not been there at all.

Pawel moved a little. He shook himself free of the stupor. He felt tired. God but he was enormously tired. Sleep seemed as unattainable as the stars.

He stretched and moved a little and glanced over his shoulder and saw the bear behind him. On his feet, enormous, with arms outspread.

He went sideways for his rifle as the bear came on like an expresstrain through the undergrowth and the undergrowth exploded with this crashing sound and the bear roared and the highpitched yell came from everywhere, out of the trees and shrubs and bushes and rotten vegetation as well as out of him, and a rifle went off and thunked distinctly into flesh and the bear went by at a dead run on his four feet like a monstrous cannonball with breath whistling.

God. *Jezu*. God.

Quick riflefire came from the forest towards Lysagora.

Oh God.

There were thrashing sounds.

God. God. God.

Pawel lay on the forest floor. He heard the beating of his heart. The rotten treetrunk smelled of putrefaction. The grass smelled of dry days without rain. The fetid smell of the bear hung there. His nostrils were full of it. The smell was like a blanket on his head. His mouth was full of the bear smell.

Soon Bogacz came along the deer track.

Bogacz. The word means riches. What grinning humorist of a God bestowed that name on him?

The little tracker came soundless in the grass. His elbows stuck out brownly through a German huntingcoat, a thing of hornbuttons and velvet trim. Goering had given him the coat (Bogacz said) five years ago in Bialowieza. He had tracked for President Moscicki and Goering had been there and Goering had been delighted with his tracking. There was no hunting, he (Goering) said, like the hunting in Bialowieza. Pawel thought about the corpulent German with contempt. He had hunted with him. You get to know about a man if you hunt with him or are a soldier with him. He nodded to the tracker. Bogacz wore a sorrowful, apologetic grin.

—Are you hurt, your honor?

—Yes.

—Where?

—I don't know.

—Don't move. Where is the pain?

—Here. Oh everywhere.

—Do not move.

—I have no such intention. I have no wish to move again.

Bogacz cackled. He looked this way and that and (carefully) not at Pawel, and scratched himself and cleared his throat and hawked and spat and considered the contents of his hands. He studied each finger separately and explored the contents of the fingernails. The little man had tact. Pawel smiled a little.

—It was close, eh?

—Yes master.

—I never heard a thing. There was no warning.

Bogacz nodded. He squatted on the ground like a large brown ape. He looked at Pawel in quick glances. Clearly he was unhappy over something.

—But you're not really hurt, master?

—No. Not really. Ah, there's nothing wrong with me after all. Everything is all right.

Pawel sat up. His breath was short and painful. Small white circles spun crazily out of the corners of his eyes like rainwater on glass in a high wind.

29

Bogacz pressed both hands against Pawel's shoulders; gently but firmly enough.

—Lie still, master.

—There is nothing wrong.

—Truly? Sometimes it is not possible to tell. The bear was close.

Pawel grimaced.

—A little rum, perhaps, master? There is another bottle in the blanketroll. Or perhaps the spirits in the bottle that is shaped like a bear?

—Later perhaps. And you may have some too.

Bogacz smiled, pleased, but there was a furtive quality about the smile. Not even the promise of rum helped to put aside the thoughts that worried him. Pawel looked at him carefully but the tracker would not return his look.

Pawel wondered what the tracker was disturbed about. The bear . . . well, he was gone. And he was not the right bear, of that he was sure. He breathed deeply. The air was cool and sweet and redolent of green things. The bear smell was gone.

—The bear, Pawel said. Is it dead?

—Yes master.

—But he was not the Old One?

—No master. He was a big one and also an old one but he was not the Old One. The Old One waits for you.

Pawel sighed. —I know it. He looked around the clearing. He was averse to leaving this place so suited for ambush. It was the only way for the man-killer to come to the river if he was, as they thought, on the southern slopes of Lysagora. But he would not come that way again if he smelled the traces of the other bear. Old, outcast animals liked to keep alone. They shunned the common trail. They shunned the company of other animals once they had killed man. Killing man was the great divide: once across it, an animal had a certain knowledge, a certain mystery. It was a compliment to the human race, Pawel supposed.

—Where is he now?

Bogacz moved uneasily.

—Perhaps he isn't here anymore. Perhaps he has gone across the mountain to the other side.

—We would know it. The animals would tell you, man of riches. Speak to me of your riches.

—Riches, master?

It was a game they played. Tracks were the riches. Pawel paid for tracks. Bogacz was paid by the number of times he discovered tracks, by his skill in following and reading them, by their relative size and by the result. It was a complicated system and it had to do with the tracker's pride. He did not lie about tracks. If he found them, he found them. If he did not, he did not lie about them.

—There were tracks but it was not the Old One. Doubtless the Old One has left the country now that there is another. But (Bogacz shrugged and looked evasive) perhaps he has not.

—There was nothing else?

—Nothing.

—You are certain?

—Yes. There was nothing else there, master.

But if not there, then elsewhere.

The small man was unhappy. Something was troubling him. He had not told everything and Pawel knew that it would do no good to ask. He would speak when ready, Pawel knew well enough.

At last the tracker said: Master, there has been a killing.

—When?

—In the night.

—While we watched here?

—While we watched.

—What was killed?

—A woman.

(So the Old One had not left after all.)

The tracker looked ashamed. He sat down on the ground and hung his head. The bear had outwitted him again. Pawel waited for the tracker to continue because there would be more; there would be the full measure of his shame to be confessed. At last the old man said: —For two days I have found no track.

Pawel nodded. This was a time for kindness and for understanding.

—I have found track but it was not the Old One's. Since I had found no track of the Old One it was to me as though the Old One was not here.

—So we both thought, Pawel said. (Old man, I share the responsibility.)

Bogacz kept his eyes down. —Last night I heard the animals talking in the forest. They told me there had been a killing. I did not come to your honor because I was ashamed. I will be glad to find another tracker.

—As good as you, man of riches?

—Yes master. Better. Yesterday I would have said there was no better.

—I say so today, man of riches.

Bogacz seized Pawel's hand and kissed it.

—We will find him, Pawel said.

He poured rum into a metal cup and passed it to Bogacz. He poured a little for himself. They both drank. Bogacz sighed.

They had tracked the bear in the first half of the first week and found the roads he used, the paths and secret galleries on the brown sides of the naked mountain, and staked out goats in the clearings and in the twilight places by the river. On the first day of the second week the bear came upon them as they were washing in the river and Pawel barely had time to reach the river-bank and to pick up his rifle and to fire without aiming and the bear skipped aside with a nimbleness no bear could muster and vanished in the shadows. They found blood in the bushes. Not much but enough. For the rest of that day they followed the spotted red trail, then lost it. In the third week they found track bypassed earlier; it was not new track. And Bogacz, who was surely a full professor tracking, a licensed diplomate of the ungentle art, grew confused, as any scholar grows confused when robbed of reference books. One thing became impossibly clear: the bear walked in the river to hide tracks. No bear could have such an intelligence. —*Next he will walk upon the water instead of in it,* Pawel said, disgusted. You had to admire an animal like that. On the third day of the third week the peasants came into the forest where they were, and the peasants brought a young goat with them and butchered it and roasted it to show gratitude. Two weeks had passed without a killing. The peasants were grateful. Goats were expensive and the peasants had little enough with which to show their gratitude but they had a dour uncomplaining peasant pride and so they brought the goat. On the first day of the fourth week, which was this week, a ewe was taken from the herding hill. The peasants came again. This time they brought a silver bullet, some hornshaped roots and a medallion of St. Hubert the Hunter. One way or another, separately or jointly in some impossible alliance, these were to help against the bear.

Pawel felt the silver bullet in his shirt pocket under the cartridge loops. He fingered it. It would be something to talk about in time. It would amuse his Warsaw friends. It was wrapped in the telegram that had called him there (an extravagance which showed the peasants' state of mind and) which they had laboriously composed, probably with the help of their priest. They had found some articles about him in an old newspaper and so knew who he was and where he hunted and how good he had been at it, which was very good, and about the Olympic riding trophy and the tigers, the elephant and the rhinoceros, the whole dead menagerie which made up his public life, and, having read this or more likely having had it read to them by the priest, they supposed him good enough for the bear and so wrote to him hopefully and laboriously about the Old One.

HONORED CAPTAIN STOP THERE IS A BEAR STOP HE HAS KILLED THREE MEN AND BOY AND COWS AND SHEEP STOP SIGNED COMMA THE GMINA OF THE VILLAGE OF PILOWKA IN THE PROVINCE OF THE MOUNTAINS OF THE HOLY CROSS STOP GOD WILL REPAY YOUR EXCELLENCY STOP.

Which was a flattering assumption that time had stood still and that he was still what he had been and that the innumerable white nights had not changed him, had not deteriorated him; that he was in fact still good enough for the bear.

Well, he was. Or was that just the ancient arrogance? He had always had it.

—*Read me the passage of the speech of Caesar to the legions before Philippi. Silence in the class. Proceed, Master Prus.*

—*Certainly, sir. And Caesar mounted the stump of a tree with the legions assembled and in his hand he held the fruit of the fields and he bit into this fruit and chewed it and masticated it thoroughly and he gestured with this fruit to show what they would do to Pompey and the legions laughed.*

—*Adequate, Prus, adequate. Now, if your clever little mind permits it, tell us what you suppose was the fruit of the fields?*

—*A turnip, sir.*

—*A turnip?*

32

—Turnip. Of course it could have been a potato but I do not think so. I feel it is unlikely that the great Caesar would eat a raw potato.

—Your imagination, however, does not recoil at the thought of turnips?

—On the contrary, sir. But we are not discussing my imagination.

—I see. And do you have a theory about this mystic gesture which Caesar used to set his legions laughing?

—Yes sir. This, sir.

—What does that signify?

—A threat of copulation, sir. Or perhaps a promise? And may I quickly forestall any commentary on my imagination?

—Prus, you have acquired an unfortunate facility for wit. You are irreverent. You are far too clever for your own good. I detect in you certain anarchistic tendencies. Were I your father I would take some measures.

—That, sir, would be impossible.

—What would?

—That you could be my father. My family has always frowned upon miscegenation.

—So, my young, rich, arrogant and irreverent friend, take this note to the Pan Dyrektor, if you please. Six of the best with a rattan cane . . .

And in the tapestry-hung apartment in Rozwadowska Street, Pawel laughed at the thought of what the poor peasants would think if they saw some of the other pictures, the ones which could not appear in their old newspaper.

The tiger skin had had a run of late. A bearskin off a genuine mankiller might give an added touch . . .

For two weeks now he had not thought about it. The bearskin, and the various uses to which he might put it, had taken ominous form.

The sun rose steadily. The morning mists cleared and the light hardened and the shadows took shape and acquired texture.

They made their way slowly through the forest, cautiously—not because of actual danger but because of the unseen that watched them and because of that which had been done which they had not prevented.

A woman was dead.

Bogacz went first, sadly. Pawel followed. Twigs whipped them both. The forest chattered in derision with a thousand voices.

Well, fair enough: You have a right to be derisive, Pawel told the forest. I have failed.

A bear was dead. It was not the right bear.

A woman was dead.

The forest has defeated me again. But not defeated. No. Say rather it has stopped me temporarily. I have been outflanked.

It has outwitted me for now but there will be other nows. Certainly I now have the determination. I have the necessary dedication. I am consecrated to a cause.

So . . . not defeated. Merely halted for a time as on the Ebro in Spain and in Ethiopia, pushed back a little; a little battered, certainly, but not defeated.

33

Defeat is only possible with an admission of defeat. I shall come back to this clearing or another like it on another day.

The village was twelve kilometers away and they made their way through the forest quickly enough despite the caution. They were in the village in late afternoon.

With the sun going—not yet gone but almost gone in a fat, orange glow above the forest—with the trees black against it and the naked mountain an ancient crone-brown there, they marched into the village where dogs besieged them. There were many dogs. Men moved about purposefully in pitchfork-bearing groups.

Before one house there was a group of kerchiefed women and from the house came the thin howling of a man who has suffered loss and the loud, open, heartcleansing wailing of a woman. This was the home of bereavement. They went there first.

The women and the old men parted before them saying nothing, looking at them with the distant peasant look. They shouldered their way through the peasants to the door. There the priest met them coming out.

—*Tragedia, Panie Kapitanie, tragedia.*

—Yes Father. How did it occur and where?

The priest pointed towards the forest wall so black against the sun. He made sounds in his throat. —*De mortuis nil nisi bonum,* but had it not been for sin . . . for sin . . .

He has eyes like a boar, Pawel thought.

All of this had a macabre quality of something many times experienced. Like walking into a room in a house where one has never been and seeing objects just so arranged and shapes familiarly beckoning, and picking up small things one knows are there although hidden from view. There was a satisfaction in the priest's voice despite the *tragedia* part of it.

Then all the women started to speak at once and the old men made grunting sounds and all of them edged forward. This one knew this, this one knew the other.

—You speak, Pawel said, pointing. The rest of you keep still.

So came the story of the killing in the forest. A man and woman going in the forest: both young, both loving. And being young they made that thing among the bushes, by no means an uncommon occurrence.

The old man who told this smiled stupidly and spread his arms.

—Well? (The foolishness of old men speaking of the foolishness of youth.)

—And then she left him, sir, to wash. (The women stirred and giggled.) And went off a little ways into the forest because she was modest and there the Old One waited.

The Old One took advantage of this modesty.

And then, of course, all of it fell in place like a bad melodrama because, wouldn't you know it, Pawel knew this girl. He recalled her modesty and remembered thinking her an uncommonly pretty girl, though sturdy the way these peasant women were. He had looked at her once, hard, in the man's way, as she crossed the river holding her skirts bunched up around her waist, and as she came through the water and the river shallowed she had, perhaps, forgotten to lower her skirts and so came towards him on the bank with youthfully narrow thighs exposed and looked at him not modestly, not immodestly, in a woman's way. Ha. Look, I am a woman. The source of your life and of your destruction.

And now, modest or immodest, sinful or virtuous, she was dead and bloodily disemboweled, and the fine thighs would never open or close for anyone again and the look would never be in the eyes again and nothing mattered to her any more.

Jezu, to be dead like that.

To be killed at a time like that.

From the embrace of life to one of death. Death while, perhaps, freshly planted life was taking root. . . .

—Who took her there?

It was, the priest explained, a man named Gosin, a man from nowhere. A bad man. A man who has no roots cannot be trusted. Where did he come from? No one knew. For all they knew he could have been a murderer or a thief. And probably was. At any rate, he had never attended mass in the church. Not once in three years.

—It would not surprise me, the priest intoned, if there had been no bear and if it was the man Gosin who . . .

—Who what?

—Well, I would not like to cast aspersions on anyone. Not even this Gosin. Who is one man to accuse another? Still . . .

—Still what?

—Well, a man without roots, a man without reverence . . .

Pawel turned his back on the priest.

—Tell me about the woman, he said.

—The innocent, the priest said. The innocent.

—What about the sin? Pawel heard the priest's smug satisfaction. —Didn't you say there was sin?

—Indeed yes. Lust and carnality and therefore destruction. But there has been a death and of the dead one does not speak evilly.

—I thought you said that she was innocent. If there is innocence how can there be evil?

—Before the sin, Sir Captain. Before the sin!

—And after death?

—The dead are innocent.

—The worms don't care about innocence or sin.

The priest made a vague gesture. He moved uneasily. He peered at Pawel with fat eyes.

—I must say, Captain, he began. I must say . . .

—Must you? Why?

The priest's black arms became windmills. —We are all God's . . .

—*Gowno,* Pawel said. Shit. He said it quietly.

The priest made a peculiar strangled sound. The peasants pressed close. They looked puzzled. A woman giggled. Someone blew his nose.

—Come, man of riches, we will leave this place. There will be fresh track by the river. We will follow it.

Bogacz sighed. He looked at the black wall of trees and the sun behind it.

—It is late, master. There is little sun.

—There is enough.

Although there wasn't and what there was of it would soon be gone and there would then be only an impenetrable darkness in which the bear would see but they would not.

They walked the dry highway for a while. It was paved with clay. Clay made a fine walking surface. Later the rains would turn it into swamp but now it was hard. The dull stare of the peasants followed them. The priest's sharp, boarlike stare followed them. He would not want the bear found and destroyed. The bear was God's own executioner punishing carnal sin.

Wait, bloody bear, wait.

The bear waits for me.

Mine Own Executioner by any name.

How quick the sun went down.

It is dark.

There is a chill.

It will be cold.

The night will bring its cold.

It will be dark and cold within an hour; the forest's several darknesses will become one.

It's time for autumn rains.

The tracks are better after rain.

Perhaps, Pawel thought, tired (becoming aware of fatigue, of that sudden weakness, and thinking sleep as unattainable as the stars), there are no tracks because there is no bear. There is neither a bear nor a village nor darkstaring peasants nor a blackrobed priest.

In Spain they called them crows because of their black robes. There was a priest he remembered from Estremadura. The priest had a radio in the belltower and spotted targets for the Kondor Legion. Loomis had spotted the priest in the belltower. The priest's Zeiss binoculars caught the sun and the sun betrayed him. Loomis told Gomez about the priest's binoculars. Gomez went up the belltower and brought down the priest and they tied the priest to a chair in the· square and shot him through the head. The priest flopped up and down like a fish after he was shot. He asked to be shot facing the church and they had done that for him. A man at dying has a right to face what he believes in. The bullet made a small hole in the skull where it went in and then the priest's whole face exploded. —*Sonovabitch,* Loomis had said. *Who notched my bullets?* The priest was quickly dead. He was one of the softheaded priests, Gomez said. The hardheaded ones took a long time dying. Gomez had taken a long time to die when the grenade exploded. A considerable amount of Colonel Gomez (formerly a tram driver in Madrid) disappeared after the grenade. But enough of him remained to die slowly and terribly and with blasphemy after the explosion. The grenade was of a type they had not seen before. Loomis thought it was a German mortarbomb. The Germans, Loomis said, had endless varieties of bombs and grenades. Just when you thought you knew everything they had they would come up with something new; they were good at that.

Pawel thought about Loomis. Where was he?

36

Loomis was an American, a journalist when he could remember. Most of the time he could not remember and became involved in what he was supposed to be observing. He had become involved in Spain. Later both he and Pawel were involved in Ethiopia. Loomis had also been involved in Manchuria. Pawel drew few conclusions from the war in Spain. He learned some new terms to apply to people. People, Pawel thought after Spain, were mean and dishonorable and avaricious and cowardly and servile and depraved and untrustworthy and heartless and prejudiced and benighted and noble and highminded and magnanimous and modest and honorable and generous and charitable and brave. In short, emerging from the Spanish conflict, Pawel knew that he had acquired neither wisdom nor nobility of spirit and that no conclusions could be drawn from conflicts.

His father, who was a colonel, could not understand this inability to draw conclusions. —*Why do you live like this? Where are you going? Do you know where you are going?* —No father. But it does not matter. —*What? What?* —I said it did not matter, father. The Colonel was an honorable man. He was disappointed. —*You must have direction, Pawel. You must have a purpose. One is not possible without the other. Without them you are a slug, a sybarite. You are a civilian!* Civilian was the Colonel's favorite expression. It denoted all the uncomplimentary things. —*You cannot merely amuse yourself with animals and women. You waste your time and talents, not to mention money.* A gentleman did not mention money. *You live to gratify yourself. You don't contribute anything. You do not wish to contribute anything. You want to live only the way* you *want to live without contributing anything. You are a pleasureloving wastrel and I do not know you.*

—*Selfish. You are selfish.*

Yes.

—*You will be punished.*

Yes.

—*You will be paid for not contributing.*

Yes.

—*You will regret.*

Yes.

But not now.

Soon; possibly sooner than I think but please not at this time.

Because I have a Thing to do.

I have a loving rendezvous in the forest and I am awaited.

I am patiently and inexorably awaited in the forest.

I am awaited by mine own old enemy, the Executioner of God. We have this unavoidable appointment . . .

Sleep.

I wish devoutly that I could go to sleep.

I am tired.

I am very tired.

Perhaps there is no one waiting in the forest. Perhaps there is nothing.

There is nothing.

Sleep.

Halt and fall out and sleep.

Rest and sleep. Can you sleep?

I can always sleep.

I am a soldier (now and then) and always a hunter and as a soldier (now and then) and hunter I can *always* sleep. Anywhere and at any time.

But a woman is dead.

A woman has been slaughtered and I am awaited.

The Old One waits for me.

At the junction of the clay road and the forest track a man waited, halfcrouched in the bushes. He was at first invisible. The river made its splashing sounds clearly at this point.

The man saw them and suddenly became erect and tall like a shadow when lights move behind it. Bogacz started when he saw the man grow in the shadow. He raised his arm. They stopped. The man came forward.

—Are you the man Gosin?

The man said that he was.

Bogacz asked to be shown the place where the bear had waited. He asked politely. He would not face the man. The young man took them to the place. It was a private place with rushes sweeping up to meet overhead to form a secret chamber like a chapel; a place for modesty and sweet remembering and for murder. Bogacz went to the river's edge to look for tracks.

Pawel looked at the man. Gosin was young and stern. His dark face was without expression.

—It was you who brought the woman to this place?

—Not this place.

—Where then?

—I did not bring her here to die.

—But to the forest?

—Yes.

—You let her come in here alone?

—She wished it so.

—You did not come to help her?

—There was no sound.

—You heard nothing? Saw nothing?

Death, after all, hardly comes unnoticed. It comes in noise and fire and acrid smoke. That is where *you* seek it.

—There was nothing.

Bogacz came back then.

—The track is not clear, master, he said.

—The tracks of blood are clear, Gosin said. We will follow that.

—I will follow those tracks, Bogacz said, and the others a little way into the forest to see the direction of the Old One. But I would not go looking for the Old One until morning. The woman is dead, after all, he said apologetically.

—Go ahead, Pawel said. I shall make camp here.

With Bogacz gone Pawel unrolled the blankets. The camp was simple. It was a matter of a moment to pitch it: a canvas nailed into the ground at two corners, two corners raised on poles. As he worked on shelter, Pawel saw

38

the other, the man Gosin, move to the bedrolls and take out the Primus and light it and take the kettle and fill it with water and put the kettle on the stove to boil. Gosin did this and sat down. He said nothing. It was as though he had suddenly made himself one of the hunters. There would be no way to drive him away.

—Can you make tea, Gosin?

The dark man nodded. Pawel took the bottle out of the bedroll. He poured a measure in the metal cup. The rum was thick and brown and smelled of islands in the sun. There would be no bears there, on the islands, but some other thing would be. There was always something.

—Drink, Pawel said. He passed the cup to Gosin. He passed a flat square of corrugated hardtack and a length of sausage and cut a thick slice off the goat's cheese and passed that too. Gosin took them, ate and drank and said nothing. He had a young man's consciousness of dignity and pride. He stared at the kümmel bottle shaped like a bear.

—Did you love her? Pawel said. Were you to be married?

There would be tragedy in this if it were so. There would be retributive justice when the bear was killed. The bear would not then be the Executioner.

—No, Gosin said.

—You did not love her?

—No.

—But you brought her here?

—Yes.

—There was no love between you?

—She may have had love. I do not know.

—But you did not?

—I did not then.

—And now?

—Now I do not know.

In time Bogacz returned.

He said nothing at first and Pawel knew that it would do no good to ask. The old man squatted by the fire and drank rum. He drank some tea. The others waited. At last the small man said: —The track is clear.

Pawel closed his eyes. —Where is he?

—He is within an hour's march. He is in a thicket of old trees and tall grass on this side of the mountain. I have gone up behind him and I know that there is no way for him through the mountain.

Eyelids close out the light and make a peaceful darkness. What closes out the Light? —What is he doing?

—Nothing, master. He waits.

He waits.

—Keep up the fire for my return.

—I will go with you, master?

—No. You have done well, man of riches. Drink the rum. Wait for me in this place.

—But I will go, Gosin said.

—You will also stay here.

—I have a need to go, the young man said.

—The Old One waits for *me*.

Pawel picked up the Mannlicher and hefted it. The weight was right for him. He loaded the rifle carefully, and slung it, and considered the bottle and its sweet brown contents. The rum was warm and sunny and inviting. The fire was inviting. The brilliant eyes of girls were open and inviting but a woman was dead.

—For you, *Bogaczu,* he said about the rum.

It was, then, cold. Not as cold as it would be later but cold enough. The river whispered and fallen timber moved in it sluggishly. The river was low. It was dark and muddy. Rushes bowed along its banks. Trees reached for him darkly.

He sensed a movement in the trees to his right and swung towards the movement feeling the rifle slip with practiced ease off his shoulder and into his hands and saw the glinting eyes. It was a goat, one of the dozen he had staked out in the clearings and in the thickgrown places by the river. The goat was nervous. It trembled. He moved on through the forest.

A moon came up and splashed its dead white light onto the forest. The sky was clear. The sky was unconcerned about the earth. Things moved and plotted and waited on the earth; there were killings and murders and small destructions within each sixty-second eternity but the sky was tall and unconcerned. When you are tall you can remain aloof.

In time he became aware that the grass and bracken and thorny twigs and rotted branches and small clumps of forest vegetation under his feet were not there anymore and that, instead, there was sand crunching yellowly and his boots trod around lumpy sandstone and the trees were smaller and thinner and the light was better. He saw the slope of Lysagora.

The mountain was gaunt and enormous in the dead white light. It stretched an infinity of meters up the careless sky. The sky was blank. It communicated nothing. Tall trees; tall sky: equally unconcerned.

It was time to rest.

He rested, hearing his heart beat up. At thirty-five he had no trouble with his heart. No. Not of that kind either. His thighs and calves were tense. His eyes were not quite clear. Things trembled slightly as he looked at them. I must relax, he thought.

I must calm my hands. I need calm hands and a steady heart. Or is it the other way round? One way or the other he would need them both when the bear came.

He scanned the naked slope of Lysagora left to right then right to left in the military manner. Bogacz said that there was a thicket. One of those thickly grassed outposts of vegetation thrust up the lower slopes of Lysagora. He found one hidden under an overhang of sandstone. It was quiet and dark. It was filled with menace. Nothing confirmed the notion of a bear in there but he thought there was one.

He circled the thicket, looking into it. Each tree, each shrub had its private darkness and these spread at the edges to run into others and somewhere in that total darkness the bear waited.

Come, bear.

I wish devoutly that you may come.

And because he was a firm believer in such things, he slipped a coin into the rotten trunk, and spilled a little water from his canteen on the ground.

I wish to meet the maneater of Lysagora, he told the old gods with formality. He wished that he could ask for a clear eye and a steady hand but the old gods did not allow two wishes.

Nothing moved.

Small things made no sound. No deer broke through to test his bad side. There were to be no more rehearsals: This time the bear would come.

Come, bear.

How to make him come?

You like woodcutters, brother bear?

You have a partiality for old men? We will get you one.

And grinning whitely in the dark Pawel retreated to prepare a stage. He checked his rifle and released the safetycatch. There would be no time for moving levers when the bear came. He placed the rifle within reach and hunted for a stout piece of healthy timber with which to simulate the sound of a woodcutter's axe. He carefully trod on a piece of rotten wood and heard it give a satisfying crack.

He began to whistle.

As an old man might whistle at night in the forest; softly enough.

—Ungh, he grunted and swung the cudgel against a tree.

Again.

Pause.

And again.

The echoes flew up the slopes of Lysagora. The forest was quiet. Pawel grinned.

Hear this, brother bear.

There is an old man cutting wood in the forest.

Is age not tempting enough for you? Is infirmity required?

He moved haltingly around the tree, simulating lameness. He broke wind, hawked, spat and made old-man sounds and hit the tree again with the simulated axe.

Come, brother bear.

The old man is tired.

See, he is resting now. The axe is still. He is old and he can't do too much. He must rest between so many strokes.

—Egh!

Hear him clear his throat.

—Oj tam.

Hear him grunt.

He is a peasant and his life is hard.

He is a tired old man.

He is unarmed, unarmored and lacks the necessary swiftness.

Pawel thought he saw the shadows move. A dark form moved in the total darkness of the thicket and crouched on the edge of it. It vanished. The bear was stalking him.

This was the only way for the bear to come. He was trapped in the thicket. The yellow mass of Lysagora hung over it like a cloud. He would come this way to reach the broader shelter of the forest. He must be made to come now. While the light was good. Pawel remembered the cloud over Lysagora earlier in the day. It could obscure the moon and shield the bear with darkness. He must be tempted into coming now.

He would come swiftly and silently out of the thicket to the right where the trees were thinner. Possibly he had already done so. Possibly he was already in position to attack but Pawel did not think so. There would have been some small sound to give the bear away.

He would break from the trees with a roar, rising on his trunklike legs in full gallop, and would crash through the undergrowth and the young trees there, and come straight through with arms extended like a lover and there would barely be time to stoop and grasp the rifle and swing with it and raise it and aim and press the trigger and shoot the bear before he was fully visible but betrayed by the sound of the attack, and the bear would be shot mortally while still unseen but he would keep on coming.

He would still be menacing as he burst through the last line of small shrubs there on the right and he would keep on coming like a monstrously animated steeple of a church on trunklike legs, and there would be ten meters at the most remaining between the bear and the man and the bear must die in this intervening space.

Come, brother bear.

Instead, the unexpected came.

The sound of the motorcycle on the river road gurgled up through the forest and towards the mountain. The river road was ten kilometers away but sound carries at night and in the forest.

Pawel sighed.

He tossed the axe-simulating stick aside. He picked up his rifle and unloaded it. He found a treetrunk to sit on. His hands resumed their shaking. A sudden chatter of nightbirds told him where the bear had gone.

He felt fatigue returning. It had been gone while he was waiting for the bear but now the bear was gone and the fatigue was back. He lit a cigarette.

Soon Bogacz came. Gosin was with him. The tracker scratched his head and smiled apologetically.

—It was a letter for your honor, he said.

—Since when does a sergeant of police carry letters? Gosin was annoyed. The motorcycle belonged to the Commissariat in Stopnica. He had admired it. He did not think it now at all admirable.

—Where is this letter?

Bogacz put the large, official-looking envelope into Pawel's hand. Pawel tore it apart and drew out the red card for all of them to see. He did not have to read it.

—It must be of importance, Bogacz said hopefully. It is not every day that sergeants of police carry letters.

Pawel smiled. He was very tired.

—Beware of sergeants of police bearing gifts, man of riches. They are like the Greeks.

Bogacz smiled, uncertain.

—It is a saying, Pawel said. A proverb.

This Bogacz understood. —Proverbs are the wisdom of the nations.

—That is so.

Gosin moved uneasily on the forest floor. He looked from Pawel to Bogacz and back again. His look asked for an explanation. He would not ask for one but his look could.

—This letter, Bogacz said. It is of importance?

—Yes.

—It does not look very big. And the color is strange.

—It is an order of mobilization and it means that the hunt is finished.

Gosin stood up and took a quick step forward. —But the bear? he said. The bear lives.

—Yes.

—Finished? How can it be finished? What about the bear?

—The bear must wait. Soon there will be other bears in the forest. There will be a variety of bears.

Gosin stared. Bogacz looked away into the darkness of the forest.

—It must be finished, Gosin said.

—It is finished.

—It must be properly finished.

—For me it is now finished. I will leave this place.

—But the bear lives.

—Let it live.

—The sergeant of police waits for your honor in Pilowka, Bogacz said. He has a little cart in which to carry your honor to the train. It is a small cart tied to the side of his machine. I have never seen such a thing.

—But it is not finished, Gosin said.

—Someone will get the Old One, Pawel said. Perhaps it will be you? Or perhaps it will be this small man of riches.

He had hoped they would laugh but no one did. Gosin turned away and went quickly down the trail. He did not look back. Bogacz shook his head.

—The Old One waits for you, he said.

Pawel swore softly. He got up and picked up his rifle. He went down the trail he had come up earlier. Trees whipped him. Whip me. The hunt is not finished. The bear lives. It waits for me somewhere. We have not kept our unavoidable appointment. There will be another.

Bogacz followed him to the camp by the river, then into Pilowka. There the police sergeant and the peasants waited. The sergeant saluted and reported. He would drive the Pan Kapitan to the train. The peasants said nothing. Bogacz said goodbye.

—Here, man of riches, Pawel said. This is for you.

He gave the Mannlicher to the tracker.

—I will not need it, master, Bogacz said.

—A man can always use a good rifle.

—I will take it, then, in memory of your honor. But not as payment. I have been paid enough in several ways.

—You were paid what you earned, *Bogaczu*. That is all.

Bogacz shook his head. —More, much more. Besides, it is not yet finished, master, is it?

—Not yet. One day we will again go after the Old One.

—I know, the tracker said. God protect your honor.

—And you, *Bogaczu,* Pawel said.

And then the motorcycle stuttered and roared and blue exhaust came from it, and small boys laughed and put their hands across their ears, and small girls giggled and the peasants stared.

Saturday, August the twenty-sixth

I THE GENERAL

The house stood on a shelf; above it an impossibly pure sky of a corn-flower blue hung like a borrowed canopy. The woods spread left and right of it like a smudge of smoke. They had no texture, shape or definition. They seemed impermanent, merely imagined, as though someone had spread them out to dry in the sun only that morning and would come back at dusk to take them in.

The house, though, had a permanence: There was a quietness and a time-lessness about it as though it had always been there and always would be. It looked confident and calm, as though assured that time would ignore it and pass it by and leave it as a white memorial to itself.

Day came.

The General came from the house leaving the doors wide open—the interior a dark, warm place full of shadow—and stood under the portico to watch the sunrise.

There it was (he thought), like a recruiting poster or a plate out of a history book: too bright, too sharply etched. The white glare was too white, the sun so improbably red, and the bluish pinetops impossibly gallant in the breeze. The sun rose and his hopes rose with it: up, gradually, from the shadow in the red glow.

He thought they both exaggerated just a bit: the historians and he. Nothing was quite as simple as they made it out. There wasn't that much definition anywhere. Nothing was merely black or white, the choice was not that simple; there were all those greytones in between that the historians forgot about.

But (he remembered) he was no longer to be concerned about historians. They were no longer a part of his scheme of things. He was done with them and they with him. He supposed that he should offer thanks to God except that he felt Michal's agency had been more instrumental in ending his exile. And it would do to wait until the messenger got there before giving thanks, in light of experience. Since Thursday afternoon, mobilization had been canceled twice and could be again and there was no use wasting thanks on disappointment. Now, once again, the telephone had broken up a morning, and the postmaster (no longed diffident, less self-effacing, more authoritative) had given his report and now, quite possibly, the messenger was coming.

He had not said anything about it to Lala and she had asked nothing. They had gone on about their days the way they always had, calmly and peacefully in a time that was neither calm nor peaceful nor suggesting peace, as if nothing could happen to change anything and no messenger would come. If one came he would come unsummoned and unprompted: a matter of chance that neither he nor she could do anything about. That was the way she would expect it, he supposed. His leaving, then, would be unavoidable. Almost preordained. God's will, destiny, or the laws of nature; call it what you will. Who could be blamed, after all, if lightning strikes? She would not feel abandoned.

But he had been his own *deus ex machina* and now he wondered if she knew what he had done to set the messenger in motion: the letters and Michal's intercession behind scenes. He supposed she knew; she knew him too well for any subterfuge. He was as bad an actor as he was an historian, and a deplorable deceiver. Still, if she knew, she wouldn't say anything about it; her pride would not allow complaints or accusation.

The fact of his leaving for war would not damage anything between them if he had not arranged it. War was his element, after all, and he was a soldier. She would feel no betrayal, no sense of injury, if war came for him as it did for others: an unsolicited summons. She would wait for him, her love undiminished, and he would come back to her when the war was over and everything would be as before. But he was leaving her by special request. He had written letters (thinking that he could not risk waiting for the natural course, that he would be ignored) and had not told her (hoping she would think the summons came because he was remembered with no pleading necessary), and this manipulation made it all a lie. Her pride would not allow her to take that kind of parting without bitterness.

Perhaps it was this sense of having betrayed her, or the mounting tension of the days (with war so imminent) and his artificial calmness, or the *commedia buffa* of the two postponements (the-on-again-off-again business with uniforms and mobilizations) that made the whole thing of messengers and messages seem small and unimportant, a sort of footnote. The General felt no gladness, waiting for the messenger, no more fierce anticipation. If anything, he felt a growing irritation. He stood on the porch, a heavytimbered structure built to resist time and the Polish winters. He squinted his eyes up against the sun on the mountains and hunched his shoulders forward and watched the sun climb up. He, too, was built to resist time, weather, men.

Red fire was all around; the woods rose black out of the mist and hardened and acquired texture and broke up into reds and yellows; night's monochrome was finished. The sun made mountains soft. There was a smoothness and gentleness about the land in its light.

Behind these mountains were others and others beyond them where the Germans waited. There too the sun was rising. Out it came, apolitical there as here, and as the day came the mountains lost their early innocence and pinkness. They became hard again and wild as shadow slipped off the peaks and down granite fingers and flowed into the red, wornout soil of the foothills. There were few trees to trap the shadows in the mountains. The peaks of the High Tatras are particularly dead, particularly naked, more somber and forlorn than any Polish mountains except, perhaps, the Mountains of the Holy Cross. They are pocked with old scars, pitted with old wounds; these fill with scabrous brown as the sun rises. Elsewhere, the Carpathians are a soft green wall. There is a mist in the air and a fine morning haze, and all the days look the same in their beginnings, and the sounds and the smells are the same as those of yesterday.

Nothing, he thought, ever changes here: Mountains stand still in the sunlight like waves caught at convulsion's peak by a glacial seizure and the plains are ironed out endlessly by the white of the sun, and you can see villages smoking a long way off in the flatness and small towns spring from nowhere and the shimmering steeples are like an impossible perpendicular mirage. The roads are white and straight. Along them lie things plowed up from the soil: ancient, rusty things infinitesimally crumbling.

And now a column of soldiers showed at the edge of the woods and spun out from between the trees. The soldiers marched in the dust. The officers rode horses. There were small cars with the regimental staffs. Dust covered all of them. The General watched them.

He became aware of motion behind him and turned. He saw that Lala had come out to join him. She stood near him watching the soldiers who passed tightpacked, redfaced in the dust, with boots beating out the longremembered rhythms like a giant heart.

Soldiers, he thought, are to be used. Disuse destroys a soldier. It takes away his sense of purpose and erases him.

—You have that look again, she said.

—A look?

—Like a hungry eagle. It used to frighten me a bit.

—But now it doesn't?

She knew him well, he thought: all the looks and the moods. He watched her eyes but could read nothing there.

—No. Sometimes you look at me like that. As though you wanted to remember each part of me. Each of our days and nights.

And each part thereof.

—Last night, he said, looking at the road and at the soldiers, there were troops on the road. Did you hear them?

—It has become a familiar sound.

—I welcome it. Yet I feel regret.

—Why?

—I don't know.

—Are you uneasy about what is coming?

—It will not be an easy war for anyone.

—Must there be war?

—I think so. I don't see how it can be prevented.

—Isn't there some way?

—Not now. I think there was a way but it's too late now.

—Why is it too late? It can never be too late for something like that.

—I think it can be. These things build up until they seem to have lives of their own. Then nobody can stop them.

—Something should have been done, she said. Why didn't anybody do anything before?

Five years, three months and two days earlier, he said, Pilsudski had a plan. The Old Man had been ill but his fine mind functioned. He said to the French and the British: Now. Now is the time. Let us go into Germany now, when it is time, when Adolf Hitler is not yet secure, when there are still

46

Germans alive who have a conscience, who remember war, when the Reichswehr is a bare two hundred thousand men and not too big to handle. Let the French march into the Saar and the Rhineland and disarm the Germans. Let the Poles disarm them in Silesia, Pomerania and East Prussia. Let the British help by doing nothing.

—It was undoubtedly an immoral plan. It was based upon the premise that a small victorious war was better than a large disastrous war. The British are so terribly moral, though. They voiced their indignation. Besides, they were beginning to make money trading with the Germans. The French have never been particularly moral. They would have gone along with it. But British pressure made itself felt at the Quai d'Orsay, and it is still the British who set the tone in dress, manners and politics. So they didn't listen to the Old Man's plan and soon the Old Man died and you could hear the sigh of relief from London to Berlin.

—So now there will be war.

—Yes. No one can stop the Germans now, not even themselves. They have reached a point where nothing else would make any sense. War is now the only logical thing left for them.

She looked away, then said: —And you will go, of course.

He nodded. He waited for her to go on but she said nothing more. Her face had closed; she looked infinitely calm and totally withdrawn. If she said anything about his secret machinations it would be in her own good time, he knew.

He thought about the war, wondering when it would come. He had fought in two. He knew this one would be different, infinitely more bloody, more terrible. But in another way (he thought) not so different: In the far east, in the marshes of Volhynia, in the forests stretching northwest from Lwow, the complex of wide rivers spilled in the density of the Mazovian lakes, the line would be formed, the frontier would be straight at last, and there the Grand Maneuver, that Polish specialty, could begin.

She said: —You are quite sure? There could be no mistake?

—No mistake, he said. I am sure.

—It could be just maneuvers.

Yes, he said. It could be but he didn't think so.

—It could be just another false alarm. Like all the false alarms we've had this month. It could be just another of those mobilizations that are canceled in an hour or two. And anyway, we still don't know that you will be going, do we. Your notice hasn't come.

—That's right, he said.

—It's possible that they will not call you, she said evenly. There is no reason why they should. After all, you are on the special list, aren't you?

—Which list do you have in mind? They have a number of them in Warsaw.

He laughed, thinking she would also laugh. But she only shook her head and looked at him steadily.

—The retired list.

—You mean the invalid list, don't you?

—Yes. That too. They don't take people off a list like that unless there is a special need. Or unless there is some other special reason. I think you told me once that that's how they do it.

He nodded. She went on: —So they might not send for you?

—It's possible, of course.

—But if they do, for whatever the reason, and you have to go, where will you go? And when?

—It would be quick, he said. Probably the same day that the message comes. And it would be Warsaw. Afterwards, I don't know. But it would be Warsaw to begin with.

—Oh, Warsaw, she said. Her shoulders came forward and made her back narrow. She looked away from him.

—We haven't been there for a long time, he said carefully. Perhaps it would be a good change for you. Even under these circumstances it is something different.

She nodded. —Yes, I know.

—You used to enjoy that sort of thing.

—What kind of thing?

—People, lights, parties, conversation. The theater and the galleries. I remember how you were about the galleries. The things you said about our national mania for dead art.

She smiled. —Dying, not dead. Heroic things with realistic wounds.

—Yes. The art of dying and dying as an art. I remember that. And Roman statuary. Do you remember what you said about that?

—No.

—That it was atrocious. Also very true.

—They were so stern and disapproving, those stone portrait-busts; so certain of their own virtue and so very brutal. They were much like my former friends.

—And mine.

—And yours, she agreed.

—It was good to hear you laugh at them. We could do that again if we went to Warsaw. Wouldn't you like another trip there? I think you'd enjoy it.

But she shook her head quickly and turned her face away.

More soldiers came out of the woods as they watched the road. The sun sat on the mountains like an angry red shield. The soldiers were a long column, green in the yellow dust. Things gleamed and sparkled in the dust: sharp pinpoint lights. Bayonets. Buckles. Glinting soldier things. Boots thudded. Leather squeaked. Whatever the sound there was the beating of the boots.

—You love them, don't you. He was looking at them.

He agreed that he supposed he did.

—And you look at me like that again.

—How is that?

—With this look of eagles.

He laughed. —There again are those eagles. What is this about them?

—It is the way you look sometimes.

—What kind of eagle am I with one wing? How can I fly? The crows would eat me.

She did not laugh. She studied him as though this were the first time they had seen each other.

—Also you have the look of lions, she said reflectively.

—Lions? A lion now? What happened to the eagles?

—Also a lion. A lion which has been injured. A slightly wounded lion but one still adequate for all the lion things.

—A threadbare kind of lion. Motheaten.

—But one that knows a thing or two.

—So now I am a lion, he said. I would prefer to be an eagle. Not to be earthbound. Like my son Adam with his mountainclimbing. And now Adam has learned to fly a glider, did I tell you?

. . . Not long ago (he thought, looking at the woods across the road that had the soldiers on it) Adam played in the bushes and the bluetipped pine. He had a little saber and a toy Italian carbine that puffed smoke.

Smoke and a flash.

Small peasants were his army.

—*There, by the river, the Cossacks!*

—*Where?*

—*In the bushes by the river, little master.*

—*Extended order! Sabers out! Charge!*

They slew hordes of Cossacks and Tartars and Teutonic Knights and all the legions of Sweden and Kara Mustapha and all varieties of Turks and once in a while some Prussian grenadiers. Once in a while a stray cow was chased bellowing out of the riverside mud into the fields and there were damages to pay.

—*Did you see, Father? Did you see my charge?*

—*I saw.*

—*Was it good?*

—*It was very good. But where were your reserves? And where was the cavalry maneuver?*

—*Next time, Father. I shall remember the* zagon. *I shall have the maneuver.*

—*Sweep from the wings into the center and bring your charge home.*

—*Like you did, Father? At Kiev and on the Dnieper?*

He would laugh. —*Has Grzes been telling you more lies?* Grzes told great lies about himself and the general-his-master. How they had captured that and taken this and how many Bolsheviks they had slaughtered and what Marshal Pilsudski had to say about it.

. . . And once there were tears and blood on Adam's face; his knuckles were swollen.

But that was not that long ago. That was twelve years ago when Adam was seven. He had not come home after some war in the bushes and was found in the woods sitting in the shadow of tall pines. He was red with weeping. He was not visibly hurt.

—Who has done this?

—They said things about you. They said that you were an enemy of the marshal and therefore a traitor. They are liars and I hate them.

But they were not liars.

—Oh.

My son, do not look at me like that.

—Not liars, sir?

—No.

Do not look at me like that.

General Prus thought about his son and about his wife. He had seen neither for twelve years. More like thirteen years. That is a long time: a surprising span. You do not notice time; you think in terms of days or weeks, or at most, months, and these you can manage. But all the weeks and months become years and then you look at them and see them as a huge mass pressing down upon you and you say: What is this? Where did it come from? It wasn't there yesterday.

But thirteen years. Or two or three. They have this in common: They help change nothing. Nothing changes. Nothing. What you felt then you feel now. Nothing ever changes. You love what you loved thirteen years ago. What gave pain then still gives pain. It may be a lesser pain, but it is still there. What seared before now only bruises and that is the difference. Time was no cure for anything except youth.

He looked at Lala carefully. She watched him. Curiously and a little sadly.

He said: —Why are you sad?

—I am not sad.

—Your eyes are wet. It doesn't look like joy.

—It's a small sadness, she said. Of a personal kind.

—Tell me.

—Are you sure that you will understand? Sometimes you don't, you know. I am wondering what will happen to me now that you'll be going. Is this selfish? To think about me at this time.

—I don't know, he said. Forgive me but I wasn't thinking about you. I was thinking about them (he nodded at the soldiers) and about Adam.

She smiled. —I know. But now that you are going I must think of myself.

—You're sure that I am going, then?

—Yes. Aren't you? After all, your notice is coming, isn't it?

—Yes, he said, it is.

She smiled. —It's nice to have no doubts about anything. And now that you are going and it is finished here, I have to think about myself. At least, I think I must.

—You can come with me, if I go.

She laughed. —To Warsaw? Have you forgotten what I am to those people there? A woman who left her husband to live with a man married to another. Have you forgotten what they said? How it was then?

—That was a long time ago, he said. It may be different now.

—There could never be enough time for those people to forget. No, it won't be different.

—No one will dare to say anything, he said.

—You will not always be there. Then they will dare.

The General struck the balustrade with his one fist. The old wood snapped. —No one has a right to call you anything. You kept me alive.

She smiled and touched his shoulder. —You didn't need me to stay alive. You don't need anyone. Nothing could destroy you.

—*They* could, he said.

—They cannot touch you again. You will be the General again. And there is nothing now that I can give you. What use would I be to you in Warsaw? Can we live separated from the world in Warsaw? We can't build woods and fields and mountains there to hide in. That is now over. You will be the General again and that is their symbol and there is no more room for me.

—I will still need you. That much hasn't changed.

She laughed a little; a small laugh without joy in it. —You've always known the right thing to say.

—You will be my insurance against insanity. The war will be the hardest of our wars. It will be an unbelievably bad war. I will need reassurance that there are still bright, beautiful things in this insanity. You will be my officer in charge of reassurance.

—Be serious, she said. This is serious.

—I am serious.

—You are not. You will not be serious.

—I mean it.

—Yes, I know. But it is one thing to mean it here and another to mean it in Warsaw. Everything will be different there.

—Nothing will be different. You will be with me and no one will dare to say anything.

She was quiet a long time, watching the soldiers on the road. He thought she had not heard him or, if she had, that she agreed. But then she said that both of them would have to make new plans, separately. What they had could not prosper in Warsaw. People would not permit it. What they had in the country would stay in the country; they would not be able to take it with them.

—I'll come with you to Warsaw, she said. But afterwards we'll have to think in other terms. You do see why, don't you?

He did but he would not admit it.

—I think you make too much of those Warsaw people.

—It's not just the people, she said carefully. Although they are a part of it, of course. So much has changed already and we haven't even started to pack for Warsaw. Once we are there everything else will change.

—No, he said. It won't be like that at all.

She smiled, looking away across the field towards the soldiers. —I wish I was a man so that I could love an idea. Men die and go away. Sometimes they do not go away but it is as though they had gone because what they had is no longer there. An idea lives and can be continued. I think it would be good to have an idea to follow. To believe in. It must be a sustaining thing. It is so much better than a person, don't you think? Love depends so much on its object and objects are impermanent. Each time a man leaves her, a woman diminishes by that much, I think. Soon there is little left of her. Each man who leaves takes something away.

—Women take, too, he said. No one leaves emptyhanded.

—We only chip at a man's pride, she said. We only take away a bit of a man's self-esteem, I think. That is repairable. But a man leaves a great vacant space behind him and it is not always easy to fill it.

—A man's pride is important. He is nothing without it. When you take his pride it is the most valuable thing he has.

—Women have pride . . .

—Women find replacements.

—The more she loves a man, the more difficult it is for a woman to accept replacements.

—No pretty woman is long unattended. You know that.

—This is not what I mean, she said.

—What then?

She smiled. —Perhaps love is an idea, after all. Don't you suppose? It is so much a part of a woman's life . . . all kinds of love . . . each woman has her own interpretation of it . . . each is different . . . I think the thought of being needed is the heart of it . . . Do men love like that?

—Of course, he said. Don't you know?

—I am not sure, she said. Did you love your wife?

—I loved you.

—You use the past tense, she said.

—Oh words, he said. Words. It is not what I meant. You know what I mean. I love you, you should know.

She smiled, but not at him. She seemed to be studying something within herself, considering something, weighing past loves and the present one, adding, subtracting. She looked incredibly young and vulnerable.

—We never talked about your wife, she said. I have wondered about her. I suppose every woman wonders about her predecessors as much as about her successors. Men must too, I think. I wonder if I shall meet her in Warsaw and what I will say to her. Of course, I know what she will say to me if she says anything, but I wonder what she is like. You must have loved her once.

—Why talk about her? It is past.

—It seems suddenly important to me to know about her.

—Why now? You never wished to know about her before. It is long past.

—It seems important now. I feel—you know?—a friendship for Irena.

—We met, we married and we had a son. We lived and then she left. That is all. I do not love her and I do not hate her. She is gone, it is all past, and there is no more I can say about her. I do not understand your sudden interest in her.

—I wonder if you ever knew her, she said. I suppose you did. But then do men ever get to know their women? I think they only see themselves in their women's eyes. That is why they can leave and not be hurt, don't you think?

—I don't know, he said, feeling his regret; he hadn't wanted anything like this to happen.

He thought: I regret this moment. It is ironic: the long wait and now this sense of loss. That is because I shall be leaving this house and she is in it. We will not take with us what we had here. The message will take me from it and from her. Away from shadows and oblivion but also from her. The message will have come too late because I do not need its reassurance. I have another officer in charge of reassurance. I do not need to be told that I am not finished and used up and no longer useful, a legend living in the shadows and a part of them. I have, after all, an importance, Army or no Army. It is to her. I do not need the message.

The soldiers had now come clear of the woods. They came stolidly out of the sun and past the house. A battery of field artillery rolled after them. The horses were yellow, streaked with brown where their sweat streamed down. Then came another marching column. Boots beat out the longremembered rhythms.

Prus moved a little. —It will be hot today.

—Perhaps there will be rain? It is long past time for it.

He agreed that perhaps there would be but he didn't think so. Yellow dust billowed from the road towards them. He felt her sadness reaching out to him. This was no time for sadness: Sufficient grief was coming as inexorably as the march of centuries. Months, years of grief were on the way, marching like soldiers in formation. She must not be sad before she has to be.

The mountains stood out clear and shadowless in the hot sun, their peaks delicately blue. It was a fine day, a truly fine day of autumn: She must not be sad.

—On such a day we could do many things, he said.

She agreed that the day held out promises. —What could we do?

He thought for a moment.

—We could sail to Valparaiso in a fishing smack.

—We could, she agreed. I hoped you would want to do that.

—Or look for buried treasure in Transylvania. Or sail down the Vistula on a raft.

She thought the Vistula sounded a little tame. There was so little water in it.

—The Orinoco, then, he said.

—That's better.

Presently she remarked: —You couldn't just ignore the war and not go to it?

—No.

She sighed with what he knew she hoped would seem like contentment. —I like a man who knows his own mind.

Then a small figure showed on the edge of the woods where the road rolled from among the trees. It was a boy riding a bicycle. The bicycle was red. Prus smiled, enormously amused. There was the messenger so long awaited.

—Did you expect a boy on a red bicycle? she asked.

—No.

—What did you expect?

—The Archangel Gabriel, he said, laughing. Something like that.

—It may be Gabriel in disguise, she said.

—Wingless on a red bicycle? And what about the trumpets?

53

—Yes, I suppose there should be trumpets, she said.

Instead there came the tinkle of a bicycle bell, distant and thin. It was a soft sound; too soft, he thought, to be a call to arms. But, it occurred to him, it was one.

Sunday, August the twenty-seventh

I THE CORRESPONDENT

Loomis was tired; and it seemed pointless to stay—with the party aging so rapidly and the smiles becoming a bit strained, a little wooden, and all of it a duty. It seemed equally pointless to go to his hotel. Here, at least, Miller talked.

—Yesterday I looked in a mirror, he said. And there looking at me was an obscene old man. What do you think he said?

—Well, what.

—He said he was a prisoner in a mirror factory. He said he had been trying to break out for years. Finally he sneaked into my mirror. It didn't do him any good.

—Why not?

—He forgot the secret word for getting out of mirrors.

—The word is Sesame.

—No. That's another word. The word for getting out of mirrors is Poppyseed; the stuff that dreams are made of.

—Did you give him the word?

—I did a better thing.

—It's bad luck to break mirrors.

—Ah, but not when you're a prisoner in a mirror. It's good luck then.

—How about when you're a prisoner in a whiskey bottle?

—It's very good luck then. Care to change your luck?

—You're an obscene old man. Get back inside that mirror.

—It is a cool and lovely place, Miller said. But I broke it up.

At sixty, Miller was a relic, a kind of newspaperman now gone. The new kind could have sold insurance just as well. He had been married once, divorced (in New York State). In 1930 he flew Oak Park Nellie, a Guernsey cow, over St. Louis in an airplane and bombed the town with milk.

Now someone laughed at the bar: a hearty ho-ho-ho redolent of Christmas.

—It sounds like Goering, Miller said. The jolly rolypoly Hun. I never can quite trust the son of a bitch for all his ho-ho Merry Christmas world.

—Who, Goering?

—Goering? Who's talking about him? I mean Santa Claus. He's like your father-in-law. Their names should be Maxwelton.

—How so?

—They have a bonny bray.

—You're drunk, old man.

—A little. Only a little, though. That's the thing about this business: You can always get a drink after closing hours.

He was a great old man, Loomis thought, and wished that he could take Miller and leave the German party and go somewhere else. Germans rubbed him the wrong way. They were so damn friendly. Their children were so damn cute in their leather pants. Their little pink German faces were so clean, and their damned old Gothic architecture so romantic, and their beautiful antlike efficiency so admirable; and you never knew whose destruction they were plotting next. But Miller said there were amenities to be observed. It would not be *korrekt* to depart before the Man arrived. He was not sure which of the German Men was going to be shown to the correspondents, but you could bet your sweet ass, he said, that one of them would be. Loomis would know, Miller supposed, about German amenities. They were important. They had to be observed. Especially at this time, at this kind of party. They were important not only to the Germans, who, Loomis thought, could go to hell for all he cared, but to the others there: the people who went so joyously to parties of this kind.

Our friends?

Our friends the phonies. Miller supposed that Loomis would know about them: the famous correspondents who lived on ministry handouts, and the desperate not-so-famous-common-or-garden-variety scribblers; the whole kit and caboodle. He explained: the keepers of the flame.

—Ah-h-h-h-h, he said with a wave of an enormous hand (himself huge and glowering, so fat that he appeared hidden behind a mountain with only the eyes, the fine eyes, clear and sad, watching. He sat much as a hill does, Loomis thought, hard on a flat base and immovable.

—Friend, Miller said, my ass drags. I am tired of Europe. I feel like Moses, friend, the first man with an elastic posterior. The Bible says: *And the Lord spoke unto Moses, and Moses tied his ass to a tree and walked six miles.* I feel for Moses on this night of nights. I know how he felt.

—You wild old man, Loomis said.

—Wild about Europe, that's what. What did you come here for, anyway? They have the same kind of parties in Manhattan.

—The war, old buddy.

—Which war? Are we having one? If so I haven't been invited. Didn't we fight a war to end all wars some years back against our charming hosts?

—You know which war, Ben, Loomis said.

Coming to Berlin at this time had been his idea. The office in New York had seen no need for it. They had not been sure that anything would happen. The world had circled above reality for ten years, after all. They thought the British and the French would do it again: shuck off their obligations and back away smiling. Then Roosevelt wrote to Hitler asking for guarantees that German appetites were satisfied after Austria, the Sudetenland, Memel and the Czechs, and Hitler read the letter in the Reichstag, rattling off a long list of names of countries, planets, states and geographic equations in which Germany had no interest (all to the thunderous laughter of the deputies), and William Shirer cabled his report about the reasonable nature of Hitler's demands, and the foreign bureau chief said: —*All right. I guess the budget can stand it. But you had better come up with a war.*

Loomis left the same day. He was in Paris on Friday, August 25. Next morning he boarded the Eastern Express at the Gare du Nord and was in Berlin shortly after noon. The city burned with color. Great banners hung in the Fehrbelliner Platz and along the Kurfurstendamm. The air was thick with tension. He could almost feel it. News came that the Polish border was closed, then that it was not, then that it was, and finally Loomis drove to the Friedrichstadt to find out for himself but no one seemed to know anything. A fat young SS lieutenant, named Libesis, told him (with tears in his eyes) that the war had already begun. It was a terrible disgrace for him not to be in it. He had enlisted in the SS Waffengrenadiere because he thought that he would thus become one of the first to cross the Polish border and raise Germany's banner from the mud and plant it in the land of the enemy and now look what happened: The war was on and he was in Berlin. It was patently unfair. Loomis made sympathetic sounds. On Sunday morning, he sought out Miller in the Adlon Bar and Miller reassured him. —*No war. Not yet. Don't worry, Billy. You haven't missed anything except a lot of German parties. There's one tonight you'll have to come to anyway.*

All of official Berlin seemed to be one tense, excited party. After Paris the contrast was startling. Paris had been almost black with gloom: The City of Light seemed asleep, life slowed down. In Berlin the excitement was impossible to contain. They talked of nothing but the coming war. They still believed that Hitler would get them all they wanted without war, but no one doubted that within a week Deutschland would march. Cadence of martial music crashed from loudspeakers. *Sieg Heil! Wir zogen gegen Polen.*

—That war, Miller said. Only God and Hitler know when that one will start, and neither is talking. At the moment, friend, we're having Neville Chamberlain's Pax Britannica and everybody flies a lot of planes and talks a lot, but it's been clear since April there will be war. No one knows what kind of war it will be or when it will begin, but there is little doubt that we'll have one. Now that the Germans have Czechoslovakia, their border with Poland is seventeen hundred and fifty miles long. You will admit that this is a marvelous assault line. With all your military experience you have to admit it. The Germans will, since they so clearly can, take advantage of this opportunity. They are remarkably good at taking an advantage. They have never been known to miss an opportunity. They will attack from every possible direction. They will come, my sources inform me, south and southwest and southeast out of East Prussia, east from behind the Oder River, north and northeast from the new Czech acquisition. They will come slowly and methodically and relentlessly in their German manner and will go hell for leather for Warsaw the way they have always done. What they find so attractive about Warsaw beats the hell out of me. I never thought it much. Can't get good bourbon anywhere in Warsaw. But you know your Boche. Once he gets an idea in his square head you never get it out and they've had this one about Warsaw for nine hundred years. The Germans are, after all, traditionalists.

They haven't changed their way of thinking or doing things in a thousand years. And that gives them credit for nine hundred and thirty-nine years when all they thought about was slaughtering each other. They've never looked kindly on military innovations. They've never been known to gamble on anything. They are remorseless and persistent and they never do the unexpected.

—You're a bitter old man, Loomis said. But I love you.

—Fine. But I know what I'm talking about. Maybe I haven't seen as many wars as you but I've seen a lot more politicians and it's the politicos who make wars. And when you get a crazy politician who's also a German . . . Jesus H. Christ, hold onto your head. This is going to be a honey of a war.

The *why* of it was also known and understood, Loomis thought. The Versailles Treaty (ending the war to end wars) made sure of this one. It was absurd, of course, to blame this coming war entirely on that treaty. Germany's humiliation was not that important. The Germans had been humiliated many times before and had always recovered in their German manner. But the treaty brought about new borders. New states were formed. These were to be insured by a system new to Europe: a plan of collective security dreamed by a man who was not a European, who was an austere, idealistic President of the United States. So far so good. Then the United States became the first nation to repudiate this dream and shatter the illusion of security. With the dream gone, except in marble theory in Geneva, the British got into the act with their oldstyle frontier insurance: individual security based on alliances and balance of power. It was a fine system when there were huge powers to balance in Europe, but these were now gone. Instead there were some little nations which were not designed for the fine old system. And so you have it, Billy Loomis; another fine war. Just try to write *that* for your fine old paper.

—And I'm going to be right in the middle of it, Miller said. I'm covering the whole thing from the Adlon Bar.

Loomis laughed.

—Not me. I think I'll go to Warsaw.

—Can't get a decent drink in Warsaw.

—Can get good wars, though. First-class wars.

—The hell with it, Miller said. What do I care about a European war? (His fine, clear eyes were sad.) Let's not talk about wars.

Loomis laughed a little.

—Don't you like wars, Ben?

—No. They are immoral. Immorality gives me indigestion; I am too old to enjoy it. Wars make me wonder if I am, indeed, fashioned in God's image. I'd like to think I am; a nice, benign, fat God who likes to drink. Do we have any gods like that?

—No. We have different gods.

Miller sighed. —Yes. Well, I suppose one God's as good as another, but I miss the fat friendly gods. What do you suppose ever happened to them?

—They went on a diet.

—Well, maybe. It's sad. I suppose it's all connected with this business of getting on the head of a pin. You couldn't get many fat gods on that.

—It's the angels, Loomis said. It's angels that hang about heads of pins. Not gods.

—Those damned angels, Miller said. They fuck up everything.

Miller had bought a copy of their hometown paper. It was the usual upstate New York daily: not good but good enough. They had both worked there at one time. The paper was owned by the Otis Publishing Company, which was owned by the First National Bank of Drubal County, which was, in turn, owned by Owen Otis. This, Loomis thought, ought to make me happy. I am married to Mr. Otis' beautiful daughter. I am glad that Mr. Otis has money and that he has a daughter. It ought to make me happy.

—What does the Great Sheet say?

The headline said that the police chief would be fired. It was a black authoritative headline. Elsewhere were stories about seminary students electrocuted accidentally, a boy who had lost his dog, and a reunion story about Jewish refugees.

Miller said: —Listen: *High Tension Wires Fall, Injure Three Students,. One Is Killed.* Does it move you, friend.

—Wong's bowels move, but Wong no move.

—*Four Friars Fried* would make a wonderful headline.

—*Frivolous Writer Fired* would be the subhead.

—And how about the rest in verse? *Future friars, faithful fraters/ Found their frocks in frightful tatters/ Wires taut with highest tension/ Scorched that which I cannot mention.*

—*Let a conclave now inquire:/ Is it fair to fry a friar?*

—Oh Christ, Miller said. Christ that's wonderful.

—Let's write the papers in verse from now on, Loomis said.

—Oh my, Miller said. Wouldn't they like that? Wouldn't they just love that, our Presbyterian publishers?

—They'd love it, Loomis said.

—Wouldn't you love it?

—I'd adore it. If it was rich enough I'd marry it.

—Your father-in-law would love it. It is to be supposed the stockholders would love it. It would give tone to our sheets. It would give them culture. We're all so cultured nowadays. Wouldn't that be the thing to give the papers culture?

—Don't give it, Loomis said. Sell it. Otherwise you'll never get the publishers' approval.

—What? Even our highminded, civicminded publishers?

—Specially our publishers.

—You shatter my illusions, Miller said. I am shattered like a shattered mirror. There is nothing quite so shattered as a shattered mirror.

—Unless it is a publisher pinked in the vitals.

—Those long, leathery, pendulous vitals. What d'you suppose they use them for?

—They make purses out of them.

—Used to be a man could read these sheets and feel that there were still men here and there who stuck above the crowd, the grey herd: men with big, swinging vitals. Oh Christ, I love that word. Now there is nothing but mediocrity. A bloody great sea of it, spreading like the sad, grey monochrome of winter. The shitty miasma of mediocrity. Here, there, everywhere. Dehumanized, unfertilized and Christ so thoroughly organized. Oh my, but I remember other times. Friend, am I making sense crying in this shitty wilderness?

—You are, friend.

—You read me loud and clear?

—Loud, clear, over and out.

—No shit, friend?

—No, friend. Wong no move.

—Are we together then? Shoulder to shoulder in the wilderness? Keeping bright the dying flame? Onward and Upward? Excelsior, then. Let's march on City Hall and set the chief on fire.

—The chief is fired, friend.

—Again? Who went and did and fired my chief? The chief of all my joys and my delights? Nobody's dared to fire him since I fired him in the old, old days. Your honored pa-in-law chained me to a desk and took away my vitals. Because I was not the coming man, you know: the pusillanimous ambassador of the bright new world; the happy harbinger of tidings of gladness and joy. The dinner partner, boon companion of memowriting editors and other coming men. Member of the sergeants' mess, as it were. Some such sweet journalist is now the happy harvester in my garden. Long live ubiquitous mediocrity. Ah, me, it's time I died.

—Hang on awhile longer.

—Ah me, but I remember other times.

—Like Oak Park Nellie?

—There was a female for you. A little bovine, true: somewhat bucolic. Not brilliant, indeed, but what a character. A soul to warm a man and comfort him. What dainty little hooves, what melting eyes. Ah, and that tail; what feminine swishing was there in that plane. That was a story. I have many stories. I have a marvelous memory: like an old rewrite desk full of old tear-sheets, broken pencil stubs, lonely galoshes with holes in them and all that friendly, useless junk. Perhaps you'd like to hear another story?

—No mirror stories. No Maxwelton stories, Loomis said, laughing.

—Don't blame me for Maxwelton. George Washington's to blame. He was the father of the Great Mule: the American Jackass.

—He was the Father of Our Country, Loomis said, laughing.

—In 1785 the King of Spain sent George two full-blooded Andalusian mules. This was a mark of esteem, I suppose. Until that year jackasses were restricted to the court of Spain and we came mighty close to getting none. In 1776, you see, on July twenty-seventh, a Private Tom Hickey got himself strung up in Brooklyn for trying to shoot George. He missed and won, instead, the honor of becoming the first American soldier executed by the Army. Think of the possibilities if he had not missed.

—No jackasses here today?

—None.

—I don't know, Loomis said. They'd find some way in.

The party went on, interminable. He supposed that you could call it a success, as you could call the newspaper men and women there successful. But that, he thought, would be debatable. It was a matter of semantics. It was a matter of your point of view.

The war was coming: He was sure of it. He could read it in the shining eyes of the Germans. He could hear it in the click of their heels. Everyone talked too much and drank too much and said the witty, the expected things and the orchestra played Lehar and the *Blue Danube Waltz* and no one said anything about the coming war.

Later Miller drove Loomis to the train. The train was delayed two hours as, again, there was uncertainty about the Polish border.

Was it closed? Was it open? No one seemed to know.

—You ought to take it as an omen and stay here, Miller said. This is where the story is going to be.

—The press handout, the communiqué, Loomis said. You write your war your way and I'll write it mine.

Miller shrugged, sighed. —One thing, Billy. Don't become involved. Remember, there's two sides to a war. Righteousness is not necessarily confined to one uniform. No rule says that the good guys are all on one side and the bad guys on the other.

—I'll remember.

There is so much to remember. Shirts, socks and memories neatly stacked. All clean and starched and ready to put on. All ready to face new days in. I'll remember.

—Well, there's your train. Take care.

—And you too take care.

—Oh, I'll take care, all right. But you take special care. For Chrissake don't become involved. It's just a war.

—I won't. I don't get involved anymore.

—All right. I'll see you in Warsaw.

—You?

—Oh, I'll get there.

—With the Germans?

—Why walk when you can ride? Sure, with the Germans.

—Have a good war with your Germans.

—And you with your Poles. Tell them not to drop bombs on the Adlon Bar.

Then the train moved and clanked and gathered speed and steamed out of Berlin and headed east towards the Polish border. It was full of Germans. They were in uniform, mostly officers. Most of them were young. They were terribly excited and talked too much and laughed loudly and smoked many cigarettes. They were clean and roundcheeked and smelled of leather and cologne. They had no doubts about the coming war.

One of them looked into Loomis' compartment as he pushed by several others in the corridor and he smiled and came in and introduced himself. It was the fat SS lieutenant who had wept when he thought that he had missed the war. —My name is Libesis, he said. We met in Berlin. Do you remember?

Loomis said he did.

—It seems that there was no war after all. It had not yet started.

—But now it will?

—Of course. It is impossible to prevent it now. We shall be fighting within days, perhaps hours. It is a magnificent feeling, I can tell you.

In his behalf you could say that the lieutenant was not a typical SS officer, Loomis thought. He was articulate and he had probably gone to college and he still had a certain collegiate charm. He was probably an idealist. Loomis wondered how long his ideals would last.

—Congratulations, Loomis said.

The German took him seriously. —Thank you, he said. Thank you very much. Are you going to the front?

—I am going to Warsaw, Loomis said.

The German looked surprised. —Well, he said. Well. Perhaps we will meet there. I too am going to Warsaw but (he laughed) not by train.

—Why walk when you can ride, Loomis said.

He wondered what the German would do if he spat in his eye. He wished he were a Spaniard or a Pole so that he could spit in the fat young German's eye. A Pole or a Spaniard can do such things. An American cannot.

—Why not? the German was delighted. Why not indeed? This is the twentieth century, after all.

Loomis laughed. To spit in someone's eye is to express an opinion. It is to take sides and to become involved. I will not be involved. Not this time. Besides, spitting is a dirty habit; you can get fined for spitting in a train.

—The Führer said that the first day of this war will be the first day of the twentieth century, the German said. We are the standard-bearers of the twentieth century.

—Congratulations, Loomis said.

—Thank you, the German said. It is a marvelous feeling, I assure you. We will bring the twentieth century to the world. It is a great responsibility. We will destroy the nineteenth century once and forever. This war will be the last great struggle between the nineteenth century and the twentieth. This is our great gift to the world. The world will never forget it.

—I am sure, Loomis said.

—These are proud days for Germans. We bring the future. We destroy the past. The outcome of this war is as inevitable as the victory of the future over the past. I know it. I feel it. I have been told it and I believe it. Do you believe it?

—I am an American, Loomis said. Americans never believe anything.

—As an American, you are of the future. You are with us. You will see what we do and you will believe. No one can stand astride the path of progress. No one can defy the inevitable. And we are as inevitable as the twentieth century.

—Yes, Loomis said. You are the standard-bearers.

Loomis closed his eyes. He found that he was trembling. Outside, in the corridor, someone began to sing.

—*Treue, treue, auf dem Tod*. Faithful unto death.

The train ran through the evening to the east. High clouds of dust obscured the roads beside the railroad tracks and trucks and guns and tanks moved like great iron beetles to the Polish border.

The newspaper which Loomis was reading said that there would be no war. Dahlerus had flown to England again with Hitler's new proposals. Hitler was anxious to keep the British out of the coming war. The British leaped at every opportunity to talk. They had tried all summer to talk Hitler out of beginning the war and they were still at it. One headline said: SWEDISH INTERMEDIARY FLIES TO LONDON WITH NEW GERMAN PROPOSALS. Another said: RIBBENTROP, REDS DRAFT SECRET TREATY? Another said: GERMAN HONOR GUARD GREETS BRITISH ENVOY IN BERLIN. Another reported the cancellation of yet another mobilization of Polish armies. It was an English paper. It said unkind things about Poles, who, by mobilizing, were provoking the Germans.

Night came and robbed the world of substance and filled it with shadow. The express rolled across the flat, moonlit plain of eastern Germany, where motors hummed and blue flames of gasoline exhausts flickered beside the darkened roads and men came aboard at stops and these men had no doubts about the coming war. Shortly before dawn the German lieutenant left the train, and eventually all the Germans left it, and when the train rolled into Poland in the morning it was almost empty.

Monday, August the twenty-eighth

I THE SOLDIERS

The old woman was weeping as she crossed the road towards the convent wall, and Antos, who was the youngest and most curious and the most aware, said: —What is she weeping for?

—I don't know, Surma said. Maybe she's just old.

—Maybe she's weeping for us, Stas Guz said. He laughed and Antos also laughed and Surma spat into the dust.

They were sitting on the ground with their backs against the convent wall, their legs outspread and their collars open. Their hands picked at things and scratched at things or just lay on the ground beside them. The sun was three hours old. It warmed the convent wall and them. They waited to be fed.

They had come there in the night when the white August moon painted the town silver. It was a little town. Their horses were down by the river. Their carbines were stacked in the churchyard across the road. They were hungry and young and looked forward to eating and to seeing new things and looked in awe, now and then, at their new leather boots.

Wasn't it time to eat? Yes it was. Antos felt the hunger that came faithfully each morning. He felt good. Hungry, true, but also good. This was a fine day coming and it was fine to be a soldier and to have new leather boots and to have spurs on the boots like a lord.

He felt so good about it that he laughed.

—What are you neighing for? Surma said.

—I feel good.

—You want to feel something good feel this, Surma said.

Guz laughed and Antos also laughed. He didn't feel good about Surma or the way he said things. There were things about Surma that made him itch.

Surma said things that made him want to scratch and clear his nose and button up his coat and go away. Surma made him want to wish he weren't there. But it was time for laughing: He was young and the morning looked good.

He gave Surma one quick sliding glance but Surma was not laughing. Surma never seemed to have much to laugh about. He had deserted from the regiment in Trembowla soon after they were drafted into it, and had gone back to the village, which was not the village of Antos but a larger, richer, newer village, almost a town, and he had been found there by the fieldpolice and had been brought back and Antos thought, as everybody thought, that Surma would be shot. Weren't deserters always shot? He had heard something about that.

But they were not shooting deserters that summer. There had been a number of desertions with the harvest season hard upon them and no one in the villages to take care of it except the old men and the women and the girls, and the young men said, —*Well, nothing's happening, is there? The German hasn't come. When he does we will give it to him. Right? We'll give him a good one. But until he comes what's the use of being away from the village? Who's going to take care of the harvest and the girls? Somebody's got to.* So there were desertions.

Then there was this MO-BI-LI-ZA-TION. This was a fine word. It was a new one Antos had learned since he joined the Army. It was the word that put him in the Army. Well, they kept changing things around. One day they had this MOBILIZATION and men came into the regiment with their bundles and grins and with their village food, and then the next day it was all off and the officers were swearing, and then in a day or two it was all on again. This was another reason why there were desertions. —*Well now, look,* the young men said. *If they don't know if they want us or not, well, they can't need us much, can they? So let's go home till they make up their minds.*

Antos thought that Surma would be shot. Pan Szef—that terrible man with the mustache and the red face and scars and the silver chevrons of God—said that deserters were always shot. *Trach, trach* against a wall. They all expected Surma to be shot and this made him a hero. All of a sudden everybody was the best friend Surma ever had. Everybody knew him. They all expected the shooting. Hadn't Pan Szef said it? But Surma was not shot. He got out of it. Surma always got out of everything. Perhaps it was because he came from a bigger village, almost a town, and knew about things. Antos wished he knew how Surma did it. He gave Surma another quick glance but the soldier's face was closed. It didn't say how Surma did anything.

Surma got out of being shot and came back to the squadron and now he and Antos and Stas Guz and the whole squadron (and the whole regiment, by God!) had come to this small town where there was a railway track, and they sat down to wait for the train. They didn't know where the train would take them. What mattered was the thought of the train itself, not where it would take them. Antos had never ridden in a train.

A train.

He grinned.

Poof, poof, poof. Woooo-wie! We-are-go-ing-we-are-go-ing, woooooooo!

—Listen you, Stas, he said. How is it in a train?

—Ha ha, Surma laughed. The shitnose don't know about trains.

—Ha ha, Stas Guz laughed. He didn't know about trains either.

—Why, you shitnoses, Surma said. What do you know? Do you know about anything? You don't know about trains and you don't know about shit. Though maybe you do. Shit is all you know about. He laughed. *Gowno,* he said. That's what you know. Do you know about this?

He slapped himself on the thigh. The others laughed. Antos thought, Well, yes, that's true. I don't know about it. Stas don't know either, I bet. But it don't do to say so. No. Never. Surma would laugh again. The thought of Surma laughing made him want to scratch. Surma didn't laugh much, but when he did, God, it made you itch all over. Surma now . . . Surma knew about everything. He had lived in a town for about a year. You get to know about things when you live in a town. You wear shoes all week in a town, not just on Sundays. It don't do to tell Surma you don't know about It. Or anything. No.

—Oh, he said. That. Everybody knows about that.

—And everybody knows about trains, eh? Surma said. And what about motorcars? You ever ride in a motorcar? All you know about It is what your hands told you.

Which was true. And because it was true and he wasn't much good with words anyway and because he was afraid of making Surma angry and afraid of making Surma laugh and ashamed of admitting that it was true about the hands and because he didn't want Stas Guz to think he didn't know about It (although he was pretty sure Stas didn't know about It) he grinned and looked away and scratched himself.

Well now. What do I know about It?

A little but not much.

He and Kazio (the priest's boy) and the fat boy from the tavern used to go to the river on Saturday mornings. They would go down real quiet in the rushes and sit in the water with only their heads sticking out (but covered in the rushes) and they would wait for the girls to come and wash themselves. The girls came down on Saturday mornings to the river and then you saw things. Not much, true, but something. There were always young men in the rushes and the girls knew this, although they pretended that they didn't know. They would laugh and giggle. God, they would laugh and giggle, and their funny high giggles made his hair stand on end, and his eyes bugged as he looked for them in their rushes across the river, and there were white things and pink things and shining wet things in those rushes, and there was all that giggling.

Girls, Holy Father; they did an awful lot of giggling.

And then after a while the rushes would open and one or two of them would come out swimming in the river, and some of this white would show where the water was clear, and the other girls would call out to the swimmers, —*Hey, Marys, take care the Water King don't get you,* and giggle some more.

All that giggling.

His hair would stand on end and he would blink fast trying to see the white in the clear water, and Kazio made strangled sounds in his throat and the fat boy made funny breathing sounds, and he supposed that he too was making sounds as they watched the girls swimming in the river. And once in a while one of the swimmers would stand up in the water (but always facing where the other girls were) and there would be a quick white back displayed with that sharp incurve where it went in at the sides that made him choke and swallow water and all the other girls would hoot and giggle.

But about It . . .

Well, all right. He didn't know.

He supposed that there was a lot he didn't know about; like It and trains and motorcars and what a telephone was for. He knew about telephones as something you talked into. He had asked about the wires on the telephone poles. But what a telephone looked like or what you said into it or why you would want to say anything into it he didn't know. He wondered what he would do if he ever had to talk into one of them. He wondered what it would be like, and what it would be like in the train and what it would be like to do It. He scratched himself and moved his booted foot in the dust so that the spur made marks there. The spur dug little furrows in the dust. He made several such furrows. He moved his back up and down the convent wall to scratch it. He felt hungry. He felt warm. He felt good.

Soldier.

He was a soldier now.

And soldiers got to know about everything sooner or later. Even the girls looked at him once or twice and giggled when they saw him the first time as a soldier. The Wolnys' Marysia gave him a good hard look. That look made him want to do something. It made him feel like he was sitting in the rushes. Yes. Phew! It looked like a hot day coming.

Well now.

He was a soldier now.

And he was hungry.

And he felt good.

And then the old woman came out of the churchyard, weeping, and he gave her a slow look, the way you look at old people, not caring much because old people are no longer any good for anything, and he asked what she was weeping for, not really caring, and Surma spat into the dust.

They sat in the dust waiting to get fed, waiting for the train to come, and they looked at things like the old woman, and the smoke of the fieldkitchens in the orchards, and ants and bugs, and the officers striding here and there and laughing in clear young voices, and once Pan Szef went by (on his bent legs that Surma said were straightened on a barrel) and gave them a hard look that made them stop moving and scratching and damn near breathing too, and they heard a bell ringing behind the wall in the convent.

—Dingding ding, Guz said, like the bell.

That Stas. He could make any kind of sound.

The word was IM-I-TATE. It was a new one he had learned since he became a soldier.

—Imitate the older men, the lieutenant had said. *If you don't know what to do, do what the older men do. Maybe that isn't much of a training program but it's the best we can do. Maybe you'll learn something that way. I don't know. Maybe it'll do you some good. Watch them and do what they do.*

Stas Guz could imitate anything. He could even walk on bent legs and

65

look like Pan Szef although that was a fearful thing to do. Now Stas imitated the convent bell. Antos laughed.

—Imitate the train, he said.

—Woooo-woooo, Stas Guz said.

Antos laughed.

—You stupid shits, Surma said. You apeheads. You goats' assholes. What are you neighing for, Antek-the-Stupid?

Surma spat into the dust. Surma did a lot of spitting. Antos supposed that Surma was the best spitter in the squadron; best in the whole regiment, by God. He could hit a fly two meters away. He was a good spitter and he knew about things. He had a hard, used look. Antos got a hard, used look to come up on his round, unused, nevershaven face. He spat in the dust and looked sideways at Surma. Surma didn't say anything. He had unbuttoned his jacket all the way down and pushed his shirt open and his white, meaty chest hung out like a girl's. At least, Antos thought, the way I *think* those things hang out. He would find out about that now that he was a soldier. He would find out about a lot of things.

Antos got up and stretched. He dusted off the seat of his breeches where the leather patch was sewn, rubbed his long new boots against the upper portion of his trousered legs to get the dust off them, and looked down behind him at his spurs and wiped them off with a rag he took from inside his shirt. He pulled the short, tight cavalry jacket down on his rump, and straightened the jacket a little and buttoned his collar, and felt the cavalry braid bite into his neck. He walked across the road into the churchyard.

There were many soldiers in the churchyard. There were, he informed himself, four squadrons of lancers and the machinegun squadron, and that made it six hundred soldiers of the cavalry. That was a lot! He had never seen six hundred of anything before. Well, it would take a lot to beat the German. His father had been in the Tsar's army in the other war. He had a helmet with a spike on it hanging in the house. The German, Antos' father said, was a natural soldier. You could tell him to do something and he would do it. You could tell him anything. That was because the German was stupid. You could make a fool out of him without any trouble. It was like the legends about Old Nick the devil. Old Nick was always out to get your soul. He got you to sign things called a *cyrograf* with blood. Once you signed in blood he figured he had you. But you always got around Old Nick in the legends and you could always make a fool out of the German. Still, for all that, Antos' father said, the German was a good soldier. Antos was glad there were so many soldiers in the churchyard. It would take at least *that* many to kill all the Germans.

The soldiers kept away from the graves in the churchyard. This was good. Graves were for dead people. You didn't want to fool around with *them*. They would come out and haunt you like the *legionista* in the song.

The soldiers kept away from the graves but sat and lay around them, and walked among them, and their shiny carbines were gathered in little stacks neatly in a row along the churchyard path. Their saddlebags and packs and sabers and bayonets and lances and steel helmets and caps with silver eagles on the front and messtins and canteens and overcoats and blankets and saddles and saddleblankets and straps and bridles and chains and stirrupstraps and thongs and grenadebags and gasmasks and rationbags and waterbags and gloves and polishingrags and brushes and knives and forks and spoons and belts and saberbelts and cartridgebelts and the sweet-sour smell of them, that was like a thatched roof thick with dew drying in the sun in the morning or like bread when it is fresh, lay all around them.

Shining things all around.

Antos never knew that there was so much of anything anywhere. He could not get over this. This was more than he thought he would ever see all in one place at one time. And he had all of it.

He had one or a pair of everything like the other soldiers. Boots, spurs, gloves, a saber, overcoat and the other things.

And he had a horse.

It was *his* horse.

It was big and brown and not at all like the small horses in the village. God, if he could only ride into the village on this horse.

He called the horse Zloto, which means gold. The horse had some other name in the squadron list of horses but Antos called it Zloto. He spent hours cleaning it and combing it and touching it and stroking it. It was *his* horse. Now he wondered about Zloto and if the horsehandlers had given him enough to drink.

Zloto was down by the river with the other horses. They were being watered. Antos thought he had better go down there and see that Zloto got his share of the river. It wasn't much of a river and there were many horses in it.

He went around the graves to where his gear was stacked and got a cube of sugar from the pack and licked it a little and would have liked to eat it but he put it in his shirt for Zloto. This was the first piece of sugar he had ever had. He got it for Zloto. Pan Szef had given him the sugarcube. That had surprised him so much that he forgot the thanks. It was as though God had spoken to him. Antos had washed and combed and cleaned Zloto as soon as he dismounted in the little town. No other soldier had yet begun to clean a horse when Antos was finished. Pan Szef went by and looked at Antos and at Zloto and Antos became nervous, the way he always did when Pan Szef was anywhere around, and Pan Szef put his hand in his pocket, which was not sewnup like Antos' pockets, and he took out this piece of sugar and gave it to Antos. Also, he nodded. Antos didn't know what to do. He didn't know what to say. It was as though God had smiled at him. So he said and did nothing. Then Pan Szef started shouting at the other soldiers. He called them sons of whores and footsoldiers, which, Antos had been told, was a terrible thing to be called in the cavalry, and Antos forgot the cube of sugar. Now he remembered it and got it for Zloto.

He went around the stacks of carbines, the ammunition and machinegun carts, to get to the river, and as he passed the stack that had his carbine in it he stopped to look at it. It awed him and mystified him. He had never fired it. It was a beautiful thing, this carbine. And it was his. Like Zloto. There was dust on it. He brushed the dust off with a rag he took out of his shirt. At once more dust came to settle on the carbine. Antos sat down on the ground beside the stack of carbines and brushed off the dust. As he was getting up to go to the river with the sugarcube the whistle blew.

Pan Szef came down the path between the graves blowing his whistle. Beside him and a little to the rear of him walked the Pan Porucznik. Pan Porucznik was a tall young man with a brown face and little stars on his shoulderstraps. He smoked a cigarette in a small yellow tube. He knew a lot of words. He had taught Antos this new word, this IM-I-TATE. There was also a Pan Kapitan in the squadron but Antos had never seen him. Pan Kapitan was an officer of the reserve and had not yet joined the squadron. It was all the fault of the MO-BI-LI-ZA-TION; it was off again. Antos worried that perhaps the Pan Kapitan would not join the squadron and then he would never get to see him. This was a famous Pan Kapitan. He was a famous hunter and had been in many wars and everybody knew him. You could be safe in a war with an officer like that. You could do great things. Without the Pan Kapitan, Pan Porucznik was the chief of the squadron and Pan Szef was (Antos was willing to believe) the chief of the whole Army.

Antos joined the ranks forming among the graves. Stas Guz stood on one side of him, Surma on the other. The sweet-sour smell of soldiers was around them. They were put into the position of attention, then they were turned and marched *raz, dwa, raz, dwa* with spurs jingling to the orchard where the fieldkitchens were waiting.

The fieldkitchen had a wonderful new smell. There was also a smell of horses there, and of soup. Antos got soup and a piece of hardtack and sat down to eat it. The soup had meat in it, and *slonina,* and barley and potatoes and an onion. Pan Porucznik made a face when he tasted it. Antos wondered about that a little. But there was no time to wonder much about anything. He was too busy eating soup. It was the best soup he had ever tasted and he got some every day now that he was a soldier.

Back home . . . well, it was different there. You didn't get much meat in your soup back home. Home was a small village in Polesie, a country of woods and wet fields and little streams and thatched roofs where autumn blazed red and yellow along the riverbanks. It was a place of colors and small sounds made by animals; and of smells. There were many smells; each of them good in its way. There were the fields and the wet grass and they had a fine smell. There was the hay in the barns and that had a special smell of its own. There was the smell of the thick black earth, and of the water, and of the old trees in the woods and the rushes by the river. There was the smell of horses and cows and chickens. All this was home. It was his father up before dawn and bedded down long after the sun went down. It was his mother and his sisters and their cooking smells. It was the smell of cabbages and potatoes and acorns and the green smell of open cooking fires.

His mother making soup.

Not much meat there; mostly cabbage. Sometimes potatoes and often a mash made of corn, but mostly cabbage. Cabbages were plentiful and cheap. Potatoes could be sold for more than you could sell the cabbage. As for meat, well, what meat was there? Cows, pigs and chickens. Who would kill one of those just to eat? How could there be eggs to sell and milk to sell and shoat to sell if you killed them? So you didn't kill them. You got them to eat when they died but you didn't kill them.

And there were other things you didn't kill at home. You didn't kill spiders because they brought luck. You didn't kill the mice because they were the horses of the little people and the little people kept your home from harm. You were especially good to the storks because they brought prosperity. You got cartwheels and you nailed them flat on top of poles and stuck them in your yard so the storks could come and make their nests there. You were good to swallows because to have them in your roof was a sign of goodness. Everyone knew that swallows stayed away from the roof of an evil man. You never found a swallow in the roof of a Jew, did you? No. Well now.

But then you didn't have a Jew in such a little village. The bigger villages, especially the Ukrainian villages, would often have one. He would buy up the eggs and milk and shoat and potatoes and even the cabbage. He would buy up the cloth the women weaved. He would sell beads and metal pans and rosaries. If you worked hard for him for a day or two you could buy some vodka. In Antos' village they didn't have a Jew and had in fact (he remembered) once held a *gmina* meeting to look into it. Having a Jew was . . . well, there was a lot to be said for it. There were the beads and pans and rosaries, to begin with. The Jew could write letters. All the boys in the village could read and write, and some of the younger men and women, but few of the old people knew about letters. The Jew could do their letterwriting for them. And there was more he could do. Perhaps he could open an inn.

An inn turned a small village into a market place as everybody knew. There was a lot to be said for getting a Jew. But there were other things that made the getting of a Jew not quite so good. It was well known that swallows kept away from a village that had a Jew in it. The swallows were the messengers of the Holy Mother. Antos' village had been fortunate for many years. The crops were good enough and there had been no floods, droughts or any other visitations. The village was clearly protected by the Holy Mother. How would she like it if the people got her Son's murderer to live among them? The old men of the village didn't think She would. So Antos never did find out about Jews or how you went about getting one (thinking for many years that there was a place somewhere, like a store, and that you could go there and get yourself a Jew) or what they looked like, until he left the village and became a soldier, and had his photograph taken with Stas Guz and Jozio Prosty and Stas Sztych from the machinegun squadron by a photographer in Trembowla. This photographer was a Jew: a small, pale man in a black robe and white socks and cracked shoes and sidelocks who made him laugh. He didn't look as though he could have murdered anyone but that was the thing about a Jew: He could make himself look anyway he wanted.

Well. But this was not a time to think about such things. This was a good morning. The sun was up, warm, and the soup was hot, and the hardtack was soft and smelling of white flour (once he had soaked it a little in the soup) and he felt good; he felt really good, and he was glad he was a soldier.

Home in the village they were used to soldiers. Each year some young man would go off for his year as a soldier. And he would come back to the village in the Soldier Year, and he would walk about, and nod to the not-as-lucky youths without saying anything, and he would talk with the older men like an equal and sit with them in the evening *before* the sun went down. Everyone else would still be working in the fields but *he* would not. He would be talking to the old men like an equal.

All these young soldiers looked older with their heads shorn bald and in their uniforms. Antos wondered if he too looked older. He thought he was about seventeen years old, although he wasn't sure. He thought he probably looked old now that he was a soldier. He wished that he were back home with his uniform and his horse and saber. They were used to uniforms there, true, but not his uniform. His was a *cavalry* uniform and he had a saber. They had seen him in the uniform but without the saber. They had not seen that, and they had not seen him on Zloto with his spurs and saber. He was the only man in the village to be taken into the cavalry. Antos wished he were home in the village, riding down the short village street on Zloto, in his boots, with his spurs and saber.

One time, that time in Trembowla, Stas Guz, who was the orderly for the Pan Porucznik and polished the Pan Porucznik's leather boots and his silvery saber, borrowed these boots and the officer's saber with the little white and silver saberknots and a pair of Pan Porucznik's parade trousers with the broad stripe down the sides, and they had smuggled all that into Trembowla, where the Jew took their photograph. He took one photograph of all of them (Antos standing between Stas Guz and Stas Sztych, and Jozio Prosty on a chair with the saber and the saberknots) and then he took a picture of each of them alone so that each could wear the officer's soft boots, and the trousers with the stripe, and hold the officer's saber. Antos sent this picture home: himself alone, in the soft boots and striped breeches, leaning on the saber.

He thought maybe his mother would show the picture around among the other women. He thought she would. His mother was like that. She would show off the picture to the other women. And maybe the Wolnys' Marysia would get to see the picture. Yes. She would see it. Himself in striped breeches and with saberknots.

Antos wished that he were home now by the river. Ha. But he wouldn't hide in any rushes anymore. Ha! He was a soldier now. He would reach right down in there, in the rushes, and say, Well, what is this, and he would pull Marysia out of there and . . .

. . . And what?

Well, anyway . . .

He ate a bit of hardtack and ran his finger inside the messtin to get out all the soup. He went down to the river where the horses were, and found Zloto and gave him the sugarcube and patted his neck.

The horse gave him a soft, warm look and neighed a little.

So. You are glad to see me? *Ej tam,* golden one. Take the sugar. Good? I will have more someday.

The horse sniffed the palm of the soldier's hand and nuzzled his shoulder. Antos put his face against the warm, brown neck and rubbed his face against it. He could feel the living warmth of the animal. Heh, Zloto. You and I. You and I. We will show them, eh?

Then other soldiers came down to the river and took the horses from the horsehandlers and led them back to the churchyard. Windows and doorways in the houses near the churchyard filled with heads and people. This was more of a village than a town, but it was a big, rich market village with an inn. It was bigger than any that Antos had seen. That is why he thought of it as Town. The houses were of stone and brick. Some were of wood, but not many. They were roofed with slate, not straw and boards. There was a clean smell in this village, and the people were clean, and the old men and women and the giggling girls walked about the long village street and gave bread and fruit and cheese and buttermilk to the soldiers. Antos wished he could say something to one of these girls. But he felt ashamed. He didn't know why he was ashamed except that he couldn't help looking at the front of their shirts where they stuck out. Things bounced about in there as the girls walked. Antos began to feel hot and uncomfortable and started to comb Zloto's mane and tail. This didn't help. The tail and the mane made him think of the hair of the girls. The girls wore their hair in long plaits like dark and golden ribbons. Antos found that he was plaiting Zloto's tail. He became angry. He combed out the tail and led Zloto to the churchyard where the other soldiers were saddling their horses. He saddled Zloto and strapped his equipment to the pommels of the saddle, and pushed the saber and the carbine into their proper places under the saddle, and leaned on his lance (hearing the soft flapping of the red-and-white pennon in the breeze), and then he heard the whistle of the train.

Zloto neighed softly and turned his head to look at Antos.

—It is the train, Antos said.

—Wooo-wooo, Stas Guz said and Zloto stared at him.

Antos laughed.

Stas Guz laughed.

Surma said —*Gowno,* and spat onto the ground.

Pan Szef blew his whistle.

The soldiers backed their horses into ranks. They pushed the horses carefully around the graves and the little crosses. Still, some of the horses trod on graves and the soldiers cursed.

The village people started waving at the soldiers. They also stared at the train. For all of its size, the village was a village and not a town and trains never stopped there. This one was stopping there. It was something to see.

The train whistle came again, loud this time. Antos shivered.

Stas Guz no longer imitated the whistle of the train.

—Attention, said Pan Szef.

Pan Porucznik said something to Pan Szef and Pan Szef saluted. Pan Porucznik walked off to where a small group of officers were standing. The officers were quiet. The younger ones were smiling. The older officers looked like Pan Porucznik when he ate the soup.

Antos felt that he too was smiling. He wondered why the older officers did not smile to hear a train coming. Some of them looked worried about something. He wondered what they could be worrying about. What was big enough to worry an officer when even Pan Szef had to click his heels when they went by? But it didn't do to worry about officers. Hey lancer! You worry about your horse and your gear. That's what you have to care about. You worry about that, not why officers aren't smiling.

—Platoons in a column of twos from the right, said Pan Szef. From the right: forward, march!

Antos led Zloto. He held tight to the bridle near the horse's head. He felt the beating of his heart and of his horse's heart. Stas Guz led his horse beside them. Surma led his horse behind them. Stones rattled underfoot and spurs jingled. Small chains jingled. They walked to where the train was waiting. The train was long. Antos could not see the beginning of the train. Its head was hidden around the orchard. Antos led Zloto up some planks into a wooden car. The car was as big as a house. It was dark. Stas Guz and Surma led their horses in. Then five more horses were led in. They were officers' horses. The horses of the officers did not know the lancers' horses. They snorted and looked at each other. They smelled each other and moved around a little. They were ill at ease. The car smelled of potatoes and of canvas. The soldiers brought straw for themselves and hay for the horses. The hay smelled of woods and fields and streams and rushes in the sun. Surma threw his overcoat on the hay meant for the horses. Antos pulled some of this hay away to save for Zloto. Horses did not like to eat hay on which a man had slept. Antos spread his overcoat on straw. He sat down. His heart was beating. He looked at the horses. The horses looked at him: dark in the dark of the car with their green eyes gleaming. A warmth and a hot smell came from the horses and the hay.

Soon now they would be going. In a train.

Well now. A train. Antos Mocny in a train.

Where? It didn't matter.

He wished his father could see him. He wished Marysia could see him. He wished the world could see Antos Mocny in a train.

Then the train moved a little.

Then it shuddered.

There was a loud noise like anvils and hammers and heavy things falling. Like thunder in summer. Like thunderbolts in the woods by the river.

The train shook. Then moved again.

Then it moved faster.

And kept on moving, and moved faster, and the village slid slowly, lazily past the open doors of the cattle car, and then the orchard slid by and the girls and the old people waving in the orchard, then the river where the horses had been watered and the churchyard and the churchsteeple flicked by and vanished and then the train was past the village and it was in open fields and then the train was flying.

Flat fields roll by.

Woods, villages roll by.

The train passes everything. It goes by everything. Everything falls behind the train and is as though it had never been. The train passes countries and continents and worlds. It ticks off worlds with the measured flicker of telephone poles.

Antos watched the world through the open doors of the cattle car.

Click, click clicketyclick.

Ra-tA-ra-tA on bridges.

The world slips by and falls behind and the train goes on.

We-are-go-ing-we-are-go-ing-we-are-go-ing!

A long ride.

Somewhere in the swaying length of the boxcars a song begins and is picked up from one car to another and is passed on to the next and then another song is begun at the head of the train before the first song dies in the last of the swaying cars and that new song travels the length of the train and another follows.

O moj rozmarynie rozwijaj sie . . .
Bloom little flower on my soldier's grave . . .
Bloom
On the grave
Of my soldier.

It is a sad song but all these songs are sad, these songs of peasant soldiers.

The sun climbed and stayed motionless for a little while, then dipped to the west. The train headed into the sun. The sun retreated as the train came on. Shadows grew longer in the fields, grew deeper. The train went on. And on. And eventually it stopped.

This is a stop to feed the men and horses, to water the horses and to count the men who wake with sleepy faces and crumpled faces and smeared faces without form or definition and push things into place and tidy things and hide the worn strap or the dingy buckle from the eye of the inspecting officer who is counting them.

—What is this, lancer? Whose saber is that? These reins are too short . . . this mane is two centimeters too long . . . waterbuckets dirty . . . these nostrils have dust in them . . . this one is inflamed . . . what the hell is that? In the name of the Living Christ will you tell me? Is that the tail of a lancer's horse or the tail of a cow? This buckle is rusty . . . grease this saddle . . . saddlesoap this strap and soften it . . . blankets are to be spread and hung, not folded! There's rust on this saber! Get those burrs off that mane!

The lieutenant sees an overcoat spread on hay. He is about to say something about it, to chastize, but checks himself. This is a young lieutenant. He sees himself as a Leader Beloved by His People: stern, manly, just and soldierly but also kind. That is how he sees himself. He sees his soldiers as his children who must be patiently guided. He feels that he has shouted enough. He looks away from the overcoat on the hay. But, he says to himself, they know I saw it. He sees a lancer hook his foot under the offending overcoat and kick it into the straw where it belongs. The lieutenant smiles: They understand, these children. The lieutenant is twenty-four years old and he has much to learn. He leaves the cattle car. He smiles. He has been stern but kindly.

There are the three soldiers in this cattle car, and two of them look at each other and grin and scratch, and one procedes to imitate the lieutenant and the other, the very young one, giggles nervously. The third soldier, who is older and whose face is used and crumpled and defined, spits hugely at a fly, which escapes through the open doors. The fly wings westward toward wondrous smells and settles on the rim of an iron kettle splashed with moisture and falls in and eventually drowns. The three soldiers congregate around the kettle and receive their meal and soup and hardtack and wander off to eat it. There is a colony of faces around the three lancers: soldier faces which are sleepy, the anxious faces of the officers, and the hopeful faces of civilian men and women looking at the train. Some of these turn to the lancers and ask politely, rather anxiously, if this is a strictly military train or if, for a small consideration, he or she (the civilian) might be allowed to board.

Because they have a need to board this train.

So many trains these days are reserved for soldiers.

The lancers eat and wander back to their cattle car and there the lancer who imitated the lieutenant says: —Listen. We will have a passenger.

—What?

—We have room for one, don't we?

—But it is forbidden.

This soldier, the one who says that it is forbidden, is so young and tall. His face is round and smiling and unworn. He listens to his friend talk about some passenger. He does not quite understand. He does not wish to seem uncooperative. A great deal has happened to him all at once and he can't quite keep up with all of it.

—There is a girl up there on the trestle, says the other soldier. She has been waiting for a train for two days.

He pauses but the others do not comment. One spits. The other stares.

—She has a basket of good things to eat. She takes this basket to her husband who is an artilleryman in some hospital in Krakow. Her husband has something wrong with his stomach. He does not eat much.

Now the others listen. The older of the listening pair nods his head and narrows his eyes and spits reflectively.

—We will take her in, says this oldest soldier. —Who knows when she will find another train, says the soldier who had found the girl. —It is against the regulations, says the young soldier. It is forbidden.

His young friend laughs. The older soldier spits. —And so were apples in the garden of Eden.

And so a plan is made and certain preparations involving the shifting of hay and straw and a screen of overcoats are also made, and when the train moves and shudders and lurches again and there is this banging and rattling and thundering to which the young soldiers are by now accustomed, three heads and three pairs of arms extend from the open doors of the cattle car and a girl is caught under the arms as the train creeps up onto the trestle, and the girl is lifted into the train as it thunders over the trestle and she is ceremoniously seated on a throne of hay: flushed, laughing, out of breath. Her eyes are shining and her cheeks are flushed. Her cheeks are like little round apples. She is fresh and young and clean. Her linen shirt is starched and clean. She laughs (a little embarrassed, not quite sure about things, but grateful) and the soldiers also laugh. They make much of her.

The train goes on.

Ra-tA-ra-tA on bridges. Clacka-clacka-clacka-clacka.

Past towns where men and women lean from windows waving. Past crossings where columns of peasant carts wait and the drivers wave.

Towns pass, and woods and fields and rivers, and eventually the day.

Night comes.

The cattle car is dark with no light in it. The night is dark and stretches from one end of the world to the other. It is an infinity of darkness. The night is warm and the horses radiate their own special warmth. Gradually talk ceases and there is a silence. In the new, spreading silence the thudding of the wheels and rails carries monotonous warnings.

In daylight (Antos thinks, looking across the darkness, hearing the thundering warnings) it was pleasant to have someone near; someone who had not killed anything or anyone or would kill anyone, who was not a soldier, who laughed so prettily and smiled and listened and spoke quietly and gently, who smelled of woods and fields and sunlight and the gentle smells of home, who shared the contents of the little basket—sweet bread and milk and cheese and cherries and an apple and homemade *pierogi* with potatoes and cheese and with cabbage—who had a freshness and an innocence which curbed the tongue, who could be told (and was) of hopes and dreams and, yes, fears too, who nodded and turned soft understanding eyes at their troubled faces and murmured small womanwords. But now it is dark.

The horses breathe and move in the dark corners.

They radiate a terrible compelling heat that excites the imagination, that is like no heat from any other source; not like the warmth of the sun, which is clean and white, not like the heat of fire, which is comforting, but the scarlet heat of animal blood, which testifies to the urgency of life. This is indeed a living, an oppressive heat, and as the horses move and sniff and their delicate nostrils flare, there is in this flaring of the nostrils further testimony. The eyes of the horses gleam green in the darkness and the green of the iris spreads into the whites and makes the eyes enormous.

And now the soldier who had laughed and said the least in daylight, who amused the young woman with feats of longdistance spitting and whose lined, blurred, self-indulgent face had remained closed, proposes sleep. The soldiers prepare straw bedding for the woman. They are quiet. She is also quiet. She and they are listening. The straw of her bedding is fresh and smells of riverbanks and sunlight. The soldiers creep under the walls of the cattle car, into their dark corners, and there pretend to sleep and make breathing sounds and harsh snoring sounds and restless dreaming sounds and are also listening.

And now the young soldier becomes aware of his own tired, unused, unaware body and the imagined curves and textures of the woman's body and the mysterious concavities and protuberances so close that you could just stretch out your hand . . . and he thinks warm, chaotic thoughts and tries to suppress them and then no longer tries. And now the soldier who had proposed sleep creeps forward silently towards the woman and touches her and whispers to her and at first she does not understand. She watches the face of the whispering soldier and this face is suddenly no longer blurred but has definition. The woman makes a small sound and shakes her head and backs against the wall of the cattle car and now the whispering soldier pulls her down in the straw and the woman screams. The woman twists and struggles and beats her small fists against the soldier's chest and face and head and now another soldier comes up and joins the other, and the young soldier stares and hears the woman screaming and he can't stand this sound and so comes forward and puts his hand across the woman's mouth and she bites into it, and he feels her hands claw at his neck and something tugs and jerks his head forward, something snaps, and then, because the hand is bitten and bleeds jaggedly, he makes a fist of it and hits the woman's mouth. The woman is momentarily quiet. The horses mill about in their dark corners. There is shrill neighing and snorting and rattling of hooves on the floorboards of the cattle car, and there is a confusion of sights and sounds on the straw pallet, and there are strangled sounds and tearing sounds and hoarse breathing sounds and thin yelps and thin cries and thrashing sounds and sounds of things scraping and then there are no more sounds and the silence is back. In time the horses quiet down, although they do not quiet down entirely. They sniff the violent odors. The train flies on and the night flies on and eventually it passes and the day returns.

In daylight the soldiers avoid each others' eyes, avoid the stained white form halfburied in the straw, and there comes awareness and realization and fear of consequences and shame and bitterness and silent self-recrimination, but mostly fear, and a strange silent conference is held in the cattle car. And then as the young soldier with the bitten hand vomits upon the floorboards of the car and shudders as though ill, the two other soldiers pick up the body of the woman, who moans a little. At this the younger of the two drops the woman's shoulders and they come down against the floorboards and he steps back shaking his head and pointing. The older soldier shouts at him, and hits him in the mouth, and the younger soldier picks up his share of the woman's body. They swing her by the feet and arms and throw her through the doors.

The body flies like an obscene bird through the air, turning a tattered cartwheel, slowly, lazily, with a white shirt hiding the head and face, and smacks against the ground of the embankment and rolls down to a dry road-side ditch and there comes to rest sprawled and outspread. It is found there within the hour by the advance guard of a battery of field artillery. The gunners stare at it and cover it, and find in the tightclenched fist of the corpse a metal disk such as is worn by soldiers and notify their battery commander. The corpse is covered with a saddleblanket and rides aboard a caisson with the marching battery until a town is reached and in this town there is an office of the Posts and Telegraphs and a message is sent.

So that when the train halted and the soldiers led their horses from the train and unloaded their packs and saddlebags and sabers and bayonets and lances and steel helmets and caps with silver eagles on the front and messtins and canteens and overcoats and blankets and saddles and saddleblankets and straps and bridles and chains and stirrupstraps and thongs and grenadebags and gasmasks and rationbags and waterbags and gloves and polishingrags and brushes and knives and forks and spoons and belts and saberbelts and car-tridgebelts, all in the sour-sweet coffeesmell of soldiers that is like fresh dew drying in the sun on thatched roofs or like newmade bread, and when Antos took his Zloto from the train and brushed him down, and cleaned him, and tidied him, and pressed his hot, fevered face into the warm neck of the horse, he was arrested.

He was tried, found guilty and condemned to be shot.

I   THE JEW

It was too hot to talk.

Berg heard them on the stairs, the incredibly steep and narrow stairway that was like Jacob's ladder sprung from the dark well of the underworld.

Boots: ironshod, authoritative.

Their clattering command.

Voices: booming hollow in the stairwell.

Dullpounding drumbeat of fists on a door below. Soon they will come here. Soon they will try the door: The doorhandle will go gently down and up again, and the knock will come and the door will squeak against the bolt and they will break down the door and be inside.

Berg felt like laughing. He also felt like crying.

He looked at Mendeltort, wondering what Mendeltort was thinking. He wondered what Mendeltort would do. Whatever it was it would be something terrible, something terrifying. Perhaps the sound of a thousand rams' horns will come. Perhaps the walls will tumble down. It would be something that only Mendeltort could do; he, Berg, could never dream of doing such splendid, terrifying things.

He, Berg, was small.

Zydek. Little Jew.

The Polish word for Jew is *Zyd.* But nobody used that. It was always *Zydek, little* Jew; a sort of petname, half contemptuous and half amused, for something small and harmless and ridiculous and inconsequential. It was a good name to hide under: No one did anything bad to small, amusing and inconsequential things.

Mendeltort, though.

He was not amusing.

He was not harmless or inconsequential.

He would do something splendid and terrifying now that They had come.

Berg wondered what Mendeltort would say and do and what he was thinking but Mendeltort did not say what he was thinking nor did he say anything else, and he did nothing and there was no sound of rams' horns nor of walls tumbling. Mendeltort stretched and lay back on his bed and looked out of the window. Also, he broke wind.

—Well, Berg said, nervous. They have come.

—Who? Who? Where? Where? Rosenblatt said. He stood up and took off his hat and sat down and put his hat back on again. He giggled. Berg thought about Rosenblatt's propensity for giggling. He tasted the word: propensity. A natural inclination or bent. A favorable disposition, a liking. Also bias. Propensity was also bias but not in this sense. In the Rosenblatt sense propensity was an irresistible impulse to be ridiculous. It was an explosion of a protective mechanism designed to amuse. If they laugh at you they will not fear you. If they do not fear you they will allow you to survive.

Berg thought about propensity and about other words he liked. He thought that he probably knew all the word origins and their romantic stories. This did not add to his stature in the Quarter, where the important words were *Ooshoovor, Oosfeelor, Ootsdorkor* and a man's stature was measured in terms of survival. —*Survive, no matter what,* Papa Berg said. *There are always two ways out of everything.* But now the only way out was Mendeltort and what Mendeltort would do. Berg trembled in anticipation of what Mendeltort would do. Meanwhile, Rosenblatt indulged in his propensity.

—Who? What? Where?

—*Glina,* Mendeltort said. The police.

Glina means clay. Berg wondered about the origin of the word as applied to the police. Perhaps it meant police because the thought of the police turned his knees to *glina?* Berg blinked his eyes fast and felt a headache coming on again. Rosenblatt made a sound like a train when it takes on water. His eyes bulged. Berg began to sweat. He watched Mendeltort and wondered what Mendeltort would do.

They were in Mendeltort's room above the Untenbaums' on Solna, a dirty street in a Quarter of dirty streets and pushcarts and hot cobblestones and shrillness and dead, despairing smells. Berg listened to the footsteps on the stairs. Soon they will come upstairs. He tried to draw no attention to himself, watching Mendeltort.

Mendeltort lay in bed and did not move. His eyes were closed. He is supine, Berg thought. That is the word for it. There is an attitude of death about him. He looks as though he had died by violence in the night. He looks as though he had been run over by a steamroller or been exploded into an infinity of Mendeltorts by a charge of dynamite. He is scattered all over the bed. He appears to be alone in the room. Soon they will put their shoulders to the door.

Berg looked about the room. It is no more than a storage place for Mendeltort, he thought. Mendeltort takes such rooms about with him from place to place and pitches one each night at the top of a steep, evilsmelling staircase and stores himself in it.

The room is like an Arab's tent. The tent of a nomad. Mendeltort is a nomad. But Jews are not nomads, are they? No. Is Mendeltort a Jew? Yes. Mendeltort is a Jew; see he has possessions. There is a halfchewed apple on the chair beside the bed. Last night Mendeltort had talked about the chair. —*It is no longer functional or recognizable,* he said. *It no longer has identity. Identity is the most important of all things but this chair has none. It has abandoned all pretensions and aspirations and it has no more dignity. It is an ancient piece of furniture, much abused. It is the Jew of the furniture world; without a shred of former pride and elegance, a threadbare thing decaying of its own inability to resist decay. It has been straddled by whores and sneakthieves and men with crumpled, fugitive faces and it has groaned under gross men and conspirators and it has shuddered under the weight of hastily packed suitcases and illicit bundles and it has been stood upon by a suicide and it has been a weapon for assault and now the chair has given up; it has surrendered and spreads its legs and is prepared for disintegration.* Rosenblatt giggled. —*I can fix it for you. See? A patch here, some wire there.*

I'll stuff it with straw. Mendeltort looked at Rosenblatt as he would at a putrefying corpse.

But Mendeltort had even more possessions. —*I am an affluent Jew, you see,* he said. His smile was unpleasant. —*And affluence and security are the answer to everything, are they not?* Beside the apple on the chair was a sock. It had a hole in it. There was a spool of thread with a needle stuck in it. —*I am a thrifty Jew, you see,* Mendeltort said. *And thrift is the key to accumulation, is it not? Wealth is tranquillity, don't you agree?* Trembling, Berg agreed.

There were papers on the chair that had been scribbled on and a piece of *Bryndza* cheese made of the milk of sheep and there was bread and a jug of water and dust and waste and devastation. —*That is all my Jew of the furniture world is capable of supporting,* Mendeltort said.

Berg heard the voices in the Untenbaum's apartment. Someone was laughing and someone else was making vigorous denials. He looked about the room. Nothing was permanent about it. It was an obviously rented room, used not a lifetime but an hour at a time; a room which had seen only artificial warmth, fabricated love, and if it had seen life at any time it was an imitation. No Jew has such a room.

Downstairs someone was shouting. Downstairs the sound of boots was loud. Mama Untenbaum would get a headache with all the shouting and all the excitement. Berg felt his headache mounting. He hoped the aching would not fill his eyes. He did not want Mendeltort to think him a weeper.

—They will come here, he said. Mendeltort said nothing. —What will you do?

—What do you think I will do? Mendeltort said.

He has teeth like white spade blades, Berg thought. Small graves can be dug with them.

—I don't know, Berg said.

—What would you do?

Berg grinned and shook his head and spread his hands. Mendeltort watched him.

—Would you resist?

Berg trembled. He wished he would stop trembling and that he had courage. He wished the earth would open up and swallow him up. He wished for an earthquake and for bravery. Survive. Survive no matter what.

He looked down at his hands. They were thin and pale and ineffectual. They were like Mendeltort's chair, he supposed.

—Survive? he said.

—You earn survival, Mendeltort said. It is not a right. It is not guaranteed. It is not an umbrella you buy at Melnick's. All you are guaranteed are the attentions of Aprikozenkranz.

Rosenblatt giggled. —What? What are you saying?

—That the day is warm.

—Oooof, Rosenblatt said. Phew. Warm? It is hot!

—But, then again, it isn't.

—Yes, Rosenblatt agreed. It is cooler than I thought. I mean for a hot day.

—Such heat is unreasonable, Mendeltort said.

—Oh, Rosenblatt said. His eyes began to bulge and he hiccoughed. —It is hot enough to melt. Such sun. Have you ever seen such a sun?

—Cloudy, though, Mendeltort said. He watched Rosenblatt without expression. Rosenblatt fell into a paroxysm of giggles.

—Yes yes. Cloudy.

Mendeltort laughed. He pointed at the giggling man. —A camel, he said. And yet a whale, although it could be an airplane. You . . . little . . . Jew!

Rosenblatt flapped his arms about and giggled and his eyes bulged. Berg felt his stomach turning over. He felt that he might vomit. He wished he had not eaten Mendeltort's *Bryndza* and that he had courage. He could not look at Rosenblatt, whose mouth hung open and whose hands flew about like terror-stricken birds.

—Resist, Mendeltort said. For you I should resist?

—Please, Rosenblatt said. His giggles came in squealing bursts. —Please.

Berg heard the laughter of the policemen coming up the stairs. One was telling a joke of some kind and another laughed. Berg looked at Mendeltort and at the door and wondered what would happen.

There was one window in the room; it was cracked and filthy. Sunlight seeped through its speckled greyness. Even the sun was diffident before Mendeltort. It lighted up his face, which was huge. His face resembled a crumbling block of granite. It was composed mostly of cheekbones and a beard and eyebrows that jutted over his eyes like the thick, black roots you see over the Vistula down by the Praga bridges where it is deep. Berg looked into the eyes of Mendeltort. They were the yellow eyes of tigers. Such eyes had not looked out of the face of a Jew in generations. Mendeltort did not look like any Jew Berg had ever seen. He did not look like anyone from the Quarter. He was not pale and his eyes were not myopic and he did not blink. He did not wear the smile of the Quarter. He was not diffident. He wore his hair cropped short and he did not say *nu*. He did not wear the black uniform of his people. Above all, he was not afraid. Berg supposed that Mendeltort had never been afraid of anything, or agreed with anyone with whom he disagreed, or been polite to anyone whom he did not like, or had ever felt like weeping or had a headache, or ever felt the wonderful warmth of self-pity or ever carried any kind of private Wailing Wall inside him. No one could call Mendeltort a *little* Jew. He was two hundred and fourteen centimeters tall, seven feet give or take an inch, and that was taller than any Jew had stood in Europe in several hundred years.

Berg waited for the thing that Mendeltort would do. Now was the time for it.

He heard the boots outside the door. He heard a muffled sound; a short complaint about the steepness of the stairs. They would be looking at him through the keyhole. Soon they would try the door. Soon they would break the door down and be inside.

He looked at Mendeltort.

Mendeltort did not move.

He could not look at Rosenblatt, who was shaking and weeping and could no longer control the muscles of his body and who disgusted him.

—You little Jew, Mendeltort said to Rosenblatt.

—He cannot help it, Berg said.

Mendeltort looked at him. —You have found a courage?

—No, Berg said. I do not have courage.

—Giggling pig waiting for the slaughter, Mendeltort said to Rosenblatt. Each word was an expectoration. This is for me, Berg thought. Why is he doing this for me?

—He cannot help it, he said. We are not as you are.

Mendeltort watched him curiously. There was a small smile on his giant face. It was a fleeting thing, this smile. —Are you a Jew?

Berg trembled. He tried once more to help himself with words. Words. Words were no good for anything! Still, he tried.

—It is a matter of size, he said. That is all.

—Size? Mendeltort said. Size? What was the size of David?

—David had courage, Berg said.

—David was a coward. There is no such thing as courage in a little Jew!

—No, Berg said. You cannot say that.

—You disagree? With me?

—No, Berg said. I do not disagree.

—Pig! Sniveling coward! *Zydek!* (This to Rosenblatt.) And then to Berg: —Do you know why he brought you here? Can you follow the motivations of a human vulture? Giggling vulture!

—He cannot help being as he is. He is what he is and I am what I am and you cannot change us and perhaps that is not so bad.

Mendeltort looked at Berg, grinning. Berg was afraid. The yellow eyes of tigers measured him. —Courage, Mendeltort said. Such courage.

—No, Berg said. I do not have courage.

—You disagree with me.

—No. Only he can't help it.

—Do you think that the day is hot? Mendeltort laughed.

—Yes, Berg said in whisper. He was sweating. He smelled his fear. He thought: I shall be destroyed. The *Oonsaneh Toekehf* kept running through his head. In years past and every year on Yom Kippur, the Day of Atonement, he said it in reverence and awe, sampling the beauty and the poetry of it and the awesomeness of it. Now conscious of the dreadful import of the words, conscious of his weakness and smallness and his insignificance, he clung to the last words of it.

Ooshoovor, oosfeelor, ootsdorkor . . . but penitence, prayer and charity can avert the evil decree.

If it was not too late for penitence then he was penitent. Survival tempted me and I fell. It was wrong to fall. Even I have a duty to the world.

If any charity remained to be performed then he performed it. I offer charity to Rosenblatt. I loathe him. Am I like him? Are we all like him? I shall be charitable and save him from disintegration.

What prayers were there? There were many prayers. Jews have a prayer for every possible occasion. But I have said my prayers. The time for prayers is past.

—It is hot, he said. You will now tell me that the day is cold and ask me to agree? It is hot. It is not cold. I am what I am but the day is hot.

—Go close the window, Mendeltort said. He was laughing. —It is getting cold.

—No, Berg said.

—You don't agree, Mendeltort said. You hold an opinion. You are a sorry-looking *Zydek* with a head like a thin whore's buttock and your *peysy* gone and a nose like an anteater with catarrh and eyes like all the Hebrew sorrows but you hold an opinion about the weather and you state it firmly. (He grinned enormously. He stretched.) A man who has such courage does not need my help. Don't you agree?

—I do not know, Berg said. I did not want to come here.

—Then why did you come?

—I do not know. I had a headache . . .

Mendeltort laughed. —For headaches there is *aspiryna*.

Berg nodded. His head was filled with hammers and with sounds. He moved his head carefully so as not to disturb the hammers, not to agitate them. He heard the knock: authoritative on the door. He looked at Mendeltort. Mendeltort closed his eyes and crossed his arms behind his head.

He said: —Open the door for them.

. . . who by the sword, and who by the wild beast . . .

Berg drew back the bolt.

. . . who by strangulation or who by lapidation . . .

He unlocked the door and opened it.

. . . Ooshoovor, Oosfeelor, Ootsdorkor . . .

There were two policemen.

One was fat and redfaced and sweated heavily and made attempts to dry his face with a red handkerchief. The other was thinner. They were elderly policemen and they were out of breath.

—Phew, said the fat policeman.

—Ooof, said the policeman who was thinner. How come you *Zydki* live so close to heaven?

—Is there a Berg here? Morys Berg?

Berg looked at Mendeltort. Mendeltort did not move. He did not say anything or do anything and gave no sign that he proposed to do anything. He appeared asleep.

—Mendeltort? Berg said. Mendeltort?

The huge man opened his eyes and looked at him.

—What are you going to do?

—Nothing.

—Nothing?

—Nothing.

—You said you would do something.

—Rosenblatt said it. Mendeltort closed his eyes again. He grinned. —You know their saying about the promises of a Jew?

Berg looked at his hands and at the policeman. He was terribly afraid.

—Well?

—I am Berg, he said.

—Well, then. Come on, said the fat policeman.

—We've wasted seven days looking for you.

—Six, said the fat policeman. Six. Not seven.

—Six, then.

—You are worried? Why do you worry? said the fat policeman. Jews have two ways out of everything, don't they?

The policeman laughed. Berg nodded cautiously. He did not wish to agitate the hammers in his head. His head was filled with varieties of multicolored pain.

—Consider, said the fat policeman. You have alternatives. Either you will be sent to the front or you will not. If you are so sent it will be unfortunate for you perhaps, but the alternative remains. Either God sends you a bullet or he does not, and again you have alternatives: Either the bullet hits you or it misses. If it hits you it will not be good. But even so you have alternatives. Either the bullet kills you or it does not kill you, and but one bullet in a thousand kills a man. If it does kill you, it will be unfortunate, but your alternatives remain: You go up or you go down.

—Two ways out, said the not-so-fat policeman. Up or down, there are the two ways out.

—If you go up you do not have to worry, said the fat policeman. If you go down, well, that would be unfortunate but, again, you have the alternatives. Either the Devil will be hungry or he will not. You have two ways out.

—Either he will eat you or he will not, said the thinner of the two policemen.

Berg nodded.

—Two ways out, said the fat policeman. You understand? Always two ways out.

—So if he eats you you do not have to worry, said the thinner of the two policemen.

The policemen laughed.

Berg watched them.

He looked at Mendeltort and Rosenblatt and at the policemen.

—*Gowno*, he said. It is too hot to talk.

He went down the long, evilsmelling staircase and the policemen followed him. Outside the sun was shining. Birds made spring noises. The cobblestones were hot.

Wednesday, August the thirtieth

I   ADAM

They rested for some hours on the Weissturn, looking down at clouds, gulping the thin, cold air greedily, quiet after the effort of the climb. Around them was a marvelous land of floating powderpuffs and curdled oceans where lesser peaks squatted like confectionery icebergs in spunsugar bowls.

You could look down and dip your hand in them, Adam thought; they seemed that close: an innocent white world without sound. Somewhere below was the murderous North Wall they had climbed that morning, a mass of granite like a giant icefloe turned on its side. There the wind sobbed like lost souls and howled like the tormenting devils and leaped at them out of the crevices and tunnels in wisps of cold, wet mist.

—Do you have anything like this in Poland? Kuno shouted. He looked at the white peaks with their yearlong snow, the shining glaciercaps, and laughed, shaking his head. He was an Austrian and he didn't think anyone had anything as beautiful as that.

—Of course we do. We have everything you do.

—Everything but the yodel, Erich said, laughing.

He yodeled and Kuno also yodeled and Adam tried it but it didn't sound much like a yodel so he started laughing. They all laughted then, looking down the easy, southern face of the mountain: a wrinkled greenbrown mass of scrubpine and humped billows of deadfall and fallen timber spilled like yellow matchsticks. Below that was the valley now hidden in clouds; a gentle rampart. They would make the descent later in the afternoon.

—So much for Polish yodeling, Erich said.

Kuno laughed. —Of course. The yodel is Austrian.

—The Swiss also yodel, Adam said.

—Well, if they do it's just an imitation. Ours is the genuine yodel; everyone knows that.

Adam and Erich laughed and Erich yodeled. Kuno looked upset. He drove his mountainaxe savagely into the glacier ice. The clang of steel on granite rang clear as a bell.

—The Swiss. Fat moneychangers. Has anything good ever come from them?

—Cheese and the Red Cross, Erich said. He laughed.

—Watches, Adam said. The League of Nations.

—That's not theirs. That farce is an American invention. The Swiss just keep house for it.

—Well, they do yodel, genuine or not. There's even a sort of yodel in the Polish Beskids. You can't copyright a sound and good lungs.

But Kuno said that no, he didn't believe it; the yodel was Austrian. —Don't tell me about any Polish yodels, he said. I will not believe it.

—All right, I will confess.

Erich laughed. —You have sinned?

—I am without sin but I will confess about the Polish yodel.

—Speak, my son, Erich said. He was the oldest of the three. —I give you absolution in advance.

—We have no such thing. We leave our yodeling to the Swiss.

Kuno laughed with immense contempt. —They march for the Pope.

They went down to the soft green slopes below the clouds late in the afternoon, drunk with its beauty and their own wild spirits, leaping like goats and shouting in the deadfall, with the wind rough in their faces and the sun still hot. Then they were in the valley and the town, tallspired and gingerbreaded like all the towns in the Salzkammergut, and it was time to stop. They punched loose the iron buckles of their mountainbelts, and piled the rope, and drove their axes deep into the pitted block rolling up against the wall of the inn, and stacked their rucksacks and went in for the young goose and cucumber salad and the pungent wine. Adam looked at the others' faces: deep redbrown from the wind and the sun, glowing in the warm room. Even Kuno's pale mask had color. Erich grinned at him. Adam hummed. Erich was his friend. He wished that things could go on as they were without ever changing. But things were changing even now; everything was changing.

That autumn, even nature seemed to lie. Nothing seemed real, everything was unnaturally calm. Nothing important was as it had been; there was no warmth in anything.

The weather was magnificent, of course, the way it is in the Tyrol and the Salzkammergut that time of the year. The country burned with color. It was all red and gold and the incredible green of foothills in clean morning air. The sun burned hot on the mountains; it eased the harsh bite of the wind.

But this seemed somehow artificial, a sort of mask. There was a tension and a breathlessness about the country, the way it is in the high glaciers before an avalanche when everything (rocks, boulders, deadfall, piled cloud) is absolutely still and the air trembles. Even the mountains held their powdery breath.

In the youth hostels and the lodges where they stayed there were arguments in highpitched voices. Angry words. There was talk of war. The rights of Germany to this and to the other. Intolerable wrongs. Place in the sun and national destiny. Duty to the world. The march of progress, the iron boot of history. You couldn't tell anyone who and what you were; they would catch the soft Polish accent and ask: —*What are you?* and you couldn't tell them because to tell them would be to bring down a silence that was worse than all the angry words.

And so: the shrug and lie. Nothing is truly good if you have to lie. It's not a good feeling to carry to the mountains on a difficult ascent.

Adam went on, pretending that the good clean feeling that had always been the heart of mountainclimbing for him, that made him feel at home and welcome in the clouds, above the dark valleys, was still there and that the trip was good. But it was not good. He knew it. He wondered if Erich also knew it but he couldn't ask. Because he knew that his friendship with the laughing Austrian was also changing. When the trip ended that would also end.

He looked at his friend and he looked at Kuno. The Austrians carved their birds with fierce concentration.

—Ah, this is good, he said about the food. (That, at least, was true.)

—You liked that, eh? And what about the wall?

—It was a good wall. Better than anything we did this year.

—Better than your Gerlachowka?

—I don't know. You tell me.

Erich grinned at him. They had first met on the chimney of the Gerlachowka in the Polish Tatras where Erich tried a lone ascent and was caught by darkness. He took a tumble there, fairly hard, on the shelf that cuts across the north-central buttress just below First Peak. He lay all night unconscious with a broken leg, and Adam found him and fired the necessary flares and waited with him until consciousness returned and brought him down the cliff-face to the Hala, where the ropesled waited.

—Less bumpy, anyway. One of our best. I can't imagine why the better clubs don't climb here. The north wall of the Weissturn is as good as anything I've seen.

—It isn't fashionable enough, Kuno said. Not sufficiently expensive. But it'll all change someday, you can bet on that.

It had been difficult enough to please all of them; five hundred meters of sheer cliff, sparkling granite flutes smooth-polished by wind, without a good traverse of any kind, and then the naked chimney thrust like an arm up through the clouds. There the wind drowned shouting.

It had pleased Erich. He had led the ascent. He had done brilliant work. He would have every reason to be pleased, Adam thought, and wished he didn't have to tell the others that the trip was over.

—Well, it's your turn tomorrow, Erich said. I left you a good one. If you can take the Weissturn from the northeast buttress I'll concede that you're a mountaineer. Nobody's done it yet.

Adam smiled. He didn't want to disappoint his friend.

—I've been thinking . . . Why do you climb? he said.

—Good God, why do you?

—The altitude. Somebody told me that you can't hate anyone at six thousand meters. They said that twenty thousand feet was the quarrelsome altitude. Another thousand feet and the best you can do in the way of hate is a sort of mild disapproval. It doesn't seem to matter there.

—How very nice, Kuno said. And how stupid. How high have you been?

—Don't worry, Erich said. He's been high enough.

—Yes, but how high?

—He did Scafell, for God's sake. Central Buttress is about his mark. Why do you want to know? You haven't done enough rockclimbs to know a scramble from a plate of eggs.

—I only wondered if he played a harp, Kuno said. He looked at Erich with a cold white smile.

Erich shrugged and looked away. He no longer smiled. Some of the warmth seemed to leave the room. Outside, the sun went down in a red rush behind the mountains.

So there it was again, Adam thought: the feeling that you didn't want to take up to the mountains. But one way or another you couldn't get away from it this autumn.

He thought about Adrianne and (because, until now, you couldn't think of her without thinking of Erich) also about the Austrian. The thought of Adrianne made his mouth dry up. She was now on a train, somewhere north of them, coming down from Vienna, and what were mountainclimbs and friendships and friends' disappointments when compared with that? He had a choice, yes; but there was no choice. Adrianne had promised to meet him that night in Mariazell.

He wondered about her insistence on time and on place. Why Mariazell? Why today? It meant the end of the painstakingly planned trip and that, of course, meant a bitter blow for Erich, who had done the planning and to whom the expedition meant much more than to the rest of them. He had been careful to explain to her about the trip: how he and Erich (mostly Erich) had planned it all year, and what it meant to him and Erich (mostly Erich). The trip was to be something of a final contest. He and Erich had climbed, separately and together, in so many places and had argued so often (only half in jest) about who was the better mountaineer, who had the stronger nerve, the higher skill, whose planning was better, that finally Erich had demanded this examination: a month-long assault on the little-known glaciers of the Salzkammergut, where neither of them had done any climbing and would have no advantage. It seemed a fair enough test and promised fine climbing.

There wasn't much more left, for either of them, to learn about rockclimbs at this point. Both were very good indeed, Adam knew, but there was a difference. Because while he, Adam, climbed for altitude, and was becoming quite well-known in that tight, exclusive circle of mountaineers who wear the badges of famous clubs, who like to disappear up a giant, mistshrouded complex of peaks a mile in the sky for weeks at a time (in carefully chosen teams . . . by invitation only . . . with expert porters), Erich climbed only for technique and style. He got as much out of a good cliff a half-hour's ride from Baden (he said) as he would from the traverse of some monstrous rockface in the Himalayas. The ultimate spires and pinnacles of earth did not interest him. Or, if they did, he would not admit it. Certainly (although he would not say it among climbers) he knew that he would never stand higher above the sea than he had stood already. The glittering white peaks of the Salzkammergut offered a challenge to technique.

But Adrianne had not, apparently, understood the importance of the trip and had said, in her cool, positive, English way that it would have to be *this* time, at *that* place, or nowhere at all.

—*Of course, if you would rather climb a silly mountain than be with me* . . . The implication was that mountains were very much less eternal.

It wasn't much of a choice, Adam thought: not when you considered the lasting qualities of mountains and the fact (never voiced, always thought about) that you had never had a girl before and, in particular, a girl like Adrianne. Adam had thought himself a minor satellite in a universe where Adrianne was the sun.

It was, at first, impossible to believe that this girl (so poised, so very much pursued and so remarkably controlled) at whom he must have made five thousand asinine, enamored faces, would meet him anywhere. Why him? It was impossible to believe that she had suggested it. But here he was, waiting in Mariazell, and there she was, coming down from Vienna. . . . All that remained was for him to tell the others that he was not going on with them after dinner, that the trip was over and he was staying here.

He could picture Erich's disappointment and delayed the telling. He wondered what had gone wrong between Adrianne and Erich. She was the daughter of a British consular official and went to school in Switzerland (arts and humanities and poetry writing) and everyone thought that she and Erich would be married. Certainly, they had gone everywhere together. But something had, apparently, gone wrong, because they had not married and did not see each other anymore and there she was, on a train, coming down to be with him, Adam, in Mariazell, as she had so often come to other places where Erich was climbing.

Adam wished he could ask Erich what had gone wrong between him and Adrianne; indeed, if anything had. But Erich no longer mentioned her and there was no good way for Adam to ask. He ate the roast goose and drank the wine and wondered how to tell the others. They would go on that night, of course, and might go on climbing, but the whole sense of the trip would be gone for Erich, who would not forgive it. Adam wished the trip didn't have to end. But, he supposed, that fall everything was ending one way or another.

Then dinner was over. Erich sighed and grinned and said (looking across the debris of the birdbones and the cigarettes stubbed out like little question-marks on the plates) —This is the best of all times. There will never be another time like it.

—Why? Kuno wished to know. One time is like another. And, anyway, there will be better times; you and I both know it.

—In that sense, yes, of course. But I meant in the sense of friendship and of being young. Nothing can replace that. It takes this, you see, to climb mountains—it takes that kind of heart.

Kuno laughed. —Purity of heart? Innocence? We will all lose it very soon, believe me, those of us that still carry it. It is a stupid burden anyway.

—Still, I wish it wasn't necessary, Erich said. I wish this trip or another like it could go on indefinitely. What do you think, Adam?

—We could plan something like this for next year, Adam said cautiously enough.

Kuno looked at him with contempt. —Next year? Who knows what we will have next year? There might not be a Europe next year, eh? Not as you know it, anyway.

—It'll be here, Erich said. And we will also be here.

Kuno looked at the whitecapped mountains, smiling to himself. —Shall we? (His eyes did not smile.) I shall be here. Erich will be here. But where will Adam be?

—Here or elsewhere, Adam said. Let's not talk about it.

—Why? Kuno said. He laughed his quick, thin laugh. —Next year the war might come. And then where will we be, pure hearts and all? What will we be doing?

Adam looked at him carefully. He did not know him well and did not like him. Erich had recruited Kuno Saal for the expedition because they needed three men for the north wall of the Weissturn.

—Shooting, I expect, Adam said.

Kuno went on laughing. Erich did not laugh. His eyes were on the mountains. He kept his eyes turned carefully away from the others.

—Germany doesn't want war, he said to the mountains. Everyone knows that.

—Ah, but what about our Polish friends, Kuno said. (And then to Adam, angry:) How long do you think German patience is going to last?

Adam said nothing then. He felt his throat dry up. Also he felt immense relief. He knew that now the trip was really over; it was all done. No matter how much longer it could have gone on. He felt a gratitude of a kind for Kuno because now he could tell the others what he had been unable to say for a week.

—German patience can matter only to the Germans, he said, feeling cold.

—You must be joking, Erich said. A poor sort of joke.

—Perhaps I'm only losing patience. Do you think Germany has a monopoly on patience?

—Don't talk like that, Erich said.

Kuno laughed. —You see? You see how it is? And you talk about friendships—the best of all times. There will be time for good times when we have taught the world respect for Germany. When we have set to right all these intolerable wrongs. Until then we should have nothing but anger, Erich. And (looking at Adam, smiling:) contempt.

—No, Erich said. Not yet. We still have our mountains. Anger's not something you want along for that. Let's drink more wine and talk about that.

—No, Adam said. That's all over now.

Kuno went on laughing. He put his hands together as if praying. —Oh Adam. Did I hurt your feelings?

Erich made a quick, impatient gesture. —Enough, Kuno. Never mind that, Adam. It's just the times. Tomorrow when you take us up the Weissturn it will be all right. Hey! (He pointed to the mountains, whitetopped behind the windows in early moonlight.) Look at that. Doesn't that make everything all right?

—It's over, Erich, Adam said. I'm not going on. It has nothing to do with Kuno or what he is saying.

—But why? For God's sake, man, you can't be serious!

—I am meeting someone. There is a girl coming down from Vienna.

—A girl . . .

—Yes. Adam shrugged. Kuno went on laughing.

Erich stared from one to the other. —Is this a joke?

—I am not joking.

—That's out of the question! We planned it for a month! You just can't be serious.

—Oh, but he is, Kuno said, laughing to himself. Look at that serious face.

—I'm sorry, Adam said.

—Oh, Kuno said. Such sorrow.

Erich said: —It is a joke, of course. I don't understand it.

Adam shook his head. He closed his eyes and thought about Adrianne. Kuno went on with his small, happy sounds.

—And so a girl is coming down to meet him, Kuno said. I wonder who she is? Have you wondered, Erich? Of course, perhaps there is no girl at all. Perhaps our Polish friend has simply run out of gas. Is his pack too heavy?

—You can have the pack, Adam said.

One-third of their supplies was in it.

—Thank you, Kuno said. Thank you *very* much.

—We don't need it, Erich said. We have enough in ours. But to leave us like this, after we had planned so much more than a week, that is to spoil much more than a trip. Is that worth sleeping with a girl? Change your mind, Adam, and come with us and we will all forget what was said tonight.

A new chill came into the room then, and it was not because the mountainclimb was over but, Adam thought, because this surely was the best of all times and it was already ending, and soon it would be gone and soon it would be only hazily remembered as something that might have been. . . .

Adam shook his head.

—So it is over, Erich said. That's more important?

—There are always mountains.

—I am not speaking now about the mountains!

—To me it's more important.

—Perhaps it's too cold for him on the mountains, Kuno said. He will be warmer here, eh?

—There is nothing like this, Erich said, looking at the mountains.

—Some things are, eh? Obviously they are. Hunting is good too, did you know, Erich? Perhaps we will have good hunting soon in Europe. I wonder where our Polish friend will be when we go hunting.

They had been a long time eating. When the meal ended, Adam went out with the others to watch them strap on their equipment. They did not look at him. Their eyes were on the slopes. He was no longer with them or of them; they did not speak to him but only to each other. They talked about the ascent from the northeast buttress but Adam knew they would not attempt it.

They marched off down the hill to the valley floor and took the road to Reichenau, black against the moonlitwhite of the gingerbread street, and Adam watched them until they disappeared among houses. Later he saw them small on the road where the slope lifted it out of the town, and then they were gone. Then there was only the greying whiteness of the mountainpeaks.

He heard the whistle long before he saw the train—a thin sound lost in cooling air—and he came out of the waiting room stamping his boots. The sound was faint when it came again. He looked at the mountain out of which the train was to come.

—On time, the stationmaster said. He was pleased. —*The Herr* is leaving?

—I am meeting someone.

Now the whistle came louder and lasted longer.

—The train is now entering the tunnel, the stationmaster said. It will be here in exactly three minutes. The tunnel is two kilometers long and the train goes slowly because of the animals.

An Englishman, a German and some Austrians came out of the waiting room. The German and the Englishman wore Tyrolean hats. Adam looked at the white peaks where the clouds were moving and at the black tunnel mouth. There was no sound from the mountain. He waited for the sound to come.

—Where will the first class be? He slapped his sides. He was cold. He hoped Adrianne had not been cold on the train. But perhaps the first class was heated.

—There is only one first class, the stationmaster said. It is behind the locomotive. That way it stops before the waiting room, of course.

—Why of course? said the Englishman.

—It is always so.

—Where is the first class? the Englishman said. Behind the locomotive. Why behind the locomotive? It is always so. Will it snow tomorrow? *Natürlich.* It always snows on Thursday. These Germans. God.

—Austrians, Adam said.

—Is there a difference?

—There used to be. They have a sense of humor. At least they used to have.

—I say, are you leaving too?

—No. I am meeting someone.

—Pity. Thought we could share a compartment. Now there'll be only these Germans.

—Austrians, Adam said.

—Yes, of course. Pity.

Adam looked at the steel lines, clean and white where they touched the tunnel mouth. The moon was on the mountains. It made the iron silver. The train whistle came then, loud and urgent, and the thud of the wheels came and the low thundersound that the train pushed out of the tunnel with the black smoke, and then the train rolled out—a threecoach comic toy with a green toy engine.

—On time, the stationmaster said. It is always so.

Then the train reached the far end of the platform and the engine was no longer a green toy but a snowflecked mass of German steel, steam, black smoke and sparks, and then the engine whooshed past and the coaches came and eventually they stopped.

The priest was the first out: a round man, small in a round black hat. His shoes showed wear. Two brownshirts jumped out. Out came three women in cloth coats and kerchiefs. They carried baskets. Warm smells came from the baskets. No one else came out. Adam walked the length of the train looking in the windows but he could not find Adrianne. She had not come.

He could not understand why she had not come. She said she would come if he broke up the trip. He broke it up and she had not come. She said she would. If you say something, that you will do something, you do it, don't you? But she had not come.

Then the train moved and gathered speed blowing steam and black smoke and then became a green toy again and then that too was gone and the rails were still.

—Perhaps your friend will come on tomorrow's train, the stationmaster said. There is another train tomorrow.

—Perhaps, Adam said but he did not think so.

He went back to the inn, to the room for which he had had such hopes. He held a series of imaginary conversations with Adrianne and suddenly felt foolish. After a while he went downstairs, where there was a bar.

Some men were drinking at the bar. One was a one-armed man. Another had teeth like a horse. They were poorly dressed. The one-armed man reminded Adam of his father. He did not want to think about his father. His father was living in the old white house with a divorced woman. She had been married to Professor Karolewski. Adam knew about the professor, who had been a minister of something at the time that Adam's father lost his arm. His father had lost more than his arm at that time. Adam was willing to forgive his father many things but not the *skandal* of the divorced woman.

He could forgive him his treason of 1926. The General had ideas and ideals and these, perhaps, had made such an act excusable. Certainly, Uncle Michal, who also had ideals, had not found it necessary to be involved in treason. But perhaps these ideals were different for his father. The *skandal,* though, was inexcusable. It was a disgrace. Adam did not wish to think about any of that.

He went into the bar and sat down at a table and waited for someone to come and bring him something and eventually a waiter came and brought him a beer. He drank the beer, watching the men in the bar. There were several men. They were mostly elderly and roundfaced and pleasantlooking. Some had white mustaches and all had red faces. There was a lot of robust laughter. There were songs. The beer came and went and the laughter followed and Adam thought that he had never seen such pleasant, friendly people.

Then the two men, One-Arm and Horse-Tooth, looked around and saw him. They talked quickly to each other and got up and came to his table.

—What will you drink with us?

—I don't know. Yes, thank you. What are you drinking?

—Schnapps. Can you drink schnapps? How old are you?

—Not very old.

—But how old? I do not mean to be impertinent but we were just saying that you looked like a man who would know how to drink. It takes a man, after all, to drink schnapps well.

—I am nineteen, Adam said. I will have schnapps.

—Ah, what it is to be nineteen, Horse-Tooth said.

—It is not so good, One-Arm said. It is only that the problems of nineteen are small when you are done with being that. In their time they are bad enough. I remember when I was nineteen. That was, of course, many years ago and many snows have melted on the mountains since that time. I may not look old but I am long from being youthful. Would you believe that I was a grandfather?

Horse-Tooth shook his head. —Impossible. Wouldn't you say, young friend, that it was impossible?

Adam, politely, agreed.

—Ah, but I was in the Great War, One-Arm said. Would you guess it? Of course, it was not against the English. I lost my arm on the Russian front.

—In a cardgame, Horse-Tooth said.

—A Cossack cut it off.

—Are you a Russian? Horse-Tooth said. Where are you from? Personally I have warm feelings about the Russians. I am a great admirer of the Don Cossack choir.

—I am an Englishman, Adam said. He didn't think Adrianne would mind the lie. He wished he didn't have to lie about being English but being English was still a safeconduct in a country that lived off rich tourists.

—I have a splendid feeling for the English, One-Arm said. Also, of course, for the Americans, although they do not know how to live. Of the two, I would much rather be English if I could not be German.

—You are German?

—We are all German now. I am Austrian, of course, but that is merely a technicality of birth. Now that Greater Germany is one again we are all Germans.

Horse-Tooth confided that he also had warm feelings for the English. —They know how to live. They are gentlemen. You can depend on them to do what they say.

—Have some more schnapps, One-Arm said. He filled Adam's glass. —It's not as good as whiskey but this is a small bar, it has limited resources. Austria is not a rich country like England.

—But it will be soon, now that we are all Germans, Horse-Tooth said.

—*Prosit,* One-Arm said in the north German manner.

—Heil Hitler, said Horse-Tooth.

—To which party do you belong in England? One-Arm wished to know.

—I don't know, Adam said. I've never thought about it.

This was something he had heard Adrianne say; it had appalled Erich, who took his politics seriously. He had been a group leader in the Hitler Youth when it was still illegal, when Germany and Austria were still separate countries, and then a student in one of the Napola schools for future German leaders and now he was a cadetofficer of some special kind. Both he and Kuno Saal had beautiful black uniforms and boots.

—In Germany we all know what we are, Horse-Tooth said; he sounded superior. One-Arm smiled at Adam in a conciliating way and kicked Horse-Tooth quickly under the table. Horse-Tooth winced. Then he, too, smiled at Adam.

—I hope you're not offended? I didn't mean to offend you of course.

Adam said that he was not offended.

—In England and America they do not have to know, One-Arm explained. You do not have to know anything when you are rich and respected. It is not important. It is sufficient to be rich without being anything else, eh? That is something that we have not experienced in Austria.

—But, Horse-Tooth said, we will now that we are Germans.

—Still, if I was an Englishman, One-Arm said, I would be a Conservative. That is the party of the gentlemen. Germany has many friends among the Conservatives who understand our rights.

They drank more schnapps. Adam felt warm. He smiled.

—You like the schnapps? One-Arm was solicitous.

—Yes. It is very good.

—Ah, the friendship grows? It is warm now, eh? That is how it should be. My friend, England and Germany will never go to war again against each other. That was the great mistake of the other war. When we march east again it will be with England. The future of the world demands that the two greatest nations in the world march shoulder to shoulder.

—Let's drink to that, Horse-Tooth said.

—But the schnapps is finished.

—I'll buy some this time, Adam said.

—Ah, you see? Now we are allies. But it is more economical to buy schnapps by the bottle.

Adam said that he would buy a bottle. He felt warm and he was grateful for this warmth to his two new friends.

—Are you staying long in Mariazell? Where are you staying?

—Here at the inn.

—You travel alone?

Adam explained about the interrupted rockclimb. One-Arm grew grave and made cautioning sounds. —I would be very careful about traveling alone. The world is full of unscrupulous men, my dear young friend.

—Rascals, Horse-Tooth said, that would rob you.

—Yes, even now when there is order and correctness in the country, and the country has its pride again and knows its destiny, there are still men who would rob you.

—If they can, Horse-Tooth said. If they can.

—Oh, Adam said. He laughed. He felt marvelously well. —I know about that. I can take care of myself. I keep my money in my moneybelt.

—Capital, Horse-Tooth said. What better place for money than a moneybelt?

—Oh, he is an experienced traveler, One-Arm said. One can see that.

They refilled his glass and their own and drank and again refilled the glasses. They drank a long time, laughing, and cheered him when he spilled his liquor and said that it did not matter in the least. The liquor was easily replaced by refilling the glass; as for the wet table, someone would mop it up sooner or later. Soon Adam reached for his glass and knocked the bottle over.

—I'm sorry, he said. Let's buy another bottle. I spilled it so I shall buy it. All right?

—Now there is a gentleman, One-Arm said. I really admire that. Now we shall really drink.

—But we must have a toast, Adam said.

—Of course, didn't I say that we were gentlemen? To what shall we drink?

—To friendship, One-Arm said. Is that all right?

—That's beautiful, Adam said.

—The King, Horse-Tooth said. We must drink to the King if we are gentlemen.

—And to the Queen.

—And to Edward and to Mrs. Simpson.

—And to being rich, Horse-Tooth said. To not knowing anything.

—To friendship again, One-Arm said, laughing.

—That is the best, Adam said or thought he might have said. Because he was no longer sure of what he was saying. But that was all right. Everything was all right. It didn't matter about Adrianne. Or the mountainclimb. He didn't mind about anything, not even his father. The General was a traitor, everybody said it. It was a lie, of course. —*They are liars and I hate them.*

—*But they are not liars.*

—*Not liars?*

—*No. Do not look at me like that.*

But it didn't matter. Nothing mattered. He felt powerful and strong. He flew above it all in his glider, soared above it into an innocent world where there was no sound of any kind.

It was marvelous to fly in a glider high above everyone who said things. It was like climbing mountains. These good friends seemed to understand.

—Why couldn't Erich understand? he said or thought he said. This was the only time she could come. She couldn't come at any other time. She said: Is it so important? What's so important about a climbing trip? Whose trip is it anyway? It is Erich's. It is important to Erich to prove that he is better than you. It won't do anything for you, only for Erich. Why help him prove a point? Why trouble yourself about him? Why get involved in his emotional problems? And I said, all right. If this is the only time for you. I shall tell Erich. Don't tell him, she said. Don't tell him till you get to Mariazell. I said,

Why? But she only smiled. He would not start the trip if he thought he would not finish it, she said. I want him to start something and not finish it, she said. I want his plans to go wrong . . . want him to know what that feels like. Do that for me and I'll come to you. All right, I said, and then she did not come.

—You cannot depend on women, one of them said.

—That's it, Adam said. *Exactly.*

Everything was marvelously clear. But his voice seemed distant and coming from some other corner of the room. He wondered what his voice was doing in the corner. When he was in primary school he used to be put in corners after fights. There were always fights. Some boy always brought up the subject of the General. Adam fought anybody who said anything about the General. It got to be so that if a boy wanted a fight he would walk up to Adam and say —*Traitor,* or —*Your father is a traitor,* or —*The General is a traitor,* or they would talk about the woman who had caused the *skandal.* They would get their fight. Adam fought hard and tried to hurt the boys he fought. He kicked and punched and hit with books and inkstands and rulers and pencil-cases. He stabbed with pens and gouged with pencils. He was always bloody. It would always take several teachers to break up the fights and then Adam would be ordered to stand in a corner. And now his voice was standing in a corner. Why? It had not done anything. It had not fought or injured anyone.

Poor silly voice.

Adam giggled.

—Come back out, he said.

And then he didn't hear himself at all and he didn't hear the others and the ceiling was a marvelous white canopy like snowflakes rapidly revolving.

During the night he woke to find himself alone in the great bed, huge out of all proportion, with the featherbed and the pillows in marital proximity. The bed was enormous. It was a stadium more than bed. He had had hopes for it; high hopes, he remembered.

The bed filled the room. It crouched on massive black legs like an animal. No sacrifice had been made to it. It had not been fed.

He had hoped Adrianne would like the inn and think it picturesque. He had planned several man-of-the-world monologues about it. The inn had green shutters and was, in point of fact, a replica of all the other inns in the Salzkammergut; not at all unusual.

He woke cold with the featherbed fallen to the floor, wondering why he was in bed in all his clothes. Then he remembered Adrianne and that she had not come. He remembered Erich and the trip. He didn't want to think about that—it was a form of treason—so he closed his eyes. He tried to force sleep to come back. It would not come back. He got up. His legs were rubbery. His head was full of bees and his mouth was parched. His mouth felt as though an army of small peasant boys had run barefoot through it. He thought that if, perhaps, he started now he could catch up with Erich in a day or two.

He packed his things in his shoulder pack. He could not find his watch or his fountain pen. The snaps were torn off his moneybelt. The pouches were empty. He searched the room and his clothes but the money was gone. He could not find it. He remembered the bar and the drinking and the men.

He ran down the stairs but the bar was closed. Only the porter dozed there. The porter was polite. He said his two friends had left after putting him to bed.

—I have been robbed, Adam said. Where did those men go?

—Robbed?

—Yes. Those men robbed me.

—Ha ha ha, the porter said. Of course. Could it be otherwise?

—What?

The porter was no longer polite.

—So you were robbed. And, of course, all your money is gone. Everything.

—Yes. Some Deutschmarks, nearly two thousand French francs and my watch.

—That is everything?

—Also my fountain pen.

—And the bill, of course, is still unpaid?

—How can I pay? They took all my money.

—So it comes to that again, hey? The porter shouted. Do you believe that I was born yesterday? That I descended from the moon?

—Listen, Adam said. Call the police. You have more policemen in this country than you have people. Call the police and make them get my money.

—Of course, sir, the porter said. At your orders. Oh, I shall call the police all right. Have no fears about that. But tomorrow! There is time for arresting thieves and swindlers tomorrow! Now go to your room and stay there. You'll get no featherbed tomorrow, I assure you!

The porter followed Adam up the stairs and locked him in his room. He took away the key. Adam sat on the bed. He felt remarkably alone. He was used to feeling more or less alone but this was a particular loneliness. Outside his friend was on the mountains. The mountains were white and shining in the moonlight.

In time he felt fatigue and sleep creeping up on him; but he knew that he could not afford to sleep. With morning the police would come. He had to be gone long before they came.

He opened the window. He breathed the cold air. The night was clear. He threw his pack far out into the street. He followed the pack.

It occurred to him suddenly that he was a fugitive. He did not know where to go or what to do but he did not worry. He decided to head east toward Hungary. The General, he remembered, had friends in Budapest.

It also occurred to him that he was many kilometers inside Austria and that distances were enormous when you were alone. When you have friends to walk with, time passes quickly.

Climbing the hill above the town he looked back at the toylike gingerbread in the moonlight. The scene was beautiful. It was a fairyland that children might imagine. He turned his back on it and worked his way rapidly up the easy slope to the high ridge that ran above the town, along the valley, to the next peak, and so on to the next, where no one would look for him or question his accent. Soon the wind caught him and it was, then, like flying. He wished he had his glider to fly to Hungary.

He hurried, pushing harder, straight up with the gaping black crevices and the cold wind expertly ignored, until clouds came and hid the moon and the darkness stopped him. He was too good at rockclimbs to go on when he couldn't see. He was too tired to go on, anyway, and lay down among the scrubpine, wrapped in his quilted jacket. There was a wind. He lay a long time listening to the wind.

That night it rained. When he woke in the clean-washed air, he buckled on his pack, went on. He marveled at the beauty of the new day coming up in the Salzkammergut.

Thursday, August the thirty-first

I MICHAL

The situation map stretched across the entire west wall of the underground chamber. It was in shadow. Lights were dim in the War Room and the fans were still.

Outside the sun is shining and there is peace of a nervous, uncertain kind but, for all that, a peace. Here it is dark, he thought, and peace is no longer possible. The map showed war. It was, of course, expected. Feared, foreseen and expected but not really believed. There was no doubt about it now. Events were moving. The war was marching up with giant strides and even its conclusion was assured.

—I never quite believed that it would happen, Michal said. I suppose I hadn't wanted to believe in war. I thought about it the way we all thought in these last few months, in terms of family; where shall I send my wife and when? But I never thought the war would really come. I knew it yet I did not know it.

—There is no doubt now?

—For good or evil we are finally committed.

He made a troubled gesture, staring at the map. His brother moved, impatient.

—Are you that surprised?

—No. But it was the idea of it, don't you see? It did not seem believable. You know a war is coming and you know that it will be a terrible and bloody war, and you have fears and anxieties about it even though you know the outcome.

—That, of course, you can't really know.

—What? Ah yes, of course . . . Michal didn't want to tell his brother what he knew. Well, anyway, you feel the spirit of the country and you say that you are not afraid of anyone and that if, indeed, this war is inevitable you will not die cheaply. You try to accept this inevitable prospect but you are a human being, after all, a civilized man, and you can't accept, without protest, the *fact* of war. And so you question it, and review its antecedents, and you

97

say: Here, at this point, it could have been prevented, and at that point it could have been avoided, and you know that none of this is really true. Still, you review the situation. You try to understand. If anyone is to die, you say, he has a right to understand. That, after all, is justice.

—Justice is a word.

—And words are cheap, is that it?

—Yes. And a dispute with our kind of neighbors can't be resolved with words.

—That's clear now. But you have to try to live calmly and normally in a world that is neither calm nor normal no matter how absurd that seems. So you pretend that you can. You do anything you can to help the illusion.

Michal thought that here, in Poland, there had been less of that oblivious bliss that had chloroformed the world: If it came to fighting, he knew, the country would fight. But he had not wanted to think about war, or consider it, or give it shape and substance by planning for it, as though it was too hard to part with the established order, too painful to upset the daily schedule of small routines.

—So, purely as a human being, you see, I had to ask: Why war? We live as others live. In a country much like any other. Filled with hard sins and virtues, no better or worse than anyone else . . .

Janusz Prus smiled. —There is one difference. Our love of country. No other country I know of has this love spread so broadly, through all levels of society. So deep that it is almost superstition. To touch us there is to call out greater strength than life. It lets us die with gladness. Who knows if there would be a war if we were Czechs or Frenchmen? Perhaps it could have been avoided then.

—I wish we were Frenchmen. This rationale of ours is too tragic to be a source of happiness.

—But in the end it comes to this: Life is only worth living if you have something for which you would die.

—That's too much pride for a world that understands only entries in a ledger.

—Would you have it any other way?

Michal sighed. He shook his head. He stared at the map.

—No. Of course not. The choice is obvious. I can't believe in a world without honor.

The General shrugged. —Hence war.

—Still, there was an illusion. France and England stopped our mobilization only two days ago. It helped me think that perhaps a miracle would happen.

But Janusz Prus was not listening. Michal supposed that this strange brother of his, this tall, one-armed general who trampled on intangibles at will, had never listened to anyone. He is like Pawel, he thought. It is almost as though *he* were Pawel's father. There was the same unconcern with what was proper and expected. The same derisive courage. The thought of Pawel made him wonder where his son was. He looked at the map, at the small blue flags. Janusz was counting them. There were fifteen blue flags on the border and fifteen deep inside the country. There were eighty-one red flags that had grown in a scarlet forest between Germany and Poland. Sixty-one spread like a crimson pool from the Carpathians to the Baltic Sea. Twenty bled in thin lines back into Germany. Sixty divisions poised to strike and twenty on the way.

—And we have fifteen? the General said. *That* doesn't seem believable to me.

—In three days we hope to have fifteen. We don't have them yet.

Michal's voice was flat; it communicated nothing. —In thirteen days we will have thirty. In ten more days we will have thirty-nine.

The colonel stared at his brother across invisible barriers. There was between them a curtain of time and attitudes and aspirations.

Michal wished his brother had not come to see him at the staff that morning. It had been a particularly bad morning with the ambassadors of France and Britain arguing with the Marshal. They wanted him to cancel the mobilization, which was finally on. Michal had been afraid that the weary Marshal would once again bow to the wishes of the politicians. He came close to it. He almost canceled the mobilization. But, somehow, the staff had got the Marshal through the morning without another cancellation. The aerial photographs of von Reichenau's panzers parked nose-to-back for forty-seven miles southwest of the border had been a help. Parked and waiting. Poised like an arrow aimed at the underbelly of the country.

Michal wiped sweat off his neck and forehead.

If I never did anything else (Michal thought) I saved our infant mobilization. That, at least, is something. I stole seventeen hours from the British. It is not much but something. It is my contribution.

He, my heroic, larger-than-life brother, does not know what it is to wrest seventeen hours from the British. He knows what it is to attack and defeat and conquer and to be brave and to be loved and followed but he has never torn seventeen precious hours from the British.

Seventeen hours mean a regiment formed, a troop mounted, a brigade put aboard a train. It is not valorous. It is not magnificent. It is not an item for history books. But it is *my* contribution: a gift of seventeen hours' life for the country which will shortly burn. It is the sort of accomplishment my heroic brother would not know about.

The battle of the conference room. The charge of argument. A barrage of memoranda, followed by an attack of reports. The enemy counterattacks with counterarguments. Bring on the reserves. Attack. God is on the side of the strongest mouth. It is a deadly battle. The good generals Faury and Carton de Wiart live in the Marshal's pocket. Each time he puts his hand in it they scream: Provocation! Under no circumstances are the Germans to be provoked. They must not be angered. They must not be disturbed or interrupted.

The colonel did not wish to think about the allies and the conferences. He did not wish to think about the Polish War Plan and all its assumptions. He had considered both a thousand times. There were altogether too many assumptions in the War Plan. It was assumed that it would rain and that the allies would eventually come. It was assumed that the soldier, the legendary *zolnierz,* would do his duty. He had always done it. This was the only assumption that could be safely made.

The plan was the old Pilsudski Plan of 1934, taken from the archives in August, dusted off and reviewed. It was, perhaps, not designed for the coming war. It was, perhaps, unrealistic in view of the assumptions. But it was the only plan possible: It would have to suffice.

Michal studied the map and the growing scarlet areas at the sides of it. So much would merely have to suffice in the coming days.

Involuntarily, in his mind, the flags translated themselves into men. Human beings. Who slept and ate and waited and looked for shade. Who sweated in the hot sun and ate dust. Who thought about home. Whose armpits itched and whose bellies rumbled. Who had not slept well in the hot dry night.

But, he thought, an officer of the General Staff cannot afford such sentimental luxuries. These are not men. These are divisions. Think of them in terms of Grand Units and Tactical Divisions and Corps and Army Groups and Groups of Operations and forms without shape or face and not in terms of men who grin and scratch and look for shade and you will maintain your equilibrium. Think of them as men and you will fall apart. Because you can see *all* the flags and you know the assumptions and you know about the allies, and you can calculate the degree and probability of falsehood in these assumptions, and you can calculate the times required to bridge distances by armor, and you know that the sum total of these calculations means death for the men, and you have put them there and you know what the real odds are.

The small blue flags were so pathetically few. So many red flags on the map. A fly crawled in the lower left-hand corner of the map. Von Reichenau's massed armor blocked its exit south through the Carpathians. It turned north. It was not discouraged. It walked through Krakow and into Silesia. The Silesian Division of Sadowski barred its way. The fly set off for Czestochowa, the Holy Place, the place of miracles. There is a monastery in Czestochowa. It contains a painting of the Virgin Mother. There have been several miracles effected by this painting. Now is the time for miracles. The fly brushed past Janicki's Seventh Division strung out before the Holy Place; it skirted cavalry and walked into the outposts of Rummel's Corps of Lodz. The small blue flags were spread thin. There were many gaps. The fly chose one, went north. It crawled through Wielkopolska and Kutrzeba's soldiers of the Poznan Army. Then through Bortnowski's Torun Army up to the coast, the sea, Danzig and Westerplatte—a tiny blue pinpoint in a sea of red. It turned off into Germany but a forest of red flags and pins barred the way. This was Guderian's armor. The fly turned south. It went back the way it had come, southward along the border back to where it started its walk on the map: the territory of Antoni Szylling's Krakow Army. With five divisions it was the biggest of the Polish armies. Half of it, though, was theoretical.

Where was the rest of it?

In barracks, east. Taking off workmen's smocks and peasant shirts and laughing and trying on unfamiliar uniforms and walking biggrinned and self-conscious into barracks yards with loaves of freshbaked village bread in pockets and flowers in buttonholes and hatbands, and reading red cards and saying: —*Well, see you in spring when all this is over,* and waiting for red cards that had not yet come.

If only there were some fortifications . . .

Fortifications made war orderly. But there were none. There were only men. The fortified zone of Silesia had been sold to the Germans sketch by sketch only three months earlier. A cartographer who needed money to cure his syphilitic wife sold every meter of it. It had strained the nation's budget to build it. How the French and British screamed! The French could afford screams. They had the Maginot. The British could afford to scream, Michal thought. They would fight to the last Frenchman, as usual.

Damn them. Damn them to hell. I hope they feel this war.

—I would forgive your British friends all their sins if only they had allowed us our mobilization, Michal said.

—We have it now. It might not be too late. When will the war begin?

—Tomorrow, according to our people in Berlin. The British think it will begin on the fifteenth.

—Tomorrow? That is . . . what? The last day of August?

—The first of September.

Michal tried to control his hands. They had begun to shake. He felt his brother looking at them. He put them behind his back. The right side of his face began to twitch.

—And what do *you* believe? The General's voice was hard.

Michal tried to control the twitching muscles of his face. It was important to maintain composure and to appear unconcerned. He tried to match the General's assurance but his voice betrayed him.

—An hour before you came here I was with the Marshal and the ambassadors. It seems that these days you cannot see the one without the others. They wanted us to cancel the mobilization. They swore the Germans would not move before the fifteenth. They have begun new negotiations with the Germans and threatened to advise their governments to cancel the guarantees to us if we went on with the mobilization. The Marshal refused and ordered all troops into line. Say what you wish about Smigly-Rydz, I know you never liked him, but he did this one thing: He was strong this morning. We are to reach full combat readiness by 0100 hours tomorrow. Do you know what we expect on line at that time? Since the mobilization started only yesterday we shall have eight divisions and three brigades of cavalry on sixteen hundred kilometers of line. You must forgive me if I seem upset this morning. I can see that you are disappointed in me. But I believe that our men in Berlin are right and theirs are wrong and that we shall be fighting when the sun comes up tomorrow. This is sufficient reason for being upset.

The General stared at Michal. It was as though the older man had slapped his face. His face was gaunt and dry.

—What shall we have the day after tomorrow?

The colonel looked through notes. His voice was dull. It was as though he were reciting the minutes of an unimportant meeting.

—By the twelfth hour of the day it is expected that the Army will reach forty-five percent of readiness for war. Mobilization of the first stage will be sixty percent completed. Concentration will be thirty-five percent completed. Of our total 1,700,000 men and 50,000 officers we will have fifteen divisions of infantry, six cavalry brigades and three and one-half battalions of National Defense volunteers to meet, stop and hold for ten days sixteen panzer and motorized divisions and forty infantry divisions which we have already identified on the border. Thus you can understand, perhaps, my lack of composure. But we have definitely identified eighty-one German divisions either on the border or on the way to it. We know that they assigned 4,000 aircraft and

3,700 tanks to Operation White. Operation White is their name for this war with us. They have been working on it since April of last year. They have, you see, the advantage of not having French and British allies.

The General frowned and made a quick, impatient gesture and Michal struggled to compose his voice.

—You are impatient with my doubt, Michal said. You have no doubts even now, and I have no doubt about the spirit of the Polish soldier. I have no doubts that he will do his duty. But no one likes being murdered; no one likes to be condemned to death or asked to commit suicide for no good reason. I think our allies have condemned us. They have asked us to commit suicide and to destroy ourselves, and this, I think, is reason for dismay.

—We have faced odds before. It has been bad before. It is not the first time.

—It has never been like this before. The colonel closed his eyes. He tried to force the image of men from his mind. Men who trusted leaders and waited and hoped and who believed. Men who would fight and who were condemned. Men who would be erased.

—Sacrifice, the colonel said. It always comes to that in the end, doesn't it? But there must be a reason.

—There is.

—I do not believe it. I do not see the need for national suicide. I see why we must fight, don't misunderstand me. I do not see why we should be condemned.

—Look, the General said. We have lived as soldiers. Politics has never been a part of our lives. This is no time to ask the whys of anything.

—I ask it, Michal said. His voice was calmer but his hands still fluttered like the twitching eyelids of an old dog. —These small blue flags are men. I put them there each day. They are only there because I put them there: alone and naked and exposed. My little flags are 270,000 soldiers and 36,000 reservists and 12,000 cavalrymen, or 318,000 men. They are men, after all, you see. There are 199 men to one mile of line, always supposing that there will be a line, or, reduced to its ultimate absurdity, one man to each twenty-six and a half English feet along 1,500 miles, provided we all take a rifle, including the Marshal, and line upon the border. I cannot help thinking of that border and the men on it. I see the 3,700 tanks on it. I cannot help thinking that there could be a million more men on it if we had mobilized a week ago. That one week would have saved us. We would not be condemned.

The General made another of the quick, hard gestures as though to brush his brother's uncertainties away.

—Don't you believe in victory?

—No. We have lost this war. It was lost long ago in the Battle of the Budgets, our impossible frontier, our own Byronic unpreparedness, our faith in other people's word. How much of this is our fault and how much a classic, atavistic wish for self-destruction, I don't know. But, since you ask, no, I do not believe in victory.

—Then you should resign.

So simple, then?

Michal found that his hands no longer trembled and his face was still, and his voice was calm when he began to speak.

—I disappoint you. This is not what you would expect from your former adjutant. From your brother, perhaps, but not your adjutant. This is not the way you did things in the Ukraine in 1921. Those were brave days. These are different days. These days the fate of nations is not decided on some gallant battlefield but in a conference room halfway around the world. You mentioned war plans. Well, we have a War Plan. Our allies have also planned a way to fight the Germans. It is unfortunate that their plans and ours do not coincide. Do not look shocked; it is easy to explain. Not easy to understand, perhaps, but not at all difficult to explain. We will begin at the beginning, and the beginning is a conference in Paris in March of last year. There the British and French staffs met to plan a joint war to resist the Germans. They decided that the Germans would attack France in 1942 and so they planned a ten-year war with all the fine British attention to detail. The war was to be a defensive war. Neither the French nor the British were to attack the Germans anywhere at any time. That was left for others to do. They expected that the Germans, the Italians and the Japanese would attack simultaneously, that the Germans would attack England by air and France on land. The Allied plan was to hold fast in France and in the third year of the war to attack the Italians in Africa. In the sixth year of the war the Italian mainland was to be invaded but Germany was not to be attacked at all. The British fleet was merely to blockade the Germans. The second part of the Allied war plan was, and still is, to interest America in joining the war. The British have much contempt for the Americans but they cannot win a German war without them. They came too close to losing the Great War to forget that. Russia was also to be bribed to fight the Germans. I do not know the nature of this secret bribe but I leave that to your imagination. Thus the plan was to be a huge holding action until the Russians and the Americans could be propagandized into fighting and winning the war. All this time they did not consider Poland as a factor. They made their plans without considering us at all. And then came the political guarantees to Poland and they had to count us in on their plan. And here we come to climax. Now you will know why I am disturbed. Perhaps you won't be so terribly disappointed after all.

Michal again wiped sweat off his face and forehead. He stared at the map. He did not look at his brother's face.

—At first they would not meet with us, he said. They made many excuses. But we insisted and finally there was a meeting in Paris this April and we insisted that they give some thought to us and finally they did. The British said they could do nothing for us and did not attend the meeting. The French argued but finally agreed to attack Germany on the third day of the war. It was to be a small attack. But on the fifteenth day a full-scale offensive against Germany was to be begun by the majority of French land forces. According to a separate air convention signed by the French and the British, air attacks against Germany were to begin on the first day of the war so as to draw off the Luftwaffe from Poland. This is the agreement. This is the basis of our war plan: to hold until the French invade the Germans.

His brother stared attentively. —Were there conditions?

—There were, of course, conditions. We were not to provoke the Germans or start the war ourselves. We were to wait until we were attacked, then hold until the allies came.

—Yes. The General was thoughtful, but still undisturbed. —Can we do it?

Suddenly Michal laughed.

The General looked at him curiously.

—Why do you laugh?

—Wait. Later. Let me go on about the War Plan. The French have today one hundred and ten divisions. They have as many tanks as the Germans and some of them are bigger and better than anything the Germans have. They are capable of a great assault. They and the British have an air force almost twice the size of the Luftwaffe. They could crush the Germans today if they wanted to. Look at my map and see how many divisions the Germans left to face the French. Do you see them? Seven. Seven against one hundred and ten. Does this look as though the Germans expected the French to attack them? Does it look as though they expected our allies to move? Does it, perhaps, suggest that the French are going to come to our aid? Or does it suggest that we have been betrayed? And is that sufficient reason for loss of composure? Is it enough to justify a certain lack of faith in victory? Perhaps you are now a little less disappointed in your old adjutant.

Now it was the General's turn to say nothing and to look silently at the situation map.

—I have been unfair to you, Michal said. For this I am sorry. I have played a little game with you and this is not fair. But it is the sort of game that has been played with us and I wanted to show you how it felt to be the object of the game. The French (he said, suddenly serious and professionally cold) are not going to move. Marshal Gamelin has issued a secret order to his General Georges. In it he orders a limited advance with three divisons on the third day of the war. If these divisions find any resistance, even outpost resistance, they are to return at once to the Maginot Line. That is the extent of our allies' assistance. That is how they mean to keep their word.

—Is this true? The General's voice was hollow.

—Yes. Do you know where we learned of this directive? Our secret service stole it from German staff files. The Germans know they have nothing to fear from our allies. They have been given their permission to begin the war.

—The Marshal knows about this?

—Of course.

—Then we are really alone and the Germans know it.

—Yes. We hope, of course, that our allies will move eventually. The Marshal believes it. We are to hold the Germans until our allies come, the way the Belgians did it in 1914.

—And if they don't come?

—Then there is one thing we can do. We've always done it well. We must put up such an incredible fight that Poland will be remembered in the future. That is what matters, after all. That the peacemakers remember us when they sit at the conference table. That they are not allowed to forget how this war began.

—We are to die with noise, is that it? We are to make such a great sound in our fall that we shall be remembered? Do you know what you are doing? What kind of war is this?

Michal passed his hand over his face. His voice was noncommittal.

—One way or the other the country will survive, he said.

The General laughed. —And so to bed, he said. Sabers out! Line from the right at a trot! Charge! So that some gentlemen at some future time remember something that died and bring it back to life. Do you believe they will bother to remember? Do you think anyone will care in ten years' time what we do here today? How vast a sign must we blaze? How huge must be the sound of our annihilation? Do you still think the world has a conscience to which one can appeal? Are we, in short, to die on speculation?

Michal said nothing then. Was there no other way? Yes. There was, of course. There are always alternatives, aren't there? Humanity always has a choice. One can arrange a compromise with providence and sell an idea in exchange for safety. . . .

—There is no other way, he said.

The General nodded.

Michal said that perhaps the French could be induced to come.

The General laughed. —Ah yes, the French. He spread his fingers in the French military salute. —The croissant and the apéritif. Do you remember? Are they still a part of the Polish War Plan?

—They have to be. There isn't any plan without them.

—And rain? Of course you are counting on the rain?

—It always rains in August and September.

—So you've made God a member of the General Staff?

—He'll do as well as any one of us, Michal said.

Again he saw the faces of the men who would begin to die tomorrow. Some of them he knew, the field commanders: the precise Kutrzeba (always wrapped in details, enmeshed in plans and theories); Bortnowski with the leonine head and posture of a Caesar (the task assigned to him in Pomerania was near impossible); the courteous, knightly Szylling; the nervous, mobile features of Przedrzymirski, who spread his thin Modlin group between Warsaw and East Prussia in the north; Rummel, commander of the Lodz Army on the Warta River, an arrogant, overbearing martinet contemptuous of anyone's opinion but his own; the self-indulgent Fabrycy, who was to hold the Carpathian passes in the south . . . He knew them all. Can they hold back the red sea, halt the inevitable? Can they and the other men whose faces he would never know hold out? Or if they fall, can they assure remembrance?

Michal faced the map again. He wanted to attack it, to tear it down and crumple its bland, noncommittal face.

—Maps, he said. Scale portraits of earth seen from above. Everything is calm on maps. Everything is peaceful. Everything is in its correct position. That is how God sees it. That is where God makes his mistake.

—Our battleline is on the border, the General said. That is a mistake. We should at least pull back to our riverlines.

Michal laughed a little.

—We can't do that. There are, you see, political considerations. There can be no retreats until the French and English declare war.

—What have they got to do with it? They won't be dying out there tomorrow. It is our Army that could be saved today by a retreat. This isn't politics any longer. It is war. There is no place for politics in war. Its conduct is a soldier's business and there is no room in it for any but military considerations.

—There is in this one, Michal said. Don't you understand?

He would not, of course.

Michal looked at the darkened face of his younger brother, the brave and brilliant leader of legendary raids when with a thousand horsemen he could, and did, hold back great hordes of Bolsheviks pressing westward. What simple wars those were! How clear the situations! Here was your side and there the enemy's and you drew up your men and pointed with a saber and shouted charge and the trumpets played and the lances swept down beside the horses' ears and in the thunder of hooves and the cries of men and the clash of sabers the future of the Nation was resolved.

But who was friend today and who was enemy and who was ally; who stopped mobilizations and who did not intend to help? Who made speeches in the House of Commons while a nation died? Who gave the empty guarantees that brought about a war and then stayed back to watch? Not simple now.

And there was Brother Janusz looking like a thundercloud.

Not simple now!

There were the sabers and the lances and the cheering infantry; there on the map where the blue flags faced the scarlet sea, and there the simplicity and the faith and the belief and the narrow horizons between flatpressed ears of a horse or across the out-thrust edge of a bayonet. Not here. Here there was the map. Here the political considerations. Of how to make their allies come and fight. Of how to make two great and noble nations keep their word. Of how to make death meaningful.

He said: —You are right, of course. We should be withdrawing to fight on logical positions: forests and riverlines. Oh yes, I know. Even with this magnificent map of mine, which is so orderly and precise, with the reports from the border, which are too confident of tomorrow, with his unawareness of the chaos which will begin to grip the country tomorrow: roads, bridges, rails bombed . . . communications down . . . all of western Poland on the move eastward . . . Smigly-Rydz knows the line is too long. We do not have the men to hold it. It is outflanked now, before the first German soldier has crossed the border. Don't you think he knows? Don't you suppose he can see it, even on my map? Why do you think he ordered the Army to fight on the border instead of some logical riverline like the Vistula and San and Narew? Oh yes, I know, we can't abandon the richest half of our country without fighting . . . a matter of honor as well as economics. But there are also political considerations. Look (Michal's voice was steady), the weather is insane. It's real Hitler weather. The sun has burned our fields as hard as concrete. The Germans will cross our rivers with their tanktreads dry. They will be tearing us apart with pincers bigger than our total forces. Of course the answer is an immediate withdrawal! It is the only answer. It is the logical thing to do. But we must abandon logic. We must induce our allies to enter the war.

—By dying? The General's voice was contemptuous.

—Try to understand. In Paris they are rioting today against their commitment. In London there's a cabinet crisis. The British want negotiations. Dahlerus has brought them new letters from Goering. The London merchants have forced Chamberlain to send Sir Neville Henderson with offers to Hitler. They will be talking while we will be dying. They will talk on unless we can encourage them to enter the war. What effect would a Polish retreat have on them even before the war began? Or on the first or second day of the war? Would they be encouraged? They are casting about for some way out of their commitment. Can we encourage them by showing them how strong the Germans are?

—What will our dying do?

—It will shame them. There are honorable men among them. They will point out this shame.

The General shook his head. —This is no war for me. Give me men and I will know what to do. I will lead them and we shall fight and it will all be clean. But this is nothing that I know about. This is simple murder.

—It is not murder yet, Michal said. It will only be murder if the French don't come.

—You know they will not come.

—Eventually they will and so will the British. And they must come before it is all finished here. We must shame them into it and into remembering.

—Do you believe they will?

—I no longer believe in anything, Michal said.

1 THE CORRESPONDENT

The room was one of three above a stable. The stable had copper gutters and iron rings and the warm influence of horses. It had a cool, damp cellar smell. He thought it would be good for sleeping in the fall. This town got hot in autumn, he remembered, and September would be here tomorrow.

There was a smell of dust in the place, and of things a long time unused. Sometimes this was old leather heavy with reminiscences, or dry harness and green brass and copper rings. Sometimes it was the sad suggestion of arid land and things that grow and are not harvested. It was no place to hurry to at night.

Loomis had rented the carriagehouse from a woman who ran a summer restaurant in Marymont. She had bought the house from a man who had been an ambassador in South America and had, apparently, looted the hemisphere of ponchos, blankets, earthenware, moronic-faced gods and a bas-relief of St. Anthony being tempted.

The woman had Mexican furniture. It stood, incongruous, on pink marble paving under stained-glass windows. The effect, he thought, was one of terror that even the marble would not prove durable enough.

The woman said the house had cost forty thousand rubles in the old days when Warsaw was still part of the Russian Empire. She regretted the passing of the old days. Her name was Vogel. Her parents and her husband's father had come from Germany. She said she didn't have to work but wanted to keep busy. Everyone must keep busy, she said. Loomis said he didn't need to work but wanted to keep busy. She said she thought he would be happy there. All her guests were busy.

The house was in a one-way street of stables and carriagehouses. The street rose steeply and Loomis' apartment was at the highest point. It commanded a really splendid view, and perhaps this was why the little balcony had been built outside the tall bedroom casement window. All of the houses were attached to stables by archways, mostly Gothic. Each had a cobbled court. There were no sidewalks in this part of town. Those who had built the houses had not wanted those who could not afford to ride to walk there. Frau Vogel rented only to foreign visitors.

Loomis unpacked.

Each time he dipped into a suitcase he brought up not a shirt or sweater but a face, an hour on a hillside, the crackling sound of bullets in the Pyrenees. Nimi had seen these things as he supposed they really were: cloth and metal. She called it childish to keep them. Why keep old things? She said that she was being realistic. Women are realistic. That is good; someone has to be practical and realistic. But surely not all the time, not about everything.

There was a mottled stone from the Ebro River. He had gone to the Ebro on a bet to get it. Pawel Prus had lost the bet. The champagne cork was from the Ambassadors' in Madrid. With the binnoculars they had watched women bathing off the Llobregat. And in the metal box that had held English cigarettes were three metal things on ribbons—one red, one green, one white and blue with a red stripe centered—a set of captain's bars (U.S. and tarnished), a button, and some pale shreds of Players Navy Cut. These things meant something now and then; not much, really not enough, to show for all those years.

It had not been easy despite a number of advantages. He had inherited money from his mother and married a great deal more of it and had a name which, in his small town, had a measure of importance. Despite this he was largely homemade, a product of his effort (having gone to work in the Otis cityroom after school, and then to other towns, to other schools and cityrooms where names, he hoped, were not important; where he could make his own way). He reached a certain peak, a small professional eminence from which to look down. It was a comfortable little platform; from it he could disparage less glamorous professions. But there was something not quite clean about it because the glamour was artificial and shoddy and the work trivial, and all of it an excuse for an empty bank account. He was visibly unimpressed with the bylines and the casual way in which the mayor's name could be dropped, and the casual reference to drinks had with (and on) this or that politician, and the fierce gossip about absent members. The little eminences were so jealously guarded, the small heights so bloodily defended. There was a saying he remembered: that a newspaperman seldom caught the six-fifteen, but that when he did finally get home he had things to say. He wondered who invented that facesaving nonsense. Dull people who told dull stories about painfully dull and frightened little lives. He thought: There must be something wrong in this lack of appreciation. He wondered why he couldn't see the marvelous nature of the work, why he even found something sinister about it, why he thought of cancer cells multiplying. What could be dangerous about it, after all? What difference did it make what anyone thought about it, how close they thought they sat to God's right hand? They were, after all, such unimportant little oracles, small, frightened men trying to cast a shadow.

His office and his wife were both several thousand miles away. These miles were, in themselves, a form of independence. He thought: Well, here I go again being disloyal and unkind. That seemed to be his greatest fault in work and marriage, dissatisfaction with the fact of it and a lack of kindness. He had that ruthless cruelty, Nimi used to say, the inability to compromise. Well, maybe once he had it but not anymore. Somehow the large issues tended to disappear and the small treasons were explained away. He liked to think that he was kind and patient and forbearing and that he had courage. But somehow the little battles of the day were never quite won, the strong decisions not strong enough and the kindness took a permanent vacation.

Meanwhile there was marriage. Christ, marriage.

If only it wasn't such a constant effort. If only it wasn't so committing. If there was some way to give it a rest, to take time out from it; some way to send it out with the carpets for a beating, to hang it out to dry.

It could have been all right, he supposed. And if I could have stayed what I was, being what I was, and if she could have been what she wanted to be but never was, I would not be here now. Here, or anywhere where she was not.

But that's it about marriage: There is too much of it. There is too much of being married and not being anything else. There is no way for anyone to be what he wants to be. You are what you have to be, and know it, and that's the worst of it.

There must be more to marriage than bills and bridge and cocktails and child psychology and amateur dramatics and tennis (and Nimi's innumerable instructors) and more cocktails and visiting and being visited. Otherwise, why would people do it?

Well, he thought, it was all right at first. There was that urgency about it and it was good, then, really good, the way it can be. So where did the good feeling go? Who killed it? Where did selfishness and cowardice begin?

If there had been some way to talk about it, to explain without hurting, it would have been all right. But truth is spoken only twice in marriage: in the beginning, when there's this urgency for being married, and at the end, and then it's too late to say anything.

Oh Christ, marriage. Sweet fruit of love. Where does that go after marriage? What makes it what it is and where does the love go?

He went on unpacking. He took off his clothes and put on his robe and slippers and brought his shaving gear out of the smallest of his five suitcases and stared at the framed photograph of his wife, who smiled up at him from among the socks, shirts and military brushes. The brushes had been her idea. His tight, clipped mustache had been her idea. Nimi had altogether too many ideas involving her husband. She was a small, compact, energetic woman; marvelous on the tenniscourt, he remembered. She was also marvelous at a cocktail party, magnificent while presiding over dinner, not so magnificent in the kitchen and less than first-rate in bed. At least, he was careful to correct himself, not in *his* bed. She was a bright, courageous, emancipated college girl and it was not her fault that she was still just that after fifteen years. Some girls do become women, Loomis supposed. At least I think they do. Most don't. Nimi won't. It's not her fault. It's just the way things are. What things?

He thought about home. Home was a bright, beautifully organized apartment furnished and planned and bought and paid for by his wealthy wife. It was a part of her, and each time he entered it he had a feeling that he was violating some part of her, entering sacred precincts where he had no right to be. It was a secret, private place, all hers. There was something a little furtive about the way he entered the apartment. It was not anything he cared to think about now, thousands of merciful miles away from Nimi and her bright apartment. But you can't get away from it, can you? Never. Those hungry walls go with you where you go.

Loomis was in the bathroom with the water running when the knocking came. At first he did not hear it, then he did. Yes? Who was there? It was the houseboy. Pan Korespondent was wanted on the telephone.

Out of the bath and dripping down the corridor back to the room. Large blots of water mark the trail. Cold with the windows open. The robe is soaked.

—Hullo?

It was Pawel.

—*Arriba comandante!* Death to the Moors and the Tercio!

—*Muerte a Franco!*

—*Avanti Mussolini!*

—Up yours too, old friend, what a time to call.

—Were you in bed? With anyone I know?

—Alone and in a bath, *Pawelku.*

—My condolences.

Loomis laughed and he heard Pawel laughing.

This was a good sound. It was good to hear. It was like all the times in Spain and in Ethiopia when there was so remarkably little to laugh about and there were such frequent opportunities to lose one's perspective and laughter was so terribly important. Laughter prevented a serious involvement. Serious in the sense that one was committed, that one began to feel the way the natives felt about their war: losing the precious capacity for emotional detachment, the oh-so-valuable cynicism that made life amusing.

There had been such times, frequently. And there was always Pawel at such times to laugh and comment and amuse and to make seriousness absurd. It was good to hear this particular laughter.

—I got your message, Pawel said. My landlord is impressed. He looks upon me with immense respect now that he knows I am an intimate friend of a famous correspondent.

—Your landlord is an asshole, Loomis said.

—Agreed. His young, impressionable wife agrees. I have frequently managed to impress his wife but I could find no way to impress him. Now, I am sure, he will reduce my rent.

—Congratulations. Are you coming with me to the Bristol?

—The Europejski. The reception is at the Europejski. That's where the Foreign Ministry does all its celebrating. That's where they introduce their usual *figura* of importance.

—And which particular *figura* is on show today?

—Who knows? Don't you know?

—No idea. That little fellow from the press department, Swiderski, merely said that I would be surprised.

—Well, are you ready? I have a car to take us to the Europejski.

—*Minuta,* fearless hunter.

But the *minuta* became three, then five, then fifteen, then thirty-five, and when Loomis came into the street Pawel was not there. Either he had not yet arrived or he had stepped into one of the cafés. Loomis looked for him. Then he asked for him. First he asked the porter.

—*Nein, mein Herr.* The porter was icily polite.

Another man started to say something and walked away with a melodramatic clenching of the fists.

—A man of thirty-five, tall, dark like a gypsy?

—*Nein, mein Herr.*

—You, sir, can you help me?

This young man's lips trembled and he clenched his fists and God, yes, you could almost see the patriotic fires blazing. He wore a button of the OZN in his lapel, which made him a patriot indeed. A red mobilization card peeked from his pocket like a handkerchief.

—Pig! German pig! he said. He spat in Loomis' eye.

—You little sonovabitch, Loomis said and hit him in the nose.

The patriot flew backwards and landed on the cobblestones. His nose sprayed blood on Loomis.

—*Gwalt! Policia!*

Someone caught Loomis by the right arm and someone by the left and several persons shouted and a handsome distinguishedlooking gentleman hit him on the head with a rolled umbrella. Loomis fell down. The gentleman with the umbrella aimed a few ineffectual blows. The young man with the button got up and kicked Loomis in the ribs. Blood from his face cascaded onto Loomis.

—You little shit, Loomis said and punched his kneecap. The young man shouted and fell down again. The gentleman with the umbrella lifted it overhead like a twohanded sword, but the porter and some other man caught him up under the arms and bore him, with legs churning furiously, out of sight. The young man with the broken nose got up and limped away.

All of this lasted less than half a minute. One moment the street outside the Vogel house was loud with shouts and oaths and the fat thud of falling bodies, there were yells and blood and outflung fists and descending umbrellas; then there was nothing.

—Are you all right, *mein Herr?* It was the silverhaired porter, solicitous, amused. —I trust there is no permanent damage to your head?

—Kiss my ass, Loomis said in English.

—Pardon?

—*Küsse mein* . . . oh, the hell with it.

—You are not a German?

—No, I'm not a German.

—Sir, our apologies but it is the times. The times are difficult, you understand.

—Help me up.

—Your suit, sir . . . I am truly sorry.

—I am also sorry.

—If you will telephone the laundry before nine o'clock it will be repaired and cleaned before evening.

Loomis felt like laughing. He wondered if the buttonbearing patriot's blood, now sweet and sticky and vaguely evilsmelling on his face, could be considered the First Blood of World War Two. Spilled in defense of hate in the name of love. Dedicated to hysteria. *Battle of the Vogel Stoop* would make a lovely headline. And the conclusion. There must be a moral conclusion. We are all so moral nowadays. Something about Never Again or Lest We Forget, a proper and respectable American conclusion about the war and the evils thereof. Mustn't forget the gentleman with the rolled umbrella. Hell hath no fury like a noncombatant. Who said that? Wounds cleaned and stitched by nightfall if you telephone.

Ribs ache. The little shit must have had steel points on his shoes.

Then Pawel came. At first Loomis did not recognize him: tall boots with spurs, tight breeches, short cavalry jacket with the high, silverbraided collar. But the face was the same: saturnine, amused. The careful stride of the hunter was the same.

—What happened here?

Loomis laughed. The porter handed him a handkerchief. There was much blood. The young man must have had a vast supply of it.

—They beat me up.

The porter said it was an error of identity.

—They thought I was a German. There was a brisk engagement. At first I was outflanked, and, as in the best scenarios, things looked black. But virtue triumphs. Since my heart is pure I had the strength of ten. And now that the relief column has arrived from Zinderneuf let us stack arms and sing songs of the Legion.

Pawel asked if Loomis had been injured.

—Only my dignity.

—Each time I see you, *comandante,* you have blood on you.

—It is the times. But have you noticed? It is always someone else's blood.

They went upstairs, where Loomis changed his clothes.

There were few other correspondents at the party and, certainly, there were no Americans, who, wisely and according to instructions, had stayed in Berlin.

There was a brittle little woman from a French magazine. There were her poodles, which looked much like their overmanicured mistress. There were two Englishmen who looked superior, and a laughing Swede, two secretive Russians and a little Jap. There were Italians in and out of uniform and a British officer with an eyepatch. This man was easily recognizable as Carton de Wiart, head of the British Military Mission in Warsaw. Loomis knew him slightly. He wondered where Faury was. The Frenchman was never far behind de Wiart, a faithful shadow. Most of the other guests were Poles: journalists and colonels without ribbons and quick pale young men with lacquered hair who looked like caricatures of Joseph Beck. There was a handful of glittering young women from the theater.

As the party went on, Loomis had the feeling that he was attending a last rite. He wondered if the others could tell how he felt about them. Certainly they knew who he was and where he had been. Spain was the bloody end of one republic and he, Loomis, witnessed all the bloody ends.

He wondered if they thought of him as some kind of vulture, the running-mate of death. But if they did, they gave no sign of it. Everyone was exceedingly polite and Miller was quite wrong about the bourbon; they had quite a bit of it at the Europejski.

Loomis felt hypocritical.

Thinking that he could escape for a while and not be missed, away from their politeness and his own smiles that were not warm enough, he went out on the balcony. It was quiet there and cool. Streetlights beamed whitely. A fat barrage balloon flashed dingy grey or silver. He heard the Vistula, then saw it: There a stray beam bounced off the balloon and lit the water with a thousand fires.

Lazienki Park was black, a jewelcase with pinpoint lights strung through it, a great blaze of it at the Belweder where old Pilsudski used to live. Then there was more light: the city (Krakowskie Przedmiescie scarlet and blue in neon; Nowy Swiat and Marszalkowska, elegant avenues; the blue coolness of the Saxon Gardens, the white finger of the Prudential building thrust sixteen stories up from Napoleon's Square); then blackness where the Vistula slashed through like a saberstroke, then more light from the Praga across the river, then more black night.

All was strangely quiet; so perhaps they knew.

He saw through a curtain of a kind: the smoke and fire of Madrid and Barcelona and his firm resolution not to become involved. Not again. Miller was right: I am an American and what do I care about a European war? It is merely copy.

But he saw the barricades and the overturned streetcars and the uprooted paving stones and the shallow graves dug in the streets in the cold damp soil among the steel pipes, and students with air rifles, and the dead horses. That was the worst of it, he thought: the horses. They, at least, are always innocent.

He thought about war. Did he really have an instinct? Could he smell wars coming? And why did it always have to happen to people he liked?

At times he thought that there was something wrong with him: It was as though wars followed him, as though he brought them with him like a plague.

Question: If typhoid fever can be carried by a carrier why not the germ of war? Answer: No answer. Perhaps this time I'm wrong.

Certainly nothing seemed to have changed in Warsaw. It was as he remembered it from 1926: The park was black and the town was bright and the river ran through the town into the night and north into the Baltic Sea at Danzig and ended there, and wars and Germans were many miles away.

The peace and quietness of the town confused him a little. He thought (with a sudden fear, a touch of anxious panic) that, perhaps, there would be no war. There had to be one. He needed one. It had become increasingly difficult for him in New York. Of late his assignments had become less and less important and this and that was said about his drinking (which was not

113

unusual) and this and that about his competence (in view of his drinking) and this and that and the other about his professional achievements. . . .

A well-reported war would be very useful. It would erase the small doubts left behind in New York. They were still not important doubts; no one who mattered had said anything. But when enough fellowscribblers started talking in their happily derogatory vein, more ponderous voices would join the chorus.

He breathed the night air and smelled the roses in the garden. He smelled the sweet smell of chestnuts and he heard the river. He heard trucks and saw their yellow lights unfold across the park, distant and cool. The moon was yellow. It threw a dead white light on the water. And now a woman came out of the shadow under the balcony, where, he supposed, the garden door still was, and walked across the small lawn to where the artificial lake began; some stray light touched her. It was pale light. Her face was hidden but he thought it would be, probably, a pretty face, one that had looked into mirrors and knew that it was pretty. He saw the red glow of her cigarette. She wore a cocktail dress of sorts, some shiny stuff that left her back and shoulders bare. In that dress with all the other darkness she looked fragile and small.

She walked up to the artificial lake with the cigarette crooked at her shoulder and stopped there. Contemplating what? Tomorrow's dinner was arranged. Tomorrow's breakfast was still problematic but God takes care of pretty girls. The Lord would provide.

He supposed that she was well aware of the picture she made: fragile, appealing in that light. He thought he had seen her before. One of the actresses inside? One of the glittering girls with long hands sitting with ankles crossed at lunchtime at the Bristol, in that same cocktail dress or one like it later at the Quid Pro Quo. Her eyes would slide unfocused over her escort's shoulder. Later she would have dinner and the *koktajl*. What a revolting word that was. Later she would be more amenable to this or that. Or perhaps the other.

He was sure he had seen her before. Certainly the pose with the cigarette was familiar. He had seen that introspective stride before. She stood above the artificial lake looking, herself, artificial, with arms crooked, back curved, and a little belly thrust out towards the water, her neck bent.

Moonlight was yellow. It lighted up the garden. He was about to say something, make some sound to break the spell of some garden-girl-water-moonlight-roses premonition when a large shadow detached itself from the black shade under the balcony and became a man walking firmly.

Something about him was familiar. Loomis had seen that lurching stride before, as though the man was uncomfortable on the ground, as though he was not used to feeling earth under his boots. He saw the silver braid snaking on the band of the military cap he carried: a general officer. Man, braid, cape made an impression on him. Moon, distant traffic sounds, shadows and the river and now the stalking dark figure in the military cape.

A breeze came suddenly.

It blew back the cape and bared a shoulder and Loomis saw the sleeve pinned up under the multicolored blaze of ribbons. The General came up beside the woman. He spoke quietly. They were too far for Loomis to hear them but he could see the man's angry gesture. He urged the woman to do something. Her answer fell monosyllabic and flat. They were like puppets on the lighted stage of the garden. The soldier puppet gestured with one arm. The woman puppet shook her head. The soldier puppet urged, explained, pointed to the building where now a blaze of light and sound poured from the room where the party was. She said something in a low voice and shook her head. Her shoulders rose and fell. The General looked at her a moment, then nodded slowly, as though a great and difficult decision had been made, as though something conclusive and irrevocable had been decided; then left her and went back into the shadows the way he had come.

And now the girl was again alone and the garden was momentarily quiet. She stared into the water. She took a step up on the balustrade that separated the artificial pond from the tailored lawn. And then she laughed. She stretched her arms and gave a skip, one-two, like a child. Then she spread her arms wide with the palms out and up to the moon or to the dingy grey balloon and spun around and saw him, Loomis, while she faced him in the spin, and stopped with arms outspread, looking up surprised.

There were two things that he could do. Speak to her or go. One or the other was expected. He threw his cigarette away. It arced towards her. He went back inside.

—Where were you? Pawel said.

—Out on the balcony.

—They were looking for you.

—There was a girl there in the garden. I was about to talk to her when a man joined her. They quarreled about something. I think I witnessed the breakup of something romantic. The man looked familiar. He was a general and he had one arm. Do you know any one-armed generals?

Pawel looked at him curiously.

—There is my uncle. You talked to him in 1926.

And then, all of it fell in place. The curtain lifted. The lurching stride and the pinned-up sleeve found their proper groove among recorded memories.

Of course!

He had been promised a surprise.

It would be Prus, of course, the legendary raider, the Genius of the Cavalry Maneuver. So they have brought him back. For what? To illustrate national unity in the face of war?

Loomis laughed.

Pawel looked at him curiously.

—I though he was dead, Loomis said. I had this idea. And the girl?

Pawel shrugged.

—She is his, he said.

Well, yes. Of course. The General would have a girl. He would insist on living even in oblivion. Still, the professional questions had to come:

—Not his wife? She looks too young to be his wife.

—Not his wife, Pawel said.

—What then? A mistress?

He would, of course, have a mistress. His kind do.

—Why must you classify her? Pawel seemed annoyed. —Must everyone have a label? She is a girl and she is his. For me that is enough.

—She must be brave to come here, Loomis said, but Pawel said nothing.

A hot wind blew in off the Vistula and flapped the curtains. The curtains were black and new and hung with a foreboding. The windows were white-streaked with tape crisscrossed against concussion. Outside flowers grew.

Loomis felt tired. He was immensely tired. It was the true fatigue of sleep-lessness combined with tension and foreboding and gnawing excitement. He heard the forced, unnatural gaiety in the room and saw it exercised and now the General was back and now he had no doubt that he was right, and had been, and that there would be war.

And, either because of the champagne drunk without caution or the late hour or the tiredness or through a combination of the three, he saw the party guests as skeletons. *Le Danse macabre.* The pretty girls will not be pretty when the bombs explode; the gallant gentlemen will stink and rot.

Then the two poodles went barking out into the corridor and the French-woman ran after them calling *Taisez-vous! Méchants!* and the gay people were amused, and the huge, ornate door was opened and swung in and General Prus came in. The girl was with him. Talk died as though sabered.

One moment there was sound: seas of it beating in every corner of the room, in waves of baritone and tenor and contralto with now and then a high soprano laugh against the ceiling with the cherubs on it. Then this appalling silence.

The General marched in. The girl walked a little to the rear of him. She walked motionless from the waist up, holding her shoulders back as though without this conscious balancing they would fall. Her eyes were steady, fixed on nothing. Her smile was painted on. Her face had the familiar whiteness remembered from the garden.

Then, just as suddenly as it had died, the sound resumed: sibilant mur-murando. Heads craned. Hands pointed. Mouths bent to ears to whisper.

—How could he . . . at this time! The urgent bitterness in the man's voice made ice. Loomis turned. He saw Swiderski at his elbow. Some junior replica of Beck was with the little man from the press department. It was the replica that spoke.

—Doesn't the old fool have any sense? Couldn't leave her alone for a moment, I suppose. What will the foreigners think?

—You must expect the unexpected with this man, the little politician said.

—Yes, but at this time . . . at this particular time! What kind of an im-pression does that make? What will Carton de Wiart think? What will the ladies think?

—The difference between you and Prus is that he would not think what you are thinking, Swiderski said. It would not occur to him.

Indeed, the General marched into the room as though to the drumming cadence of an absent drummer, unsmiling but polite enough. The crowd surged forward. He moved through the crowd as though it were not there. The Frenchman Faury and General de Wiart made room around them and waited for him. Swiderski came up beside him, bowed, and spoke. The General nooded. Loomis was too far away to hear but he could see.

He watched the girl who stood beside the general. Her small triangular face was closed. Her smile was painful.

Around her and the General formed a circle of curious, whispering faces: disdainful female faces and the frank, brutal faces of calculating men. They had her there on that floor, Loomis thought, naked and unarmed. Their eyes slid over her like hands. The women's eyes stabbed like talons.

He marveled at her quiet dignity. Mistress or not, she was the only woman there, he thought.

He thought she looked at him briefly and so he bowed, the way the others there should have bowed but didn't, but when the bow was done and his back erect, she was looking elsewhere. All right. He shrugged. It's your game, we'll play it by your rules.

—Proud little bitch, he said to Pawel. But better she than I, brother. Better she than I.

Pawel said nothing.

—Why did he bring her here?

—Because he was invited, Pawel said.

—He was. She wasn't. That's clear enough.

—To you, perhaps. To him it wouldn't be.

—She knew, though. You can see she knew.

And then he told Pawel what he has seen from the balcony: the urgent gestures of the soldier-puppet and the girl-doll's refusal and the small pirouette of freedom she had made above the artificial lake. She was so free, so thoroughly liberated in her spin, he said. But then she changed her mind. She must have changed it because here she was, with him and yet so very much alone in that watching circle, holding her shoulders up.

—She would have done better to have stayed outside. They'll tear her up in here.

—Perhaps she wants to prove something, Pawel said.

—To whom? These people? They need no proof. They have tried and condemned.

Pawel shrugged and reached for yet another of those ubiquitous small glasses of champagne. —You are the man who makes his living from human reactions. I do not understand anything about women beyond the physical but I know pain and determination when I see it.

Pain, determination indeed. —You Poles with your incurable romanticism, Loomis said. Always attributing so much more to women than they are worth. You almost had me doing it, you know? I started thinking all kinds of melodramatic thoughts about her, thanks to your unholy influence: the way she held her shoulders, small pirouettes of freedom and so on. Good God, you'll have me bowing from the waist in one more minute.

—Is that so bad? Pawel said. He laughed.

—It's un-American, undemocratic, reactionary and downright dangerous.

—Long live America, Pawel said. He laughed. —Long live democracy and progress and the age of reason. Three cheers for Modern Times. But could we not have all of that and also kindness?

—Kindness is weakness, they say in Berlin. What will you fight them with?

Good manners? Friend, kindness is on a permanent vacation; this is no time for kindness or the gentle things.

—It is precisely such a time, Pawel said.

And possibly because of something in the cavalryman's voice, or because the atmosphere in that room was so unreal, or because he could not forget the small sweet gesture of total acceptance that the girl had made as she looked at him in the garden—with arms outspread and palms up to the moon —Loomis looked at her. Finding her in that crowd wasn't difficult. There was space around her.

No one said anything to her. Some men, few women, smiled. If they caught the General's eyes on them while they looked at her, they smiled. It was as though a cold glass wall had grown between the girl and them and she was an exhibit.

She must have known that it would be like this: in this country at this of all times, in this place, at this sort of party. Why had she come after her gesture of determined freedom? He thought he knew. Still, the professional questions had to come. He moved towards her and the General and the small, military group around the General: de Wiart, Faury and the Polish colonels. Swiderski saw him and spoke quickly to the General so that when Loomis and Pawel reached the group they had all turned to look at them and dressed their faces in small, inviting smiles.

The girl had not turned. She stood as she had stood before: holding her shoulders up, her face closed. She smiled at no one and at everyone, looking at nothing, and Loomis felt both pity and an admiration and wondered why he did.

There was the courage, yes. And the determination and the pride. And these deserved respect. And there was more, some other quality that he did not immediately recognize.

He bowed to her. Swiderski introduced them.

—Madame Karolewska (a small smile there, the same as all the other smiles) . . . General Prus (calm, suddenly amused) . . . General de Wiart (cynical detachment) . . . Colonel Faury (ebullience tainted by a secret knowledge) and Colonel Prus (white line of cheekbone, haunted eyes and nervous mouth rigidly controlled).

—Mr. Loomis . . . Captain Pawel Prus.

The General said: —I'm glad to see you again. Welcome to Warsaw.

Loomis said that he didn't think the General would remember their last meeting. Or himself. So much had happened since then, after all. There were so many years between the meetings. The General laughed and nodded at his pinned-up sleeve and said he carried a reminder of the meeting. Or of the circumstances of the meeting. One way or another, he said, it was not something that he could forget.

—As I recall, we talked about the military families of Europe. You have an example of one here: myself, my brother and my nephew. . . . How are you, boy? (This to Pawel.)

—Well, sir, thank you. Good evening, father.

—Good evening, said the Colonel.

They talked but afterwards Loomis could not remember what anybody said. No one said anything about the coming war. De Wiart talked about the shooting in Polesie: That autumn the wild ducks were particularly good. Faury wanted to know if Pawel was, indeed, the man who had defeated the champion of Saumur in the Olympic riding trials and said that this was *formidable*. Swiderski made small sounds and smiled a lot and asked that Pawel's father meet with Loomis in the morning. The Colonel said that he expected to be very busy in the morning. The afternoon? He also thought that he'd be busy in the afternoon. The crowd moved in and out around them and occasionally threw up a new face and a new set of hands outthrust for shaking. Then the crowd split the group around the General and Loomis found himself in the small space reserved for the girl.

He said he thought the party was quite good. What did she think? She said, politely, that she thought it was.

—You must go to a lot of things like this, he said without thinking. You look at home here.

She looked at him steadily, in a friendly way. When he said nothing more she shook her head. He could see now that she was older than he had thought when he first saw her in the garden. There she had been girllike and small and vulnerable and terribly appealing. It was the kindness of the lack of light. In the bright glare of the ballroom she was older and the fine skin was, perhaps, not so fine and the small fugitive wrinkles crept out beside her eyes.

—This is the first affair of this kind that I have been to in several years, she said carefully.

He said that he would never have believed it.

—Why? Because I know how to hold a champagne glass? Because I'm wearing shoes?

Oh no. Of course not, he said in retreat. He had meant it as a compliment, he said.

—I know how you meant it.

She was not angry; more amused than angry. It was, perhaps, an amusement born of anger; she was beyond anger, he could see that. There was the slurred trace of pain under the mockery in her voice and there was something that could have been fear or perhaps a terrible disappointment, and the tight edges of her smile slipped a little then, and her eyes were veiled as though she had stepped back into herself for safety.

—I didn't mean anything like that, he said. I only meant that the General is an important man and must be in demand.

—The demand is recent. He became important to these people only yesterday. For thirteen years few of them even knew he was alive.

He admitted that he himself hadn't known it and that he had wondered, now and then, what had become of Prus.

—We lived in the country, she said. There were no receptions there. And no need for them or for the people who give them and go to them.

He said it sounded like a quiet life.

She said it was. There had been time to think; it was a peaceful time.

—Did you like it? Is that what you like?

—Yes.

He said he hadn't thought she would like the quiet and all that. It seemed too much like death or premature retirement. —And you seem so alive. How could you stand thirteen years of quiet?

She laughed.

—It wasn't thirteen years and it wasn't always quiet. There was a calmness and a certainty about it and I wasn't alone, and I could live the way I wanted to. Quiet when I needed it and all the excitement that I wanted. I think quiet is not the proper word for it.

What was?

—Peacefulness, she said.

He said he was surprised to hear her say it. He said he would have thought she would be bored with living in the country.

She looked towards the General and shook her head.

—No, she said. She had not been bored.

He thought that she would cry; there was that effort being made to control emotion and, certainly, here was an opportunity for crying. But there were no tears. If she had wept about her loss (whatever it was) it was all done and no more tears would come. Instead, she laughed.

—You've asked so many questions. Will you answer one?

—Of course. Unless it's very personal.

—Have you ever had a peaceful life? I don't mean uneventful and motionless and dull. I mean a life in which you can combine pleasure, excitement and the joyful things with peace of mind.

The joyful things?

—No, he said. I haven't.

—It isn't boring. Only a coward would think that it was boring. Only a coward would be afraid of that kind of time.

He said that he would try it the next time he lived somewhere in the country. —But you are talking as if your life was over.

—Oh no, she said. Nothing is ever over if you have something in which to believe: a firm patch of ground. You can replace what has been lost if you have this faith in an absolute idea. Perhaps you can't repair and rebuild but you can replace.

—Now you sound like a woman: practical.

She laughed. —I have to be.

He said that sounded bitter. But then, he supposed, she would have reasons for bitterness.

—I am not bitter and really not practical enough. But there is a certain sort of peace possible with that kind of thought.

—Peace, he said mocking gently. It is wonderful.

—Peacefulness, she said.

Loomis laughed and put a hand to his face. He felt peculiarly stirred and rejuvenated and at the same time older. Her calmness and controlled vitality, her unexpected thoughtfulness and lack of bitterness, stood bright and distinct in the near hysteria of the crowd. Their modulated murmurs were a mask. She did not wear one. She was herself and said so to the crowd: Look, I am a woman. I have no other aspirations.

Listening to her and to the murmurs of the crowd, he felt his weariness again. That was the trouble with everything, he supposed: He was immensely weary. Of Nimi and himself and of the way that everybody lived at home, with their pale prejudices and lack of courage to invite commitment, where the little daily treasons made betrayers and betrayed equally contemptible, and only *self* was important and any other love (of man for woman or for country or for an idea) was a vulgar joke. He had missed Europe, which was so familiar with its enormous loves and hates (equally unreasonable) and monstrous persecutions and its history of gigantic treasons and passionate destructions. He felt a tightness in his throat when he thought of reason and being reasonable, and of the loss of stature and of manhood that a man would suffer in the name of reason. And suddenly he wanted love and hate on an enormous scale with nothing withheld. And he felt panic: a momentary thing. It was safer, after all, to be reasonable.

—I'd like us to be friends, he said.

She looked surprised. —Of course.

—There are too many people with whom one can't be friends. It's like back home. There are so many people there who talk a good friendship but that's as far as it can ever get. They have such wonderful conversational attitudes about it.

—There are many such people here too.

She watched him carefully, her hand with its empty champagne glass still cocked defensively at her shoulder. He took it from her and exchanged it for a full one from a tray carried by a passing waiter.

Someone laughed. He turned to see who laughed and why they were laughing. Was it at him? But there were many laughing people at the party; their small gay cries crossed each other under the chandeliers.

—I don't like these parties either, he said. I don't like this kind of people and what they like to think. I think they are afraid of something they don't understand. That's why they must destroy everything that is a little different.

—Aren't you ever afraid of anything?

—No.

She laughed.

—Why are you laughing?

—Everyone is afraid of something.

—Even your friend the General?

—He has his private fear.

—I am sure he would never admit it to anyone. Especially to you.

—Neither would you.

—A man isn't supposed to be afraid.

—Why not?

He said he didn't know. He drank champagne. He listened to the laughter of the people at the party. She said that she was sorry if he was upset. She didn't want to upset him by anything she said.

—I'm not upset, he said. But we don't have to talk like that. I haven't done you any harm. And I don't really like to play with words; they're valuable to me: I make my living with them. And as I said, I'd like us to be friends.

—Why?

—I'd like to know you better. I am not used to women who are brave.

She shook her head and looked at the General and said that she was not at all brave.

—Then why did you come here? You must have known how it would be.

She said she knew. But courage had not much to do with it.

—Why did you come, then?

She laughed.

—This friendship you propose isn't very old.

—And I should mind my own business, is that it?

She nodded, smiling. —Yes.

The party ended shortly afterwards. The General was the first to leave and she left with him. He watched them go, feeling a resentment. He listened to the avid crowd: the coarseness of the laughing men and the soft, murderous innuendos of unsmiling women.

And suddenly he felt no sympathy for any of them anymore.

War. Let it come. Let them stink and rot. I will not be involved.

The breeze ballooned the curtains. Outside sirens blew.

The evil portent of disaster floated in and suddenly the sounds of jollity were gone and gaiety flew apart like fog hit by an autumn wind and he could see the many fears in the room: gaunt under glittering chandeliers. Men bit their lips. The mouths of women trembled.

He went in search of Pawel, found him and said he thought that it was time to go. It had been a long day.

—Have you had enough?

—Quite enough.

—And you have no more questions about anything? Not even about my uncle's beautiful young woman?

—No questions.

—I am glad.

I WESTERPLATTE

Dinner was quiet on Westerplatte.

Even Lieutenant Leon Pajak, the youngest and the most ebullient (being four months married), said little, listening to the sound of celebration coming in from Danzig. Bands smashed out martial rhythms there, crowds cheered. Tanks rumbled on the ancient cobblestones.

Pajak looked at the major and all the other officers laid down their forks and looked, but the major went on with the roast pork and beans and potatoes and did not look at them.

There was excitement despite the silence round the table, an air of expectation, a certainty born of a feeling that the times of waiting were about to end and that the time of that for which they had waited was about to come.

Major Sucharski was in a contemplative mood. He contemplated imminent destruction and at such times a soldier takes stock of past and present and the near future. There is, of course, no distant future to consider. He adds up assets and liabilities and balances the red against the black and closes his personal account and prepares for the inevitable. He is calm and assured and at peace and he knows that he had done all that there was to do and that what is about to happen is the climax towards which his life and career have pointed all the years and he knows that he may never read the final tabulation.

This is a calm and wonderfully peaceful moment. Major Sucharski savored it.

He thought about his men: handpicked professionals, volunteers; an outpost in a sea of Germans.

He thought about Danzig, listening to the happy roar of it. The irony of Danzig: Polish for generations and now so terribly German. He thought that Westerplatte was a proper setting for an outpost of this kind, being a peninsula. We are, he thought, truly like a ship in a sea of Germans.

All month Danzig had undergone an orgy of decorating: tall poles with banners and heraldic shields, wreaths, triumphal arches. Whom were the Danzigers awaiting? The major had few illusions about Danzigers. He knew their expectations.

Sieg Heil indeed!

He went on with his dinner calmly, and eventually the other officers returned to theirs.

He looked at them and at once they put their forks away and looked at him: Franciszek Dabrowski, captain of the 29th Kalisz Regiment, thirty-six, tall, hard as iron, with the dry, uncommunicative face of a professional, son of a retired general murdered by Russians in the other war; Pajak, twenty-nine, son of Kielce peasants, allowed to marry in this bachelor garrison only because he was on loan from the 4th Regiment of Legion Infantry and due to return to it in a month; Warrant Officer Gryczman of the 3d Legion Regiment, a chevalier of the Virtuti Militari, a hardhanded peasant who could never be an officer because he lacked the prescribed education; Second Lieutenant Zbigniew Kreglewski of the Gniezno Regiment; Dr. Slaby, physician, a captain in the 5th Mounted Rifles; and Second Lieutenant Stefan Grodecki, a construction engineer from the 2d Air Regiment.

—How do you find it? The major pointed at the pork.

—Very fine, sir, Dabrowski said. The others nodded, watching.

—Then eat. Why look at me? I'll never win a prize for beauty.

One of them sighed. They bent over their plates again. The major watched them for a moment and smiled to himself.

The pork was truly good. It came from the major's farm behind the new administration building. The men had wondered about this farm at first: tall rows of corn, banks of potatoes, thirty-six pigs reproducing with comforting regularity, a cow, a horse for plowing. They shrugged it off as part of their odd major's madness. Certainly they had thought him mad at first. When he arrived on the peninsula in March, the year before, he began to build. Up went a variety of storehouses, garages, an administration building, guard and pump houses, toolsheds; down went trenches for a new storm sewer. Somehow there was no pipe to lay in the trenches but they remained uncovered. He changed the quiet face of Westerplatte with a seven-foot wall which screened all these activities from the German suburb of Neufahrwasser one hundred and fifty meters across the Martwa Wisla.

The soldiers scratched their heads. These were peculiar buildings. Why concrete? Concrete was expensive. And why brick them over? And why did all of this take place at night?

And what mad buildings: windows so narrow that a man could hardly put his arm through them (the major talked about Egyptian architecture and the way thick walls and narrow windows kept out the summer sun); steel doors and shutters forged in the major's smithy; underground storehouses and concrete cellars (to keep the food cold, of course); crates of plumbing supplies locked underground. (*For those storm sewers . . . if we get the permits.* Somehow the permits never came.)

Before 1914 Westerplatte had been a pleasure beach. It was a sandy strip of land jutting one kilometer into the Bay of Danzig along the Neufahrwasser, some twenty acres of sand and small pine and romantic dune and sun-warmed pebble. An ancient fort stood on the neck of it.

The Versailles Treaty, which partitioned Danzig, gave this to Poland as a coaling station. It was to be Poland's access to the sea. The Poles built their own seaport at Gdynia: the biggest in the Baltic, put up in fifteen years. Westerplatte remained unimportant. A company of Polish soldiers were allowed to live there as a token of Polish control over Danzig. The Danzig Poles (teachers in the Polish schools, railroadmen, Post Office staff, port commissioners and deputies to the Danzig Council, youth and social workers) used it as a gathering place for national holidays. There the Polish flag was flown.

The Danzig Germans were allowed inspection privileges to see that Westerplatte remained no more than that. As August neared they paid their visits once a week. The French and British military missions also sent inspectors to see that there were no violations of agreement, no fortifications, no provocation of the Germans. Inspectors found no violations. The Poles did not provoke the Germans by fortifying anything. The buildings? They were merely buildings, after all. A little thick, perhaps, a little heavy, but wonderfully insulated against the sun. The old fort was razed to the ground on German insistence and the inspectors were content. They laughed about the Polish major and his pigs, his trenches, his unfinished pipelines. Typical Polish *Schlamperei,* was it not? Inefficiency. *Der toll Major . . .* a sentimental Polish peasant keeping pigs to remind him of his home. *Natürlich.*

In March the major called a night alert.

The soldiers of the garrison watched as the brick veneer fell away and loopholes appeared, and small coal cellars scattered aimlessly around the beaches became concrete bunkers, and hidden generators whirred to light and ventilate underground rooms, and they manned the unfinished sewer trench across the neck of the peninsula and understood why no pipe had been laid in it.

Behind the trench they had put up another bit of their odd major's madness: a whitewashed picket fence of Bessemer steel.

The Germans had found this the most amusing. (—*Is the Herr Major afraid his pig collection might stray into Danzig? Ha ha ha.* The Major shrugged, grinned stupidly. —*Into Danzig or from Danzig; what is the difference? Pigs have no business coming among people.*)

Captain Dabrowski got a look at the stored pipe and plumbing: four Brandt (81-millimeter infantry) mortars, sixteen machineguns, twenty-five automatic rifles, two antitank guns and, glory of glories, a 3-inch Russian cannon!

Then Sergeant Grabowski of the Light Artillery understood why he had been asked to volunteer for Westerplatte. He had known the major a long time. The major had sought him out in the garrison of Lwow and asked him to volunteer. Grabowski did not like this duty very much. The work was hard, there were no leaves or passes into town, the garrison lived like monks in a monastery—some change after Lwow, the gayest, most carefree city in the Commonwealth! *Tfui* on such duty. But the major asked and so Grabowski came. Pay was bigger here. Food was as good as that of the guard company in President Moscicki's palace in Warsaw. But there was no artillery and to Grabowski a garrison without a fieldpiece was like Rome without a Pope in it. *Tfui* on such a life! Dogs have it better.

The gun was put together in a garage which fitted it exactly.

—Mad, is he? Grabowski said to Sergeant Bierniacz, a mortarman who had been lost without his tubes and suddenly had four. Listen, you, Bierniacz. They should all be mad.

Bierniacz, taking iron lids off four concrete fruit cellars, agreed.

From that night to this night, which was the night of August 31, 1939, the little garrison stood watch. Each night half of it manned the bunkers and the trench. Each night, sometime after dinner, Major Sucharski walked about his little kingdom.

And so this night, having finished dinner, listening to the roar of joy and greeting coming from across the bay, hearing the thunder of tanktreads, hearing the brassy growl of military music, the mad *Sieg Heils,* he said goodnight to his officers and went outside.

He was a quiet, stocky man, dwarfed in darkness. He had never married although there had been many opportunities for it . . . sometimes too many. Sometimes he wondered if he should have married, if he should have passed on his name. But, then, the name had no particular significance. Henryk Sucharski was the son of peasants. He was born in the village of Grzeboszow in the Tarnow district and had worn soldier's clothes since his sixteenth year. His great-uncle had been the Senator Bojko about whom many arguments had raged. Henryk Sucharski hardly knew his famous relative. His home and family was the Army. It seemed family enough.

Certainly he had devoted enough love to it, although the Army is a stern and heavyhanded mother, sometimes hard to love.

It was never quite clear to him why he became a soldier. A war was being fought and suddenly there were men in arms who wore an eagle on their caps, and this was the eagle his mother had taught him to follow: the White Polish Eagle that was a forbidden symbol, as white and scarlet banners were forbidden. All of the Tarnow district was in arms. Long columns of peasants wound into the towns to put on the caps with the eagles, and one day his mother took him by the hand and led him to a man who handed out the caps and said to him: —*He's small. Only fifteen. But maybe he will be of some use to you.* And to Henryk she said: —*If you disgrace this badge, don't come back.* He did not disgrace it but never went back.

In 1920 he won the Virtuti Militari in an assault with two infantry companies on a division of Budyenny's Cossack cavalry. Then he became a captain and went to Warsaw, where for a strange, unreal, impossible year he was attached to the General Staff: lost in the silent corridors. Something was planned for him but he never discovered what it could have been. Somehow he must have offended some important person. In 1935 he was sent to command the 35th Infantry Regiment in Brzesc, and in March 1938 he came to Westerplatte.

Walking about the sandy strip after dinner he had no illusions about peace and war and such things as survival and duty. He contemplated imminent destruction.

He thought that he had managed to prepare Westerplatte for what was to come. He was at peace. The night was quiet. There was a cool, moist breeze off the sea. The night was truly marvelously quiet. He heard the Germans singing.

Since mid-August, the port of Danzig had fallen into a strange, foreboding sleep. The docks and slipways were still: No keel moved to mar the glistening black mirror of the bay. But three days earlier the mirror swirled and leaped under the screws of a fearsome visitor: The battleship *Schleswig-Holstein* sailed in with twelve destroyers to anchor one hundred and fifty meters off the sandy strip.

Grabowski had watched with wonder the four 28-centimeter naval guns and ten 150-millimeter guns mounted in battery on the battleship.

Aboard the battleship was a battalion of German naval officer cadets just back from the summer's training cruise in the eastern Baltic.

Major Sucharski heard the singing and the laughter of the Germans. He heard their conversation. They were so close that he could throw a pebble at them from the beach. They sang of *Deutschland* and *Heimat* and of *Sieg*. They sang that song about the grieving mother.

Voices: young, confident in the still night.

Across the bay in Danzig the major heard the wild arrival of the city's other guests. *Sieg Heil . . . Sieg Heil . . . Sieg Heil . . .* and then the murderous strains of *Deutschland über Alles!*

Before the major and his officers sat down to dine, one of his radiomen brought in a message picked up on German shortwave: *Die Gäste kommen über die Brücke.* The guests were indeed coming across the bridge: General Eberhardt's armored columns out of the Third East Prussian Army were crossing the pontoons put up by Danzigers in July. He heard their motors and their tanktreads and the tumultuous greeting.

The major passed along the bank of Martwa Wisla with the black warehouses of Neufahrwasser behind it. A great white beam of light fell on him suddenly. The Neufahrwasser lighthouse seemed to be stuck. Light bathed each crevice on Westerplatte, showed each blade of grass.

He passed in this white light along the backbone of the sandy strip where railroad tracks etched the white sand. The tracks led from the loading basin at the northern end of the peninsula to the iron gates set in the major's wall at the southern end. Barbed wire was rolled along the loading basin. The polished helmet of a Danzig SS man gleamed there.

The major looked into Bunker Two facing the basin with a light machinegun.

—Awake in there?

(A smile. Teeth glow in the dark. A cigarette is hastily crushed against the concrete.)

—Yes sir! We'll get that one over there with the first burst.

126

—Oh, you will, will you? The major laughed. —You do that, soldier, and you'll never see the outside of a guardhouse.

The gunners laughed.

—Well, sir . . . if something was to happen. I mean if they start something, that schnitzel eater will shake hands with Bismarck.

The major smiled, went on.

Bunker Four covered the tracks and the sea and half a kilometer of beach. It was too much for one machinegun crew but it would have to do. Yes. It must do.

The major thought about his men. —Damn few, he muttered.

Too damn few but possibly too many for what was to come. Most of them would be in the trenches at the southern neck of the peninsula and so the major went there. He passed the antitank fence. The two quickfiring tank guns faced the railroad gate. Platoon Sergeant Lopatniuk greeted him there. The pigfence that had so amused the Germans glowed white.

If they send nothing extra heavy, this should stop them, the Major thought.

Bunkers One and Five covered the fence and the hundred and fifty meters of trench dug in front of it. The major walked on. Past the motor gate and the Danzig SS patrolling on the other side. Past the trench where Pajak's young, eager heroworshiping face looked at him smiling.

The major looked into Bunker Five, where Platoon Sergeant Adolf Petzef reported his crew alert.

—How is it, Petzef?

—Quiet, sir. We are ready.

—Yes, said the major.

He went on.

Poor Petzef. With a name like Adolf he took some heavy jokes these days.

Almost within sight of Bunker Six, the great two-story administration building where his quarters were, the major stopped before a soldier who lay on the ground wrapped in his greatcoat. The night was chilly. The breeze was moist and sharp. The pipes of mortartubes peeked from the ground beside the sleeping soldier.

—Bierniacz, are you asleep?

Clearly he had been. But he was instantly awake the way an old soldier becomes when caught asleep.

—No sir! The bastards on that boat won't let the saints sleep.

The major laughed. —Don't you like their singing?

—I have heard better at a Jewish *szabas.*

—When did you ever see a *szabas, Bierniaczu?*

The sergeant grinned. —My father's name is Bernstein. He sings worse than they do.

The major nodded. He went on.

He wished he had not eaten pork. Roast pork upset his stomach. He slept badly after eating pork. Besides, he could not help thinking about infant children when he saw young pigs. They were like sucklings and the sucklings, in turn, bore a terrible resemblance to the human young. There had been a day in the Ukraine in 1920 when a village burned and little corpses roasted in the ashes . . . No. The major shook his head. He would not think of that. Not now. Not on the threshold of his personal accounting.

He had ordered the piglets slaughtered when the radioman had told him about the Danzigers' guests thundering into the city.

—*Let the men eat,* he had said. *Give them a dinner that they will remember.* (Let them nibble roast pork, the crunchy skin, the thick white flesh of the little pigs browned in their own juice.)

He wished that he could have given a real party for the men. With women and good Danzig vodka that had gold flakes floating in it, and *zakaski* and yes, by God, fiddle music. But you don't give parties in a sea of Germans.

The major passed the garage door, whispered: —Grabowski?

A shadow rose. The gunnery sergeant showed beside the oily mouth of the artillery piece. —Sir?

—Your men awake?

—Yes sir!

—How is the cannon? Do you have your targets?

The cannon gleamed with oily lights in the darkness. It pointed at the lighthouse.

—She is a sweetheart, said Grabowski. We can have her outside in thirty seconds and firing in thirty-five.

—Well, keep awake and watch.

The major turned towards the big two-story bunker. He wondered how long Grabowski would have left to live after he wheeled his sweetheart out of the garage. Not very long. How long? A minute, two. The *Schleswig-Holstein* wouldn't give him more.

The major went inside the bunker and into his room. This was the telephone control room. He and Franciszek Dabrowski slept here; their pleasant little villa in the sands was shuttered and abandoned.

The major took off his cap and boots and coat. He contemplated the removal of his trousers.

No. Leave them on. You do not know the hour nor the day. He lay down in his shirt and trousers.

Young Pajak worried him. Nights of sleeping in the cold, moist trench had given the lieutenant a touch of the grippe. He had coughed at dinner.

His wife will give me hell, the major thought. I'll move him here tomorrow.

The gentle whirring of the dynamos lulled the major. He picked up the book he had been reading for a week: *The History of Westerplatte and the Port of Danzig.* A date leaped at him from the fluttering pages:

September first.

Hmm. Interesting.

On September the first, 1577, the starving garrison of Hetman Zolkiewski, abandoned by the king and the country which had sent it there, surrendered Westerplatte to the Swedes. Danzig was saved by the patriotism of its good merchants loyal to their country.

The major put the book away. He looked at his watch. It was two A.M. It was, then, another September the first.

I wonder what the day will bring.

The major fell asleep.

War

War, being the province of danger, requires that courage be, above all things, the first quality of a warrior.

Friday, September the first

I WESTERPLATTE

It was the pork, of course, which brought on the dream: a fantasy of twisted shapes, vague forms of black and grey in torment; some murderous conflict of the inarticulate and the unidentifiable.

Nightmare.

Major Sucharski dreamed that the world was ending.

There was a fearful crash and he awoke.

Concussion sucked the air from the room. It threw him off his cot.

Nightmare!

Outside the world turned upside down: Trees flew like birds, birds fell to earth like leaves. The day was grey with smoke and dust and flying soil and an unending sound. The sound was all around and did not recede or in any way diminish but went on, madly, incredibly, constant.

—The Schleswig-Holstein, Dabrowski shouted. Blood came from his ears.

The major looked at his watch. The crystal was broken. The time was four A.M. He heard machinegun fire and the dull bumping sounds of mortars.

And then the ringing sound. His ears? The telephone.

—Yes!

—Lieutenant Pajak reporting. Wall and gates dynamited. Am under general attack. Have opened fire.

The major ran into the other room, the telephone and radio communications center. The bunker swayed like a ship at sea. He fell down once, got up.

White faces stared at him.

He smiled to keep calm.

—Well, boys, it's come.

The air was grey with dust and chips of concrete. He could hardly see the radiomen and the telephonists. Someone lay on the floor in blood, moving and moaning a little.

In the far corner of the room Corporal Burda cleared the coding table and now two men lifted the moaning man onto it and Dr. Slaby came in with his instruments. Soon there were screams. There were no anesthetics. That smuggled shipment had been confiscated by Danzig inspectors.

The major settled down to work.

He telephoned the bunkers. None had been hit and the major wondered how anything could live untouched in the grey world outside. There the SOUND lived. There the sky had fallen.

The major telephoned the trench.

—Leon? How is it with you?

—Good, sir. We are holding them. The young officer's voice was shrill and he was out of breath. —God, sir, every German in the world came through that wall!

—Yes.

Hmm. Must make him calm. —Tell me about it. First tell me, are they still coming or do you have them down?

—They're down, sir. They punched through the wall and have machine-guns shooting down on us. They have a cannon in the gate. They came in with grenades at first but Adolf Petzef stopped them from Bunker Five. Now they've gone back behind the wall.

—Then you are all right. Good. Don't let them get into your trench. What are they?

—Soldiers, sir. Danzig SS.

—Not Wehrmacht?

—No sir. Just Danzigers. There were about two hundred of them at the start.

—You have done well, Leon. Keep them outside.

The major telephoned Bunker Five and asked for Petzef. Soon the old soldier answered.

—Thank you, Adolf, the major said. I understand you did some work this morning.

—Men work, the soldier said. He laughed.

—It is good work.

—Towards the Glory of the Fatherland, the soldier said.

Glory and Fatherland.

It was the ancient formula with which a soldier answered compliments, received promotions or decorations. It was the ritual. Outside, the other ritual was beginning: the formula of death.

But now the crashing sound drew off a little and the headquarters bunker no longer swayed, and the lamps were still, and dust came down in great, speckled circles and settled on the floor.

The major drew a breath.

It was time to see what was happening in the world outside. The Army would be fighting now along the entire border, that vast arc of plain and forest and mountain that separated Poland and the Germans.

The radio stuttered broken messages, warnings, alerts.

. . . I have a warning for the Warsaw district. Air alert . . . the Krakow district . . . Lwow . . . Torun . . . Poznan . . .

The entire country, then, was under air attack.

As minutes passed the major pictured for himself the larger stage: the country in flames, reservists crowding into barrackyards. And suddenly, without warning, he saw the longago, near-forgotten day. He saw the woman with her hand tight on the hand of the boy, and the woman said:

—He is small but maybe you can use him for something. And then she said: —If you disgrace this badge . . .

Someone was shaking his shoulder. It was Dabrowski with a bloody rag about his head.

—There is word out of Danzig, he said. They telephoned from the Post Office. They said they are under attack but are defending themselves in the lobby. There are fifty-five mailcarriers and students there. The SS are attacking with flamethrowers. The Germans are rounding up all Poles and hanging them on lampposts. They said they can hear our fight and pray for us. Then the line went dead.

—Yes, said the major.

He thought about his friend Dr. Mendyk. Dr. Mendyk, the witty, shrewd Polish member of the Port Commission whose house had been surrounded by Danzig SA since mid-August. Bridge was his passion.

He saw the great, jovial head bowed down, the rope extending . . .

—Anything else?

Dabrowski pointed to his head. He could not hear. His eardrums were broken. The major shouted and Dabrowski nodded.

—Oksywie radioed a report to Warsaw. We picked it up on shortwave.

Oksywie was the never-finished naval base farther up the coast. Colonel Dabek, the Little Oak, commanded there . . . another friend.

—Yes?

—They are on fire. Two hundred bombers are attacking. There are so many bombers that two have collided. A cruiser and six destroyers have come in from the Baltic and are shelling them. Colonel Dabek has been hit in the spine but retains command. The torpedoboat *Mazur* has been sunk in shallow water but the crew is on board and still mans the guns. The trawler *Mewa* beached without a crew. A near miss with a five-hundred-pound bomb blew the crew overboard. Divebombers wrecked the seaplane base at Puck. Great crowds besiege Colonel Dabek's quarters asking for arms. He is forming a battalion of pikemen since there are no rifles for them.

—Did you say pikemen?

—Yes sir. They are resetting peasant scythes to make spears.

The major nodded.

—And elsewhere? Have you anything from the country?

—The radio is confusing. They are fighting on the entire border. The Germans are bombing every city from the air. The Allies have not declared war.

—Thank you. He noticed the captain's pallor. Blood ran free through the bandage and stained Dabrowski's shoulders. —Did Dr. Slaby take care of your head?

—He is too busy now.

Indeed the little doctor was.

The major looked towards the corner where the surgeon worked; the corner out of which came the howls and shrieks and blasphemies, the rasp of saw on bone. He had not noticed these sounds before.

All at once he became aware of the silence outside. The air was still. The sun burned scarlet in the dust cloud.

Dabrowski caught the look.

—They have stopped shelling, he said.

Then the rattle of machineguns came from the gate and the dynamited wall. Attack!

The second assault on the peninsula went in at seven A.M., Corporal Burda noted in the major's log. Three companies of Danzig SS and SA, covered by machineguns, attacked the trench. General Eberhardt had offered his Panzer troopers to the mayor of Danzig but the mayor had refused. (He had said: —*Today the Reich welcomes us to her breast. We come to her in blood as befits Germans.*)

The air was so still that the major heard each shout as the Germans came. They breached the wall. Pajak's machineguns and Petzef's crossfire from

133

Bunker Five stopped them in ten meters. In half an hour the assault was over. The SS fled.

Then the SOUND came again.

The air leaped and the trees turned over. The bunker swayed and a lamp came down. The bulb exploded.

The sound, in that close, dustfilled, rocking space was like the blast of an artillery shell. So soon? Is death to come so soon?

Dust filled the major's eyes. He saw white faces strained towards him. The sight sobered him, calmed him. They depend on me. I must be calm.

He opened the outside door where the air was brown with upflung soil and learned against the doorframe and lit a cigarette. His hands, he noted, were steady.

The major felt the air turn as the explosions came. He watched the southern end of the peninsula where sand hung in a permanent cloud above Pajak's trench and the explosions had an almost tangible solidity. He saw red flashes through the dust: the muzzle blasts of the battleship's artillery.

Then new sounds came.

Across the Martwa Wisla, in Neufahrwasser, the Germans hoisted ninety-eight machineguns up on the warehouse roofs and a light cannon opened fire off the lighthouse. It took time to hoist it up there. They must have done it in the night.

The major wondered how long anyone would last in that firestorm. Not long. He remembered a longago time in Brzesc and Grabowski's eyes. There was love in them. For him. The old soldier loved him. The old soldier had come here because of him. Now he would die for him.

—Tell Grabowski to get his sweetheart out and clear those roofs, he said.

—His line is dead.

—A messenger then. Volunteers?

Corporal Burda ducked out of the bunker and was immediately hit. A cannon shell came from the lighthouse, hit the ground, bounced like a tennis-ball and struck him in the back. The upper portion of his trunk sailed to the right and vanished in the shellhole. The legs churned on, tripped, sprawled.

They were like empty trousers.

Rifleman Maslowski was running through the door before Burda's bloody legs were still.

He gained the shelter of the mortar pits, fell in headfirst. Then Bierniacz jumped out of his concrete shelter and ran for the garage. Bullets kicked up the sand around him. He fell, got up, ran on, shouting. Grabowski heard him. Grabowski had been watching. His crew wheeled out the Russian cannon and the squat barrel fired immediately. The range was simple: pointblank at a hundred meters. The second shell hit squarely on the lighthouse roof. The German cannon flew up like a twig, turned and fell in the sea. Then the top of the lighthouse buckled inwards and a column of dust shot up into the air.

The major saw Grabowski wave his arms and point to Neufahrwasser and the crew seized the cannon by the tail and spun it round to face the German suburb. At once the barrel rocked and a plume of fire showed on a warehouse roof. Five rapid shells set another roof on fire. Black figures showed there. They leaped into the water. Grabowski's cannon swept the German gunners into the water and the warehouse yards. They scrambled off the roofs. Soon Neufahrwasser burned and the roofs were quiet.

How long? My God, how long?

It was too long.

It was against all probability. It was unreasonable that the gun could live so long.

Dust shielded it.

The thick grey clouds flung up by the enormous naval shells were like a smoke screen.

The red blaze of the muzzle blast glowed in it.

It betrayed the cannon.

And now the *Schleswig-Holstein* turned her batteries on Grabowski. The major saw the sergeant fall after a near miss. The gunner got up. The crew picked up the tail of the fieldpiece and aimed the cannon at the battleship. Their first shell brought a scarlet glow on the grey ship's deck. Then the earth heaved about the cannon as ten shells landed around it. The earth rose in a wall. It fell. The crew was broken, dead. But Grabowski lived. He got up, dragging his legs behind him. He pulled himself towards the gun, loaded it, aimed while the earth rose round him once again, then came the red flash and the battleship's bridge flew in the air. He fired again and one of the ship's great 28-centimeter guns swung up and pointed skyward.

The major shouted for three volunteers.

—Who'll help him? Do you want him to sink that ship alone?

Five men jumped up. They stopped inside the door.

—He's gone, sir.

In the hole that gouged the sand where the gun had been there was some twisted iron.

A piece of something like a brownish cloth lay strangely folded at the side of it.

The German shells hammered it, beat into it. Soon there was nothing in the crater and still the shells came. The crater grew.

And then, again, the silence and the dust drifting earthward and the machinegun fire from the gates . . .

Attack!

Now the officer cadets came off the battleship and stormed the trench. But the respite that came when their huge cannon dueled with Grabowski had given Pajak time to dig himself out of his caved-in trench. Bierniacz, back at his mortars, zeroed them in on the gate and the Germans fell in sections, in platoons. The sand was red with their blood, white with their bodies in summer uniforms.

Red and white. The forbidden colors of his childhood.

The major watched from the door of Bunker Six.

The Germans came and died.

They broke.

They ran.

The battleship began to fire again.

Gryczman reported that Pajak was hit.

Soon two riflemen crawled in carrying the lieutenant on their backs. The young man's face was white. His left leg hung on a strip of flesh from his crumpled hip. The strip broke as they lifted him upon the table and the leg, in its long boot, clattered on the floor.

The major thought about the young man's wife. It was a foolish thought. She will be angry. This is what he thought. I did not take good care of him. The trench is damp. He coughed last night at dinner.

Six riflemen held the lieutenant down while Dr. Slaby sawed at his hip.

That last illicit load, the major thought: an operating table, morphine and bandages. The Germans found it under the rations. They confiscated it.

Suddenly he looked up, as though to question someone or something, as though to register complaint.

At first he thought that he was ill, delirious, seeing what was surely not there to see. He *could* not see what he saw.

Sometime during the morning three shells had torn away part of the bunker roof. He had not noticed it. There had been so much sound. So many shells. Now he saw the sky.

The sky was blue. Small, silver planes began to wheel in it.

He listened to the wailing sound as they came down on him, and he heard a new note in the explosions. The flat, dry crack of land artillery joined the hollow booming of the naval guns.

Someone brought in the bottom of a shell.

—An eighty-eight, Major Sucharski said. They must have brought a battery to Haubude.

The great guns of the *Schleswig-Holstein* continued to fire.

Time passed. He measured it in moments, because each moment brought fresh men onto the bloody table where Dr. Slaby worked. The surgeon was scarlet from head to foot. His hair was caked with blood.

Time passed.

Shells came.

Bombs came.

Men died.

The guns grew silent at eleven P.M.

This time it was the sailors off the German ships with what was left of the cadet battalion, the Danzig SS and German police. Three tanks preceded them.

Sergeant Lopatniuk held his gun crews until they could count the rivets on the leading tank. Then the two antitank guns fired. The first tank rumbled as the shells exploded deep inside it. The second lurched into the whitewashed fence and hung upon it, burning. The third turned back and hid behind the wall.

And now the Germans halt, and lie down and refuse to move, and officers run among them shouting, and Gryczman cuts them down as though they were tall rows of wheat and this was August, not September, and the Germans fall and build a new wall for the major.

And now searchlights go on in Neufahrwasser and the peninsula becomes a white sheet of scorched sand pocked with craters.

It looks like the surface of the moon.

The major watches as the sand leaps and trembles in the craters as the explosions come. Waves of sand lap against the bunker wall like a sea. The bunker rocks and sways. The major feels blood on his cheek. It is not his blood. His ears ring. The ringing sound goes on. The telephone?

—Yes?

—Gryczman, sir. They've broken off the attack. They've gone behind the wall.

—How are your men?

—Cheerful, sir. Hungry. They will do.

—How is your ammunition? Grenades?

—We are short of grenades. We'll get them from the Germans. How is Lieutenant Pajak?

—He died this afternoon.

Gryczman said nothing then.

—Call me again, the major said. Count the dead Germans. Tell the men how many.

Gryczman's men, collecting German handgrenades before the trench, counted seven hundred and fifty-five corpses. Before they managed to regain the trench a new assault began.

—Gryczman, sir.

—Yes?

—They have begun again.

The major looked at his watch. He had forgotten that the crystal was broken and that the hands pointed to the hour of attack, the hour of dawn.

Four A.M. was an eternity ago.

(Dabrowski's watch still ticks. The time on it is twelve-fifteen A.M.)

It is September the second, the major said. There was a note of wonder in his voice.

The men looked at him. Some grinned. So the day was over.

It was over.

It was done.

And they were still alive.

I THE CORRESPONDENT

Loomis woke in his comfortable apartment staring at the peculiarly red light in the windows, wondering about the light and about the sounds. He had a clear recollection of the sounds, and perhaps that was what had wakened him.

First there had been something like the rushing of a black express. Then mercifully distant thuds and rattles like November wind sliding on corrugated iron sheets. Now from the west came a hollow drumming softly puncturing the remote horizon.

There was a gentle motion in the room as he got up, as though a large bird had flown outside and brushed a window with its wing. Then the explosion came. Everything shook just a little and the windows flew in and splintered, and the jagged sounds rushed in.

There they were: familiar.

Masonry and glass spilling on cobblestones. Up in the sky the pulse of motors. He heard the sighing of lowflying planes. Somewhere a horse was screaming.

He ran out on the tiny balcony. It faced the Saxon Gardens. The trees were buried in mist. The day was rising.

After a moment he heard another roll of distant drumming and another. The air shuddered. He felt the concussion. He thought: War. It had come upon him unaware. He was asleep and the war had come.

Last night, he remembered, there had been a party. Last night he had witnessed the humiliation of a pretty girl. And now, without transition, the world was exploding.

The mist began to rise. He saw the smoke. Outside the frame of it the day was blue. A bird sang and the horse continued screaming. Outside the smoke the sky was beautiful and clear.

He thought: I am awake.

He felt chilled. Mornings are cool in Warsaw in September. The days are hot and arid but the nights are cold and mornings carry some of their grey chill. Someone said something in the street and someone else laughed.

They can still laugh? This is their funeral. Why are they laughing?

Then Loomis became aware that he was standing in his shorts out on the balcony. He never used pajamas. Someone was pointing at him, smiling. Well, what the hell. When horses scream while birds sing and the sky is blue and there is glass and masonry in the street and smoke in the sky and windows burst and shred curtains and when the world stands on its head and thumbs its nose at the absolute a man may wear his shorts out on a balcony.

Still, the proprieties . . . He pulled the shredded curtain down and wrapped himself in it.

He caught sight of himself in a long mirror miraculously unshattered inside the room, a tall, heavyshouldered Caesar with greying hair, then turned back to the burning city. He could see the fire and black smoke rolling over Praga, and searched for adjectives which he would later use.

War. It was impossible to believe in it.

The day had promised nothing new.

It was to have been filled as any other day with small affairs, small matters of living. He was to have lunch with Pawel at the Europejski. Pawel was leaving for his regiment in the afternoon and even that phrase, strangely outmoded and a little foolish, seemed normal and routine. He was to arrange to get an interview with Pawel's father later in the evening after a session with Swiderski at the Information Ministry. At night he was to visit friends. All of this suddenly lost its sense. The air shuddered as though ill. The sounds of war came from the thick carapace of smoke.

The day's plans were useless. All the plans of all the days now would be useless. Life, as these people knew it, as they thought of it, was over. Another world was being given birth.

He heard explosions, felt concussion, saw the fires. New worlds are born in fire.

He picked up the telephone, asked for a pot of coffee from the kitchen.

All his impressions of the day before (the sights and sounds of Warsaw: roses and chestnut trees and antiquity, the old man with the rolled umbrella, blood and the young man's broken nose, the General's dark face with the light gone from it, the champagne so readily available and Pawel smoking endless cigarettes, and siren wails and windows taped against concussion, and the cold emptiness in the girl's eyes, her absolute aloneness in the crowd and the small, free, abandoned pirouette on the brink of the artificial lake) fell into place and added to this moment. They had been the signs.

He shook his head.

He waited for the coffee. It would come, of course: War or no war there are amenities for nonparticipants.

Always afterwards he would be able to say that at the moment he knew the war had finally started, he was drinking coffee.

It would sound good, said that way: as though war was a casual sort of thing, an adventure of a kind in which you could take time out for coffee. And it wouldn't offend anyone, disturb anyone. And those of my friends, Loomis thought, who somehow managed to avoid wars, to miss them, and who continued to live comfortably and to make money, would not need to feel envious or regretful about missing them, or uncomfortable hearing how this war began. It was the best possible war story; it didn't lose you any friends.

And his friends (he remembered without pleasure) were particularly sensitive. They were intelligent, they were hardworking educated North Americans. They talked compassionately about orphans and about the brutality of war. They were uneasy about Hitler and Stalin and the Democratic Party and worried about the younger generation and socialism and they were sad about the demise of the arts. They were against vulgarity and for democracy. They found it hard to understand why he became involved in European and Asiatic madnesses. None of these were, after all, America's concerns.

Ordinarily, he would not have become involved in anything, he supposed. But there was that first time. There always is, he supposed. It is like ceasing to be a virgin. You get it once and then you find you have an appetite for it. He would not have become involved in anything if it had not been for that unfortunate first time. The first time had come at a bad time for him.

He was then twenty-nine and at the point of becoming forcibly unmarried. Nimi wanted to divorce him.

The news had come without warning. It was a letter like any other of her letters (written infrequently every summer from the Cape), with the same sloping writing, the same impatient, restless script sprawling all over the pages. She wrote that she was sorry, really sorry, but that he would understand. *If you are anything it's intelligent,* she wrote. She had met someone else; no one he knew. She was very much in love and love was like that, she wrote: Either it came or it didn't and when it came there wasn't anything that anyone could do about it. Who is to blame, after all, if lightning strikes? She wanted to get married and for that she needed a divorce. She supposed that he would give her one: quickly, without any fuss. Fuss was unnecessary and vulgar. Well then, would he?

By God, he thought then, I will not.

Because he wanted her to know his hurt. Because he was unable to believe that this had happened. It happened all the time to people he knew. His friends were constantly getting married and unmarried and it had gotten so that you no longer knew if you should ask about their wives or husbands when you met them (evolving that new, safe, can't-go-wrong, inoffensive phrase,

How's everyone? because everyone had the proper number of fathers and mothers and others he could not divorce).

But not me, Loomis had thought.

These things did not happen to him.

We are different, my wife and I: We are not like the others.

After a while the shock, the pain that is forever, the pain you can't live with, grew less and there was a hollow emptiness where the pain had been, and something had to be found to fill this hollow-gutted void and so he looked for something with which to keep busy, something in which to immerse himself and (possibly) drown. And then, later, because it didn't matter then, and Nimi had not shed him after all (writing another one of those letters to tell him so), he kept on joining those who had some war to keep them busy. It had become a habit of a kind and he continued to involve himself in other peoples' conflicts.

This time, though, I will observe; there have been altogether too many involvements.

Later he went to the railroad terminal. He thought he might find Pawel there; obviously there would be no meeting for lunch. It seemed important to find Pawel and to talk to him, to (as he told himself) make Pawel laugh, make his seriousness absurd; a turnabout sort of thing. At least, he told himself, that's why I *think* I have to talk to him. Seriousness is danger.

He picked his way carefully among the legs and boots. They sprawled like logs on the platform, in the waiting rooms, dangled from windowledges, off benches, out of doorways, stood stacked on stairs, protruded from sheds and from behind mysterious crates, wrapped in khaki puttees and shod in hobnailed leather. Vast crowds moved in the terminal.

The glass in the great vaulted roof was gone. Girders hung drunkenly. There was smoke. The air was full of shouts. Men called each other. They shouted numbers. There was the grinding rattle of hobnailed boots on broken glass and the stamp of iron riflebutts on concrete.

—Sixth Company here, someone shouted and

—Fourth Company here, someone shouted and

—Form up, form up, hurry up, someone shouted.

And the legs and the boots moved and untangled and slipped off the windowsills and the stairways and scraped on the platform and grated off towards the shouting voices and at once more legs and boots spilled out to take their places.

Also there were civilians. Great crowds with anxious eyes and wet eyes and eyes brimming with excitement, looking bright and soft and delicate in summer colors beside the hard, dull drabness of the khaki. These were mostly women.

(A boy was arguing bitterly with a young officer.

—But listen, Julek, I have to know: Will you be all right?

The officer had a high nervous laugh. His uniform was new.

—Of course. Don't worry. It won't last long, you'll see.

—But listen, please, don't be angry but (he blurted out) did they teach you how to fight?)

Loomis pushed through the crowd. He looked for Pawel. He could not see him anywhere. There were tall backs to look at till the men turned. Loomis tripped, almost fell over a pair of legs; he smelled the sour-bread smell of soldiers.

—You in a hurry? Watch where you are going.

It was a soldier who spoke. Loomis looked down at him. The man was short and grotesquely broad. His face was all flat planes and cheekbones and contemptuous eyes. He smoked a pipe with a long mouthpiece. Several other soldiers sat pressed against him under the waiting-room wall.

—Maybe he is hurrying to sign up, another soldier said.

—Maybe he is hurrying to the Bank Narodowy to count his money.

—Watch where you're going, said the soldier with the long pipe. He spat yellowly between Loomis' shoes.

—You tell him, Kublarz, said another soldier.

Loomis went on. The terminal roared with shouts, whistles and the clash of couplings.

Earlier that morning a highexplosive bomb had pierced the glass dome of the terminal and burst inside the cloakroom of the station restaurant. A group of people stood amid the ruin. They were Jews. The woman was still weeping. The man and the boys were done with that. The man's lips trembled in some prayer. The younger boy stared fascinated at the older boy with the thin, harassed face under the too-large cap with the silver eagle, the thin hands nervous round the barrel of a rifle, the neck a thin stick in the too-wide collar of his uniform.

Behind them stood two military policemen impassive in steel helmets.

—A-a-a, a-a-a-a, the woman said, weeping. Her hands went out to the boy in uniform. His face had softened at the sound of her weeping. The old man prayed. The boy stared at his brother's rifle. He licked his lips.

—A-a-a-a, the woman said.

The soldier smiled.

—Quiet. Be quiet now, he said gently. Be quiet.

—Morys, can I touch your rifle? the small boy said.

—Hold it, the brother said.

The small boy grasped the rifle. The woman continued to weep. The man prayed. The soldier smiled. His cap was tilted low over his eyes. His mouth was thin. You could not see his eyes under the shadow of the tilted cap.

Loomis went on.

A redfaced major in a uniform too small for him, the tunic of an unfamiliar cut, oldfashioned, reminiscent of Loomis' last visit to Warsaw, ran out of the buffet. He ran into Loomis.

—*Burdel!* he shouted. This is a French whorehouse! This is not a war. This is not transportation. My train was to leave at five! It is almost noon! What kind of way is this to have a war? How can you have a war if they can't get you to it? Do you know where you can put such an organization?

Loomis tried to pass. The major caught him by a sleeve.

—Are you an official? Do you know anything about these trains? Can you get me a locomotive and some cars? I have a battalion to move, don't you understand?

—No, Loomis said. I am an American. Correspondent.

The major swore.

—I am looking for a Captain Prus, Loomis said. Do you know him?

—Last time I heard of one he was a general of brigade. I think he is dead. You get me a train and I'll get you any number of generals, dead or alive. There are some officers around the stationmaster's office. Perhaps your dead captain-general is there. Good luck.

—And to you, major.

—Luck, the major said. I copulate with it. It's the train that's important. If you should hear anything about my train . . . my name is Tarski . . . the Fortieth Regiment.

Loomis went on.

He saw Pawel when he least expected him, leaning against a wall under a great bronze clock, a too ornate throwback to another era, that now hung by torn cable and straining rivets out of the wall. The twisted hands pointed to the time the bomb had dislodged it: five-fifty-five.

—*Arriba comandante,* Pawel said.

Sunlight curved off the ruptured bronze mass above Pawel's head and slanted cruelly into his face. He smiled into the crowd beyond Loomis' shoulder. The smile lacked warmth or any necessary brightness.

—I hoped you'd be here, Loomis said, wondering about the unbright smile. You look very martial.

—The regiment rides at dawn, eh? Well, not these regiments.

—No trains?

—No trains. It seems they've been bombed to pieces somewhere else.

—I never thought much of your Polish trains.

—Not like Italian trains, eh?

—Nothing is like Italian trains since Mussolini made them run on time. We are all impressed back home by Italian trains.

Pawel laughed abruptly.

—You shouldn't make unkind remarks about Polish trains. Don't you know that you shouldn't speak ill of the dead?

—I forgot. I am a vulgar, unmannerly American. Besides, where I come from no one says anything unkind about anybody until they are incapable of answering back.

—We, on the contrary, make the loudest noises when we're in no position to open our mouths. I think your way is better. It doesn't guarantee a bloody nose.

They walked along the platform.

—You'll be all right, *Pawelku,* Loomis said. Where are you going?

—Nowhere, obviously. But if we ever find a train we are going west. At least, that's where I'm supposed to go. Why don't you come with me?

142

—Not this time.

—Not interested this time?

—Yes. But it seems different this time. Ah but (he tried again) this time I want a comfortable war. How about you? Don't you remember how we used to do it?

And Loomis knew that he had said the worst possible thing. But Pawel didn't seem to hear or, if he did, to care what Loomis said. His eyes were on the crowd of uniforms, moving swiftly, and he waved to another officer who came up to them. They talked in French so that Loomis wouldn't feel left out but, for all that, he felt an intruder.

Having found Pawel, he had wanted to wait with him for the train, to see him off, but now he didn't want it. He felt conspicuous and lost. He wanted to go.

—Well, I had better go, he said. Goodbye, *Pawelku.*

—*Arriba,* Pawel said

His hand was cold. The clasp was strong but mechanical and brief. Loomis moved away as quickly as he could.

He went back the way he had come, past the wrecked toilets where the Jews no longer stood, past the crates and the bundles and the stacked cases where men sat and lay and stood and sprawled and cursed him when he tripped over their legs, and so out of the terminal into the street.

Men hurried there. There was a roar of traffic and voices and much dust. The crowd was grey, flecked with browns and greens and the violent young colors of women's summer coats. In it rumor grew and multiplied. Some man, magnificently drunk, waved a squarecut bottle and shouted: —On to Berlin! Hurrah! He tripped, fell and disappeared. In the street a troop of cavalry waited, grinning, while a young officer harangued the crowd to make room for them.

—Berlin next week, someone said and

—Have you heard?

—A thousand English tanks wait in Romania and

—Two hundred French planes landed in Okecie yesterday and

—The French are marching on Berlin and

—The Foreign Legion came ashore at Danzig . . .

Loomis saw Pawel's father pass in the crowd, where small girls handed flowers to soldiers. One child pressed a bouquet into the colonel's hands. He threw it from him as if it were hot. The child ran away, crying.

On to Berlin!

Glass crunched underfoot.

Suddenly the crowd hesitated. It stood still. Necks craned up. Arms pointed. Loomis heard the soft, low humming in the west, a murmuring that faded in and out like radio in bad weather.

The sky had a peculiar steely quality as if the blue of it was not enough to show how innocent it was. Across the pale expanse of cheerful brightness moved rows of glittering objects like wintering geese.

Then the sound was heavy and insistent and the street bellowed with a hundred voices, the shriek of horses, shouts, curses, calls, blasphemies, the grating drumbeat of frantic feet and hooves and it seemed that the old houses held their breath and the glittering echelons wheeled slowly, lazily, as though with time to spare, and fell with infinite assurance one by one towards the town. Little black things like broken pencil points came tumbling down end over end.

Then the sound of war was there and fire was there and windows tinkled out despite the tape and a great moaning sound came from the town as the planes nosed up from their dive somewhere east of the Praga bridges. There fighters caught them and the bombers spilled out in all directions like the opening petals of some evil flower and at once the sky was filled with whining, hurtling shapes and white streaks of contrail and black exhaust and eventually black plumes of smoke that ended in fire like a falling star. Soon these were many.

The sky no longer held its optimistic blue; it blurred with smoke. Smoke twisted over Wola and Zoliborz and the green fields of Mokotow. Okecie Field glowed in the smoke like molten metal. A sound like giant waves crashing ashore came from the smoke.

It was a long time ending but eventually it did and the planes were gone and smoke hung in its thin, pathetic veils again and underneath this funeral veil the blue sky was inviting.

Then the streets filled again with the quick crowds.

And the city burned.

The great facades slid down into the street and left the houses naked and exposed, betraying rows and stacks of rooms with all their private parts no longer hidden: the portraits and the overstuffed furniture and the ridiculous bathtub dangling by a pipe, the swinging toilet chain and the marital bed, all in the forest of shredded wallpaper waving like seagrass.

And soon the sky sank down on all of it.

Later that night, unable to sleep despite the bourbon, Loomis went out on the balcony. The sky was red. The city glowed. Where the night was black across the river small mounds of suburb pulsed like coals.

I wonder what it looks like from the air, Loomis thought.

I ADAM

Adam woke to the sound of military bands marching in the streets. There were shouts and some singing. He did not know how long he had slept and at first he did not know where he was.

—What, he said, and, Where, feeling the fear of confusion. His face was wet. His ears felt as though a fire burned in each of them.

He saw the ceiling. It was white and now the red light of the setting sun turned it into a pitted pink like a cheap confection. The bars in the windows made black streaks on it.

He heard the click of the opening Judas but kept his head averted. He tried to breathe as though asleep. Now he knew where he was and he remembered his questioning and knew why his ears burned and wondered which of the policemen was looking at him through the little circle in the iron door. He wondered if the big one with the flat ears would hit him again. This made his stomach tighten in a knot and he moved up his knees despite himself. At once a voice behind the door said: —He is awake.

—I would wake him all right, said another voice. I would so wake him that he would never wake again.

—Ha ha, said Voice One. Then Reinhardt would wake *you*.

—He's a thief and a fugitive and a Pole. He is a spy. Does that make him special?

—Don't ask me, *bubi*. Ask Reinhardt, it's his baby. Now go tell Reinhardt his special is awake.

The Judas clicked shut and presently footsteps went away. Adam felt all his muscles relax. He was wet with sweat. The day had been hot and the night was barely beginning. It had not yet lasted long enough to cool off the concrete. Later it will be cold, he thought: but not yet.

He got up and got the metal pitcher off the floor and poured water into the metal cup and drank the water and sat down. The water was warm. It did not make him feel any better. After a while he lay down again.

He had come into Reichenau, a small town of steep roofs and many gables and shutters and the crisp cleanliness of soil and air so typical of the Salzkammergut, and at first he thought that it was market day, there were so many people in the street, and then he remembered that it could not be. It was a Thursday. Still, there were all those people. They were excited about something. They wore the looks of expectation and, yes, here and there, also anxiety, but mostly this kind of eagerness. They wished to know if something had begun yet and if it was true that there had been a radio broadcast about it earlier in the day. Someone asked him and he said that he did not know and the man's eyes became grave with suspicion and he asked where the young *Herr* had come from and where he was going.

Adam supposed that he had lost his head. He began explaining about the rockclimb, talking too loud. His accent softened the gutturals. Someone noticed this and asked about the accent of the young *Herr*. Where was he from? America, he said and knew that he should not have said it because the accents of Americans are well known in the Salzkammergut where so many of them come to ski and to eat young goose with cucumber salad and for the festivals. Besides, just about everyone in the Salzkammergut has a relative in America. When he told them that he was from America they became very quiet. His loud voice and soft accent had brought about the forming of a small crowd. Also he was nervous. He thought about the unpaid bill in Mariazell. He had never been good at looking innocent when he was guilty. He had always managed to look guilty when he was innocent and now, feeling himself a fugitive, thought he probably looked as guilty as a murderer. He began to stammer, tried to walk out of the crowd but the crowd detained him. No one laid a hand on him, in fact the men made considerable effort not to touch him, but, somehow, whichever way he turned he faced a wall of faces and could not pass. It was as though he was the axis of a wheel and when he turned the wheel turned with him. Eventually, of course, the crowd interested the ubiquitous policemen and the policemen asked to see the passport of the young *Herr*. The young *Herr* could not produce the passport. It was in Mariazell under the counter of the reception desk. One does not search for passports while jumping out of windows with the bills unpaid. The policemen took charge of the young *Herr* and took him to jail and later questioned him and the big one hit him. Then several others hit him and made him stand in a corner with his trousers off. Eventually he told them who and what he was and they sent for his passport and verified his story. Then they took him to another town, a bigger one, with a new concrete jail building, and questioned him again. They wanted to know why he said he was an American when he was a Pole. And what he was doing in the Salzkammergut during the war. What war, he said and they told him. After that he said nothing but it was too late.

His questioning had gone on most of the afternoon and the policemen kept slapping his ears with their open palms. Each slap was like a pistolshot. Soon he could not hear their questions and that made them angry. They beat him with belts and with rubber truncheons and with thin metal rods. The rods seemed designed for this purpose. They inflicted pain without cutting the skin. He fainted several times and this also annoyed the policemen. They put him into a cold bath every time he fainted.

There were, he remembered, five policemen in the room with him. One was the big one who slapped ears. Another was an expert with the metal rod. One did not contribute anything to the questioning except by shouting: —*Liar! Give it to him!* each time Adam said anything (including his name). He sat behind a small table in the corner eating his lunch. This was thick bread and butter and a sausage he took out of a rolled-up newspaper. He would take a bite out of the sausage, wave it like a truncheon and shout: —*Liar! Give it to him!* and take a bite out of the bread and butter. After a while he found something interesting to read in the greasy paper and took no further part in the questioning. The fourth policeman was a small man with glasses who took notes. He covered page after page of scribbled testimony whether Adam said anything or not. He smoked innumerable cigarettes. The fifth policeman searched himself for crabs. He had his trousers open under the narrow window and searched and scratched and cursed and once in a while shouted something at the bespectacled policeman. All of them, except the thin one who took notes, smoked cigars. The small room was blue with the smoke. There was little in the room: a chair with straps on it, a sort of billiard table with more straps, a metal cupboard where metal rods were kept, the small desk where the fat policeman was eating his lunch and the two bathtubs, one steaming and one with ice caked on the surface. Each time Adam fainted the policemen threw him in the icy bath and once, to make a surprisingly painful difference, into the hot one. Then they would put him back on the billiard table and ask more questions. They wanted to know the object of his mission. They wished to know where he had hidden his demolition charges.

—*What charges?* The dynamite with which he was to blow up the tunnel in Mariazell, of course. It would have to be a lot of explosives because to blow up the tunnel called for the demolition of the mountain. So where was it? Who were his associates? Where was the dynamite concealed? —*Oh, not the mountain,* Adam said. *It is so high. When you walk along the high ridge in the wind it is like a glider, high above everything, and no one says anything, you are alone.* —*Liar! Give it to him!* —*What?* said the big policeman —*Do you know about clouds?* Adam said. —*Liar! Give it to him!*

. . . And the soft humming downcurve of the metal rod.

146

—If not that tunnel, which one?
—What was the mission?
—Who has it now? The charges!
—Who helped you?
—Where did you report?
—And the charges. Where did you hide the charges?

He was then very tired and no longer felt the blows except as something which sounded like pain: the humming of the metal rod and the dull thud of it across some drumhead. They were insistent about charges. Charge! He said it the way he used to say it under the bluetipped pine along the Wiselka. Sweep from the wings and bring your charge home. *—Was it good, Father? Did you see my charge? —Very good, but where was your maneuver?* Next time . . .
—Who helped you?
—When did you come?
—What was your mission?

The scarlet sounds of pain followed each question. You could count to three in the time between the end of the question and the beginning of the pain. Question. Count. Pain. But there was no longer pain, only the sound of it.

Time passed.

Question.

—Where are the charges?

Eins . . . zwei . . . drei . . .

The sound of metal curving through the air and the thud across the distant drum.

—Where did you hide your parachute?

One . . . two . . .

Oblivion.

Shock of ice.

—Who helped you?

Count to three.

—What was your mission?

—I . . .

—Liar! Give it to him!

The silver hum of metal rods descending.

The questioning ended towards the end of the afternoon. It had not lasted long, but a man spreadeagled naked on a billiard table forms unusual conclusions about the passage of time. To Adam the end of the afternoon was the end of centuries. A man arrived to end it. Adam did not see the figure properly; his eyes swam unfocused on the whitespeckled ceiling. But he saw the edge of a uniform which was different from the uniforms of the five policemen. It was something like the clothes Adam had seen hanging in Erich's apartment. The new arrival gave an order and said various uncomplimentary things about the policemen and the policemen hurried to get Adam off the billiard table. Clearly they did not understand any more than he did. The fat policeman had the look of a puppydog who confidently expects a lifetime of bones and gets the end of a boot. The fat policeman and the expert on the metal rods were sent for a stretcher. The policeman who was eating sausage (—*Liar! Give it to him!*) said something about jurisdiction and authority and civil crimes and time of war and the irregularity of something and was silenced by one word from the man in black.

The policeman hurried to put Adam on the stretcher. He supported Adam's head. Each of the other policemen took hold of one of the four handles of the stretcher and they carried him to a cell. There they rolled Adam gently onto a bunk and left him. They said nothing to him and next to nothing to each other. They said words like *political* and *special* and *How-were-we-to-know*. The bespectacled policeman patted Adam's head. Presently a doctor came and applied ointments. The doctor grasped this and that, and felt the other, and took deep soundings with his stethoscope. He was a jovial, elderly physician. He made several jokes. He commented on the resiliency of youth. Then he produced a syringe and filled it and gave Adam an injection and presently Adam slept. When he woke in the cell, to the sound of the singing in the streets, he did not know how long he had slept. He did not think it could have been long.

He sat up carefully and felt his body with both hands. Nothing seemed broken. This and that hurt, this and that were blistered, but nothing grated under his fingers, nothing bent, no bones protruded. He wondered if the questioning would resume now that he was awake. He wondered about the mysterious Reinhardt the guard had talked about. He wondered what would happen to him. He supposed that he would be shot. Then he got the drink of water from the metal pitcher and lay down on his cot.

He thought about his execution.

He supposed that they would take him out tomorrow into the courtyard. There would be the blindfold and the cigarette: That was the way it was done in the books, and it made no more sense than all the books he had read, but then nothing made sense anymore. He would be shot as a spy, he supposed; certainly the policemen had talked about spies. He wondered if there really was a war between Germany and Poland. But perhaps they would not shoot him in the courtyard. They could shoot him in a cellar by the light of flashlights. That is the way the Bolsheviks shot people, according to Grzes. Grzes had told many stories about the Bolsheviks. He wondered if the Nazis and the Bolsheviks had this in common.

He did not wish to be shot either in the courtyard or in the cellar. He wished to be alive.

He waited for the footsteps of the policemen. He waited for the questioning to resume. He wondered what he would have to do to remain alive. He heard the noise of military music in the streets. There were shouts, songs and cheers. There were many cheers. The parade lasted a long time.

But no one came for him that evening. No one bothered him. The fat policeman (—*Liar! Give it to him!*) brought him cabbage soup. Later one of the others brought black bread and coffee. Neither policeman said anything to him. They didn't look at him. The fat policeman was particularly careful to stare straight ahead, as if to look at Adam, to be reminded of his availability, would cause him to lose control of himself.

148

Clearly, the policeman had been disciplined about the questioning. His rigid back and carefully averted eyes and thin mouth and whitening line of cheekbone all said that he was forbidden to indulge himself further. Adam drew little comfort from this. He knew that the mysterious man in black, the officer who had miraculously intervened and stopped the questioning, could have it started up again anytime he wanted. Adam did his best to make himself inconspicuous while the policemen were with him.

Later he got up and had a little of the soup. He couldn't drink much of it. The soup was cold and greasy but it was also salty. The salt burned in the broken corners of his mouth and where his teeth were loose. His throat felt tight. Each other bone and tendon and muscle and nerve end seemed to house unsuspected quantities of pain: innumerable small aches, little agonies.

He lay quite still on his cot, watching the darkening red sky outside his window, listening to the sounds. The pounding thumps of military music drew off and became a tinny mutter in the distance, but there were other sounds: the cheers and the shouting. He heard parts of a speech punctured by the shouting, the voice metallic, booming: A loudspeaker, he thought. The words were all the bitter words of the nightstops in the mountainlodges but there were other words as well. Their tone was triumphant.

War . . . if there was, indeed, a war between Germany and Poland . . . confused him. The concept was too broad. He couldn't fit it into the narrow, red and black confines of his cell. But he knew war meant that there would be no consulates to make inquiries about him. If that was so, he was indeed alone. True, he was no stranger to being alone. His mind worked well . . . best . . . when he was alone. But here were all the elements that made aloneness terrible: pain, fear and fear of pain . . . lack of reason.

What did they want from him? And why should it happen to him anyway? All he had done was to leave an unpaid bill in Mariazell. He was willing to confess that guilt. And that was all. But no one mentioned that. They talked about dynamite and spies. (—*Liar! Give it to him!*) It was impossible that they would think he was a spy.

But there had to be something. He went carefully over everything he had heard through the Judaswindow and knew that unpaid bills had nothing to do with what was happening to him. The jailers called him special and political. It was ridiculous, of course. He had never been interested in anything political. But that was what they said.

There had to be some way to show them they were wrong. Somebody had to listen. Clearly it would do no good to talk to the fat policeman (—*Liar! Give it to him!*), but the new man, the officer in black, would possibly listen. Somebody had to listen while there was still time. Because he had no doubt that, unless he made the Germans understand their terrible mistake, something more would happen, something infinitely more dangerous than beatings.

It had never occurred to him that he might not be good about facing pain. He had never thought about it, but now he did and he became afraid. He closed his eyes tight and tried to force the thought of pain away from him, and the thought called up new agonies from his imagination. Oh (he thought) not the quick pain of blows, no, not that kind. That comes too fast for anticipation and dulls itself in time. Each blow is an anesthetic of a kind, each makes the next easier to bear. Yes. So . . . not that kind of pain. But the imaginative, slow pain of protracted torture. That is terrifying.

But then he (thought) if he could make somebody listen, make them believe, there would be no more pains of any kind. The whole thing was a huge mistake. The Germans must have thought he was somebody else: a case of mistaken identity. That sort of thing happened every day. And he could show them their mistake if someone would listen. Erich could tell them who he, Adam, was and what he was doing in the Salzkammergut and how ridiculous it was to think him a spy.

That was the answer, of course, the way to end the nightmare, although he wasn't quite sure what would happen afterwards. War probably meant that he would be imprisoned somewhere. But there would be no more fat policemen with their metal rods, and no more pain, and nothing to withstand or to endure, nothing to prove to anyone about ability to face pain, and there'd be time to think of something to improve his lot. It was a marvelous fine thought. Erich would tell them!

He tried to imagine where Erich might be so that he could tell them where to look for him. He didn't know which way Erich would take now that the trip was over. He would have passed through Reichenau, heading north, if he was still following the time schedules of the plan. Adam thought it likely; Erich always liked to follow a plan. It occurred to Adam that Erich's anger, his great disappointment, was due as much to the disruption of his plan as to the interrupted rockclimb. He would follow the plan as closely as he could.

Adam smiled, carefully, because of the pain. Soon now the nightmare would be over. In a way he regretted being out of danger . . . but only in a way. He felt so relieved that he laughed, a quick laugh, like a bark. His mouth was swollen; he could not laugh well. But he would laugh later, he thought, feeling remarkably content.

He thought about Adrianne (no longer angry or disappointed but still puzzled), wondering why she had not come to Mariazell. War may have had something to do with it, he thought. But it wasn't likely; he didn't think the English would come into it. If you tell someone, after all, that you will do something, you do it. A man stood by his word, no matter what happened. But perhaps it was different for a woman.

He went carefully over everything she had said to him in Vienna the day she had telephoned him in Erich's apartment, the day before he and Erich and Kuno Saal had set out on the trip. It had been a fine day, the best he could remember for a long time. A quick rain had washed the air clean shortly before noon and the sun was hot.

Erich was out, making the last arrangements, when she telephoned. Yes, he said into the telephone, Erich would not be back for some time. She said she knew it. What was Adam doing? Nothing, he said, surprised. She also wasn't doing much of anything, she said. It was a shame to waste the afternoon . . . it was so beautiful . . . would Adam like to take her for a walk? Later they could have coffee with whipped cream and nutmeg.

Why, of course, he said, thinking for one quick moment about Erich. But then, perhaps, it was over between her and Erich. And anyway it would be only a walk in the park and coffee. . . .

Good, she said. Her voice was warm; there was laughter in it. It made a promise of a kind. He loved the rich sound of it. He waited for her at the main gate to the park, feeling his heart pound, his hands moving in and out of his pockets without him doing anything about it, thinking about clocks. Time seemed to have gone on vacation; it passed impossibly slowly. He thought the clocks were laughing at him. But, at last, she came—smiling and very much at ease, cool in the hot sun like the marble women in the fountains—bright-patterned like a flower field but severely tailored; simple straight lines commanding attention. Several men looked her way and Adam thought his chest would explode. When she came up to him, still smiling, and put her hand in his, the men looked at him curiously. He felt immensely tall.

—*Well*, he said, *here you are. I had just about given up on you.*

She laughed and put her arm through his. —*Oh? Am I late?*

—*Not really. I just got here myself. There's a tremendous lot to do before the sort of trip we're going to take.*

—*I thought you said you weren't doing anything.*

—*What? Well, yes, I did. I was doing something but it was nothing that couldn't wait.*

—*Not that important then?*

—*Well, no, I suppose not. I mean it was but it could wait. Why are you laughing?*

Now when he thought about it, Adam wondered if that was the way it always was: that men and women always lied to one another about what they were thinking, to make things pleasant. Things had certainly been pleasant that day. The sun shining. Redgold in the park and silver in the fountains. Silver and white, because of the stone nymphs and bigbellied mermen. Jets of gossamer spun by gardeners' hoses. She called the gardeners *small gentlemen of the gravelwalk, indefatigable spiders.* Their multicolored hose-sprays, she said, were silver filaments that made a web to trap the sun.

—*That's very beautiful*, he said. *But then, of course, you write poetry.*

It's not mine. I read it somewhere. (And, picking a dead flower:) *Look at that. I hate to see the end of summer. I walk so crooked in the cold months. Damn winter, stupid damn snow. I hate it.*

—*There won't be any snow for two more months.*

I hate the cold. I hate grey days. I hate to see the end of the beautiful bright days.

—*They do come back.*

—*But not this year and the wait's so long. And if you listened to my father you would think there would be no more years after this one. I hate to see things end. It's just too depressing.*

—*What things?* he said, thinking of Erich.

—*Why, all this of course.*

—*Yes, I suppose it's hard for you.*

She (quickly): —*What is?*

—*What you are saying. Losing the bright days and so on.*

She laughed. —*You're sweet. You really are a sweet boy.*

—*Oh, I don't know. I'm not as innocent as all that.*

She laughed. —*Of course. I didn't mean it that way at all. Listen.* (And she swung around on his arm, facing him, her hair spilling all about his necktie.) *I have a marvelous idea. Let's make an alliance. A private pact of mutual support against the cold grey days. You and I, independently of any international agreements. The first to be attacked by the gloom of winter can summon all help from the other.*

—*Done.*

—*Your word, sir?*

—*Right.*

—*No matter what other commitments we might have. An unconditional pact of mutual assistance.*

—*Right.*

To seal the pact, she kissed him. Later, while having coffee, with the sun going down and the quick crowds spilling from the sidewalks, and Adam laughing, Adam being witty, Adam telling the urbane stories of evening hours, she said some words that led him to say others and then, suddenly, it was all arranged about Mariazell.

He couldn't quite believe it. He thought he had misunderstood her somehow and so said (cautiously): —*Wonderful. I'll get the rooms for us.*

She laughed. —*Rooms? It's you I'm coming down to see. Unless you'd rather that I didn't come.*

—*Good God, no,* he said. *I mean yes, of course I want you to come.*

—*For a moment I doubted your enthusiasm. You looked so solemn. You're still looking solemn.*

—*I don't feel solemn. I'm astonished, that's all.*

—*Why? Because you find that I like you as much as you like me?*

—*Good God, do you?*

—*I've always liked you very much. I've thought a lot about you. I've wished that I could know you better. But there was always Erich.*

—*Yes,* he said, suddenly remembering. *Erich, of course.*

—*You know how he is.*

—*Yes.*

—*But that's all finished now. Now there is nothing to get in our way. Oh, I'm so looking forward to my trip. But you're still looking solemn. What's the matter, Adam?*

He shook his head, troubled. —*It's Erich. I keep thinking how bad this will be for him.*

—*Bother Erich! It will serve him right.*

—*He is my friend.*

—*And we are allies, remember? Don't I have your word? Of course, if you'd rather climb some silly mountain than be with me . . .*

There could be only one answer and he gave it, anxious that she should not think him ungrateful or lacking in enthusiasm, an indifferent lover.

She smiled, content. —*I knew I could depend on you.*

He went on to assure her that, of course, she could. Always. In every way and all circumstances. She said, again, she knew it. Later he saw this as a doubtful compliment at best. But when she said it (smiling to herself, leaning back in her chair with an odd air of triumph, her smile sliding, with her eyes carefully averted) he heard it as an accolade. Bells, trumpets and artillery salutes couldn't have made him feel more richly praised.

He took her home. (She said: —*Have pleasant dreams. Sleep well.*) Sleep was impossible, of course. He walked a long time through the darkening streets and, later, in the glare of neon, seeing nothing. He didn't want to go back to Erich's apartment. At least not right then. His thoughts were chaos: pride, immense happiness and a touch of guilt. He didn't think he should be quite that happy when he remembered Erich and the trip. But, he thought, perhaps it will never come to that; perhaps some way out will present itself in time or, if not, perhaps there will be some way to make amends, later, for wrecking the trip. One thing he knew: Erich could never be allowed to know about Adrianne. Nothing could make amends for that; he would not forgive it. He would not be able to bear being supplanted or replaced.

Well then, if he was not to know he wouldn't be told. And, Adam thought, laughing a little, even if told he wouldn't believe it. Any more than Adam could believe it. He had no guarantee that the night was real.

He went on, laughing quietly to himself, aware of people stepping carefully out of his way, people annoyed and amused, and other people, in huge, silent lines against the walls of houses. These turned white faces towards him and then, quickly, away. He wondered why they stood there. There were no theaters in that part of town. And then he was in front of the Polish consulate general, looking with a quick warmth at the white-eagle plaque with its crimson background. It was long after office hours but the place was busy.

He watched the silent lines work their way gradually into the brightlit lobby, symmetrical white faces, anxious eyes. These were the Jews. Of course. He had seen them before. They were like rows of slowly moving trees growing each day from early morning until late at night beside the consulate. Every consulate had its own sad softly murmuring forest of Jews about its doors; fearful, intense, desperately hoping for a foreign passport, waving their faded proofs of citizenship, stuttering freshly learned phrases to convince. A few would leave laughing, incoherent, clutching the passports. Most left as they came: with hopeless eyes. Next morning they would stand at a different consulate reading dictionaries.

Adam went up the steps, past the agitated lines, feeling the angry eyes, the enormous hunger. He could sense the huge resentment when the doorman, seeing his passport, made way for him. He couldn't understand why they hated him.

The doorman's voice was hoarse. —*Stand aside there, please. Stand in line.*

But the lines doubled and tripled on the steps and small men darted in under his widespread arms and when he turned after them others pushed inside.

Hands reached out for Adam. —*Five thousand for your passport . . . —Ten thousand . . . —Do you want diamonds? —Listen, I have a Rubens . . . genuine antiques . . .*

He wanted desperately to get away from the hands. He felt that if they fastened onto him they would tear him apart. The desperation was tangible; fear, despair and envy made the grey men and women unrecognizable, unhuman. And suddenly the lines broke and flowed around the doorman up the steps and into the hall and a score of white fists flew up holding sheaves of banknotes and jewels flashed like weapons in the too bright light.

—*What will you take? What will you take?*

He ran inside, pursued by their voices.

—*For God's sake, mister, you can get another . . .*

White faces. Mouths like wounds.
—*Stand back there!*

He didn't know why he had come into the consulate. Certainly he had no business for the clerks, whose cold eyes and impatient, manicured hands combed with elaborate disdain through the dog-eared papers of the frantic Jews. But he had felt a curious lack of ease outside, as if his small guilt about Erich had made him particularly alone in the foreign street. And then he had seen the familiar symbol on the plaque: the silver emblem of his father's cap and buttons. His childhood world had revolved about them and him.

It had been long since he had thought at any length about his father. But now, suddenly, needing the warmth of his boyhood, wanting to feel the General's two hard hands on his cheeks, the bite of silver buttons, and to smell the comforting metalpolish and the leather, the floodgates of his memory lifted.

These were the fondest and the most stubbornly remembered recollections of his boyhood, when the shining, uniformed man with hard hands (that could be so gentle about his small head) was as much a symbol of reverence and love and authority and belonging as the white eagle on the plaque outside; when both were, indeed, interchangeable in the boy's mind. The General was each hero that he read about. Adam had no trouble in imagining how they looked or how they moved or how their voices sounded. His father was Stefan Czarnecki leading winged hussars across the Baltic into Bornholm, and Wisniowiecki holding Zbararz against the Tartar Khan, and Jan Sobieski scattering the Turks outside the walls of Vienna; each of them had the scarred, familiar face and the warmclasping hands. His father was to him the sum of everything magnificent and awesome: kind, strong and indestructible, protecting and, seemingly, eternal. Nothing (the boy had thought) could ever change this natural order of things. It was as permanent as the sky, as enduring as the country whose history he read in his father's face. Poland—the word itself—was best understood if compressed into the familiar figure so that he went about each national holiday with the enthusiasm of a family birthday. Nothing meant more than an approving nod and smile from his father; each disapproval was a tragedy.

He had long schooled himself not to think about the General, to lock him from his mind. But sometimes, when he was particularly tired, or particularly disturbed, or conscious of a transgression of some kind, the quick, bright thought returned. (If I did this and that, what would He think? What would He do in such and such a situation? If He could see me now, would he feel proud?) And so the rockclimbs: innumerable times of doubt while he inched along some giant cliff-face in the thin, cold air, with the high winds howling like all the devils in the precipice below, in the great quiet, with the difficulties mounting and fatigue a tangible quantity like the piled-up, white clouds, immeasurably heavy, and with the first, hot licks of fear. The question, then, is: Is it now? Is this to be the time? Because the wrong decision can make it so. And so, eventually, the moment of the last possible decision: on and up or safely down, either way irrevocable. He would say nothing if I backed off, but . . . And is there enough strength and enough light? And is this the time? There is still time to work my way back down. And the hands move and grope for the new, unsuspected fingerholds, and find them, and the trembling arms and thighs grow steady, and the mind clears and there is a new determination and the choice is made. Up. And then it is done.

And, being done, there is the long rest in the difficult, thin air, high above the doubts and difficulties and the black rockwall sliding away into the cellar of the earth, and the quiet laughter. It is derisive laughter. Because, of course, He wouldn't ever know the choice or the decision. So mock it. He saves his smiles for his woman.

But, mocked or not, it would come back in those marginal moments: the lean, hard face with the calm, softening eyes, the smile and the fraction of a nod: —*It was good.* Warmth then; a marvelous, fine feeling.

He felt no warmth in the marbled lobby of the consulate under the glittering chandeliers, with the desperate slow lines moving past the tables and the desks and the cold clerks.

He had to make a special effort not to think about the General, who would find little to be pleased about that day and nothing to approve. Well, not quite; he wouldn't be entirely disapproving. No. He would have a small smile about Adrianne: a measure of approval. That was all right: a part of being a man, becoming a man. The General would know more about that than most other men. But the way that Adam was going about it would wear less well with him. The business about Mariazell and the trip and Erich. The need for subterfuge. It was not clean enough; a kind of betrayal.

But what of that? He felt the sudden bitterness, the so familiar yellow taste. Let me, too, have a little taste of treason. Perhaps it's in the blood.

Someone asked him what he wanted, who he was, and he muttered something about having come to register with the consulate for mail. He had reported his arrival the week before but, he said, he wanted to make sure they had him on the books. His passport? Certainly. Visa'd through Switzerland. The clerk looked through it with a magnifying glass, compared signatures and numbers in the register. (—*We have a dozen forgeries presented every day.*)

—*How long do you intend to stay in Germany?*

—*Austria? About a month.*

—*Austria, Germany, it's all one. The same devil. I wouldn't stay that long.*

—*Why not?*

—*The situation. We are advising all our nationals to go home. If I were you I'd be on the morning train.*

—*I can't do that.*

—*Why not? I strongly advise it. At least, leave German territory. You came from Switzerland?*

—*Yes.*

—*Then go back there. At least for a few weeks.*

—*Impossible,* Adam said.

He felt a growing sense of irritation, aware of the envious eyes of others (those without passports or a hope of one), and wished them all to the devil for making him feel guilty and conspicuous. But this was no help. The cold clerk with the back of his smoothpolished skull carefully presented to the greyfaced wall, with his filingcabinet approach to their anxiety, made him feel ashamed. It was as though it was particularly important now, at this special time, to prove that the white eagle on the plaque outside meant something after all. That it could perform the small, required miracle. Salvation.

But there could be no miracle here, he knew well enough. More than anything, he wanted to leave, to get away from the animal eyes of the unpassported.

—*Well?* the clerk said. *Will you go home tomorrow?* Then, urgently: —*There won't be anyone to help you if anything happens. Do you know what can happen? Do you know what I'm talking about?*

—*Everyone knows about that.*

—*Listen, don't be a fool. Get out while you can.*

But Adam shook his head. It was impossible, he said. And he was not a fool; he knew what he was doing. He turned on his heel then and walked quite blind, angry beyond reason, out of the building and into the street. Would all his hopes, he asked (of himself and of the glittering, spangled boulevard, and the quick crowds there), all he believed in, always be betrayed?

He asked this now, lying on his cot, watching the dark ceiling of his cell after sunset, hearing the measured tread of the guard and the occasional click of the Judaswindow. Yes, he said, contemptuous, I am still here. The prisoner has not sprouted any wings.

The cell grew colder and his aches returned; dark pain of bruised bone and broken tissue, expertly induced.

Saturday, September the second

I THE HUNTER

On the bloody poster done all in red and scorched black and violent white, a soldier plunged a bayoneted rifle into a talon hand that reached with hooked claw fingers for the earth and grasped it and buried in it. Above the hand was the downthrust bayonet. Below it in flaming white, jagged and leaping like fire, was the word *Nie!*

It was, he thought, too soft a word to deny anything to anyone. More than words was needed.

The poster was new, a week old at most, but already ragged. It was torn and scorched and blackened and curling away from the wall. The wall stood in a pile of blackened stone, and chickens wandered by it and made disconsolate noises in the rubble. In the field a biplane lay stupidly on its back and soldiers were cutting up its canvas for souvenirs.

Pawel felt cold.

He put the collar of his greatcoat up and felt the scraping, powdery touch of somebody's dried blood on it, and smelled the acrid odor of singed wool.

—Here? he said. Is this the place?

The peasant nodded. He reined in the pony and the cart stopped rolling and Pawel got off it carefully, feeling his joints stiff and his back sore, and took up his haversack and the mapcase and the binoculars and the blanketroll.

—God will repay, he said.

Sometime. Somewhere. God always settled his accounts.

—Go with God, Sir Captain, the peasant said.

He made a soft sound with his lips like a kiss; a gentle urging. The small horse pressed forward. Soon the wagon was around the ruin, gone in the darkness, and Pawel was alone.

He was cold. It was not the crisp cold of mountains and of forests that he felt. Not the greensmelling chill. It was the damp, penetrating cold of morning in the flatland where every sound and smell is clear and defined the way the colors of a watercolor are defined when the artist first touches the paper with his brush. Later the colors run into each other. Later they blur. But when he first touches them to paper they are distinct.

He buttoned up his greatcoat. He felt hunger. Yes. God, I could eat.

It seemed impossible to believe that only two nights before this one there had been champagne and caviar and *zakaski* and pretty canapes and duck stuffed with apricots, and even in the train (poor, blasted, burning heap of metal) there had been Courvoisier (the Brandy of Napoleon) and Bisquit and twelve-year-old Zubrowka and hard, dry sausage and fried chicken offered apologetically by the little Air Force officercadet and *pasztet* that an unknown woman thrust at him for the journey (with a quick handshake and the head rapidly averted to hide emotion). The redfaced major of infantry had had some cigars.

But that had been last night. Before the train crawled up on the embankment outside Janowiec—a long, iron animal festooned with men who clung to handrails and footboards and couplings and lay on roofs like cordwood and who flew off the roofs like broken puppets when the planes came and the bombs came down until, finally, in the quick, omnipresent clatter of machinegun fire and the shriek of rending metal and heaving floors, the stricken animals leaped off the embankment into the fields and burned.

And then the screams. Men burning. Horses burning. The terrible sweet smell.

And the planes coming back again and again and the machinegun bullets pinging in the wreckage.

How red the sky became.

He had been drinking the Brandy of Napoleon —*Towards the greater glory of the Fatherland* and —*For the honor of the regiment* and —*To victory* and —*To the laughing gods of war,* tilting his head back while the major laughed and the cadet munched chicken and the light artillery officer said something about lancers and how it didn't matter whether they were drunk or sober because, as everyone knew, they had horses and these were intellectual giants compared to their masters and would get them home, when suddenly he felt himself rising in the air and the ceiling came towards him in a great airsucking sound and he was catapulted out of the train window and flew, birdlike and surprised.

When he recovered consciousness his head was bloody and the train was burning. The fields were redly bright. Things lay there: men, horses, ruptured crates, haversacks, helmets, valises; all equally inanimate. Some man ran past (head in hands, eyes staring) howling. Soon the peasants came.

He got up to help them with the fire. They tried to put it out and get the men out of it. They could do nothing about the horses. The horses had been in wooden cars at the head of the train and these burned quickly. But there were men to take out of the burning metal cars, and so they worked to pry and pull and tug and lift and hoist and tenderly remove, running back into the fields when the planes came round and down again with pinpoint lights twinkling.

Somehow, somebody had set up a machinegun behind the embankment, and soon another gun was firing from the field, and suddenly one of the small, sharpnosed planes was in the field and sliding drunkenly toward the trees. The pilot climbed from it and crawled toward the trees on his hands and knees. The peasants ran to him and surrounded him and their feet moved up and down rhythmically and when Pawel got there the pilot in his black leather coat was strangely flat and boneless.

After some hours, either because all the men had been taken from the burning train or because they were dead, the screaming ended and it was quiet and there was only the fire and the sweet, thick smell reminiscent of a boar roast.

He left it then. On foot, aboard a stolen bicycle (found in a ditch with no live owner near), in a passing courier truck, in an ambulance, and finally picked up by a Kasubian peasant with a laddertruck (piled high with sweet-smelling hay and oats, bringing fragrant memories of summers in Volhynia where his grandfather lived his strange antiquated life), he pushed northwest by backroads in a sea of refugees flowing east. By nightfall these were an unbroken stream stretching two hunderd kilometers, a silent, hurrying mass bent under bundles, behind wheelbarrows, in carts, taxicabs, aboard firetrucks and garbage trucks, in carriages, on foot; a great greybrown serpent crawling down the roads, the Poznan Highway, through the paths and along dikes in endless, shapeless motion crosscountry across fields: an exodus. All of western Poland, Pomorze and the Poznan region were on the move. The tide swirled, persistent, unreasoning, about Army units stalled in its path and unable to move, trampled them, pushed them ahead of itself, with an occasional group of police or border corps or uniformed officials fruitlessly trying to channel the flow. The human sea caught them, carried them off. Supply wagons, trucks, even batteries of artillery were flung off the roads.

The sky was red with distant fires. The night air shuddered to the roar of returning German aircraft. In the south, Gniezno, first capital of Poland, glowed like a giant coal. In the north and east, Bydgoszcz burned and Inowroclaw burned. From time to time a fighterplane or the everpresent Stuka fell from the sky and swept the roads at treelevel and emptied its guns.

When day came the crowd thinned out and spread over the plains as the sky filled with the drone of motors and endless box formations of Junkers and pencil-like Dorniers and fat Heinkels flowed east. These ignored the roads, but the fighters were busy.

The Kasubian peasant finally brought his cart within sight of Znin and presently a brown sign at the roadside said that they were entering Lubostron and there a nervous sentry aimed his carbine at them and presently Pawel showed his orders to a weary adjutant in a gamekeeper's hut.

The Second Squadron lay across the fields in Jablonna, the Place of Apples, and there the old peasant left him.

Pawel pushed his forearms deep into the pockets of his greatcoat and marched into the village.

He smelled the rubble and he smelled the soldiers. They sprawled in the village street and in the orchards and in the barns. He breathed the sour, curdled smell of sweat and lubricants and urine in the ditches, and leather and dewdamp wool and metal, and coffee hot in a metal cup (which, he thought, was the most intoxicating of all campaign smells), and he heard the pre-dawn sounds.

Whistles blew. A clatter of messtins. Hobnailed boots. Spurs with their cruel ornamental rowels.

A platoon of two-man TK scout tanks tested its motors under the appletrees and a blue wind rose and blew straw off the roofs, and there were laughter and calls and shouts of command and other shouts that commanded nothing, and men cleared their throats and yawned and hawked and spat and urinated and broke wind and scratched themselves and stretched (groaning, grinning) and above all of this there was the steady, inexorable murmur like an ocean: eighteen hundred voices of a cavalry brigade speculating on what the day would bring. Not, Pawel knew, about death or victory or defeat or any of the other grandiose, conclusive things, but Will there be fighting today? and, if so, Where? and Will we get into it? and How many Germans will there be? and I heard they all have tanks! and Some of them weigh *ten tons!* (followed by derisive laughter) and I swear to God! and When will the soup come up? and Whose boots did the cooks use today to make the coffee in? and How far will we go today? and How long are we staying here? and speculations as to whether chemicals were put in the coffee to make an erection impossible and whether or not this would wear off by the time leaves were available again, and when they would ever get leaves.

He came around the corner of the ruin and saw four flat Polesian faces staring at him from under helmet rims. The four men scrambled to attention. All had carbines. Their boots were clean and they were freshly shaven and their cartridgebelts were full. Some dozen meters away from them sat another soldier, without a cap or jacket. He did not look up when the others rose. He stared into the rubble, at the chickens, and made small sounds at them. Another soldier sat beside him and this one made chicken sounds now and again as though to amuse the other. The four armed men looked at them, embarrassed.

Pawel didn't have to ask anyone to explain the scene. He wondered why the soldier was going to be shot. The soldier didn't seem to have lived long enough to have done much of anything except be; and soon he wouldn't be. There was about an hour left before sunrise.

One of the four armed men stepped forward and reported.

—Firing party. At your orders, sir.

The soldier who was imitating chickens looked up and sighed and opened his mouth and closed it rapidly and stared at Pawel. The soldier who was to be shot said nothing. He made small, friendly noises at the chickens.

—I am not here for the execution, Pawel said.

The armed man stared.

—Where are the officers of the Second Squadron quartered?

They were, the armed man said, to be found in the house of the *Wojt*. But, if the captain forgave him, when would the executing officer arrive?

—In time, Pawel said, and then about the condemned soldier: What did he do?

The corporal looked bewildered. —I don't know, Sir Captain.

—What squadron is he from?

—Ours, sir, I have the honor to report.

—Who commands the squadron?

It was the Lieutenant Lenski who was, the corporal was sure, to be found in the house of the *Wojt*. The house of the *Wojt* was near the mill. The mill was near the big apple orchard. The apple orchard began at the end of the street. The Sir Captain would have no trouble finding it, the corporal was honored to report.

Pawel nodded. He answered their sudden clash of heels and presented carbines with a careful salute. The condemned soldier did not look at him.

Pawel entered the orchard and soon he found the village headman's house, with tightly blanketed windows through which light crept out. A sentry crashed his heels for him and presented arms.

It was a whitewashed house of mud and stones and a little timber and the roof was thatched. The dark interior hall smelled of straw and cabbage: dry and hot even in the nightchill. The sun would soon be up. When it was up it would burn down like yesterday's sun and the air would appear to be on fire and it would be hard to breathe.

But, perhaps, there would be wind today. Even a breeze would do; it would be good if there was one, Pawel thought. In the mountains and the forests there was always a cool breeze. The air was fresh and crisp and it was a joy to breathe it. A man felt hard and tightfaced and tall in the mountains. Here there was nothing but dust and burning air and flatness and a sea of emptiness and a man felt small. This was Pomorze, the spit of land between East Prussia and German Pomerania: a gaunt place. It was a hungry land without green things.

Pawel wished for the crisp chill of the mountains.

The lieutenant had been looking at his watch.

He was pale.

—We had best get on with it, he said.

Underensign Gzyms lit a cigarette. His hand trembled.

—What time is it? said Underensign Gzyms.

—Call me sir. Address me properly, the lieutenant said.

Underensign Gzyms put out his cigarette. He rose and brought his heels together.

—Because we are at war and we are going to shoot a man it does not mean that discipline can be relaxed. On the contrary, now is the time to affirm it.

Now is the time to observe the regulations. Now is the time to be particularly correct. It is a matter of responsibility. It is now four o'clock.

—Thank you, sir, said Underensign Gzyms.

He sat down. He lit another cigarette. He inspected the ceiling.

Underensign Powaga stood up and brought his heels together.

—May I speak, Sir Lieutenant?

The lieutenant nodded.

—When does the sun rise, Sir Lieutenant?

—It rises at four-forty-five, Sir Underensign. It is almost that time.

—Thank you, sir, said Underensign Powaga.

He sat down. He was eighteen years old. His upper lip trembled.

—Where is the priest? the lieutenant said. He should be here now. Has someone gone after the priest?

—The sergeant-major has gone for the priest, Underensign Gzyms said. He stood up and brought his heels together. —Sir!

He sat down. He dropped his cigarette.

—He should be here now, the lieutenant said. It will not be correct without the priest. Why couldn't he get the regimental chaplain? The chaplain is a priest.

—The chaplain went to Gniezno, said Underensign Powaga. I am very sorry.

—What did he go to Gniezno for? He should be here for the execution.

—I don't know, sir, Powaga said.

—Perhaps they are having executions in Gniezno, Gzyms said. He stood up and brought his heels together. —Sir! He sat down and lit another ciragette.

—They have priests in Gniezno, the lieutenant said. They have an archbishop.

—They wouldn't get an archbishop, Powaga said. Would they, sir?

—How do I know? How do I know who they would get? The lieutenant looked at his watch. —Where is that priest? Where did the sergeant-major go for him?

—There was a priest in Lubostron this morning, Gzyms said. There is a beautiful Gothic church there. It is said to be three hundred years old. I saw a priest there in the morning. Perhaps he is still there.

—Why shouldn't he be? Lieutenant Lenski looked at his watch. —He should be here now.

—Sir, Gzyms said.

Lieutenant Lenski looked at him.

—Why must that man be shot?

—What? What? Do you question orders?

—Rape is a civil crime, sir, Gzyms said. This is war. If he must die there will be many opportunities for it. The sergeant-major says this man is a fine Ulan.

—He is no Ulan! He is a former Ulan. He has been convicted of rape by a court-martial. Do you know what rape is, Underensign? It is disgusting!

—Yes sir, said Underensign Gzyms.

—You surprise me, Sir Underensign, Lieutenant Lenski said. You are no longer a student of architecture, Underensign. You are a junior officer. Can you remember that you are an officer? That carries a responsibility!

—Yes sir.

—Thank you, Underensign.

The lieutenant wiped his forehead with a handkerchief. The room was hot. The windows had been screened with blankets and these kept out the air. The lieutenant looked unhappily at the windows.

—So now you know why former Ulan Mocny must be shot.

The lieutenant wished that he were anywhere but where he was. He remembered former Ulan Mocny. Mocny means strong. Former Ulan Mocny was not strong. He was young. It did not seem possible that he would rape anyone, or hurt anyone, and he was clean and he kept his horse clean. Pan Szef (of whom Lieutenant Lenski was secretly afraid) swore by former Ulan Mocny. He said the former Ulan could not rape anyone. He said he spent an hour talking to the soldier (the former soldier) and that he didn't think the young man knew one end of a woman from the other. He didn't know what anything was for or where you put anything and, in fact, Pan Szef said, laughing, if he had raped the woman she would not have suffered anything except discomfort if she sat down hard. It was not possible for Antos Mocny to rape anyone. Rape is like everything else, Pan Szef said: You have to know what you are doing.

But there was the identification disk in the woman's hand. That and the physical evidence. That and the testimony of the battery commander who had found the woman. That and the former Ulan's inability to explain. And there was the verdict. And that was an order. And he, Lieutenant Lenski, always always executed orders.

And then, suddenly, miraculously, like a divine intercession, like a marvelous incomprehensible gift of heaven in which the lieutenant devoutly believed, the door opened and the blackout curtain blew apart, and cold night air came in and a man came in, and this man was sweatstained and unkempt and in need of a shave and he had dried blood on the collar of his greatcoat and on his cheek and his coat was burned, and on his shoulderstraps he had the three stars of a captain and he said that he was the commander of the squadron and would someone please get him something to eat.

And the lieutenant was no longer responsible.

The woman put the black bread and the sweetsmelling creamcheese and the jug of sour milk on the table, a thing of coarse pine boards greased and polished by generations of exhausted peasant elbows. She pushed his mapcase and his pistolbelt and cap and his binoculars roughly aside as though they were of no importance, as though they were toys, child's aftersupper playthings, and he a child at feeding.

—Thank you, madam, Pawel said.

She laughed, embarrassed, covering her mouth. Her teeth were yellow and her breath was bad and she had a great scarlet face like an angry moon and arms like a man. Her hands had the texture and the color of a crust of bread.

—Madam! Me?

She was, of course, a peasant, and such words as *pani* or madam or lady had never been addressed to her. She worked hard and her life was difficult.

She would not know about ducks and apricot stuffing. She would not know about the Brandy of Napoleon. Oh but, he thought, you could see she liked it: This was the first time, perhaps, that anyone had called her anything but mother. Therefore he smiled as though this was, indeed, a Warsaw drawing room, and spoke to her as if she were that kind of hostess. She, in turn, made her voice gruff: —It is simple. It is only bread and cheese. But (and her voice was suddenly soft and shy and girllike) if the Sir Officer will eat it will be an honor.

Pawel cut bread and cheese. He drank the milk. In the far corner of the room, where the holy pictures and the handwoven tapestry made the guest-corner of the house, someone sighed. It was a sigh of immense relief. Someone else laughed nervously and Pawel wondered why they were so nervous.

Eating, he looked at them: his officers.

Janek Lenski (it was he who sighed and now smiled and looked at his watch and at the door as though expecting someone) was twenty-four years old and two years a lieutenant. He was (Pawel had been told) the son of peasants from the flat fields and soft rolling plains of Volhynia, the sweet-smelling blacksoil country where peasants harvested two crops a year. His father had two sons and, being a peasant, sent them to the two institutions that meant most to him: the Church and the State. Lenski became an officer, his brother a priest; somewhere during this process of transformation from peasant to officer, Lenski acquired the -ski at the end of his name, and now dreamed of acquiring fame, renown, medals, and a general's insignia.

Powaga was a baby freshly promoted out of the Corps of Cadets. His baby dreams were formless. No one could tell Pawel anything about Powaga. Gzyms was from Lwow, an architecture student of some promise.

He ate and they watched him and Lenski went on looking at his watch and at the door. Soon a rooster crowed. The tension in the dark peasant room became unbearable.

At last the young lieutenant got up and cleared his throat. —Sir, he said formally. Panie Kapitaine! If I may interrupt . . .

Pawel looked at him and Lenski became confused. He glanced at his watch and at the door and at Pawel's food. Pawel waited.

—It is now oh-four-four-five hours and it is time for the execution. We are having an execution. It is a soldier, I mean a former soldier, condemned because of rape. We are to shoot him when the sun comes up. It is almost time.

Pawel remembered the silent soldier by the blistered wall, the one who had made friendly noises at the chickens. And now he understood why Lenski had seemed so marvelously relieved when he had turned up. Pawel was now to be the executioner. Still Lenski remained nervous. And he was, he went on to say, terribly embarrassed. He offered an apology. There was no priest. The squadron sergeant-major had gone to Lubostron after a priest but was not yet back. The sergeant-major was certainly taking his time. And here the sun was rising and the cock had crowed and it was time to get on with the execution and there was no priest and regulations called for priests to shrive the condemned man and to be present at the shooting and you could not have an execution without benefit of clergy. Death must be sanctified by God as well as men or it becomes murder. The lieutenant said he thought the captain ought to know. As secondincommand it was his responsibility to inform the captain.

Pawel laughed.

The lieutenant stared.

Gzyms lit another cigarette, lost it, retrieved it, and Powaga (being the youngest and the most bewildered) coughed nervously.

—Cancel it, Pawel said.

—Sir?

The lieutenant was astonished. One cannot cancel a military execution.

—Postpone it, then, until you find a priest. Don't you think there will be priests tomorrow?

—It is hard to know about priests, the lieutenant said.

—But what do you think?

—I will try to find one, sir.

—You must be sure, lieutenant. You would not want him to be shot without a priest?

—No sir. It would be incorrect.

Pawel laughed.

—Would you like to be shot without a priest, lieutenant?

—I do not think I would like to be shot with or without a priest.

—Neither would I. And what about the soldier?

—There is still time. I will try to find a priest. There may be one somewhere in the village.

—Well then, lieutenant. Find him. There is no reason for you to be nervous.

Then a headquarters messenger came in. The brigade was to be on the road in half an hour.

I ANTOS

In the grey light, the first pale artificial dawn that precedes the sun, Antos felt cold. He smelled the acrid reek of dewdamp rubble and the thick smell of soil, the tired, dew-washed red-and-yellow earth of Pomorze that was like no earth-smell he knew about.

He fingered the soil: It was poor.

—See how poor this earth is, he said. Stas Guz agreed. It was, indeed, poor earth compared with Volhynia and Polesie. Compared with Polesie it was very poor. There is not much about Polesie that is rich except the earth.

—One crop a year, Stas Guz said. He sniffed the earth and crumbled bits of it between his fingers. It powdered easily.

—It is not good earth.

Stas Guz sighed and made cups of his hands and blew into them. He had long given up imitating chickens. He had made chicken sounds, at first, to amuse Antos, who was soon to be shot. But Antos did not laugh and so Stas gave up imitating chickens. He warmed his hands with his breath. His breath was white in the nightchill, in the grey light.

—It is cold, he said. Are you cold?

—No, Antos said.

—Well, Stas Guz said in a troubled way. Well. He sighed and blew into his hands. —It is cold, he said. Then he looked at Antos, who did not look cold but who soon would be. He picked up a small stone and tossed it at the chickens.

Antos made small friendly sounds at the wandering chickens.

—Earth does not smell good here, Stas Guz said. What can they grow in such earth?

Antos scratched his head. He said he thought they might grow wheat, but only the one crop a year.

—It is not like home, Stas Guz said. Both soldiers sighed about that. —This is poor land and everyone is poor. They have not even an inn in this place. We have one in my village.

—Is there a Jew in it?

Stas Guz nodded. He made an angry motion with his hand. Obviously he knew about the Jews. Having an inn in the village was a good thing, and a good thing to talk about. You could be proud of a village with an inn in it. But then you had to admit that you had a Jew. This took some of the pride away.

—Then you do not have swallows, Antos said. We have many of them.

—We have swallows. They come every year.

—How can that be?

—They come, Stas Guz said stubbornly.

—You do not get the swallows in the roof of an evil man, Antos said. Everyone knows that.

—We have them, Stas Guz said.

—Even the Jew? Don't tell me that. I will not believe it.

Stas Guz thought about that. He scratched and blew into his hands. He tossed stones at the chickens. Then he agreed that, perhaps, there were no swallows in the roof of the inn, or the Jew's store, or the factor's office. —But there are many in the other roofs.

Also storks. There was a multitude of storks in the village of Stas Guz.

—Then you have a rich village, Antos said. He sighed. —Mine is not so rich.

—The house of the *Wojt* is of stone, Stas Guz said.

This also was something of which one could be proud. And one did not have to spoil it by admitting the possession of a Jew. Other things to be proud of and to talk about were a school and a church, but for those things it had to be a big market village, almost a town. Neither Antos nor Stas Guz could claim one of those.

—The father of my grandfather was *Wojt* in our village, Antos said.

Stas Guz said nothing. Antos supposed that there was little Stas Guz could say after that. His grandfather's father was dead a long time before Antos was born but the fact of his village office remained. The older men still bowed to Antos' father because of this. Stas Guz could not improve on that. Antos looked at his friend and felt sorry for him.

—But his house was not of stone, he said. Also it burned down. And, well, your village is a bigger village, everyone knows that.

Stas Guz nodded, smiling. He looked at Antos with a gratitude of a kind.

—You have a fine meadow, he said, and you are close to the river. For a small village your village is a good one and your land is good. There are a lot of fish in your river. We have to buy our fish.

—There are rushes by the river, Antos said. Girls swim in there.

—Ha, Stas Guz said. He sighed. He looked away. He scratched his ear. He looked at the fingernail with which he had scratched it. The chickens made sounds and Antos looked at them. He pointed his finger at the rooster. The rooster was old and looked tired. He looked lost in the rubble. The chickens flocked around the rooster but he did not seem to be much help to them.

This is the rooster that will crow when the sun comes up, Antos thought. He wished that he had bread to give to the rooster. Maybe if he had bread he would not crow in time. Maybe if I wrung his neck he would not crow. But he thought that he could not wring all the necks of all the roosters before the sun came up and that, anyway, it was not true what they said about the roosters, that it was their cry that called up the sun. The sun would come up no matter what he did. He felt cold. He had not felt cold before but now he did. It was the thought of the sun coming up that did it.

—How old do you think he is? Antos said about the rooster.

—I don't know, Stas Guz said. He is a grandfather, you can see that.

—He has lived a long time, Antos said.

Stas Guz also looked at the rooster. Both soldiers watched the bird with their fingers opening and closing. They did not talk about what lay closest to their hearts: the dawn and what would happen when it came. It was not necessary to talk about that. When it came, it would come.

The goat dies but once, Antos thought.

—Listen you, Stas, he said. Do you have bread?

—I have hardtack.

—Better feed the hens. They don't look like they'll find much here and the rooster isn't any good anymore.

Stas Guz took some hardtack from inside his shirt and broke it up and threw the crumbs to the chickens. They all started eating, except the rooster. The rooster looked at the grey light in the east and ruffled his feathers.

—This is about the hottest summer I've ever seen, Stas Guz said. He took care not to look at Antos. —I don't know when it's been this hot.

—Should rain soon, though.

—Yes.

—Should have rained a long time ago.

They were quiet then, and the chickens were quiet, and they listened to the small talk the others were making: the four soldiers and the corporal behind the wall. They talked in low voices and they did not laugh. They waited for the sound of the officer's boots in the street. They waited for the sun to rise.

Somewhere close in the darkness, in the apple orchard, a horse snorted and another neighed.

—*Zdrow, zdrow,* someone said. The omens were good for the day: The horses were making the good-omen sounds.

—Listen you, Stas, Antos said. Have you seen my Zloto?

—He is all right.

—Is he clean? Are they cleaning him?

—I clean him, Stas Guz said. I clean him as good as you did.

—Who has him now?

—Nobody. They are keeping him for an officer.

—Is *Pan Porucznik* getting him?

—They are getting him for the *Pan Kapitan*. There is a Pan Kapitan coming today. He will get Zloto but I will clean him every day.

Antos nodded.

Stas Guz was good with horses. He would take care of Zloto. Antos wished he knew about the Pan Kapitan. He was glad Pan Porucznik wasn't getting Zloto. Pan Porucznik had spurs with big rowels that jingled. The rowels had sharp points. Antos wondered what kind of spurs the Pan Kapitan wore. He hoped they were small and without rowels.

He had looked forward to seeing the new captain, who was, as everybody knew, a famous hunter and had been in many places and in many wars, and no other squadron in the regiment had a commander as good as that. Going to war with a man like that was . . . Hey, yes, it would be good. Antos wished he had seen the new captain. He didn't think a man like that would have big rowels on his spurs.

—He hasn't come yet, has he?

—Who?

—The new captain.

—I don't know, Stas Guz said. Maybe he has come.

—Then he will come here, Antos said. I would like to see him.

—He is a famous man, Stas Guz said. A man like that, knowing about wars and people and horses, he will be good to Zloto, don't worry about that. And I will clean him good every day. Zloto, I mean.

Antos sighed and stretched. He was cold but not as cold as he had been earlier. Now the grey light grew whiter, and there was a scarlet edge to it above the trees, and the rooster raised his head and flapped his wings as though to beat away the cold, and crowed.

At once the sun burst out above the trees in the great red light. Antos looked at the red sun. He thought about blood . . . like when shoat were slaughtered back home at the market. You hung them up by the legs and you cut their throats. They gave one thin squeal and then their blood came all over everything. You tried to catch it in the pot for the sausage the women would make out of bread and blood. You put the pot right under the red mouth cut into the throat of the pig and the pig jumped on the rope and the blood sprayed on you and the men laughed to see you turning all red. Everybody laughed and the girls giggled and the blood was in your nose and in your ears and in your eyes and it was all down your chest and back.

He looked at the sun and he turned to Stas Guz to tell him about what the red sun looked like and he saw that Stas Guz was weeping and that his shoulders shook and that both his fists were in his eyes. Why is he weeping? Antos thought. And then he realized: He is weeping for me. And with this thought it came back to him like a chill why he was there and what was to happen there and who that something would happen to (which was himself) and he thought, It can't happen to me, not like that, and I didn't do anything, it was Surma and Surma should be here, where is he; and he knew that Surma always got out of everything and nothing ever happened to Surma and he wished he knew how Surma did it and then perhaps he would do it too and nothing would happen to him, and he remembered that Surma wouldn't be

167

there because he had deserted, which, as Pan Szef said a long time ago, was a terrible thing. You could get shot for it.

—God, he said. No. I didn't do anything.

And then the corporal of the firing squad came around the corner of the wall. He looked embarrassed and a little ashamed (as though what he was about to do was something bad, something punishable) and said: —Well, boy, it is time.

—No, Antos said. The sun is not yet up.

—It is up.

—No, Antos said. It is coming up but it is not yet up.

—Like it says, boy. It is up enough.

—No, Antos said. It is too little yet. It has only just come up.

The corporal put his hand on Antos' shoulder. The corporal had been in the Army fourteen years and he was thirty-two years old. Antos felt the hand of the corporal and that was all he felt.

—It will be quick, the corporal said. I got some good men. They all shoot good and we will do it right the first time. Don't worry about that. You won't know anything, it will be that quick. It will be like lightning. I got the best men in the squadron. But you got to be still and not move, see? You got to stand up straight and not move. You let your knees go, or move over to the side, or look like you're falling, and it won't be done right and the officer got to finish it. It is never any good that way. Then you got to lie there and wait for the officer and he fools around with his revolver and it takes a lot of time. All that time you wait. It is bad then. It is bad then, all right. You stand still, though, and we'll do it right. You understand?

No, Antos said. Or thought he said it, because certainly the corporal did not appear to have heard him. The corporal nodded as though something good had been agreed upon. He looked content.

—Listen, the corporal said. Do you want a smoke? You're not supposed to have one, but what the hell, I tell you. You want one you can have it.

—No, Antos said. This time the corporal heard him.

—All right. And you'll stand straight? You won't move?

—No, Antos said.

The corporal nodded. —You'll be all right. Well, let's get on with it. Come on around the wall. We've got the tank all lined up there nice and proper with the lights and all. We'll do it right for you. Come on up.

—No, listen, Antos said.

—Come on now, said the corporal. You know it's time. The officer will be along any minute. Get up now and come on.

Antos got up and the corporal put his hand on his shoulder. He pressed the shoulder gently. Antos felt that and he felt his legs begin to move. How slow they move, he thought. The corporal led him around the corner of the wall. His hand felt big and comforting on Antos' shoulder. It felt warm and friendly. He is my friend, Antos thought. I am not alone. He will do everything right. It will be all right. Everything will be all right. He won't let it happen. It wouldn't happen and he would be saved. I didn't do anything and it will not happen. Everything will be all right, hadn't the corporal said it? The corporal had been a soldier a long time. He even looked a little like Pan Szef. He had the same red face and the big mustache. Antos' father also had a mustache. Antos wondered if Pan Szef had any more sugar and, if he did, if he would give some to Stas Guz for Zloto. The thought of Stas Guz made him think of weeping, and that, in turn, made him think of the old woman who had wept near the convent wall. He had wondered then why she had been weeping. Stas Guz said that maybe she wept for them. But there was no reason for anyone to weep. Everything would be all right now. Hadn't Pan Kapral said it? But the corporal led Antos around the corner of the wall and propped him up against it. He pushed his shoulders back so that they lay tight against the wall.

—Just stand right there, the corporal said. That way we'll do it right for you.

And then the four soldiers with the rifles and the steelhelmets and the fat, full cartridgebelts (brown and shining in the new red light) got up and stood in a row in front of him, facing him, and up the street came the tinny jingle of Pan Porucznik's spurs with their big ornamental rowels, and Antos knew that no one, not Pan Kapral, not Pan Szef, not even God Himself could save him, that no one would save him, that it would have to be something bigger than God to save him and surely there was no such thing anywhere.

He watched Pan Porucznik coming up the street in the red light of the sun, and he heard the motors of the tank roar suddenly and the great light on the tank went on suddenly and blinded him.

He saw nothing then and waited and didn't know what he was waiting for and it didn't seem to matter much what it was or when it would come. And then the light was suddenly gone and presently the motor was still and the four soldiers were at puzzled ease in front of him and Pan Porucznik was walking up the street away from them.

The corporal was scratching his head. He held his helmet swinging by its strap. The corporal looked astonished. He looked at Antos with immense respect.

—May bullets strike thee, he said. His voice was disbelieving. —I have never seen such luck. (And to the other soldiers:) Have you seen anything like it?

The four agreed that they never had. All four were grinning. One wiped his head with a rag. One laughed. All looked at Antos with respect.

—This new captain, the corporal said. Do you know him, perhaps?

Antos shook his head. He did not understand anything.

—He must know him, one of the firing party said. That's luck all right.

—That is more than luck, the corporal said. That is the Devil's luck. I have never seen such a thing and I have seen much, let me tell you.

—What is the captain like? said the soldier who had wiped his head. Is he strict?

—I don't know, Antos said and the others laughed.

—Well well, the corporal said. If he says he doesn't know the captain then he doesn't know the captain. Right?

Everyone laughed. One of the firing party held his tobacco tin out to Antos. Another offered a piece of newspaper to twist the tobacco in.

—What happened? Antos wanted to know.

This set the corporal laughing so hard that he dropped his helmet. The others also laughed.

—Ah, said the corporal. He doesn't know what happened.

—The captain whom you don't know got you off, said the man who had offered the newspaper. We aren't going to shoot you.

—Yes sir, said the soldier who offered tobacco. I wish I didn't know the captain like you don't know him. It's good not to know a captain like that.

—Yes sir, the corporal said. Come on now, though. We're moving.

But now the firing squad wanted to know if Antos had known all that time that he would not be shot.

—He stood up there like he was waiting for a train, said the soldier who had the tobacco, like he was waiting for the inn to open.

—He had the nerve, eh?

—Oh, he knew. Did you know?

—Well, let me tell you, the corporal said. We were going to do it right for you. You just remember that.

—Standing there cool like that. He knew all right. Didn't say anything either. That's a bit of all right. Where are you from? (And when Antos told him:) That is only three kilometers from my village. Well, we are neighbors. Ha. Men have nerve where we come from. You can see that.

—All you have nerve for is talk, said the corporal, but he has nerve, all right.

—I'd stand straight, too, said the soldier who had wiped his face. I wouldn't move if you was going to shoot.

—Ha ha, the corporal said.

—You'd shit, said the other soldier.

—It takes nerve to stand like that. Who'd think a kid like him would have such nerve?

—That's because he is from my country, said the soldier with the tobacco can.

—Come on. Let's go.

Antos heard the laughter, and this was deep and rich and comradely, and he saw the faces and these were respectful, looking at him the way he had looked at Surma in the time that seemed such a longago time: when he was waiting for the train and Surma was spitting. Surma had gotten out of being shot and now Antos had also gotten out of it and not by deserting. And then the corporal patted his shoulder and pushed him a bit to get him away from the wall (which, he noticed suddenly, was cold and dry and smelled of fire and smoke and, yes, death too), and as the four soldiers and the corporal fell in about him Antos knew that he would not be shot.

He knew this, and then he knew what he had not known or even suspected: that there was, indeed, without a doubt, something greater than God; something that could do something that God could not do, like making him, Antos Mocny, *be*. And he knew that the name of this marvelous something was Pan Kapitan, *his* Pan Kapitan, and that he now belonged to him. Otherwise why should he have saved him?

Obviously there was something special that he had to do now that he was not going to be shot. He would look after Pan Kapitan. Not the way he looked after Zloto and his carbine and his cap and coats and saber and other equipment, but in a special way. Pan Kapitan had won his, Antos', life.

He walked up the street towards the house of the *Wojt,* with the men who only a few moments earlier were going to shoot him, in the grey light that was becoming red, with scarlet fingers spreading up into the deep blue of the sky and the nightchill going. Suddenly he was aware of a sound like summer thunder rolling in the north. He wondered about that, thinking it at first to be thunder. Then he knew what it was.

Suddenly men were running in the street, and men were shouting and whistles were blowing and horses were being led from under the appletrees and being saddled, and hooves rattled on stones and horseshoes clicked on the flat stones by the river, which was dusty and dry and waterless and looked like a road, and a courier galloped up the street in a cloud of chalkdust with his great leather pouch leaping importantly about his back, and Antos and the corporal and the others scrambled to one side to get out of the way of the horse, which covered them with dust and chips of stone.

And presently, among the flying chips of stone and chalk and small bits of yellow clay in the dust, in the changing mass of forms and faces in that dust-cloud, there appeared a scarlet face which was terribly familiar, and this face was festooned with a long grey mustache, and the face came close to Antos and said: —GET-BACK-TO-YOUR-SQUADRON-WHAT-ARE-YOU-STANDING-ABOUT-FOR-LIKE-A-PRICK-AT-A-WEDDING! and then the face split into a grin (with the teeth like a boar's tusks: yellow and gleaming) and then, as Antos trembled and thought that he might perhaps be shot after all, Pan Szef said: —So they did not shoot you?

Antos shook his head.

—It is a miracle, eh? Do you feel good about this miracle?

Antos said he did. He said he would be grateful to the Pan Kapitan and Pan Szef spat upon the ground.

—It is because they did not have a priest, Pan Szef said. If they had had one they would have shot you all right. There is your miracle, Ulan.

Antos nodded but he did not think so. He was not shot because the Pan Kapitan willed it so. What did the Pan Kapitan have to do with priests? If he could make a miracle he did not need priests.

—I am to find a priest tomorrow so that they can shoot you, Pan Szef said. I do not know yet if I can find one. Do you think I will?

—I do not know, Antos said. He was terribly afraid. This was something he did not understand and he wondered why Pan Szef spat upon the ground when he said he, Antos, would be grateful to the Pan Kapitan.

—It is like this with me, do you see? Pan Szef said. Sometimes I do not look hard for what I am to find.

Antos nodded. He did not fully understand but he was beginning to understand a little. It seemed good to nod. It seemed to please Pan Szef. He did not think the Pan Kapitan would mind if he pleased Pan Szef, although he felt that he was doing something wrong.

Why was it wrong and what was it? He did not understand. He wished he knew why Pan Szef did not like the Pan Kapitan and what would happen if they, Pan Szef and Pan Kapitan (those terrible great men), came against each other, and what would happen to him if they did. Pan Szef was a terrible great man but so was Pan Kapitan. He was a famous hunter and had been in many wars. He had saved Antos. It was a miracle. But Pan Szef could always try to find a priest.

—So now you know about your miracle, Pan Szef said.

Antos nodded.

—You understand about it? And about the priest?

—Yes sir.

—Just so you understand. NOW GET BACK TO THE SQUADRON YOU ABORTION OF A FOOTSOLDIER YOU! MOVE YOU HORRIBLE PEASANT! and Antos moved (thinking that he had never moved faster nor ever would, not even if the Pan Kapitan told him to) and he looked back once at Pan Szef and for a moment he thought that this terrible man was laughing.

Sunday, September the third

I THE HUNTER

The bursting shell ripped the soil apart with a great orange flame. A second followed it immediately. It rustled in the trees. Pawel heard the quick sound of steel plowing into timber, a soft *thunk* of a noise melodious as a tuning fork, and with the sharp intake of his own breath came the explosion in the treetops. Almost at once there was a melancholy sigh behind him and, turning, he saw Powaga slip sleepily off his saddle and hit the ground rolling. The two orderlies swung their horses left and right to bypass the body. They were young and their faces were white. They do not want to trample the body with their horses, Pawel thought. Later they will not care. There will be many corpses later and it will not matter whether or not they are stepped upon. Underensign Powaga lay smiling and surprised on the piny ground.

Then they were silent. Other officers were coming. There were now about a score of officers in the clearing. Most were cavalrymen of Colonel Kern's brigade but there were also officers of engineers and some of infantry and some of artillery. These had joined the column earlier in the morning. Several strayed units had drifted into the column.

They were in a small pinewood fifteen kilometers southeast of Koronowo, a small town on the southern edge of the Tuchola Forest. In the Forest of Tuchola men were dying. They had been dying all of yesterday and the day before. This was the battlefield of the Torun Army of General Bortnowski, an area like a crossbow standing on its side, bounded in the west and southwest by the German border, the Baltic in the north, and by the sands of Prussia and the Ossa River far to the rear in the northeast. Three German armies had struck it from three sides: headon across the forest at Chojnice, southwest out of Prussia and northeast across the dry lakes and small ponds of Koronowo. A savage battle had been raging for fifty-two hours. No one knew exactly what was happening anywhere on the huge battleground.

They had come to the pinewood shortly before noon when the flood of refugees on the Torun highway had split the brigade and scattered it, and the thin mist, which shielded them from air attack, began to disappear as the sun rose higher. They had been on the road since dawn. Haze shielded them from planes. They heard the planes pulsing in the sky and, looking up through the pale morning mist and the mercifully granted haze, counted them: box after box of them flew east; small, silver, innocent.

The roads were full of desperately moving people. This was a silent, hurrying mass. No one looked at the passing cavalry. The mass flowed south and east with heads down and eyes averted in the dustcloud and the only sound in that white world of dust was the quick muffled drumbeat of slurred feet on the hard clay roadsurface and now and then a child's thin wail. Occasionally there were uniforms: small groups of destroyed men. These grew in number as the sound of the explosions grew. The rolling thunder of explosions grew with each passing hour. Soon it could be broken down into crumpled sounds that had their own identity. Then staffcars and ambulances joined the flow and there were corpses in the ditches. Then came the tide of walking wounded: a terrible procession bobbing up and down in tight military fours, in a silent, accusatory formation of pain. The lancers called out to the wounded: What is happening? Where are you from? But the wounded had lost interest in the war. How can you care when your wound hurts?

But words occasionally fell from this sad procession and gradually, as the morning passed, these words resolved uncertainty about the battle of the forest.

Dazed men with eyes like coalchips.

—Chojnice . . .

—The Germans drove an armored train into it. A bayonet attack captured the armored train. Imagine, they announced the train at the border the way they announced the freight train every day for the past ten years. Then that thing came in . . .

—Sepolno . . .

—The armored column was eleven miles long . . .

—Treason at Koronowo . . .

The mass pressed in among the horses. It burrowed into ranks as though seeking shelter. It pushed against the horses. It threw the horses and their riders into the ditches. The horses reared and the soldiers shouted. The horses neighed and screamed and fell into the ditches. Children wailed. The drumbeat of the dusty feet rolled in the white chalkcloud. By noon the brigade had ridden ten kilometers and stood fast, caught in the crowd, and the crowd rolled over it. The colonel gave orders to dismount. Men were dismounting anyway to hold the horses. The crowd had burrowed into the brigade and split it. Farther back, the supply wagons lay upturned in ditches and the gunners of the brigade troop of horse artillery fought the crowds with clubbed carbines to protect their cannon, and there were screams of horses whose legs snapped when they fell into the ditches and there were the quick shots which silenced the horses.

The colonel's face was white with dust but his mouth was wet. His eyes were bright. Sweat had turned his uniform black under the arms. Four shells in quick succession landed in the trees. A horse screamed and the colonel swore.

—They must have an observer, he said. They could not shoot like this without an observer. Where do you think he is?

—A steeple is a good place for an artillery observer, Pawel said.

He pointed to where the steeple of a church rose white above the treetops two miles north of them.

From where he stood in the clearing he could see through the thin screen of pine the yellowbrown flatness of scorched fields and the blond bristle of stubble where the corn had been. The earth was dry and cracked. Beyond the field began another belt of woods, etched blackly against the lighter background of the Hitler sky that had no cloud across it. The white roof of the steeple rose above the trees and, as he watched, he thought he saw the diamondlight of lenses catch the sun but he was not sure. I would be there, though, he thought, if I were the observer. The priest in Spain had also been betrayed by sunlight on his lenses.

He watched the steeple for another flash but no more came. He thought about the man inside the steeple. Or the woman. The Germans used them also for that kind of work. Women, men, priests, nuns, policemen, schoolgirls.

He was conscious of the hungry feeling, the old feeling of the forests where he hunted.

He thought that he could cross the stubbled cornfield without being seen if he kept the pathetically wilted ricks between him and the steeple. Then through the woods to the village and into the church. What then? Grenades? Quick but impractical. The man or men or woman in the steeple might have a hostage. Probably the priest.

The rifle, then, and cunning. First a shot for a warning to the watcher in the steeple and then a war of nerves. Once he or they broke from the church, the ambush.

—I could go after him, he said, looking at the steeple.

—Are you sure he's there?

Not knowing was a part of it. He could be there or elsewhere. But Pawel thought that he was in the steeple.

—It is almost a tradition with artillery observers.

—A good one would ignore tradition, the colonel said. He would be in a tree.

Pawel agreed that a tree was possible. If the observer was in a tree and not in the steeple, Pawel said, he could also find him.

The day was hot but on the clearing floor there was shade and coolness. They were comfortable enough. The German spotter had been inactive for some minutes but now came back to work. He brought in single shells at intervals of half a minute, scattering them to parallel the highway. Some shouts followed one of the explosions.

The colonel listened to the shouts. He looked at his watch and at the generalstaffmajor and then at the steeple. More shells came then, closer, and the colonel swore. He swore in Russian and in Polish. These languages are marvelous for swearing. There is a word in each of them for every foulness in every other language and then there are combinations of foulnesses, hybrid words, transpositions, graftings and amputations; whole new languages in which to voice displeasure. There was no way to measure the depth of the colonel's displeasure judging by the words. He spoke at length about the family of the artillery observer and the behavior of his household pets. He analyzed his diet and his private habits, speculated on the function of his boots on cold winter nights and the thumb of his glove in summer, bestowed upon him a number of diseases and combinations of diseases, dismembered him, examined each part separately and voiced doubts about the virginity of everything born and yet unborn.

All the while he spoke he kept glancing at the generalstaffmajor, as if his displeasure was at least as much with the generalstaffmajor as with the German artillery observer.

Now a new group of officers came into the clearing.

Colonel Kern began to swear softly, listening to the screams of wounded horses on the road behind them.

—Do you think he is in the steeple?

—It is a good place, Pawel said.

—That is the way to fight a war, the colonel said. See how they do it, these Germans. You have your coffee and *kuchen* and you talk into a telephone. It must be very comfortable to be a German soldier.

—They also have tanks, said an infantry major. And also airplanes. But they were not very comfortable in their tanks at Koronowo yesterday.

Lenski laughed. It was the short, clipped bark of an anxious seal. Gzyms stared at the dead Powaga, who stared at the sky. Pawel told the orderlies to carry the corpse away. The orderlies looked fearfully at the treetops. They were afraid of the shells that sighed among the branches.

—You, Pawel said, and you. Take the Pan Underensign to the wagons.

—But . . . said the taller of the orderlies. The other orderly said nothing.

—Take him up, Pawel said gently.

—We are afraid, the other orderly said with dignity.

—Everyone is, Pawel said.

The orderlies picked up the corpse by the arms and boots and took him off to the wagons where the shells were falling. After they had gone, Pawel sat down on a fallen pinetrunk. He worked on the dust that had caked around his mouth and the corners of his eyes. The sun was high and hot. It would be a hot day. He wondered why the colonel and the officers had come into the clearing, and whether the brigade had finally received orders, and where they would go to fight the Germans, and how long it would take the Germans to find the range for their heavy guns. Judging by the way the shells were falling it would not be long.

—That is the way to fight, the colonel said. You get up not too early, not too late, in time for coffee and cream and the little cakes. You eat your breakfast and then the trucks arrive. All right, gentlemen, everybody aboard. A little ride in the fresh air. Up to the front. Here we are; everybody out and wait for the tanks to come. Sit down there in the shade where it is cool. Then the tanks come. All right, *meine Herren,* a little stroll before lunch, if you please. But please take care. Nothing rash. Nothing foolish. We do not wish anyone to be hurt. We have the tanks and airplanes, do we not? So why take foolish risks? This goes on until the *fajfoklok,* eh? The evening hour of *kuchen* and coffee. Eight hours worked. The trucks come back. All right, away we go, back for the schnitzel and the little cakes. And you, you Polish tramp, fight the tanks all day, then drag your ass forty kilometers through the night and fight tanks in the morning. No dignity in being a Polish soldier.

The others laughed but not the generalstaffmajor, a remarkably neat and tidy officer with very clean boots.

Now the colonel looked at Pawel and at the generalstaffmajor.

—You don't agree with my analysis of this war?

—I most heartily agree, Pawel said. He watched the whitehaired colonel carefully.

—Our visitor does not agree, the colonel said.

They looked at the generalstaffmajor.

—That is because he is a man of dignity, said the infantry major. I was formerly a man of dignity but I lost my dignity at Koronowo.

—What happened at Koronowo?

—A very conclusive thing. I will tell you about it as soon as I have recovered my breath and my dignity. I left them both this morning on the road from that place.

—Our visitor could not have been there, the colonel remarked. He has both dignity and breath. Also, it appears, a very bad cough. (The colonel's voice softened and his eyes became sad.) It is now finished at Koronowo?

—To the last man.

—All of the Twenty-second Regiment?

—Every man. We were too late to help them.

The colonel stared at his hands. He shook his head. —First Chojnice, then Sepolno and now Koronowo. How did it happen this time?

—In the same way. They could not go through us and so they went around us. A German from Koronowo led them around the ponds behind us and they came in from the back.

—So now the front is broken?

—Yes. At Koronowo.

—And elsewhere? Do you know anything about that?

—Only what I heard, sir. We're still holding Chojnice but that won't last long. All of Guderian's panzers are attacking there. General Drapella's people are still fighting north of us around Sepolno. They're on a railroad embankment, if that's any help. The panzers have run over them so often that they're ready to break at any moment.

The colonel made a brief, impatient gesture. —Nothing good anywhere, eh?

The major sighed. —I understand we did well this morning on the Ossa River.

—Where the devil's that?

—Behind us, sir. Up towards East Prussia. The Germans got a corps across last night but General Boltuc's group threw them back this morning. It's all grenade and bayonet work up there. It's a slaughterhouse. But the Germans don't have any tanks up there so maybe we'll hold them.

The colonel said nothing, then. The infantry major went on talking about the massacre at Koronowo where, he said, the corpses lay piled eleven deep and the Germans had used two divisions to break one regiment.

—I'll never forget it. . . . But where are you heading, colonel? Where is the new line to form?

Kern shrugged. —I've no idea. Why should I know more than any other Polish commander? None of us know what's happening half a mile away.

Then he laughed abruptly. He nodded towards the generalstaffmajor.

—That gentleman has our orders. At least I think he has them. He looks as if he had the orders for all of creation. But if you were to ask me privately I'd tell you those orders won't be any good.

—Why not, sir? Pawel asked.

—Because they were made on the basis of the situation as it was, or might have been, an hour or more ago. That is no longer the real situation. In this war there is no way for us to keep up with the situation. And that's why we're getting the stuffing knocked out of us no matter what we do. Whatever we do, it's always too late for the situation. But I know one thing: We won't go anywhere unless we can take out that artillery observer.

—The Germans will be here before long, said the infantry major.

—All the more reason to blind that damn artillery. They'd stretch us all in half an hour once we leave these woods.

(And then to Pawel, quietly:) —Get rid of that observer.

Pawel nodded.

—How long will it take you?

—An hour. Maybe two. That village looks much closer than it is.

—We shall be riding soon. You'll have to join us elsewhere if you can't do it in less than an hour.

With angry glances at the generalstaffmajor, Colonel Kern listened to the passing shells and their echoing explosions.

Pawel left immediately, taking the two young orderlies who had been afraid to carry the body to the road. Gzyms followed them. Gzyms was depressed about Powaga's death.

—It was such a stupid death.

—It's all stupid, Pawel said.

He didn't want a heartsick man along on the hunt, but he didn't want to add disgrace to Gzyms' sorrow by sending him back. He let him come, setting a rapid pace. It was getting late. He looked at the sun, as a hunter, judging its position. The sun was high and hot, the way it had stood many times for him: high and disinterested in the sky while he prepared for ambush. Soon it would dip. Then the light would go. Then the many darknesses of the woods would be one. Then the light would be shut out and he would be alone. It would be good to be alone, like that, in the neverending dark. The sun hung motionless. But the position of the sun would not apply to this sort of hunting, he thought, and laughed catching himself at it.

—I mean the way he died, Gzyms said. There was no sense to it.

Pawel smiled a little. And because he wanted to help the young man over the pain of his first violent loss, he said: —If a man must die it's better if it's quick and easy. Powaga didn't know what happened: alive one second, dead the next. That way you don't have time to regret anything.

—But to die like that, Gzyms said. Without having done anything to make it important.

—Tell me about him. Where was he from?

—He was from Sarny. There is absolutely nothing in that place. I used to laugh at him about it and he used to blush. He was such a damn baby.

—It's not a bad town for a little one, Pawel said. I was there some years ago when what I needed most was a little quiet. I liked it well enough. There were some pretty girls there, I remember.

—But there is nothing *in* it, Gzyms insisted. There isn't even a theater in Sarny, and the dogs go to sleep in the main street and there is no electricity. It is as bad as Rowne. Do you know that place? Lieutenant Lenski comes from somewhere near it but it is different for him. You see, the lieutenant knows who he is and who he wants to be and he has a dream. Powaga didn't have anything. The damn kid. There is no sense to it that way.

—Would there be more sense in Lieutenant Lenski's death? He is not much older.

—Why yes, Gzyms said, surprised. He knows what he wants. He wants to be a general. He wants to capture some machinegun nests and to be decorated.

—And what do you want, Underensign?

—I want to build a skyscraper in Lwow.

—Why?

—Because there isn't one. Warsaw has one and it's the one thing those damn *Warszawiaki* have over us in Lwow. It's not as though it was much of a skyscraper, either. Only sixteen floors. Can you call that a skyscraper? More like a cloudtickler. I want to build a real one in Lwow.

Then they were quiet for a while, walking through the dry woods toward the field that they could see through the thin screen of trees before them. Shells sighed above them like melancholy freightcars and burst along the road. They were too far to hear the cries of wounded men but they could hear the shrieking of the horses.

He stopped the others in the last stretch of the woods and went on by himself to where the small shrubs ended and the field began. These were broad fields with few folds of land in them, but there were the usual hayricks and these would give protection of a kind. They would conceal the hunters from the quarry while they crossed the fields. Also there were shellholes of earlier bombardments and craters of aerial bombs dropped the day before. These too would serve. And there was smoke, the miraculous, ironic gift of the German artillery which had set grass and cornstubble afire with short shells.

So we shall go: this way past this hayrick and this shellhole to there. It will not be difficult in the smoke. His own shells make the screen for us.

Pawel beckoned to the others. He told them what he wanted done; how they would cross the fields into the next woods that looked so cool, inviting and unshelled, with the white steeple of the church innocent above them, and what would be done in the woods and how they would go, and who would first go into the village and where the rest would wait and what the rest should do while they were waiting. There could be several Germans in the woods; they had dropped parachute diversionists, he had been told.

The orderlies stared and Gzyms was attentive. One of the orderlies looked familiar in a vague, uncertain way, and Pawel wondered briefly why the boy stared at him so intently. He thought that he had seen the boy somewhere before. He had been in the clearing, true, but Pawel thought that he had seen him earlier. The boy was listening to him as if to an oracle. Well, well, he's young. He would have better oracles if he were not.

They went into the field in a rough formation of a wide diamond, with the orderlies out at the flanks, Gzyms in the rear and Pawel ahead. They walked quickly and quite erect through the smoke, which hung black and acrid between them and the sun. Where the smoke wavered and grew thin, or where the breeze blew this screen apart, they ran hunchedover for the shellholes. After a space there were many shellholes. There was a coolness in them. Of earth and ripped-up soil: the sweet brown entrails of pastureland laid bare. And in one shellhole there was a peculiar dampness, a coolness moist on his face and chest. Blood. Something had come into the shellhole, had bled and had gone again, leaving the blood. It was as though the blood came from the soil.

Soon enough they were among the trees with the field behind them. They listened to the sudden silence which fell on the woods and the fields and the other woods where the shells had been falling. The shells no longer came. Smoke seeped through the fields where cornstubble burned. It was dry and it burned like paper.

The village lay some fifty meters ahead. Pawel saw the houses: well-shored walls of whitewashed wood, blank windows, ornamented roofs. It looked bypassed by time. But it was silent and this deadly silence was proof that war had come to it. No dogs barked. Nothing moved. The only sound from it was the dull, measured clacking of a shutter swaying against a frame. They moved towards the village through the trees and stopped on the edge of the wood to look down into it. The village seemed swept clean of life. The homes were abandoned. A dead dog lay near the steeple of the church, incongruously flung up on the roof by some explosion. Beyond the village was a willow grove.

At first they didn't see the boy in the church door. He sat there quietly, partly hidden in the shadow, working in a notebook. He was young, no older than the youngest orderly, Pawel thought, but built like an athlete. No peasant boy had this gloss of youth. He wore a knitted white athletic shirt and short grey pants and he had taken off his shoes and socks. His arms and legs were muscled and tanned a deep brown. There was no sign of anybody else in the long village street.

—There is our visitor, Pawel said.

—That boy, sir?

Pawel laughed quietly. —He is no younger than you or Powaga. Or that young orderly.

Gzyms looked unconvinced. —It seems to me, sir, he is just a boy.

—Well, he could be.

Pawel signaled to the others and all of them rose and moved down the embankment to the village. They walked in a wide line with their carbines ready. The boy looked up and saw them and, for a quick moment, looked startled. Then he smiled. He rose and brushed his long hair out of his eyes and watched them come closer. His hair was babyblond and white in the sunlight. His eyes, when he looked directly into Pawel's eyes, were blue and confident.

—Well, young man, Pawel said. And who are you?

—I'm from the village, the boy said. He laughed. —Right from here.

—Good. Then you'll be able to help us.

—Yes sir, glad to help.

Pawel peered into the dim shadows in the church behind the boy but he could see nothing. The boy laughed again. He stepped aside so that Pawel would have an unobstructed view. Nothing suggested danger in this place but Pawel felt danger. He slung his carbine carefully across his right shoulder and lit a cigarette. He felt eyes watching him. Watch me. I am doing nothing. I am at ease and unsuspecting. He offered a cigarette to Gzyms.

The street was empty to the left and right of him. The dust lay somnolent. The shadows were opaque. He motioned to the others to take cover in the shadows, away from the sun. He felt his heart beat up and thought, This is the one, looking at the boy.

—So you are from the village, he said.

—Yes sir. I've lived here a long time, on and off.

—You speak well. You must have gone to school in town somewhere.

—Yes sir. That's what I did. But there is no school now.

—No. Of course there isn't. Where do you go to school?

—The Jesuits at Hyrow, sir. It's a fine school.

—Well, it's a hard one, Pawel said. And far from here. What are you doing here?

—I came to stay here with my aunt and uncle. School wasn't starting till next week.

—Where do your parents live?

—I have no parents, sir, the boy said carefully. His eyes were confident and knowing.—Hyrow is for orphans.

—Ah, so it is. But aren't you a little old for Hyrow?

—Oh, I look older than I am. I am sixteen. And then, of course, I work every summer. I work on road construction. And then, before school starts, I come down here and stay with my aunt.

—And with your uncle.

—Yes sir, the boy said, surprised. You can go down and ask them, if you like. They live by the stream right here behind the church.

—Well then, we'll go and see them in a while, Pawel said. Perhaps your aunt will have something we can eat?

—Oh yes, the boy said, laughing. She'll be glad to feed our soldiers. Our brave soldiers.

—Thank you, Pawel said. Have any Germans been through here today?

—Germans? Oh no. I would have seen them if they'd come through here. Are they coming here?

—Oh, I expect so. And where are all the people?

—Gone east, the boy said. He smiled. —They too expected the Germans.

Pawel nodded. He drew on his cigarette and watched the smoke curl outward. He walked back to the other soldiers and stretched and spread his arms and yawned and took off his cap and said (softly, not looking at the others):

—Listen. This place stinks of Germans. Be careful. Watch yourselves. I think we're being watched. Soon now I'll go into the church as if to pray. One of you go behind the church. There is a small house there beside the stream. Knock on the door and see who is inside. Ask for bread and milk. Then get the people from the house to come to the church and bring food with them. Tell them that there are many of us and that more are coming. Another one had better walk up and down the street. Don't stare too obviously. Just look around. And you (to the youngest orderly) just sit here and pretend to sleep and watch this boy.

Gzyms said: —Is that boy the observer?

—Yes, Pawel said. But he isn't alone. He is too calm to be alone in an enemy village. Make sure you see that aunt and uncle of his when you go to their house. Then, when they're here with the food, go back to the house and look around.

—What shall I look for, sir?

—Communications wire. There is no wire hanging from the steeple. They must have put the radiotelephone somewhere else. Look at your feet as you walk. Kick the dust. Look in the streambed and in ditches. Don't make it obvious but find me that wire.

—Yes sir, Gzyms said. The others nodded. They looked tensely up and down the street.

—Easy, Pawel said. Relax. Don't make it so obvious. We don't want anybody getting away from us. We don't want to alarm anybody. Do you understand?

—Yes sir, they said in chorus.

Pawel turned away. He walked back to the church and to the boy, who watched him coming with confident eyes. He smiled. Pawel nodded to him and went inside the church. The nave was dark and cool. It was a small church, empty. Pawel climbed the short ladder to the steeple and looked out. He could see the far woods across the fields and he could see the smoke of trees set ablaze by the artillery shells. The observer had stood here, in the steeple, and his elbows had been placed so, on the narrow ledge, and he had spotted the fall of the shells and corrected them. There was no other place in the village high enough to rise above the trees. Pawel looked at the floor in the steeple and along the ledge. The wood was old, rotting in places. It was scratched and stained by years of weather. There was no trace of any kind to show that an artillery observer had crouched there earlier but Pawel knew that an observer had been there.

But where were the glasses? And where was the essential radiotelephone? The observer didn't need it in the steeple if he could call down his corrections to another. And there was another, Pawel was sure. He had no proof that the boy was lying but he knew he was. It was the feeling he got in the forests when he could find no track but knew that the animal was there. A cold feeling better than a sign. He looked down from the steeple at the small house squatting darkly beside the dry streambed. A barn stood beside it. He watched Gzyms come to the door of the house and knock, and smile and speak politely to the woman who opened the door, and after a while the woman and a man and Gzyms left the house carrying bread and cheese and apples and a large stone jug. The man filled the jug from the stream, carefully dipping it away from the moss. Once he dropped the jug and filled it again, looking carefully around. The woman stood straight and impatient. She said nothing. The man made small sounds as he filled the jug. Gzyms peered self-consciously into the stream. Pawel smiled. He listened to the silence of the village. It, like the silence of the woods, would not tell anything to an unskilled ear, but it did to his. Because there is no silence which is really silent. Even the dead communicate. Trees talk and dust can whisper about tracks. Where did they hide it? Pawel asked the village. And soon the village told him and he knew.

He climbed down from the steeple. Outside, the boy smiled at him. Pawel nodded. They watched Gzyms and the old man and woman come around the corner of the church. The soldier in the shadows across the street got up and scratched his head. The other soldier stalked like a nervous crane down the street towards them. He couldn't be more obvious if he tried, Pawel thought, smiling.

—There are my aunt and uncle now, the boy said.

—Very good. (Then softly, without looking at the boy:) Why did you lie about the Germans?

—What? The boy stared. There were no Germans here. . . .

—They went east, past your aunt's house, past the stream. You can see a long way off from the steeple, as you know. One of the halftrack drivers ran into the stream where it curves beside the road. You can't see it from here but you can see it from the steeple. How many were there and when did they pass?

The young man rose but Pawel motioned him gently down again. —I will give you one chance. I will forget that you are out of uniform before the others get here. Tell me now, quickly, who you are and where the radio-telephone is hidden. Otherwise I will hang you in ten minutes.

—You're wrong, sir, the boy said. I am not a spy.

—Wrong answer, Pawel said, but I will ignore it. Again: When did they pass and how many were there and where were they going? Quick!

—I don't know anything, the young man said. He stood erect and his face was hard. His mouth was thin and white and his eyes were confident.

—Have it your way, Pawel said. He waited for the peasants and the undersign to come with the food. —Good day, mother, he said to the woman, and to the man, Good day, *gospodarzu*.

—God be praised, the man said.

—For ever and ever. Your nephew tells me that some German tanks went through here half an hour ago.

—I said nothing! The young man shouted. Nothing! I didn't see tanks.

The woman said nothing.

—Well, *gospodarzu?* How many Germans were there?

—Germans, sir?

The old man shook in terror and in doubt. He looked at the woman. She kept her face cold and away from him. She looked at the dark door of the church. The boy stood angry in the door. —They don't know anything! he shouted.

—Old man, Pawel said. Do you want to hang?

—Hang sir? The old man's voice was low. They could hardly hear it. —Hang, sir?

—How many tanks were there? Which way did they go?

The old man shook his head and looked at the ground. He looked imploringly at the woman. The woman kept her back straight and stared straight ahead. Her mouth was a tight line, lipless and colorless. It was lost in the wrinkles of her face.

Pawel sat down on the bottom step of the three leading to the church. He looked at the sun. It had moved while they were in the village and now hung straight overhead, yellow above the steeple. Gzyms looked at him, uncertain.

—Those people, sir . . . are we sure?

—We're sure.

—They seem all right to me. Stupid, perhaps. Frightened. But they don't look like the enemy to me.

—Do you know what the enemy looks like, Underensign?

—Well, no sir. Not exactly. But these are just people.

—Germans are also people, Underensign. They are as patriotic in their way as we are in ours.

—But sir, how do you know? I mean, they look all right.

—They are the only people here.

—Still, sir . . . some proof. It would be terrible to make a mistake.

—There will be proof. Go and search the house and look into the barn. Take one of the men with you and search that streambed. It's getting late and we must be going. The Germans who went through here can't be far away and they'll be sending couriers back before long.

Gzyms and the older orderly left for the peasants' hut. Pawel ate the peasants' bread and cheese. He tasted the water. The youngest orderly, the one who seemed familiar, looked at him in awe. The peasants and the young blond man stood silent. The woman and the young man were erect. The old man kept his head down and his shoulders shook.

It was the orderly who found the wire in the all but dried-out bed of the little stream, carefully hidden under moss. The wire had been in the water for some time. The soldier followed the wire to the barn, hauling it up hand over hand out of the dust that hid it, and in the barn the wire led him to the freshly slaughtered body of a pig and in the carcass was the telephone. In the house, under the eaves, was a light machinegun and ammunition and a case of German handgrenades.

Pawel felt nothing then, neither pleasure nor sorrow. It was like all the other times in forest clearings: Once dead, the animal was small and therefore pitiful.

He watched the sun move. He listened to the faraway cannonade of an artillery bombardment. Long rows of German planes droned overhead.

—What are you going to do? the young man said. He stared straight ahead. He brushed his hair nervously out of his eyes. His voice was still calm, still assured, but he no longer smiled. The old man fell on his knees and began to pray. The young man looked at him with contempt. The old woman said nothing.

—There isn't much I can do, Pawel said. What would you suggest?

The young man pulled his shoulders back and advanced a foot and placed both hands on his hips. He looked slowly at Pawel and the other soldiers.

—You can surrender, he said.

Pawel raised his arm and let it drop. —Don't be ridiculous.

—Yes. You should surrender. The war is almost over anyway. That is the only thing for you to do.

—You're either very young or very stupid. That is not the only thing to do.

—I'm serious, the young man said.

—You are ridiculous. Keep quiet if you're going to be ridiculous.

—It's you who are ridiculous, Captain. Your position is ridiculous. Why can't you see it? Your war is lost and you still talk about going on with it. You can surrender to me now. Your position is absolutely hopeless. Absolutely. Our Third Panzer Division went through here this morning and you are cut off from the east. There is no way for you to rejoin your people. And even if you did, what good would it do you? Tomorrow, the day after, you'll be prisoners or dead. The war is almost over. Today, tomorrow, it'll all be over. End it now for yourselves. Lay down your arms and I will accept your surrender.

—I can't surrender to a sixteen-year-old boy, Pawel said.

The young man laughed. —I am twenty-one, I am a German officer. My name is Otto Jeshonek, Lieutenant, Special Services Detachment of the Reichswehr. I can accept your surrender as a brother officer.

—You're not in uniform, Pawel said. And these others, the man and the woman, are they also German officers?

—There is no point in being sarcastic, the German said. You're not in a position to make pleasantries. No, they are not officers. The man, in fact, is not even a German. The woman is of German origin. They are, of course, both under my protection.

—Of course, Pawel said. Well, let me think about it for a while.

—You don't have much time. I suggest that you surrender at once. Our infantry will be here in an hour and then I might feel less inclined to give good conditions. I give you this opportunity now, Captain. Later I may be less generous.

Pawel laughed. The German flushed and the others stared.

And now some peasants came out of the woods where they had hidden when the Germans first passed through the village. They stood about the street away from the soldiers. They watched the German and the peasant couple. Most of them were old. They made no sound of any kind standing in the street. Behind them came more soldiers: cavalry pulling their horses through the underbrush, their lances catching in low branches and their faces hot.

Pan Szef came to report. He had brought up two squads and horses for the captain and the men already in the village. Also there were new orders. The brigade was to ride in the opposite direction, northeast, to Chelmno, a town on the Vistula. There it was to join half of General Bortnowski's troops and cross the Vistula to form a new line.

Pan Szef had heard that a fleet of barges would be brought from the mouth of the River Brda to meet the army gathering at Chelmno. The fleet would float down the Vistula and meet the troops and ferry them across. Without these troops safely across the Vistula there was no way to stop the Germans here in the north, now that the front was broken at Koronowo.

The brigade was not going to move until nightfall. The early mists had cleared and, though the artillery had grown silent, nothing lay between the earth and the German bombers. The colonel had hidden the brigade in the woods. When night came they would ride to Chelmno.

—Those bastards, Pan Szef said, looking at the sky. Those bastards fly there like it was their own.

The captured German smiled. Blue eyes, bright and innocent like the sky,

184

smiled a conciliatory smile. Pan Szef asked who this was and Pawel told him and the sergeant-major smiled terribly and clasped his hands together. —Well now, he said. Well now.

—He wants us to surrender to him, Pawel said.

Pan Szef spat and the other lancers laughed.

—Down on the ground, Pan Szef said. The German shrugged his shoulders and sat down.

Pawel stood apart from the other soldiers. He watched the German and the peasant couple who had aided him. The German smiled. He was not afraid, though not as confident as he had been. He said, once more, that the war would be over soon. So why go on with it?

—*Alles kaputt,* he said in a friendly way.

—*Alles kaputt,* said the orderly in imitation of the German. He imitated the highsounding whistle of an approaching shell so well that both Gzyms and the German ducked their heads. Gzyms shook his fist at him and the German laughed.

Pawel did not say anything. He looked up at the impossibly blue sky and at the silver chevrons droning overhead. Soon they would see the men and horses clustered in the village. He motioned the men into the woods where the green canopy would shield them from the Hitler sky. He told Gzyms and the youngest orderly to stay in the village.

—Watch the road, he said. Let me know if the Germans come.

Gzyms lit a cigarette with a shaking hand. —What will you do with . . . them, sir?

—They have to hang.

—Yes sir. But must *we* hang them? Must it be us?

—We caught them. They are ours. Would you rather have them hanged by somebody else?

—I don't want them to be hanged at all. It doesn't seem like we should do a thing like that. I mean, two peasants and a boy. It doesn't seem right.

—Right, Underensign? What is right in war?

—Well, I don't know. But I didn't think it was like this. I mean, what kind of enemy is this?

Pawel turned from him and walked after the column of soldiers, prisoners and horses that moved into the woods. Three soldiers carried ropes coiled over their shoulders. One carried a stepladder. He halted them in the cool shade of a yellow clearing.

The German asked once more what Pawel would do. To him and to the peasants. He was, he said again, a German officer. He was a prisoner of war.

Pawel shrugged his shoulders.

—I must protest, the German said. I know what you are thinking. But the fact that I am out of uniform is a technicality, a mere technicality. Don't you see? It is the man who is important, not the suit he wears.

The German brushed his hair away from his face. He had long, nervous hands. Pawel looked at them. Perhaps the German was an artist of some kind. The German's eyes were bright and intelligent and, now, less confidently blue. The eyes of the lancers and the silent peasants were hard and hooded as they watched the German. Pawel wondered which of them would do the actual hanging.

There were small drops of sweat along the babywhite hairline of the German. His long hands fluttered. Pawel wondered what kind of artist the German could be. Perhaps he played the piano.

—What is the use now, anyway, the German said. The war is almost over, surely you know that. Our panzers are far behind you now. You are now surrounded. There is nothing for your brigade to do except surrender. The last chance you had of getting across the Vistula has been lost to you.

—We will get across.

—How? Will you fly? Our Third Division will cover the crossings. Guderian's panzers are down from the north. They are already at the Vistula. Listen to me. Surrender now and be done with it.

But time was passing. Yes. Time passed. It was late. It was time to finish off what had begun when the shells first came. The shells no longer came. The day had a particular stillness in the clearing. Nothing moved. There was no breeze of any kind in the woods. The air was still.

If only the sky weren't quite so innocent and the sun so bright. If only there were clouds. Skies should be overcast at a time like this. But there were no clouds anywhere in Poland, Pawel thought. It was German weather.

The German was no longer confident. He smiled his conciliatory smile. His voice broke now and again as he talked about the end of the war.

—Isn't it true? Isn't it all over?

—Not yet, Pawel said.

The German rubbed his eyes. It was as though he was asleep and wished desperately to awake. He pulled at the soft corners of his mouth. He rubbed his neck. Someone sighed. It had gone on too long.

—It isn't over yet, Pawel said gently. Do you understand?

The German stared at him and shook his head. He made a small sound. It was like a sob. A horse neighed in the woods. A twig cracked. You could hear the knuckles of the German. The German's hands were twisted in each other. They were good hands. You could do fine things with hands like that. Paint. Play the piano. Write verse. Perform surgery. Love and make love. Comfort. Pick up telephones. Point. Beckon to the shells. Salute.

—Take two men, Pawel said gently. Get a rope and hang him.

The sergeant-major drew himself erect and his face swelled. The veins stood out on his neck and his face grew red. His eyes bulged. He clicked his heels. The German tried to press himself into a tree. He could not get away from an old peasant who sat at his feet. The peasant moved each time the German moved. The peasant sat like a huge grey dog at the German's feet. He stared into the boy's eyes as though they held some secret to be read. He was an old man and death was not that far from him and, perhaps, he wanted to see death so as to know it when it came for him. Death would be in the boy's eyes if anywhere.

The sergeant-major beckoned to two men: the one who imitated things and another lancer. The lancers came up quickly and stood near the German. They were ill at ease. The German made small animal sounds. The old grey peasant stared into his eyes. The peasant's mouth was open. The sergeant-major spoke to the peasant and gave him a push. The peasant did not move. The sergeant-major kicked the peasant out of the way and put his hand on the German's neck. He caught the German by the collar of his singlet. At once the German leaped as though this was a signal of some kind. The collar of the singlet tore and most of the thin cloth remained in the sergeant-major's hand. The sergeant-major swore and grasped the German's neck with both hands. It looked as though he would strangle the German. He was very angry. The German screamed, once. The sergeant-major hit him in the mouth. The German fell down beside the tree. The treetrunk was black. The German's skin was white and babylike beside the black trunk. The German put his hands up and asked: —*Warum?* Why? The sergeant-major pulled a piece of wire out of his pocket. It was communications wire. He turned the German face down on the ground and pulled his arms behind his back. The German said: —*Warum?* He held his hands obediently behind his back and the sergeant-major wired the hands together. The German said: —*Warum?* He began to cry. The sergeant-major spat into the ground. He looked around like an artist searching for the best place to set up his easel. He pointed to a tree. One of the lancers who had brought the rope climbed into the tree. He tied the rope to a thick branch. He jerked the rope. It held. He made a noose in it. The lancer with the stepladder set it up under the noose. He looked at Pan Szef. And now the two remaining lancers tied the German's feet securely with a strap. It was a bridlestrap. They finished and stepped back and the sergeant-major stepped up to look at the knots. He pulled them this way and that. He was satisfied. He jerked his thumb towards the tree and the two lancers picked up the German by his arms and knees and hoisted him up onto the stepladder. The German was weeping. The lancer on the branch slipped the noose around his neck. He made it tight. He worked his way back to the fork of the tree and held onto the trunk. The sergeant-major said: —Now! and the two lancers yanked the stepladder. The German fell. He dropped down quickly until the rope stopped him. The rope was short and it snapped taut about his neck. It snapped his neck. You could hear the snap. The German who was no longer a German, who was no longer anything you could love or hate or frighten or condemn to death, swung stupidly under the branch. His body turned in little circles. He was dead. The sergeant-major wiped his hands on the seat of his pants. The lancer in the branches climbed out of the tree.

The German swung slowly underneath his branch. It was his branch now. It was no longer the branch of a tree in a wood near the village in a province of a country which could dispute the ownership. It was the property of the hanging German.

The clearing lost its silence then.

Pawel became aware of the flies. They hummed about the German cautiously. They showed no respect. They did not care about propertyrights or ownership. They settled on the German's white hair and his shoulders. Sooner or later everything became the property of the flies.

And now the sergeant-major pointed to the peasant couple. The lancers moved towards them. Pawel looked at the sun. It hung disinterested in the branches. It would be unconcerned with what happened here. Darkness, when it came, would erase the day and clean the earth of stains.

—These are civilians, Pawel said. He listened to his own voice and didn't recognize it. —At least get their names.

The sergeant-major asked the questions: Name . . . age . . . place of birth . . . guilty or innocent. He waited with his pencil and a notebook.

The old man said nothing. He held his head low as though unable to look into anybody's eyes. He had the look of a child who had broken something and would now be punished. The sergeant-major asked his questions and the peasant smiled the small shy smile of a little boy and closed his hands and opened them but did not say anything. The sergeant-major spread his hands and looked at Pawel. Pawel looked away. And suddenly, as the sergeant-major said, again, Guilty or innocent? the woman started shouting. One language didn't seem enough for what she had to say. She shouted German, Polish and her husband's dialect. She was a German, she said, from German Pomerania and had worked in great houses before the Great War. Her man was a groom there. He brought her east. She married him and lived with him and, yes, loved him, but she could never stand life with the people among whom he brought her. She had no family now except the man. Her two sons were in Germany, her brothers were there, maybe they were dead now. Death was everywhere, murder everywhere, nothing was safe, nothing was secure, nothing sacred. She cursed the soldiers and Pawel and the sergeant-major and the Army. She shouted for five minutes, maybe more.

When she stopped her terrible monologue the sergeant-major said: —Guilty or innocent? This was the formula of military justice but it meant nothing. Nothing depended on the answer. Everyone knew what would happen. —Guilty or innocent? No answer. There was, instead, the anger of the woman. —Guilty or innocent? The question came, monotonous, inexorable, as if played on a human phonograph. The woman took deep breaths. Her words lost coherence.

—Guilty or innocent?

The old man jabbed the woman lightly in the side with his elbow as though to say: Tell them, why don't you. They want to know something. Why don't you tell them? Obviously you know.

—Guilty or innocent?

She seemed to understand the pressure of the elbow. She turned dilated eyes on Pawel. Her pupils were enormous. Her mouth was open but her teeth were clenched. She shouted: —Yes! I am guilty, am I? Am I? Yes!

The sergeant-major nodded and wrote in his notebook. He looked at Pawel and Pawel also nodded and four lancers came to stand behind the man and the woman.

—We'll use another tree, the sergeant-major said. That oak over there. Get the ladder up against the tree. Get the ropes up.

The woman was still talking. The man muttered quietly: small words of clumsy love with which to soothe the woman. She did not seem to hear him. Her voice went on in the same, chaotic monotone: saying nothing. And suddenly she stopped. She was silent but Pawel still heard her. The lancers led her and the man to another tree.

The old man and the woman stood under the tree, saying nothing. Pawel wondered if they would say anything more before they were killed. But then, he thought, they had the look of people married a long time and so, perhaps, they would have nothing more to say.

The lancers stopped them on the edge of a small fold of land, a concavity that looked, for all the world, like an ancient crater and could have been: a yawning little chasm under the chestnuts. The chestnuts were still. There was no breeze of any kind. No one said anything.

A soldier propped the ladder against the oaktree, a solitary oak among the chestnuts in the clearing. The soldier with the ropes climbed the ladder and tied the ropes to the thickest branch. He swung himself on the ropes with a stupid smile. He jumped down. The silence became heavy.

The old peasant watched, looking as though he would have liked to bury himself in the ground. He looked ashamed, like a child. He resembled Nietzsche with a sharp, pointed nose, a mussed moustache and red hands. The short, coarse peasant hands closed and opened, closed and opened. Pawel thought that he could see tears in the peasant's eyes but perhaps it was only the way sunlight fell. The old man did not look as though he could remember how to cry.

The woman . . . ah, the woman, Pawel thought: she has finished with living. There are such people (he was sure, then) who cease to be alive even though their hearts beat and their pulses throb and breath enters and leaves their lungs and legally they are still counted with the living. But after her outburst she was no longer alive. He knew the look: the wide eyes blindly glued to something an infinity away, seeing nothing. In her mouth she held a blade of grass. Around her head and shoulders she wore an enormous shawl embroidered with red flowers and green leaves. She held it tight across her chest with both hands. She stood like a grotesque, lumpy statue with feet grown deep into the earth.

Then Pawel understood what Pan Szef was saying; something about a priest. There was no priest to shrive the condemned pair. There was a faint tone of mockery in the sergeant-major's voice, but Pawel did not hear it. No one knew if the condemned pair wanted prayers but they could not be robbed of the opportunity.

Pawel looked at the condemned pair. He did not think that they wished to pray. Perhaps the man would pray if someone told him to, but the woman was done with all that. When you are dead what difference does a priest make? She was already dead. Still, he had to ask.

—Do you want to pray?

The condemned pair did not say anything.

—Give them ten minutes to pray if they want to.

The peasants did not pray. The sergeant-major shrugged. He spoke to the woman. She turned her head with incredible slowness to look at the sergeant.

The clearing had become completely light. The sun was clear of the trees and moving to the west horizon. Pawel could see the woman's face: her brows were black and thick, her mouth was colorless; around her lips ran innumerable wrinkles, like the painted rays of light in the holy pictures of peasants.

Her face was like the earth, mapped by thin lines of wrinkles; the same grey, parched earth that spread in the field. The face showed neither fear nor pain. Only her lips were moving as she chewed the strawblade.

With slow, careful precision she turned her head to look at her husband. She looked into his eyes. He moved his hands towards her but she did not take them. For several moments he held his hands out towards her. She did not offer hers. The old man's back was turned to Pawel and he saw a shuddering begin between the peasant's shoulderblades. The shuddering grew. The old man laid his head on the woman's shoulder like a shamed small boy.

He wept quietly, nervously. His tears seemed to flow past the woman. She stood calm and straight. His head had found a steep, uncomfortable perch on her shoulder. Her face was turned towards him but she no longer looked at him; she looked into immeasurable distances beyond the man, through Pawel, into nothing.

Without emotion, she moved to the roughbuilt ladder under the oaktree.

When she moved, her husband's head lost its resting place. He lost his balance and ran forward, stupidly, staggering after her. He wept silently. He wiped his nose with his hand. Then he fell down and did not move.

The sergeant-major climbed up on the ladder. He motioned to the woman to come up; she tried but it went badly. She tried to hold her shawl at her breast with one hand and the ladder with the other. She could not do it. She changed hands and still it was no good. Somewhere in the watching crowd someone began to curse.

The sergeant-major gestured impatiently. The woman made another attempt to get up beside him but could not steady herself on the bottom step.

—Take off that kerchief, mother, the sergeant-major said.

She nodded slowly and took off her shawl. She folded the shawl as though to keep it bright and tidy for some other day. She put the shawl carefully on the ground. Under the shawl she wore a coarse, white shirt. Her shoulder-blades cut thick, rounded ridges in the cotton weave. The ridges were like spadeblades. They were a testimony of hard work, a peasant's life. Her hands were square, the fingers twisted with arthritis; her bare arms were brown to the point of blackness. These were no woman's arms that Pawel knew about. They were not recognizable as part of anything alive. They were like branches of a stunted oak. He watched her as he would watch a tree that had acquired independent motion.

She was now on the ladder beside the sergeant-major. She held her shirt closed at her breast with both hands. The sergeant-major looked once more at Pawel, made a quick, mystic gesture with the noose about the woman's head, jumped off the ladder and kicked it away.

The woman swayed forward as the ladder flew out from under her, much as a bird would do in taking off from the limb of a tree, and hung, momentarily unsupported by either rope or ladder, then dropped, swung; her hands flew up to her neck. She tried to grasp her neck. Then, as though having changed her mind, she did not grasp it.

Her hands dropped. They swung beside her as her body swung. She moved like a great white pendulum from side to side. She spun around the axis of the rope: a whirling nightmare. Her body shook with quick electric tremors. Her head dipped, her face fell forward and her hair slid across her face so that all of the face except the mouth was hidden. And then the mouth, with its frame of radiating wrinkles, opened wide.

Pawel watched the revolving body of the woman.

He could not move his eyes away from it. The woman swung in ever-narrowing circles. The rope creaked. Pawel did not feel the sun. The sun had lost the power to give warmth. It hung above the clearing like an incandescent bulb.

The sergeant-major caught the woman by her ankles and pulled twice. When he released her feet they swung towards each other.

And now the soldier who had brought the ladder and the soldiers who had brought the ropes went to get the man. He lay on the ground as though dead. He was like a rag cast into a ditch, splayed out and smeared fatly into the soil. The soldiers caught him by the arms and pulled him to the ladder. His bare feet dragged along the ground behind him. The feet were turned inwards. They made two thin lines in the dust.

For one brief moment it looked as though he would stand erect beside the ladder but when the soldiers let go of his arms his knees bent outward and he fell into the little chasm under the branch of the oaktree.

The soldiers jumped in after him and pulled him out. They struggled with the limp old man under the swaying body of the woman. The sergeant-major cursed.

—Hold him under the arms. Get him up here. Steady!

But the old man kept slipping out of the soldiers' arms and sliding back into the ancient crater.

If they don't hang him soon, Pawel thought, I will start to shout.

Several men took a few steps forward as though to help the struggling soldiers in the ditch. Some began to walk off into the woods.

The soldiers finally got the old man up against the ladder. They had to climb the ladder with the old man like a sack between them. They held him up while the sergeant-major put the noose around the old man's neck. As soon as they released him, and jumped off, he slumped on the top step of the ladder, kneeling as though to pray after all, and hung with his toes on the ladder and his knees in space.

The sergeant-major got off the ladder. He looked at the kneeling man and scratched his head and looked at Pawel and spread his arms. Then, with great gentleness, he took away the ladder. The kneeling man hung straight now. He swayed very little. It did not seem to matter to him whether or not there was a ladder under him. The sergeant-major touched the gnarled feet of the hanging man apologetically. He gave them one slow tug.

Then there was sound. Peasants cleared their throats. They began muttering to each other. Someone laughed. Someone sighed heavily. The old peasant, who had stared so hard into the German's eyes, was the first to slip away into the woods. One by one, the other peasants followed. The lancers looked at each other. They said little. They did not look at the three corpses swaying in the clearing. One muttered something about horses and walked behind a tree. Pan Szef stared at the hanging German and then at the peasants. He wiped his hands on the sides of his pants. His hands left greasy marks. He chewed a blade of grass: the blade moved up and down. Then he spat out the grassblade. The lancer who imitated things pursed his mouth. His tongue curved in his mouth to make a sound. It was the short, sharp click of a snapping neckbone but nobody laughed.

And then another sound: men running through the undergrowth. A call. Pawel shook himself free of his stupor.

—Captain, sir! The Germans are coming.

It was the underensign and the orderly who had watched the road.

—Where from? How many?

Gzyms was out of breath. —We saw dust on the road. There is dust in the east and in the west but the dust in the east is moving very fast. . . .

And now the underensign made a sound: not quite a sob and not quite a gasp but a compromise between the two.

Does he at last begin to understand? Pawel thought.

He looked at the young man searching for words that would encourage him. But Gzyms did not look at him. The hanging corpses' feet swung in little circles.

In the village, the shadows of the afternoon had begun to spill, sliding like pitch down treetrunks to form pools of black among the roots. Pawel halted his men at the edge of the woods. He went alone into the village. The hard-packed clay of the street still burned under his boots. His legs felt strangely weak. It took enormous effort to move them. He was aware of a sour taste gathering at the roof of his mouth. He took off his cap in the dark doorway of the church, surprised at how long it took him to get his arm and hand up to the soft round peak. The inside of his cap was wet with sweat. The cold, damp air of the church felt like ice after the white sun in the street. The church was dark. It smelled of incense and sweat and Sundays, and old boots greased with animalfat, and dust. It did not offer hope or consolation or forgiveness. Pawel began to shudder. His shoulders shook. He could not stop the shuddering. Stop. Now. Control yourself. But he couldn't do it. He wanted to get out of the oppressive, accusatory darkness. The ladder, then: up to the trapdoor in the steeple floor. For light and sunshine. But he could not push up the trapdoor. He stood on the steeple ladder shaking like a dog. He bit his hand to stop the shuddering and pressed against the ladder. Up. Push. The trapdoor moved and fell and light came down. He went into the top of the steeple running with sweat. At first he could see nothing. White pinpoints ran across his eyes. He leaned on the weathered ledge, breathing deeply. And soon the pinpoint lights ran out of the corners of his eyes and he could see.

At once the flatlands to the east unfolded before him and distant smudges on the edge of vision became woods, and the white road ran among them twisting and dipping into hollows. It crossed a small stone bridge spanning an irrigation ditch. The fields to left and right of it were flat and brown. Beyond the bridge a mass of dust boiled up above the trees. The road was hidden there behind the trees. The dust flew high and quick. Whatever threw the dust into the sky was moving quickly. It was too far away for sound to come and tell him what it was. Still, Pawel thought, the riders in the dust moved far too quickly to be numerous.

In the west a larger, slower dustcloud mounted in what seemed like an infinity of miles to the far horizon; an endless yellow monster creeping east with, now and then, a bright gleam blinking like a malevolent white eye. This would be infantry patiently pacing out the miles. Their cloud rose more than ten kilometers away. Pawel didn't think the column would reach the village before night.

Ah, but the others: the quick cloud. They would be past the small stone bridge in another hour and in the village in ten minutes after that. These could be ambushed, killed and left to greet the infantry in the dust. He wondered what lay under the quickmoving dustcloud. It was most likely a courier detachment or a staffofficer with escort or a commander going to a conference. Somewhere ahead the panzers raced Bortnowski's weary infantry for the river crossings. It would be good to know where the panzers were. It would be good to know if the panzers were racing for Chelmno. The courier, if there was one in the quick cloud, would have maps and orders. Thinking of maps, Pawel thought about his father: There was the avid expert of the map, the highpriest of order and delineation. Hail to the map and to orderliness and efficiency. He wondered what his father would think if he saw him now: having ridden from nameless and unmapped point A to a mysterious B without sense or reason, plotting an ambush in a church.

The light machinegun to be mounted here, the riflemen here, men with grenades to wait inside the steeple, just in case. It could be quickly done. Pawel went down into the church and out into the street. There Gzyms and Pan Szef waited for his orders. Gzyms smoked a nervous cigarette; he would not look up into Pawel's eyes. Pawel told them quickly what he wanted done.

Gzyms said: —Sir, may I speak?

—Yes. (Kindly; there was time for both kindness and understanding.)

—An ambush, sir. What way is that to fight? Like criminals in the night . . . out of bushes . . . hiding . . .

—It's the best way.

—How can that be? It's cowardly . . . it's as if we were afraid. It's not the way a soldier is supposed to fight.

—It kills the enemy. That is all that matters.

—There must be more to war than killing enemies. I mean, if that is all there is, why do we do it? Hanging peasants, shooting out of bushes at men who don't expect it, that's simple murder, sir. There must be more to it than that.

Ah, but there isn't. There is only murder. Pawel searched for words with which to explain but found none. He motioned to his orderly to follow him and walked down the road towards the bridge. The yellow dustcloud ran towards him through the woods.

I ANTOS

It was, perhaps, halfway through the afternoon when the Germans came. The captain's watch had stopped but he could tell the time by the position of the sun. The white bulb, hung in the pale blue overhead, had shifted westward. Antos supposed the captain could tell anything. He, Antos, also could tell the time of day. His stomach rumbled, so he knew that it was time to eat, and soldiers always ate at the end of day, didn't they? So now it was midafternoon and the day was ending. His stomach and his captain told him so.

He looked carefully at the captain to see if the Pan Kapitan would say anything about eating but the captain looked with narrow eyes and a strange smile down the road, and tilted his head, and did not look as though eating would interest him at all. Antos sighed. He wondered if the captain had to eat. A man like that; who knows? Maybe he didn't have to. I do, he thought.

I'd like to. Hardtack carefully wrapped in paper among the grenades. No soup to dip it in, true, but there was water. It would be good. He risked another sideways glance at the captain and felt suddenly ashamed. This was no time to think about his stomach. Soon now the Germans would come and there would be killing and surely at a time like that a man should not be listening to the rumbling of his gut.

Keep quiet, Antos told his stomach with formality. I am ashamed of you. A rumble like the passing of a train across a trestle came in reply. The captain turned his eyes away from the road and looked at Antos. Antos hung his head. He brushed dust off his carbine with his hands. The captain smiled and nodded towards the road where it dipped into the other woods. Then Antos knew that the Pan Kapitan had heard the Germans.

A sound like many bees came from the east where the road turned in among the trees, dipped into a hollow and came out again no farther than a meadow's length from the first house. It was like bees and yet it wasn't. Bees had a good sound. This, getting louder, had a hard sound. And now a tremor ran along the earth before the sound, and Antos felt this tiny quaking of the earth and he too shivered thinking that this was like the coming of spring storms back home: the stillness and the rumble far away and soon the fire and lightning, and the roll of thunder.

The sound of several motors rolled towards them. Antos looked quickly at the Pan Kapitan. The captain smiled and then it was all right. Antos also smiled and then grinned and nodded towards the sound. It would be all right.

—You hear them?

—Yes sir, Antos said.

—I don't think they have a tank. I think they'll probably have an armored-car and several motorcycles and possibly a truck. Do you hear the cycles?

—Yes sir. Loud, aren't they?

—That's all they are. Don't let them worry you. A motorcyclist is a naked man. He can't do anything until he gets off his machine and once he's off it he is just a man. Don't let the noise impress you.

—No sir, Antos said.

He wondered what it was to be im-pressed. This word, like im-itate, was another new one. Whatever it was, he would not let the motorcycles do it to him. But he was frightened by the loud noise coming from the road. He heard the popping rumble of the motorcycles and the higher, sustained noise of something else.

—There will be motorcyclists in the lead, the captain said. Don't worry about them. Let them pass. The others will take care of them in the village. They have an armoredcar. They also have a truck. Don't even think about the armoredcar. I'll take care of that. Throw your grenades at the truck . . . or it may be a staffcar.

—Yes sir.

The sound of motors was now close.

It was a roar now, no longer a rumble, and not at all like bees or even thunder. It was coming close. The hollow where the road dipped filled with the roar, and the sound changed where the road rose out of the hollow, and then the sound spilled out, like water from the millpond back home in spring after the snow has melted, and in the flood of it (with the earth shaking now, not trembling) in a mass of dust that looked almost solid, they leaped out of the hollow and were *there*.

Dangerous animals, machines. Out of the ground. Grey. Not men but iron ghosts. Eyes like huge bowls of glass. Bulging yellow with the sun on them. Heads of iron. And the rest all grey and squat and hunched around the roaring mass of motorcycles. The machines floated in the dustcloud, cut off by the dust at the rider's knees. The sound was enormous. Perhaps it was the sound that kept them up, suspended in the dustcloud that spurted up and boiled between the invisible road and the riders' amputated knees.

Holy Mother of God! Queen of the Crown of Poland! Wounds of the One True God!

Antos felt his eyes bulge and strain towards the coming Germans. He felt pain in his hands and looked down at them and saw the knuckles of his hands white and his fingers flattened around the warm brown carbine stock. The handgrenades looked like corrugated eggs piled innocently in the dust.

What do I do now? There is something that I have to do. What is it? Antos could not remember what he was to do now that the war was with him, face to face, coming forward with its stuttering roar on amputated legs.

There were four motorcycles with two men on each. The machines moved slowly. Each motorcycle had a small car fixed to its side and yet another German sat in each small car. The men, who were men after all, strange and not manlike but nevertheless men, sat stiff and cramped on their machines. Their heads moved in short turns round and round. They looked carefully into the ditches on both sides of the road. They had short carbines strapped across their backs and these were yellow-tinted with the dust and soft-looking and furry and not at all dangerous. Like branches of a tree with dust on them.

Antos watched the squat, nervous, curiously animated shapes aboard the machines come closer. They looked very strong. They looked nervous. Antos wondered why they should be nervous. There were a lot of them and they had the machines.

Behind the motorcycles came an armoredcar. It was big. Bigger than the cars in the reconnaissance platoon back at Regiment. About twice as big as the TK tank they had brought up that time he was going to be shot. The snout of the armoredcar was shaped like a coffin. A coffin with six wheels. Antos supposed that the car could go real fast if it wanted to. Six wheels, that was a lot. The more wheels you put on a machine, the faster it would go. Wheels were like legs, weren't they? A man had two legs and a horse had four and which could go faster? Antos wondered how many wheels there had been on the train. He looked sideways at the Pan Kapitan. The officer's eyes were halfclosed and his mouth was thin. This is the way a wolf looks when he is waiting for the calf to come close to the woods, Antos thought. And now there was a small smile on the captain's face.

He had pushed his carbine from him and lay with the small smile on his face close to the rough stones of the well. His face was dark in shadow. It was always dark, almost like a Gypsy's, but in the shadow it was almost black. Why did he push the carbine away? Antos thought. What is he going to do? He looked carefully at the captain but the officer did not look at him. The captain watched the Germans on the road.

They came on steadily enough. Turning their faces this way and that:

watching. Will they see us here? Antos thought the Germans would see him and the captain. He did not see how they could help seeing them. Even with the dust.

The Germans on the motorcycles rode past the well. Dust boiled up from under their machines and swept over the rampart of the well and over the captain. For ten heartbeats there was no captain and Antos was alone. What now? But then the dust settled and he saw the other: It was all right then. He wondered if now was the time to shoot at the Germans but the captain gave no sign. Antos supposed that he had better wait until the captain started shooting Germans. The captain would know when the best time was.

But now the Germans on the motorcycles were well past the *zagroda* and into the village.

They didn't see us, Antos thought. He felt like laughing. He wondered why the captain let them pass.

And now the armoredcar was abreast of them with a small German in black leather and a round, soft cap sticking up out of the top of it. The German had a white cloth round his neck and he kept pulling it up over his mouth and nose but it slipped down every time he did it. He was so busy with the cloth that he did not see them any more than the others did. Antos looked at the captain to see if it was time to shoot and then remembered that he was not to be concerned about the armoredcar. The captain had said that he would kill the car. He watched the armoredcar go by, and saw its back with small square cans piled on top of it, and behind the car there was something else drowned in the dust. What was it? Antos looked at it. It was a little car. It was like no car he had ever seen. Four Germans in big helmets sat in the small car. They looked as though they sat on top of each other. The car had a flat nose that curved downward so that it looked like a small dog sniffing at the road. The Germans looked cramped in the little car; three of them were big.

Ah, but the fourth one! Antos looked at him and started laughing. He almost dropped his carbine. He put his hand over his mouth and looked at the captain but the captain gave no sign of any kind. Antos looked at the fourth German and tried not to laugh.

This German was so little he almost wasn't there: a thin straw of a man and old. His little face was all crumpled up and his collar came up to his ears and his big helmet sat on his head like an upturned bucket over a wilted cabbage. His nose was sharp and pointed and stuck out from under the helmet as though to point the way. He had a lot of gold twisted into small ropes on his shoulderstraps. These came up in a point about his ears as though the helmet was so heavy for the little German that the shoulders could not keep it up and had collapsed under the weight of it.

Was this the enemy? Antos could not believe it.

The others, yes, they looked like enemies: big and bullnecked and wellfed and dangerouslooking with round, hunched shoulders and flat faces. But the little one? A puff of autumn wind would blow him over!

And now the captain got up. He did it marvelously quick. One minute he was flat on the ground, down in the dust and near invisible, then suddenly he was upon his feet with the small smile now wide, and in each hand he held a handgrenade and his right arm swung back and then forward and the handgrenade sailed prettily over the little car and, before it landed on the back of the armored car among the little cans, the other handgrenade was also in the air. It fell between the cars and the small car nosed over it.

Bang-O!

The back of the armored car disappeared in yellow fire.

Smoke.

Somebody squealed like a dog hit with a stone.

Bang-O!

The little car jumped up as though someone had kicked it in the nose. Out came all the Germans: head over heels, round and round in the air with leather cases and small round cans and bags and bits of rifles and pieces torn out of the bottom of the little car. The air filled with these. It was full of Germans. The Germans rolled along the road when they landed on it. The bits and pieces fell on top of them.

And now the Pan Kapitan was running down into the road with his carbine going and Antos got up and also ran to where the Germans were. There was a thin sound in the air that was like the sound an old dog made one time in the village when the fat boy from the tavern hit it with a stave and broke its back. But there were no dogs in the road, only Germans. One was down on his knees and his face, with his hands somewhere under him, and a long green rope trailed from under him as he tried to hump his way along into a ditch. Another sat with his legs straight out in front of him with his face in his hands as though he were weeping. His hands were red and more red fell from between his fingers and splashed between his legs.

Antos passed them both and ran to the car. The little car was empty. It was flat on its nose with the front wheels splayed. The howling come from somewhere under it. And in the ditch behind it sat the little German.

The old man had no helmet now. His thin head was bald. His face was brown and wrinkled. He stared at Antos and Antos stared at him. The little gold ropes were gone off the German's shoulders and most of his coat was also gone and his pants were torn. The German got up and began to explain something carefully to Antos. He pointed to the road and to himself and to where he had come from and also to the village. The sound of rifles and grenades and of machinegunfire came from the village. The German pointed to the burning armoredcar and to himself. Antos looked at him and scratched his head. He supposed that he should shoot the German. But how can you shoot somebody who isn't doing anything? The German should be doing something. He should be trying to get that enormous pistol out of its leather case. But the old man did nothing except talk in a squeaky voice and point at himself. He saw Antos looking at the pistol and, holding his pistolhand away from himself, began to take his belt off with his other hand. All the time he explained something carefully in his high oldman's voice. Antos knew that he had to do something with the old man. He looked for the captain, who would surely know. But the captain had run behind the motorcyclemen into the village. There was nobody in the road except Antos and the little German. The German looked like an officer. Antos drew erect and clicked his heels. At once the German drew erect and stopped explaining. He said something in a sharp voice.

—*Grate-grate-babble-babble-babble.*

Antos scratched his nose.

—*Grate-grate-babble?*

Antos grinned at him.

The German was erect and angrylooking and he was buckling his pistolbelt around himself again. Antos was sure now that the little German was an officer.

—Now, just you take it easy, sir, Antos said. No use getting angry.

—*Was?*

—No use spitting, either. Just take it easy and you'll be all right.

The German stared at him with furious eyes. What was he angry about? Antos supposed he had better take the big pistol away from the German. Antos sighed and pointed to the German's pistol.

—You'd better take that off, he said.

The German shouted something. One word was familiar. It sounded like the German tried to say he was an officer. And that he wouldn't give up his pistol. What now? Antos thought that if he punched the German in the nose he would give up the pistol fast enough. But he didn't know if he could punch an officer in the nose. Even a German. He didn't think Pan Kapitan would like that.

—Well now. Now here. I got to have it, see? Pan Porucznik said so. And Pan Szef. I got to do what they say, see? Take off that bloody cannon.

The German raised his arms to the sky. He made swearing sounds. He hit one old brownmottled fist against another. Then he stared at Antos as though he, Antos, was an animal.

—Officer, he said. Give . . . officer! Understand?

Well, there was nothing for it. Antos shrugged. He didn't want to make Pan Kapitan angry but there was nothing else that he could do. Well, what the hell. If only the old man would behave himself.

The keening howl still came from the little car. The German who had wept with blood and the other German, the one who spilled entrail on the road, were lying still. Fire came from the armored car. There was a smell of burning meat. The sun was high and hot. Antos sweated. He wanted water and he wanted to eat and couldn't get on with it because the old German wouldn't co-op-er-ate. The old man was a nuisance, Antos thought. Well, perhaps the captain won't be so angry.

—Old man, he said. *Dawaj pistolet!*

And then he swung his carbine by the barrel and brought the brass butt down on the old man's head.

The old man's head exploded. He fell down. Antos looked at the old man in the torn grey blouse. He nudged him with his boot but the old man was dead. He was very flat on the ground. His false teeth had jumped out of his mouth and lay on his chest like a decoration.

—Well, Antos said.

Well.

He hadn't meant to kill the old German. He looked at his hands and his carbine. They were red and sticky. He dropped the carbine and stood in the hot sun saying: —Well.

From the village came the highpitched rattle of machinegunfire and rifleshots and the flat crack of grenades. Antos listened to the sounds of the fight and looked at the dead German. He said: —Well, again, and stepped back until his back was against the back of the small car. He felt the torn steel sides of the car cutting into his coat; stepped away and picked up his carbine. He dusted off the carbine and wiped the sticky red buttplate with a piece of paper. The car was full of papers. A quick breeze came out of the woods and lifted up the papers. The papers and the smoke from the burning armored-car flew about the fields. Antos slung his carbine on his back and walked to the village.

The fight in the village didn't last long. The lancers had shot the German motorcyclemen off their machines as soon as they had roared into the village. A few Germans had run into the church. The lancers got them out of there with grenades. It was all over by the time Antos walked into the village. There were dead Germans lying in the street and behind the church. The sun was low in the west and the street was red.

Soon afterwards the sun fell out of the sky. It was as if the day had been too terrible to bear, the smoke too nauseating, and as though this smoke had drugged the sun and sickened it.

The captain spoke to Pan Szef and Pan Szef gave an order. The lancers got their horses from under the trees and rode them out of the woods into the village where the spilled Germans lay flat in the dust. Now, with the day gone, the dogs came from the woods. The dogs were hungry. They started pulling at the Germans. The lancers rode through the village and across the grey field where marmots whistled to each other and small fieldthings moved. More lancers joined them in the fields. They rode northeast and then due east and then north again. Ahead lay Chelmno and the Vistula and the fourth day of the war.

Monday, September the fourth

I ANTOS

The shells were passing overhead.

Wrooo-wrooo-wrooo—like a flock of geese.

They flew close to the tops of the trees, so close and there were so many of them that they made a wind among the branches and it was then even more like birds going up. Leaves fell, red and yellow, on the resting men. Neither the men nor the horses paid much attention to the passing shells because shells, even in such numbers and so close, were no longer new, and these shells unlike all the others that they knew about did not come among them but passed on overhead and burst where all the black clouds were: behind the sandy hills by the river.

At first they speculated about the shells, their size and number. Stas Guz said he thought maybe a whole artillery regiment was shooting. Stas Sztych said maybe it was two. But Pan Szef said it was a lot more than that, a whole lot more. So why didn't they forget about it and shut their stupid mouths and get some sleep? Eh? It could be the last time many of them would get a chance to sleep and wake up at the end of it. It would be the last chance for most of them if the boats didn't come.

—So go to sleep, Pan Szef said. It's an order.*

Well, all right then, they said and lay down and snipped out their cigarettes (those that still had some) and closed their eyes. And fuck the shells, they said, feeling like old soldiers, wise and old and knowing about shells. And fuck the sergeant-major they said (when he couldn't hear them) and went to sleep.

Antos didn't sleep. He listened to the shells and wondered why the boats hadn't come. He watched the Pan Porucznik walking up and down. The lieutenant looked nervous.

They had ridden all night to get to this place; first the small group that Pan Kapitan led, then more men and horses, then the whole squadron and the regiment and some other squadrons: many men and horses. The men were tired and fell off their horses and nobody stopped to pick them up because there was no time. And now they had come to this place, about an hour's riding from the river, and they stopped because (someone had said) there were a lot of Germans between them and the river and these Germans had caught a lot of infantry soldiers on the riverbank and there were no boats.

They were in a thin wood astride the Chelmno road with the broad riverbed of the Vistula on their right. There was no fighting in this place. North and south of them there was a lot of fighting. They waited to be led up towards the fighting, where the boats were supposed to be. Pan Kapitan had gone up to that place to have a look at it. They waited for him to come back and tell them about it.

Antos wondered what kind of fighting there would be. Also he was hungry. He wondered if he would kill anybody in the fighting. He knew what it felt like to kill a man. It felt like . . . nothing. That was the secret of it. Like when he hit the old man in the road. Somebody said the old man was a general. His head popped like a turnip. Who would have thought a general would have a head like that?

Antos didn't believe the old man was a general. But everybody said he was, a real general with maps and papers and stripes on his trousers, and Underensign Gzyms was angry with Antos and called him a murderer and Antos thought (then), Well, here it is again, but Pan Kapitan won't let them do anything to me even if the old man *was* a general. Because I didn't want to kill the old man. Who would have thought he'd have such a weak head? Still, he was worried just a little. Pan Underensign Gzyms took away his carbine and said that Pan Kapitan would have him shot. —*I should have shot you on the spot, you swine,* he said. *God, what a disgrace.* But nothing happened. Pan Kapitan didn't say anything about it. Antos thought about that and wondered about eating. He listened to the shells. He watched Stas Guz, who slept. He poked Stas with the toe of his boot.

200

—Hey Stas, he said. Imitate the shells.

Stas woke, sighed, looked at him.

—Wrooo-wrooo, he said.

Wrooo-wrooo-wrooo went the shells above the trees.

—A while back I was up the road, the corporal said. That's where the Ulans of Malopolska are lying. They said they were up north yesterday and it was bad there, they said. They tried to get across the river without boats and the Germans killed three hundred of them in ten minutes. They trapped two of our infantry divisions up there without boats.

—That doesn't look so good, Antos said, the way Pan Szef would have said it.

The others nodded.

—Yes, the corporal said. You're right there, Antos. It's going to be a sonofabitch, all right. Specially if we have to go through those Germans without infantry.

—Maybe there won't be any fighting, Stas Guz said. Maybe we'll just lie here and wait for the boats.

—Ha, Antos said. He spat. Some of the others laughed. They heard calls among the trees and looked towards the sound and saw the officers moving among the pines to where the colonel was sitting.

They looked at the officers the way soldiers do, quietly and trusting enough but with a touch of fear. These were the men who knew what kind of fighting it would be, who could say to *this* man, Go and fight, and to *that* man, Stay and hold the horses, and who decided in that way which man would wake tomorrow after sleep and which would not.

And so . . . this ap-pre-hen-sion he had heard about. A kind of fear: like standing under a linden tree during the summer storms back home, wondering where the bolts would fall. On me? Not on me? It wasn't up to you.

The sun moved then. It hung itself among the treetops and made the branches black. Morning was well begun. The shells flew overhead and the leaves fluttered and a small wind came off the Vistula. The smell of it was fresh. Many new officers came into the clearing where the colonel sat. They stood very straight before the colonel, but oh, Antos thought, they don't want to stand straight at all; they want to lie down and go to sleep and never wake up. They kept well away from the colonel as though they, too, were only common soldiers and he the only officer among them.

It had not occurred to Antos before that officers were like other men. They were *officers* and you stood straight before them and didn't look at them and you did what they said *because they knew;* they were never wrong and made no mistakes. Hey yes, lancer (he thought, surprised), you do what they tell you. But now they looked as though they didn't know any more than he, Antos Mocny, knew. About anything.

—Ha, Antos said because he was surprised.

—What do you think, Antos? Stas Guz said. How's it going to be?

He didn't know, of course, but the officers looked solemn and he thought that he couldn't go far wrong by saying that it would be bad; one way or another a lot of men and horses would be killed.

—It'll be bad, all right, he said. That's what I think.

Stas Guz sighed and the others nodded and Bartek-the-Stupid said: —Bad, bad, as though he had thought of it first and Antos looked up to where Pan Szef was sitting and thought that Pan Szef had smiled a little but he wasn't sure.

—That's what I think, he said. It'll be bad if we got to go up there without infantry.

—You're right there, boy, the corporal said. It's no fun making an attack without the infantry. It's one thing if the footsoldiers make a gap for us and we go through and raise hell, yes sir. That's what we're for. But it's something else for us to go it alone.

The corporal grinned at Antos in a friendly way. The others nodded. The corporal took a packet of tobacco out of his breastpocket and carefully spilled some black leaves on a piece of newspaper and rolled the paper into a small tube and put it in his mouth and lit it. The tube flamed like a torch. After two puffs he put the fire out with his thumb and finger. He didn't offer his tobacco to anybody else. Nobody thought he would. Because that's the way it's got to be in war, Antos thought; you got to look out for yourself. Who knows when more tobacco comes your way?

Antos looked at the others who lay among the trees, some sleeping like Pan Szef told them to, others waking, others awake and sitting up and looking at the officers. They didn't look like anyone he knew. There was Stas Guz, who didn't look like anyone Antos could remember, thin, burned black by the sun, his face split by sores; Jozio Prosty from the machinegun squadron, with teeth like a sick dog's protruding from his black mouth, his hands shaking. Once, long ago, Antos thought, we had a picture took in Trembowla by a Jew. When? And there was Bartek Dryblas. Stupid Bartek who was surely the biggest man ever to come out of Polesie, where everyone is small. He looked like he was riding on a dog no matter how big a horse they got for him. He was, as Pan Szef used to say, the stupidest man in the regiment (*After you, shitnose, that is*), in the brigade, by God. *Duren z Durniow,* a fool, the Holy Father of them all.

Ha, yes. He was a fool all right. Antos grinned. He spat. At once Stas Guz and Bartek also grinned and Jozio Prosty spat.

That Bartek. One time before the war Bartek fell asleep in a horsestall and the horse got mad at him and kicked him in the head: one-two. Bartek talked about a sore head for two days and then forgot about it, but the horse went lame. Another time, at night, in village quarters on maneuvers, Surma set fire to the straw where Bartek slept. Bartek got burned. He wasn't angry, though. Maybe he didn't believe that anybody would set fire to him; or maybe he thought it was a punishment from God for his dreams. Or maybe Bartek had his own reasons for not being angry.

And there was Corporal Mus. Pan Kapral Mus who looked like Pan Szef. Yesterday, he had been in charge of the firing squad. And there was a lancer with a wart whom Antos didn't know, and another lancer, a small man who had lost an ear, and, farther off, there were the officers. There were a lot of other men around but Antos didn't know them. They were from other regi-

202

ments that had come in for the river crossing. There were, maybe, a thousand men in the woods and a thousand horses. And there were (someone said) twenty thousand men already by the river, waiting for the boats. There were a lot of Germans with a lot of tanks around those men trapped on the river-bank, and there were more Germans behind *them,* and nobody knew if the cavalry was going to try to get across the river by itself or if it would go up and attack those Germans.

Antos watched the officers. The colonel's face was red. His eyes were red. He looked like he was weeping blood. Antos thought: Like a holy picture.

And now he saw that Pan Kapitan had come back. He had lost his cap and his uniform was dirty and the sleeve of his coat was torn and he limped a little. The captain spoke to the colonel and the colonel nodded and drank from a little silver bottle and motioned to the officers. The officers got up and stood very straight. It was a hard bright moment and Antos also waited. Because something would happen very soon.

It won't be long now, Antos said.

—Maybe they're just talking, Stas Guz said. Maybe they don't know what's going to happen any more than we do.

—And maybe the Pope isn't a Catholic, said Corporal Mus. Maybe fat dogs don't fart.

—I had a dog once, Bartek said. He wasn't fat, though.

—Christ but I'm hungry, said another lancer.

—He was real smart, though, Bartek said.

—So maybe he had you and not you him, said the corporal.

—And he didn't fart much, Bartek said. His voice was triumphant.

—He didn't have to with you around, the corporal said.

—When did we last have something hot to eat? the lancer with the wart wished to know. He scratched his wart.

—It was the other side of Krakow, said the small lancer. We got *kasha* with *slonina,* remember?

—That was in Jablonna. We didn't get no *kasha* outside Krakow.

—He was a real good dog, Bartek said. But he was thin.

—I could use something now, said the lancer with the wart. Hey, how about a stew? I could go for about half a kettle of it.

—They'll cook you up a stew in just a minute, said the corporal. He nodded at the officers and then towards the fields behind which were the sand dunes where the Germans waited.

—Hey Antos, Bartek said. He grinned sleepily like a child. —Tell us how it was on the road with the general.

—He was an old man and he didn't want to take off his gun, Antos said.

—Yeah, Bartek said. He grinned and edged closer to where Antos and Stas Guz were sitting. —He wouldn't take his gun off.

—So I hit him one.

—And his head went pop like a turnip, Bartek said. He had heard the story many times, although not from Antos.

—Yes.

—I never killed a general, Bartek said.

—Maybe they've got a few behind the sand dunes, Antos said.

—They're all lined up there waiting for Bartek to stick 'em with a lance, the corporal said. Everybody there is a general, see? And they're sitting around right now saying *Himmel,* Bartek is coming with his lance, we better get the hell out of here.

—Yeah?

—You bet, the corporal said and everybody laughed.

Antos laughed too. He felt good. Hungry but also good. He didn't feel good about the fighting that was coming but only (he told himself) because he didn't know ahead of time what kind of fighting it would be.

This made him nervous. He didn't want to look like he was nervous, like Pan Porucznik, who stood behind the other officers with his hands behind him. The hands were pulling at each other and twisting about and the lieutenant's shoulders moved. He kept moving his shoulderblades under his coat. Nossir. But, still, not knowing made him nervous.

Well, he said without saying anything. Well. It won't be long now.

He got up and stretched and yawned and scratched a little, and tried to look as if he didn't care about what the officers were saying, and walked off slowly, kicking pinecones. He walked this way and that so that the others wouldn't think anything of it and then he was behind the last tree by the clearing and then he could hear.

He got a good look at the captain, who was drawn and pale. He had been shot high in the leg and Antos could see the red-grey rag tied under the torn trousers. It didn't look like a bad wound but it would get worse if it wasn't washed. Antos thought he'd better do something about it as soon as the officers were done with their talking. He counted the grey faces of the officers. They looked tired. Their eyes were redrimmed and their mouths were slack. The colonel looked as if he had had a drink or two: His eyes were bright and his mouth was wet in a grey, dusty face and his mustache dripped. He wiped his mustache with a beautiful white glove.

—Well, we're all here, *Pawelku,* the colonel said. How is it up there?

—Not good, sir, I'm afraid. There are two groups of Germans between us and Chelmno: infantry and panzers. The panzers have ringed our infantry on the riverbank and made a shooting gallery out of them. Our men are being killed in hundreds in a huge field with their backs to the river. They're waiting for the boats.

—How many of our men are up there?

—Two divisions, sir. Colonel Worobej and General Drapella brought them up last night to make the river crossing. Guderian's panzergroup caught up with them this morning. It's a slaughterhouse. Our people are trapped between the panzers and the river and they can't get across without boats.

—And the boats?

—There will be no boats. They were coming downriver to met us at Chelmno but the Fordon bridge fell upstream and blocked the river. The fleet is all jammed up against the Fordon bridge.

—Fordon? Where's that? a light horse major wished to know.

—It's a small town a few kilometers upriver from Chelmno, the colonel said. It's not much of a town, as I remember. But they did have a fine steel and concrete bridge. Is that what fell?

—Yes sir, Pawel said.

—Was it bombed?

—No sir. Some people said our engineers panicked and blew it yesterday. Others say it was sabotage. A priest told Colonel Worobej it was an act of God. God who, in his mercy, wished to shorten the war.

—Yesterday? Then why didn't they stop Worobej and Drapella from reaching the crossing? Why weren't we turned away?

—Apparently no one told General Bortnowski that the bridge was down. The light horse major swore. —Just what the hell is this? Boats . . . bridges . . . infantry . . . Guderian. Is there or isn't there a crossing at Chelmno? Are we riding there or are we going to sit in these woods all day? My orders were to bring my troop to the Vistula at Chelmno. Nobody said anything about any bridges at Fordon or anywhere else. Who are you, anyway, Captain? Where did you spring from? How do you know so much about what's happening ten kilometers away?

The colonel gave the major a slow, careful look.

—A little less noise, if you please.

—I have my orders. I have a right to know when I am to be allowed to carry them out.

—Most commendable, Major. And now, if you're quite finished, perhaps Captain Prus can give us an idea of the situation. I sent him up to Chelmno to see what was happening. Did you get all the way up there, *Pawelku?*

—Yes sir. I talked to Colonel Worobej on the riverbank.

—How did you get past those two groups of Germans you told us about?

—I swam past their lines. One man can do it. Still, they spotted me. There was some shooting.

—Apparently they're bad shots, the light horse major said. I still don't understand about this bridge at Fordon. What does it have to do with crossing the Vistula at Chelmno?

—Enlighten him, the colonel said. Be quite sure he understands everything. Then perhaps we can get on with what we have to do.

—Yes sir, the captain said. He put his hand against a tree, swaying a little. Antos thought that he would fall but he kept his feet. That wound must be worse than it looks. Blood seeped lazily out of the grey rag down the captain's leg. The captain kept his leg turned away from the others so they wouldn't see it.

South of the town of Chelmo on the Vistula (he explained), about halfway between that town and the mouth of the Brda River, is the town of Fordon. It is a place of quiet unimportance. But it had a steel and concrete railway bridge and this bridge was blown up. Whatever the cause there was this effect: The Vistula was blocked. Nothing could go down the Vistula past Fordon. The bridge was now a dam and it did not occur to the citizens of Fordon to inform the Army. True, as the citizens finally explained, there was no good way to inform the Army. But a boy on a bicycle could have gone to the Torun highway, where Army couriers passed, or a man in a rowboat could have gone to Chelmno, or a man on horseback could have gone south through the woods to the railway.

No one told General Bortnowski about the fallen bridge. All night he had hurried his infantry divisions to the Chelmno crossing. There was no bridge at Chelmno, but General Bortnowski had prepared for that. He had hidden a great fleet of boats, tugs, pontoonbridges, riversteamers, punts and barges in the thick rushes where the Brda joins the Vistula above Fordon. He gave the order for the fleet to meet the infantry at Chelmno. The engineers put the fleet in motion. It sailed into the Vistula, entered the steep banks at Fordon and stopped, and all the tugs and boats and barges and ferries and floating bridges piled up against the fallen steel and concrete. An officer in a rowboat finally got to Chelmno to tell the trapped divisions there would be no boats.

—We could say that among the wreckage piled against the bridge lie, also, all the hopes Bortnowski might have had of salvaging his army, the colonel said. Is that right, *Pawelku?*

—They think so on the riverbank.

—It's that bad up there?

—They have one ferryboat. They are ringed by panzers. They lost twelve thousand men in three hours this morning. General Skotnicki is bringing the Pomorska Cavalry Brigade down from the north. He too thinks there will be a crossing. So that, sir, is the situation. The infantry is being massacred by the river: two divisions, about twenty thousand men. Between them and us are the Germans in two groups: infantry and panzers. The infantry is digging in to face us. They know we are here. They'll try to stop us if we try for Chelmno. But we can cross the river at another point.

—Where?

—The peasants told me about a ford two kilometers upstream. I checked it. It's shallow; we could cross there if the colonel wishes. But Colonel Worobej told me, up on the bank at Chelmno, that if we could take those panzers in the rear it might save his people.

—Skotnicki will attack them from the north when he gets to the river.

—Yes sir.

—When do they think up there Skotnicki will arrive?

—Not before afternoon. He is still half a day's riding away.

—Do you think Worobej's and Drapella's people can hang on that long?

—They've made seven counterattacks this morning. Colonel Worobej didn't think they could survive the morning without some diversion.

—So it's a question of getting ourselves safely across the river or making a diversion.

—That's about it, sir. I saw the Germans stringing wire up there and setting up machineguns. About two kilometers beyond them are the panzers in an arc before the riverbank. Our people are between the panzers and the river.

The colonel looked towards the lancers resting under the trees. He looked at the horses. He sipped a little from his silver flask and wiped his mustache with his glove.

And suddenly it was very quiet in the clearing. No one moved. Horses neighed under the trees and men stirred around them but in the clearing there was no sound of any kind.

Then Antos saw that the captain smiled. The smile was pinned like a butterfly to his face; as though those muscles were whittled out of wood.

—Well then, the colonel said. We might as well begin.

He told them what they were to do and how they were to do it and also why it had to be done in that way and not in another, and Antos watched their faces to see which would blanch or which would slip under a mask of uncon-cern that hid the deepest fear; which eyes would turn away or seek a neighbor's. But he saw none of that. If anything, the backs grew straighter and the eyes grew brighter. And if the faces remained grey, well, he thought it could be the dust.

I GZYMS

Lieutenant Lenski said: —My God, my God.

Gzyms looked at him.

—My God.

—Sir?

—God.

—Is something wrong?

—Wrong? Wrong? Why, no. Lenski thoughtfully trod upon a beetle. He looked as though he might begin to laugh or cry. He kicked small stones. Caked dust had split off from the corners of his mouth, giving him a pink-mottled leprous look.

He hit his fist against a tree. —Why? he said. Why this way?

Gzyms thought that he should answer.

—It's like he said: We have to fight through to the river before noon and there are not enough of us to leave half of us holding horses, and so combining speed with numbers . . .

—It's not true. He has another reason, Lenski said.

Gzyms shrugged.

—Don't shrug your shoulders at *me,* Underensign! I tell you there's another reason. *He wants it that way!* Why? Because it's his last chance, that's why. Because he did it this way when he was young and he'll never have a chance to do it again. A mounted charge against barbedwire and machineguns! That has damn little chance.

Gzyms shrugged. He lit a cigarette.

—Don't you understand?

—You're the professional, he said. I'm an amateur. I don't know anything about war. Now if you'd like to talk about architecture I can tell you a thing or two. I can also tell you about murdering prisoners. But war? I can't tell you anything about it.

Lenski stopped as though someone had slapped his face. He peered at Gzyms as though the underensign had suddenly sprouted horns, wings and hooves, a halo and a tail.

—Respect, he said. I'll have respect, do you understand?

—Oh come now, Gzyms said. Which of us is the professional and which the amateur? This is what you drew pay for all your life. Why rant and rave now that you've got to pay a little?

He was very calm. He studied his new calmness and thought, Well, isn't this something, now? Look at me: Aren't I the perfect soldier? But (he thought) after all, why be concerned about something that can have no meaning? A man says, Hang this boy, and the boy is hanged. Another man says, Charge, and there is a charge. Old men get confused and get their brains beaten out with carbines. Twelve thousand men die in two hours charging tanks. And no one says anything about it! No one complains, no one notices anything unusual. So why choose now to be anything but calm? If nothing makes sense any more then there is nothing that can be surprising.

But Lenski wasn't calm. —You're a cold fish! Lenski shouted suddenly.

Gzyms smiled. —Oh no, he said. I am a very warm and compassionate boy. You really don't know me well, Sir Lieutenant.

—Be careful how you talk to me! Put out that cigarette!

—You're mad, Gzyms said.

But he dropped the offending cigarette and at once Lenski trod on it.

—Mad, am I?

Underensign Gzyms began to laugh.

Lenski swore at him. —Court-martial, Lenski said. 'Sulting superior officer . . . courtofhonor.

—Hang me, Gzyms said. Or have me shot, but be sure that there is a priest. Don't you know you can't have executions without a priest?

— . . . see to it . . . you will see . . . you mark my words!

—Be calm, Lieutenant, Gzyms said. You are losing face.

—You are insane, Lieutenant Lenski said. You and that drunken colonel, and everyone here: the officers, the men, the horses, these trees, these damn shells, the sky and the sun and this rotten dry earth. All of it. Everything. This is all insane!

—That's what I tried to tell you, Gzyms said.

He couldn't stop laughing.

He did not look at the brown coils of barbedwire in front of him, the yellow line of trench. He had the feeling, a complete assurance, that if he looked at them a bullet would strike him in the face.

There were many bullets. They sounded like wind whistling through the shrouds of a sailing ship: one of those tallmasted memories out of the past that sailors were trained on. In all the glittering navies of the world.

I have never seen a real sailing ship, Gzyms thought. Or any kind of ship. Or anything redolent of adventure and distant places. But I can imagine.

This whistling started suddenly when he and all the others came out from under the protecting canopy of trees and crossed the first of the fields, which, grey and billowing, were themselves like a sea trembling in the heat. Somewhere ahead an idiotboy had lit a string of Chinese firecrackers and the earth shook under the drumming of five thousand hooves and he cantered at the regulation pace in the regulation manner, both hands on the reins and saber at right shoulder, back straight, knees tight, with the wind rattling through the lancepennons and whipping the manes of horses. He didn't look ahead towards the wire and the trench and the nearing source of the whistling bullets but only to the right and to the left at the interminable line of men and horses which surged irregularly like a black and silver tide out of the woods. Other waves came behind it, black and silvertipped. It looked as though the woods had moved and the trees had torn their patient roots out of the earth and were now running out into the fields waving their yellow branches. The fields filled with them from one horizon to the other. Before them was the wire and the trench; many lines of wire and staked-in logs and the black hulls of burned-out armoredcars and tattered flat dolls thrown about the shellholes, and through the gaps in the brown coils of wire came small men bowed under mortars and machineguns who now stopped and began to shout and point at the men and horses boiling out of the woods and across the fields, and who ran and were turned back and put down their machineguns and lay down and pointed rifles at the black mass that rolled towards them and who began to shoot. Smoke moved like a fat, lazy snake above some village in the west.

Gzyms thought about his mother. She knew Napoleonic history. She told him once about the knees of Marshal Murat. They had a way of shaking before every charge. They shook so hard the marshal's feet fell out of his stirrups. —*Let them shake,* the marshal said about his knees. *If they knew what was waiting for them they'd run away and leave me.*

Gzyms looked at his own knees and they too were shaking.

—Let them shake, he said.

We are all nervous. There to the right is Lenski: pale, with a cigarette glued to his lip. The cigarette is dead. There Captain Prus with his torn sleeve flapping like a wing, swaying in the saddle. Up front the colonel with his whitegloved hand hanging down beside him like a sheathed weapon. Ahead of him dust and the smoke and the little men who lay down and knelt and pointed rifles and machineguns. They had machineguns in the gaps in the brown coils of wire. The earth shook and the wire came nearer and Gzyms felt (giggling, feeling foolish) that he was motionless and his mare a statue and that it was the wire and the machineguns and the shooting men who flowed persistently towards him on some mechanical device. And suddenly the whistling shells were gone and then a differentsounding shell arrived. (Coming our way, he thought.) Earth fountained up behind him. This was a German shell. He wanted to kick his mare with spurs and send her flying through the field and right, towards the river, to escape the shells, but this was not what the colonel had ordered. The colonel had been quite specific about how he wanted this charge to be made. They—the men and the horses—were to ride at a canter to the first line of wire and then a signal would be given. There was a reason why this charge had to go this way and not another, the colonel had said. He didn't give the reason. But it was probably (Gzyms thought, giggling, watching his feet leap about in the stirrups and his knees shaking) a military reason. He wondered if it was perhaps as Lenski had said: that there was no reason and that the colonel only wished to do it this way because this was the way cavalry used to do it and it was now the last chance he would have of doing it that way. It could be that but he didn't think so. And now the shells came quickly. The field shrank and the wire came near. Earth, logs, sandbags and men flew up like strips of paper and burst in the air. His eyes were full of running water: Small dots and circles moved in them lazily like raindrops running down a pane of glass. Through this wet mist he saw the lines spread out in open order, two long ranks, the colonel ahead with his whitegloved hand going up suddenly like a flagstaff, the flash of sun on lifted trumpets.

My God.

The first three bars of the National Anthem.

Poland Still Lives!

My God.

He could see nothing then. He felt as though this sound had fallen from the sky. It was like fire. It cut into his back. He felt the tears running down his face. Beside him Lenski screamed like a wounded animal: —Form! Form! although everyone was formed. He too began to shout in this highpitched voice of an animal in pain. The lancers shook their weapons and shouted: —Kill! Kill! Hurra-a-a-ah! and the horses, wildeyed like the men and splashing flakes of foam, stood up on their hind legs and beat the air with their hooves.

Was this the colonel's signal? If so it was a devilishly clever one, reaching back to pull the trigger of centuries. It was all there in this music: sabers and lances and trumpets and a thousand battlefields; and the enemy could be anyone: Swedes, Turks, Teutonic Knights, Tartars, anyone.

His face burned. He was burning up. He thought that shortly he would become black and fall apart like a seared timberbeam. He felt his mouth burst like a rotten blister. Heat, fire, blindness.

He shouted orders that no one heard or understood or cared about. Everybody shouted. And the terrible trumpets went on.

When the anthem ended the trumpeters did not lift their brass horns from their lips, did not break off their invocation but picked up the last recognizable note and cracked it and repeated it over and over like the maddened drumming of a fugitive's fist on sanctuary doors: the rasping, monotonous summons of the general charge that was like ice on fevered skin and beat upon the brain and drove spurs into horses' flanks by reflex.

Charge!

He struck his mare with spurs. Felt them sink in.

Ta-ta-ta-ta-ta-ta-ta-taa-a-a-a . . .

Charge!

(Shells explode but you do not hear them.)

Strike! Kill!

(Men vanish under hooves but you do not see them.)

Charge!

Kill!

Jezu! and foul obscenities.

A sound like an avalanche began behind him: hooves and the howl of fourteen hundred men. It drowned the crash of shells so that the leaping feather plumes of earth were robbed of their identity and no longer meant danger, destruction, death or anything. There was only madness: the terribly urgent *now* of it. Earth leaped towards the sky because it wanted to. The good grey earth had had enough of men and rose toward the sky to get away from them.

Shells, shouts, hooves and the tap-tap-tapping of machineguns became one great sound without any meaning.

The horses went insane; the men were already mad.

Earth flew backwards under them. Grey forms fell under the hooves and rolled away like rags pitched from a peddler's cart.

And then the wire.

Like a brown wall smeared with thorns.

Gzyms looked for some way through it and couldn't see one. The hair rose under his cap and he closed his eyes and felt the mare gather herself and leap and soar and land and stagger in recovery and gallop on.

More wires spread before him. This time a triple apron at staggered intervals. The Germans would not have had time to put that up. It was the remnant of some lost position of a lost Polish rearguard. No horse could take that.

He pulled the mare's head to the right, saw a gap in the wire behind him, and thought: There must be more! There must be! and with each word he spurred his bloodysided mare without knowing it. His hands were bloody. Blood had splashed thickly on the mare's neck. He heard the animal's whistling breath.

He wanted to stop and turn back but there were many other hooves behind him and these drove him on. Less than half the squadron had followed him across the wire. Now they galloped down the corridor between the first and second rows of it. Others had dismounted and hacked at stakes and wire with their sabers. He saw men fly out of their saddles as the bullets hit them. He saw mouths open in terror and hands grasping air.

—Left! Left! he shouted and turned his mare that way. The horsemen followed him. Why left and not right or straight ahead or, for that matter, down into the ground or up into the sky? He only knew that he had to go *somewhere* and take the riders with him because to stay in the barbedwire corridor was death, because to move meant life. And then suddenly he saw Lenski in the smoke and felt glad because Lenski would know what to do and where to go, being so professional. He was surprised to see the galloping lieutenant. Lenski had been out on the right when the charge began but now he was in front and riding towards them from the left. His face was as red as a poppyfield and his head was strangely flattened as though his hat had fallen down below his ears and for a moment Gzyms wondered (giggling stupidly) whether the lieutenant had pulled his head down into his collar like a turtle. The thought made him want to laugh terribly hard (because the lieutenant was so *damn* professional about postures and bearing and rules and regulations) and he opened his mouth to shout to the red lieutenant something about flat heads and turtles and, instead, sat with his mouth open, saying nothing. Lieutenant Lenski galloped past him and he saw that the top of the lieutenant's head had been sheared off by·the flying sickle of machinegunbullets and now a long red stream trailed behind him like the unwinding coil of a scarlet turban and the lieutenant was shouting something in a terribly high voice and Gzyms didn't understand a word of it. (But he thought: Has he captured any more machineguns? Is he satisfied?) And then new smoke boiled up under the hooves of the lieutenant's horse and man and horse vanished into it and Gzyms could not stop thinking about redfaced turtles but he no longer felt like laughing. His mare flew more than ran through the corridor of wire and it was she not he who found the first green gap in the brown wirewall. The mare took Gzyms into the gap where several hundred men and horses were galloping through. The horses ran into each other and into the wire and kicked each other and bit and screamed and became entangled and tore themselves free and galloped through the smoke into the open field beyond the wire with their red entrails like hobbles on their legs and everywhere soldiers were jumping off their horses to pry the animals loose off the wire and died under their hooves and other soldiers tried to make their way into the open field on foot, abandoning their horses, and riderless horses ran into them and fell on them and crushed them or kicked them into wire, but many more soldiers rode into the gap and through it and more and more of them burst out into the field where the machineguns worked so close to them that they could see the terror in the gunners' eyes. Men fell like puppets off their horses and either hit the ground and did not move or hung suspended in the stirrup by one leg and the horses dragged them off among the strands of wire that reached for them like hungry tentacles and scraped the riders away that way. Sometimes the riders fell directly into wire and sprawled upon it as though tired, sleeping and finally at rest. Plato or somebody had said something about that: how wars were over only for the dead and that the dead were fortunate because of it. Gzyms could no longer hear or think and he wished that he could no longer see.

He wanted this to stop.

The cries of men and the cries of horses and the wildwind whistling of the bullets.

Shells and their orange glow.

Supplications, prayers.

Obscenities: foulness heaped upon desperate foulness.

All of it was a blasphemy.

And it had gone on too long. Surely everybody would agree it was time to call an end to it.

He wanted to ride up to the German gunners and say to them: Look, this is quite enough; we all know—you and I—that it's time to stop; we've had too much of this and so have you, no matter what the trumpets said. And he wanted to shout to the German gunners that he was coming and that they were not to shoot at him because he had something to say to them which was important, which would make it unnecessary for anyone to die. But he forgot the German word for what he wished to say.

If I can only remember the word, he thought.

What is it?

Wait.

Don't shoot.

I'm thinking of the word.

But the only German words which he could remember were the one for mother and the one for God and a blasphemous obscenity.

And then the terrible brown coils and the smoke were behind him, he was in the clear before the machineguns.

Perhaps two dozen men were left of the squadron, but to the right and left of them (where, he thought, there must have been many other gaps in the terrible brown wire) several hundred other men appeared, on foot and on horseback, hurrying towards the Germans. The men and horses were exhausted, he could see that. Their mouths were open as though every animal and man had been suddenly struck down by hideous slackjawed idiocy but their teeth were clenched. Their eyes swam in their heads like the eyes of drunkards.

Gzyms looked for officers. He could see none and thought that they were all dead and did not feel sorrow, and then he saw that no officers were needed: The men formed to charge without command of officers, led by each other in a strange, sleepy slowmotion charge, and he saw (surprised) that he was not a comfortable spectator standing to the side but very much part of the performance, erect in stirrups with his saber high.

The Germans had put up their machineguns in a hurry. It would have been like that everywhere along the line of the attack: a sudden fierce attack and the Germans unready. They had not dug enough emplacements in the fields; the guns were in the open. Around them lay companies of riflemen. The dreamlike, surrealistic charge of desperately tired men on tired horses rolled towards them like the last, faint reaching of a tide that was about to turn.

A hundred meters more.

Eighty meters.

A German officer got to his feet behind the gunners.

The German officer's mouth opened and he raised his arm.

Gzyms pulled back on the reins. The mare ran on.

There was no way to stop the horses anymore. The horses had taken over command from the men and set their own pace and could not be turned and it was then as though the animals had finally decided that they too were involved in the affairs of men and had finally declared their own war on men and had now their own will and their own dark purpose and their own desire to kill and to destroy as though man could no longer tell an animal anything.

Gzyms knew that in a moment all of them would be beaten down by bullets: They were riding headfirst into a wall of iron which would rise up before them when the German officer's arm finally fell and this wall would fall on them and crush them and erase them and he searched his mind for some secret means by which the German's arm could be permanently frozen in the air or by which the interval of time between the German's first and second commands could be compressed so that what was about to happen would come quickly and be quickly over and he, Gzyms, and the rest of them, all the animals and men, would be through it and finished with it and, one way or another, no longer concerned.

He saw the German's hand go down and he heard the sound and saw the smoke that suddenly unfolded between the horsemen and the German gunners, and he bent over the mare's neck as though to hide behind it. Someone tapped him gently enough on the shoulder and someone else gave him an admonitory slap below the knee and someone else laid a hot, restraining hand upon his chest as though to push him back in line with all the others, and he thought: What is this? Wait now, what is this about? Why are you slapping me? I have done nothing.

And then he himself was inside the smoke and saw the dirty, sunburned faces of the Germans looking up at him, and their hands were raised and empty and weaponless and their eyes were wide, and he swung down once and terribly and felt the saber land on something that was neither soft nor hard but a blend of both, and he felt his hand tremble as the saber turned upon bone and then he pulled the saber up and forward in the regulation manner and he was past the Germans.

His mare took him straight to the machineguns. There were, he saw (with a strange new feeling of unconcern, a total lack of interest), seven of them: three watercooled American heavy Brownings from the Skoda Works and four light German guns without tripods. They were set up in a straight line about ten meters apart. He found himself above the center gun. Three men were taking it apart. One had become entangled in the ammunition belts and kept falling down. They tried to get out from under the mare's hooves. The mare trod on the head of the entangled German and the head was flattened. Gzyms tried to lift his saber but it was terribly heavy and he couldn't lift it high enough and he wondered what was the matter with it, whether or not the man whom he had sabered was still on it, invisible on the end of it, and if so why he didn't slide off to make room for another. He let the saber drop towards the biggest German. The German shouted and swung the barrel of the watercooled machinegun and hit the mare between the eyes with it and the animal fell down on her knees with blood coming from her ears in enormous arcs. Gzyms' saber whistled through empty air. He watched it arc prettily in the sunlight . . . turning like a stone . . . round and wet, the way they are when you toss them back into a river on a day out in the country . . . happy day . . . hiking . . . eating on the grass . . . with a thousand small suns leaping off the blade before it hit the ground. And then he himself was in the air and flying and the ground came up quickly to meet him with a hot, red smile, and the ground was not hard but soft and warm and welcoming and comforting and it reached for him and enfolded him and soothed him and he died.

I ANTOS

Antos' horse was killed in the second charge. This charge followed the first because more Germans came, or rather the lancers and the horses came upon more Germans. There was a terrible red field full of running men and there were shouts and shots and huge explosions and around those men (in *that* field) were German men and tanks and the lancers charged them.

Antos couldn't believe that his horse was killed. He had been riding it as he had been told to, with his head down and forward, and the reins in his left hand and held back a bit, and his right side turned towards where the horse was going and his saber in his right hand slashing and hacking right and left at the enemy, and he could see nothing in the smoke except the horse's head and yellow fire leaping at him from the smoke and great drumlike things went past him, and he heard nothing except the one great sound. Like an anvil beaten on his head. The horse's hooves splashed in the blood and bodies of the men and horses who had tried to go that way before he did, and he was looking at his horse's ears pressed back against the head and suddenly the horse's head was not there anymore and he was flying through the air like a bird. The smoke was like clouds. He lay a long time on the ground looking at the red hooves and the red bellies of horses going past his head and hearing the men falling around him like great plums shaken free by wind: huge rotten fruit splashing on the ground. He lay a long time thinking. He thought about his horse and the way his head was there at first and then was gone. This made him laugh. There it was: a horse with a head and then without a head. Where had the head gone? The horse had gone on without its head and fallen down in the smoke. It was a good horse, though not as good as Zloto, and he was glad it wasn't Zloto who had died. Zloto and Pan Kapitan also disappeared in the smoke. They were way ahead by now, out there somewhere where the smoke began, surely at the end of the world. He thought maybe he ought to get up and catch another horse and go after them because maybe Pan Kapitan would want him for something. But it was so soft on the ground and he was so tired and the smoke was like a blanket all around him and he hadn't gotten much sleep since the war began. He heard all the hooves and all the bodies that galloped or fell around him and this was so much like hail thundering on the strawroof back home, and hail or rain always made him so sleepy (because you couldn't work in the fields with hail big as goose eggs coming down on you, so you could sleep a little, and you got used to lying down when the hail came), that he curled upon his soft red pillow and went to sleep. Not much sleep, true, but enough to make him want to sleep some more when he woke up when the Great Sound got to be too great, or some falling man rolled too hard against him, or some parts of other men fell on him, or when the galloping hooves threw hot blood into his face. There was no part of him that wasn't soiled with blood and he wondered if any of that blood was his but he couldn't tell. Everything was all red and brown and black and all the men and horses piled in the field had this color so that it looked like there was nothing in the field except small rusty hills.

Back home the fields got this redbrown color this time of the year. The crops were in or piled in the field and when the sun went down at night the gold of them turned brown. There was time to race the ponies and to walk or to wrestle and swim in the river or to sleep under the peartree or to throw stones at the crows. There was time for talking about a lot of things. Antos never did much of the talking but he liked to listen. He liked to listen to old men talking about the past (how it had been under the *Moskal* and the German and who was worse, and how bad times had become since they, the old men, had become old, and how the young no longer had any respect for age and how all this booklearning the young were getting would do no good to anyone). And he liked to listen when young men talked about how things were going to be. They talked about how it was going to be when all the old men died, because it was the old men with their old ways that made everything bad. Antos knew there was a long way to go and a lot for the young men to change. Too many people were cold in winter and hungry in spring and the women worked like animals at the plow so that they got old and bent before they were thirty. In the towns (oh you should see them) there were people who got more to eat in one night in a fancy restaurant than a peasant saw on his table in a week, and you got water from a little thing in the wall and didn't carry buckets five kilometers from a river, and there was glass in all the windows and not the stretched skin of a fish, and all the houses were of stone and not even the biggest wind you ever saw could push them over.

It's no good when one man has everything and another nothing, and Antos thought (listening to the young men back home in the warm evenings in the good time of the year with the fieldwork done), That's it, all right: It isn't good, it ought to be different. The young men never said how they were going to change the way things were, or when; just that they would be different. And there was that word: po-li-ti-cal. It was a long word and a hard one.

But, somehow, it had something to do with making things different. You could change things with that word, the young men said, if you didn't like them.

Antos lay in the field among the rusty hills of men and horses and bits of men and pieces of horses and thought about how it would be when the old men died. Once he got up when the smoke thinned out a bit and the Great Sound drew off and the men and the horses didn't fall around him anymore. He got up and fell down again. The blood was like the frozen pond back home. But it was grey and white and cold at home and this was red and hot.

He lay in the field and thought about Marysia and about his mother making soup and he wished he had some. He thought about Zloto and Pan Kapitan and Pan Szef and Stas Guz and wondered where they were. He thought maybe he'd better get up and try to find them. It wouldn't do to keep the captain waiting.

He got up and stayed up this time and started out across the field through the smoke to where the Great Sound was and the yellow fire jumped at him out of the smoke, and he fell over men who crawled this way and that howling like dogs, and who lay still, and who jerked about like fish when you take them from the water, and over horses that screamed like men in the red field. He tried to catch a horse so he could get more quickly to where Pan Kapitan was waiting for him. There were a lot of horses in the field. Most of them were running. But some stood still with their legs stiff and wide apart and shaking like leaves, the way they do if you come under them and rub their private parts. (Antos had done that once when he was small. The horse stood shaking like an old man in winter. Sweat poured off it like rain. It shook and sweated and stood still on these stiff legs and Antos got frightened and ran out from under the horse and ran away.) When Antos came near them they screamed and tried to trample him or bite him and ran away from him and soon enough Antos gave up trying to catch himself a horse and went on on foot.

He climbed the rusty hills and now and then he came across men sitting on the ground among the corpses and he asked them if they knew about the Pan Kapitan and where he had gone. The men cursed him or shouted at him or laughed or wept or said nothing. Once he saw an officer sitting on a horse and he came up to him and saluted and reported to him the way he had been taught and asked the officer if, please sir, if the Pan Officer could tell him where to go to find the Pan Kapitan. And when the officer said nothing Antos looked up at him closely and saw he was dead. And he saw a colonel who was weeping, and a man without arms who set his saber point-up with his teeth and then tried to crawl on top of the point, and he saw a soldier carrying another soldier who was dead and the living one was crying and, as the smoke drifted away and the Great Sound became faint and then no sound at all, he saw many men walking back out of the smoke holding hands like girls, one after another like drunken men trying to get home from the market place. Their faces were small and thin and their mouths were open and their eyes were pressed tight so they could hardly see.

Then men began to come out of the smoke heading for the river. Some walked and others rode their horses and there was no order and no one said anything or looked at anything except straight ahead. The walking men held onto the tails of the horses or the riders' stirrups or onto each other. There were many of them. Antos asked them about the Pan Kapitan but no one could tell him anything. Mostly the men looked at him in passing and said something he didn't understand or their lips moved but no sound came out. Antos went on, looking for the captain. It was a hot day. There was the sun: red in the smoke like everything else that wasn't black or brown. There were many flies. Antos had never seen so many flies. He sat down on wet ground near a stream and wondered what to do. The stream made a small rustling sound. He sat there for a long time, and lay face down in the stream and drank the water that was warm and sweet and made him very thirsty and then he heard the neighing of the horse.

He knew the horse before he saw him. He didn't have to see him. It was Zloto. His Zloto. He knew that. *Zloto, moj ty!* he called and ran towards the sound and found the horse farther up the stream looking at the bloody water that he couldn't drink. There was blood on the horse all the way up to his neck and at first Antos thought that Zloto was hurt, and he stroked him and felt him and rubbed at the blood but it was not the horse's blood. Antos pressed his face against the shuddering wet flanks and the horse neighed softly. The horse touched Antos' shoulders with his nostrils. Antos stroked the horse. Then he went among the dead men and took their canteens and some of these had water which he poured into his steelhelmet for Zloto. Then he washed the horse with fresh water he got from other canteens. Then he unsaddled him and threw the bloody saddlecloth away and rubbed him down with his shirt and led him away. Many men passed him in the smoke on their way to the river. One such man looked familiar and Antos went towards him leading Zloto and it was Pan Szef. Pan Szef rode his horse and several other men held onto his stirrups. Another man rode with Pan Szef like a bag of oats across the front of his saddle. The man was Pan Underensign Gzyms. He was dead and Pan Szef stroke his face like that of a baby. Antos could not make out what Pan Szef was saying. He asked Pan Szef about the Pan Kapitan but Pan Szef didn't answer him.

—Fall in and come along, Pan Szef said.

—About the Pan Kapitan, Antos said. I found his horse, see, my Zloto here, but I can't find him. Where is he?

Pan Szef shrugged and nodded at the mounds of men and horses and the black metal boxes that were tanks before the fires scorched them and said:
—Fall in.

—I have to find the Pan Kapitan, Antos said.

—Fall in, you stupid shithead, and shut your damn mouth. About face. March.

But Antos said: —No sir, sorry sir, I have to find the Pan Kapitan, I have the honor to report. Have you seen him?

Pan Szef looked at him and his mustache moved and he reached down for his pistol but it wasn't there. The holster was empty and the saber wasn't in its scabbard and Pan Szef shrugged and nodded at the mounds about the field.

—Look for him then, he said and touched the sides of his horse with his spurs. The horse moved and the men who held onto the stirrups staggered after it and Antos went on towards the place from which all these men came, the place he had not reached in the fighting. He looked among the mounds of men and horses. He went through many mounds of dead men but there were

217

too many. Antos led Zloto to the river and swam him across. At first Zloto would not go into the river because of the dead men and horses floating down. But then he did. Good Zloto. Good horse. Soon I'll have you safe. He let the horse eat grass and sat on the bank of the river watching for the captain. The wounded crossed the river all afternoon. He didn't see the captain and thought that maybe Pan Kapitan had crossed somewhere else and would join them all on the road and looked for him there but he did not come.

But he could not be dead, Antos thought. Not a man like that.

He was too big to be killed like that, in a field, with the men and horses. He was somewhere, maybe, on some other road, going along with other men who had crossed the river, the way Antos and Pan Szef and Stas Guz and all the other men and horses and guns and carts and ambulances and peasant carts went on their own road under the hot sun. Nobody knew where the tanks had gone but they were away for some hours from the river crossing and so the squadron and many others got across the river and joined the march. There were altogether ten men in the squadron on the road. Well, that was still a lot, Antos thought. Ten men could do a lot. But he wished that there were more than that because there were so many Germans.

There surely were a lot of Germans in the world. They came and came and where did they come from? The more you killed, the more came at you. It would be a long time, he thought, before enough were killed so that he could go home. He wondered who would do the plowing in spring and how the sowing would go. But maybe by spring they'd kill enough Germans so he could go home for a little while. It was a good thought to have on the long march under the hot sun.

Antos rode a long time among many men but he couldn't tell how long the march lasted because when you're hungry and when you're tired and you do that much fighting and it is so hot and the sun is so bright and hurts your eyes so, there is no good way to tell anything.

As he rode he looked for the Pan Kapitan in the crowd. He thought that maybe something bad had happened to the Pan Kapitan and he felt bad about that because, well, if he had been there, if he had not slept in the red field, if he had gone on, he would have kept the bad thing from happening to the captain. But then he laughed. Bad? To the Pan Kapitan? He was all right, never you fear, lancer. What could happen to him? He was a great man who could do great things and he was a hunter and knew about wars so what could happen to him? Nothing that happened was big enough to hurt him. It was a good thought on the long road from the river crossing.

Tuesday, September the fifth

I   ANTOS

The men in grey sat in long rows in the field. These were the German prisoners brought from the river crossing. They looked curiously at the men in brown. The men in brown sat down on the ground or, if they were on horseback, stayed in their saddles as though it was too much trouble to dismount. No one said anything. It was very quiet. The German guns were quiet. The gunners probably didn't know where their own men were and where it was all right to shoot, Antos thought. Also, perhaps today no airplanes would come. He was glad that the guns were quiet and that there might be no airplanes.

—Well, Stas Guz said. That was something, eh? His hands shook and his voice was high. It was like a girl's.

Antos wonder what it was he had forgotten. Because there was something.

—Who would have thought there'd be so many of them? Stas Guz said. How many of us do you think they killed?

—I don't know, Antos thought he said. He had not slept. He wished he could remember what he had forgotten.

Stas Guz sighed. He looked at Antos in a troubled way. He pushed his hands into his belt and took them out again and spread them out carefully on the ground beside him and looked at them as though they were no part of him. They would not keep still.

—Who would've thought it, Stas Guz said.

Antos shook his head.

They sat on the soft moist ground of a field where a supply column had been bombed: brown pockmarked earth, discarded steel and fluttering lost papers that had spilled out of the pockets of the dead. There were many papers.

Around them, the Germans and the lancers were sitting down and talking. The Germans did not know any Polish and the Polesie men didn't understand a word of German but each nodded at what the others said, and made small sounds, and said things in reply. There were, perhaps, three hundred Germans in the field. There were many lancers. There were perhaps twenty men whom Antos thought he recognized, but many more had come into the field after the attack and many more rode through it all the time. A whole new regiment of lancers went by them smartly at a trot, and a troop of horseartillery went by with their harness jingling and the gunners sitting very straight and tall in their saddles, and then long ranks of infantry appeared: greyfaced and stiff-legged as though they had been walking a long time. All of them headed east where no guns were booming.

The Germans did not look at the passing columns. They held their heads low and stared at the ground and several of them lay down and put their hands across their eyes. Clearly they could not understand what had happened to them and felt wronged and hurt. They could not understand where all these men and animals had come from, where the guns had come from, why there

219

were still hard columns of enemies available to oppose them and why they, the conquerors, had failed to conquer; why they were sitting in weaponless rows in the furrows. Perhaps, Antos thought, they wondered what would happen to them.

From where he sat with Stas Guz and some other lancers Antos could see the officers: the whitegloved colonel who stood a little way off by himself, hard and dry like an exclamation mark on a proclamation, and some other colonel, and a major who was wounded. The major had taken off his boot and was wrapping part of a shirt around his leg. The colonel was drinking out of his little silver bottle. He stood with legs wide apart, one hand on his hip, looking at the sky as though he wanted to spit into it. His face was black and his eyes were black. There was something about the way that the colonel stood, the hard manner of it, that made Antos think that the colonel was sad. Well, yes, he would be sad. So many men and horses had got killed. Stas Guz said that Stas Sztych got killed. There he was (Stas Guz said) riding good and hard and almost through the gap when his horse stumbled and threw him in the wire and now he was dead. Pan Porucznik was dead, Antos knew well enough. He had seen him ride with the top of his head cut off as neat as you would scythe the hay back home. He passed so close to the lieutenant that the hot red splashed him. Antos tried hard to think of the lieutenant in a kindly way but all he could think of were the cruel ornamental rowels on his spurs. Underensign Gzyms was also dead. Who else was dead? Jozio Prosty, said Stas Guz. Old Jozio from the village of Stas Guz. They had a picture taken in Trembowla before the war, did Antos remember? It was a good picture. It was a pity to lose such a picture. It was a pity to lose Jozio and Stas Sztych and Corporal Mus and Underensign Gzyms and the Pan Porucznik. It was a shame about all the dead horses. Stas Guz had lost his horse, but there were other horses. Many more men than horses had been killed and there were several animals for Stas Guz to choose from. But what Stas Guz seemed most concerned about was the photograph. Stas Guz wondered if he could look for it on Jozio Prosty.

His voice shook and his hands wouldn't keep still and he looked everyway except at Antos, to whom he was speaking, and Antos wondered what Stas Guz wanted from him. Because there was something. Don't ask me anything, he wanted to say, because I know nothing. Maybe the officers know. But, he thought, if they did they gave no sign of it.

The colonel drank from his silver bottle and then held it out towards the captured German officers who were standing near him. The German officers were young. They stood very straight. They looked at the colonel and his little bottle as if they could no longer understand anything. They looked as if something was hurting them. Antos couldn't understand why they were so upset. They were alive, weren't they? That was nothing to look sick about. He wondered about that and he wondered what it was that he had forgotten (listing carefully everything that he had done after the long march: (1) dismounting; (2) unsaddling Zloto, although no one said anything about unsaddling the horses; (3) getting bunches of dry grass and rubbing the horse down a little), and he couldn't think of anything. But there was something. He thought that if he only wasn't quite so sleepy he would remember it. Then he could go ahead and do it and get it done and then he could sleep.

Antos thought that Zloto would be tired. He had run hard in the field and walked most of the night on the march from the river. The other horses stood as if they had been broken in the middle. The legs of some of them slid out from under them and they fell down. Antos touched Zloto with his fingertips and felt the horse shaking as if he had fever. He rubbed the horse and soothed him and put his face against the hot dry face of the horse and talked to him a little. The horse still needed water.

—Hey, Antos, Stas Guz said then. The Germans got water.

The lancers stood around the Germans and drank water out of their canteens. Antos told one of the Germans to give him his canteen but the German wouldn't understand. He looked at Antos with round eyes.

—Come on now, Antos said. I got to water Zloto.

The German shook his head and spread his hands and Antos hit him on the nose. The German fell down. Someone began to laugh and said, "—It's like that other time, eh, Antos? Like with the general? You will do it, uh?

And looking down, Antos saw Bartek lying on his back. Bartek's face was bloody and he was smearing blood all over himself with great clumsy hands.

—No, Antos said. That don't do no good.

—No good? Bartek was astonished.

—Come on now, Antos said to the German. I didn't hit you that hard. Hand over that water.

—What do you mean no good, eh? Why no good?

Because I don't feel good about it anymore, Antos wanted to say. Because it doesn't *do* anything anymore.

—It's no good because . . . it's no good, he said finally.

A machinegun bullet had grazed Bartek's nose and cut the end off it. Bartek crossed his eyes and tried to see the end of his nose.

—So you won't pop him one?

—Oh, to hell with it, Antos said. And then because Bartek looked at Antos as if it had been he who had circumcised his nose (round eyes hurt like a dog's), Antos said: —I only pop generals, see? That's why it's no good.

The German sat very still on the ground and tried not to move. His eyes darted from left to right and back again as if they wanted to escape but didn't know how. I didn't hit him hard, Antos thought. Maybe he tripped or something.

—Come on now, he said. Let's have that water, see? The war's all over for you, but me and my horse, we got a long way to go. This is only the beginning. We got to be moving out pretty soon so get on with it.

The German said something and put his hands together. He talked very fast. Antos didn't understand a word of it. He was tired and wanted to sleep and his head was aching. His arms and back were aching. He thought how easy it would be to pop this talking German. How come they did so much talking when you wanted something out of them? Why didn't they just do what you wanted them to do? But that was it about the Germans, his father had said. There wasn't anybody who'd pop you one faster than a German if he was on top. You never heard Germans talking when they were the masters. But if you got them down, well, that was different. You never heard anybody talk so much then. Antos pointed at the waterbottle on the German's hip and then at Zloto and made a pouring motion. At once the German understood. He grinned, then laughed and got up and nodded his head as if he wanted to shake it off his shoulders and immediately got his canteen off his belt and gave it to Antos.

—*Wasser,* he said, laughing.

—Good, Antos said.

—Good . . . horse?

—He's a horse, all right, Antos said.

He got the German's helmet and poured water into it and held it under Zloto's nose, looking at the coolness of it, almost smelling it, and wanting it himself so badly that his hands shook and he spilled some of the water. He wondered why his back and arms hurt so and he thought that it was probably because of all the sabering that he had been doing. There had certainly been a lot of that. And there would be more. He didn't think he wanted any more. He wondered how much time there was before the officers finished counting the men and horses and inspecting horses and writing things down in their little books and talking together and looking at maps, and how soon Pan Szef would come along and get everybody on their feet again and they would go on again and do some more fighting. He wondered if the airplanes would come after all. Because as surely as he stood there the airplanes would come. Sooner or later they always came when you stood long enough in an open field. And that's another thing I've learned about since I became a soldier. Yes. Antos wondered how many more things there were for him to learn.

There was the matter of girls, but somehow that didn't seem so important anymore. What was important was *not getting killed.* There was all the time you wanted for learning everything you wanted if you stayed alive. When this war is finished, he thought, I'll go home and I'll do some sleeping. Maybe I'll sleep for seven days. And I'll do some eating. I'll eat for ten days. (And he thought about the different kinds of food he had eaten at different times, the soups and cabbage and potatoes and the meat and *slonina* you got in Army soup and the different cheeses, and he thought about the food he had never eaten like what he heard about restaurants in town.) And then I'll go to town and never come back. I'll live in town and wear shoes every day and eat in a restaurant and drink tea, and I'll get a girl all right, a good one I can do things with, and nobody had better tell me where to go and what to do because there is one thing I don't have to learn about anymore and that is how to make heads pop like turnips and how to put a lance or bullet in a back. Nobody had better try to make *me* work in fields like a horse, or take my cap off to anyone or *wait* for better times.

And then, perhaps because he could almost taste the soup he would get in the restaurant (being so hungry now), or perhaps because he was so tired and his arms hurt so, his hands shook and he spilled more water and Zloto looked at him.

Ha, golden one. Drink, drink. I am sorry.

But his hands shook so that he kept hitting the iron helmet rim against the horse's teeth.

Then Zloto sighed and lay down. Antos sat down beside him. Zloto was breathing slowly. Slow and deep. The German was sitting at the horse's head and was stroking it. He was smiling at Antos and stroking the horse's head.

222

Antos felt his eyes fill with sand and the lids were heavy and he thought that if he'd only remember what he had forgotten he could get down to sleep.

Sleep.

Yes.

It would be good.

He wanted sleep: the kind that comes after a long day's work. A long day in the fields from sunrise to sunset. With the back aching and the stomach tight with emptiness. With a long way to walk home across the fields. Home: to the village that had swallows in it and storks and all the other signs of good luck . . . where the old men talk . . . no inn or market place . . . but yes, so many swallows. Messengers of the Blessed Mother. All kinds of messengers. My mother works in the fields like a horse.

He heard Stas Guz sighing and moving about and wondered what it was that Stas Guz wanted from him.

He looked at Bartek. Bartek was asleep with the blood caked solidly around his nose and mouth.

He waited for Stas to say what he wanted from him and thought about home. He thought about the picture he had sent home of himself: alone in Pan Porucznik's pants and boots and the officer's saber.

He wondered if he still looked anything like he looked in the picture. He didn't think so.

They sat a long time in the field. The German prisoners were brought to their feet and the walking wounded escorted them eastward. The German who had provided the water for Zloto didn't want to go. He stood near Antos and tried to tell him something (pointing to himself and to Zloto and to Antos, waving his canteen), but Pan Szef came along and pushed the German into line with the others and then the wounded lancers grouped around them and the long column went down to the road.

Antos was quiet and Stas Guz was quiet and Bartek woke up and wiped his nose and the blood started coming out of it again.

—What's the matter with you? Pan Szef said. You a candidate for the Red Cross or something?

—Oh how I'd like that, Bartek said. All those nice ladies. All that tea.

And then the cunning look came into his eyes. I know that look, Antos thought. It's the way we look back home in the village when we think we can put something over on the townman who buys the potatoes. The townman says so much and we say so much and nobody is fooling anybody much but that's the way to trade. Now Bartek tried his trading with Pan Szef and Pan Szef laughed.

—Who do you think you're talking to, you stupid shit? You think maybe I'm an officer? A gentleman? I drove pigs to market before you were a dirty look in your old man's eye. Don't try your peasant tricks on me. Now wipe your bloody snout and get ready to ride. As for the rest of you . . . what d'you think you're doing? Sitting around here like gentlemen taking their rest. I'll rest you! Get up and get cleaned up! Get your horses clean! You're lancers, you bloody little abortions you, you're soldiers! Get going, move, don't sit around, you've got no time for it! You'll rest good and long when you're dead, I promise you.

Stas Guz sighed, got up and went away. To find a new horse, Antos thought. He got up also and buttoned up his coat and straightened his belt. He drew his torn jacket together. He picked up his carbine and his saber and his cap. He pursed his mouth and made the clicking sound with it and Zloto pricked his ears and got to his feet. Pan Szef walked around Zloto, looking at the horse. Then he put his hand in his pocket and brought out a sugar cube and gave it to Antos. He didn't say anything. When he went away, Antos put the sugar in his mouth and chewed it and swallowed it. Then he led Zloto to the side of the road where there was grass that had no blood on it.

Eat that, golden one. I am sorry, but I am hungry and I can't eat grass. Zloto looked at him and (Antos thought) nodded a little. The horse began to eat the grass and Antos stood beside him watching the road.

Men came along the road; hundreds of men and horses and innumerable wagons flowing along the two roads east for Warsaw. Antos had never seen that many men and horses nor that many guns and wagons and cars, small cars and big cars and even bicycles, the mass looking solid and compressed under the sun. But what he looked at mostly were the men. They were like no men he had ever seen: black in face and broken and with eyes blank in purple sockets. Not far from where he stood, two human streams joined and flowed tightly together, even more compressed. They flowed past Antos and Zloto and no one looked at them, no one said anything, and he watched them pass, wondering when it would all be over so that he could go home.

I THE HUNTER

The heat was tangible, profound. The sun was enormous. It seemed as though the earth had leaped into the sky to be closer to it. It seemed as though soon, quite soon—perhaps at the hundredth mile of this march, perhaps in its two-hundredth hour—the earth would catch fire and explode. Pawel saw nothing. His eyes had ceased to look. They were like the other eyes carried along that road, he supposed, the pupils shrunk to the size of coal-chips, seeking rest and darkness and refuge from the sun under eyelids the sun pierced brutally with a scarlet glow. For a long time, perhaps an hour or two hours, and for a great distance, which might have been two kilometers or ten, he walked with his eyes shut, seeing nothing, hearing the shuffling silence of the crowd around him: the hurried hopelessness of many feet, men's and horses', the grating sound of ironbound wheels on unresisting bone. Some man's hoarse breathing urged him on.

Somewhere ahead in the strawladen carts of the dead and wounded a madman started singing: —I once had a comrade/ But a bullet flew towards us through the air/ Was it meant for him or was it meant for me?/ I once had a comrade, now he is dead . . .

No one else made a human sound.

It was no march, he thought. It was the flow of a monstrous animated sea of indistinct shapes lapping against each other, a mute army of the Nation of the Dumb. Men fell in silence and the dust choked the sound of their collapse and the moving men stumbled against the bodies without sound, and went around them and went on in the same silence, with heads rigidly outthrust and eyes and ears turned inward, each man hearing his own terror or despair. Pawel fell several times and, getting up (facing the wrong way after the last fall), he opened his eyes and saw the overturned cannon which had tripped him in a white glare. The sun seemed very near. The air quivered. The distant trees trembled like black skeletal phantoms against the whiteness of the heat, and in the faroff bend in the road where the flow began, men, horses, wagons, guns seemed to drift along without contact with the road, borne by the air like shadows.

Someone sighed harshly behind him and stumbled against him, and Pawel, stumbling in turn against the man in front of him, saw him stop and raise his arms against the sun as though the quick indignity of the blow was just too much, the final humiliation, the last agony he was going to endure. With outspread arms the man uttered a cry and straightened his redblistered back and fell suddenly, straight like a stave, fullface in the dust. Pawel stepped over him. He began to laugh.

It struck him that for all he knew he might have died at Chelmno and was now a shadow, walking with other shades into the first peripheries of hell.

And now he seemed to be walking outside himself, looking with surprise at the blackened shadow which had no lips and whose white teeth glinted yellowly, which had small pupils like the seed of poppies in scarlet eyeballs. This apparition seemed familiar, reminded him vaguely of himself, and so he spoke to it. But the only answer was a terrible hoarse breathing that might or might not have been a laugh, that might or might not have been sobbing, so he ignored it and walked beside it wondering what the devil he was doing on that road.

The road was creamy white. It flowed eastward under all those men. He wondered if he would be borne along on this whiteness if he stopped, but it seemed like too much trouble to stop his feet from moving and so he did not try. It was the road from Chelmno, and Chelmno was . . . what? It was a name, a sound, the way lips formed, signifying . . . what?

He thought it might have been a field. Certainly. There was a field, a semi-circular arena of several miles, bounded in the west by thin, pathetic woods struggling against the heat, and in and among the feverish pines were the tanks: large metal boxes of grey and black and greenishyellow lined hub to hub under a blue haze of exhausts and the yellow canopy of dust.

There was this field. And in this field were . . . what? *Sound, horror, madness* and *despair,* and twenty thousand men. The steel container for these things, the iron bounds unrolled around the field, were, of course, the tanks: the two divisions which arrived crosscountry with six hundred tanks in line. How the earth trembled. The tanks made the iron semicircle side by side. Someone had said that there were two divisions. There had been twinkling flashes and long licks of flame from each of these shimmering metal boxes. Thus there was *sound*. Within three hours twelve thousand men were dead in the field. Thus there was *horror*. Some of the twenty thousand in the field ran in great screaming charges at the yellowgrey boxes, and the charges were hopeless and the men exhausted, but the charges went on and on and renewed themselves as though the men could also renew themselves and having fallen rise to charge again. Thus there was *madness*. Others did not charge but tried to cross the river, clinging like obscene fruit to the ferryboat, the one boat worked by the old man and the boy who wept but pushed the long pole in and out of the water to make the boat creep out onto the polished mirror of the Vistula like an ungainly, trembling beetle beset by parasites; and soon glistening white plumes uprose in the water and cascaded down onto the boat, obscuring it, and eventually amid a series of near-exploding plumes came the great yellow flash that flung small figures blackly high into the air and curving down into the water, and then the plumes were gone and the boat was gone and there was *despair*.

Many did not attack or try the river but lay down and waited to be killed and were; others worked to erect horrible barricades of corpses around themselves, and scavenged in the field among the plentitude of corpses to gather them like cordwood and pile them in a bloodybrown roof over a shellhole, then slid into the shellhole to escape the shells and died when the dead settled down and slid upon them and pressed them down into the earth. Then in a cloud of dust out of the north came the Pomorska Cavalry Brigade—the Sixteenth Lancers leading—riding for the expected crossing, and the tanks parted parted obligingly before them, and enclosed them within the ring of fire and the massacre went on. Then the screaming charges were replaced by dressed orderly lines of men and horses, lances poised; officers on one flank, trumpeters on the other, the dashing General Skotnicki pointing west, shouting, the men shouting, the roar of voices in the great hurrah, and to the sound of trumpets the cavalry charged and died and fell back and regrouped, dressed lines and charged, fell back, dismounted, charged on foot, remounted, charged on horseback, died, fell back, regrouped and charged again and broke through with seventy-five men in each hundred dead, their general wounded. There was no hurrah then.

There was a kaleidoscope of tangled flesh and iron and dead horses and wounded horses and riderless and insane horses and red tanktreads and blood and burning iron and smoking tanks and burning tanks and explosions of gasoline and oil and blacksmoke and whitesmoke and dead men and dying men and men who crawled and limped and lay still and men who prayed and who blasphemed, men who thrust and sabered and fired rifles and grenades, the shouts of men and the screams of horses, the howls of men who burned and the shrill yipping of men who were killing others. And then the mortal stillness.

What was left began to cross the river, dazed, holloweyed. Some men sang songs, others muttered prayers or laughed or wept or made strange animal sounds. Some lay down among the corpses and went to sleep. One elderly major calmly cut his throat. Nearly a hundred men walked into the river and drowned in it (walking slowly, carefully, one by one, and drowning one by one). Some men stared at the officers and shook their heads and walked off and were never seen again, but by the time the day ended and the red sun sank in Germany and the blood in the vast amphitheater of the field of Chelmno became brown, nearly two thousand men were across the river.

If Pawel had had the power to deny that scene he would have done it; and, indeed, he found himself, stiffly motionless with arms upraised on the white road, staring at the sun; but someone slid into his back and then slid down and, looking down, he saw the grey upturned face and the knowing eyes of a corpse. He pushed on into the crowd feeling neither urgency nor purpose. He went on.

Past angry sunburned necks and backs. Among the shimmering white bayonets. And suddenly he thought, Where am I going? and Why am I going? and What am I going there for?

He turned, elbowing through the crowd into the ditch, then out of it and past the embankment up the small slope to the milestone. He straddled the hot white stone like a horse and stared at the road.

An hour passed; the stone was rough and hot against the galled, bleeding lower parts of him, and his shattered leg, but Pawel clung to it as the only permanent object in the field. The silent flow went on, the air and the roadbed and the ghostly files quivered as before. The sun burned. Men moved and fell. Horses fell. Guncarriages spilled into the fields. Men slid into the ditches. He did not know them.

A redhot cannonball brushed his leg and he saw the head bouncing away from his wound and saw a man settle down on the hot soil. He appeared to sleep. He was strangely flat and his red back was bulging with enormous blisters among which flies spread blackly. Pawel wanted to move his wounded leg from under the corpse but he could not move it. He could not turn his eye away. Both his eyes had become one red eye and he could not turn it away. By the white pain boring into the hollow between his nose and forehead he knew that he would soon have sunstroke and waited for it, calmly as though dreaming.

But now the shadow, the same shadow which had marched beside him on the road, came off the road and drifted towards him with the same stifflegged lurch from side to side, straight up towards the milestone with scarlet eyes in the black face. There were no lips there. The yellow teeth were brilliant in the black face that had no light in it. It came stubbornly up the slope towards the milestone with arms stiff at the side, and the legs rigid, and Pawel suddenly stood up and shouted: —No!

—No!

—Go away!

—That's an order!

And because the burned man kept on coming he ran down the embankment and away.

Nearby was a field hospital under canvas. Streams of wagons drifted to it from the north and the northeast and the southwest, where the battles still roared distantly; strange, dazed men walked to it with shirts and puttees wrapped about their heads. Wanting help for his wounded leg, wanting news, wanting to find out what he should do, Pawel went there.

His shoulders ached and his leg was burning. Each step was a grating agony. His epaulets were torn away and he had lost his cap and he was dusty and unrecognizable. Still, the aidmen fell silent when he walked in.

—Do you have a telephone? he said. Is there a field telephone in here?

—Who are you, the doctor said. Who in hell are you and what do you want?

The young doctor's uniform was crushed and he was covered with blood.

227

He was dead tired: Pawel could see that. He could see that by the way the doctor leaned against the tentpole. The doctor talked into a field telephone.

—Listen, he said. Don't send any more. I have no way of knowing where you can send them. It does not concern me. I don't have anything here to do anything with and there are only three of us left and we cannot do anything for anyone. Yes, I know this is a hospital. Yes, I know the wounded have to go somewhere. No, I don't know where you should send them. Listen, don't send any more here. We cannot do anything for them here. Don't you understand?

The wounded lay about the floor of the tent. The floor might have been grassy once. It was now red mud. The wounded lay under brown blankets in the bloody mud. They were quiet. Their eyes were glazed. Most of them had an arm or a leg or a hand or a foot missing. Their faces were grey except where mud stained them.

One of them, who might have been young and who had red hair, kept saying: —This is the Seventh Regiment. This is all there is, sir.

Another chuckled happily with a wideopen mouth.

—What do you want? the doctor said. Where are you wounded?

—My leg and foot, Pawel said. But they'll be all right. I want to use the telephone.

—Why not? the doctor laughed. Why not? I can do anything for you if you are not wounded.

All this time more men were being brought into the tent and others were being taken outside. Outside, a long caravan of horsedrawn ambulances and small trucks and peasant carts and city taxicabs and even one great, thundering garbage truck deposited the wounded and waited for the patched and grey-faced and amputated men to be taken out of the tents. When refilled, the carts and cars moved east, bumping and lurching on the road; with each lurch the bloody cargo howled.

—Where are they from? Pawel said. What division is this?

—This is the Army, the doctor said. He was laughing and tears ran down his face. —This is the Army of the Sovereign Commonwealth of Poland and soon it will be a prison camp. So if you are not badly wounded and your legs are good, I suggest you make your use of them unless you wish to be a prisoner.

—Be calm, Pawel said, and answer me.

—Calm. Certainly. The doctor laughed. —Let us all be calm. He slid down the length of the tent pole and sat down heavily in the blood.

—Stand up and control yourself, Pawel said. Stand up!

—Oh come now, said the doctor. Shall I salute? He raised his bloody hand to his forehead, looked at it and suddenly retched.

Pawel leaned over and methodically slapped the doctor's face. In the confined space, in the near silence of the wounded, the blows had the sound and effect of pistolshots. The doctor's eyes sprang open. He got up. He leaned against the tentpole but he was erect.

—This is the battlehospital of the Ninth Division, he said. At least it was the hospital of the Ninth Division. I am not sure what it is now. Sir, he added slowly.

228

—Explain, Pawel said. His voice was calm and precise and much like his uncle's.

—They stopped sending Ninth Division men yesterday. Perhaps there are no more men in the Ninth Division? I don't know. Now they are sending everything. We have everything here. We even have a sailor. Where do you suppose he came from? I don't know. We have a pilot and we have some Germans. There is everything here except doctors. Also there is a lack of drugs. Men keep coming. They keep sending them here. Is there no end to them? How soon do you suppose we will run out of them? I hope it is soon. There are only three of us left here. There were fourteen when we came here last week, and there were nurses and all that. Some of them were pretty. One was really quite surprisingly pretty. But now there are the three of us. Doctor Malewski shot himself this morning and the old fat one, I don't know his name, a gynecologist from Warsaw, a gynecologist, can you imagine, well, he went away somewhere last night and so there are the three of us left. I don't know, there are too many wounded. How many do you suppose they will send here? Well, no matter, no matter. We cannot do anything for them except cut and wrap, cut and wrap. What is the matter with you, Captain? Where are you wounded?

—I am all right, Pawel said. It's not much of a wound.

—Well, that is very good, the doctor said. That is excellent.

Some bearers brought another load of wounded into the tent and laid them carefully on the bloody earth. Pawel knelt next to one of them, no more than a boy. —Where are you from? he said. What division are you?

The soldier's eyes were clear and he was smiling.

—Well?

—Oh for God's sake, the doctor said. Can't you see he is dead?

Two stretcherbearers picked up the boy and took him outside. The bearers put the boy in a peasant cart where seven others were lying. The wounded moaned in the cart. The peasant watched the men in the cart. He chewed a blade of yellow grass.

Inside the tent the doctor stared at Pawel as though he had not seen him before. He passed his hand over his forehead.

—We can't take you, he said. I can't do anything for you. Walk south towards Poznan, or east with the others. Just follow the walking wounded. You will find a hospital somewhere. You can't stay here. We can't take you here.

—I am not badly hurt, Doctor, Pawel said. I think I will manage.

—Well, that is good.

The bearers brought more wounded into the tent. The doctor shook his head and went to work. He looked at each of the men on the stretchers and at those who had no stretchers but who were laid carefully on the wet ground. He wrote on small bits of paper and tucked the paper into the breastpockets of the wounded. He passed out tags to the walking wounded and they tagged each other, laboriously writing down what the aidmen told them. One of the wounded was an old sergeant of the border corps. He was a Kasubian. He spoke with the lilting, incomprehensible dialect of his people and as the doctor leaned over him to tag him the Kasubian said something softly. He said it over and over. He was dying and the doctor knew it; these were the man's dying words but no one understood them. The doctor held the Kasubian sergeant's hand for a moment. Then he went to the pole in the middle of the tent and picked up the telephone.

—For God's sake, he said. Will you please stop them from coming here? Will you please do something about cleaning this place up? Will you please send them somewhere else? For God's sweet sake will you please do something?

Pawel walked outside among the walking wounded. The air was fresh. It was hot and dusty and choking but fresh after the myriad stenches in the hospital tent.

The walking wounded sat on the grass, in the dust, waiting to go into the tent. Their wounds were wrapped with shredded shirts and footcloths and puttees. They had come a long way and now they sat in the dusty grass in the hot sun waiting for the aidmen to come for them and take them into the tent. Each time the flaps of the tent lifted, the wounded stopped talking and looked up, but the aidmen only went to the carts to take out the other wounded. As the littercases arrived in the carts, brought from the leveled forest of Tuchola, and the chaos of the Ossa River, from up north in the Corridor and the slaughterfield of Chelmno, from the choked lakes around Koronowo and God knew what other battlefields, these walking wounded lost their turns to go into the tent, and waited, and now and again one died. Others talked, waiting.

—They say we lost two thousand men in a quarter of an hour.

—There are many madmen in the Army now.

—I was on the staff. Definite information. The French are marching on Berlin. Oh, you will see.

—Nearly all the fieldpieces and all the officers. Same in our battery. All the officers and nearly all the horses, but what can you do? We hauled the guns ourselves.

—A general told me that we would have to hold for at least two hours and so, yes, since he said so, we did, but no one came and well, how long can you wait? He said two hours.

Pawel went back to the road. He walked east on it. Later he thought that he had fainted several times. There were long stretches of his march that he could not remember. There was hunger and thirst and exhaustion and the enormous sun; there was the pain in his wounded leg.

He knew the bone was broken: He could feel it move. It grated. The pain no longer pulsed as it had earlier; now it was constant. It was a hot, sharp pain. But the bleeding had stopped.

The German rifleman had done his work well: a difficult shot off the riverbank at three hundred meters. The bullet went in high and up into his hip as he dived underwater to get past the pickets. But it was not the wound itself that caused the pain. He had made his way with it all the way to Chelmno and back to the clearing and it had not been so bad; no worse than other wounds. It was the fall off the horse in the field at Chelmno that had shattered the bone. He had got through the wire in the first charge, close to fainting but keeping his saddle, and he would have got through the second charge as well (the one against the tanks that trapped the infantry), but a near miss with a cannonshell exploding overhead lifted him off his horse and threw him. A dead man and his horse fell on top of him. He was unconscious for what he supposed had been several hours. Then pain and consciousness returned, and fever came.

Now he went on, feeling oblivious of his rebellious body and his exhausted brain. He had neither slept nor eaten for twenty-four hours. For two days war had enveloped him, a pulsing sun had eviscerated him and now he was no more than a tenant in his own body, vaguely aware of it as the self-propelled vehicle which carried him to its own mysterious end.

All his life he had been vaguely puzzled by why it, life, had been given to him and what he should do with it: that big, ribbonwrapped gift that came without solicitation and without instructions as to its maintenance or use. It was unreasonably given. Why, even a senseless chattering piece of metal like a light machinegun came fully equipped with literature on its various parts, its many small components itemized and illustrated and explained and the apertures where oil was to be poured labeled. But no rules or diagrams were provided for the great machine so gratuitously given to man. And after you seared it over the testing flame of all available emotion and hammered it on the anvil of all your senses and pulled it soundlessly across the taut extension of all your nerve ends, it still remained undefined and unexplained and remorselessly yours.

Certainly there were rules and instructions for the living of a life invented by men and institutions which had specific goals of their own, but these merely twisted life to fit their ends. Religions, politics, moralities—all hopelessly inadequate.

He had looked into them all and lived at times surrounded by props, and these had given nothing and explained nothing and he could find no sense in any other reasoned order, and finally, out of sheer fatigue, he had become what he was: a winner of trophies gained too easily, a hunter of animals and women (all his too easily), making his own manual out of eccentricity. Peacetime military life was a grand vehicle for eccentricity, but only to a point. It gave a time table and a daily schedule, and if one took the rules with a grain of salt and if one did not let the symbols and the shibboleths impress one, life could be lived enchantingly: up late and gambling late and drinking deep and gazing deeply into the eyes of women. He held the cup out and the women took it and he invariably said: —*Why don't you take off the rest of your clothes,* to appear interested, and often they did and, from time to time, he did feel rich and complete.

Then, one day, he woke late, even later than usual, which was very late, and he was fully dressed in bed under his pajamas (the white shirt stiff and starched and the tie orderly), and on his chest stood the Napoleonic chamber-pot filled with banknotes, the proceeds of a lucky night, and next to him lay some small shape negligently gathered in the morning hours and he rose and everything was bright and clear and pinklooking and he walked through the window, pot in hand, and fell four stories. The chamberpot exploded and money flew but he awoke again to hear the doctor say: —*Not this one. Death does not come that easily for those who look for it.* There was then something of the knowledge he was after.

But, still, the precise direction continued to elude him. He seemed always to go, as now, without any idea of where he was or how far away his goal might be. Mercifully, fever was clouding his brain, rounding off some of the jagged edges of his pain, but he did not think he could go much farther. South of the road he saw a field filled with the bombed remnants of a transport column: men, animals, pitted earth and papers; so many papers. He wondered why there were always so many papers in a field after an attack. Some men sat in the field and farther south he saw what must have been a group of officers and at the side of the road under trees a lancer was feeding grass to his horse. It was so quiet then along the road that he could hear the working of the horse's jaws. He went on towards the lancer. The lancer stared at him. He shielded his eyes from the sun. Pawel didn't think he had ever seen this ragged dustencrusted man before, more shadow than man . . . but he must have, yes, because—wouldn't you know it?—the man began to run towards him, tripping over others who lay in the ditches and at the side of the road, and the man was laughing.

—Well now, the lancer said. Well now, sir. And he went on laughing.

When Pawel fell the lancer picked him up and carried him carefully to the side of the road, and put him down in the dry grass and cut off his boot and unwrapped the leg and shook his head over it, no longer laughing. He talked to Pawel but Pawel didn't hear him.

Pawel slept.

He thought he saw many familiar faces: He thought he saw the colonel. He thought he saw the sergeant-major's cold eyes looking into his.

And then the sky. Hours of white sky with the white sun turning in it, and a jogging and jolting under him and the dry dust of crushed straw in his nose and throat and the dull clip-clop of hooves and a creak of wheels.

The Barrier

---

*Courage is of two kinds: First, physical
courage, or courage in the presence of
danger to the person; and next, moral
courage.
. . . The two combined make up the perfect
kind of courage.*

Wednesday, September the sixth

I THE GENERAL

Sleep was impossible. The General woke. He listened to the tinny sound of windows tinkling out into the street below and to the drone of motors in the sky. There were explosions: It was the dawn bombardment. Shadows of distant fires weaved about the ceiling.

He woke and looked at Lala, thinking that she looked exhausted and unwell. He had awakened several times during the night; once, when he woke, he found that she was gone. The only sign of her was the indented pillow with its delicate ornament of warmth and smell. He called to her, suddenly afraid that she had done something to herself or left him. She could not leave him; he was leaving her. But then he thought: She is probably restless. She would not want to sleep. The room was hot and the bed too narrow and the red fires of the burning city made the walls obscene.

He woke from a dream in which red shapes moved in sluggish motion like a sea of soft clay, under the wires of a telephone stretched on stalklike poles. He heard the humming of the wires. The dream quivered like jellied sand. Into this mass indistinct projectiles thudded. The mass gave under them. It was tideless and therefore not a sea but, perhaps, liquid sand. The darts probed it and vanished into it. The holes the darts tore became mouths.

He woke with sweat on him, staring at the scarlet windows. He wanted water, cigarettes, but could not move, exhausted and running with sweat like water. The waves of sand shifted behind his eyelids and the dream went on. The darts pelted. Their thudding was a constant sound. He heard it while the nightmare ebbed for the second time.

This time he woke in a room grey with a pale morning before dawn, with the night gone and the dream gone but still with him somehow because the thudding of the darts was there like a muffled drum. It resolved itself into the pounding of her small, tight fists in the pillows. She muttered and shook as though ill. Once she cried out like a child. Her face was wet. She lay like one dead, like a rag, with arms and legs spread as though discarded. Her fingers closed and opened and the hands, jerking up from the wrists, pounded the pillows.

She had thrown off the sheet and lay naked on the crumpled undersheet, her body wrapped in a dull sheen of sweat, cruelly exposed. He thought: I should not see her so completely naked with her mouth gaping and her eyelids twitching; no one should see anyone like that. He touched her gently and went on to wake her. She moved against him.

Sometimes when they had quarreled or she had bad dreams he would wake her like this. It would take her long to awaken. She came up to wakefulness out of deep sleep. She did not always know where she was. He would touch her and shake her gently a long time and usually this would lead to love when she was wide awake and he was then curiously aware of her as more than just a small body under his; it was the usual body with its usual complement of

235

planes and curves and soft shades, but more like a part of him. It was good then and he half expected it this time as she moved against him. But soon she drew away before fully waking.

—I did not, she said. I did not.

—Of course not, he said, gentle and surprised.

—I said I never would again.

—Wake up, he said.

—It is no good to cry. It does not do anything.

—Of course.

—What should I do? (She was still only half awake.) Should I beg? What is it one should do?

—Wake up, he said.

—They never tell you what to do, she said.

—Come now. Wake up.

—Why? she said, waking. What time is it? Are you going now?

—It is early yet. But you are having a bad dream.

—So I am, she said.

—It is better to awaken than dream like that. There is no rest in a bad dream.

—Yes.

—So I woke you.

—Thank you.

—It is better so.

—Yes.

—What did you dream about?

But he knew. She did not have to tell him.

Soon she turned from him and put the sheet about her and fell asleep again. Now she slept quietly, with arms crossed on her breasts and her mouth open a little. He touched her, thinking: How thin she is. I could close two hands around her thigh if I had two hands. He tried it experimentally with one, then circled her wrist with a thumb and finger. Gradually, so as not to wake her, he moved away from her and closed his eyes and slept.

The patient knocking on the door cut through the web of sleep and he woke, groping up from blackness, thinking, as he came out of sleep, that he was waking in a room elsewhere, a cool and lovely place, with the sheets cool under him although twisted. Perhaps, he thought, I am only waking because the sheets are twisted under me.

I wake uncomfortable but feel pleased. I hear her pleased, contented breath and I feel her breathe. No need to look there. I know her. I know what she looks like in satisfied sleep after love. Last night we drank hock at the Trocadero.

But he imagines that she wakes and he meets her eyes looking into the windows into which he is looking at the grey morning there. This is the best part of the day; the hopeful hours, Michal used to say.

Gradually the golden colors of morning come to us but not between us. How can anything come between us? Nothing could. Will it? Never will. This

236

is the way it was supposed to be, the way it never was before. Expected sometime, yes, but not found. Now found. Now good. There is this wonderful assurance about the *now* of it. And I say to her, this wonderful assuring new part of me: —*Do you remember last night the waiter who kept smiling at us?* —*When?* she says. —*Last night.* —*He had enormous teeth,* she says and kisses my shoulder. —*No,* I say, *that is not what I mean.* —*What then?* —*I means as though he knew.* She (sleepily): —*Knew what?* —*Nothing; it was just a thought.* —*You do say such strange things in the morning, darling.*

—*Do I?*
—*Yes.*
—*How are you?*
—*Lovely, darling. You?*
—*Lovely.*
—*I like to hear you say it.*
—*Lovely.*
—*What shall we do today?*
—*Perhaps we could go out.*
—*Not in the snow, surely? It is snowing.*
—*Then we cannot go out.*
—*Do you mind?*
—*No. Do you?*
—*Enormously.*

The teeth were large and yellow, he thought, remembering the waiter. The waiter wore white gloves rolled back a little and in the angry red space of flesh between white glove and snowy cuff showed the welts of fleabites. He had said something to her about that: something about how typical this was of their country; old welts under a snowy cuff; white gloves to hide the fleas. She had laughed. New gloves to hide old fleas. He did not remember the inn nor which town it had been. It was one of those towns in the southern moutains where they had gone their first winter. It was a fine winter and it snowed a lot. The white new snow covered the old country. He thought the waiter smiled because he recognized what they had. Like any explorer he thought that his discovery was recognizable to all. She, woman, thought that the waiter smiled because he recognized him.

—*He knows who you are.*
—*Do you think so? It has been a long time.*
—*Do you mind?*
—*Not for me. I don't mind for me. But I mind for you. There has been enough done to you.*
—*Nothing has been done that matters. If I have you it will never matter.*
—*They did not spare you very much.*
—*They must do that, don't you see? Otherwise what would become of their shibboleths?*
—*They did not have to do that much. It is because of me, I think. The politicians had to have a circus of this kind.*

She laughed. —*How do you throw a lion to the lions?*

He laughed. —*Not a prime lion. The pelt is worn and somewhat worse for wear.*

—*An excellent pelt and a wonderful prime lion.*

237

—They would have spared you much if it wasn't for the politicians.
—It will not matter if I can have you.
—Still, I am sorry about the politicians. They are little people.
—Nothing can happen to me if I have you.
—They are like festering sores. They are like fleas. Old pelts pick up sores and fleas here and there. It is a sort of occupational disease.
—We are done with them now, she said.
—Yes.
—We do not have to think about them.
—No.
—They will not have an opportunity to do anything again?
—Yes.
—None of this will matter or be at all important unless you leave me.
He laughed. *—Then it will not matter.*
She laughed. *—Look, it is snowing again. Does it ever stop snowing in these mountains? Does it ever do anything except snow?*
—Not very often, he admitted.
—Is that why we came here?
—Do you mind?
—Perhaps that is why the waiter smiled after all.
—I'll have to be very careful, he said. *Very careful. You've given up a great deal to be with me. If I ever broke faith with you and went back to them you'd be too alone.*
—You could never break faith with anyone, she said.
The knocking went on patiently; gentle and insistent.
Morning had come: golden in autumn with the red of fires obscured by the clean new sun. The sun slid on the calendar. He had not touched it for three days. That date was marked in red. A Sunday? Then this was Wednesday, the sixth day of the war.
She slept or seemed to sleep.
He lay beside her, feeling remarkably alone. He was with her and yet alone, bitterly conscious of this solitude, and thinking that no matter what happened now, no matter whether he came back to her the next day or the following year or the year after that, he would never be with her again, having left once.
—Panie Generale!
The gentle but persistent knocking on the door.
—Are you awake, sir? Are you up?
Yes. He was up, he said. Or if not exactly up, if not exactly on his feet, soon to be so. He would be up shortly and dressed a little later, smiling sternly but kindly in the military way, as though this day was just like any other and nothing had happened.
—Sir, General, sir!
Old Grzes was blessed with a transparent voice. He could hide no feelings; guilt, love, hate were equally exposed. And now excitement.
—What is it?
—The General is wanted on the telephone. An urgent message from the staff. (And then, loudly:) Just like the old days, sir.
Not quite like the old days.

238

Tell them . . . to go to hell, he thought. Tell them not to bother me today. General Prus is unavailable today. He has died. He has flown an eagle to the moon. His mouth feels as though he has been eating government newspapers. He has no longer any influence and it is not like the old days. He has broken faith with his woman.

—Tell them to wait.

He felt enormously tired, as though he had not slept at all, as though his presence in this bed was accidental. He looked at the silent woman who was now, surely, not asleep but kept her eyes closed and her head averted, the woman he was abandoning. He rose up on an elbow and stared at the pillows and at her. Her skin reminded him of apricots. His skin, he thought, was like a piece of paper. It was dry, brittle. Old. He felt old, used up. He did not feel confidence or strength. He could not understand why he was so tired. It must be the insufferably cheerful morning.

That lying sunlight.

Gradually, with his face averted from her averted face, he got up. He called to Grzes, softly so as not to wake her although he knew that she was now awake, and soon Grzes came to help him with his arm. He put it on. Grzes was proficient with the straps. He helped the General dress. Soon the General composed his face, tightened the disappointed muscles, and went out into the hall where the telephone was waiting.

He picked up the receiver. —Hullo?

—Janusz?

It was Michal. His voice was tired and dry.

—Yes.

—Can you come here at once?

—Do you have orders for me?

—Yes. You'd better come here as quickly as you can.

—What is it?

—I can't tell you now.

—But you have orders?

—Yes. I've sent a car for you. It should be there soon.

—Can you tell me where it's going to be, the action?

—No. Not on the telephone. We can no longer use the telephone.

—I understand. How soon would I be going?

—At once. Can you go at once?

—Of course.

—There are others who can go instead. Glabisz has just come back from the north. If there is anything that would make it impossible for you to leave at once you must let me know.

How circumspect he is, the General thought. How carefully he avoids mentioning her name. How obviously he disapproves. He always disapproved. It is not my lack of political acumen that he has resented. It is my love for her.

And then he saw her (thinking of her) as she was when he left the room. He smelled the sweet citrus smell and saw the white globe of a shoulder, thin somehow. It moved him. A shoulder is defenseless, seen like that.

—I can go, he said.

—I have to warn you about one thing. You may not have the opportunity to come back to Warsaw. So if there are any, ah, arrangements that you have to make, make them now.

Arrangements.

Yes.

The General felt the pity and the sorrow. He said that there were no special arrangements that had not been made.

I can go.

There is nothing to keep me from going. There is nothing to which I am so enormously attached that it would break my heart to go, to leave it, injure it.

Oh my love, there is nothing.

—I am quite ready, he said. As long as it isn't another party for correspondents.

—No. You will never be asked to do that again.

The General laughed.

—Thank you. Thank you very much. I am glad there's something else you people think me fit for.

He heard the click of the receiver as Michal hung up.

The general felt an itch in his right forefinger and thought about scratching it and didn't do it because this was the wooden hand, the imitation, and everybody knew it, and he himself knew that it couldn't itch although it did. The hand surprised him now and then even after all those years. It had its tricks too. It was a beautiful hand, much more a gentleman's than the other, the one that was replaced, although the salesman who had sold it to him had tried so hard to match the real with the unreal. No one had told him that you couldn't do it, the general supposed. The salesman had at first proposed twin hooks like claws and an armpit motor which was the latest thing to come from Germany. The general said he didn't want an armpit motor. —*All I want*, he said (he remembered), *or rather all my wife wants is an arm that looks like one. It doesn't have to feel like one because she'll never feel it. It doesn't have to work because I no longer have to. But just so that it looks like one. That is enough for her.*

The salesman showed him several arms and hands. What did the general think? There was a painted rubber arm with little golden hairs. —*Now, that's a lovely arm,* the salesman said. —*Yes,* said the general. *But my hair is dark . . . was dark.* —*Well, there are also arms with dark hair,* the man said; he would get some. —*No,* the general said, *don't bother.* (And he thought at that particular moment of his son, Adam, then a boy, and his questioning eyes, and of his darkhaired wife saying so politely: —*You didn't think of him then, did you? Why think now? It is too late for thinking now and for being sorry.* —*I am not sorry,* he said to his wife. *I will never be sorry for doing what I had to do.* —*Well then,* she said, *what more is there to say?* —*Nothing.* —*Nothing,* she said. *I could say, I suppose, that this is what we've always meant to you: nothing. I won't say it, though. It is enough for me to know that there is nothing now.* —*I want to see him now and then,* he said. —*Why now?* she wished to know. —*Because he is my son.* —*Oh my dear,* she said. *How wrong you are. He may have been yours once, but not now. You don't*

240

need wives and sons, you know, or don't you know? And he said: —*No, don't bring me rubber arms with hair, bring me a wooden arm, a forearm from the elbow down. I don't much care if wooden arms are out of style; perhaps I can revive the fashion. After all, I am . . . was . . . a national monument, you know.*

He was warned that it would take some time before he was accustomed to the straps and that, at first, he would have trouble with them at night and in the morning but that no doubt he could find someone, probably had someone, who would help. —*With what,* he said, feeling the weight of the wood hanging from his elbow. —*Why, sir, the straps,* the salesman said. This was an arm with straps and shoulderbuckles, a very fine product even if not the latest and the best. Perhaps an armpit motor after all and claws of stainless steel . . . *Goddammit, no,* the General said. —*Well, yes, of course, sir, the General knows best.*

He bought the arm with straps and shoulderbuckles. The fingers were half-closed, the indexfinger curved, the palm turned in. When held across the body (the salesman said) the hand gave an academic sort of look: alert and intelligent but also dignified. A black glove, he said, would give that *interesting* look like eyepatches or duelingscars, that sort of thing. He sold a glove. It was black and shiny and now a part of him, the general supposed.

No feeling in it as in me.

But now he felt the itch in the curved forefinger and thought: Well, they really make it realistic for you, these German craftsmen, and yes, I did find someone, didn't I, to help me with the straps. Her fingers were so gentle on the stub of elbow.

In the apartment there was another silence, the kind that comes from having nothing more to say, with everything already said, everything concluded, and no new words available.

He thought, I'm sorry, as he looked at her. I don't want to hurt you. I have no wish to do this but it must be done.

She asked when he was going and he said that it would be at once.

—Where will you be?

—I don't know. The front is breaking in the north so perhaps that's where they'll send me.

She did not ask if he would be coming back to Warsaw. She asked if he was packed and supposed he was.

—Grzes will pack what I need, he said, surprised. She nodded and said nothing. She looked at him openly enough, but he could not look at her withdrawn face. Still, he thought, I must try; it cannot end like this. It was too much to end like this, the short words and the withdrawn love and the difficult coldness.

—I will be back, he said. We must begin our retreat very soon or it will be too late to save anything. I will be back in Warsaw very soon, perhaps in a week. Will you be here?

—Yes.

She said that she had no plans to go anywhere else. There was no other place for her to go.

—Go to my father's house, he urged. You'll be quite safe there. It's a small village and the house is comfortable and the old man is not much trouble and it's far from anything important that they would want to bomb. I think that in a few days Warsaw will be under siege. I'd like to know that you were out of it. Will you go there?

—No.

—I want you to go there.

—No! I have to start to live by myself again. I am not going to start it in your father's house.

—You don't have to do anything like that.

—Oh yes I do, she said.

And then she made a gesture that he did not entirely understand. It was as though she wished to reach within herself to gather something and bring it out and offer it, but found that it was gone, that it had already been given away.

If only she would cry, he thought suddenly. But she was dryeyed and withdrawn, having cried before. If only she would say something . . . anything . . . even the bitter words, so that the guilt, or the sense of it, would be less, and you could leave on a note of indignation, so that the necessary sense of righteousness would be there like a crutch, like your bright motives. But she said nothing. It had all been said: all the appeals and pleas and explanations and, yes, the begging, all the attempts to make you understand, and to extend, in turn, an understanding. If only she would strike out physically to make the other pain less. But she did nothing. She had committed so many of her resources and reserves that she had nothing left now that it was over.

He thought that he had given back what he had taken but he wasn't sure. Perhaps at first he had. Perhaps he hadn't given long enough. Perhaps he had taken much more than he had given. And perhaps the fault for her nakedness and emptiness, now that it was over, was hers, after all. Perhaps she had given more than he was able to replace.

What was she thinking? That one life was over and that another life would have to begin? That one went on, no matter what happened? She had been part of him and he the center of her world for so many years. And now the core was gone. She would replace it, he knew well enough. But how or with what or with whom? This thought, like all the others, was unbearable.

Because you didn't want to be replaced as you didn't want to do any replacing. Because you thought that you could have both her and your bright motives and that you were not deserting anyone; that, in fact, this leaving was noble and that no one's life was being destroyed; that it was duty and your high sense of it that ennobled it.

But was that so; and, anyway, was anything true?

Motives: the war, of course; your sense of duty. And should a person who has given love ever be betrayed, no matter what the motives? Where was *that* duty? Ah, he thought, it's an adjustable ideal.

You do what you want to do no matter how brightly polished the ideal. You make the motives fit your wishes. You find the words and phrases and justifications to cover up the simple fact of self.

Take that to war with you.

And suddenly you know how that other man felt, poor Professor Karolewski with his musty smell, from whom you took her in the first place. He had been replaced and now you would be replaced and in your case it was by your wish and you felt a fool. And because you had never thought about him before, or wondered what you had done to him, or wondered what (if anything) he had felt, and because you didn't want to shoulder that additional guilt and because you didn't trust the brightness of your motives, you didn't want to think about it now. . . .

He moved towards her, to take her hand and to say something. He had to find the words, to soothe and explain; to tell her that the leaving was not permanent and that he was not deserting her in Warsaw, where she had no friends and never could have, and where she would always be alone because of what she had been for him and with him. But these were not the words which came.

—Listen, he said, Why are we doing this? Nothing is changed. Nothing has happened to change anything.

She shook her head, said nothing. She did not walk with him into the hall. He swore abruptly. His footsteps sounded angry on the stairs. Outside a smart young soldier waited for him with an open staffcar. They drove to the staff building on Rakowiecka Street while gutted buildings rocked and slid into the street and sirens wailed, and he knew, listening to the harsh sound of collapsing buildings, that time could not be stopped and that he would never be able to go back to anything.

Fans whirred. They moved the stale air. Great chips of concrete crumbled off the ceiling and fell down on the officers. The War Room shook to the sound of near explosions.

The General rubbed his hand across his face.

—You look ill, Michal said. Are you all right?

—Yes.

—I have orders for you. It may not be what you expect but it's the best I could do for you.

—What is it? he said, irritated. Pins to stick into maps? I am no good at that kind of war.

—It is a battle group, Michal said. Are you good for that?

His face was suddenly blurred and his features moved as though about to melt, and the General turned to wipe dust from his eyes. Yes. Am I? I don't know. —Yes, he said. Where? When?

—You must go south at once and block the way from the southwest. The Germans have beaten Rummel on the Warta River. The front has collapsed.

—What shall I stop them with? A miracle? Or shall I drown them with our usual rain?

Michal shook his head. His eyes were vague and he had not shaved for several days and it was clear that he had not slept. His head, grey with dust and unshaven, looked like a dirty tennisball.

—Why not, he said. That is the tradition.

—I'd like something a little firmer than tradition.

—Go to Radom and Kielce. Take command of the Radom garrison. There should still be one there. Take all troops you can find. There will be many. There are several thousand reservists in Radom and Kielce. Their mobilization orders were for later in the war but the men came early. It's been like that throughout the entire country: reservists pouring in without orders and nothing that we can do with them. They've been waiting for action since the war began. Take them, take anyone, salvage what you can off the roads. Bar the road at Kielce until the rest of Rummel's army can get out behind you. Bortnowski's remnants are also coming east. Kutrzeba is bringing his men out of Wielkopolska. You must stop the Germans until we can get everybody out and bring up the reserves.

—It's too late to salvage much of anything, the General said. Two days ago it would have made more sense. What changed your thinking? Don't tell me our allies have started their offensive.

Michal made efforts to control his hands but they flew apart each time he brought them together. He was immensely tired. The pupils of his eyes were like black grains of sand.

—No, no offensive. They did declare war on Sunday afternoon. They almost had a revolution in the House of Commons but they did go in. Once the British went in the French had no choice. But there is nothing much we can expect from them for several days.

—But you are still expecting them to come?

—Ah . . .

The colonel made a brief, conciliating gesture.

Looking into his brother's grey face the General felt pity: We are all tired, the strain is enormous. We have been driven within sight of the glass barrier. Each one of us contains this brittle limit of endurance. I am impaling him on broken glass. He said: —Forgive me.

Michal gestured vaguely. It occurred to the General that vagueness in Michal was something new; the Michal whom he knew had been a cold, decisive officer, a good one. You could always tell a good one no matter how tired he was. How dirty and unkempt. How close to the barrier. Michal is vague and looks old and the fires are gone from his eyes.

—I'll go at once, he said. There is no way to hold Kielce. It is in the open. But I will put up a line on the Zagnanski Pass. Look, here, on your map, north of Kielce begin the Mountains of the Holy Cross, and here is Zagnansk and a quarry and the pass. Is this far enough to the south? What do you think?

He knew, but wanted Michal to abandon vagueness.

—Yes. Oh yes, Michal said.

—And about Kielce? Do you agree?

It did not matter whether anyone agreed.

—Oh yes. Absolutely.

Michal spoke as though he neither knew nor believed what he was saying. The glass barrier, the General thought. He stared at the map. It loomed an evil grey in the dim, quaking light of the War Room. Dust made all flags grey on it and at first he could not see where the German strokes ended and the Polish lines began. He blew the plasterdust away and suddenly the scarlet thrusts leaped out and blue lines crumbled as though with this one breath he had changed the course of history. The map was streaked with scarlet in the south where Reichenau's tanks were coming through the Piotrkow Gap. The gap was enormous. He had had no idea of the extent of the defeat. Kielce lay at the southeastern tip of the scarlet gap and behind the town lay the yellow masses of the mountains. Beyond them lay Radom and the Mazovian Plain and Warsaw and the nation's heart. This was the center of the Polish line. The line bent back like a bow. Its arrows were scarlet. South of this thin neck in the wooded slopes of the mountains, rolling in a great scarlet sea eastward along the northern foothills of the Carpathians, the German army of List and Slovak divisions pushed against Antoni Szylling's group. North and northwest of the neck Kutrzeba marched his fresh Poznan Army towards Warsaw. North of Kutrzeba the stricken Bortnowski pushed southeast to avoid a sack. Behind them, along the vast semicircle of the border, the enemy stabbed redly.

Here and there blue flags grouped. These would be new divisions forming. In the far north and deep south blue arrows showed counterattacks. Thin blue lines fed new troops westward from the quiet eastern provinces; the red flood pressed on. He was to hold the flood.

He felt his eyelids fall. Electric fans lulled him with their whisper. Dust clogged his eyes. He felt ancient and immensely heavy and crushed by the map and devoured by it. The glass barrier, he thought, and, looking through it, found his brother's eyes on him. There was sorrow in them and pity and something he could not immediately define: perhaps an envy of a kind; something like that.

—How long are we supposed to hold the pass?

Michal said: —A day and a night. The Twelfth Division will be ready in twenty-four hours. It will relieve you at Zagnansk or (Michal blinked his eyes and made the troubled gesture) elsewhere It will most likely be elsewhere.

—Can you promise me any help?

Because it would be needed.

Michal became evasive. He looked at the map. He said that yes, hmm, possibly the Twelfth Division . . . it was a really remarkable division and would, against all probability, all logic, all military precedent, be ready in a day. He did not look at the General as he promised this remarkable division and suddenly the General was struck by a feeling of complete unreality, as though all of this was a grey, silent dream, the product of a tired, overheated brain, and he laughed. The sound was explosive. Other officers stared. Someone dropped a box of colored pins.

—I have a marvelous name for this division, the General said, laughing. I will call it the Miracle Division. It should be commanded by the Archangel Michal. I think he would make a remarkable commander. And while we are mobilizing the Miracle Division do you think that we could requisition rain?

Michal nodded absently. He did not seem to have heard anything. He said Oh yes, looking at the map, and Of course, and We will send you, and suddenly stopped and his mouth closed and he looked surprised. He swore. The General went on laughing.

—Why blasphemy? Is there to be no Miracle of the Zagnanski Pass? No divine intervention?

Michal said nothing. He made stricken gestures. And so the General turned to the map again and looked at it and watched the Piotrkow Gap through which a flood was pouring.

—How did that come about? he asked. How did they get across the Warta?

—Luck, Michal said. Luck and the kind of man who can recognize an opportunity. And seize it.

Such a man on the morning of the second of September was General von Reichenau, commander of the twelve-division Tenth German Army in the south, who was to push Rummel's four divisions slowly eastward, bypass the four southern divisions of Szylling's Krakow Army and form an anvil against which the Fourteenth Germany Army of List was to smash Szylling with twelve more divisions. But this was not what Reichenau did. He set out to build an anvil; luck handed him a hammer.

Late on the first day of the war, after an allday battle with Szylling's northernmost division outside Czestochowa, Reichenau's panzer corps of Hoepner (First and Fourth Panzers) stumbled upon a gap of some thirty kilometers between the armies of Szylling and his neighbor Rummel. They entered this gap and stopped, confused. Hoepner had orders to drive east and to flank Szylling from the north. He sent the Fourth Panzers there. But he could not resist the temptation to unleash the First Panzer Division, the Mother of German Armor, in a magnificent gallop northeast, where the mass of armor disappeared in a cloud of dust. The Fourth spent the rest of the day fighting the stubborn Polish Seventh Infantry Division, drew off before midnight and also disappeared. The rest of Reichenau's army, helped by six divisions borrowed from von Blaskowitz, pushed slowly against Rummel's line. Five of his divisions fought Szylling's incredible Seventh Infantry on a forty-kilometer front. The day ended in chaos. Reichenau did not know where Hoepner was or what he was doing but he was reasonably sure that the fiery Hoepner was not going to make an anvil for anyone out of his troopers. With Hoepner gone, Reichenau had no heavy armor, and without an armored battering ram before it his infantry fought badly. It was time for caution but Reichenau pushed on. He was not disturbed by Hoepner's disappearance.

Michal thought that von Reichenau should have been disturbed. It was not neat enough, it was too chaotic. (—It was the sort of *Schlamperei* they expect from us, Michal said.) A real soldier would have been disturbed and would have halted and withdrawn and waited for reports and made his own reports, and would have exercised some caution in view of the chaotic situation and would have failed to win the day. But Reichenau ignored Hoepner's disappearance. He remained confident. And so he should have: Even with an abbreviated armada his army outnumbered his combined opponents by two to one while List moved against Szylling from the south.

—So that's how it started, Michal said. It went all right at first; our people did well. But then, listen to this, I think it must have mystified the *Herren*. You should have heard their reports that we picked up on shortwave. They thought our people had gone mad.

Because as the day ended and the fury of the fighting passed and insanity abated, and the redstriped somberfaced staffs concluded that the day would not be one of brilliant victory, amazing reports came to von Reichenau. His enemies were dwindling by the thousand. They were abandoning the whole line that they had so bloodily and stubbornly defended. And there was more: It looked as though the Poles, driven insane, were biting their own tail. Round came their guns, the regiments faced about, and soon their guns began to shell their own positions in the east. What was it? Madness or a trap? Perhaps a mutiny. None of the Germans could understand it. They didn't know what to do.

The explanation came from Hoepner soon enough. He had found himself in the open and had run out, without knowing that he did, behind Rummel's army and cut it off from the Warta River and seized three undefended bridges and now, embarrassed, he wondered what to do because nothing remained between his tanks and the flat plains of central Poland, Lodz and Warsaw, and there was no way for him to come back.

If it was not Reichenau who commanded there, it could have been all right. The Poles might have got the bridges back. But it *was* Reichenau. And Reichenau did not react the way he should: observe, note, pass on reports and follow the timetables of the plan. He followed instinct and turned his back on Szylling (wiring apologies to the furious List) and ordered everything he had, including two panzer divisions he had borrowed from List's army, against Rummel.

And so began the second battle of the Upper Warta: an insane thing with three Polish divisions attacking east, a German panzer corps defending westward, and seven more German divisions attacking the flanks and rear of the attacking Poles.

—You can imagine how it was, Michal said. Can you picture it? A three-way slaughter rolling in the plains. There could be only one end to that kind of battle. There is now nothing, except Rummel's remnants under Thomme, between von Reichenau and Warsaw. Nothing big enough to cause him any trouble. It's only due to the miraculous confusion of the Germans that they have not come. We, for a change, are not confused. Rummel was good enough to tell us in person that he was beaten on the Upper Warta. He has been 'separated' from his troops and is having breakfast upstairs at the moment. He will shortly be placed in command of Warsaw. This, I think, is an excellent reason why you should go south and stop the Germans before they get to Warsaw. The front is cut in half. Unless we plug that opening for two days we'll never get our border armies out. What's left of Rummel's army is going to make a stand in front of Piotrkow. If you plug the other end of the gap we might have enough time to get the others out. Kutrzeba has an untouched army still in Wielkopolska.

—And what is happening elsewhere?

—Elsewhere. Hmm. Elsewhere. (Michal grew confused. He passed his hand across his face and blinked his eyes.) Bortnowski has been beaten in Pomorze. He is in full retreat. The best part of his army was trapped and massacred at Chelmno. There were even some desperate cavalry charges . . . in this day and age. Well, anyway, some of his men got out. He's joining Kutrzeba.

—What about Westerplatte?

—They are still holding out. So is the coast defense force on the Hel. If we can last another week perhaps our allies will decide to come.

—Yes. And perhaps there will be rain? Or some other timely miracle?

—We could use one.

—Rain, allies, miracles!

He left to requisition what he would need at Radom: maps and the like. He would have liked to requisition strength and freshness and youth and, yes, why not, rain too, but they were unavailable. He was told whom he could expect to fight on the Zagnanski Pass. The Second Panzer Division was coming there from Czestochowa and the Fourth Light was in the area and there were some armored SS troops and a Slovak mountain brigade.

Michal caught up with him before he left the staff. His face was open and he looked ashamed. He pressed the General's shoulder.

—Forgive me, he said. It is the fatigue.

—I know.

—I am tired of promising miracles. But it is a habit. I speak like this twenty times a day. There is no end to the promises I make. I am the Marshal's maker of promises. You have heard of rainmakers? Well, we have promise makers. I make them to everyone to whom I transmit an order.

—There have been orders, then? He controls the battle?

—The Marshal has finally begun to control the land battle. It is late, I admit, but it is progress. We are making progress, you see. We are no longer waiting for Allied permission to save ourselves. We are to regroup and counterattack and make marvelous maneuvers. It is progress. We're even talking about an offensive.

There was nothing that he could say to this so the General said nothing. Michal went on. —What we need most is time to draw a breath. To buy time we need divisions. All I can do is promise them when I transmit orders. I have forgotten how not to promise miracles. I have formed this habit. I should not say to you that you will have help unless I am sure, and, of course, I am not sure. There may not be anything to send. But, on the other hand (Michal grinned suddenly and made a burlesque imitation of his vague, apologetic gesture), we may find something and, who knows, we may even get the Twelfth Division ready in two days.

—Good, said the General. Now both men laughed. —I will expect the Twelfth Miracle Division. I will expect its arrival in a rainstorm.

—We can send you a rainstorm, Michal said. We are mobilizing one.

—I can depend on this?

—It is a promise.

—But after consideration I would not like to have the Archangel Michael. Perhaps you can find work for him on the staff.

—Most likely, Michal said.

—He could make rain.

—Or promises?

—He would be good at that. He could take charge of air operations. Could he make our allies fight?

—Ah, now you ask too much, Michal said. You line commanders have lost all sense of proportion.

—Well, he could scorch their tails with his flaming sword.

—Certainly, Michal said, he could do that. But if you will agree, it might not be enough.

Later, accompanying him to the car, Michal was quiet. Both men were quiet, then, with the laughter gone. Both were surprised at having laughed and, somehow, ashamed.

The sky was clear. There were no clouds. The sun was white. A plane droned overhead: Polish, judging by its thin, stuttering motor.

The General looked at it. He thought about Adam; he wondered where Adam was and if he was still alive. He had tried not to think about him, as if such thoughts were a part of peace, inadmissible in wartime. But the small, gliderlike Polish fighterplanes reminded him of Adam. He could not help thinking about the boy when he saw them. Adam flew gliders and would have been drafted to fight in the air if this had been an ordinary war, the kind where there was time to draft recruits. The General listened to the thin, feverish droning of the fighter and, for a moment, he was sure that it was Adam who piloted the diminutive steel bird.

—Have we lost many aircraft? he had to ask.

—About sixty percent of everything we had. Two hundred in five days. Michal's voice had kindness. He looked at his brother's hardened, noncommittal face carefully and kindly.

—They don't have much chance up there. But they've done better than anyone could hope. They've downed 540 German aircraft so far. . . . Were you thinking about Adam?

—Yes. I know this is no time for private worries. But . . . He shrugged, looking at the plane droning its small circles overhead.

—You are a hard man, Janusz. I wondered if you'd ask.

—I've tried not to wonder. This is no time for anyone to think like a father. Thoughts like that disarm a man, do you know?

—Of course.

—But I can't help wondering if he is all right. He wasn't drafted, was he?

—We took no recruits. Perhaps later. If the war lasts longer.

—Ah, later. If the rain comes and the Allies move.

—He isn't in Warsaw. I talked with Irena a few days ago. She told me Adam was away, climbing mountains with some friends somewhere. She said she thought he was in Switzerland. She plans to go there too.

—She would, of course.

And suddenly the General felt a touch of shame. There was relief, of course, that Adam was safe; but also shame, as if it were a kind of treason for any Pole, no matter what his age, to be safe at this time. No one should be safe. And because he was ashamed of his immense relief, he said: —And Pawel? Do you know anything about him?

Michal shook his head.

—His brigade is gone. Some of them were trapped at Chelmno. Some are coming down into the southern pocket. I don't even know if he ever reached them. With everything collapsing there is no way to check the whereabouts of individuals. Will you ask for him when you get to Radom? He might be there, somewhere.

—I will.

He wanted to tell Michal not to worry, not to add to his enormous burden; because a man like Pawel was not easily destroyed. But was this still true, any more than anything else that he had believed?

They shook hands. It was time to go.

—Go with God, Michal said.

—You still believe in God?

—I must believe in something or I will go mad. And so I tell myself that He is still there, that He has not abdicated. But, you know, it is like everything else that I say these days: I can't believe it.

—Yes.

—So, go with God.

—For lack of a good infantry division?

—For that lack.

They drove south through Wilanow and Piaseczno, where the pleasure beaches and excursion grounds were quiet now and abandoned and the woods were still, taking this back way to avoid the refugees and lost transports and bewildered animals that were sure to be clogging the main highway into Radom, but there was no way to avoid refugees on any road. Each road carried its own river of despair: an endless caravan of people, carts and cattle.

The car worked its way slowly through the columns. The driver kept falling asleep. Once the car left the road and hit a milestone and the radiator burst. The young driver woke and looked surprised and grinned stupidly watching the steam. Later the General drove and the driver slept. The thin humming of highflying German planes was a lullaby. In time, the streams of refugees thinned out and were replaced by soldiers in retreat.

The General didn't know how long the drive lasted. Once he fell into a sweating, restless nightmare that resembled sleep but was not sleep and brought no rest. He woke from this to see a dead, burned pilot in a leather coat and thought that it was Adam, and also thought that it could *not* be Adam because Adam was his son and he could not be dead like that: senselessly burned and alone at the side of a road.

If the boy was in Switzerland, and safe for now, he knew he should be grateful. He had kept careful track of him through the years . . . school . . . gliders . . . mountainclimbing . . . all of it. Michal reported all of it in his many letters. He had felt pride when he read about the gliders and the mountainclimbing and wondered, now and then, if Adam had a girl. He wondered what kind of man his son had become and what, if anything, he thought of his father and if the two of them would ever feel more than this curiosity.

There was a time, after all, under the bluetipped pine, by the Wiselka . . . surely that meant something. But it was a time without Lala and that made it not quite real, dreamlike and unimportant; part sleep, part nightmare, like the road.

He drove like the somnambulistic author of this nightmare, thinking of Adam and then of Lala and feeling nothing, desirous of nothing. It was all gone. She had come with him, as he had asked, and what he had pretended was a new beginning had quickly turned into the end. Still he had gone through all the motions. There had been the difficulties about the apartment. There were innumerable apartments whose wealthy owners were patriotically leaving for the country on the threshold of war. But it seemed that despite this plethora of apartments they were hard to find.

Oh, not for him. There would have been no difficulty about finding a magnificent apartment for the General. Happy to be of service, General. But in view of this and that and, yes, the other, the General was sure to understand . . . most difficult . . . regrets. Proud to accommodate the General, of course, but if the General permitted an observation . . . No? Well, no offense was meant, of course, no offense. It was so difficult to find a suitable apartment, suitable for what the General had in mind.

And then the invitations. For him alone. He did not go, of course. Lala said nothing about the invitations. He ignored them until the party at the Europejski, where he had gone on orders. He had insisted that she come with him.

—They would not dare. Nobody would dare!

Oh, but how do you fight a smile? How do you parry the thrust of an eye, the slashing stroke of a back turned and a hand not offered and a word unsaid? She took herself and her love away.

And suddenly, while the enormous sun burned through the thin cloth of his cap and the dust billowed fatly and the dimeyed figures scattered in the dust before the car and the car drove past the bent red necks and the wavering battle guidons and the bayonets askew everywhichway under the very near sun, he too wished that he could do this: remove himself from the war, since he could not offer everything.

He could do it still: ask for and receive a discharge, being an invalid, and find what he had lost when she withdrew her love.

No one would think badly of him if he left the war. Bortnowski had offered his resignation after the massacre at Chelmno. Rummel had left his army on the bloody road from the Upper Warta. No one thought badly of them. And if they did, would it matter? The world was ending anyhow.

And suddenly their home was there: the whitetimbered house, a corner of his room, a gleam of blue wallpaper and the checkered pattern that every morning turned the floor into a chessboard. Her bed had one leg shorter than the others.

There it was: the room. While in the other he could hear her moving. It was an extraordinarily clear and peaceful picture and he tried to hold onto it, but the next moment he felt a soft touch of air moving past his neck and the windshield exploded in a hundred fragments and something knocked persistently on the side of the car and, when his vision cleared (with the picture shadowed, interrupted), he saw that the young driver sitting erect beside him no longer had a face. He heard the echoes of the shots: an automatic. The sniper must have seen his badges in his Zeiss binoculars.

The driver fell out of the car. The General drove alone.

It occurred to him that in this war roads did not exist to speed transport but to hinder it. All day the car edged through the exodus. Finally, at Warka, he abandoned it. He requisitioned a horse from a farmer and galloped cross-country. Wind whipped him. The thud of hooves on dew-wet grass was long remembered and he listened to the comforting, familiar creak of saddleleather and thought of the other times, the charges and marches and maneuvers when this was the only reality, the only consideration, and men and animals matched men and animals and not machines. He drove his horse on until the animal foundered but he was then on the outskirts of Radom and the walk was short. Time was also short. In the south rolled the dull echoes of an artillery bombardment and over Radom wheeled flights of Junkers-88 dive-bombers: straddlewinged Stukas. Smoke rolled over Radom. In the smoke: the crack of explosions, the rumble of collapsing buildings. Fire. Scarlet chaos. Streets filled with men, mostly terrified civilians. Some of the refugees were soldiers. They wore the badges of Rummel's shattered regiments. Others were reservists waiting for assignment. They had been waiting since the war began. They bivouacked in small groups under tents of overcoats and blankets, under overturned carts, in doorways and courtyards. A few wore uniforms. The rest were in peasant coats, mechanic's smocks, overalls, street clothes. One man, in riding boots and a turtleneck sweater, wore an African pith helmet. The sprays of flowers and blossoms pinned to their lapels were wilted. Shrapnel and bomb fragments fell among them and masonry fell on them and their pathetic shelters vanished in dust and shattered timbers, and each time they reassembled after an avalanche of bricks and mortar they were fewer, and each time an officer showed in the streets they trailed behind him, like homeless dogs, begging for rifles.

—For God's sake, sir. That is all we want. Give us rifles. Lead us. Tell us what to do.

It was the booted man in the pith helmet.

—Wait, the General said.

—I have waited since Friday morning. Since the first day!

What could he say to this grotesque apparition who wanted to fight? The General felt sweat beading on his forehead. He had thought there was no more sweat or any other moisture left in him. He had thought that it had all boiled out of him in the hot day under the everpresent sun, that he had been cooked dry and emptied like a wineskin, yet now he sweated.

He had to say something. The man's eyes were insistent. What could he promise him?

—Later, he said, feeling inadequate. Spread the word and be ready. I will call on you later today.

Scorn spread at once on the man's face. Clearly he had heard this many times in the past five days. These were not words that he could believe.

—Later? (The man began to mouth obscenities.) Tomorrow perhaps? When the Germans come? Is that what all of you want? Have you sold us to the Germans at so much a pound? Don't you want anyone to stop the Germans?

Somehow the General lost the man in a new shower of bricks and mortar and a new dustcloud. He escaped in the dustcloud.

At the *komendantura* there were no sentries at the door and no one inside. Doors hung open. The floors were littered with paper and halfeaten food. From somewhere in the bowels of the building came a great rumbling voice raised in anger. The General ran down the stairs towards the cellar. The cellar door was open. Inside someone shouted in a deep voice and someone else made ineffectual bleating sounds. Two soldiers stood outside the cellar door. They listened to the sounds coming out of the cellar. The soldiers grinned at each other and rolled their eyes towards the cellar door. They gestured to show that someone inside had lost his mind. They jumped apart when they saw the General and the General pushed his way into the cellar between the now rigid soldiers.

Light from an unshaded lightbulb struck him, then swung away. The bare, wildswinging light without cover cast sharp black shadows on the opposite wall, a paperlittered desk, dust. Pale light seeped through the sandbagged windows. Behind the desk sat a fat, elderly major of the *intendentura* whose face was grey and mottled and corrupt, whose eyes sagged and who made bleating sounds. His spectacles had fallen off and hung from one ear, aslant his face, giving him the look of an insane owl, a great drunken bird beating against the night.

The other man was a major of infantry. He was enormously broad. He had a red face and a long grey mustache and a dirty grey bandage on his head and he was shouting. He held the elderly major by the front of his tunic and shook him. The elderly major beat the air with pudgy hands. The swinging lightbulb cast alternate palls of darkness and white light on their faces so that they seemed to be taking turns at peeking out of darkness: first the white, softmottled face, then the red one.

—I will eat you! I will tear your head off! the redfaced major shouted, and the elderly fat major bleated: —Cossack! Anarchist! You are strangling me!

When they saw the General, the redfaced major dropped the elderly fat major, who fell into his seat like an animated sack of potatoes and screamed in a high, woman's voice about assault and charges and courts-martial law and criminal proceedings and officers' courtsofhonor and duels and satisfactions and insults and provocations and redfaced barbarians and seniority and years of service and respect due his years of service, and at the point of his appeal for justice in view of his years of service the General cut him short.

—Explain, he said, cold. You have thirty seconds.

—Madness, the major bleated. Murderer. Assault. Unprovoked. Unjust. (He could not find his breath.)

Was he the *komendant* of the town?

Yes sir, the major had the honor to report. Oh yes indeed. And as such he was entitled to respect. His years of service . . .

Was he the *komendant* of the garrison of Radom?

—Yes, General. Well, that is to say . . .

—What is there to say?

That is to say that there was no garrison, the major hastened to explain. Oh, there were men, yes, at least he thought there were, but he could not say whether or not they could still be considered a garrison. There was a battalion of the Ninety-third Regiment at Radom, but the barracks had been bombed every day and now the major was not sure what was left of it. There had also been some headquarters troops and the *komendantura* staff but the staff had gone somewhere and no, the major did not know where the men had gone, and here he was alone, with the Germans coming, and now maniacs were running in with impossible demands and all of this was just too much for him.

—In all my years of service, General. In all that time, I have never seen such a state of affairs.

It was, the fat major said, impossible. It was unbelievable. Someone should review the situation. There should be inquiries. There should be an official investigation. He would personally render a report. —Maniacs! Anarchists!

—Enough, the General said. Now *you* speak. Who the devil are you?

The redfaced major with the mustache suddenly sat down. It was as though all strength, all hope, had suddenly ebbed from his body. It was as though his bones had melted. The glass barrier, the General thought.

—Stand up, he said. Report!

The major rose. He brought his hand up in salute as though his arm had moved without his will, almost despite his will. His eyes were scarlet. Still, his voice, although suddenly hoarse and low, was firm enough.

His name was Tarski. He had brought two battalions of the Fortieth Regiment into the town for rest and replacements. The regiment had been attacked by aircraft and almost destroyed. He had collected fifteen hundred men and brought them to Radom. They had come in before dawn and were now lying about the railroad yards waiting for food. They had not eaten in two days and many of them were ill. Most of their equipment had been lost when their train was bombed.

The major had come to the *komendantura* to requisition food and medical supplies and to obtain replacements. The *komendant* of the town and of the garrison refused him the supplies. He would not issue them without a written order from his superiors. There had to be a written order followed by an official requisition form followed by an official receipt. As for replacements, well, Major Tarski could not have those either. The reservists in the town were part of the replacement pool of the Sixteenth Division. They could not be assigned to any other unit. It was perfectly understandable, perfectly orderly. The Sixteenth Division was on the Ossa River in the north, or had been there, and unless General Boltuc asked for these replacements they could not be given to anybody else. This was the correct procedure, was it not?

The redfaced major had finished speaking and now stood silent while the fat elderly major asked whether or not the procedures were correct. The redfaced major looked suddenly tired and not so broad. He seemed to have shrunk within himself. His eyes were like thin, bloody slits in his scarlet face. The heavy stone walls of the cellar shook to near explosions. Screams of the dying and the wounded came in through the sandbagged window.

As the elderly fat major told about the reservists his voice shifted to a higher pitch. —What can I do? They are a sea! They come all day and all night without orders, without a place to report to, and I cannot feed them or arm them or do anything with them. I have no orders to do anything with them. There is this wonderful enthusiasm to fight, to do something. But what can I do? Are wars fought with enthusiasm? Are we no longer bound by discipline? Are orders and correct procedures no longer necessary? Some of the men have been on the road from as far as Krakow. There are more than ten thousand of them in the town. And there is not a rifle to be found between here and Kielce, and now this redfaced maniac comes in and assaults me, and I am the *komendant* of the town and of the garrison, and is this just payment for my years of service?

The major of the *intendentura* had clearly lost control of his command and of himself. The two soldiers who had been laughing outside were quiet now, with heads poked into the cellar to watch the show. Their mouths were open.

The elderly fat major waved at them to make them go away but they paid no attention.

—There are no rifles here?

—No sir. Nothing, sir.

—Nothing.

—Well, not exactly nothing, sir, the elderly fat major said. His flaccid cheeks were trembling and now pink splotches of color appeared in them. There was the battalion of the Ninety-third Regiment in town and it had rifles and there were undoubtedly some rifles that had belonged to the dead and wounded. But really, if the General allowed a comment, the major had had little time to worry about rifles. There were reports to make and forward to Warsaw and there were administrative details to complete each day and God only knew where the *komendantura* staff had got to. He could not do everything alone.

—But there are men?

—Yes sir. Oh yes.

There were the men in their bewildered thousands, the fat major said. It was impossible for an officer to walk the streets without becoming besieged, importuned. —They threw stones at me yesterday, he complained. I have not heard of such a thing in twenty-five years of service!

A sound like laughter came from the redfaced major. The fat major ignored him.

—What don't they want? Holy Mother, General! They want rifles and uniforms and boots. Some only want a cap with an eagle. But do they have orders? Do they bring me an authorization? What can I do? Am I the Quartermaster General? Am I the Marshal, to issue equipment without authorization?

—So you have done nothing? For that you need no orders, is that so?

The General did not see the fat major clearly. A red haze seemed to obscure the man. It was compounded of fury and pain and disappointment and disgust. The General wished to strike, to destroy this ineffectual man. Then reason came. Nothing was anybody's fault. It was a different war and the rules were all different and it was like no war the elderly major would remember. I also am a stranger to such wars: of papers and political decisions, of arrangements made by telephone with distant unseen men while the walls shook to the sound of the very near explosions and men died without reason, uselessly, under avalanches of stone and mortar.

No quick bright flash of purpose here, no hooves thundering on grass. The enemy kills from a distance and the friend kills from an even greater distance and there is no way for a fighting soldier to feed and arm his men without authorization.

The General turned to the redfaced major. —Are you tired? he said. How tired are you?

The officer stared at him.

—Answer me!

—I am not tired, sir.

—You are now the *komendant* of the garrison and of the town. Issue all food and all supplies to your men and to the reservists. Issue them uniforms and arms. Organize them into companies. Post patrols on the roads and collect all men in uniform they find on the roads. Arms? I will get the arms. Are there bicycles? Horses? Send messengers to intercept retreating columns on other roads. I want five thousand men on the Zagnanski Pass before noon.

—Sir, I protest. (It was the elderly fat major.) This is injustice! Sir!

His glasses fell off his face and broke on the floor. The fat man groped for them.

—Sir, this is without precedent . . . years of service . . . no authorization . . .

The General ignored him. He straddled a chair as though it were a horse. He drew the telephone towards him and began shouting into it.

There were rifles in the arsenal at Deblin and he ordered them delivered the way a woman orders groceries delivered, and there were three clean blue-smelling antiaircraft quickfiring Bofors to be had in Konskie, and in Suchedniow he had passed some shellshocked cavalry wandering about the fields, and in the Hall of the Veterans of the Bolshevik War (a war of quick bright purpose, of thundering hooves, of ultimate decision delivered with a saberstroke) three Russian Maxim guns stood in glass cases, and the military museum of Radom had the ammunition for these impossible antiques, and every man in this gamethick land had a rifle which could be collected and aimed at human game, and three more machineguns could be gouged out of the broken wings and body of a downed PZL fighter near Skaryszew, and a battle group could and would be formed and led to stop the Germans.

Later, when hoarseness drove him from the telephone, he left the redfaced major shouting into it with great oaths as he identified himself as General Prus: —Blood of a dog! The rifles must be sent at once! Authorization? I will give it to you: fifty staves laid across your bare ass. Is that authoritative enough? Is that sufficiently clear?

Borrowing a car from the director of the state match factory (despite more protests), the General drove to the Zagnanski Pass. The road was narrow, pocked with bomb craters, littered with broken transport and flycovered bodies in the ditches. The General took the fat major with him to Zagnansk and left him in the village to find guides. He climbed the piney ridges in the sun, which burned the combustible dry soil.

Clouds.

There were clouds above Lysagora. But the General did not think that rain would come. The thought of rain made him taste the dust on his parched, cracked lips.

He walked through the woods along the ridge. It was a hot, forbidding place: hilly and wooded, but the woods were dry and held no moisture. It was a dark place full of shadows and even the shade was hot. Yellow light fell in streams through the blazing autumnal canopies of leaves and dry pine branches and slid about the rotten, powdery logs underfoot and the tangled vegetation. It was said that even bears lost their minds in this place and turned upon men: the hunted became the hunter. Soon, now, the Germans would come.

The General climbed to the top of the quarry, which was the highest point of the ridge where he would fight his battle. Sandstone lay there hewn into blocks great enough to construct pyramids, to raise obelisks and memorials that would defy all time. Sun bounced off them in white waves of heat.

He shut his eyes for a moment, being so profoundly tired and wanting to shut out the sun, to keep it out, to exclude it from the dry pores of his body, and wished that Grzes had come with him from Warsaw, because Grzes, the old soldier, would either have a flask of spirits somewhere about him or would know where to steal one. He could well use artificial stimulation. It would revive him. It would bring back the taste of brandy drunk after long-remembered victories. But Grzes had stayed in Warsaw. His age had kept him from the Army. He had grown red in face and his mustache had quivered and bright tears had gleamed in his eyes and he swore terribly but the medical officers had been unimpressed and refused to talk about enlisting fifty-year-old corporals with sick hearts. Afterwards the old soldier had been terribly ashamed and had hidden in the kitchen.

I could use him now, the General thought.
Rest too. Food?
And food perhaps.
He did not think he could chew any food. Water, then? Water: the thought was cool and fresh and it evaporated in the heat as quickly as it came.
There had been no time for rest and no time for food; perhaps at some later date . . . Time: That was what he had come to buy on the Zagnanski Pass.

From where he stood he could see the two hills left and right of the road about five kilometers apart, and the forest stretching brownly east and south-east as far as he could see, and above the forest hung the yellow-white brow of Lysagora, the Bald Mountain, the place of witches. This was the battlefield-to-be. Crows wheeled in cawing, anticipatory arcs over it. For them there would soon be both rest and feast and drink.
He found a small, conveniently low stump to sit on and closed his eyes without wishing to close them, as though the simple act of sitting had triggered some mechanism in his brain that shouted: Rest. Lids fell, the white glare vanished to be replaced by scarlet, pierced by the slanting beams of the remorseless sun that fell, with almost tangible solidity, through the piney branches and the taller greenleaf ceiling, and at once he saw his bedroom in grey morning light. Lala in the familiar silk robe was holding her small machine for making cigarettes. The picture was still. He savored it: the play of light on her fingers about the machine, the spilled tobacco shreds in her silk lap, the sheen of hair and white curve of her young neck and the small shadow her nose made on her far cheek—all terribly familiar. But he seemed to be seeing her as through a barrier of glass, and as he watched her making her two-hundredth cigarette he wondered whom she was making it for. He, obviously, would not be able to cross the invisible barrier to smoke it. And why was she wearing her silk robe in the afternoon? It must be afternoon if she was making her two-hundredth cigarette.
Now and then he shook his head and opened his eyes and saw the luminous, quivering blue sky through the leaves, and when he closed his eyes the picture immediately returned. It, and she in it, were frozen as though caught

in a cloud of chemical vapor which paralyzed all motion. All was stone: wall and its optimistically blue paper, girl; and only the light trembled flamelike on her fingers.

He sat like that for what could have been hours but was, in all probability, seconds, hearing the soft sounds of the forest and the louder crackle of large bodies moving in it, and the dull rolling thunder of artillery firing south of Kielce. Soon the fat major and the tracker came.

He heard the major tripping on the forest path. The major's glasses had been broken. He came heavily through the bushes, led by a small brown man in a huntingcoat. The fat officer was wet with sweat. The tracker moved lightly through the bracken as though floating above it. They stopped at a respectful distance from the General and watched him.

I must look like Rodin's *Thinker,* he thought, or *The Young Napoleon.* Or *The Emperor at Austerlitz.* We had, this morning, the red sun of Austerlitz, and what a fine, military picture we all make: the General with his chin in hand staring into the distance, planning victories, communing with the God of War, the staff respectful in the background. Fit for a history book. Or for a painting to be hung in the Museum Wojska. This made him laugh. That dissolved the picture.

—Yes, he said to the others. They came forward.

—This is the guide, the major said. His name is Bogacz. There were some others but they would not come. This one wanted to come.

The major looked longingly at a treestump and the General told him to sit down. The tracker squatted on his heels. He was small, almost freakishly delicate. His face was burned a deep brown by the sun and wind. His hands were competent around the butt of a Mannlicher rifle. He said nothing, waiting for the General, and soon the General spoke:

—You know this place?

The tracker nodded. He stared calmly into the General's eyes.

—You know the paths and the tracks? You know the crossings through the mountains?

Again the nod.

—Do you know what we must do here?

—I have waited for you, the man said suddenly.

—For me?

—For you or another like you, master. I wished to help.

—Tracker, we will need your help, the General said. The Germans are coming. We must stop them here for a day. We do not have as many men or machines as they have, do you understand? You and the forest must help us.

—No one can come through the forest who does not know the paths.

—And you know them?

—Yes. And they do not. They will not have machines to help them in the forest.

—We will destroy their machines on the road and in the fields before the forest, but when they come into the forest after us there must be no way for anyone to take them around us. They must meet us wherever they go.

—Yes, the small man said. I will show you where this can be done.

—Let us go then, the General said. Show me where we can ambush them.

The small man rose in one swift motion so that for a moment it seemed

258

that he had not been seated at all and turned and walked into the forest. The General followed him. At times the tracker vanished around thick clumps of towering bracken, or strayed to left and right to stare into sandy patches that covered quicksand. At times he stopped to listen; he smelled the hot air, fingered it. They walked a long time. The General wondered if Major Tarski had gathered enough men. He wondered if he had put them on the road already. He wondered what would happen if the Germans came before the men arrived.

From time to time they came out into clearings and these yawned brightly in the sunspeckled corridors between tall trees. There jasmine was yellow. From one such clearing the General looked northward and saw a thick white dustcloud heavy above the road to Radom. Steel glinted in it. Soon the men would come. He followed the guide and noted in his mind's eye all the clearings and quaking morass and the deadfall of timber and stone where men could barricade themselves and turn the forest into a greenandyellow fortress.

There was a gauntness and a darkness about this place despite the sunlight and the green of bushes, and the occasional soft branch of a pine brushing against his face had a musky odor which he could not define immediately. It could be old fur laden with dust, or some other thing vaguely redolent of danger; the thing eluded him. He asked about the smell and the tracker told him.

—It is the smell of bears, he said.

—In this place? (It seemed too low, too near the road for bears.) I did not think a bear would come so far down the mountains.

—There is this one bear, the tracker said, looking hard into the darkness of the treewall. He walks here and elsewhere. He walks where he wishes. I have learned all his paths and all his roads, and I know that if he wished to come here or into the road he would do so.

—The road would frighten him, the General said, but the tracker said no.

Nothing would frighten this bear, he explained. The path they trod now was the private road of the mankilling bear, the Old One, the Mankiller of Lysagora. No, the tracker did not think the Old One would be afraid of anything.

—Has he been hunted? the General wished to know.

—Yes, several times. And also he has hunted.

—Perhaps you will see him. Shoot him if you see him. We need meat for the men when they come.

The tracker shook his head but said nothing. Clearly he would not shoot if the bear came upon him and the General wondered about that but not for long. The white cloud of dust was high now on the road and nearing and the General told the tracker to guide him there quickly. They came out of the forest into the road and soon out of the dustcloud came a Radom taxicab and stopped and Major Tarski got out of it to report.

Five thousand men were on the way, he said, all armed. From Radom the remaining companies of the Ninety-third and the battalions of the Fortieth, and three thousand men out of the reserve pool of the Sixteenth Division, and one hundred and fifty-eight men who were all that now remained from Colonel Janicki's Seventh Division. Leading them was a Captain Pelz, a sapper. Major Tarski had brought him in the taxicab. The General had not heard about the destruction of the Seventh Division. He had known Janicki, the commander of the divisional infantry, who had taken over the division from its ill commander. How was he? Captain Pelz didn't know. He was a small, slim officer in his late thirties and he looked very tired. He did not know what had happened to Colonel Janicki but the division was destroyed. No help would come from there, then.

—How were you destroyed?

—First we were hit and then we prayed and then we committed suicide, Captain Pelz said.

He laughed. His eyes were dull with shock.

—When the war began we lay across a series of small hills west of Czestochowa, a stone's throw from Germany. We covered forty miles. There is nothing unusual about that, I expect. It is impossible to cover forty miles of line with one incomplete division. We were supposed to tie in on the right with some cavalry of Rummel. On Friday morning we were attacked by five divisions of Reichenau, four of them armored or motorized. Divebombers. Tanks. They came in lines of four hundred at a time. In seven hours they had run us over. We marched northeast for the rest of the day and fought five battles and we marched at night and yesterday morning we got to Czestochowa and here we prayed for rain and miracles. As you see, sir, there is no rain and I imagine there will be no miracles.

The captain laughed his stilted laugh again.

The General thought about Czestochowa, the Holy City, home of the monastery which houses the miraculous painting of the Virgin, Mother of Christ and Queen of Poland, under whose particular protection Poland is said to be. In the late sixteenth century the painting had been slashed by a Swedish soldier and had bled.

Here the Seventh rested. —Rest, what a word, the captain said. What a miraculous word that was to us. But of course there were no real miracles anymore and so there was no rest.

There was no food and they were out of ammunition and the wagons had been lost in the nightfight with tanks and it had been a long time since anyone had seen a fieldkitchen with a smoking stack, but rest is a good substitute for food, is it not? And, who knows, perhaps in this holy place a small miracle might occur, like perhaps an unscheduled delivery of a shipment of manna, and the men might eat.

—So we thought, believing, Captain Pelz said. Colonel Janicki was wounded and in fever. No miracle appeared but the Germans did. The Fourth and Fourteenth German infantry divisions began to attack. They had, of course, their usual divebombers. We had, of course, the usual hunger and no ammunition.

The battle lasted all day, with houses changing hands several times and each street, square, courtyard, garden fence, wall and gateway a place of bitter carnage. Men did not merely die; they were exterminated. Where they fought nothing lived. There was no miracle. The holy city fell before midnight. The Germans drew back and did not follow the Seventh Division on its night march out.

—We walked about a mile into the darkness, the Captain said. Colonel Janicki, who had been wounded several times, fell into a coma, saw visions and fainted several times. About a mile from Czestochowa we walked into a tank regiment of Hoepner's Fourth Panzers, the same people who had run over us the day before. In the darkness they took us for Germans and stopped to ask for directions. We attacked. It was a short battle, perhaps an hour or two. The panzers were destroyed. Colonel Janicki put us on the road again and there began an insane march with German tanks driving out of side roads to join our column and German companies and ours walking behind each other in the same direction until someone recognized who the other was and each milestone was a battlefield that began as surprise and ended as slaughter. No one took prisoners. It went on like that until perhaps four o'clock yesterday morning. Then a wounded cavalry officer of Rummel's Wolynska Brigade was brought to the colonel and told him that Rummel was off in the night and beaten and that we were the only Polish unit between the Germans and General Szylling's rear.

Rummel's troops, the cavalryman reported, were falling back in the general direction of Piotrkow and Tomaszow and farther north towards Lodz. They were badly shocked. But they had untouched depots and if the Seventh joined them it would be fed and rearmed and put in the reserve and rest for a day or so. Rummel had fought well to the front of his prepared positions so that all his supplies were intact. The other alternative for the Seventh Division was to march on to Janow, a small town on the Wiercica River where clouds of dust during the day hinted at a concentration of tanks. This was undoubtedly a German force preparing to come down on Szylling's rear the next day.

—We were about five thousand strong then, Captain Pelz said. That is, five thousand bayonets and sabers. There was no way to inform General Szylling that his flanks were gone. We were cut off from him and there wasn't one radio in the whole division. But the colonel thought that if we fought the Germans at Janow someone would hear the sounds of the battle and warn our General. We went on to Janow. No one challenged us. The town was shuttered, the streets swept clean of anything alive. Dogs barked, that is all. But from the woods around the town came the smell of hot food and the clatter of messtins and laughter and conversation. You know, General, the whole ghostly spectrum of sound that a mass of soldiers makes. This was the panzer corps of Hoth, in from the north. We went into them with bayonets straight off the road. They did not expect us. The work was quick, as is the way with bayonets, and in two hours we had cleared the woods. And then the First Panzers, who were the only people to hear the sounds of the battle, came in from the south and shortly afterwards it was all finished.

Captain Pelz did not think that many men had survived. He had gathered a company of all arms and marched them to Wloszczowa, where they commandeered a train and drove it into Kielce. Then in a commandeered excursion coach they came to Radom and there Major Tarski took them off the road.

—So here we are, sir. The Seventh Infantry Division. I imagine I am now a divisional commander.

And now the first ranks of his men went past: grey in face, bloody and incoherent. Some sang. Others were silent. No one looked at the officers at the side of the road. Behind them rode some cavalry on gaunt horses. The men slept in the saddles. Then with much sweat and grinning and self-consciousness came a small group of elderly men in longremembered uniforms too tight for them. These were the Veterans of the Bolshevik War with their three ancient machineguns. The General looked at the major. Tarski shrugged. —They insisted, he said. More soldiers followed, and a troop of horse artillery went by and the three Bofors guns pulled by taxicabs. From Suchedniow came a small medical detachment. Major Tarski said that another fifteen hundred men would arrive from Kielce.

Then out of the shimmering dust cloud came the cadets of Deblin, the Air Force pilots' school beyond the Vistula. The last two classes had been hastily commissioned and sent to flying squadrons. These were the starting classes. They had good skyblue uniforms and marched magnificently, singing a marching song.

All were young, the oldest could not have been over seventeen, and their small, pinkcheeked faces were lost under the deep rims of their helmets. There was a banner with an eagle at the head of their column and each company had a guidon. It was a brave sight. It was the sort of sight that acts like a drink of water on a hot day. The General thought: These boys, going up to fight, to die for the only thing that is worth dying for . . .

He rose and saluted them, and the other officers also rose and stood saluting and the tall Air Force lieutenant colonel who led the column commanded an eyes-left and six hundred pairs of young eyes stared at the General.

—They brought the rifles from the arsenal at Deblin, Major Tarski said. His face seemed redder than before and his mustache moved up and down. His voice was particularly gruff. —It is the entire academy. I think they are too young. I think they should not be here.

—Who has a better right than they? It is their future that will be decided.

—But they are children, sir!

—There are no children anymore. There may have been once but now there are only men and women, only Poles and Germans. Do you understand?

He watched the cadets until dust swallowed them at the bend of the road.

Thursday, September the seventh

I THE WALNUT

He had fallen asleep and the war was lost. Sometime during the night, between the fortieth and the forty-first shuddering groan, the hundredth muscular contraction aimed at displacing the explorer ants, the war had slipped between their fingers and fallen with a hellish crash and was now lost. He had closed his eyes for only a moment and the war was lost. The soldier called the Walnut had lost it.

He struggled to awake because a monster squatted on his chest breathing fire. He was hot. And thirsty.

His first thought was: a spider. But if it was a spider astride his chest it was the biggest of all spiders, the holy father of them all. He was entangled in a monstrous web and some foul, hairy thing was strangling him, sucking his blood. . . . But it was only the heat, after all, reaching for him with a hundred small, tenacious tentacles. His pores pumped out a sticky moisture. Where had the air gone?

The soldier Walnut struggled to awake. He felt that he should say something, apologize, explain. He felt badly, so badly about the war. He had not meant to lose it. If only he wasn't quite so fat, he thought, so soft and plump and so ridiculous. If only war was something you could argue like a case. Your Honor, excellencies, I submit. My client has just claim to victory in this war; the right is on my client's side. All the nobility and chivalry, the breeding and quality is here. My opponent, the antagonist, is ignoble, Sir. He . . . they have no humanity. Sir, they are soulless. It is after all a matter of justice, Sir. Justice. My opponent has shrugged off all human decency. He obeys no rules. Ah, Sir, worse yet: He makes his own rules. On my client's standards are engraved God, Honor, Motherland. On the opposition's: *Ein Reich, Ein Volk, Ein Führer*. The right has always triumphed, Sir; it must triumph. Otherwise what is the use of moral law? Why proscribe evildoing unless it is punished? It has been so for nineteen hundred years. And You are with us not against us, Sir. The archbishop said so. (I heard him personally, kneeling in the ninety-seventh rank in the cathedral square, while he blessed the standards.) We had, Sir, his specific assurance, his personal guarantee that You were on our side. Well, Sir, in view of the above . . . what kind of verdict is this?

Meanwhile, the murderous heat.

God, thought the soldier Orzech (Walnut) Orzechowski, I must stink. All this sweat. Is there no end to it? Kula, that dirty peasant, hasn't washed in fifteen sweaty days. Why in God's name did I share his blanket?

He struggled up from under the blanket, pushing the bony bare rump of the man snuggled up against him. He couldn't quite remember where he was. He didn't know where he had been yesterday or where he was now and, certainly, he did not think he would be anywhere tomorrow. But he knew that he had lost the war.

And it had all begun so well. The bands had played such fine music and the crowds had wept and laughed and waved and the girls had come running with flowers, sticking green fragrant sprigs into their rifle barrels and draping their knapsacks with garlands so that the whole column of new-made soldiers took on the aspect of a Bacchanal. The soldiers laughed, shaking their heads and nodding at the noncoms, who walked grim (but with heads averted so as not to see this breach of discipline), and they accepted the fruit and the sweet things thrust at them. Oh it was marvelous. His tunic was too tight and he sweated horribly.

But that was not unusual. He had always sweated at the slightest provocation. At the university he had had a variety of names. Walnut was the least insulting. It was, after all, only an abbreviation of his proper name. But there were others: Tub, Bottomless Pit, Fountain, Cataract. He had sweated all his life; his life, he supposed, could be measured in gallons of sweat. He had literally floated through his law examinations, swum through the orals. He thought that he would flood the courtroom if he ever got a case. He thought that he was the fattest and wettest soldier of the Polish Army; certainly in the Warsawski Okreg. And to think that he might have been an officer! With his education he should have been an officer. Any man who had matriculated was sent to an underensigns' school, but there his grossness and his sweatiness, that twin nemesis, combined with his argumentativeness, had defeated him. Sweat, my God how he sweated. His knapsack had weighed a hundred kilos at the least even without the garlands, and his white, plump feet had quivered with every parade step, and the strain of keeping his rifle in line with those of Kula, Sowinski and Berg had paralyzed his arm. But it was such a marvelous beginning.

And at the railroad terminal before they went into the cars, when they were still loading the cars with straw for them to sit on, the relatives were allowed to come forward and surround them with their Sunday-suit smell of camphor and their anxious pride. His father hugged him and kissed him. The old Pilsudski badges and medals and the thread-bare Legion tunic squished against his sodden coat. —*Proud, Proud,* the old pharmacist said. —*Oh darling, oh my little boy.* (This from his mother.) *Be sure you change your socks and send the laundry home at least once a week. And remember, it can be cold in the mountains. Do you remember how cold it was at Zakopane when we went there? And if you get a cold or feel a fever be sure to drink some tea with rosemary and lemon.*

—*My soldier,* the father said. And Walnut exploded in a tidal wave of joy and patriotic fervor and perspiration. Look at me (he said to himself, bathed in a sea of joy and pride and sweat, blinded and glistening with all three, gasping for breath and happy, so happy, while his fat feet whimpered on the cobblestones). Look at me! How will the blue and black ribbon of the Virtuti Militari look on me? His one regret was that he had been marching in the middle and that it was Sowinski the Bolshevik who had got kissed by the flowergirls.

A marvelous beginning!

And it looked as though it would continue well at first. The regiment rode in the train and the train stopped at Radom and the regiment got out, much as a manyheaded monster might, with wiggles and jumps and scratchings and undulations, and it marched into the barracks and the people cheered. And there it stayed and waited. Then one day someone said that the war had come, that he had heard it on the radio. Someone else said that there was no war. Then bombers came and someone said that the planes were ours and it was an exercise. But when the first bombs fell on the barracks, even Kula, the stupidest man on earth, knew that it was no exercise. Many were killed that day. Many more the next day, more the next. They did not have to die like that: on their cots in the barracks, listening to the bombs falling. But no one told them what else to do. They were not allowed out of the barracks. So they stayed in the barracks and heard the bombs fall and died under them. In Walnut's barracks they had pushed mattresses into the windows to keep the shrapnel out.

And then the strange redfaced major came and talked to the officers after the latest raid (the one that flattened the kitchens and the storehouses) and the regiment was put on the road and Walnut was amazed to see how small the regiment had got to be.

They marched and then they came to some woods and went into the woods and lay down and someone told them to put blankets on themselves so that the planes would not see them and here they were.

Where?

He did not know where they were and it didn't matter. The war was lost. It had to be lost. Sometime in the night, Walnut was sure, the war had been lost and soon the Germans would come up from Kielce and take them prisoners. It was all over. It was impossible to believe. He thought that it could not be over, not like that. It could not just stop like that. It was like no war he had ever heard of or read about. Nothing had happened to him! He had stayed in bed with his mattress in the window! He couldn't remember anything. He wouldn't have anything to tell. No stories! He had not been given any medals.

No! The war was *not* over, it couldn't be. Wars did not end like that. There had to be something special about the last day of a war; perhaps the sound of trumpets in the sky or a great light or perhaps a great voice from heaven talking about swords and plowshares and pruning hooks. But the only light was the searing whiteness of a September sun, and the voice was Kula's.

—Hey, Kula said. Look up there, coming over that yellow mountain . . .

Gentle as a dragonfly, the silvery aircraft circled high above them. It would not bother them, he thought. They were no longer a military objective.

—Let's cover up, hey? He might see us. Hey, Walnut, you fat slug, cover up your belly. Do you want him to see that white mountain from up there?

—We are no longer a military objective, Walnut muttered.

Still, he drew the blanket high around his neck.

Not for a moment did he stop sweating. Oh, but this was ridiculous! This was not just a heat; it was a disease! He had dreamed that his house was on fire. He thought: I must get my clothes off. His cotton shirt was wet. His boots were squelching cups of grease. His puttees were long, stinking rags wrinkled and wet.

He looked about him, dazed by the incredible white sun. There they were in the cabbage field, Kula, Sowinski, Ryms, Kalinski, Kleinert, Ulanko, Maly and Berg, covered with blankets and tarpaulins, with grimy feet and arms and pockmarked shoulders sticking up among the cabbages. Most of them were naked under their coverings but he had not been able to force himself to take off his clothes. Kublarz had drawn away from the others (being older) and found a small bush to lie under to smoke his pipe. (Jezus! If only I had thought of that. He has shade. Yes, he sweats there, I can see that, but it must be cooler. It looks cooler.) Kublarz smoked and played with a cabbage. He bounced it up and down like a ball. Plump green cabbages in a parched field. Someone must water them. Water: That's it.

—Who's got some water?

—Germans will give you water, Kleinert said. You just wait a bit.

Ryms and Kula laughed. Kula laughed at anything. Ryms laughed at anything that Kleinert said. They had both lived in Silesia before they came to Warsaw and for two days now they had talked to each other in their Silesian dialect.

War. Was this war? Someone had handed it to them to do something with and it had slipped between their fingers and fallen with the awful crash of ten thousand china plates somewhere in the north and in the south and now it was lost. With nightfall the Germans would came and take them prisoner. For two hours there has been no sound of artillery in Kielce.

Heat, God. If only I didn't sweat so much.

Walnut looked at the others: nine men under blankets in a cabbage field; reservist soldiers, civilians in uniform who only two weeks earlier had been reading their *Kurier* and their *Dziennik* (and in the case of Sowinski, the Bolshevik paper) and with their feet on the table had yelled for their dinner. He made the tenth. Ten boys on an outing. Eight city-wise Warsaw boys and two Wilanow peasants. Ages ranging from about twenty for the *Zydek,* Berg, to forty-eight for the shaded, comfortable Pan Kublarz, the pipesmoking player with cabbages. The venerable pipesmoker had driven a waterwagon in Nalewki and sold water to the Jews. Kula was a peasant two meters tall and broad and bright as a barn. He had come to Warsaw with his boots slung around his neck and had tried to wash his hands in the flushtoilet and complained about the soap going down the drain every time he tried to get it off his hands. Sowinski: a garage mechanic from the Wola works. He had once been jailed and liked to point to his missing teeth as proof of political awareness. Ryms was a printer. Kleinert was a waiter at the Europejski and could turn a smile on and off like an electric light. Ulanko was a stable groom in Wilanow. Maly was the owner and operator of a sodawater stand in the Lunapark.

Then there was Berg, a Jew. That was enough of an occupation. Nobody knew what Jews did, and who cared, anyway? Jews were Jews and they lived their own lives and what they did with them was their own business. In the headquarters company Berg was a clerk but he didn't even know how to write Polish. He was made a clerk because nobody thought he would be good at anything else. Also he spoke German. Also he kept his mouth shut. Also he was good at leaping to attention when anybody higher than a private came into a room. And finally there was himself, Private Orzechowski, the Walnut, the Cataract, the Bottomless Pit who had been the *Akademik* Orzechowski, bachelor of laws soon to have been doctor of jurisprudence and perhaps magistrate; soon to be prisoner of war, a number, an animal in a human zoo.

The soldier Walnut Orzechowski thrust a white arm out from under his blanket to wipe a wave of sweat off his neck. He watched the German plane. The German plane flew carefully high. It flew in large circles, unhurried and unharassed. The German had a lot of time.

—What do you think he is thinking up there? Maly wished to know.

—He is thinking about going home and drinking beer, Sowinski said.

—He is thinking about the last time he climbed in a girl's bed, Kula offered. That's what I am thinking and I can't remember what it's like anymore.

—Look at the son of a whore, Kalinski said. Walnut did not know Kalinski or what his occupation had been. Kalinski had come from another company to fill out this *druzyna* of clerks and orderlies. —Look at him. He flies up there like he owned the sky.

—Maybe you think you own it? Sowinski said.

—Well, I got more right to it than he has. He's got his own sky in Berlin.

—You own what you can take, Kleinert said. And nobody's chasing him off this one.

266

—That's right, Ryms said. You can see that all right.

Tension relaxed and the ten faces calmly turned skyward and watched the German plane.

—It is a spotter plane, Kleinert said. There was reflective satisfaction in his voice. —The Germans got planes for everything, see? Different job, different plane. That's what I call organization.

—They got lots of barbedwire for prisoners too, I hear, Kalinski said. And they got a big cage in Berlin with Kleinert written on it.

—Have they? Have they now? Kleinert began to laugh and, after a while, Ryms also laughed. It did not look as though Ryms knew why Kleinert was laughing. Kula laughed too, of course.

—Look at him fly, Kalinski said. His voice was disgusted. —Where the hell is our Air Force anyway? I paid a lot of money in taxes to buy an Air Force.

—You know where it is, Kleinert said. He laughed and pointed to a field where a burned-out RWD trainer lay with a broken back like a tired pre-historic monster glad to be finally dead. —It's all fucked up. Like the rest of us. And we had better all get used to it.

—Used to what? Kula said. There's one thing I'd like to get used to right now before I forget what that thing here's for.

—That's what you drive the cows home with, Mally said.

—A lot you know, Kula said, but he was offended. He turned his back on the other men and pulled the blanket over his head. —A lot of smart city pricks, that's what you are. If you're so smart how come we lost the war?

Nobody said anything then and Orzechowski felt a sinking feeling in his stomach and he felt ashamed. He still felt that he had lost the war, that he was personally responsible.

—It's no crime to lose a war against them, Kleinert said. Look at what they got. Look what we got. Anyway, maybe it won't be so bad. There's lots worse places to be than in a prison camp.

—You're telling me? Sowinski pointed to his empty jaws. You're telling me about prisons? Nobody's getting me in any camp.

—Lot you can do about it, Kleinert said. The Germans will come and take you and that's all you'll know. And then they'll chop your balls off for being a Bolshie.

He laughed, warming up to the subject. Ryms also laughed. Kula sulked and did not laugh this time.

—And then they'll get the little Jew here and they'll chop off his nose. You'll look like a human, Jew, with a chopped-off nose.

—And what will they do with you? Kalinski said suddenly. His voice was quiet and suddenly aware. —I'll tell you what they'll do. They'll give you a black uniform and a nosechopper. You'll like that, eh? I bet you'll like that.

In the silence which followed, with Kleinert saying nothing but staring at Kalinski with saucer eyes as though suddenly facing a dangerous animal with himself defenseless, the Walnut felt a cool breeze, a new thought, and the thought intrigued him. He began to turn the thought over in his mind and looked curiously at the sputtering Silesian. The other men also sat up to look at the Silesian. There was a complete silence in which the new thought enveloped all of them.

—Hey! What's the matter with you? Are you all crazy? Kleinert laughed but without amusement. Maybe the sun has fucked up your brains. You are all crazy.

Kalinski laughed and fell back on his blanket and put his arms behind his head and looked at the sky. The German plane still wheeled its cautious circles there. One by one the other men turned away from Kleinert. Some lay down. Others began their own conversations. Kula began to scratch the fleabites on his belly. Berg looked at the ground. Maly spat. Ulanko pulled up a cabbagehead and sniffed at it. Kublarz lit his pipe, which had gone out. Ryms laughed and stopped abruptly. Kleinert turned over on his belly and put his chin across his folded arms. He was with the others in the cabbage field but he was alone, and the academician-soldier Orzechowski inspected this thought.

Because it had suddenly occurred to him that this field was not a field at all, and the cabbages were not cabbages and the woods were not woods and the evil-looking yellow mountain was not merely a mountain; that all of it, in short, was Poland and he a part of it. You do not think about your country as anything but a place where you live, he thought. It's not a thing to think about. It is something which is there, which has always been there and which, presumably, always will be. You are a part of it and that makes you a human being, since you have an identity. It is the most economical way to be a human being. You do not have to explain anything to anyone: You know what you are. It is for the others to explain: the Germans and the Russians and the Czechs and all the others who somehow missed the good luck to be born into this obvious always-there world. And suddenly this is not there anymore. It is flat and broken like a beatup old plane and you can see all of it stretched out before you. You can see the ribs of it and the gutted entrail and this great, broken thing is suddenly important. It is the most precious thing you have and somehow you must keep it whole because you cannot live without it. You watch Kleinert feeling cautiously for a replacement for this lost great thing, tasting new thoughts, new vocabularies, cutting himself off from this fallen body that he was once a part of, and you know what it is that you have lost.

You have lost it with the war and suddenly it becomes important that the war go on. It can't be over now. Now it has importance. But it is lost, is it not? Yes. And the field is a cabbagefield after all, and the woods are trees, and the big yellow mountain is a lot of sand.

The soldier Walnut got up suddenly and the blanket fell off. Kula turned with a curse and pulled it up again. Maly looked at him with wide eyes. Kalinski went on looking at the sky with a thin smile. Ulanko had pulled the cabbagehead apart and now pulled up another one. Kublarz smoked his pipe. Ryms smiled. Kleinert did not do anything. Berg got up and faced the fat soldier.

—Hey, get down, Sowinski said. Get your fat ass down. Do you want him to see us?

The German plane still circled overhead.

—It is all over, Ryms said. Eh? What do you say, Kleinert? The Germans won't bother with us now. All we got to do is not bother them.

—Get down anyway, fat-ass, Sowinski said, nervous. Get down. He'll see, I tell you.

—Where are you going, Walnut? Maly said. You going after water?

—Get down, you stinking hero, Sowinski said. You'll bring a basket of eggs down on us! Get down, Berg! Get down both of you!

The soldier Walnut looked at Berg and the Jew stared at him.

—You coming with me, Morys? Walnut said. Berg's name was Morys, he suddenly remembered, and he was a student of semantics.

The small Jew did not say anything. He nodded. He began to button up his uniform and fasten his puttees. The soldier Walnut buttoned up his sodden coat. He got his rifle out from inside the blanket and began to work the bolt. He felt numb. One by one the others in the field sat up and watched him. Ryms laughed nervously. Kleinert drew the blanket over his head. Ulanko dropped the cabbagehead and his mouth fell open. Kula pretended to snore. Kublarz smoke his pipe and watched.

—What are you doing? Sowinski's voice was shrill.

—He is going to be a hero, Kleinert said from under his blanket. A bloody great hero now that the war is over.

—What are you going to do, Walnut? Maly said. What do you think we should do?

The soldier Walnut shook his head.

—I don't think anything, he said.

—I thought you intellectuals were always thinking, Sowinski said.

—Not always, Orzechowski said.

—And what do you think you're doing, you little Jew! Sowinski shouted. You going to be a hero too? You want to win the Order of the Herring with Sourcream Cluster and an onionring? Are you crazy? I'm going home. That's what we should do!

Berg said nothing. He had slung his rifle and now drew the broad Polish bayonet that was so much like a Roman sword. He tested the edge of it with his thumb. He did not look at anyone. His eyes were narrow in the shade cast by his helmet rim.

—Well, you ready, Morys? Private Orzechowski slung his rifle and picked up his pack. Berg nodded. He held up the bayonet; sunlight made it silver.

—They are going to be heroes, Sowinski said. They are going to go and kiss the officers and fight some Germans.

Berg scabbarded his bayonet with a sound that cut Sowinski short. Sowinski spat and looked at the ground.

—Where do you think we should go? Berg said to Orzechowski.

—There is a company of the Seventh Division on the road. I saw it when they brought us here. Let's go there to start with.

—Good, Berg said.

—Maybe they will take us, the Walnut said.

The Jew thought that they might. The others listened to them and said nothing. They were quiet and did not look at each other. They looked at the Walnut and at Berg, first at one, then at the other. Kublarz drew on his pipe. This was the only sound.

—Listen you Walnut, you Berg, Maly said. What are you going to do? I've got to know.

—They are going to get their ass shot off, Sowinski said. Can't you see that, you stupid shit?

—Watch who you call stupid, Maly said but without conviction.

—The war is over and we can go home and nothing anybody does is going to make any difference and they want to be heroes now. Bloody heroes. It's enough to make a man shit, I tell you.

—Leave them alone, Kalinski said suddenly.

—You too?

Sowinski turned on the prone smiling man. —You going to be a hero?

—Watch who you call a hero, Kalinski said. And leave them alone.

—You going to make me?

—I could. Leave them alone.

—It's enough to make a man shit, I tell you.

—So shit. But leave them.

—Shit, Sowinski said.

—For the sake of Christ, shut your trap, Kula said. How can I sleep?

—You lump! You stupid oaf! Why don't you go and be a hero? Why don't we all go and be heroes and go and kiss the fine officers who make wars and then keep a man lying on his ass in a barracks while the bombs come down. I'll tell you why! It's not our war, never was. It's a rich man's war. We got to look out for ourselves. We got to go home. Don't you want to go home? You, you fat hero, you, little Jew, don't you want to go home? What you want to do this for? Huh? What for? What's the use now? What's it going to get you? Berg, you don't even talk our talk! Was it so good for you in Nalewki you want to die for it? If you're such a hero how come the MPs had to put you on the train in Warsaw? How come you were a week late coming in? I know about you bastards. Hey (he turned to the others, his eyes triumphant), you know what they're doing? They're fucking off. They're going to go up the road and fuck off! That's what they're doing. Heroes! Shit! Some heroes.

He looked around the circle of downturned faces but no one said anything. Only Ryms met his eyes, wondering. Kula seemed to sleep. Kleinert had disappeared under his blanket. Maly stared at the Walnut and at Berg, first at one, then at the other. Ulanko picked at a cabbagehead. Kalinski had closed his eyes and did not smile anymore. Kublarz smoked his pipe, saying nothing.

—Is that what you're doing? Maly said.

—No, Walnut said.

He was terribly embarrassed and dropped his rifle in the dust.

—What, then?

The Walnut shrugged. His fat shoulders heaved and a waterfall of sweat bounced off them and fell among the cabbages and on Kula. He looked at Berg and the Jew shook his head. Berg wasn't going to tell them. It was for the Walnut to tell them if anyone was going to tell them. He picked up his rifle.

—Is that what we should do? Maly's voice was anxious and afraid.

—I can't tell you what you should do. How can I? Who am I to tell?

—Somebody got to tell us.

—It won't be me, Walnut said.

—See? Sowinski said. See? It's like I said. They're fucking off and we ought to get our ass out of here just as fast. Let's haul it home right now.

—That's not what I said, Walnut said.

—Then what did you say? Didn't he say I was to tell you, eh? Sowinski swung his head around to take in the others, but they did not look at him. They looked at the soldier Walnut and the soldier Berg. All except Kula, who pretended to snore, and Kleinert, who was no longer with them or of them, and Kublarz, who smoked his pipe. The others looked at the men who were getting ready.

I could tell them, the Walnut thought. Maybe I ought to tell them. Maybe that's the way to pay for losing the war in the night. But am I right? Is anybody right? Maybe they should go home like Sowinski says, maybe that's what we all ought to do. Only I can't do it because the war isn't over. It is not yet finished. It's lost, yes, I ought to know that, but it isn't finished. The whole is not yet finished while we remain a part of it. It is only finished when all the parts fall away like rotten fruit off a dead tree. The first words of the Anthem came to him then: *Poland is not lost while we yet live.* He fumbled with his rifle and almost dropped it again. He was terribly embarrassed.

I am not a demonstrative man, he thought. I am not a sentimentalist or a superpatriot. Words like that embarrass me. I have never thought about them, never considered their meaning. They were words to be sung by Boy Scouts and men at patriotic rallies. They were to be avoided or to be smiled at. They were nineteenth-century words redolent of lances in the sun. They belonged to heroes of the type of Prince Joseph Poniatowski who covered Napoleon's retreat from Leipzig and, having lost, jumped in the Elster River and shouted, *God has entrusted me with the honor of the Poles; I will give it to Him alone.* Foolish? Grandiose? Childish? Antique and now ridiculous? I don't know. I am not going to drown in the Elster River. Nobody has entrusted me with anybody's honor. It is just that they gave me a war to fight and I didn't fight it, and it is not yet finished, and the great tree is not yet down while we hang onto it. No one can tell anybody else a thing like that.

He fastened the straps of his helmet and watched Berg adjust the cap with the silver eagle. Berg had removed his helmet and slung it on his pack, and now he put on the cap with the eagle. His rifle hung across his back. Now he was checking his cartridgebelt. The soldier Walnut remembered that each of them had been given only twenty rounds of ammunition and one handgrenade. He wondered if that meant that he would kill twenty Germans. Twenty men seemed like a lot for anyone to kill.

He watched Berg fingering his ammunition and then, suddenly, the Jew went up to Sowinski and reached inside the mechanic's blanket and hauled out his cartridgebelt and slung it on his shoulder. Sowinski did not say anything. Berg took Maly's belt and then Ulanko's. The Walnut flung the blanket off Kula and took his belt. Then he took Kalinski's. Kleinert had a full cartridgebelt but he did not want to touch anything belonging to Kleinert. He felt the extra weight of belts and ammunition and he felt new waves of sweat cascading down his sides. He went among the men and took all their grenades. He had never thrown a grenade, didn't know how to prime it. But he thought that someone would show him when they got to wherever he and Berg were going.

After that he stood still. He sweated. Jezus! He looked at Berg and the Jew looked at him. Why didn't I meet him before? the Walnut thought.

Where was he? Why didn't we meet?

—Well, Morys?

—All right, Berg said.

—Down by the road, you think?

—Or on the hill. There are a lot of people on the hill.

—Or in the quarry?

—Anywhere, Berg said. His hands moved in little arcs the way Jews' hands move. —Anywhere. Where do you think?

—I think by the road. What do you think?

—All right.

Berg brushed sweat off his brow. The gesture cocked the cap.

—By the road, then.

—Let's go, then.

You all ready?

—Yes.

They helped each other to adjust their packs and set off across the cabbage-field towards the woods. Behind them no one said anything and they did not turn around to look at the silent men. Above, the German spotter plane made one more lazy circle and flew off towards the west.

I THE GENERAL

He thought the sun unusually cruel and sought the green of the clearing where the soldiers lay.

To get to the far clearing where the riflemen of Captain Pelz, some of Major Tarski's infantry and some dismounted cavalrymen made up a reserve battalion, the General had to cross the road. The tracker Bogacz still walked beside him. The sun pressed down upon them in this barren street which led from nowhere to nowhere and which seemed to rise and fall like a sea in the hot sun.

Before him was the quarry. The cadets lay among the great obelisks of sand. Below them, to the right and left of the opening between two small dunes, the Bofors guns made an antitank ambush. The woods behind him and to the left now held other ambushes plotted and planned by the tracker: barbedwire and pits, deadfall and sharpened stakes cunningly concealed. The small man really knew the forest. The General looked at him and smiled and the tracker smiled and both men waited for the elderly fat major to catch up with them.

—This heat, the major said. Oh my God.

The tracker helped the major cross the ditch.

—In twenty-five years of service I don't remember such a heat, the fat major said.

—Perhaps there will be rain, the General said.

—No, your honor, Bogacz said. There will be no rain today.

—You are sure? The General laughed. How can you be sure of anything?

—I only know what the animals tell me. I heard them in the night.

—What did they tell you?

—About rain?

—Yes.

—That there will be no rain today, Bogacz said. Maybe later, maybe some rain later, but not today.

The General laughed. He was surprised to hear himself laughing. His voice was unnaturally high. I must be careful, he thought. I am close to the glass barrier. But rest was impossible and so, in order not to think about his need for it, he said: —You are a man of talents. With such talents you should be a general. I cannot make you a general but you can be a colonel. Do you want to be a colonel? You can be my colonel in charge of animal intelligence.

—How can I be a colonel? Bogacz cackled. I cannot read.

—Do your animals read?

—They read the winds and the air. They read that.

—That is all you need to read for me. Nothing else is worth it.

Still, Bogacz said, I do not think that I would wish to be a colonel.

—Why not? The uniform is pretty.

—I do not have the head to be a colonel.

—Then be a marshal. You do not need a head to be a marshal.

Bogacz grinned and looked sly. —If I was a marshal, then your honor would have to do what I would say?

—That is so.

The General was grateful. For a while he had not thought about being tired.

—Then I would say that we should not fight the Germans.

—Are you afraid? He did not think the tracker was afraid. What was he, then, if not afraid? —Would you give them the forest? I do not believe it.

—They would not have it long. (Bogacz thought a little.) They are like wolves in winter when they are hungry. One falls and they tear at him and, tearing, are themselves torn a little. Then they drink their own blood and tear at themselves. Soon they are eating themselves and do not know it. Just wound them and they will eat themselves.

—It is a good plan but we do not have time, the General said.

—Then kill their leader. Wolves always have a leader. Kill him and the others will become confused and this will give you time.

—Assassination? The General laughed. —You propose this?

—It will give you time, the tracker said stubbornly. Then he grinned. —But I would only say to do this if I was this marshal.

—Maybe you'd better be a colonel, the General said.

—I do not think I wish it.

—Then be a major. Majors are just as good as colonels and sometimes better.

—If your honor wishes, the tracker said. I will be this major. (Then he grinned again.) And then I could tell your honor what the animals say about the Germans.

—Oh? The General laughed. This time his laugh was stronger. —They have opinions about Germans as well as about the weather?

—They say something about them.

—What do they say?

—They say the Germans will be here soon. The Germans have come into the outer woods and are coming quickly.

—How soon?

It would be good to know how soon and where.

—An hour, two. Bogacz looked sly again and cackled. —The animals do not have fine watches like the Pan General. They do not know about minutes and hours.

—If you are right about this you can have the watch, the General said. You have more than earned it.

Bogacz smiled and nodded.

They stepped into the road and there the sun struck them and dust rolled up their bodies and enveloped them and made talk impossible. The General looked at the sky. It was so pale as to be nearly white. The sun was white in it. Soon planes will come. Then the tanks will come. Then it will begin.

I THE WALNUT

They came off the field and into the woods. He had hoped it would be cooler there. The airless dankness of the forest settled about them and pressed them down, still in the peculiar silence of this day which had begun so mysteriously in the field. There was a total lack of sound as though the forest and the mountains and the sundrenched road all held their combined breaths. No breeze. No movement in the air. Total stillness.

Some men crossed the road below. Berg and the Walnut stopped for a moment to look at them, wondering if they should go down to the road to ask them—these three men who moved with such obvious difficulty through the white heat of the naked road—where they should go, what they should do, who would want them. But it seemed like an enormous distance to cover, a superhuman effort to make, and so they did not do it. One of the men on the road was their *komendant* from Radom; they recognized him despite his yellow covering of dust. Another was the tall, thin general with one arm. He had sat by the road earlier in the morning when they came down from Radom. The third man was a little brown civilian. They watched these three men cross the road and the forest absorbed them. Then they went on into the forest, themselves hunchbacked with effort.

Trees were tall here and thick. Undergrowth spread a jagged, tangled net waist-high before them. They pushed through this for some time, saying nothing. Walnut wondered if they had lost their way and would now wander about the forest in circles as lost men did. You could die of exhaustion within touch of water, wandering in circles. This thought unnerved him. His legs folded under him. He sat down. At once the white, dehydrated log on which he sat turned brown with his sweat. Berg went on for some time alone, not knowing that he was alone, then turned and came back.

—It is the heat, the Walnut said. He could not hear himself. Sharp pinprick lights floated about his eyes. The straps of his cowhide knapsack cut into him like whitehot wire bands. The sun revolved whitely. Everything revolved. He gestured at the sun and Berg nodded.

—We could rest, he said.

—Are you tired?

Berg looked at him steadily. His eyes were narrow under the shaded patch of forehead under the sodden peak of his fieldcap. They widened. Clearly he was tired but he could go on. Walnut could not. The Jew considered this; you could see him thinking.

—Yes, he said. I am tired. Let us rest a bit.

—Thank you, the Walnut said.

—Well, I am tired. It is hot, eh?

—Yes.

—Perhaps we will find water.

—Ah. Water.

—Yes. Maybe farther on?

—You could go on, the Walnut said. I would in your place.

—No, Berg said, looking at him. I am tired.

And then as though to prove it he unbuckled the various clasps and straps and hooks that hang about the body of a soldier, that seem to contain him and hold him together, and all his heavy packs and belts and tools and bags fell with a dull thud onto the pine floor and Berg sat on them. They sat quiet, each thinking.

The air was marvelously still. Nothing moved down on the forest floor. The dead pineneedles were dry and slippery. They no longer had the smell of pines. They had no more identity, and, looking at them, the Walnut thought that, indeed, that is how it would be to be dead: One would no longer have identity, one would be nothing. It occurred to him then that he too could be killed. He smelled the dry smells of the woods. They entered him and filled him and he felt a longing to retain them.

I do not wish to be dead, he told the forest.

Being dead is the end of everything.

Is anything worth this fact of being dead?

From where he sat he could see the clearing gleaming ahead in greens and yellows and the red of the leaves heaped in it, and a jasmine smell came from it, and a white brightness shone in it. Where he sat the hot shade pressed about him darkly.

It occurred to him then, for the first time since he had stood up in the cabbagefield (filled with the brightness of the thought, the new idea), that he had done something irrevocable. He could not go back to the field. He had charted a course. There is no returning or rerouting possible with such a course. It must be followed to its logical conclusion.

He smelled the jasmine and wanted very much to remain alive. The pineneedles were dead. It was unlikely that he would ever be a doctor of jurisprudence. It seemed unlikely now that he would be a number in a human zoo. It seemed possible that he might become the needle of a pine. It was possible.

What was Berg thinking? He wondered.

But Berg did not say what he was thinking.

Then he felt the heat swell and looking up at the revolving white disc of the sun he saw that it had moved and now looked down directly on the path where he and Berg were sitting. They should be moving on.

—We should go on, he said. We should find somebody before the Germans come.

Berg looked at him. He said: —Yes, and he looked down the path they had made in the undergrowth.

—All right?

—All right, Berg said.

Neither man moved.

Then Berg said: —Do you want to go back?

—I don't know. Do you?

—I don't know.

—Why did you come? You did not have to come.

—I did, Berg said.

—Why? It is like Sowinski said: Was it so good for you, back in Warsaw?

—This is the only way for me to survive. You showed me how this can be done.

Survive? The Walnut did not understand. Survival means life and that is back in the field among the cabbages, he thought. The certainty of survival is there; here there is only lack of certainty. He said: —I do not understand. I had no choice about coming but you did. I do not understand what you mean about survival.

Berg shrugged his shoulders and spread his hands. —It is a matter of alternatives. There always are two ways out, two choices. Either the Devil eats you or he doesn't, that's the way it goes. I had no choice in the field. Here I have my two alternatives. Even in being killed there are alternatives. There are two ways for a man to die: on his feet and on his knees. I will die on my feet. In that I will survive. If I am not killed then I will have earned survival. It's something to earn. In the field, even if nothing happened to me, I would not have survived. It is really simple but it did not occur to me before you stood up in the field. When you stood up I saw there could be a choice and then I made mine. For this I am grateful.

—I too am grateful, Walnut said. Well, shall we go?

—Perhaps there will be water, Berg said. It would be good to find some.

They rose and began to fasten their equipment on again. The sun had moved and their path was dark again but in the clearing ahead the sun was bright and the yellow smells were strong. They were almost ready when the first sound came to them: a soft crackle in the undergrowth behind them, a snapping of a twig on the path they had made. Other sounds followed. Someone was coming up their path and then they heard a muted concert of sounds: the low *ungh* of effort, the dusty explosion of rotted logs collapsing under feet, the quick break of a branch. There were several men.

The soldiers looked at each other with round eyes. Walnut tried to remember the password for the day and then remembered that no password had been given them. He tried to remember how to say hands up in German and then remembered that he was not to say hands up but to shoot. He wondered if the sweat-brown log on which he had been sitting would stop a bullet. He got behind it and lay down. The log did not shield more than a half of him. He pointed his rifle down the path and then remembered that it was not loaded. He sat up and could not get his cartridgebelt unfastened. Berg had vanished in the brambles across the path, but he could see the barrel of his rifle. The barrel moved up and down as though the man was shaking. His fingers shook and he could not undo the fastenings of the cartridgecase. The

276

footsteps were close. The men were close. Sweat blinded him. He could not load the rifle. He stood up and drew his bayonet. And then the first of the advancing men came around the bend in the path, from behind some trees.

They walked in single file, without order. Kublarz came first, with his coat unbuttoned, his hands in his pockets and his rifle slung upside down behind him. He smoked his pipe. Maly came behind him, He wore Kleinert's black leather cartridgebelt and used his rifle like a crutch. Ulanko followed Maly. After an interval Ryms followed Ulanko. The four soldiers came up to the Walnut. No one said anything. Berg came out of the bushes and the six soldiers stood in a rough circle looking at each other.

Ulanko sat down on the log. It steamed a little and, sitting on it, Ulanko looked as though he was being cooked. Maly stared at the Walnut. His eyes were round, his mouth open, his smile conciliating, and he was out of breath. Clearly he wished to say something but he did not know what. Ryms looked at the ground. He stood a little apart from the others. It was odd to see Ryms without Kleinert's face bent close to his ear On the ground a bullbeetle was dragging a leaf. Ryms prodded the beetle with his boot and the miniature bull drew back and raised its head and pointed its horns at Ryms and pinched the air with them. Ryms sighed and trod on the beetle. Kublarz took his pipe from his mouth and tapped it out into his hand. The hand was hard and callused and brown and the ashes made white streaks on it. Kublarz wiped his hand carefully on his coat. Everyone watched him gravely. Kublarz lifted the pipe and gestured with it. The pipe described a halfcircle in the air and prodded it; it was the gesture of a concertmaster, Walnut thought; it had a mystic quality like a magician's incantation.

—It's a long way up here, Kublarz said.

The four soldiers looked at the sky and at the path and at the clearing at the end of it as though to compare the various distances. Maly and Ulanko nodded. Ryms looked back along the way they had come as though expecting someone. The path was empty. Ryms looked at the dead beetle.

—We got some hardtack from a man in the road, Kublarz said.

—There's a lot of people down there now, Maly said. Refugees. Maybe ten thousand of them. It's like the Lunapark on the maids' day off.

—Man down there had hardtack. Gave us some.

—Lot of people down there, Maly said. You can see the road from back there a piece. Full of people. They say the German got to Kielce a while back.

—He'll be here soon, Kublarz said.

He took a piece of hardtack from his pocket. —Want some hardtack? He held it out to Walnut and to Berg. Each took a piece and put it in his mouth. The hardtack was dry. They had no saliva and could not chew the hardtack. Their throats were parched and stiff. They put the hardtack in their mouths and made chewing motions.

—It's no good without water, Maly said.

—We have no water, Berg said.

—A smoke is as good as eating if you got no water, Kublarz said.

—I do not smoke, Berg said.

—Try my pipe, Kublarz said. It is as good as eating.

He passed his pipe to Berg, who took it carefully. He passed Berg the tobacco can and a box of matches.

—Spit into the tobacco and roll it in a ball. That way you'll have more smoke, he said. See? Good, eh?

Berg nodded. His eyes were watering. The tobacco was strong.

—Well, here we are, Kublarz said.

—Good, good, the Walnut said.

He had not expected them to come.

The others waited for him to say something else. When he did not they looked at each other (all except Ryms, who looked back along the path) and Ulanko sighed and Maly said, —Well, here we are.

—Are the others coming? the Walnut said.

—No, Kublarz said.

—I thought Kalinski would come, Berg said. I was sure he would come.

—His kind don't come, Kublarz said. Don't you know that? His kind talk but they don't come: That's the kind he is.

—Yes, Walnut said. Sowinski wouldn't come either. Is he still in the field?

—No. He went north. He said he would go home. Kleinert went south. Kula is in the field, though. He didn't want to go home and he didn't want to go with Kleinert. I think he is asleep but I also think that he'll show up here once he's thought about it. Or when he gets hungry. Ryms came, though. I thought he'd go with Kleinert.

They all looked at Ryms, except Berg, whose eyes were closed. The big Silesian blushed and stared at the beetle.

—How come you didn't go with Kleinert? Maly said. You're both from down there, aren't you? *Kameraden* from Silesia.

Ryms shook his head. He kicked the beetle. His face was a deep crimson.

—He thought you'd go with him all right. You could see that. You always do what he says. He is your *Landsmann*, eh?

—Not always, Ryms said, staring at the beetle.

—What do you mean; not always? Either he's your *Landsmann* or he isn't.

—Leave him alone, Kublarz said, and Maly grew quiet. —Well, here we are, Kublarz said again. What do you want us to do?

They all looked at the Walnut except Berg, whose eyes were closed and who leaned against a tree; the pipe had gone out and he seemed glad of it.

—Who? Me? The Walnut stared. —I don't want you to do anything.

New waves of sweat suddenly poured down his cheeks and down his brow and he was blinded by them. —Why should I want you to do anything?

—Somebody's got to say what we're to do, Kublarz said.

—Not me. The Walnut found it difficult to breathe. —I'm not in charge here.

—Somebody's got to be, Kublarz said.

—Not me, the Walnut said. Not me. Why, that's ridiculous!

—Well, we come here because of you. Maly said gently. You see how it is?

The four newcomers stared at the Walnut with attention. Their faces were grave. They studied his face and it occurred to him that he knew that look. It was the way soldiers looked at an officer: the quiet, speculative look that was half trust and half uneasiness. —Not me, he said. I can't tell anybody what to do.

—You just got to say where it's going to be, Kublarz said. Once it starts it'll make no difference who says what; everybody's too busy. I know, I've been in a war. But before it gets going somebody's got to tell the rest where to be, and what to do. That's the way battles go. That's all you got to do: find the place we're going to do it.

—I can't, the Walnut said. Me in charge? Why not you? You've been in a war. Don't you men want somebody who's been in a war? I don't know anything about it.

—I don't think fast enough, Kublarz said. Man that's in charge got to know how to think. Me, I'm all right driving a team, but my horse thinks more than I do. Now you find the place for it and tell us where to go.

Maly and Ulanko got up and straightened their uniforms and came up beside Kublarz on the path. There was just room for the three of them to stand in line and Ryms had to stand alone in the second rank. The others came up barely to his collarbone. He looked over their heads into the Walnut's eyes. His own eyes were calm and placid and infinitely trusting, and suddenly the Walnut saw him dead.

God no, the Walnut thought. I can't do it. Neither this nor anything of this kind. I want to be alive and smell the jasmine. I do not want to be like the needle of a pine. I cannot make the decisions that may make them die.

—Somebody else has to be in charge, he said. Let Berg be in charge.

Berg shook his head weakly. He had sat down on the ground under the tree and leaned against it trying to breathe. His face had the tint of old leaves.

—Let us go up across the clearing and find an officer.

—No time, Kublarz said and pointed to the road.

Walnut looked where the teamster pointed but at first he could not see anything through the green wall of trees. Sweat blinded him. He thought that shortly his sodden clothes would rot and fall away and leave him naked. The others' uniforms were dry. The glaring sun had dried the sweat on them, but even this terrible white sun could not cope with *his* sweat. He felt that he was melting in the heat. He felt his flesh floating away. He saw the wall of trees and the yellow flash of the distant road between them and then he saw the distant dustcloud above the trees.

At first he did not understand the meaning of this dustcloud. All Polish roads were dry and dusty and ironhard this September. Then from the road came a faint sound like the sound of seashells, as though a tide were gathering in the distance, as though an ocean of some kind were coming in: tentative at first, then swelling.

So soon?

—Perhaps it's the people you saw on the road . . .

—On tanks?

Kublarz took his pipe from Berg's hand and relit it.

A rumbling sound like the quaking of the bowels of the earth came from the dustcloud. It swelled and grew and boiled up off the invisible white road and stretched into infinity and there was no end to it and no beginning.

The Walnut brushed the sweat off his face. He looked at the others. Kublarz had buttoned up his uniform and turned his rifle the right way up across his back. He put his pipe away. Maly had stepped back and now stood beside Ryms. Berg stood in Maly's place. Ulanko stood next to Berg. His Adam's apple moved up and down. He clutched the dark seams of his trousers.

—All right, the Walnut said.

The clearing. It was bright and there was color in it. The sweet smell of jasmine came from it. The path was dark and dead pineneedles crumbled underfoot.

—The clearing, he said.

And then the sound exploded. The Bofors guns fired from their ambush and the dustcloud swirled as tanks drove left and right out of it into the fields with motors roaring, and then a myriad of red-and-yellow lights twinkled in the dustcloud and shells hummed overhead and in the choked sound of their explosions came the first screaming of the wounded.

Ten shells and forty echoes crashed around him and rolled rattling among the pine. The earth leaped. The sun spun in a lazy arc. Wind flung him down. He was no sooner down, smelling the hot dry soil, the dead pineneedles, the pale moss, the marvelous coolness of a secret spring accidentally uncovered, a sudden glorious weightlessness, a lack of flesh, than hands reached for him softly.

It was the Jew bending over him. His thin face was now gaunt and yellowly transparent. It was streaked with smoke. It looked like something children might carry on Witching Night. But the eyes, yes, they were solicitous; the black, moist eyes of the Jew were infinitely sad.

—Walnut? The voice was distant.

Why were the eyes sad? What was there to be sad about? The day was ending; clearly it was ending because the white sun had receded and turned a streaked, veined pink. It was almost gone in a red glow. Now the sun was red. Red clouds hung heavily over it and the earth under it assumed varieties of crimson hues. In that illomened light the Jew's face had the tint of fever.

But presently his eyes sharpened and he could see objects in the scarlet sky: hot shards of metal splintering like sickles and whirling into men, the hurtling shapeless weights (all jagged angles and razorsharp planes) that turned heads and limbs into scarlet blots, blossoming cataracts of earth like redbrown fountains, the flying trees, pine tossed so negligently upward with twisted rifles and bits of men; and then the redrimmed shellholes in the steaming earth.

Night approached imperceptibly; the red day was ending.

Sleep.

He closed his eyes. The jasmine smell was strong. The earthsmell (of dry moss and deepburied moistures and powdered leaves and dead, slippery pineneedles) was good and welcoming and soothing and blotted the scarlet shapelessness of the dying day.

Sleep. It would be good. Now it would be good. The sun was going and the heat was gone and heavy flesh had melted and there was this marvelous, miraculous coolness, and in *this* sleep nothing would be lost, nothing had been lost: The scarlet world and flying pinetrees and quaking lumps of scarlet shapelessness were proof that nothing had been lost.

Walnut smiled, grateful.

Sir, does this mean that I have proved my point? Are you postponing your irrevocable verdict? Were you moved by my eloquence to reconsider, to weigh once more the merits of my client's case? Of course, Sir! I had no doubt that you would! I could cite precedents, of course. The Western World saved at the siege of Vienna in fifteen-something, where, incidentally, it was my client's horsemen who rode across mountains to keep a promise, to scatter and erase forever the power of the Turk. And then in 1920, in the case of Bolshevism versus Civilization, the two-year war my client fought alone to keep the East where it belonged, namely in the East. These, Sir, are precedents I could cite to show how proper and how right my client's claim is. But I am confident of Your Justice and Your Mercy, Sir, and need no precedents. Oh yes, I know, my client has committed sins. Who has not? Who can point to my client's sins and say: I am innocent of such? Sins of arrogance and pride and the abridgement of the rights of others. Who has not done this? Whose civil record is spotless? Who is so pure that he can say to You: *They* have sinned, destroy *them?* You are a just and terrible Judge but not devoid of mercy. It is to this great Justice, this infinite Mercy that I appeal, we appeal, excuse me, my client and I. Judge us on our merits as well as on our demerits.

We have done evil and we have done good and the best that can be said about us is that we have served Your world as well as most. We are no better in our imperfection than others, no worse than others. We live. We lay our case in your just and merciful hands expecting nothing from You except

Justice and

Mercy . . .

And the red sun came down suddenly and trod upon his chest.

Friday, September the eighth

I THE CONQUEROR

From the woods came the last of the conclusive salvos and Libesis was drunk. He appeared suddenly around the corner of the white stone building where the ten prisoners had been kept before their liberation by the salvos; an improbable fat wraith, a corpulent avenging spirit out of some irreverent parody of Schiller, waving a squarecut bottle. The bottle glinted in the pale light. It spilled a colorless liquid that the light made silver. Libesis pointed the bottle at Erich and at Kuno Saal like an MP Feuer and said: —Bang!

He dropped the bottle in the soft yellow dust and made a mock-tragic gesture with his hands and laughed and suddenly sat down in a small puff of dust as though the wire had been drawn from him; as though whatever it was that had kept him erect had suddenly been removed.

After a while he began to sing.

He sang *Deutsch mein Bruder* and the *Treue, treue* of the Hitler Jugend and the *Liberation of the Humble.*

Then he pointed a finger at Saal and said: —Bang! Liberate the humble. Then he giggled.

He got up in a clumsy fatman's way like a cow lurching upward and stumbled in small circles to the apple orchard where the firing squad was resting. He tripped and thrashed among the bushes and cursed and eventually fell down. Erich looked to see if the squad was laughing at the fat lieutenant. It would not do to have the SS laugh at officers. But the SS were not laughing. They were eating apples. They were careful not to laugh at the drunk lieutenant.

—That pig! Saal said. He looked at Erich with colorless eyes. In daylight it was possible to see some pale blue in Saal's eyes sometimes; that is, if the light was right and one looked hard enough and tried to find it. Of course, one did not try hard or often. Men were not supposed to look into each other's eyes. The eyes are the mirrors of the soul, Erich once had heard, and what man wanted to see another's soul? Men were supposed to look into the eyes of women, and this was proper and correct and the way it should be. There was no danger of seeing a soul in a woman's eyes. If they were eyes like Adrianne's they would be touched with *Schadenfreude,* that cruel quality that finds amusement in misfortune.

This was no time to think of Adrianne. But thoughts of her kept intruding. He thought about the trip in the Salzkammergut and the way that had ended. It would have ended anyway, he supposed, with the war so close. War had been closer, then, than any of them had been capable of feeling. But in late July there had been a relaxation of the tensions and short leaves had been available and he and Kuno Saal had taken one for the Salzkammergut trip. The trip had taken them to out-of-the-way places and they had not found their recall letters until the war had started. Erich had been angry then, he remembered. But it was not the interrupted trip that mattered now; it was the thought of Adrianne and the way she had laughed.

He had explained to her so carefully about the blood. It was important that the blood be pure and undiluted with the weaker strains and there were, after all, those French and Italianate strains blending with the Anglo-Saxon, and, my God, everyone knew what that meant: Negroid Arabs and Jews included, enough to poison the blood of generations. What kind of German mother would she be? None of this meant, of course, that they could not be lovers. She could still go to the mountains with him and to the lesser rockclimbs, and it could all go on as before, unchanged, pleasurable, and all she could not have was marriage. She had not understood. He had thought she might not, and was prepared for tears and protestations and, possibly, suicide, but he was not prepared for her wide-open, disbelieving eyes and the puzzled shake of her head and her sudden laughter.

She pointed at him (sitting serious and intent and now outraged by laughter, and trying to make her understand what was so very simple) and she laughed.

Erich clenched his fist and hit it into the palm of his other hand. She would not laugh now. This was a time of war and now he was in Poland taking the war to the land of the hereditary enemy.

Soon the sun would be up and the last of the firing squads would come back with the woods silent and dark and secret behind them and day would come and the war resume.

Erich wondered what it would be like to kill a man. This was the proper climax to a year of study and drill and exercise and lectures in Party dialectics and Clausewitz and history of civilization and of the Nordic races and philosophy and logic and comparative religions and the theory of race and the testament of the elders of Zion and ordinary history and history of the German State and history of the Party and the life of the Führer and history of the SS (who were not, as a civilian might suppose, merely policemen but a magnificent state within the state, an order of knighthood dedicated to the Principle and the first line of defense of civilization against the Bolshevik anarchy), and exercises in the military arts (the goosestep and saluting), the repair and maintenance of Benz armored cars, elementary tactics, the theory of military discipline, field sanitation and courts-martial procedure, rules of evidence, markmanship and the care of feet, endurance, and the care of the twenty-seven pieces of SS equipment; and there was the vigil before graduation.

He ran the gauntlet of Alsatian dogs and stood twelve hours at attention under burning torches in the yard of the medieval castle which was the home of the Ordensburg at Bod Toltz, and when the sun broke through the morning clouds above Bavaria he was graduated: a Knight of the Order of Blood, Fahnrich of the SS, first line of defense of civilization.

And now he waited for war to resume and he breathed the smoke from the rubble, the halfburned timbers damp with dew, dust and the rich fecundity of foreign soil.

He thought about battle and its sounds which thundered in the woods around the bald mountain. The tanks and trucks of the Nordland and Westland regiments of this division, which was the First SS of *Waffengrenadiere,* which was the offspring of the legendary Leibstandarte Adolf Hitler, the Führer's bodyguard, had rolled derisively past the waiting column of his regiment, the Ostland Regiment, all day yesterday and throughout the night. The Ostland Regiment was the divisional reserve. The men of the Nordland and Westland regiments now knew what it felt like to kill a man.

Erich had come close to finding out what it was like, whether he could do it properly and whether this action of snuffing out a life would change him as he thought it might. Because that morning, although it could not properly be called a morning with the sun still down, there had been executions. Twenty-two deserters had been shot. Each company of the regiment turned out a firing squad. The squads had volunteered but the officers drew lots. The squads divided the prisoners fairly and took them to the woods and shot them. Later some Landswehr soldiers were to come to look at the corpses.

The prisoners had arrived in the night. They were Landswehr soldiers. One, who had stuttered and rolled his eyes idiotically and finally urinated in his trousers, still wore the markings of the 80th Landswehr on his collar. He did not look like anything Erich supposed a German combat soldier would resemble. The man disgusted him. —*These are not Germans,* Obersturmführer Dietrich said. He addressed the firing squads and the assembled officers. The officers were still to draw lots for the command of the firing squads. The black eyes of Dietrich burned into the prisoners. Erich wondered why the prisoners did not explode. The Obersturmführer stood tall and proud and brooding and unmarked above the prisoners. Erich watched him and his palms became moist. The prisoners also watched him. They did not seem to understand what was about to happen. —*They have lost the right to call themselves Germans,* said the Obersturmführer. The prisoners looked at each other and at him and also at the ground. —*They have spat upon their heritage . . . soiled the flag . . . they are an insult to the Fatherland and must be washed away in blood. It is your duty to avenge this insult . . . to raise the flag from mud . . . so that no no man can ever point to Germans who were afraid to die.* Obersturmführer Dietrich stood erect and proud: a real *Waffengrenadier,* a veteran of the Kondor Legion which had fought in Spain, with two medal ribbons on his chest. He was the only officer in the company who had medal ribbons. His dark face was beautiful and stern, Erich thought. He could not take his eyes away from it. The burning torches cast red shadows on it. The face was red and black in the light of the torches. The ribbon of the Iron Cross was red and white and black. Erich wished for the red and black ribbon to lie on his chest and he felt weak and his knees trembled so violently that he almost fell. He looked at the prisoners, who were weeping and not weeping, who stirred and who were still, who had been stripped of rank and buttons and epaulets and honor and manhood and human dignity and human rights, and one of them tried to stand up and talk, kicking at those who grasped at him to pull him down, and shouted: —*Swine! Brotherkillers!* You *go there . . . try it . . . bayonets . . . ah, you swine . . .* as hands finally dragged him down . . . *Cowards! Brotherkillers!* Saal reached him in one screaming bound and kicked him in the mouth. Then lots were drawn for the command of the firingsquad. Libesis drew first. He was deathly pale in the red light of the flickering torches. His hand shook and he closed his eyes. Saal and Erich drew next. Saal threw his straw furiously at the ground. He trod upon it. He glared at Erich. Erich showed his straw. It was a short one. He could not command the firingsquad. He felt a sudden great relief and was, at once, ashamed of the relief. He could not stop his knees from shaking. Libesis had the long straw. He showed it and Saal stared at it. Dietrich nodded then and said: —Sieg Heil! —Sieg Heil, shouted the company, and Dietrich marched off in the dark, his slim, willowy back swaying like a girl's.

—*You cheated,* Saal said.

Libesis stared at him. He held the straw as though it was an instrument of death pointed at his own heart.

—*You cheated,* Saal insisted. His mouth was wet and his hands clutched air. —*You drew first. You had two chances against my one. You knew the straws. I hate you, Libesis, you cheating swine.*

—*Oh no,* said Libesis. *No. No.*

He made a move as though to hand the straw to Saal and Saal clutched at it but it slipped from Libesis' hand and fell. Libesis looked at Erich. His head shook from side to side and sweat ran down his flaccid cheeks. He walked away.

At first they thought that Libesis had gone to report Saal's insubordination and Saal said: —*You saw it. He dropped the straw. He threw it away. You were witness to it.* But when minutes passed without Libesis' return, and the firing squad grew bored and stamped its feet and whispered and the prisoners once more sat down, and a messenger failed to find the fat lieutenant, Saal smiled and picked up the straw and said: —*You see? You see? You see what he did? I have him now!* and took command of the squad and marched the prisoners away. His squad was the first back with the work done.

Saal's face was a pointed mask like the paper faces children make up for masquerades. There were no colors, no lines, no shades. There was no expression. In black dress uniform at graduation Saal had looked like a corpse. In the greengrey shade of twilight, in field uniform, he was a shadow.

Now he turned the masklike face toward Erich and said quietly: —He should be shot. He refused an order. You saw him. You were there. I shall ask Dietrich to call a court of honor. You will testify.

—Perhaps he was sick, Erich said.

He thought of Dietrich and his knees trembled. He sat down on the threshold of the white stone house. He wondered why Libesis had looked at him as he walked away. He wondered why the lieutenant had refused the straw. I have to know, he thought.

—Sick? Sick? He is an insult to us all. Intellectual pig.

—Be quiet, Kuno.

Perhaps if Kuno Saal was quiet he would understand. He had liked Libesis. Libesis talked a lot and laughed a lot. He talked more than he laughed. Sometimes it was not easy to understand what Libesis was saying. But it all sounded so authoritative, so wise. It sounded as though it should be understood. And now this . . . this with the straw. Why? He would have to find him.

—You like him, don't you? Saal said.

He laughed quietly.

—Be quiet, Kuno!

—Do you like him as much as you like Dietrich?

—What?

—Ha. I know you do. Oh yes. You didn't grow up the way I did. In the gutters. Sleeping in a packing case in a cellar. My mother on her hands and knees. Scrubbing. No food. Stealing. Doing things for old men. You don't live like that and then not know. I know.

—Be quiet!

—He is your friend, eh? Your so good friend? Saal laughed without a sound. —You like the fat lieutenant. He laughs a lot. He talks the High German you understand. Perhaps you really understand each other? You people with seven-room apartments! What do you understand? Did we make the revolution so that you could have fourteen-room apartments? Libesis. You. I know what made him sick! Do you understand? Don't worry. I will make him sicker. He will go on his hands and knees to me!

Erich looked at the resting squad to see if they had heard, but the SS were paying no attention. He could see them vaguely black under the apple trees: Schuppanzigh, Schreiber, Schindlecker, Bar, Nickel, Mataushek and Dietzel. They were eating apples. Bar had his submachinegun apart and was cleaning it. Nickel threw applecores into a small clump of wild grass and gorse, and someone, it was Schreiber, said something that made the others laugh and picked up a large lump of clay and threw it into the gorse bush and there was a soft, dusty thud as the clay exploded against something solid and a voice that sounded like Riemann's roared: —*Heilige Testament von Teufel!* and soon Scharführer Riemann charged out of the bush pulling up his trousers.

This was as he had imagined war to be. Horseplay. Comradeship. Hard laughter of hard men. But now new dimensions had opened up and these he did not understand and he felt that if he did not understand them, did not find out, the war would not make any sense.

He felt chilled. He got up. He stretched and shook himself and stamped his feet. His feet were cold. His knees seemed made of ice. The earth was warm from yesterday's hot sun.

—Where are you going? Saal said. To talk to the fat lieutenant?

—The posts, Erich said. Someone must check them.

Saal laughed. —Ah yes, the posts. Would you like me to come with you to check the posts?

—No, I can do it.

—Yes. You can check the posts. But it is so dark. Will you find the posts in the darkness? Perhaps you will lose your way and get lost in the orchard? I think I will go with you to look at these posts.

—No, Erich said. You stay here.

—You don't want me to go with you, little Erich?

—You should be here, Erich said. He felt cold throughout. Even his brain seemed frozen. —Someone should be here in case Dietrich wants one of us.

—Wouldn't you rather be here for Dietrich? Saal laughed.

Erich walked away.

Erich walked in the cold darkness before sunrise. He thought that he should whistle. He thought that if he whistled a little under his breath he would feel much better about Libesis and Saal and what Saal seemed to say, about the executions and the new dimensions, and so he tried it but it did not make him feel any better and by the time he reached the blackened wall at the end of the village, the small ruin that had the old Polish poster on it, he thought he felt worse than he had ever felt. And then, because the thought of war had done it before, and the wondering about the change that would come over him after killing had made him feel good in the past, he tried to think about war and to wonder about what it would feel like to kill.

Certainly no one had been killed in taking this village. The Poles had not defended it. The regiment was still coming into it. Scholtzberg's light panzer squadron had turned off into the woods, Linz's had stopped in the fields where a Polish biplane lay in the cabbages, the heavy squadron of Reincke's Mark II's and the new Czech III's stood in the village street. The tankers had the motors going. They had put small tin basins on the hot rear plates so that they could heat water to wash. The *Grenadieren,* who had come in first and thus had the best places in the apple orchards, slept or ate apples. Still to come in was the antitank company, the field artillery battery, the signal troops, the NSKK service troops and the regimental staff. Erich wondered if this day they would see some fighting. He was anxious about it. It was humiliating to be in a war and never fire the beautiful thirty-two-shot MP Feuer slung on his hip. Yesterday's savage fighting had been distant music. The night's battle in the quarry was a fiery mystery. The Ostland Regiment had not received its baptism of fire. It was humiliating to sit in a ditch while the Westlanders and the Nordlanders rode through with tank commanders up in open turrets, laughing.

At the end of the street where the rubble lay thick, Erich turned into the field and then into the orchard. He walked among the trees. It was dark there and the fruit smell hung heavy. He looked for Libesis, and could not find him; eventually he walked right into him, a dark mound under an apple tree.

—Libesis?

—Umph, said the fat lieutenant.

—Are you sick?

—No. Are you?

—No. What is the matter with you?

Libesis turned his face up. It was white and pasty. It looked like the reflection of the moon in water.

—Nothing is the matter.

—Well, Erich said.

Libesis laughed. It was a harsh sound without joy in it. —Be specific, Fahnrich. What is well? And what leads you to believe that anything is well? Have you had an intelligence report on the subject? Have you questioned prisoners? Was there an Order of the Day issued about it? Is this what they taught you at Bad Toltz? How did you get to be an officer anyway? Stand at attention, Fahnrich. Report!

—Fahnrich Sonnerling reports, Erich said, feeling stupid. Heil Hitler!

—Heil, Libesis said.

—Fahnrich Sonnerling begs permission to speak to his superior officer.

—Permission denied, Libesis said. He laughed. —And what do you think of that?

—What? Listen, Libesis . . .

—What? Stand at attention! Speak when you are spoken to! Report! Erich felt cold.

—Fahnrich Sonnerling reports . . .

—Nothing! Fahnrich Sonnerling reports nothing! Fahnrich Sonnerling is a piece of shit! Right? Don't answer! That was a rhetorical question and only rhetors have the right to answer rhetorical questions. Besides, it isn't true. Right? Careful! That was another rhetorical question and you almost answered. You must watch yourself, Fahnrich! You have to be careful. I notice in you a lamentable tendency to answer rhetorical questions. That is a serious breach of military discipline. It is also in contravention of Party dialectics. Never answer questions! Never ask them! If you want to advance in the Party and in this Army and reach the grand and glorious authority of an Untersturmführer never answer questions. Particularly if they begin with the word *Why*. That is not a German word. It was planted in the language by the insidious French. If you want to survive within yourself never ask this question. *Why* is the secret weapon of the French. Right? Watch it!

—*Jawohl*, Herr Untersturmführer, Erich said.

—That's better! That is excellent! That is the only truly German phrase in the German language. Did you know that? Silence! What did I tell you about rhetorical questions? Fahnrich, don't you have any sense? Don't you know a rhetorical question when you see one? Are you unacquainted with the German language? Good, very good. You are learning about rhetorical questions even though you know nothing about the German language. Remember *jawohl!* It is the only truly German word. Everything else is a secret weapon of the French. Stick with *jawohl* and you will reach great heights.

—*Jawohl*, Herr Untersturmführer.

—Well, very good. And since we are on this tack, and discussing language, let me tell you about another ancient German phrase. The phrase is *zum Befehl*. Do you know what that means? Answer. This is not a rhetorical question.

—*Jawohl*, Herr Untersturmführer.

—What does it mean?

—It signifies a soldier's willingness to execute an order.

—Execute, Libesis said. Execute the order.

—*Jawohl*, Herr Untersturmführer.

—Bang! Bang! Bang! Execute the order. Did you say something? Nothing? Good. In fact excellent. Fahnrich, I have hopes for you. You are excellent German officer material.

—*Jawohl*, Herr Unter—

—Yes, *Jawohl*. Of course. And also *zum Befehl*. Very good. You are superlative material. Let me tell you what you are so that you will understand. You are a German, right? Very good. Not a blink this time. You are a German and you have a fondness for children and dogs and caged canaries and you are a contemplative man, a sentimentalist singing of *Heimat* and *Mutter* and innumerable combinations of the two and you admire Franz Lehar, and the operetta is an art with you, and you admire craftsmanship and you take pains and you despise *Schlamperei,* and you *do* possess a sense of humor, and you possess a limitless capacity for self-delusion. You trust your leaders, you have followed leaders since time immemorial. It is your nature to obey. You were never so pleased as when your newest leader, Our Führer, Leader of Our People, said, and I quote, *I have not been imposed by anyone upon this people. From the people I have grown, in the people I have remained, to the people I return. My pride is that I know no statesman in the world who, with a greater right than I, can say that he is the representative of his people.* Heil Hitler. You are obedient and disciplined but you are not a machine. In you there is something of the second Ludwig of Bavaria with fabulous dreams of empire embracing the world, geopolitical fantasies of intercontinental colonization, the founding of a new order to guard the Holy Grail. You are an intellectual column of statistics, an artist, a musician, a dreamer, a righter of intolerable wrongs. You are constantly out to right intolerable wrongs. And with all this what are you? I will tell you. I am glad that you did not try to answer. You are a German, and that is a blend of a *petit bourgeois* and a social revolutionary with a primitive imagination steeped in the nineteenth-century mysticism of Gothic romance. Dostoevsky might have created you! You are a caricature of Wagner, Nietzsche and Schopenhauer translated in terms of a new century: an age of mathematics and precision and timetables and timeclocks and efficiency experts and Swedish ball-bearings and of orderliness and of the deification of technology. *We are a race of dreamers,* says the good Herr Goebbels, *but all we have to do is hear a military band pass in the distance and we form columns.* Right?

Erich stared.

—I asked a question, Fahnrich! Libesis roared.

—*Jawohl,* Herr—

—Silence! Attention! *Die Fahne hoch!* You are the Fahnrich of the twentieth century? Where is your standard, standard-bearer? And do you suppose anyone can lift it from the mud? Do you really suppose it?

—I don't know, Erich whispered. He heard his voice from a distance and at first did not believe that he had spoken. He watched Libesis' face collapse like a white balloon suddenly unbound.

—Nobody can, Libesis said, but he was no longer speaking to Erich and probably not to anyone, not even to himself, Erich thought. He felt a sour taste at the back of his teeth. His tongue was thick with it. He wished that he had not gone after Libesis. Libesis sat on the ground and blinked with little eyes. His face had the color and consistency of a yellow cream cheese.

—What do we bring? he said. And who would want it? You, Fahnrich, do you know what you represent? Do you know what standard you are carrying? What? No. You wouldn't know.

Just then the sun rose in its orange glow. The sudden light was like a blow. Erich blinked in this light. It was like awakening from a nightmare. He turned and walked away.

He walked as though mesmerized and barely heard the snickering sound of a submachinegun being made ready to fire and the startled *Wer da?* He mumbled something and was quite surprised that no shot came his way. Half his mind was turned like a great inner ear to the dark orchards, hearing the shot that did not come from there, as he had expected it to come.

He passed through the drysnapping corn stubble in the field and saw, as though in a continuation of a dream, the ghostly, soundless arrival of Krasberg's battery and its unlimbering and not even the red and yellow fire and the too near crash of the first salvo woke him.

Krasberg said something to him, laughing. It sounded like *Grüss Gott.* Krasberg was religious. He had yelled *Feuer!* and then said *Grüss Gott* politely and in friendship. Erich made a gesture of greeting and went past the battery into the village.

He thought about Libesis and his incomprehensible words. Libesis had been drunk, of course. Earlier he had been drunk. But was he drunk when he talked his treason? And was drunkenness an extenuating circumstance? And what was friendship? And what was duty? And where did friendship end and participation in treason begin?

There was an answer to be found to this. One man would know. And with a feeling of relief that made his knees weak and his breath come quick, telling himself that all he wanted was an answer, a reassurance, that it was all a matter of loyalty and duty and patriotism, and that it did not involve a betrayal of anyone or a sacrifice of anyone or a surrendering of anyone in a bribe, that he did this because it was a *manly* thing to do, he turned towards the quarters of Obersturmführer Dietrich, where lights still glowed despite the blackout blankets.

I THE GENERAL

Night passed, and before anyone had time to notice it, or wonder where it came from, the sun was high and white again and burned down and sucked up the air. In its merciless glare the flying pinetrees assumed the size of ships' masts and the crash of bursting shells and bombs was an enormous sound.

Each shell burst in a multiple of four as the sound echoed in the pines and through the sandstone slabs piled in the quarry. One landed and exploded near the General, making his legs jerk. Someone gave a high, sensitive cry of agony like a small, delicately organized animal being disembowled, and Prus said Aha to himself, and thought, Someone has been killed, and watched the battle.

Down on the road, between the two flattopped dunes that flanked it like decapitated sentinels, a tank burned hollowly. The rumble of its bursting ammunition lifted it off the road in little squatting froglike jumps. It tossed flames through the hatches and its short gun smoked like an indolent cigarette glued to the mouth of a corpse.

Pines burned to right and left of it and up the sandy slopes that rolled away from it ran groups of riflemen with the white sun burning on the outthrust tongues of their bayonets. Farther yet to the right rose the massif of the quarry, which towered like a tall ship above the boiling sea of smoke. There the attack was strongest. There Slovak soldiers and SS men had secured a toehold on the sandstone ridge and lay behind pinktinted slabs of quarried stone stabbing out with little pinpoint flashes of automatic-rifle fire into the counterattacking companies. And now, as he watched, the outspread lines of the attackers heaved forward, lurching up the slope, and falling and getting up and, in those scarlet instances, not getting up but remaining still and grotesquely spilled on the suntinted sandy soil. He heard the wild, drawnout hurrah as the foremost of the small black shapes reached the great slices of stone where the enemy lay hidden and climbed across the barriers, bringing their bayonets among the enemy. He watched the flashing arc made by the bayonets as they went down and up, down whitely with the new sun on them, up redly with the new blood on them, and he wondered: Who are they, these inexhaustible black shadows? Certainly they could not be men. Men die and these were indestructible. Men fall and sleep and are fatigued and tremble with exhaustion and are hungry and feel fear and disintegrate within that box of fear; these must be battalions of shadows so laboriously collected on the roads before the chasing armored columns caught up with them, bolstered by companies of reservists who, without weapons or uniforms or food or rest or orders and equipped only with enthusiasm, had lain about the crashing streets of Radom and of Kielce since the war began, and whom he had collected and brought down to the quarry. More men ran past him on the path towards the quarry. The sun made them quiver. Or was it he who could no longer see in the white glare?

The General rubbed his eyes and watched. He was aware of not having slept or eaten in two days. He wondered where his own limit of exhaustion lay: the fragile point beyond which a man cannot be commanded, a point where neither persuasion nor orders and threats nor fear of death or punishment or disgrace can have any meaning. And when it was reached . . .

He watched the attack, feeling hollow. Aware of his own fatigue, he imagined the exhaustion of the attacking soldiers. The slope was now clear of running men; the only men there were the black still ones, the motionless contribution to the art of war tossed so carelessly onto the earth. The running men were in among the rocks, stabbing, thrusting, clubbing, murdering; and now among the slotted heaps of stone, stray enemy soldiers appeared. Some backed off coldly to the edge of the precipitous quarry, turning, shooting until the bayonets reached them. Others ran shouting. Some were flung down the precipice, others leaped there. Others raised their hands and knelt and fell under the flailing riflebutts and bayonets. There were shots and shouts and cries and supplications and broken bits of pleading and appeals and curses and defiant howls.

All of this carried clearly to the General. He stood on the edge of the woods. They thickened behind him. There the shells fell rainlike to thin out the woods. Trees flew and soil leaped. Men died. But they could not be men. Most of them had neither slept nor eaten for seventy hours; the sound of bursting shells enveloped them, cut them off from the earth, the sky and each other and locked them in tight, airless isolation boxes in which they moved like sleepwalkers. The dead lay still. The living moved as though in a disembodied dream, as though what was happening was familiar, as though it had happened many times before and was not surprising. All faces seemed familiar, but when he stared at them or at any object (the heaped brass casings of shells, the strayed, footless boot, the headless helmet rolling on the ground, a strip of brown puttee, a twisted rifle, the paper that always littered battlefields—pictures, letters, wrappings, envelopes, soiled links with a peaceful past) he was struck with their novelty.

His ears heard nothing and his eyes dimmed through peering into smoke; he moved as though detached from his own body, but his orders were concise and clear and the shocked shapes who reported to him drew up and calmed themselves and moved off with precision to carry out the orders. It occurred to him that nobody was afraid of death because nobody understood it.

He did not know how long the battle had been going on; time found new subdivisions in events. He did remember that sometime during the battle rain had fallen. It was so unexpected, so startling, so much like the rain of other times (almost as though rain, too, were a part of peace and sanity and not an event that could occur in war), that men scrambled up out of holes, from behind fallen trees, from under stones and overturned wagons and the smashed Bofors guns, from under and behind the corpses they used for parapets, and ran for cover, and the General too turned to seek shelter from the rain. He felt a desperate fear of becoming wet.

In moments the rain was over and the soldiers looked at each other and giggled stupidly and made shamefaced motions, and it was only by looking into the caved-in faces of the corpses, where the water lay as if in basins, that he could tell that the momentary downpour had been heavy. It had put out the fires. But the sun burst out at once and dried out the forest in a moment in white clouds of steam. New shells immediately started new fires going. Sometime after the rain the Germans brought up flamethrowers and set the western woods on fire.

When did that happen?

What day was this?

It was impossible to say whether there had been days or nights. It seemed to him that one endless period, a nightmarish day of a thousand hours, was in progress; dark sometimes, yes, sometimes light, always incomprehensible. War wiped out normal subdivisions of time, substituting its own impossible measurement; distances were also telescoped by war, so that the whole arena (the burning streets of Warsaw, the red road with the faceless driver bubbling up his life, the desperate madman in the pith helmet, the innumerable wounded, the houses sliding down into the streets, Michal's dusty face, the dark map in the quaking vault, the black face of the pilot in the leather coat) was now squeezed into these woods and this quarry.

His eyes stared at the sky, in which the sun revolved in evershrinking circles. It had dipped to the west, he noted, so perhaps there were still sunsets. He did not know how many there had been.

He heard the rattle of rifle and machinegun fire and the flat crack of handgrenades nearing in the woods. There was fighting in the inner woods. Dead men lay piled thickly in the clearings. The wounded lurched past him bent under their burdens of pain. Exploding handgrenades punctured his thought.

The General wondered about time and about what the date was, which day this was, whether the battle had been long enough. He had not been sent there to win battles but to gain time. He peered into the smoke, a darkness not relieved by the great torches of flaming pine, and heard the cries and shouts and the thin howling of the shells above him and the crash of their explosions in the trees.

What day was this?

—It is the second day, the fat major said. His face was caked with blood and the eyes stared blindly. He could not see without his spectacles. The major's hands beat against the air. His head turned anxiously this way and that like a trapped animal. There were shouts close behind the near trees and the words were German.

—I think this is a Friday, sir. The eighth of September.

So there were still days.

He remembered waking the Sunday before in Warsaw, and being surprised that there were no bells. It seemed that there had never been bells on a Sunday. There were explosions. The sound of bombs, the wild, Satanic howl of shells summoned men to worship.

But now the fat major grasped his arm. He bubbled words and peered into the General's face. The major's face shook like dry flour settling in a bag.

292

—Germans, the major said. His voice was high. His eyes were without hope.

Yes, Major? What was the major saying? Slower, please. Slower. I am very tired. And please pronounce your words correctly. Do not mumble so. And stand erect. Always be erect. Animals walk on four legs but men are erect. That is the difference, do you see, between animals and men. An upright man is an honorable man. An honorable man need fear nothing, can fear nothing, does his duty.

—Thirty-six hours now, the major said. Such hours . . . Germans in main positions . . . attack from the road . . . (What was that?) No word from Pelz . . . the cadets killed to the last man, pardon, boy, in the woods . . . can't hold the quarry . . . (What was that?)

—Nothing can stop them. What can stop them? We have lost!

The General closed his eyes to shut out the sun. The sound of rifleshots and German shouts was close. The crack and whistle of grenades and screams and the dry rattling of rifles, pistols and submachineguns had replaced the crushing roar of the artillery.

He turned so suddenly that the major, who had pressed his face almost into the General's chest, fell over backwards. The General walked off into the woods. There among shattered trees lay the reserve battalion. The men lay motionless on the ground. Tired, grey, they seemed to be covered by some incredible ringworm: tattered and bloody. They stared about as though seeking a familiar face. The officers rose and came towards the General. They moved jerkily like puppets. Each movement of arm or leg was executed with an unbearably slow precision. They watched the General. He listened to the sounds of fighting below the ridge. Time. It was his time now: The time of commanding was over and it was the fighting time.

—We'll go now, he said. He picked up a rifle. He began to walk through the woods towards the sound of fighting. The officers fell in about him and the men rose. No one said anything. The woods were burning. They moved through the burning woods. Pinetrees lay about like toys. Men lay among the pines. The General pretended that he could not see how hard it was for them to get up. Officers moved as though drunk. He felt as though he was about to collapse. Thinking. It becomes a slow, painful process. Each thought requires a terrible concentration. Do not think. Move. Behind them German shrapnel broke through the leaves. A man ran past the General with the eyes of an insane dog. He held an arm high in the air. The wrist was torn off. It pumped blood. This trailed behind him like a flag. In his other hand he pulled a rifle. Blood. Slippery needles of dead pine.

The General's temples pounded and he felt his eyes straining to leave his head. At each step men tripped and fell. Other men hoisted them up, pointed them the right way and pushed them. The battalion of shadows moved on. Then there was yellow jasmine underfoot. Corpses to step over. Flies clustered greenly about empty eyes. Red sockets in black faces. Trees. These thinned out at the top of the hill. They broke over the crest of the hill like a silent sea, poured down. Old, dry pineneedles made them slide and then everyone was running.

—Down!

Down the slope through the thin woods. Bullets whine in the yellow clearing. Some men lie there, scattered, halfburied in the jasmine.

Thirty meters more of thin trees to pass.

—There they are! Forward! Hurrr-aaah!

—HURRR-AAAH!

Now he is shouting fullbreasted and the fatigue is gone and he is running with a dead man's rifle and bayonet outthrust before him like a lance and seven hundred voices pick up the shout and the shout is enormous. Before them, coming to them, are the Germans: strange grey men in deep helmets that rob them of faces coming up the slope in froglike jumps close to the ground like a horde of flatheaded reptiles; toads after summer rain. The ground is covered with them; there is no end to this field filled with the toad-like figures. Seven hundred bayonets point at them, extend towards them, hold out death to them, and the waves collide. There is one vast scream that is also a clash and suddenly the picture splinters into a thousand smaller, individual prints, and men crash into each other, and grapple, and climb onto each other's backs and shoulders, and clasp each other like bears and roll downhill in clawing embraces and bodies fly like pitchforked sheaves. A face appears: grey, twisted, mouthing silence. The white blade of the bayonet crosses it and the eyes turn upward.

—HURRR-AAAAAAAH!

At the foot of the slope a fat German officer rallied men around him. They ran to him and formed around him shoulder to shoulder like a picture out of the Thirty Years War: fit for historybooks. They moved off spraying bullets left and right, with bodies falling off this larger body at every step. Then a huge soldier sucking a dead longstemmed pipe fell on them with a flailing rifle like an iron club and behind him poured a mass of men with swinging riflebutts and bayonets and the mass exploded and splintered off and again a hundred individual combats took the place of one. The German officer threw his empty submachinegun away from him and picked up a dead Pole's saber and laid about himself with that, then jumped clear of the mass, shouted: —*Ich liebe Deutschland* and put a handgrenade to his mouth. The grenade blew his head off. Wetness splashed the General. Then from the bushes and small trees on the right a tank crawled tilted on its side across the slope. It stopped and the gunmuzzle swung and a red flame came from it and a shell soared high into the woods. At once men climbed onto the tank. They pushed their rifle barrels into slits and openings and hammered out the perspex glass and shot inside, and, as a broad Silesian shouted: —*Raus! Raus!* (hammering on the turret with a broken rifle), the lid swung up and a small, sandyheaded youth raised his incongruous arms up out of the metal monster. At once his head exploded under boots and riflebutts.

—HURRR-AAAH!

Blood and the white crushed tissue and the sandy hair smeared on hot steel plates. He cannot look. He turns his head. At once the heat evaporates and he is cold and the sun's rays bounce off his body without piercing. A boy brings him the German's papers. A map. Lines of attack included. Fire plans. The Order of the Day for the First SS Panzer Division. Paybook. The corpse is a lieutenant, aged nineteen, from Munich. Letters. The usual picture: round, smiling woman, proud old man, small girl with white pigtails and the young lieutenant. Behind them the Karwendel Alps purpling in the morning.

Why must there always be the picture? This is a field of battle, a place for the dead and those who made them dead. Why must the smiling living intrude? The red and grey mass on steel plates steams slowly in the sun.

—HURRR-AAAH!

The General thought that the round objects which softened under his boots were heads and it was with a feeling of intense surprise that he saw they were cabbages. Cabbages? It did not seem possible that anything could still grow and live; but these *were* cabbages, and they were in a cabbagefield running for the new line of woods, which grew darkly before them. Poles and Germans were now intermingled. Many pursuers overtook the slower among the pursued and died, surprised, shot in the back. The big Silesian who had hammered on the tank raised his clubbed rifle above the head of a slim, wildeyed German officer and was at once shot in the back by another German. He, in turn, died at once under the bayonet of a thin soldier with a yellow, smokestreaked face who pitchforked him into the back of an enormously broad Pole with a dead pipe who was strangling a palefaced officer, who, thus reprieved, jumped up and ran off with strange cries, bounding like a hamstrung horse across the field. Then the field cleared. The mass of men vanished in the next line of woods. There the shots and the cries and shouts and screams faded away and then the field was clear and he was alone and grew aware of silence.

Here and there in the littered field, among the mounds of twisted, bayoneted corpses, among the gibbering wounded and the twitching not quite dead, men moved on hands and knees like blind and dazed animals, bleeding and eventually dying in shapeless scarlet heaps that could have no relation to purpling mornings and round smiling women.

He had had several lines of barbed wire strung among the thickets and had had round pits dug and had had the men drive sharpened stakes into the pits: excellent ambush. Several hundred men, mostly Germans, now lay in the pits or hung with the wire coiled around them like snakes. Many were alive. One bent against the pull of barbed wire on his disembowled belly and carefully drew a pair of heavy wirecutters from his boot and thoughtfully snipped the wire, and the tight strand whirred up and around and beheaded him. Many had fallen into the pits and had been pushed deeper by the pressure of new bodies on their backs and hung upon the stakes, which pierced their chests and limbs and bellies, still leaping in the pits like fish drawn out of water. This quaking mass filled the pits to the brim. Hundreds of hands and fingers clawed upward through this mass of writhing dead and living and reached about like the upturned legs of spiders, grasping convulsively at everything, attaching themselves to anything, so that men who were not dead, who were wounded and crawled blindly onto this human quicksand, were seized by these desperate tentacles and dragged down. Over all wheeled an enormous cloud of crows cawing in voices that were no less human than those of the men sucked down into the pits.

Two thousand men died in half an hour.

He wondered about Bogacz, the tracker. Had he survived?

And now the sun was setting. So there still were sunsets?

—Two thousand men. It is impossible.

The fat major blinked up from the ground. He sat crosslegged on the

295

sodden soil. In his hands he held a dozen pairs of spectacles. He tried them on one by one. He swore and wished to know if there were no farsighted Germans in the world. —Are they all nearsighted? Is this possible?

Out of the darkening woods men began to come into the field.

The sun dipped redly. Crows flopped down heavily into the field and lifted up cawing as the men came in among them from the woods. The pile of maps, papers, documents grew at the General's feet. The men were impossible to assemble. They came back to the field shouting and leaping. Some danced wildly. They were laughing. They hit each other on the back and shoulders and clasped each other like lovers and rolled drunkenly over the corpses. They fell into blood and over corpses and into the grasping pits. All wore the terrible uniform brownness of moist blood splashed with tufted greyness. They crossed the field like drunken men. The slope where the charge had started began to slow them down. They could not climb the slope. They began to fall; one by one, then in groups, then in companies. Everyone fell where he stood as though scythed. It was as though a silent, invisible machinegun had begun to fire. They slept as soon as their heads struck the slippery soil.

It was the glass barrier.

The General began to laugh.

The glass barrier! He was suddenly completely alone: the only man erect in a field of prone men who were either dead or dying or asleep. He thought that if he woke those who could be wakened—if he could tell the living from the dead—and asked them, Why are you here? What are you fighting for? they would answer: Sleep. It occurred to him that there were only two true horrors in war: the hour of waiting for an attack to begin and interrupted sleep. A man never can get used to these. The pounding came back to his head. His temples filled with lead.

And then he saw that he was not alone; a man was coming towards him across the piled corpses. He saw the terribly white face of the man and wondered: What is there to be horrified about? It is only a battlefield. A field of decision. The man came on. His eyes were enormous. He was a young man, a volunteer. He brought orders and a message from the staff. Far to the west Piotrkow had fallen. There fresh divisions had come from the Reich to crush the last of Rummel's regiments and now roared through the falling night northeast for Warsaw. The General was to fall back with his men and form a new line for the morning.

He felt that he would not be able to move. Nothing would move him now. —Don't they have anybody else?

The messenger stared at him and at the piled corpses. He said: —Are they all dead?

—Is this not enough? the General said. The glass barrier is broken, don't you understand?

The messenger stared at him and shook his head. The General felt his mouth shake. The messenger stared at the piled corpses and the sleeping men. —Is everybody dead? But who will stop the Germans?

Who indeed?

Shades from another world . . . sleepwalkers . . .

The General moved. It took huge effort to turn his head. His legs trembled. His head jerked as though unhinged. The papers trembled in his hands . . . *line for the morning* . . .

He said: —Where is the line to form?

—Before Suchedniow, General. It is some twenty kilometers north.

—I know where it is.

The messenger stared at the silent field. His mouth opened and closed like that of a fish.

—Is everybody dead?

—No. Not everybody.

The General felt the order the way a prisoner feels the point of a bayonet in his backbone. He moved. He began to shout. The voice was hoarse and unnaturally high. It was the voice of a tired old man, he thought. It grated as though dragged across small bits and pieces of broken glass. The shards of the glass barrier, he supposed. The General shouted: —*Officers! To me! Officers!* Soon these arose. They began to come to him across the field. The redfaced major . . . Tarski? Some such name . . . came like a drunken man. Pelz did not come. Pelz was dead in the quarry. The Air Force lieutenant colonel was dead with his cadets. The fat major came. He had found some glasses. The metal frame was too big and the glasses kept falling off his nose. Soon a trumpeter came. The thin music of the trumpet drifted among the dead and sleeping men. Those who could, rose; the machine began to function. With dreamlike slowness the battalions formed.

I ADAM

The thin screams of the Communist came from the cell along the corridor, punctured by the familiar thudding of the metal rods. The Communist no longer screamed in time to the rhythmic thudding, and Adam wondered how much longer the man could go on. He wished him new strength and (oh, so fervently) additional resistance and an immunity from pain so that he would be able to go on, every night, making his terrible thin sound.

Don't stop, my friend, he told him with formality. You are my salvation. Without your pain and its dreadful sound I will be destroyed. You are my clock and calendar; between us, you and I are fooling the Germans.

He wondered if prayers would help, if he should beg God to keep the Communist alive . . . make him, perhaps, immortal. He wished it devoutly. But his thoughts were slow and the effort to control them, to direct them at all, was so immense. And, anyway, how do you pray for Communists, and wouldn't they resent it? Would prayers do more harm than good? And to whom could you address prayers for them?

He listened to the fading cries, imagining the morning. The Communist began screaming shortly after midnight. He kept it up, more or less, most of the night. But by morning—at least it seemed to Adam to be morning—the thin, unwavering sound lost much of its vigor. Soon there would be no sound at all at night and so no way to tell that night was there, and time would be erased, its passage unmarked, and then there would be nothing but the chessgames with which to mark days.

Ah . . . but he didn't want to think about the chessgame; it went on anyway, unending, whether he was awake or sleeping. But now he had the measure of the game the Germans were playing.

He lay with tightclosed eyes, not quite awake but no longer sleeping, pretending that his eyes were open and that he could see. He saw a corner of blue sky through the imagined window, with, perhaps, a cloud or two moving slowly at three thousand feet, and the bucolic sun cheerfully unconcerned and the hard shape of mountains. He heard familiar sounds: birds and the rattle of wagonwheels on the cobbled street . . . klaxon horns. It still astonished him when his eyes were open to see no window and to hear nothing. Lately he had been hearing things quite clearly when his eyes were closed. There was no window in the whitetiled room; only the huge white bulb recessed in the ceiling filled the room with everpresent light. There was no way to tell when the nights ended and the days began without the thin screaming.

He lay quite still, estimating minutes. It was no longer easy with his brain so remarkably dull, so completely tired. He waited for Reinhardt, or one of the others, to come with the chessboard. They would come soon enough, he knew. His hand moved mechanically about a chessboard he imagined somewhere at the level of his chest.

This way and that; aimless. In time with the thudding of the metal rods. The rhythm was a metronome like Reinhardt's cane tap-tapping on a bootheel. Whether awake or dreaming.

He knew he wouldn't win the game, whichever it was: the real game they forced him to play every hour, or what they *said* was every hour, and the game he went on playing when asleep. Eventually he would lose. They said it was inevitable and he believed them. But he still tried to win it. But each time he tried less hard. He wondered what would happen when he no longer tried. But that was something that he couldn't bring himself to think about, no more than he could think about what would happen when he no longer had the screaming Communist to mark the nights for him.

You are my secret weapon, he told the tortured man. I shield myself with you. In the days before the Communist, the Germans had come close to winning the real game they played. . . .

He forced his face into the strawfilled, dusty pillow so that the Germans (if they watched him in some way) would not see his smile.

Let them still think that I believe their version of time.

A particularly heavy blow silenced the Communist, and in the sudden silence Adam couldn't move. He could not think at all. There was cold terror and total fatigue. Thoughts wouldn't stand still long enough for him to read them. When he did focus his mind on them, saw them as words, they slipped sideways and away, like diving shapes of birds, before he could identify them. He could feel fear, a separately diluted apprehension that had nothing to do with the chessgame but went back into the bottomless past and violently forward into a shapeless future. Fog. He was groping in a thick, yellowgrey fog where nothing had definition or solidity. He was sure of nothing.

He felt enormously heavy, awake or asleep; each movement was slow, on and off the chessboard. Each effort was final but, of course, it wasn't. It couldn't be. Too many questions were unanswered. He knew he was being rushed headlong into a monstrous wall of time; the crushing contact was as inevitable as darkness at night; but, still, something had to be done to prevent this collision, to slip past the rushing obstacle and flow on, safe in the yellow fog, on the other side.

Something had to be done but he couldn't think of anything, at least not for the moment. Thinking, in fact, had become just about impossible. Nothing seemed left except to hang onto such reality as still remained and wait. For what? He didn't know, of course. It was, then, like that time long ago, possibly in another lifetime lost somewhere at the bottom of the black well, when he flew a glider and lost control in a sudden downdraft and watched the earth come roaring up towards him with its innumerable trees and spires and curling arms of smoke reaching so violently upward. It was death extended; a matter of no terror because for terror there must be the ability to think and to imagine. In the flat spin there was absolutely nothing except astonishment and then impersonal curiosity, as though he had stepped quietly outside himself and the glider to watch unconcerned. There seemed no need to do anything; he waited patiently, aware of mild curiosity (Is this the time? Is it to be now?), and felt totally frozen in the narrow cockpit while earth and death spiraled hand in hand towards him, watching with that odd, diffused intensity as his feet moved to save him on the rudderpedals, countering the spin, and then the beautiful gull-like craft rose under him and hoisted him away from the onrushing wall of earth turned on its side.

No conscious movement could be wished then. As now. And, for a moment, he wondered whether he was still asleep, dreaming the game that made it necessary for him to move, or if this was, after all, one of the real games. He had not understood the purpose of the games at first and almost went under. Ah, but (he thought, awake now, opening his eyes) that was before the nights of the thin screaming, in the days before my friend the Communist.

My so-good friend.

The game of chess began on his first day in the whitetiled room, which was the third day of his imprisonment, two days after his capture and the questioning by the five policemen. At those times when his mind surprised him by functioning at all (a halting, stuttering process at best, like an abused motor), he looked back with a sense of loss at the simple beating (—*Liar! Give it to him!*), the bathtubs and the billiardtable and the rods. He was no longer sure how long ago that was; there had been several days or, possibly, weeks in the windowless room, when he had been taken out of the context of time, before the nightly torture of the Communist. Time had blown up then. There had been nothing but the game and intervals of sleep to mark time's subdivisions. He thought he would go mad.

He had been sleeping, he remembered, and woke unconcerned, although aware of the sharp agonies housed in his beaten skin, wondering what the Germans wanted from him and what they would do. He didn't think they would do much; this was the twentieth century, after all—men didn't torture each other anymore. He heard the rasp of locks and the hard click of iron heeltaps on the flagstone floor and then a hand shook him, neither gently nor brutally, as if not really caring whether he woke or not. The voice was equally disinterested. It told him to get up. He did and stood, waiting, peering at the Germans through the lightless gloom of his cell. Two Germans in black uniforms, with the turnkey obsequious behind them. Adam was pleased to see the uniforms; they were like Erich's, not like the policemen's. He nodded to show he was ready and they took him quickly by the elbows and marched him out into the corridor, up and down steps to an old cobbled courtyard and so into a car, saying nothing.

He had a quick glimpse of their young-old faces, hard and unmoving as if carved from stone, eyes hidden under the sharpslanted peaks of their black, silverbraided caps, where a death's-head glittered. They did not look like Austrians; here was all the humorless efficiency of Germans: flat ears and bronzed line of cheek and jaw and bulge of neck, supremely confident. He sat between two of them in the back seat of the car, behind two others, feeling less comfortable about his future prospects. If they were Austrians he would think about beginning a conversation of some kind; there were amenities to be observed if, as he thought, they were officers. But the motionless carved profiles flanking him, and the stiff backs and rigid necks in front of him, invited no comment.

In time the drone of the motor and the whine of rubbertires on asphalt lulled him and he dozed, careful not to let his head fall on the shoulder of a flanking German, then woke and tried to look through the opaque glass of the carwindows, eager for landmarks. A slow, disinterested voice told him to sit back and keep his eyes forward. He peered between the shoulders of the driver and the officer beside him, seeing trees and night. They drove a long time, very fast, first up and down serpentines through mountains in a corridor of trees, then through a long, flat valley and small towns over a river. Armed men in pillbox caps and ridingboots waved them on, past other traffic, over bridges. Telephonepoles measured the miles. Small towns and gardens and a light, white mist across the fields. No lights except the stars. Blueblack night split apart by the white road fleeing in the headlights and the great black Opel Admiral with stiff scarlet pennons unfluttering on bumpers. Everything drew aside until they were past. Then they were coming into yet another town, bigger than the others, winding down in highgear from the hill above it, and here the streetsigns and the market place told him where they were: Wiener Neustadt, he knew it at once.

He thought that this was, probably, their final destination; an administrative center a long step up from the jail facilities of any Reichenau. Here he would tell his story. There would be an intelligent officer to hear it. And then they could find Erich and confirm it. And then . . . well, it was no use thinking about that. Something else would occur to him when the time came. He had no doubt that everything would turn out all right. He looked forward to getting out of the car and stretching his cramped legs and eating. He found he was hungry. He peered forward eagerly through the windshield, waiting for the big car to stop.

But the car went on and soon the town fell away at the bottom of another hill, and then there was another, and the white road carried them on through the black night. It occurred to Adam then that the Germans could be taking him to the Hungarian border. Wiener Neustadt was on the way to it; he had planned to take that route himself out of Reichenau. And, certainly, it made sense that they would deport him; what use was he to them? Only an embarrassment, proof of misunderstanding. He tried to make out the roadsigns that fell away behind them but it was too dark. Eisenstadt might be next, and then into Hungary through Sopron. He had come so close to convincing himself that he was going to be put across the frontier that he felt shock when they drove into Berndorf before dawn. He thought, at first, that they had lost their way in the dark and turned to say something about that but the closed faces of the Germans changed his mind for him.

In Berndorf they stopped to refuel the car, then went on. Then it was Baden (Erich's summer home) on the way to Vienna, and then Mödling. Vienna would be next, he knew, uneasy about it. His apprehension mounted as they drove into the town and the various good alternatives that he had considered fell one after another. The great streets rolled by with their roar of motors and harsh clang of streetcar bells and the ululation of klaxon horns, teasing the prisoner with their freedom. One building looked particularly familiar, although there was something wrong with the facade . . . mudstains and broken windows behind a Swiss flag and, yes, the plaque with the white eagle was ripped from the wall. And suddenly Adam felt a special fear, a particular loneliness, as if this battered, shuttered consulate behind a neutral flag was the last, lost friend. No one to help him now. Total aloneness. What had seemed permanent and unshakable was broken and hollow. He felt nausea begin deep inside and the start of tears. He fought to control them both. The German beside him saw him looking at the consulate and laughed. And now the Germans in the car came to life a little; they yawned and stretched and dusted their knees and shoulders and adjusted belts. They straightened their caps. Adam kept his head down until the car stopped. He didn't need anyone to tell him where he was.

In the old days, in the impossible-to-imagine time when Vienna was Austrian and its indolent, easy life flowed with such unconcerned gaiety among the coffeetables and there was charm and wit and time for everything connected with the two, and thoughts of Germany and Germans were best expressed in jokes about *Ersatz* and dull minds and deplorable manners, the Hotel Metropole was one of the best. Adam had stayed there. In fact, coming this last time into Austria, he wanted to reserve a room there and could not understand why Erich had laughed. (—*Oh, you wouldn't want to stay there now. The management has changed.*) The Germans had taken over the hotel for the Gestapo, some government department. Now an enormous scarlet flag with a swastika centered in a white circle hung limp in autumn heat from the flagpole over the bronze-and-marble entrance and uniformed sentries in black polished steelhelmets and white gloves held bayoneted rifles.

—*Raus.* (This from the officer who sat beside the driver.) They all got out. —*Inside.* Inside were marble coolness and tall ceilings and smoothshaven, softvoiced men with clean fingernails—all of this so familiar in this place except for the black and green uniforms in infinite variety, the holsters and the boots—and long white stairs and doors with polished handles shaped like kissing dolphins, and sentries helmeted in oxidized black steel to open the doors and then an anteroom. The yellow dolphins part and come together. The room was lit with brilliant yellow light and everything in it was either white or yellow: walls, ceilings with molded cherubs, carpet, tightdrawn draperies, Louis Quinze furniture (delicate chairs and desks with yellow handles on the drawers and yellowgold and white upholstery on the sofas), a crystal chandelier reflecting the light, the white and the yellow, so that the blackdressed men at the desks captured all attention. They were enormous in their blackness and total lack of color. Adam felt infinitely small. Each of their movements was sharp and distinct and therefore magnified; nothing they did blended with the background, there was no complementing darkness behind them to soften anything. Their effect was one of size, power, precision, cold efficiency, absolute ruthlessness and total assurance.

There Adam's escorts left him. An officer waved him to a bench. The bench was hard. The officer read through papers in a scarlet folder. The folder lay like a colossal bloodstain on the leathertopped desk. Adam felt ill and hungry and terribly tired. His hands shook. He could not control them. He wondered what would happen to him in this place which he had liked so much in the old days. He could see nothing which could reassure him.

At last the officer put away the folder and spoke into a telephone. —*Yes sir,* he said. *At once.* Then he took Adam through another door.

Brightness stopped on the threshold as if brutally thrown back into the anteroom, so that Adam stood, blinking in the dimlit gloom, until the officer motioned him inside. The lamps were heavily shaded with a dark velvety material. A thick, redbrown texture lay across the ceiling; it seemed to press down on the deepstained paneling and the dark pool of carpet and the furniture (all oxidized black steel and darkbrown wood and black upholstery, episcopal and solid) and made the room small, ageless, permanent and warm. Nothing suggested violence; dark tones and a medieval mustiness made the room comforting, as if this was the private study of a benevolent great-uncle whose eyes were bothered by strong light. Here was a refuge of a kind from the violent white brightness.

Adam held his breath, expecting a sudden flood of light to strike at him out of the dark corners like a fist. But the enfolding darkness remained undisturbed and soon he could distinguish the shapes of desk and tallbacked chair and the man in it and then the man behind the desk nodded at the officer and the officer left them.

They looked at each other for several silent minutes, Adam and the man behind the desk. The man smiled, content. He motioned Adam to a leather chair and said: —*Good morning,* and sat back, relaxed and very much amused, and Adam also said: —*Good morning,* wondering what was happening and why nothing was as he had imagined it to be. He understood absolutely nothing. Perhaps he was asleep. A clock clicked slowly like a metronome in his brain. The soft black leather seat came up around him like a vise.

—*Are you surprised?* the man said. A calm, authoritative voice, but pleasant enough.

—*Yes,* Adam said. *No. Yes, I suppose I am.*

—*What did you expect?*

He didn't know what he had expected. Everything and nothing. He thought that he had pictured everything possible, from more bathtubs and metal rods to burning splinters under fingernails and thumbscrews. Grzes had told terrifying stories about torture, and historybooks and legend told more, and the literature of Europe carried racks to spare. Certainly he had not expected anything like this: the gently chiding but benevolent voice in the refectory, the dark solidity of a confessional. He said he didn't know what he had expected.

The officer made a small, chuckling sound pardoning ignorance; a mild sin at best. —*I'm sure I know all the stories that you've been told about us. They are seldom true. Halftruths, if anything, spread by jealous people . . . Jews . . . malcontents. We've learned to live with slander. Envy and spite are staple fare for anyone who has a role to play in history. Ingratitude is often the paymaster of those who are brave enough to bring a new order. And so we wear our crown of thorns with dignity. History will prove us right.*

Adam said nothing; indeed, there seemed little that he was expected to say. He was aware of hunger and of aching tendons. The German looked at him closely for a while, then looked at some papers on his desk. The room was warm, enfolding. It occurred to Adam that he had not eaten anything since Mariazell; the soup served by the fat policeman hardly counted. The dark shapes in the room began to sway a little. He closed his eyes. The beating of the metronome was loud behind his eyelids. He listened to the measured voice and thought he smelled incense and soon the sound of clock or metronome was the huge sound of bells beating in time with his heart against his bruised ribs.

—*My name is Major Reinhardt,* the voice said, firm but benevolent. *I have a job to do where you can be helpful. It is an opportunity for you to do a great service to us, to Poland, to your father and to yourself. It is the sort of opportunity that a spirited, patriotic young man would dream about. Have you had such dreams? I am sure you have. You've read so many books, heard so many tales, in which courage, devotion to a principle and love of your country led you, so far only in imagination, to greatness and the love of everyone who matters to you. Who can resist a dream like that? Who could refuse such an opportunity? You're being asked to play a role in history. I am sure that you will not refuse. You look surprised. Well, that's understandable; how many of us are picked by destiny? And, of course, you're tired, very tired. But you'll be able to rest comfortably soon. I only wanted you to see that you are among friends. We will have many talks and I am sure you'll see where your duty and opportunity lie. I envy you that combination; you are lucky. Not many of us have it drawn as clearly. Are you listening to me?*

—*Yes,* Adam said.

—*Listen as carefully as you can. I know you are tired, but do your best. Relax and listen. It will only be a little while longer and then you'll rest. I know you are tired.*

—*Yes,* Adam said.

—*A long trip, tension, uncertainty and fear . . . They are depleting, particularly fear. The wondering what will happen . . . the alternatives . . . pain, fear of pain . . . the future twisted into a questionmark . . . and in the end a warm room and a promise of everything that one ever wished for. You are a lucky young man, Adam, don't you think?*

Was he? He didn't know, but he supposed he was. He felt as if his body were falling away, absorbed in the tight grip of the leather chair, in the good warmth. Ease and contentment of a kind and a lack of pain; drowziness, a sort of sleep where he was perfectly aware of sounds and shapes but not concerned with their significance. He heard the words without listening to them. He listened to the beating of his heart as if it came from the end of an impossibly long stethoscope with himself at both ends and only mildly curious.

Meanwhile, the voice: —*The world is seldom just to the deserving. Appreciation is often delayed. But, sometimes, destiny can upset the rules when a corrupt, old order is destroyed. Then the deserving and misunderstood, who had been victimized and condemned by the corrupt order, can be exalted and resume their proper place in history.*

(—*Liar! Give it to him!*)

—*You're smiling. Are you thinking about the war? It is a tragedy that Poland and Germany have to fight each other, but it is not as bad as it might be. War, Adam, has been slandered. It is the tool of history. We are at war, true, but it won't last long and you and I can help to make sure that it has only positive results. The war will burn out old corruption, erase all injustice, and when it is over a fair new order will be built. Old, trusted leaders must be found in Poland to help guide the new. . . .*

And then he told Adam what he wanted from him.

—*Your father, Adam. Where is he?*

(What?)

—*We need your father. When the war is over . . .*

(—*The charge, father. Did you see my charge?*)

—*To form a friendly government of cooperation . . . lead Poland to a partnership with history. No other man has such authority, such a following . . . has been so illtreated.*

(—*They called you a traitor.*)

—*Poland will rally to him and through him to us. And you must help us influence your father . . . and not as a hostage. . . . We're very lucky to have found you . . . and you too are lucky, aren't you? You will be treated as a guest, not as a prisoner, if you cooperate willingly and enthusiastically. You would be ineffective unless enthusiastic. But I am sure you will be happy to cooperate in time. Time is of the essence, Adam. You will see, in time, who your true friends are.*

(—*Liars. They're liars. You are not a traitor.*)

—*War has confused you, Adam; the fact of war. Perhaps you think your side is automatically defined. But this is not a war of countries but of ways of life. . . . This war is a tool of justice righting wrongs . . . against corrupt men in the pay of England . . . for progress and new opportunities. . . . It is a wonderful opportunity for you.*

(—*Not liars, then? Not liars . . .*)

—*It is England's war . . . Jews and corruption, Bolsheviks. . . . For Poland, following your father, it can be a blessing. We are your real friends.*

The voice went on, reasonable and authoritative, and the metronome or clock beat out its soft, hypnotic rhythm, but Adam wasn't listening to one or the other. It was all clear to him then: what they wanted from him. The dimlit warmth was no longer comforting, secure; the sharp pains returned. It was so clear with all its hidden irony (obvious to him but hidden from

304

the German) that he wondered what the German officer would do if he laughed aloud. Would he go up in a cloud of smoke like any other tempter? Spitting sparks, perhaps? It was more likely that he'd call in experts with their metal rods. There would be no time to explain that the prisoner who was not a prisoner, hostage who was not a hostage but guest (who was quite willing to be treated as one), was not laughing at his captor-host or at the situation; there was, indeed, nothing amusing about either . . . or about the additional batteries of pain that would be sure to follow. But the idea that he, Adam, could influence his father, that he could be any kind of hostage, a pawn in a political blackmail that affected Country and Honor and Duty as his father saw it . . . ah, it wasn't even amusing enough to risk a laugh; it was ridiculous.

He supposed that, given a reasonable choice, some task that he could do, he might have weakened in time and done what the German wanted. It was conceivable that he would weaken under pain . . . pressure . . . whatever they used. Time, as the German said, was probably important in making prisoners pliable. But *this*. It was impossible. And, of course, the German wouldn't know it was impossible. And that was where the irony lay: He could never be a hostage for his father, even if he tried.

They had it all worked out so well, these Germans, in their German way. Needed: One traitor with a name great enough to rally a nation. Each man has his price. Hostage + Pressure = Price. You offer Price to Man and you obtain your Traitor. And what better hostage is there than an only son?

Ah, but, he thought, forcing back the smile, not for that man. He has too much contempt for his own flesh. Perhaps a different hostage. The woman, perhaps? Although even that would be insufficient. Certainly not me, even if he loved me.

He did not laugh and worked to control the collapsing muscles of his face but some of what he thought must have showed because the German's voice was suddenly cold.

—*You find it amusing?*

—*No*, Adam said, feeling particularly cold.

—*Perhaps you need time. I will give you time. In the end you will come around to my way of thinking. It would be better for you if you cooperated from the start.*

—*Yes.*

But he didn't know specifically what the German wanted, and so he asked. And it occurred to him that he should never let the Germans know how bad he would be as a hostage. He didn't know why he shouldn't tell them except that it seemed an advantage of a kind.

—*Specifically? Very well. We want you to cooperate with us, as one of us. That is as specific as I can be now. It would make my work considerably easier. We don't need your cooperation to treat you as a simple hostage. Is that much clear?*

Adam said nothing.

—*You are already working for us, whether you know it or not; we have taken steps to have your father notified of your whereabouts. That should give him something to think about, don't you think?*

—*Yes,* Adam said.

—We could leave it at that. In fact, Adam, we can rule Poland with or without your father. But with him it will be easier for everyone concerned: us, Poland, you, your father, everyone. Think about that.

Adam shrugged then. He knew it would be no good even if he told the German what a bad weapon he, the German, had in Adam as any kind of hostage. Reinhardt would not believe it.

—It is up to you to make the right appeal to your father. And you must do it from conviction. Without it, our approach to him is not sufficiently friendly; it lacks the necessary warmth, it is too much of a demand. Without your help we are reduced to threats, and I deplore threatening until it's absolutely necessary. I see that you are not yet ready to cooperate. You don't see where your duty lies. I will give you lots of time to reconsider.

Time, yes; that was the answer here. In time some way out would present itself. Adam knew that he couldn't do what the German wanted and he wished he had listened to the consulate clerk before the trip to Mariazell and that he had left Austria. Now, even if he refused to cooperate, he would still be a kind of weapon for the Germans. But, with time, he would think of something, some way out.

—Yes, he said. *I need more time.*

His cell, although the Germans said it was not a cell but an infirmary, was whitetiled and windowless and always brightly lighted. They left him there, alone for some hours, then brought in food. He slept. When he awoke they had brought in a chessboard for his recreation. . . .

He supposed the games had gone on for several weeks, possibly even months. The Germans brought the chessboard every hour, and each game, they said, lasted exactly two hours, after which he would sleep until it was time to resume the game. At first he made attempts to keep track of time; he thought he must have played a thousand games with Reinhardt and Reinhardt's assistants. In the early days, when he thought about it, Adam supposed that none of them needed two hours to beat him; he was not very good at chess, not at all expert. At first he tried to shorten the games so that he could sleep, but no matter what he tried the game would always last two hours. They would be playing, he and Reinhardt or one of the others (unintroduced, silent, impersonal as surgeons), and then a guard would come in and say: *—Time,* and Reinhardt (if it was Reinhardt who was playing with him and, unlike his assistants, talking to him) would nod and point with his blacklacquered cane to the piece he wanted moved and the guard would step forward and move it and the game would end. Then the guards would take out the chessboard and Reinhardt would say: *—See you in sixty minutes.*

Adam would sleep then. He would dream. His head became a silent cinema; the program never changed. He dreamed a chessgame where the chessmen grew to human size and acquired features and these were recognizable as people he knew. Sometimes they had the features of his father and sometimes his uncle, and there was Reinhardt and Erich and Kuno and Adrianne (always the white queen) and the various guards. The faces were not always the same but he was always there: small on the enormous black-and-white board, propelled this way and that. And always he was white and had to start the game and the surrounding chessmen were invariably black and threatening, and these animated black obelisks forced him to shuttle back and forth across the board, chased him and cornered him and, no matter which way he turned, they would be facing him with cold, careful eyes. Each time they cornered him he would be awakened. Then the real chessboard and chessmen were carried in and either Reinhardt or another German came in and the new game began. Each time the game ended, and it was time for his sixty-minute dream, he closed his eyes in terror. Because he knew that he would wake only if he managed to stay on the enormous chessboard. Only the pieces on the board escaped. He waited on the board (dreaming) and hoped that no one would begin the game, watching the cold faces of the black chessmen across the board. But then the thudding rhythms would begin and he would have to move because he was white and it was always the white pawn that began the game.

Time had lost all sense, then, in the first days. It had no discernible beginning and, certainly, no end that he cared to think about. It passed incredibly fast in a headlong rush marked by the chessgames and the intervals between them. He had thought that months were going by, that seasons were changing, and he drifted, mindlessly caught in that river of time, spun this way and that, with nothing on the shore to mark either distance or direction, and each day (or what he thought was day) Reinhardt's persuasion was harder to resist; he could find fewer inner arguments to refute the German. (*—Where can you turn, Adam? What can you depend on? Who won't disappoint you? Now you are in check, but where can you turn? You need a guiding force; it's terrible to be so very much alone. You have friends, Adam, if you would only see it. . . .*) This made a kind of sense with nothing else dependable. And what was right and wrong began to slide into each other like lanternslides overlapping. (*—Who is your enemy and who your friend?*) Reinhardt provided the sole reality; all else ran through his hands like water.

And then one night he heard the first thin screams, a measured interval, and distant thudding so far away along the corridor as to be almost part of the nightmare, something imagined. Certainly the Germans did not seem to hear anything. But then, he thought, perhaps they were accustomed to such sounds and no longer heard them. He tried to shut out the thin sound at first, but it persisted; the rhythm of pain went on like a clock, with terrible precision, and he began to count the beat of scream and rod through an interval between the chessgames, then through the first game and another interval, and so on through games and intervals that, he had thought, marked the passage of several days. He didn't know when he first began to count the beat as seconds and then added up his seconds to acquire minutes. He strained his ears, then, not to miss one sound, and marked the minutes with a fingernail scratch on the paint of his metal bunk: one vertical stroke for every thirty measured screams and thuds. He could hardly stop himself from screaming in time with the passing minutes. His mind focused totally on counting the sounds and the mad river of time slowed and acquired landmarks on the shore.

Time, as the Germans marked it, was a fraud. The chessgames did not last longer than thirty minutes, and the intervals were sometimes only fifteen minutes long. At first he didn't want to believe that Reinhardt had lied to him, that he had speeded up the timeriver. Why should he? But the faint sounds proved it. He counted them while pretending concentration behind the chessboard and sleep between the games. He had to be quite sure, and, in time, he was: For reasons of their own, probably to bewilder him, the Germans had invented their own, private time, where hours became days and days were weeks. When he was sure of this he almost gave himself away. He laughed when Reinhardt said: —*See you in sixty minutes, Adam,* and went on laughing like an idiot to cover up. He could hardly wait, then, to throw himself down on his bunk and begin counting, and, sure enough, in fifteen minutes the guard came to wake him. He laughed then, too, but the guard said nothing. Perhaps he thought that Adam's mind was going or that he was tired, too tired to control tears, laughter, anything. After that game Adam hid his face in the pillow and laughed a long time. He had not understood the purpose of the games at first, but now he did. He thought that as long as he knew what was being done and kept it from the Germans and let the Germans think that he was still confused, lost in the insane flow of their accelerated time, and as long as he could laugh at them, privately in his pillow, he could resist them.

He worked out the exact length of the nightly torture (picking night for no particular reason except that it was the dark time of childhood fears and so, perhaps, the right time for screams and metal rods and lack of mercy) and timed the six-hour interval of beating and fixed the starting time at midnight and the end at dawn. With these to fall back on he had his points of reference; he could keep track of time. The whole geography of the day could be mapped from them. Perhaps not perfectly, but well enough. It was like being lost in mist on the high peaks, with the stars shrouded, in that total silence several kilometers up above the valleys, motionless on a ledge with the banked fog sloping down to the deep well of the world (fantastic shapes of fog moving about him then), when every footstep could edge him over the lip of some crevasse and so on down the sheer wall of darkness into nothing, with the fog moving suddenly to show familiar constellations or the faint hooting of a shepherd's horn marking the world below; everything falls in place then to map the darkness.

He gave the tortured man an identity, needing to picture him; he could not ask about him without betraying his source of orientation. He decided that the tortured man was a Communist. Somehow the words for torture and Communist had become synonymous, and, anyway, a Communist would be someone the Germans would beat. He pictured him as tall and thin with unfleshed ribs and white face and eyes blank under torture, spread on the flat cross of the billiardtable, and he held several imaginary conversations with him to comfort him and to sustain him and to give him strength. It is a matter of relaxing everything, he told him frequently, of not anticipating pain. Adam had learned a little about that in Reichenau; he hoped the Communist knew how important that was.

Conserve your strength, my friend, he told him formally. I depend on you. Without you there is nothing: a brightlit chaos of hurrying time worse than any darkness, nothing to hold on to.

Be brave, he told the silent man with the torture ended and the dawn marked and the Germans coming down the corridor with their foolish chessboard. Time . . . it is so important. It will bring some solution.

He lay quite still in the white glare of the lightbulb, in the white room, waiting for the Germans.

I THE CONQUEROR

They ran twenty kilometers all the way to Kielce. Night overtook them. Erich fell several times, tripping over corpses, and then when they were out of the woods and off the field and there were no more corpses to trip over, his own terror entangled him. He thought at times that he was flying; certainly he did not feel earth under his boots part of the time. He had thrown his MP Feuer away in the field. Now he stripped off his helmet and gasmask and binoculars and mapcase and his pistolbelt and threw them away and then he stripped his coat and emptied his pockets and still that did not seem enough; he was still too heavy and too slow, he thought. Branches smashed into his face. Brambles tore his boots and his trousers. He bled in a hundred small places and did not feel anything. He ran. Everybody ran. The bloody woods seemed to be running with them through the night amid strange howls and shrieks and the gurgling sounds of men who were being murdered in a scarlet twilight.

Libesis was dead.

Scholtz was dead.

Reincke was dead.

Somewhere in the broad woods Dietrich was also running.

—Aa-a-a-ah. A wounded man crawled through the undergrowth clutching his head with both hands as though afraid that it would roll away if he let go of it. I should stop and help him. Yes. Erich ran. The mad eyes of the wounded man pursued him.

It began . . . how? How do such things begin? Was it Bad Toltz and the *Ordensburg* or the training fields at Vogelsang or those bloody purple mornings in the Karwendel Alps? Scholtz used to talk about the purple mornings. He was from some town where they made violins. Mittel-something. Young Scholtz. We are all young but he was truly young. Too young to be a lieutenant, everybody said. Too young to be dead. A big Pole stamped his head to pieces. They crawled up on the tank and Scholtz came out and they stamped on his head. Like a dead bug. A cataract of madmen leaping down the slope. Hacking. Stab. Cut. No time to shoot. Shoot what? How do you shoot an avalanche? Clubbed rifles. Bayonets. Everybody running. Screams and shouts. —*No!* he shouted. *Stop!* It is not the way it is to be. This is not what I thought it would be. This is not what they said it would be. —*It is all wrong!* He looked for Dietrich, who would know how to stop the avalanche of madmen. . . .

Running he thought of Dietrich, who was also running. Everybody ran. Well, not everybody. Scholtz did not run. He was dead. Libesis was dead. Libesis had got the men together and built a sort of walking *castel* out of them and led them back down the slope while everybody else (Dietrich, Saal, himself, the regiments) fled howling through the woods with the madmen riding on their backs.

The flash was white and yellow.

Blood.

So much of it suddenly uncorked.

Libesis had settled down slowly like a balloon with the string untied and the air escaping. First his knees bent outwards and he sat between them and then he sat on the ground and the blood shot upward out of the neck, which looked like the jagged end of a broken bottle, and Libesis began to deflate. Then he died.

Erich ran. He fell, tripped, got up, ran, fell, got up, ran. Dietrich ran. . . .

I saw his slim back weaving among the corpses and thought: Stop! you should not be running! This is not the way. This is not as you said it would be. Or, if it was not you who had said it it was someone like you. This is not what a man does. A man does . . . what? I don't know. But he does not run like this: weaving among dead men with his hands about his neck.

And suddenly the longbarreled Erstalt was in his hand and pointed at Dietrich and he began to shoot, laughing, at the running man but, ah, wouldn't you know it, the big Pole who had stamped on Scholtz's head ran into the bullets. . . .

You shoot to kill a man, to erase him, to wipe out your disappointment and disgust, to make things in you whole again, to rebuild your love, and the bullets go into a man who, if not struck suddenly from the rear, would have smashed the man at whom you are shooting, and your bullets save your target and prolong its life.

Erich laughed, running.

He put his hands across his ears and ran.

He walked about the streets of Kielce with seven thousand other men who had, somehow, ceased to be human in the night. Three thousand more lay in the woods. He could not assemble them. The soldiers stood, walked about, sat in the cobbled streets. Some slept. Some went in and out of the houses. They were bewildered, buttonholing strangers, turning their yellow faces towards officers; their black eyes were vacant.

Somewhere a madman screamed at measured intervals. From time to time some man would start to curse and shout and throw grenades through the nearest window. No one restrained him. Once an old Pole came into the street and several SS ran to him and ran him down with wild shouts and knocked him down and stamped on him.

Erich left the streets and went into the park. The park was small. He sat under a statue of a soldier who waved a saber over some object. Nothing made any sense. Shots and the explosions of handgrenades echoed in the streets. The streets were narrow. They were like empty grey valleys. Someone would come eventually and there would be order. Several hundred men lay around him in the park. Most lay with faces pressed into the grass. Their heads were cradled in their arms. Some walked about and laughed and talked, as though all this was routine, but if anyone stopped them and asked them anything they shook their heads and walked away.

310

Soon night came and it was cold. It cooled the park and chilled the iron bench where he sat. A light mist and a bluegrey haze drifted about the park. The park, the trees, the men quivered in the haze. He closed his eyes and at once the red glare of the forest burned in his eyelids.

Libesis held the grenade to his mouth for what seemed like an eternity and Erich thought: Throw it. Why doesn't he throw it? Throw it and save yourself. They will remember what you did and what they did: They ran, you did not. Oh, they will remember. So throw it, Libesis. Hurry. And the hand moved back. Ah, why don't you throw it? But the hand remained cocked behind the fat neck, past the pendulous grey jowls, and suddenly the white and yellow flash came and uncorked the body. . . .

He thought of Libesis and his betrayal of Libesis. He did not understand all that Libesis had been saying, only the gist of it, and when he reported the incident to Dietrich he got it garbled, torn between his duty and his liking for Libesis, and Dietrich, sensing his confusion, smiled and said: *—You say the lieutenant was drunk. Perhaps that explains it. It is a serious breach of discipline, nevertheless, and you have done right to report it to me, Fahnrich. We shall have to watch the lieutenant.*

It was impossible to know what Dietrich meant by watching the lieutenant. Dietrich made notes while Erich spoke and Erich believed that something would shortly happen to Libesis. He felt like a Judas. He wished that he could take back the words he had spoken to Dietrich. He waited, momentarily, for something to happen to the fat lieutenant.

And then Libesis had died, horribly. That had happened. But had something happened before that, after all? Why hadn't Libesis thrown the grenade? Erich shuddered.

The moon rose higher. It must have been well on its way to midnight when the Polish prisoners were brought into the park. There were perhaps seventy of them. They walked close together and kept their eyes down. They took careful steps among the SS men who lay about the park.

At first no one said anything or appeared to notice the arrival of the prisoners. Erich looked at them and felt nothing. He was not interested in prisoners or in battles or in anything. He was still thinking of Libesis, and his small wounds began to pain him. A hundred small scars formed. Each burned with its individual fire. Erich moved on the cold bench with some difficulty. He paid small attention to the prisoners. He thought he probably hated them. They came on in a compact group, seventy men with their hands in their pockets. Some wore overcoats slung on their shoulders. Their uniform coats were dirty and unbuttoned. They walked carefully and smiled strange slight smiles and their necks were bent forward as though they expected a blow in the back of the neck at any moment. Then all the SS men in the park began to get up and to look at the prisoners. Erich also got up. He looked at the smiles of the captured men and he began to hate them. The smiles reminded him that he had run. This was clearly not the intention of the prisoners. They smiled conciliatory smiles. The crowd of soldiers who had run from the red pits began to walk beside the prisoners. The crowd began to mutter. Erich found that he too was cursing the prisoners. He found that he was picking at the fresh scars on his arms. The mutter of the crowding SS men rose and then the crowd roared. These were no longer soldiers held by discipline but a savage mob. It gave the savage roar of a dog chained on a chain which was both too short and not strong enough. Fists rose and shook. The prisoners pressed against each other and some became pale. One started shouting something in Silesian German and tried to run into the crowd of uniformed savages but the nearest SS man seized him and threw him back among the prisoners. The man fell down. The prisoners walked carefully around him. The man got up and shouted: —*Ich bin Deutscher!* But the guard kicked him in the small of the back and pushed him among the other prisoners. The crowd blocked the way and the prisoners stopped. They pressed close to each other. They were careful not to look at any of the Germans. And now hands and fists reached out of the crowd and began to hit the prisoners. The prisoners shielded their heads with their arms. Some drew their overcoats over their heads. They pushed against the arms hitting at them and suddenly someone in the crowd shouted terribly and a grenade sailed above the prisoners and fell among them and, as the explosion shattered the compact group, the crowd fell on it. In moments, the prisoners were a mass of heaving brown cloth with arms and legs thrusting out of it.

Erich felt as though someone had spilled a bucket of cold water over his head. He shouted: —Stop! I order you! These are prisoners! And someone laughed into his ear and he turned to see black eyes filled with madness.

—What prisoners, Fahnrich?

It was Huneker, the sergeant-armorer of Lenz's squadron. —What prisoners? Do you see any prisoners? Hey you (to another man) do you see any prisoners?

And the man shouted: —What? What? and kept on stamping on the brown rags underfoot.

Erich ran out of the park and into the street. It was a long street. It was narrow. The windows were blank and sightless like the eyes of corpses. Behind him he heard shouts and the pounding of many feet running into the street out of the park. He ran to the end of the street, into a small *Platz* with trees and benches and a statue of a man on horseback. The horse had a thick neck and enormous testicles. The rider held a cross in front of him. Several thousand Poles had been assembled around the statue: men, women, children, Jews in black coats and foxfur hats and beards, workmen and peasants. In the light of torches they hummed like anxious bees. Soldiers and SS men stood around them holding burning torches. More SS stood in the streets that led into the *Platz*. Something was about to happen; he could smell it. But what? No one seemed to know. Major Streisslinger, the regimental liaison officer with the Wehrmacht, was arguing with Dietrich.

—What is this, Untersturmführer? What are you going to do? Why are these people here?

—I am Obersturmführer! Dietrich shouted. Obersturmführer!

—Ober-, Unter-, what do I care? Who gave the order to assemble these people?

—I did! And as for what is going to happen, why they are here, well, we'll see. We will see!

—This is irregular!

The major was unsure of his ground. He was an Army man and he was not to interfere with matters outside military jurisdiction. The SS were soldiers and yet they were not. It was a hell of a situation. The SS officer was his junior and yet he might be a member of Brandt's special staff responsible directly to Himmler or Heydrich. Brandt's men could give orders to almost anybody. Erich watched the major's dilemma.

—This is irregular, the major said. I don't care for it.

—You don't have to care. These swine are here because I want them here, and that's enough for you to know. This is SS business.

—Then it's on your responsibility? As senior officer I must know whose responsibility is involved.

—Yes! Dietrich shook with anger.

—But what will you do?

—What? What? We'll see!

—Well, it is your responsibility. The major mopped his forehead. —I disassociate myself. Is this understood? I am not to be associated with any of this. It is irregular.

The major turned and walked away. He pushed his way through the SS and soldiers and got into a car. The car drove off. Erich made his way through the soldiers to where Dietrich stood. Kuno Saal squatted on the ground beside the Obersturmführer. Between them and the Poles lay a small stack of corpses. Erich wondered how they had got there. The corpses wilted: a mound of puppets, wooden arms and legs raised stiffly, yellow faces shining like wax. On top of the mound lay the corpse of Riemann. It was strangely flat and boneless. It bore an enormous bayonet wound in the throat. The slashing bayonet had almost severed Riemann's head. Scharführer Riemann grinned hugely at the innocent white moon with this great new mouth.

—This must be paid for, Dietrich said.

—What are you going to do, Dietrich? Erich had to know. Quickly he told the captain about the murder of the prisoners. The men had gone insane in the park and murdered all the prisoners. —They tore them up like rags. It was incredible. I recognized Huneker. He disobeyed my orders.

Dietrich did not seem to hear. He stared at the Poles.

—They will pay, Saal said. All these here.

His throat was twice its normal size and his tongue was black. A Pole had tried to throttle him in the field. His voice was now like gravel poured over glass.

—Every one of them, Erich said. I tried to stop them but Huneker refused to obey me. It was appalling!

—Yes, Dietrich said.

Then he began to shout: —You damned swine! You will pay for this! You love this Polish soil of yours? All right! You will have your full of it! We will arrange it, that I promise you. We will fill your bellies with it until you choke!

Saal giggled, choking. He held his throat with both hands. Blood from the crushed cartilege and torn tissues in his throat caked in the corners of his mouth.

—Swine! Dietrich shouted. Bastards!

—What do you want from us? a Pole shouted. His German was fluent. He took two steps outside the crowd. He was tall. His hair was white and he wore riding boots. Erich came up beside Dietrich. He smelled the sweet, acrid stench of the captain's sweat. It occurred to him that Dietrich was afraid. He touched the shoulder of the Obersturmführer and Dietrich looked into his face. The eyes of Dietrich were black and enormously enlarged. They were like glassy pits that went down into nothing.

—You see? he said. You see?

—What are you going to do?

—I mean them. Do you see them? Do you hear them? Do you see how they treat us? Would you say that this was the attitude of conquered slaves?

Erich felt fear. He was cold again, the way he had been in the park when the crowd began the murder of the prisoners. He did not know what was about to happen but he was afraid.

—They must be taught, Dietrich said. We will teach them fear. We will teach them that to speak to a German is death unless they speak on their knees. The Reich will last a thousand years, but they will not see it. Their children may not see the middle of it, but their grandchildren will see it and they will remember the lesson that we will read tonight. (Suddenly he laughed.) Where is Krasberg? He is religious. He should preach the sermon. Do you know where Krasberg is?

—No, Erich said. Listen, Dietrich . . .

—He is probably dead, Dietrich said. He can't read the lesson. Can you read lessons, Erich? You used to talk a lot to Libesis and he knew everything. And where is Herr Libesis this morning?

Libesis is dead.

—So. He is dead. Did he finally draw a straw to his liking?

Dietrich began to smile and Saal laughed, clutching his throat. Erich shook his head. They knew how Libesis had died. They had been there. At least at the beginning they were there. At the end, when Libesis had held up the handgrenade, they were running for the woods. It seemed suddenly terribly important that they should know about Libesis.

—He blew himself up with a handgrenade, Erich said. While you . . . were running.

Dietrich looked into Erich's face. It was a long, hard look. —*Ach so,* he said. With a handgrenade.

—While you were running, Erich said.

His throat was tight. He knew then what would happen.

Saal choked out another giggle. The tall Pole still stood in front of the crowd. Dietrich stared at the Pole. The Pole took one step forward and stared at the Germans.

—And do you see them? (Dietrich stared at the corpses.) Do you see Riemann? Do you know that he was with me in the Kondor Legion and before that in the old Freikorps in Silesia? You should have seen him in Alenstein in 1936 when we cleaned out the Jews. He used to laugh a lot. Look at him laughing now.

—It is war, Erich said. Was it? He did not know. He knew what would happen and he was afraid.

—War? You have yet to see it.

Dietrich looked at the Pole. The Pole stood very still. He seemed like yet another statue in the square, a monument dedicated to total lack of motion.

—Yes? Dietrich said.

His voice was soft and low. Kuno Saal looked up at Dietrich and chuckled again. With each chuckle fresh blood came from his mouth.

—Yes?

—What is it that you want from us? the Pole said.

—Do you see? (Dietrich turned to Erich.) Do you see how innocent they are?

—They died in battle, the Pole said. Did our men not die?

—Oh, they died. Indeed they died.

—More will, Saal said. (He could not say much.)

—We did not kill them, the Pole said.

—Oh but you would, Dietrich said. Indeed you would. And they are dead, are they not?

—What is that to do with us? We did not kill them.

—That is true, Dietrich said.

—We were not there.

The Pole stepped forward and came closer. Dietrich's voice was reasonable. Erich began to think that perhaps he had been wrong to think that something terrible would happen.

—Soldiers die, the Pole said. Yours, ours, everybody's. Is it not their business?

—A part of it, yes, certainly, Dietrich said. His voice was amiable.

—Well, the Pole said. He smiled.

—Only a part of it, however, Dietrich said. He stepped up to the Pole and struck him in the face. He hit him across the face with the barrel of his MP Feuer. The Pole fell backwards across the stack of corpses.

—The other part is killing! Dietrich shouted.

Kuno Saal shouted and fired at the Pole and the Pole jumped up. Saal fired again and hit the Pole in the lower belly. The Pole gasped and sat down. He sat on Riemann's flattened chest. He looked at his abdomen where the small hole was. He held the wounded part carefully, gently, and blood ran through his fingers and between his legs. Saal shot him in the head. The Pole sighed and slid towards Riemann's feet. Then he lay down carefully on the corpses. His face turned towards Riemann's smiling throat as though to whisper some secret into it. At once the crowd screamed. It rolled against the cordon of SS and soldiers that walled it in.

—Now! Dietrich shouted. You will have your fill. Eat it! Choke on it!

He emptied his submachine gun into the crowd.

Saal also shot into the crowd. Bar licked his lips and began to shoot. Then Nickel started shooting, then Schindlecker, and soon everyone opened fire.

A woman ran towards the open gate of a house. She carried a child under her arm like a loaf of bread. She hooted like an owl: —Hoo-oo-o, a long howl of terror. The sound had nothing human in it. At once iron fingers drummed a tattoo on her back and dust puffed upward between her shoulderblades. She went on running and fell headlong against the wall. The child rolled like a football. It landed at Erich's feet. He picked up the child. He looked at it. It was dead. He dropped it.

Swine! Murderers!

Dietrich had lost his mind.

He ran among the Poles hitting them with a spade. Where had he got the spade from? Erich felt that if he knew where Dietrich had got it, it would explain everything. Nothing else could explain what was happening, so perhaps that would.

The front ranks of the crowd collapsed, and men slid and fell and tumbled backwards with wideopen mouths and bulging eyes and the scream of the crowd was enormous. The crowd boiled against the cordon of the guards. It broke through the soldiers and ran for the safety of the houses. The guards tried to catch the crowd but it was like water. It flowed between their fingers. It escaped. And suddenly the guards no longer tried to catch the crowd. The guards began to shout as the crowd was shouting and they began to fire into the crowd and to hit out with anything that fell to hand.

It was a nightmare. It could not be happening.

Erich felt his mouth go slack and his jaw unhinge and hang loose as in sleep. He turned to seek the company of others; he could not stand and watch this alone; but there was no one behind him anymore. All the SS and soldiers and the Slovaks who had not run off after their own massacre in the quarry, and all the madmen who had followed him out of the park where the prisoners were killed, were in among the Poles and Jews in the square. How many were there in the square? Perhaps ten thousand. More? Perhaps more. It did not seem so terrible when you thought in numbers. When men died in thousands you didn't think of them as people.

He could distinguish no faces. This victim was a crowd which had no identity and, since there was no identity, there was no victim! And, therefore, no murder!

The mass hacked and was being hacked and was, in all respects, like an animal which consumed itself.

The SS seemed to have gone mad.

(Their eyes are black but they see nothing with them. All the compressed pain and fury of the battle, the pass and the forest, the terror of the black field, frustration of defeat and shame, the barbed wire and the grasping pits, the stabbing bayonets, and God only knows what private horrors have broken loose and they are mad.

Blood flows.

They are drunk with it.

They are no longer men; there is no discipline, they cannot be commanded to do anything but kill.

They laugh and shout and are insane and kill and they are being killed because the crowd defends itself. It has hands like the grasping pits had hands and the crowd grasps its killers and upends them and hauls them howling into its depths.)

And suddenly he had to stop this. He could not stand the sight and smell of it. Libesis would have tried to stop it. Black smoke blinded him as the houses across the square began to burn. Parts of the crowd had splintered off and reached the houses. The crowd had slammed the doors against its killers and the SS threw phosphorus grenades through the lower windows.

He ran towards the soldiers, shouting.

—Stop! Assemble! Stop! I order you!

They went on with their work.

He grasped arms, shoulders, slapped faces. He tried to turn the men around and push them away from the crowd. Someone tripped him and pushed him from the back. He fell. A riflebutt exploded in his temple in a thousand stars. The last thing that he saw was boots.

When he recovered consciousness he was alone. The soldiers were gone in the smoke that blotted out the square. He lay across the body of a woman. There were many bodies. Around him houses burned. Fire made the square bright as in daylight. A timber crashed into the corpses, scattering sparks and fire, and soon the smell of burning flesh came through the black smoke.

Erich got up.

He ran out of the smoke, away from the sweet smell and the corpses and the madness of the square. His feet kept sliding out from under him. He saw someone propped up against a wall. The man stood with feet wide apart, shoulders against the wall and hands straight at his sides. His head hung down. It was Krasberg. He looked stupefied.

—Krasberg!

The man looked at him as though both he and Erich and everyone in the world were out of their minds.

—This must be stopped! Help me stop it!

He had to shout into the artilleryman's ear. The crash of rifles and machinegun fire, the clatter of falling masonry and timbers, explosions, the screams of Poles and the shouts of Germans drowned his voice. He pulled the artilleryman into an archway.

—We must stop this.

His voice squeaked and at first he did not recognize it. —It must be stopped.

—Why? Krasberg's round, pleasant face swayed from side to side as though he was drunk. —It is too late.

—Come on. Help me to stop it.

—Everything is too late. There is nothing to be done.

—We can stop it, Krasberg! You outrank Dietrich. You can make them stop it!

—It is too late to stop anything, Krasberg said.

—You are a Catholic, a religious man. You go to church and pray. You believe in God. How can you believe in anything and allow this to go on?

Krasberg smiled. He seemed calm and untouched by anything.

—Ah, but you see, I don't believe in anything. (He had the strange, sweet smile of a drunken child.) I have discovered there is nothing to believe in. There are no faiths and no philosophies and there is nothing but the blue emptiness of space. A man is alone. There are no props. But I think that it's good for a man to know that he does not have to believe in anything and still live, still breathe and go about his business. (He went to the gate and looked out. The screams and shouts went on. The massacre went on.) You can't do anything, he said. You can't stop that. They have a thirst for blood, you see. They do not care about their lives, you see, either now or in the thereafter, except, of course, that they still don't know that there is nothing thereafter. And so how can you make them care for the lives of others?

—And you, Krasberg? What about you?

The artilleryman began to tremble. He tried to stop the trembling. He pressed his hands flat against his thighs. The knuckles grew white. But despite this the hands leaped away from his thighs and flew about like terrified birds. His face grew vacant, like an idiot's.

—I am terrified, he said. I am constantly afraid. I hate death and I hate dying and I am afraid of dying and being dead and I am afraid of the war. Right now, I am more than afraid. Erich, we are all dead men.

He stood away from the wall and his hands flew up like wings. He tried to bring them down again and then to make them reach out towards Erich. He made small sounds. Erich turned from him and ran into the square. Some men stood there, resting.

He recognized Huneker in front of them. Huneker was a dandy and the women liked him. He always dressed himself as though for a wedding and smelled of pomade. But now his uniform was foul. There was blood on it. Mud and strange yellow greases. He stood with feet so wide apart that he seemed to be about to do a split. He leaned forward as though a wind was blowing in his face. Red streaks of fingernail scars crisscrossed his face. He swung an Erstalt by the barrel in his hand.

Erich ran to him, slipping in the blood.

—Call your men to order! Assemble them.

Huneker stared. His eyes were like the small eyes of a pig. His face was soft and womanlike. He had the small, petulant mouth of a child.

—Don't you hear, Huneker? Assemble your men.

He thought the sergeant had not understood. He thought he would give him time.

—Eat me, the sergeant said.

Now it was Erich's turn to stare. He thought he had misunderstood the sergeant. The sergeant caught his trousers by their bloody front. —Right here, *bubi,* he said.

—Huneker!

The sergeant laughed.

—What are you up to, Sonnerling? Are you trying to make a monkey's ass out of me?

—I order you! Call off this butchery!

The sergeant spat between his legs. His piglike eyes were red and dangerous.

—Where do you think you are, Fahnrich? he said. What do you think it is? A highsociety picnic? Do you see anything with which to play croquet? You are an SS man now, you little shit. A Fahnrich, no less. So be an SS man and cut out this Good Samaritan horseshit. You call this butchery? You have yet to see it. It was your comrades who were butchered in the pits.

—That was war! Erich shouted. This is murder!

—War. Murder. Don't you know the words! Huneker shrugged. His fat cheeks dropped small flecks of powder. —Dietrich gave the order, *bubi.* You don't like it, you go see him about it.

Erich reached out and caught the sergeant's Erstalt and, without thinking, without considering anything, he wrenched it from Huneker's hand and brought it up and down barrelfirst across the armorer's scarred cheek.

—I am an officer, you swine! Do you understand?

The sergeant caught his face with a shout of pain. He spat out teeth. Blood welled up between his fingers.

—Assemble your men! You'll rot in Magdeburg for this!

The sergeant doubled up and clutched his jaw. —Oh, *bubi,* he said. You are dead.

Erich pressed the pistol against the sergeant's ear.

—At once, he said.

Huneker straightened up and drew his whistle from his pocket. He put his swollen lips around it and blew on it. The SS paid no attention. Huneker threw the whistle down and sat down on the ground.

—You blow it, he said. I hear you're good at it.

—Pick it up, you swine, and call your dogs off.

—Oh *bubi,* I will kill you, the sergeant said.

But he picked up the whistle. He put it in his mouth and blew; his face twisted with the pain of it. I wonder if I broke his jaw, Erich thought. Blood and spittle came from Huneker's mouth. Erich felt a strong desire to laugh. He found that he was giggling. Huneker looked at him and blew the whistle. Soon one or two men came and stood around them.

—All your men, Huneker, Erich said. Everybody.

The sergeant got up. His hands traveled stupidly about his belt, to and from the empty holster.

—Blow your whistle, Huneker, Erich said. One or two men began to laugh and Huneker looked at them. He looked as though he wished to remember the faces of the laughing men. When he looked at them they stopped laughing and turned their backs. Huneker blew the whistle.

Now men began to come out of the smoke. They looked infinitely weary. Their arms hung at their sides, dragging along the ground whatever weapon, axe, pick, club, fragment of furniture, board they had. All of these were red. The men's hands and arms and shoulders and even heads and faces were red. They came out of the smoke and sat down. Some formed uneven ranks. No one said anything. Huneker blew the whistle.

Soon Dietrich came. He threw the spade on the cobblestones and sat down heavily like an honest workman with the day's work done. He worked to catch his breath.

—Oh, he breathed. Oh God. Is there no end to them?

Then he looked up. He looked at the gathering SS, at Huneker's torn face, at Erich with the Erstalt pointed at the sergeant.

—What is happening here?

—The Good Samaritan, Huneker said. The little Christ. That's what happened.

—I am stopping it, Erich said.

—It? What are you stopping?

—This massacre. I am taking command of the company.

Dietrich stared at him as though unable to understand. Then he turned to the sergeant-armorer. His voice was amiable, although tired.

—Your face is all torn up, Huneker, he said.

The sergeant nodded.

—Who did it? Did you pay him for it? You've got to pay them for every drop of blood they spill.

—The Good Samaritan did it, Huneker said. The little Christ here. I haven't paid him for it yet.

Dietrich looked at Erich and at the pistol pointed at the sergeant.

—Who gave the order to assemble the men? Why did you blow the signal, Huneker?

—I gave the order, Erich said.

The sergeant nodded sideways at the Erstalt.

—I am stopping this. You should not have let it happen, Dietrich.

—Stop what? Has something happened?

—The massacre, Dietrich. That has happened. You are mad. You are wild animals, not soldiers. I am taking command of the company and I will make a report about this.

Dietrich sighed and got up. He picked up the bloody spade and rested his forearms on it. He looked carefully at Erich. I am right, Erich thought. I am doing what is right and *korrekt* and expected of a German soldier. Dietrich studied the face of Erich. The face of Dietrich became, again, soft and amiable.

—A report? You wish to report something? Has something displeased you? Huneker has something interesting to report, I know, and now you also have something? Ah, won't the boys at headquarters have fun with all the reports.

He took Huneker's Erstalt out of Erich's hand and returned it to the sergeant.

—Massacre? he said. Huneker's face has been massacred, that I can see. As for the rest . . . how can you say it is a massacre? When we arrest civilians to take hostages and they attack us, can't we defend ourselves? Is that what you mean?

—You know what I mean.

—Yes, I do. But I wonder if *you* know what *I* mean. I wonder if you have considered all the consequences. Failure to carry out an order, insubordination, insulting a superior officer, sympathizing with an armed enemy, striking a subordinate, inciting mutiny. That is a lot to think about. I, too, can make reports. Huneker can make reports. What do you think he will get, Huneker? Twenty years? Thirty?

—Why not a firing squad? Huneker said. I think he qualifies.

—You think a firing squad?

—I think that would be best.

—Would you like to command it?

—I would enjoy it.

—You are a bloodthirsty man, Huneker.

—I know my duty.

—I am sure you do. But I do not think we will need firing squads or

320

reports. If we grow up we will not need a firing squad. We will begin to act and think like Germans fighting an implacable enemy. The Führer has called for terror. He said that these people are not to lift their faces from the mud for a thousand years. They are our enemies. They would cut our throats as soon as look at us. I think even Fahnrichs grow up eventually, yes, and then they are men and do the work of men and do not talk about massacres and reports. (His voice hardened. He brought his face close to Erich's.)

—Listen, Sonnerling. Get out of here or I'll have you shot. You sniffling infant. What do you think this is all about? Do you think we are amusing ourselves? We don't cut throats for the fun of it. These people are only wait-ing for our foot to slip and our backs to turn. If we don't teach them a lesson they will not forget, no German will sleep safely for a thousand years. They will kill more of us than all the armies of history. (His voice softened. He put his hand on Erich's shoulder.) Calm yourself. You are a young man yet, a boy really. There is much that you do not understand. Do you know about men and what they are? They are animals. Look at Huneker, who so wants to kill you. Huneker will kill anyone and anything. He has a pistol and both the excuse and the freedom to use it. That is all a man needs to become an animal. And is that so wrong? Every man is like that; we are all animals. Only in peacetime we cannot be honest about what we are. We cheat and scheme to grab as much as we can for ourselves. In war we can kill. A soldier kills. Learn to enjoy it.

There were some two hundred soldiers around them then and more came out of the smoke with every passing minute. There were still screams in the smoke. There were shots and shouts and detonations. Dietrich took Erich by the arm. He led him slowly to the nearest truck. There he pressed down on the klaxon horn and held the signal a minute at a time.

—You may be right, Dietrich said. I think the lesson was excessively severe. It is probably time to stop it now.

The soldiers came out of the smoke and began to form. The smoke drifted. The shouts and screams gave way to weeping. Women knelt among the corpses in the square. Erich sat down on the curbstone. He held his head in his hands.

I THE GENERAL

The General sat on a milestone beside the road, bathed in the cool white light of the moon, which made the road silver. Moonlight blackened each bush and shrub beside the road. It cast exotic shadows in the fields.

He was alone. No one was near; the last of his sleepwalking columns was long gone on the Radom road. He watched the road as though half expecting someone and it was not quite clear to him why he sat there.

The fields were still.

The air was fresh and chilly.

Somewhere a dog howled.

Shadows were motionless.

Occasionally small groups of soldiers who had wandered off to sleep among the shrubs were brought down to the road below him, and pointed northward towards Suchedniow, the Place of Dry Days, and told to march. They did not look at him in passing. Their faces were black and cut across by some muscular spasm. Teeth bared. Packs weighed them down, pressed them earthward.

Soon even these were gone. The road was empty.

Victory.

It had a bitter taste.

He knew the taste of victories and it was sweet, but this time it was bitter.

He looked across the battlefield. His battlefield. His place of victory. Four thousand men were dead. They lay in the field and in the woods in the white light of the moon. A man in death looks so remarkably alone. The quarry hung whitely above the dead men in the field. They lay in softly undulating piles that were like frozen waves out of which stark limbs protruded at irregular intervals.

Victory and retreat.

Elsewhere the day had brought no victory. Piotrkow had fallen and the flanks were gone again and the machines ground on. So . . . victory and retreat.

He sat and listened to the stillness.

Sleep.

He wanted it.

(Because, you see my dear, I am so very tired. There is this weight pressing down on me. It is so heavy. The night has this enormous weight. Darkness is heavy and a tired body has a weightlessness of its own and a fragility that cannot stand up against the weight of the night. Or perhaps it is the tired brain that has this weightlessness. Certainly. The brain. The body is incredibly heavy. It cannot be moved. Look how difficult it is to move a finger. And the feet. It is impossible to think about moving feet. They are part of the earth. They have grown roots and these have sunk deep and their great shafts go down into the center of the earth and, who knows, my dear, perhaps out at the other side like the slanted poles of a schoolroom globe. But they tremble so. They pulse. So perhaps they are not anchored in the soil. The pulse comes from the soil. It is like the quaking of a great, hard stomach. The soil is trembling and it moves the feet. I can see the trembling of the feet and feel the trembling of the soil. It is as though the earth was gorged and ill and would vomit now. As though there was to be a cleansing of the bowels of the earth.)

Sleep? Well, perhaps tomorrow . . .

He felt the tremor which had grown imperceptibly until it could be felt and then, as he opened his eyes to the brilliant white streak of the road, he saw a black mass move in the darkness, blacker than the darkness, and this mass grew as the tremor grew and then the beat of feet striking in unison transformed the tremor into a giant pulse that beat in time with the beating of his heart.

Before they had become more than a trembling blackness in the general shadow of the night, he knew them. These were the wounded.

He knew them before he could distinguish them from the other shadows;

the ghostly shapes of bushes and shrubs and torn pine twisted in the darkness. This mass did not spill hopelessly into ditches. It did not trample anyone or crush anyone or run or stumble or make sounds of terror. This was not the usual mass of terrified civilians and bellowing unmilked cattle with crazed eyes, the pathetic rivers of the panicstricken homeless. This was a wall. A black, human wall. His soldiers. They marched in step, in fours, in silence, and the wall was solid. It had the breadth and depth and the perspective of defined corners. There was no sound from it beyond the measured drumbeat of boots in the dust.

He looked at them.

Heads wrapped and swaddled like grotesque baskets of dirty laundry. Stiff legs: monstrously animated pylons stamping rigidly. Spotted cocoons for arms.

He wanted to say something.

He rose to say it and could not find the words. No word had been invented for what he had to say.

He watched them.

Some recognized him, nodded. Some smiled. The smiles were black in the white, moonlit faces.

All looked at him.

He stiffened slowly. He felt the cold stiffness crawl upward along his legs and body as though this cavalcade of pain could, and somehow did, transform its rigor through the trembling earth to his feet, and they, in turn, to legs, and they to back and brain. All feeling left him.

When they were gone, finally swallowed up in darkness, the sad, slow creak of wagonwheels replaced the drumbeat footsteps of the marching wounded. A low hum trembled in the air. He recognized it as the joint, mute groaning of the badly wounded. And then the creek of wagons and the hum were also gone.

It seemed to him that the earth still trembled, that the quaking would go on forever and that, surely, all earth everywhere would be trembling from then on, and he looked into the darkness where the carts had gone and could not control the motions of his body.

Radom, the quarry and the mad drumming of artillery shells exploding, bombs and the pool of yellow jasmine in the clearing, the red sockets in the black face of the pilot and the black smoke of the burning woods, and the charge and the tank that had come too far forward aslant the hill: He saw them all. Instantly they were there: the soft, pale head of the Bavarian towhead mashed under hobnailed boots, the man who held his torn wrist in the air like a scarlet flag, the mounds of dead, the pits, the dancing puppets on barbedwire strings, the silent march . . . Eyes right!

And then he saw that he was no longer alone.

Someone stood beside him: the last grey shadow from the column of the wounded. It was the redfaced major. His redrimmed eyes blinked like those of an insane owl.

—What happened, General? Why are we retreating?

The man was quivering as though ill. His face was slate-grey in the moonlight.

—After such days! Such fighting! So much death!

The General listened and the major shouted.

—The Germans are beaten, sir! They are all dead, all finished here. They are like cordwood, like the grass. Why are we leaving and where are we going? Why are we giving them these woods? The country? What will be left for us? What will stop them?

He shouted and his face quivered and great tears splashed his too-large greatcoat collar and he grasped the General's arm as though it was the only solid object which would not give way, which would, somehow, support him. The General looked for words. They were somewhere, he knew. They had to be. Everything depended on finding them before the barrier broke. And suddenly dark doors swung open and corridors unfolded one by one and he felt the last barrier crack and splinter within and something lifted him up and carried him off, away from the road and the night and the black field and woods and the vanished column of destroyed men and, feeling nothing, thinking nothing, aware only of the words which suddenly came from him, he shouted:

—Years! A thousand Polish years, you understand? That will remain! That will stop them!

He did not understand what he said or why he said it. He shouted this because he had to shout something. Anything. He felt that this was the answer to everything. Everything that had been and would be: Poland, their lives, the days of the war and all the days that had gone before and would come after.

That did not die.

That was too much to die; to be killed.

History, time powdered in infinity . . . (How could he say it?) . . . everything.

I WESTERPLATTE

The day was scarlet. Red sunlight filtered through the black canopy of smoke and dust and turned the pitted, pockmarked sand of the peninsula an orange-tinted brown. It was as though a giant lid of dirty redbrown glass had been suspended over Westerplatte to shut out the natural brightness of the sun, altering the colors.

Under this lid the air was still. There was absolute silence. This silence, first in more than two hundred hours of absolute sound, pressed down like part of the remorseless lid. It took his breath from him.

Major Sucharski could not think in it. His head filled with the lack of sound to which he had become accustomed and this was worse than the sound itself, because at least in the terrible sound of War, which was Death, there had been Life or some proof of it. In the still silence there was proof of death.

The major walked through the silent redness to the gate. He fell several times. There was no area larger than the square of five meters without a shellhole in it. His boots grated in the silence on the pitted sand. He did not recognize the sound at first. It seemed like a lifetime since he had heard the sound of his own footsteps; it was a strange experience to be aware of footsteps and their sound after moving without footsteps for a lifetime. The grating sand reminded him of the squeal of rats along the loading basin.

But there were no more rats on Westerplatte, he remembered. No pigs. No animals of any kind. There were some human animals but they did not move. Nothing moved as he walked towards the gate. There was nothing along the way except blackened stumps of small pine and the craters. Often the craters overlapped and made twisted waves in the baked clay. Some of them sent small spirals of smoke into the redbrown canopy. Men lay in some of them. They peered with scarlet eyes out of blackened faces towards the gate, or what used to be the gate in what was the wall. They lay in little metal pools that gleamed bloody red in the strange light. It was as though each of them was bleeding, as though life was ebbing from each one of them and they accepted it.

But blood no longer had that color, he remembered. All colors were altered under the giant lid. On Westerplatte blood was brown or black. There was a lot of it in the ruins of the bunkers. The scarlet pools in which the men lay in the shellholes were the empty shells of bullets with the red light on them. Some of the men lay buried in the metallic pools up to their shoulders. They pointed their narrow, dust-encrusted eyes towards the gate. They did not look at him or wonder why he walked erect in this strange, moonlike landscape where nothing moved erect and lived. They peered towards the dim rubble of the wall and gate over blackened riflesights. He supposed that they no longer saw anything except that gate and what would come from it. Nothing would come from it anymore, he thought.

He walked, falling into craters and clambering out, feeling nothing, his head filled with the pain of the enormous silence, his body suddenly conscious of the wounds in it. Behind him walked Aniolek. The name means Little Angel. My guardian angel, the major thought and suddenly saw the sentimental religious picture that had hung on the wall above the communal bed where he had slept with his brothers as a boy: a frightened child being led across a plank bridge over a raging river by a longhaired, whiterobed figure with wings and a halo. Aniolek had no wings. The thought of the clumsyfooted soldier with wings and a halo made the major's shoulders shake. Any child guided by Aniolek across raging torrents would have cause to fear. Aniolek fell into every crater they came to. He tripped over every jagged lump of steel halfburied in the sand. He was not very bright. He had been chosen to walk with the major because of his size. Aniolek was the biggest soldier still alive on the peninsula. It was important that the Germans see him and the flag he carried. The flag was white. It was made of the white silk shirt of Dr. Slaby. It hung over the back of Aniolek's shoulder like a furled pair of wings. The major hoped that it would protect them until they reached the Germans at the gate. Thus, he thought, my Aniolek is really my *Aniol,* since what he carries has suspended sound and death and the raging river of steel cascading on the sand.

How quiet it was with the sound gone.

Major Sucharski wondered what the time was. He wondered about the date. He thought this might have been the seventh of September but he was not sure. Days, nights . . . they had rolled into one long, interminable column of minutes and seconds. They had no end and no beginning but flowed into each other like the many overlapping craters underfoot. They were marked by events, not clocks or calendars. Thus on the first day Pajak died. Poor Pajak. I did not take good care of him. He died under the knife of Dr. Slaby on the coding table. Was that before or after the roof fell in and we saw the sky? The sky was blue. It was the last time that it had this strange, unnatural color. Soon afterwards it became red. Everything was red. The floor was red with blood under the coding table. Later it became brown and black, but first it was red. It was slippery and red but rubble soon took care of that. You could crawl in the rubble without slipping. It was the last day that men walked erect. Afterwards they crawled. It was the last day that they heard human voices, because on all following days the sound outside made speech impossible. They used sign language and screamed into each others' ears after that.

Thus the first day could be called . . . what? The Day That Pajak Died. But was that fair? So many died. Burda was disemboweled and cut in half. It was the day of the terrible duel between the battleship and the old Russian cannon. Who fired the cannon? Major Sucharski could not remember the name of the artilleryman. It was as though he had forgotten his own name. He could not understand it. What was his name? At any rate the man was also dead. So many died. Thus the day could be called The Day of Duel with the Battleship by an Old Friend Whose Name I Cannot Remember.

That was the first day. The second day marked the beginning of the scarlet twilight. The first shells of that day arced into Westerplatte with the first rays of the sun. Two other warships had tied up beside the *Schleswig-Holstein* and turned their guns on the peninsula, and in . . . what? Twenty minutes? Thirty? The sun was obscured and the lid descended and cut the peninsula off from the remaining portions of the world, where, it could be presumed, the sun was still yellow. The second day was also The Day of the New Sound. It had cut clearly through the crushing roar of the bombardment: highpitched and plaintive like the screaming of an animal gutted alive for some pagan ritual. There was no need to do more than look upward to see the source of the new screaming sound. The ceiling of the bunker was the sky. Down through the scarlet twilight came evil-looking Stukas with bent wings and crooked, out-thrust understruts like the reaching talons of a vulture. They came so low that he could see the goggled faces of the rear gunners as the divebombers pulled up and drove into the murky red-brown cloud. Then the explosions came and earth flew and walls collapsed and soon the bunker of Adolf Petzef disappeared in a flash of orange light and Corporal Magdziasz ran in with redness pumping from where his right shoulder should have been, screaming: —*Petzef is dead.* And then a mortar tube sailed in and crushed his skull. The second day could thus be called The Day of the Stuka or, perhaps, The Day of Vultures and the Screaming Sound or The Day That Petzef Died, but many died and it would not be fair to pick one man out of them all to name the day after. It was the day on which the men sang in the burning bunker. Someone began a song, a strange, harsh sound tainted with madness and hysteria, and everyone else picked it up and the major also moved his lips to the words of the tune he did not remember and the singing calmed the men as they lay under the falling bombs and watched the wheeling Stukas. One hundred and twenty-seven bombs fell that day on the peninsula. One blew the storage vaults apart. Water was gone before evening; at dusk the generators were hit and electricity failed. The major had machineguns dug into the ruins of the old French fort and fire from that rubble stopped the Germans when they attacked at midnight.

The third day was the Day of Fire. The Germans did not come onto the peninsula but fired eleven thousand shells into it during the day and night. They lined the banks of the Neufahrwasser with thirty giant searchlights which dispelled the night. Light . . . fire . . . the sound of chaos and destruction . . . that was the third day. It was also a day of hope, or renewed determination, as the surviving radio brought the news that England had declared war on Germany and France would soon follow. A three-day debate in the British House of Commons had ended when twenty young Members of Parliament screamed denunciations at Chamberlain and his merchant backers and the frightened appeaser gave way and washed his hands Pilatelike and gave word for negotiations with Germany to end. Radio Stockholm brought the news to Westerplatte, and at first the men looked at each other as though feeling the shame of England personally: to be forced to keep one's word, to be browbeaten into fulfilling obligations, that was shame, that was lack of honor. But still, the English were now in the war and soon the French would follow and then the giant French and British fleets would sail into the Baltic. —*Now we are not alone,* the Major said. (It was then, he supposed, walking to the gate, also The Day of the Illusion.) That night three Polish trawlers sailed into the Bay of Danzig and tried to ram mines against the *Schleswig-Holstein.*

The fourth day was The Day of the Cadets, because at daybreak the officer-cadets aboard the battleship, with two tanks and a company of Danzig SS men, launched an attack on the Peninsula. They were beautifully dressed in white, well fed and rested, and charged enthusiastically after a twenty-four-hour artillery bombardment which should have left nothing but corpses to oppose them. But Gryczman's men destroyed them in an hour and shortly after seven o'clock in the morning the Germans sent in men under a flag of truce to ask for thirty minutes' cease fire to collect their wounded. In that time Gryczman, Aniolek and Corporal Lakowiec went out to collect ammunition from the German dead. It was most fortunate that German 7.9-millimeter ammunition fitted Polish weapons. No more attacks came on the Day of the Cadets, but two new bombing raids by planes, and seven hundred naval shells, crushed the rubble where the defenders lay.

The fifth day was the Day on Which Lakowiec Began Howling and The Day When the Last Rations Were Issued and the night that followed it was The Night of Fire. The day began with an attack by Wehrmacht regulars led by the special Pionierlehrbatallion from Dessau, who were flown in by air from Königsberg in the night. They attacked with flamethrowers and mine-throwers. The bunkers crumpled and dust filled them and choked the crews and the crews died burning. It was the day on which a fragment of a shell severed the spine of Corporal Lakowiec and he began to howl like an animal and this sound became a part of the other: the crushing sound of bombs and shells and exploding mines. Somehow the all-day assault was beaten off, but only seventy men, all wounded, were left alive on Westerplatte when the red day fell into the Baltic and the glare of searchlights announced the coming of the night. It was The Night of Fire because the Germans drove a train of twenty tankers onto the peninsula and exploded them and burning gasoline and oils covered the sandy strip from end to end. These waves of flame flooded every shellhole, each crevice and fold of land. They poured through the shattered doors of the bunkers and through the loopholes, into the ventilators of underground storage rooms, into trenches, ditches, lapping behind each stone. What was left of the pinewood blazed like a giant bonfire and in its scarlet glow burning wounded screamed. Into that vast sea of flame fell the heaviest of all the German bombardments: the ships and the artillery in Neufahrwasser, batteries of heavy mortars, railroad guns from twenty miles away, forty batteries of field artillery, and minethrowers hurling ten landmines a minute threatened to scatter the peninsula into the bay. Indeed, flaming oil flung out by the explosions did set the sea on fire so that the burning strip seemed to grow and spread and twist and change its form.

At dawn a second train of gasoline was pushed into the thick red smoke, but Sergeant Lopatniuk blew it up with the last shells of his remaining anti-tank gun and the burning lava poured into German trenches. It was the Germans' turn to burn and scream and leap flaming into the sea, and the wall of iron fell once again on Westerplatte. Soon the command bunker, where reserves of ammunition and all the wounded lay, was a smoking heap of rubble. A landmine blew in the walls of Bunker 1. Men could no longer see or hear or speak but sat with eyes open and mouth wide apart. Everyone was wounded. That was the day of . . . what? Fire, yes, shells, yes, and bombs and mortars and death, yes, certainly. But these were commonplace on Westerplatte. That was the sixth day and after six days of such things it was no longer remarkable. You cannot name any of our days for the commonplace. It was, the major thought, The Day on Which Lakowiec Had Been Howling for Twenty-Four Hours. The howling of Lakowiec had been augmented by the screams of the burning Germans. There was no end to this animal howl and no end to the sound of explosion and the night brought no relief from either as fifty batteries of heavy mortars were added by the Germans. Somehow the night passed. None of them noticed the passing of the night; there was no longer any difference between night and day. The light was the same red glare of either sun or searchlights through the smoke, the yellow and orange flames were the same and the sound of explosions was the same. At dawn on the seventh day the assault companies of the Twenty-first Division and Pionierlehrbatallion resumed their attack, but this time the scorched, reeking, shattered defenses did not stop them; they beat them down with steel before they came to them. The Germans walked slowly, moving cautiously from shellhole to shellhole, preceded by a wall of artillery and mortar fire which fell an exact fifty meters before their front rank. In the front rank walked the flamethrower company of the Light Pioneers. They burned everything between them and the wall of earth fountaining in front of them, but somehow the defenders rose and somehow charged with bayonets and handgrenades and somehow the Pioneers and the companies of the Twenty-first Division were stopped. They were not driven off the spit of land. But they were stopped. They lay behind the firewall and waited for tanks and self-propelled artillery to come up and when these did arrive they rose and moved behind them and this time the Polish charge that stopped them used all the living men on Westerplatte and used up all the ammunition and all the grenades and everyone who came back after that charge had new wounds and bled and was exhausted. Shells hammered into them all night and all of the morning.

And then the silence fell.

It took time for the upflung stones and earth and treetrunks to fall back to earth, but when they did there was no sound of any kind. Slowly the dust settled and for more than two hours no one moved. Nothing moved. Great crowds of Germans lined the banks of the Neufahrwasser in total silence. —*There is no doubt that the next assault will be the last,* the major said. No one disagreed. No one said anything. The men lay in their shellholes and peered towards the gate. Gryczman had fainted with twelve wounds. Behind the ruined wall sounded the motors of several tanks. The crowds of Germans grew on the riverbank. They stared without a sound. The major stood up suddenly in his shellhole and climbed to the rim of it. No one shot at him. He walked slowly about his shrunken kingdom. Every bunker was crushed. Fewer than sixty men remained alive. Thirty-seven of them were unconscious, bleeding in their shellholes, torn, tattered, bloody, some with stumps crudely wrapped in unrecognizable strips of shirt or puttee. The major watched them, feeling nothing. He saw Aniolek in a nearby shellhole. He beckoned to him, told him what was wanted. Soon the tall soldier brought Dr. Slaby's shirt tied to the broken stock of somebody's rifle. The major looked at the surviving officers. His look questioned them. They gave no answer. He nodded and began to walk towards the gate and Aniolek fell into step behind him and hung the white flag of surrender over his shoulder.

This day would be what? —The Day That Westerplatte Fell, the Major said, not knowing that he spoke aloud. The Day of Surrender.

He walked to the gate, falling into shellholes. He saw the great crowd of German spectators surge and break into a run. They ran down the banks of the Neufahrwasser towards the neck of the peninsula. They ran in complete silence. As he walked the major grew aware of the silence. It filled his head and pressed into him. He stumbled several times under the pressure of the silence. Once Aniolek fell over him and helped him to his feet, apologizing. The major saw that Aniolek was weeping. Dirty brown tears pushed through the black mask of his face.

They passed the first rows of German soldiers lying in the sand, and these said nothing, did nothing, but watched the two Poles coming through their ranks, and some of them sat up and some leaned on their elbows and one or two stood up, but no one tried to stop the Poles or said anything to them. At last a young lieutenant came running up and pointed a machinepistol at the major and screamed for him to put his hands up and to surrender. The major raised his hands and two embarrassed Germans took his pistolbelt away from him. The young lieutenant motioned with his automatic for the major to kneel and then to lie down in the sand and when he did his pockets were turned out. Then the lieutenant led him off Westerplatte. As they passed the rows of tanks and companies of men and batteries of heavy guns lined hub to hub the major wondered: Whom are they to fight? What did they bring this army here for? Against one hundred and eighty-eight Polish soldiers on a spit of land?

The young lieutenant saw the major look at the guns and the tanks. He waved his arm and smiled as though all this was his personal property and asked a question that the major did not understand. The lieutenant was excited and his eyes were shining. He licked his mouth. He was a clean and shining young lieutenant despite the dust and smoke.

What if it had been man for man, bayonet for bayonet? What if there had been a British battleship in the Bay of Danzig? What would have happened then?

Pain filled the major's head. He had not eaten or tasted water in two days. His wounds bled. His burns festered. He counted the tanks and the guns and the waiting Germans. There were too many to count. The young lieutenant suddenly stopped smiling. Clearly he had remembered something. He saw the major counting tanks and guns, and shouted, and the soldiers stopped the major and bandaged his eyes with someone's dirty handkerchief. As an afterthought they bound his arms behind his back with telephone wire. Then someone took his right elbow and someone the left and led him.

They walked like that for some time. It seemed like a long time. The major did not think or feel anything. He concentrated on the squeaky sound of sand under his boots. After a time they stopped and the major heard the young lieutenant reporting to somebody. He told how he had captured the Polish commander. Then there was a long silence. Then a low voice, angry and suppressed, began to curse the young lieutenant. Then the voice gave an order and the blindfold was taken off the major's eyes, and his hands were immediately unbound and the two Germans who had led him leaped aside and stood at attention. He almost fell, then, but recovered.

Bright daylight blinded him.

The sky was blue.

A white sun shined in it.

He heard a question, or rather the questioning intonation of a voice. The voice was solicitous, polite: It repeated his name. —The Herr Major Sucharski? Then he saw them: cleanshaven, shinybooted officers, all wellcut tunics and mapcases and binoculars; angular faces, professional and cool.

He nodded, unable to speak.

The Germans drew themselves erect, clicked their heels. Saluted.

—I have the honor, one of them said. It is an honor . . .

He was a handsome officer in his early forties. He introduced himself. He was Oberstleutnant Hencke, commander of the Pionierlehrbatallion. He was redfaced with embarrassment and anger. He hoped the Herr Major would understand and forgive the incivility of the young lieutenant. The other officers frowned at the mention of the young lieutenant. Oberstleutnant Hencke was terribly embarrassed. —You understand, Herr Major . . . a young man . . . like a puppy . . . eager . . . no sense of what is fitting . . .

The Herr Oberstleutnant wished to apologize. He wished to be of service. He was at the disposal of the Herr Major.

—What time is it? the major said.

The Oberstleutnant looked surprised. He stared at the major. It occurred to the major that the question was ridiculous. He had not come here to ask about time.

—It is now thirteen hundred hours, the Oberstleutnant said.

—Thank you, the major said.

He had lost much blood and now he swayed. The Oberstleutnant stepped forward and caught him by the arm. His touch awoke the major. He drew his arm to his side. He felt as though he had been touched by fire. He did not wish a German to touch him or be polite or be solicitous.

—I have come to negotiate a capitulation, he said.

Hencke nodded. One of the Germans sighed.

—It is no longer possible to resist, the major said.

—Of course, the Oberstleutnant said.

—My men need medical attention, the major said. His voice was distant and he found it difficult to speak. —Can you send someone?

—Of course.

—There are many wounded. Everyone is wounded.

The Oberstleutnant nodded. He looked embarrassed again.

—How many would you say, Herr Major?

He did not look at the major.

—There are sixty.

The Germans stirred and looked at each other. The Oberstleutnant cleared his throat. He hummed.

—Of course, he said. At once.

Then he said something quickly to a junior officer, who, in turn, repeated the order to a messenger, who left at a run.

The Oberstleutnant said that he could not accept the major's surrender.

—After such heroism (he said), the only man competent to negotiate with the Herr Major is the Herr General Eberhardt. I have sent word to him. He will undoubtedly permit a capitulation with honor. This means, of course, that officers keep their sidearms and march out at the head of their troops and the troops do not have to lay down their arms in the presence of their enemy. My men will present arms, officers will salute. Then, of course, I have no doubt that the Herr General will wish you to be his guest for dinner. He is a man who appreciates the qualities which you . . . which your men . . . seven days and nights . . .

The German talked but the major did not listen. He thought the redbrown cloud over the peninsula had grown taller and broader at the base. He could no longer see the sandy spit. It lay under the cloud, which, like a living mountain, a cooling volcano, spread ever wider. A sharp breeze came from the sea and tugged at the edges of the cloud. It took a portion of the cloud away. Then it took another portion. By nightfall the cloud would be thin, thinner by morning. In a week it would be gone and soon there would be nothing to show that it had ever been.

The Siege

God! God! If they were all there—
all the generals, the admirals, the
presidents and the kings—theirs,
ours—all of them.

Wednesday, September the thirteenth

I THE CORRESPONDENT

Light came in unobtrusively, a little at a time. It did not seem as though another day had passed, a proper day with a beginning and a middle and an end: the usual dawn and hot noon and cool dusk with all their necessary hours. But neither did it seem as though there ever had been anything but war, any dreamlike fairytale time without it.

His watch had stopped during the night and the alarm clock had been demolished when plaster fell on it three or four days before. But Loomis thought that it was probably close to five o'clock.

It was sometime after the predawn bombardment. The shells came high and slow. They rumbled ponderously overhead; first in formation of a kind, grouped into salvos (great family excursions of them paired in measured intervals), then stragglers appeared (one first and then another, some more impatient and running ahead, others lethargic in the rear), and then the sound of their passing and their explosion became constant and uninterrupted and settled on the city and lay on it like a blanket of mist: a distant flashing drumbeat, hurried and irregular like a sick man's pulse. Lately—a matter of six days—the Germans had begun to shell the city every morning. Each morning for two hours, drumming a reveille before the sun came up. When the sun came the planes arrived and then the pitch of the bombardment changed. The howl of diving Stukas and the wavering drone of multiengined Dorniers weaved in and out of the splintering crash of bombs, masonry, glass and uprooted trees. There was fire then. The bombs struck indiscriminately at the town: homes, palaces, theaters, churches, schools, parks, streets, the hovels of the poor, workers' apartments, stores and warehouses, factories, orphanages, hospitals, museums; all things military and unmilitary. The shells were more selective. They fell among the plants and warehouses of Zoliborz and Mokotow and in the Wola suburb. They did not threaten Loomis in the center of the town. They merely woke him and he listened to them and knew, listening, that the day had started and that the planes would come in an hour or two.

The interlude between the shelling and the bombing was the quietest. The city lay in shock. It burned, crumbled, disintegrated, spilled its masonry like blood into the streets and was alone. The men who would later fight fires and quench the flow of rubble and prop walls and clear streets and stanch the city's wounds with makeshift dressings of timber and sandbag and firehose did not yet come to help. They lay in streets and hugged walls and only gradually took their crossed arms off their heads and turned their faces to the greying sky to listen to the silence, and the firetrucks and ambulances and shovels and pickaxes waited for the men; everything waited and the city burned.

Loomis lay in bed in the silent interval. Soon the night would drift and the planes would come. The shells were in; the promenade was over. Now was the time for planes because day was coming.

335

Perhaps the shelling was a signal for the Germans, some sort of reveille; they would be waking and getting up and stretching and yawning, and pushing cold feet into dewtight boots, and dipping cold chins and noses into coffeecups and stamping their feet, and clamping on their belts with the presumptuous *Gott mit uns* stamped into the buckle.

Perhaps the shelling was connected with the fact that streets filled with people before dawn: Soldiers marched to trenches and barricades, and the wounded drifted out of these towards hospitals and parks and schools and churches and public buildings, where, in the gangrenous stench of inattention, the wounded of the day before made room for them by dying; and the trenchdigging and barricade-mending parties of old men and youths and girls massed in the squares, and women went out in search of food and fuel, and lines stood at the groceries and commissaries and at wells, and firemen sat in drunklike stupor around their equipment, and ambulances rattled over rubble. Excellent targets, these.

The Germans had come up to Warsaw late last Wednesday afternoon, which was the sixth day of September and of the war. That was the fine thing about this war for a correspondent, Loomis supposed: You could look at a calendar and see which day of the war it was.

No one in Warsaw thought the Germans could come up so fast. They came in great numbers out of the southwest through the Piotrkow Gap, two full divisions roaring in the huge dustcloud: six hundred tanks, assaultguns, eager men flushed with victory, confident after their hundred-kilometer gallop from the Warta River.

Assault!

It came at once. It was as though there could be rest for the Germans only inside Warsaw. The tanks swung off the roads into the villagegardens and picnicgrounds of Wola and Ochota and roared fullthrottle into small huts and the greystone houses of the southern suburbs, pushed by an insane hunger for destruction. Shouting men followed their machines, jumping over rubble. They bit into the suburbs, hung on, pushed on, fought for each house and every garden fence, died, ran and came back in a fresh wave, piled up their greygreen walls of bodies, smashed in a wave of steel and enthusiastic flesh against the bayonets of General Czuma's garrison, and finally ebbed, leaving torn debris. One hundred and forty tanks destroyed, ten captured. Nine hundred panzertroppers dead.

They drew off then, late in the evening, and brought up their siegeguns and set up their schedules. You could depend on them to set up working schedules, Loomis thought, yawning, listening to the silence.

It went on like that for some days, day after day unrelieved: morning artillery and bombing, afternoon bombardments (a potpourri of miscellaneous destruction), and a particularly heavy shelling around dinnertime, then a continuous splattering of shells throughout the night. The Germans tried no new assaults until September 12. Then they attacked along the whole perimeter so that no sector could come to the assistance of another.

I went down there last night, Loomis thought, unwilling to remember the aftermath on the barricades. The stacks of massacred dead were seven men high.

Ah, but he didn't want to think about dead men so early in the morning. He didn't want to think about much of anything. It was too difficult just to get up without feeling empty; the days themselves, filled with insanity, some perverted purpose, seemed dead and corrupt.

The room was full of dust disturbed by the bombardment. There hadn't been enough time since the shelling for the dust to settle. Loomis tasted the dry plasterdust and wondered if the telephonelines had been repaired in the night and dialed the number of Swiderski's flat. The telephone rang a long time but there was no answer.

This was unusual. He thought about that (drowsily at first, then with awakening interest, prodded by instinct). He had not known the pressdepartment man to get up that early unless something important was happening, some special work to be prepared for morning release.

The light made bolder inroads on the shadows in the room and Loomis instinctively listened for the drone of aircraft motors. They should be on their way. They should be here. But the air was remarkably still. He was quite sure, then, that something was happening.

In the house across the street moved the shadows of a family—the man and woman, anyway. The man dressed and wrapped a scarf around his neck and put the gasmaskbag over his shoulder and picked up the shovel; the woman hefted a pickaxe. Morning, dear. Good morning. Have a nice day on the barricades. You too, my dear. See you tonight? Perhaps.

There were wet sounds of a curtain slapping windowpanes and the disembodied hum of traffic elsewhere, and the grating sound of boots on fractured pavement, the hundred small sounds of that time of day, sharper and clearer than later in the day: the clash of spadeblades in overhead collision (while the mostly old and very young trenchdigging volunteers walked into each other in sleepsodden formation), the dry rattle of riflebutts on cobblestones, commands, the slurred footsteps of the night's wounded, curses. And the boots. Always the patient boots.

He watched the man and woman in the window across the street. They faced each other across a table drinking coffee. In hats and boots. Gasmasks. Spade and pickaxe handy. What were they really saying and thinking?

Getting up, looking for his shoes, feeling the itch of five bathless days, brushing off plasterdust, he wondered how long the siege would last. He did not think it would last long: Surely no one believed that there were still things worth defending to the end.

Swiderski did not think the siege would last, but for a different reason. Relief was coming, after all. Warsaw was now surrounded on three sides. The Germans had finally managed to reach it from the north and had also cut the Vistula below it, but the Poles still had their three field armies in the west and these were coming back as fast as battles and the Germans and clogged roads and ruined railroads and the unmerciful hot sun in a clear sky would let them. Nobody doubted that as soon as the field army of Kutrzeba and what was left of Rummel's and Bortnowski's came to Warsaw the *ofenzywa* would begin and the inevitable miracles would start to happen. Then in some not quite clear but oh-so-ardently-believed-in manner the Germans would be driven to Berlin.

In the cafés, under the linden trees, in the food lines, the water lines, the fuel lines and all the other patient lines that make up a siege, the talk was all about the great offensive. It would be, naturally, great. No other scope could be imagined for it. There would be singing regiments and thundering hooves, waving battleflags and all the glorious panoply that civilians imagine. On to Berlin! And saltcellars and pepperpots described great sweeping movements on starched tablelinen battlefields, and ranks of matchsticks captured mounds of breadcrumbs. This was Kutrzeba and this was Bortnowski and here the cavalry and there the infantry and this cigarbutt was Guderian and this was the offensive.

Certainly, this much was true: New regiments marched through the city every day out of the east, from the undisturbed vast stretches of yellow field and black forest, the unbombed and still undemolished no man's land between east and west, the heart of Poland, or what the Poles said was their country's heart—the Eastern Lands where Tartars, Russians, Mongols, Turks, Huns, and all the other history-styled Scourges of the Lord had come with the sweet smell of Europe in their nostrils and made the land fertile with their bones. The Poles called it the buckler of civilization. Fools—as though a buckler was not expendable.

Still, they looked good, these eastern soldiers: hardhanded, heavyfooted. Big men grown hard in years of skirmish on the Russian border.

On to Berlin!

There was enthusiasm and anger and the necessary indignation and there was patriotism and determination, and these, Loomis supposed, were some of the ingredients of a victory; and if there was no motor transport to speak of, if there were no functioning railroads, if ammunition and food were lacking and there was not enough artillery, that was not the soldiers' fault.

And other facts were true. If what they said in their communiqués was true, their situation had improved a little. The German drive had slowed. The battleline was almost straight, running south out of the eastern edge of Prussia, curving westward before Warsaw and east again below it, and then straight down towards the mountains and the Slovak border. In the great bulge west of the Vistula were the hurrying field armies. The Germans no longer had automatic flanking privileges. A crisis was coming.

The Germans had come too far too quickly, an avalanche of metal pouring quicker than anyone, including Germans, had expected. Loomis thought that even the Germans would not have expected to come so far so soon. They had been in the war business a long time, and this was not their way of doing it. Chaos, confusion, luck—none of that was the German way of doing business. The Germans were professionals, after all. They were men of habit. They were the twentieth-century experts in efficiency and planning and timeclocks and precision mechanisms and production schedules. Experts don't get confused. They don't need luck so long as they have schedules. So, Loomis thought, they must be very much surprised to have so much success so badly out of schedule. They had driven so deep into the soft throat of this country out of the Piotrkow Gap that they were confused. No one had scheduled any drives from Piotrkow. The wild ride of the panzers had outrun the schedules and marching infantry and trains and supplies and all the other intricate ingredients of German warfare; these were now stretched along interminable weary miles, armorless and exposed. On maps they looked like a grey, manyheaded beast whose body could not keep up with the hungry heads. The beast was off balance. The rubbery grey necks were taut and thin and above them hung the western bulge like a ponderous axeblade waiting for the tipping fingertouch. In this bulge the Polish field armies were looking for a place to strike.

A crisis was coming. It is a thing you can almost touch, almost see. Today, tomorrow, sometime: Something would begin.

The Poles were too compressed in the iron circle of the western bulge. The Germans were stretched thin below them. And there was irony in this, Loomis thought. Because it was the Germans who had managed to concentrate the Poles, forging the axe that hung above their necks; no Polish general had been able to do it. The Germans had tried so hard to break up the Poles west of the Vistula that they had pushed too hard. They had attacked from every possible direction. But the Polish armies did not disintegrate or scatter. The German iron ring compressed them, and now, for the first time since the war began, a Polish general had many troops within reach.

It was all there, in the stories he had written and never sent, a growing mound under plasterdust on his table. He wondered, now and then, what he would do with all that dirty paper. There was no way to get it out of Warsaw.

But each day he added to it anyway. It was his record of the war. It would go on as long as the war went on, and that, of course, still had time to go: There had been no ultimate decision. A war had started, and there had been battles, and a huge three-day battle on the border ended in a complete German victory, and no Pole was chauvinist enough to deny it. No one had expected anything else. What counted (the Poles said) was the coming battle. There had been a German breakthrough, certainly, and then a period of confusion. Chaos. The Hour of Uncertainty was a good name for it, he thought: ten days of confused struggle like the thrashing of a prehistoric monster in a fog, a shapeless thing without form or name composed of roars and breaking sounds and anger, spilling itself along nine hundred miles.

But now a breaking point was coming, a decisive stroke.

He started dressing, looking with distaste at his huge manuscript. New plasterdust had fallen on it in the night. He went to the door and shouted for the houseman. There was no longer runningwater to be had in Warsaw and he wanted a shave.

He felt dirty and sweaty, and he swore, thinking as he did so that perhaps he would come across the General's girl again before the day was over. He felt a sympathy for her and wondered why. Sympathy: fellow feeling, according to the dictionary. Feeling what and whose? Well, maybe that is all it was. All it is.

He went out on the balcony; easy to do with the French windows gone. The day had come but the planes had not and this was unnatural. The sky was clean of contrail and the ragged powderpuffs of antiaircraft shells exploding. He squinted up in search of the familiar silver echelons of threes that came each morning from the west and tried to pick out the familiar multiengined drone, but there was nothing in the sky.

No planes.

No clouds.

No sun. The sun was still far in the east climbing out of Russia. It was, appropriately, red. The city lay motionless in unnatural stillness. It was as though all its inhabitants had become invisible in the night or had abandoned their town and streets and homes and favorite cafés to an equally invisible invader.

But there were distant sounds: the feverish drone of cannonfire so faint as to be almost merely imagined and more like silence multiplied several hundred times. It was like a cloud, he thought, listening to it, wondering what it was. A great battle was taking place somewhere in the west.

And then he noticed that his street was not deserted after all, that there were many men and women in it—in doorways and against walls and under trees, and that was why he had not seen them at first. They were hidden. They made no sound of any kind. They held their heads cocked to the distant sound. Old women knelt. Some old men were kneeling.

Loomis watched the day's battle from his rooftop. He climbed it with a basket of bread and sausage (solicitously packed for the American *Herr* by Frau Vogel, who was getting more German every day), and his old binoculars. They were the Zeiss lenses of 16X magnification which he had taken off the Spanish priest: beautifully precise. The battle was a wall of smoke which coiled like a grey snake about the Wola and Ochota suburbs; it moved and twitched and rolled back and forth, and poinpoint lights glittered in it like golden scales.

Occasionally a little rectangle like a shrunken matchbox fell out of the smoke and hesitated and turned and disappeared in the smoke again with little red and yellow fires twinkling about its front, and antlike things crawled in and out and wheeled tiny guns to the edge of the smoke as though it was the shoelace of a giant, a nightmare Gulliver. Other black insects ran and fell in microscopic cabbages. War was a pop and rattle and a tinny drumming; it was a show to be watched through binoculars; a matter of shapes and colors and their shifting to be remembered and recorded: the way the smoke looked solid and the way it rolled. The snakelike coils of the smoke contracting and expanding. The jeweled glitter of innumerable fires.

The city lay below him like a soldier's gear spread out for fieldinspection. So many streets and alleys and so many parks. Here the cathedral and there the museum and there the Institute of Physical Culture. The prescribed number of gas works and electric plants and an oversize *Filtrownia*. An excess of churches. Too few schools and too many churches. The one is not a substitute for the other in the twentieth century. Churches and streets and squares laid out for inspection. So many houses in so many streets and so many centuries breathing in the stone, and he, high on the roof on the escarpment above the town, detached and cynical like a god, could be critical. The city would not pass inspection. There was too much smoke. There was too much rubble and devastation in the streets. There were too many black gaps torn in it. The parks and the avenues were no longer green but brown and black and pitted with yellow clay and suffocating under their decapitated trees, and churches lacked their steeples and glared with empty windows, and broken bridges had tumbled stupidly into the Vistula as though aware of their unimportance in this dry month. The human warrens breathed heavily, closepacked under the immense hot sun.

He watched the battle ebb, and the rattling dwindled and soon enough the sun set. Night came and Germans were at rest.

Later that night, sitting in a café on the Marzalkowska, a place of snowy tablecloths and Turkish coffee purpling in the candlelight, and good Madeira and Balkan cigars with their incredible long ash, among the undespairing, animated, almost unaffected people who laughed and argued and gesticulated and were so witty and charming and looked so unconcerned, whose mobile faces blurred and shifted in the candlelight and disappeared in blue smoke like divers in water, whose eyes and voices were brilliant and reflected light like the many faceted jewels of the women, and who wore their pretty frocks and smiles and gallant uniforms as though the windows were not spilled out in the street and the ceiling were not etched with the black latticework of crumbling plaster and the dead blackout curtains were only the result of the obese proprietor's morbid preoccupation with respectability and the dark greasy stains outside the door were not the remnants of a gutted horse and the horse were not in the kitchen being carved for service and the old waiters were still the young waiters and the young waiters were not asleep under the barricades (some permanently), Loomis said:

—This is the damnedest war. And you're the damnedest people.

Swiderski laughed. —It is? We are?

—I'd say so. Try and see how this place looks to an outsider. Outside, this town, getting torn apart. The Germans are cutting up your Army into pieces. They've broken through just about where they wanted no matter what your propaganda geniuses say about it. For ten days you've been cut off from the coast. Your country is a burning pile of rubbish. You've lost half your men and about a quarter of your country, you have no railroads or highways that haven't been bombed, and if there's one bridge still standing I'd like to see it. Even you, my optimistic friend, must see that your allies aren't about to help. You've been written off. The Germans are beating on your doors and what are you doing?

—Amen, Swiderski said. He seemed very much amused. Clearly he knew something.

—Well? What's so funny?

—You, my dear outsider. You think we're finished while we haven't even started properly. Or, if we have, it isn't generally known.

—Oh, come. Be serious.

—I *am* serious. I have a little bit of news for you, my friend. You *are* interested in a little news?

—Not particularly. Of course, if you have jailed all your censors and got the telegraphs away from Army control, and if I can get one word out of this place, enough to let my boss know that I'm still alive, I'd find it interesting.

Swiderski laughed and signaled to a waiter.

—Champagne, he said.

—You've lost your mind, Loomis said.

—Have I? Ha ha. We'll see. Wait till you hear the news.

—You've captured Hitler? Somebody woke the English? The French have got their fingers out? Please, I can't wait. Particularly since I can't tell anybody about anything.

—Well, you'll have to be patient about sending stories for a little longer. Maybe a week, maybe two. But soon now, my friend, you will be able to send out a book!

—I bet.

—Still doubting? Well, we'll see who laughs best. I think I will have this fine last laugh. You see, my friend . . . you might be interested to know . . . we have begun the offensive.

Loomis said nothing and Swiderski laughed.

—Well, what do you think about that?

Loomis shook his head. —I'd hate to tell you.

—It is the end of our retreat and the start of theirs. This is the breaking point, the turning point. This is what we have waited for. Now, what do you say? Isn't that fine news?

—Oh, excellent. But tell me something, friend. When are you going to start being realistic? There'd be more news in that.

Swiderski waved his arm: a tolerant gesture. —You have no faith, that is the trouble with you. You are a cynic. That is professional, of course. But wait until you hear about it. It has been marvelous, a wonderful success. Our people have attacked on a forty-mile front. They have already destroyed one German division and have another trapped. They have advanced forty kilometers already.

Loomis sighed. —Well, good for them.

—You'll see. Oh yes, you'll see, my doubting friend. This is the critical moment. From now on everything will change.

—Sure, Loomis said.

—You'll see.

—It'll do one thing, though. It'll keep the German planes away from here for a while, and that's all right with me. I'm getting damn tired of waking up with half my ceiling in bed with me every morning.

—Poor Mister Loomis, the Pole said. He laughed, shaking his head, wiping an eye. —Such poor company in bed. But perhaps we can send you something from Berlin in a week or two.

—Sure, Loomis said. Send me Hitler's mustache.

—It's possible, the Pole said. Everything is possible.

Swiderski went on laughing.

Then there was laughter by the bar and, looking up towards this sound, which suddenly possessed a macabre quality, a touch of madness like a wedding song taped accidentally into the sound track of an old man's death scene, he saw the General's woman: very gay, and with that shortly-to-be-strained expression that meant too many thoughts suppressed and tears held back and too much conscious trying for indifference. She was pressed close against the bar. The crowd was thick around her. Their faces were insistent and pink like fresh skin on a wound. She wore a white dress with a collar and sleeves. Her face was pale, the eyes enormous. He saw her smiling and talking to the man beside her and now and then she touched the man's shoulder with her gloved hand as she talked to him.

Swiderski talked but Loomis didn't listen. He watched the girl by the bar, her pale face and animated hands, making such small gestures. She was constantly in view. The crowd moved and swallowed her, but now and then it shifted and then he could see her.

He had thought about her only once or twice since the party the night before the war began, in a passing way. But now he thought about her and the party. His interest in her then had been mild at best, although there had been that one moment of exhilaration; he remembered it. He had not thought that he would see the girl again except as just another face at parties, and next time the greeting would be less constrained, the conversation longer, because, having been introduced, they could claim a right.

But there had been something more than sophomoric speculation. He had felt . . . what? Anger? Not much of it. Sympathy of an uncertain kind kept returning. Anger meant taking sides, but you could feel vague sympathy without involvement. And so . . . sympathy. She had held up her shoulders with such determination.

There had been something about her tense insistence on indifference that made him think of Pawel. He thought that she and Pawel would understand each other, and he thought that if he could break through the outer edge of their indifference he would understand them both, would understand what made such people what they were.

He searched for her now in the crowd, then saw her. The man she had been with was gone. She was alone. Her mouth was a tight red line in her white face under the enormous eyes. He did not think she liked to be alone and wondered where the man had gone and why she was not with the General. Perhaps it was all finished for her with the General. Such things began and ended simply enough at home; they were a routine, a game of musical beds if you like. But here it was taken seriously enough. So if it was all over with the General for her, she was alone indeed. And suddenly he felt his own aloneness, not the kind that comes of being in a foreign country but the kind that says, There is no country for you anywhere; these people don't mean anything and therefore don't exist. But no people anywhere have meant anything that lasted. You are alone and always have been, one way or another, and look, here suddenly is another face trying for indifference, and this is a bond. . . .

He felt a touch of panic then. Careful! Never reveal yourself. You are alone and that is good. Comfortable. Safe. Keep it safe. That too is part of the Good Life, the uncomplicated Dream.

And suddenly Loomis wanted to get out of there. He wondered if his thoughts had showed. It doesn't do to open oneself up before anyone: They may use your open self against you. You laugh and you tell jokes, exude jollity and friendship, and you are all right. Because that is a part of The Good Life. That is what you aim for. You don't let the veneer crack, because you're all veneer. When this carefully cultivated front of a thousand smiles and quips burned in with sunlamps (with never a meal missed except by choice) begins to crack, you run. You've got to run. It took four painful years of Colgate to buy your nice veneer, and it took your rich wife (with her own veneer of kneesocks, sportscar, polocoat, and ten thousand baths) to put a gloss on it, and you are happy in it and forget that there might be something under it. Do what you've learned while buying the veneer: Run when emotion shows. A thoughtful face does not fit the Dream, and that, he thought, is the last thing that you learned at Colgate.

So he got up, and saying something about air and how he needed it in that hot room (feeling his face tight as though wooden and the salesman's smile painted like a bright insect on his face), he made his way among the tables.

White tablecloths and animated hands.

—*Pardon, pardon.*

In French. It would not do to push his way in German. Not even Colgate teaches that much gall.

—*Pardon.*

—*Certainement, monsieur. Êtes-vous français?*

—*Americain.*

—*Un pays fort beau. Et* (with a hesitant smile) *qu'est-ce qu'on dit en Amerique de nous . . . de la guerre?*

—Ah. (Make that smile solid, make it firm. Don't tell them about the latest baseball scores or the latest dancecraze or about Tommy Manville's latest wife, which is about all that *on dit en Amerique*.) *Pardon, pardon.*

Among the tables to the bar and the door beyond it.

(The bar is crowded. She has turned from it and looks for a table where she can sit down but they are also crowded. Men look up at her because she is alone and women *of good family* do not come alone or stay alone in a café. She ignores the men. Her back is very straight and her head is high. She waits for someone to get up and offer her a chair.)

Loomis wondered if she knew that no one would.

He went on to the door, glad that he had not stopped to talk to her. It would have been embarrassing.

Three steps more. Then the door. The night was cool. It smelled of smoke and rubble and dead roses.

Somehow he knew she would come out into the street. Whatever it was that she had tried to do by coming into the café (and you could tell by her careful hair and simple jewelry and animated smile that she had tried something) had obviously failed. They did not want her there, any more than they wanted her at the other party.

She looked at him in passing and went on, pulling at the belt of her light summer coat. He thought she recognized him. She had almost stopped and, he thought, would have if he had spoken or made a sign of recognition. But he had not, and she went on, tugging at the belt with one hand and trying to straighten out her collar with the other. The collar had turned inside her coat under her hair. Obviously no one had helped her to put on her coat.

—Here, let me help you, he said, coming up behind her.

She stopped uncertainly. Her face was urgent with the need for recognition. She looked vulnerable and small and stubborn and her eyes would not meet his. The sound of many trucks came from across the Vistula. They sounded close. The moon was yellow in the unobstructed sky. There was an undefined urgency about her in the yellow light—poor light that smoothed away the harshness.

And now that he had started talking to her he could not stop. It was as though he was afraid that she would turn and leave the moment he stopped talking and make him look a fool.

—We've met before, you know? We were at a party together two weeks ago. Perhaps you remember? No reason why you should, of course. It was an Information Ministry reception for foreign correspondents at the Bristol. Or was it the Europejski? A large room with angels on the ceiling and a balcony and a small garden outside. The garden had an artificial lake. You were out there at first. Then you came inside. You wore a black dress (he went on desperately). You were with General Prus and I was with his nephew.

She kept on looking at him with the same urgent look that might have been cautious or suspicious under other circumstances. He thought that he was making a fool of himself. Her collar was now out from inside her coat and she had stopped fastening her belt. She did not say anything and did not thank him for either help or recognition. His quick words bogged down in confusion.

It occurred to him that perhaps she didn't understand what he was saying. He had assumed that she would speak French. What had they spoken at the party? Either French or German. Most Poles of her class spoke one or the other, but French was preferred. It was the language he used with the General. Pawel spoke perfect English. Swiderski and the houseman at the Vogel house did better with German. He was on the point of switching to German when she lost the urgent look and seemed to come to some small decision. She smiled and nodded once and said in a pleased, polite voice in excellent French that of course she remembered him.

Her voice was firm but (he thought) when you're experienced in such things you can spot the tremor. Even when it's held back as rigidly as hers. His relief, he thought, was out of all proportion.

—Well, that's fine, he said. That's just fine. I didn't think you would remember.

She said she had a good memory for faces. It was a gift, she supposed. And . . . well . . . the party had not been successful, if he remembered. She'd have no reason to remember anybody else.

He agreed that the party had not been successful. —I didn't want to go but I was invited. The propaganda people put it on especially for the correspondents. It's one of the crosses of the business. There was no way for me to get out of it after Pan Swiderski, the little guardian angel they assigned to me, promised some sort of a surprise.

The wary look he had seen on her face in the café returned at once. Her smile vanished. Congratulations, Loomis; you're just about the most tactful bastard in the world. Well done. Oh, so well done. He groped for some way out.

—I certainly got one in the morning.

She said that war surprised everyone more or less.

She began to walk away among the sagging buildings, her face turned partly to the sky as though she was listening, and he was struck again by her pallor, which, in that harsh, undiluted moonlight, robbed her face of lines and made it smooth and vulnerable. She looked young and delicate in that white light against the scarred backdrop of drab old buildings, and she also looked brave and resolute and quite determined to remain undaunted inside and out. It was as though a secret wire bound her spine erect despite the turned face and averted eyes, and he thought: Yes, that's it, that's what Pawel had. What is it and where do they get it? He wondered if she really was as beautiful as he thought (thinking beauty to be a deceptive combination of circumstances at best) or if it was merely the result of the background-drab days and buildings, chaos, and hopelessness, uselessness and lack of purpose, against which she stood out as the only object which was not tinged with fatality, which had symmetry and line and freshness and was not yet broken.

He did not hear the whistling tremolo of the approaching shell. But then it started up somewhere near the roof of his consciousness and grew and then the shell arrived and struck the street between them.

There was a cry in the smoke and at once Loomis ran towards this sound. His mouth was dry the way it was that day when he woke up in his apartment and the war caught him by surprise.

The smoke was yellow. Under it the crater was surprisingly small, and he knew, tripping into the crater, that it was a marker shell and that soon more would follow. He fell, struck his head on stone, got up and ran (a little dizzy with the effort, dazed by the blow on his forehead) to where she had been.

—Are you all right?

She was down on her knees on the sidewalk and the raincoat had one long, vicious tear in it and her hair was wildly down across her eyes and these were not steady but she nodded and said yes, she was all right except for dignity.

—That and torn stockings, he said, incredibly relieved.

And the ruined raincoat.

Which made a form of laughter possible, and they laughed, kneeling in front of each other on the sidewalk.

And then the shells came quickly, ranging like hungry birds on the yellow smoke thrown up by the marker. He caught her arm and pulled her into the cold vault of an archway, one of those heavy gateways that lead into the courtyard of a *kamienica* and seemingly from one century to another. There they sat on cobblestones with their heads down and their hands about their ears while the shells landed in the street. One shell burst in the building over them and several others sent their sharp shrapnel rattling off the gate and the cobblestones trembled under them and the great sound of explosions, breaking glass, falling masonry, shouts and the desperate drumming of running feet (ending in explosions) compressed the air about their heads.

The shelling did not last long, but it seemed a long time. It ended as quickly as it had begun. She tried to get up when the shelling ended, but he pulled her down.

—Why? It's all over now. We can go out again.

—Not yet, he said. They'll fire another salvo in a minute.

—How do you know?

—Because I've seen them do it. They wait until everyone has come out of hiding and then they fire again. It's an old trick. They get a lot of people that way.

—They've never done it here. And everyone is going out.

Indeed, the street began to fill with hurrying people. Each doorway spilled its quota of men and women. Soon there were many, moving rapidly between the sidewalks.

—Oh, I think it's over.

—No, wait, he said.

—But this is foolish.

—Wait. I know my Germans.

—Why should they want to fire at those people? There isn't a soldier in the street.

And suddenly the air grew heavy with a sound like an enormous whisper, a great breath rapidly expended, and as the people in the street stopped and looked up and shouted and began to run, the shells came and exploded and the street became a huge black kettle in which men, women, animals and objects boiled upward, disintegrated and flew away, hitting against stone and splashing the blackrimmed yellow shellholes with their thick red rain.

She sat with her knees folded under her, her body turned towards the wall and her head down, hugging herself with both arms. Her eyes were closed as though to shut out the brilliant yellow flashes and the smoke that welled up in the street outside the gate, and her ears seemed closed to the howls and supplications that came in from the street between the explosions, and her whole face (he thought) seemed slammed shut and tightly locked: pale and motionless. He was conscious of gladness that he had been right about this second shelling. Also vaguely ashamed.

It was suddenly important that she see him this way: as one who knew and who could be depended on. It was no good the other way; as an observer striving for indifference. It was an admission of a kind. And one should never admit anything, should one? No. Each part of yourself that you give away is taken from you and is not yours anymore and presently it will all be gone if you go on sharing yourself with others.

But somehow (possibly because she looked vulnerable or because of the violence outside) he wanted to reach out and touch her and make her open up her closed face and show herself to him.

Outside the smoke and dust had blotted out the sights. The sounds hung disembodied. They were secluded then, he and she alone, pressed against the stone wall, linked by what he thought was the intimacy of shared danger. He felt no fear of any kind and wondered what she felt, and thought that perhaps he would find out if the shelling went on hard and long enough to break up her whitefaced silence. But this was not the kind of shelling that would last, he knew well enough.

—Tell me about yourself, he said to break her silence.

—There isn't very much to say, she said carefully.

—Oh, there must be. You look as though you'd have a lot to say.

—No, really, there is very little. It's all been very ordinary.

She didn't want to talk about herself, that much was clear. Because what could she say, after all? The story of her life with Prus? The hopes she had had for that (if, indeed, she had had any hopes) and their disappointment?

She sat pressed tightly against the trembling wall with her hands sliding down into her lap. Her fingers were long and thin and looked competent, and her very white face was sharply etched against the darker wall.

—I heard you were an artist at one time, he said.

He had not, but he thought she had the look of one: intense and withdrawn but also volatile, as though her restraint was no more than an artificial lid consciously pressed on to keep her closed inside herself.

—That was long ago, she said as though it was of no importance and never had been. But she looked surprised. A start if nothing else, he thought.

—Were you good at it?

—Oh no.

—How do you know?

Because it was important that she should go on. Whether or not she knew how good or bad she was, or how she knew, was not important. What mattered was that she should go on talking, and then, perhaps, he would know why he wanted her to talk. —Did you think you weren't? he said.

—Everyone said I wasn't.

He said he didn't think anyone would say that she wasn't good. Not in this country, where everyone who was in a position to say anything was so painstakingly polite and agreeable and never offered (or accepted in good grace) anything critical unless it could be roared off a political tribune or applied to a group rather than to an individual, like Jews and Ukrainians and Lutherans and the Catholic clergy and the National Democrats (if you were a Christian Democrat) and Social Democrats and Socialists and peasants and bankers and the nobility (such as it was) and the Camp of National Unity (whatever that was) and anything else that one was *not*, and neither art nor artists fell into those categories. Artists, in fact, and writers and people who did nothing more than think aloud enjoyed a privileged standing comparable with champion longdistance runners and pilots who died gloriously in international air races and the man who almost (but not quite) knocked out Max Schmeling and the woman who had almost (but not quite) won an Olympic gold medal for the sprint. They did not need success to be thought interesting. No one thought badly of them if they had some talent. And so, perhaps, she was mistaken about the criticism? Did she misunderstand?

No, she did not, she said. Because it wasn't that anyone had said she *wasn't* good. It was the way they said she *was:* politely but not understanding anything she did.

—Not that it matters now.

And she supposed that it was probable that she wasn't good and they, the people who came to her parties and talked and read and wrote but mostly talked, would know whether she was or not.

—It's different in America, I suppose. You have so many different kinds of people that you can try something different. Here we have just one group of people who know anything and they know everything about everything in every field and it's always the same people with the same ideas who decide what is good in every field and what isn't.

—We have them in America too, Loomis said. We call them critics. But no one ever called them particularly polite. In fact, the less polite they are the more their followers are inclined to trust them. It's something to do with human nature and the wish to pull down anyone who climbs above the mob. But nobody pays any attention to them if he is any good.

—It's very different here. I think I would much rather have truth than politeness. But, I suppose, the people who were so polite to me had little choice. They were my father's old friends, and (she smiled a little) also my husband's, and didn't want to hurt my feelings.

Now it was his turn to be surprised and to show it: a fair exchange.

—I didn't know you had a husband.

She laughed (a pleasant sound) and looked at him curiously.

—Why are you laughing?

—You have the look of a suitor confronted with black soup.

—What does that mean?

—It's a peasant custom. When a girl or her family reject a suitor they serve him a plate of black soup. That way nobody has to say anything unpleasant.

—I'd rather be confronted with the family blunderbuss. It's a lot less pleasant and a damn sight less cruel.

She smiled.

—Didn't you really know?

He said that he did not. That he had no idea. He didn't think she believed him, but she looked as though she wished she did.

—Oh yes. I was married at seventeen to an old friend of my father's. I always thought he was waiting to marry my mother. I think she also thought it. He was my father's age.

—No black soup?

—None. And then he married me. It was a great surprise to everyone.

—But not to you?

—To me as much as anyone, I think. But then there was so little time to think in those days. They were like these days in a way. And in the end it didn't make much difference.

—Well, he said. He had no idea.

—Isn't this what you wanted to find out?

—What? Why, no, he said.

Yes, it was true he wanted to find out about her. Certainly. But he had not expected anything like this. Not that it made any difference, of course. On the contrary! It was just unexpected, that was all.

—You don't look as though you had been married, he said finally.

He felt inept and clumsy and (he thought) he probably looked ridiculous. He thought that when she laughed she laughed at him.

—No, I wouldn't laugh at you. You've been kind and pleasant. But if you want to know something about me just ask; there's nothing I can tell you that everybody doesn't know. I am thirty-four and my husband is alive. I was married in 1922 and fell in love in 1928 and was divorced in 1929 for reasons that I'm sure you are familiar with.

—The General, he said.

—That's right.

Suddenly he felt angry.

—Because he was famous? Because he was a military hero?

—He was nobody's hero then, except perhaps my husband's, who, like all weak men, those who prefer to have others do their fighting for them, had made a piece of history out of him, a legend that he could believe. But he was strong and proud and he needed me, and I needed him, and he was interesting and alive and different from all the professors and theorists and talkers that I was so familiar with.

—And he was crippled, he said, wishing to be cruel.

She laughed. —It was only an arm.

And suddenly they realized the shelling had ended. It was over. The silence was contemptible after the sound.

She hid her face momentarily in her arms and pressed her hands against her ears, and her shoulders shook and he wanted to put his arm around her shoulders, but of course he didn't. He didn't think that she would notice it.

—It's all right now, he said. It's all over. We can come out now. They won't shell again for an hour or so. There's time to get you home before they do.

They went out into the street where the doors and gateways spilled out new crowds and where unidentifiable grey shapes crawled in the rubble with inarticulate small cries.

He took her arm and tried to guide her up the street towards the pock-marked avenue that led (she said) to where she lived: a quarter which had been fashionable once but now was not.

—All those people, she said.

—There's nothing we can do.

—We could have warned them.

—How? How do you warn people? Tell me so that I'll be able to warn everyone the next time.

—I don't know, she said.

—You can't warn anybody about anything. Nobody ever listens. Let me take you home.

She shook her head and pointed to the wounded in the street and, for the next hour, until the ambulances and carts and horsedrawn cabs came into the street, she wrapped torn limbs and covered sightless faces and closed empty eyelids. Other were also doing it. If there was nothing else that could be done she stroked foreheads and held hands. She said small words. Soon her hands were brown and her coat was bloody. He stood apart and watched her and the others, feeling uninvolved and useless, wondering at her calm competence after the show of shaking shoulders in the archway. He wondered where this calmness came from and how soon it would be all used up, and how soon she would slip from under the mask of her assumed indifference to anything that did not need her immediate compassion, and how soon she would become the kind of woman that he knew about.

Eventually the ambulances came. The dead and wounded were put in the carts. Some woman's feet hung over the edge of a cart. They made thin lines in the dust. No one paid any attention to the woman's feet.

—Come now, I'll take you home, he said.

She nodded and, after a moment, took his arm. Her high heels clicked and he thought about how different high heels sounded on cobblestones in a city under siege, with the guttural rolling of the shells so close across the river.

—I never liked that sound, he said. She thought he meant gunfire and agreed with him. But he said that he meant the clicking of high heels. —There is something false about it, the way the heels themselves are false and unnatural: ridiculous stilts. But they have an entirely different sound against a background of gunfire. They sound fragile and, somehow, reassuring.

She asked him to explain.

—It's as though no matter what happened or what horizon burned there would always be this small womansound to mock destruction. You have a feeling that when all the cannonfire is over and all the streets are torn up and there are no more houses to destroy there'll be a silence and then suddenly some girl will come out in high heels and it'll all begin all over again. That little tap-tap-tap makes everything all right. A man would need this, I would think, to keep his sanity.

She said nothing then, and they went on quietly.

Now and then they came out of shadows into yellow patches splashed on the cobblestones and then he saw again how pale she was. She had a small face like a triangle; her hair was mussed on both sides of it.

He crossed the streets she crossed and turned where she turned and soon he had no idea where he was because the street signs were mostly down or twisted and those that were not damaged had been painted over. To confuse spies, someone had explained. No one stopped them or questioned them and presently they were in front of a forbidding gate that made the tall, narrow-windowed house look like a fortress or a convent of some kind.

—This is where I live.

She pulled a rope beside the gate. A bell rang inside. And then a small window cut into the gate opened and a face looked out. The girl spoke to the man, and he nodded, looking at Loomis with reluctance. The small window closed.

—I see that, like all fairy princesses, you're guarded by a dragon, Loomis said.

She laughed a little. —That's Grzes. He was Janusz's orderly a long time ago and, lately, a sort of servant-friend. He stays down here in the porter's lodge.

—The faithful family retainer?

—Something like that, she said.

—Why isn't he away with his master, then?

—Janusz wouldn't take him. He is too old. He's here only because he was left here and has nowhere else to go.

—Like you? (He laughed to take the edge off it.)

—Something like that. You can come in if you like. I can give you coffee.

—What about Cerberus? I don't think he approves.

—You must forgive him. Because loyalty of that kind is a rare thing. Few people have it.

The stairway was dark and smelled of dampness and the stairs were steep and it was a long climb to the third floor. There was a small card pinned to the door at the top of the stairs, but she went in so quickly that he didn't have time to see the names on it. He wondered if the General's name was still on it. He didn't think she would ask him to come in if the General still lived there.

—Come in, she said.

Inside a small black cat eyed him yellowly and a dog came up without enthusiasm to smell his shoes. There was a small, dark hallway: coatracks made of horn and ornate mirrorframes and his own oddly worried face looking out of glass. The room was large. There was no carpet, but a quilt was crumpled near the enormous porcelain stove; near the quilt were an ashtray with a dozen broken stubs of homemade cigarettes, a small machine and a box of papers for making them, an old-fashioned gramophone (the kind that made you look for RCA Victor's dog sitting before the great trumpet speaker) and records, a glass and a dark bottle of something violently green. A book lay face down there.

It was a room full of suggestions, of things implied, shadows and halftones that were this and that and could be anything; and yet there was a sense of permanence about it as though a decision had been made about the way it should be. The room was clean but looked undusted. The lines of furniture and stove were simple, free of ornament, and the walls were bare, uncluttered by the usual Polish middle-class collection of incredibly bad pictures in heavy gilt frames (portraits, patriotic scenes, Thaddeus Kosciuszko, photographs of reunions, sunsets in watercolor), although white squares and rectangles on the walls showed that some had hung here. Only a handwoven *kilim* from the Halicz hung on one wall. But the quilt looked soft and there was a piano and the stunted chair yielded like down despite its very modern look of canvas and iron.

And then the animals. They were a surprise. He clicked his tongue at them. The cat ignored him. The dog (damn fool) came up with tongue lolling to have his head scratched.

—Somehow I wouldn't have thought you'd have animals, he said.

She said that animals meant a lot to her. She depended on them. She said she had always had some animal, starting with a bird (when she was small) and then two goldfish that were fragile and died. Then she had had, in succession, seven cats and two dogs; she preferred cats because they tended to be independent and a bit more selective about showing love, making their love valuable because it was uncommon. When she was small, she said, she had wanted to be a veterinarian. There was something so hopelessly small about all animals, she said.

—Elephants too?

It all depended on how you looked at them, she said. If something was dependent on you for food and care and (possibly) affection, how could you think of it as large? Elephants too were small when seen in perspective.

—And lions?

Also lions, she said. And all the other predators. Did he, Loomis, know (she asked) that all the animals were shot in the Warsaw Zoo? The day the Germans reached the suburbs and the siege began, the police shot all the animals.

—An obvious precaution.

Well, yes, perhaps. But wasn't it a little sad? Didn't he think so?

—Well, yes, he said.

He waited in that room while she went somewhere inside the apartment. The dog brushed up against him and shed hair. The cat blinked once and went to sleep. It was warm, although the room looked cold, and Loomis thought that the last shelling, that time-on-target fire that had kept them secluded in the archway, must have been longer than it had seemed, because now, as he looked at them, he saw the windows redden. Soon it would be light. Loomis was glad that the night was ending. The warmth of the room and the nearness of the woman inside the apartment and the brightening sky outside descended on him suddenly and he felt tired.

He thought of the General, who must have sat as he now sat on the saddlelike chair in this room, and about the General and this woman (seeing their intimacy), and he wanted badly to go home. He had forgotten all about the General as a man. Now he remembered him and envied him and was annoyed. When she came in he said he had to go.

—How far do you have to go?

He told her about the Vogel house on the escarpment. It was impossibly far. But (he said) perhaps he could get a ride on one of the deadcarts or the ambulances. They, like the horsedrawn cabs of peacetime, worked all night in Warsaw.

—I put some coffee on, she said. It's the last of the coffee, and, of course, there is no cream for it. But if you'd rather have a drink there is some wine. Janusz left it here. I don't drink much alone.

She knelt beside the gramophone and groped among the records. She put a record on. The sound was kind and warm but with an undertone of harshness, as though the man who wrote the music was laughing at himself for writing something kind. There was a martial beat to it that seemed burlesque, and sonorous passages that made Loomis think of the *Emperor's New Clothes.*

—What is that?

—It's *Lieutenant Kije.* Do you know the story?

She turned towards Loomis, looking at the record. Her hair came forward in bright wings and hid her face. She had washed her face and removed the makeup and wiped the traces of her work in the shelled street from her forehead and made her face small.

She said it was an old Russian scandal, the story of one of the more imbecilic Tsars who issued a communiqué citing this lieutenant for a heroic act. Only there was no such lieutenant. The Tsar just couldn't spell. So they invented one to cover up imperial ignorance. They gave him birth and life and love and friends and marriage and eventually death, and it was all there —all of it—in the music.

—All the pomp, the foolishness and hope and aspiration; all the love anyone could want. Only it's all a joke of course.

—Of course, he said.

—I wish I had some whiskey for you. You are a whiskey drinker, aren't you?

—The wine will do just fine.

—Sometimes I like it too. Most of the time I don't drink anything.

—It's not much good, he said.

Oh, she said, it was good sometimes. Sometimes it really was surprisingly good. But it was over so quickly and then it was no help with anything. She tended to do silly things (she said) after drinking and then she wouldn't be

353

able to remember and she would worry about what she did. She supposed that he would know about that. He must have known many women like that.

—Well, some, he said.

She looked so young then, almost childlike without makeup and unconcerned about her hair (not patting it or playing with it), and this too was a surprise. He could see now, in that better, artificial light with the blackout curtains drawn carefully over the night outside, that her skin was less than fine. There was uncertainty about her mouth and two small lines folded about her neck. Still, she looked childlike. So that when she reached suddenly for a glass and filled it with the wine he wanted to reach out and stop her, as though it were unthinkable that she would drink that and not Ovaltine.

He thought the evening and the night had been a mistake. He remembered his various resolutions: to take life, use it, waste none of it, and certainly not to complicate it or become involved. This girl or woman, her noncommittal apartment, her self-imposed restraint and discipline, her immense compassion, the quilt so carefully disarranged (he thought), the book face down, the animals and the warm room that somehow looked cold, all spoke of failure and a hopeless sort of determination that promised nothing new. Here were all the sad signs of defeat despite determination. He wanted no part of it.

He rose and reached for his hat on the table. He thanked her for asking him in and for the drink and for the recordplaying.

He thought as she looked at him that she probably expected him to ask if he could see her. That was, after all, the logical conclusion; part of the night and darkness and the recordplaying and the talk about Russian scandals and mythical lieutenants, and perhaps (he thought) I should make some gesture towards her, perhaps a small attempt to kiss her, something like that.

He asked if she would like to have dinner sometime. There were still several places in the town where the inevitable horse was well disguised and where good wine and service could be found if one had dollars. That was the fine thing about dollars: They were the magic password in a city under siege.

—Yes, thank you, if you like, she said. She told him he could reach her every day at the military hospital in the Ujazdowskie.

—Are you a nurse now? That's something I didn't know about you.

—No, I'm not a nurse. I help there with the things the nurses are too busy for. There aren't many nurses and there's a great deal to do.

—Yes, I imagine there would be. Can you get away from there without any trouble?

—Yes. I don't do anything important. Mostly I just sit with the wounded and talk to them. They are so anxious to talk, you see, when they're badly wounded. It's as if by talking they keep themselves from dying.

—I think that's important.

—It's very little. And there are many wounded.

He asked in which ward he should look for her and she shook her head and said that there weren't any wards anymore in Warsaw hospitals. The wounded were everywhere, including the stairs. He should look for her and ask for her by name. Someone would know where to find her and would tell him.

—Goodnight.
—Goodnight.

Outside there was no miracle: no cab. He walked a long time through the dark streets of the blacked-out city lit with the distant glow of fires.

Thursday, September the fourteenth

I THE GENERAL

The day came violently. The sun exploded in the east as though the sky wanted to match the suicidal heavings of the earth. There was no grey dawn; black night blew up suddenly on the red horizon, the sun bolted out of Russia like a burning timber hurled into the sky by an immense explosion. It climbed the thick coils of smoke and hung suspended over Europe like a malevolent red eye.

There was a haze that morning over Warsaw. The night had been cold. The smoke was thick with the northern suburbs burning for the second day. A great black cloud speckled with red and yellow fires hung like an immense lid above the Forest of Kampinos. The forest was burning. The Germans had set fire to it, unable to cope in any other way with the men who fought their way every night, through the thin forest and the German lines, into besieged Warsaw. Smoke and haze boiled up into the sun.

The General watched the march of the western armies into Warsaw. For several days this grey mass had been coming in despite the Germans, working their way by night through the Kampinos Forest, cutting through the iron ring around the capital with their bayonets. They would keep coming as long as Kutrzeba's divisions pushed back the Germans on the Bzura River.

They came as soldiers, not as a disbanded horde. The men's beards were long and unkempt, their uniforms were in tatters, but they marched with a steady pace behind battleflags and in tight formation.

Someone said: —Who are these men? What troops are those?

—Rummel, somebody said. Thomme's regiments.

A lancer went past with yellow flashes on his collar.

—That's the Sixteenth Lancers. They charged at Chelmno. He was with Bortnowski.

The men came on and, once in a while, a few would turn out of the column and go to stand against the wall of the hospital and, frequently, two or three of them, carrying another, would take him to the wall or up the marble steps and laid the wounded man gently down and walked back to the column.

The General watched them until the sun came up and the bombers began to come out of the sun again and the dark woods beyond the German lines closed over other columns.

He went up the steps into the main hall of the hospital, then past the wounded waiting on the littered stairs. He stepped carefully around the wounded. The stairs were red, like a butcher's chopping block. The wounded looked at him without interest. They made no move to get out of his way. He asked the wounded to excuse him as he stepped over them.

A doctor shouted at a soldier on the crowded stairs. —Don't you have anything to do? Can't you find a barricade to die on? Get out of here. You are in the way.

—But sir, the soldier said. The captain . . .

—Forget your captain, do you understand? You got him here. He's still alive. At least he's not yet dead. Look after your own mangy hide, *zolnierzu!* Now get out of here.

—I got to look after Pan Kapitan, the soldier said. I got to stay here.

—Listen, the doctor said. His voice was flat and dull and immensely tired. —We have no room for mourners here. We're not equipped for it. Get out and get yourself blown up on a barricade and then we'll take you for a little while.

The stairs were slippery underfoot. The General reached the doctor. The doctor looked at him and made a tired gesture. He said: —What can you do with people like that? Ah, Janusz, I'm glad you came. (And to the young soldier:) Are you still here? Get out. Go grab a spade and start digging trenches!

—Yes sir . . .

The soldier didn't move.

—I came as quickly as I could, Tadziu, the General said.

—Good, good. I think he's still all right. He ought to be. We haven't done anything to him yet. Or for him, for that matter.

—Ah, then it isn't serious.

—Serious? Serious? Of course it is serious! But he must wait his turn. We had him here for a week before we even found out who he was. There are just too many of them here.

The doctor rubbed his face. His voice had a dreamy, detached quality as though he didn't know what he was saying but knew that nothing he could say would be important.

—I sent for you as soon as I knew who he was. I didn't recognize him, can you imagine that . . . as often as I've seen him at Michal's . . . at your home. Well, no matter. Everything is insane these days. Nothing makes any sense. My surgeons are falling asleep at the tables. Good God, Janusz, what kind of a war are you running?

—It's not my kind of war.

—No matter, it'll end some day. I'm glad you came. Couldn't Michal come?

—Duty. I have no duties at the moment so I came.

—Good. Good. It's not so good with him, you know. But come, let's go to see him. (Then he shouted:) Orderly! Orderly! (And when the orderlies came running:) Can't you get this place in some sort of order? Can't you keep it clean? Can't you get these people cleaned up?

The orderly wished to know where to put the wounded.

—Where? How should I know? I haven't the faintest idea. But get them off those stairs and get this place cleaned up. Get this place looking like a hospital. Get those stairs cleared.

—There isn't any other place for them, the orderly said. There just isn't any room.

—Good God, don't you suppose I know that? Get this place cleaned up!

The wounded watched the doctor and the orderlies with disinterested eyes. The orderlies sweated and the doctor shouted. He was a firstrate surgeon, a specialist in coronary work and (Prus remembered) fanatical about sanitation. Before the war he had been chief of surgery in this hospital. Now he was a colonel in command.

They went through the crowded corridors and stairways to where the surgeons worked. The surgeons moved like men asleep. The instruments fell out of their hands. The nurses slapped new instruments into their hands. Everything was red with blood. The wounded shouted on the operating tables. There was no ether and no electricity and the fans hung still in the reeking air. Hot air came through the windows with the flies.

The General looked at Pawel. He didn't recognize him. Pawel was ill with sunstroke and weak with loss of blood and lack of food and rest, dehydrated and burned black by the sun, and in fever. His leg was rotten with the long-remembered stench of gangrenous corruption. The blue streaks of corruption had crawled up to his hip.

There was no ether but there were four scarlet orderlies to hold down the delirious man and there was a surgeon with exhausted eyes.

—Hold him down! Harder!

—Can't you give him morphine?

—He's too weak for that. He'd never wake up.

—Give it to him. On my responsibility. Then do what you can.

—With what, sir? Anything you'd care to suggest?

—Ah . . . must you amputate?

—Look for yourself, sir. What would you suggest?

Familiar corruption.

—I'll help you hold him down.

(You hold the boy's hand a bit because you know how bright the pain will be if the blade is quick. Listen, you say: It only lasts a little while and then it is gone. There are other pains, later, but those are permanent and not a bit bright and you can learn to live with the dull grey pains. You find someone or are found by someone who makes you whole and wipes away the dull pains and makes you complete once again and then, if you have anything left in you, you hold to that someone because nothing is worth the losing of her. She is your brightness and your light and there is no more grey. Listen, this is how it is. You can lose arms and legs and you can live without them and you can be a whole man if you have her love. I tell you this and I know it, so listen well. Love . . . light . . . the words confuse me at the moment but one is like the other and they can brighten many grey days for you. Without them you have nothing, no matter how many arms and legs you have or how many other possessions, or how many hopes or aspirations or talents. So you see, you see, it doesn't have to be so bad. It really doesn't have to. It can be good for you no matter what you lose if, as I say, you have someone. A loss of limbs never crippled anyone if they had someone. This pain now, that you feel now, if you feel it, will soon be gone and then there'll be the others but there will also be someone to wipe them away. I know such a someone who will help to make you whole because that is the way she is. She has small animals which she has collected because they were hurt one way or another. She can mend any animal or man. I will let her know and she will mend you. She is good at it. Now you feel pain, I can see, and I can almost feel it; it is much like the pain I had although also different because mine came quick and bright with the regulation downswing of my saber and yours is prolonged, because this man must saw where my man cut and we must tie your arteries as we come to them before cutting further because there is no hot pitch in which to dip your stump as there was for me. Ah now, you see? It is almost gone and we are taking off our shirts, those of us who have them, and these are being torn to make the wrappings for you, and see, there is the morphine, though not much of it, to make it easier for you at the moment. You will not need it later when you have *her*. Now it is done, you see, and you will live. And she will mend you and I envy you. The wound you have is insignificant.)

—Next!

The orderlies rolled Pawel onto a stretcher and carried him away. A nurse splashed water on the table. An orderly took Pawel's amputated leg out of the bucket under the table and threw it into a small cart that moved from one operating table to another collecting the offal. The small cart and the leg, and all the other legs and arms and hands and feet and fingers and grey bone and sinew and wilting muscle and discarded flesh rolled away into the corridor, past the waiting wounded. —Get out of the way, the orderly shouted to the wounded. The wounded stared at the small cart with sunken eyes.

—Next!

The General made his way down the stairs. The orderlies had not managed to get the stairs cleared. They had pushed the wounded closer to the walls, but at once more wounded men climbed up from below and took the vacant places.

—This is impossible, the doctor said. We simply can't work under these conditions. I wish you'd do something about it, Janusz. This way we can't do anything for anybody.

—Nobody can do anything about it. It's the same in all the hospitals, schools, churches. You just have to do the best you can.

—Listen, I tell you, something must be done. It can't go on like this much longer. Do you know that we have to send for water to the wells across the park? Do you know that we don't even have any water here? No light, no water, no ether; we have nothing.

—Nobody does.

—Last night one of my surgeons fell asleep and knocked a kerosene lamp over the man he was working on. How long will this go on? I'm not a professional soldier. I'm not even a very fanatical patriot. I am a human being and a doctor and I'd like to know.

—I don't know. It will go on as long as we can bear it. There is no other choice for us anymore.

—Sometimes I think I'm going mad. It wasn't like this in the last war. This is a war I can't understand at all.

—The rules were different. Tell me, do you think Pawel will be all right?

—I don't know. I hope he'll be all right. We can't do anything for him, the way things are. (Then to the waiting wounded on the stairs:) Move aside now, come on, make room on the stairs. (And to the young soldier hiding behind the wounded:) Didn't I tell you to get out? Do you want me to call the fieldpolice? Get out! Get out! Orderlies, throw this man out of here and don't let him back.

The General followed the orderlies and the soldier. The soldier said:

—Let me go, you bastards.

—Take it easy now, said the older orderly. You heard what the colonel said.

—Some colonel, said the soldier. I got to stay here with Pan Kapitan Prus. I got him here, didn't I? They won't do him any good in this place. Let go my arms, you medic sonofabitch.

—Take it easy now.

—Let go of him, the General said. The orderlies sprang aside and stood stiff, saluting. The General led the soldier through the hall. The soldier's eyes were wet and he was shaking.

—What's your name, soldier?

—Ulan Mocny, sir, the Second Squadron, the Ulans of Polesie.

—You brought your captain here, is that it?

—Yes sir. And now the bastards won't let me stay with him. They won't do him any good in this place. They're going to kill him here if I don't stay and look after him.

—You can do better than that, soldier. Look, here is an address on a card. Can you read?

—Yes sir.

The lancer slowly read the address of Lala's apartment, written, long ago it seemed, to ensure that she be notified if he should be killed.

—Go there. You'll find a lady there. Tell her about your captain and that he is here and bring her here to him. Can you do that?

—Yes sir, I can do it.

—She will help him. She is good at that. But don't tell her that I sent you to her, understand? Just that your captain needs her. She will come to him.

—Yes sir. I'll get her. I won't say who sent me.

—Be sure of that. Take good care of your captain.

—Yes sir.

And there it was again: a loss and now a hope. That's all I can give him. That is all I had: her hands on the great wound inside me and the love of a peasant soldier.

So, down the red stairs to the marble lobby. An officer of engineers sat in the door with his face in his hands. The wounded walked into him as they came off the street but he didn't move. He did not say anything and made no attempt to get out of the way of the wounded. The General went to him and told him to get out of the way. The engineer turned an eyeless face up to him, fixed the two brown holes on him, and bared a lipless mouth. The General left him and went to his car.

He felt a tightness in his chest and throat and his sight blurred, and he leaned for a moment against the windshield of the small staffcar and the driver asked if the General was ill.

—No.

—The General looks unwell.

—I am quite well.

—I thought . . .

—Don't think.

—Yes sir.

The General got into the car and the driver put the car in gear. The General looked at the engineer officer and the waiting men. —Wait, he said. He got out and went back to the engineer. He looked into the burned, naked face as though he wished to imprint the sight of it on his memory. Then he came back to the car, got in.

—All right. Drive to the Staff.

Walking into the cold marble anteroom in Rakowiecka Street, the General wondered what the red day would bring. There was no longer any major work done at Supreme Headquarters. On the top floors in Rakowiecka Street the garrison command under Rummel, Czuma and Mayor Starzynski planned the defense of Warsaw under siege. The Marshal's staff was in Kolomyia, near the Roumanian border, and the evacuated government with its innumerable ministers (with and without portfolio, with and without honor, courage, dignity and a sense of shame, carrying in official trucks and limousines wives, children, jewels, works of art, furniture, pets, maiden aunts, Swiss francs and twenty-dollar goldpieces, convertible bonds and diaries justifying flight) was also there, and all that remained of the glittering Staff in Warsaw was the last order of Marshal Smigly-Rydz: Fight to the last man and to the last bullet. Show them in London and in Paris that we *were* worth the effort. Shame them. Make them remember us. Make them remember their treason and their obligations.

Who had betrayed whom? Who was to be ashamed? Was it the French and the English whose treachery was so unpardonable? Or was it possible, perhaps, that the fugitive ministers, wiring their reservations for Bucharest hotels, had also something for which to answer to the tired soldiers on the barricades?

Prus watched the red sun in the smoke above Praga and scanned the faces of the staggering shadows marching into Warsaw. They knew the answer as well as he and the ministers. If anyone was worth anybody's effort it was these men whose tired eyes said: We will do our duty. We know what has been done to us and who has done it, and when the time comes we will remember it. But that is for the future. If there is a future. Now there is other work to do.

The General had no work to do, but that was all right; he had not expected another assignment after the fight in the quarry. His makeshift battle group had done well enough at the Zagnanski Pass and next day at Suchedniow, where the Germans had thrown three divisions to get at the rear of the great offensive. He had held them up for thirty-six hours.

It would have been good, of course, to keep the command, but there was next to nothing left of it; when he brought his survivors into Warsaw he didn't have enough to form a battalion. The battle group was broken up among other units. As for himself, well, he had no regular command, after all . . . no permanent assignment. When some need came he would be used again, he knew, and he could wait. The Marshal had a troop of highranking officers he sent every day on special assignments, and if such work grew scarcer as the war went on (with the fronts drawing farther east, barriers collapsing before they could be bolstered, units disintegrating, and more gaps springing open than there were men to fill them), nobody could do anything about it.

It was enough for him to be near soldiers, he thought. He felt no regret, no anger at having no command. The war was not his kind; it had no need for generals. It was no war of one military art against another or even of technique against technique. Against German art, leadership, and technology there stood one solitary combatant: the private soldier left to his own devices.

The Germans had broken Poland's defensive organism with great iron pincers before it could gather itself to fight. They tore it apart in the air and on the dehydrated plains. Communications and unity of armies went first. Their destruction settled any doubts about the possible outcome of the war.

But the soldier was isolated and resolved to fight no matter what happened. In this seclusion, the lonely stand of individuals withdrawn into themselves, there was something splendid. It was the spirit of antiquity, Prus thought. War, carried on hopelessly, bitterly, by lone groups (divisions and regiments that had become complete armies in miniature), became more than anything a war of individual men. It was as though the remnants of the nineteenth century had reached into an even more remote era to find a weapon with which to fight the twentieth century. A divisional commander led his men the way his men fought: counting on no help from anyone, relying on himself alone. This war had no grand sweeping strategy, no planned maneuvers or plotted operations. Each meeting with the enemy was a head-on collision meant to be decisive one way or another. It was not guided by the will of a supreme commander: the private soldier, with his lice and hunger and beard and redrimmed eyes and bloody bayonet, fought it out by instinct. Alone, locked in himself, he formed his own military art. He understood at once that his greatest enemy was the tank and the tank's aerial runningmate: the bomber-observer. He could not hide from them and could not fight them all. The forest became his ally in the flatlands. There he could escape the observer's eye. Fighting against material odds he could never equal, he guessed at once that a sunny day meant death and he chose night as the frame for action.

Darkness and trees robbed his enemy of sight and the use of machines. The soldier wanted to fight an enemy as naked and alone as he was himself. He wished to make his loneliness the common standard. His art became the ability to bypass the German art of fire and machine and to meet the German face to face as a man. Then he became victorious. Then separated units, lost, wandering regiments, divisions without flanks or rear, went into battle with no inferior feeling. They carried with them the soldier's most potent weapon: contempt for death.

The General supposed that the offensive in the west had started successfully enough. Its start had been scheduled for the eleventh of September, but Kutrzeba had begun his attacks on the night of the eighth. He had his own Poznan Army and Bortnowski's corps and what was left of Rummel's. Of the five divisions that were supposed to begin the offensive only three were ready. Of these only two attacked. Troops that came up after the start were thrown piecemeal into new attacks.

But for all that the offensive began well enough. It surprised the Germans. They fell back fifteen kilometers the first day and twenty on the second. Their losses were heavy. The Polish casualties were, of course, enormous. Lowicz was recaptured with bayonets and Lodz was threatened, and the attacks went on, and everywhere long columns of German prisoners marched disconsolately eastward. But the columns of the marching wounded were equally long and there were no replacements and the artillery ran out of ammunition and no more came up from the rear, where the ubiquitous Luftwaffe hovered above the roads. The General wondered how long it would be before the Germans recovered from their surprise and brought up new divisions and called back their armored spearheads and summoned the Luftwaffe to those plains before the Bzura River. He didn't think it would be long. Two days? Three? Three if we have luck, he thought: but not the luck we've had since this war began.

There was no contact between the fighting corps and headquarters in Warsaw. There were, in fact, no communications of any kind left anymore, and if a messenger couldn't bring orders by car or on horseback no orders were given. No one in Warsaw even knew when the offensive started or how few troops there were to take part in it or what anyone was doing. Certainly, fresh troops were forwarded to the lines the way they would be for a battle that had not begun. Not for one that had been raging for six days.

Elsewhere, the situation was equally unpromising. The red arrows on Michal's map pierced the blue lines and swept around them and left them far behind. North of the city, the Modlin Group was in full retreat for the Narew-Bug-Vistula line of rivers and the old fortress of Modlin. They had done well the day before, attacking with cavalry and two infantry divisions. And then a lost and wandering German armored corps ran, accidentally, into the flank of their attack: One division wiped off the face of the earth, the other shocked, remnants and cavalry retreating. In the deep south, beside the Carpathians, Antoni Szylling and his Krakow Army raced German armor for the River San. If Szylling managed to fight his way through, a stand could be made on the San and the Germans halted. If. That was the guiding word.

If the reserves can form.

If rain comes and the Allies move. If the offensive's suicidal charges show the reluctant French that Germans can be beaten.

If we have luck.

Time might be slowed. Not stopped; that was impossible. But the remorseless hours might be slowed, extended, stretched, prolonged to delay conclusion. The General walked down the stairs to the War Room.

Michal worked alone in the underground chamber. There were no other officers in the War Room. The fans were still and did not stir the stale, hot air. Storm lanterns cast black shadows on the situation map. Without the

362

humming of the fans and human voices the clatter of Hughes teletype machines was unnaturally loud.

—How is he? Michal said when he heard his brother.

—I won't lie to you. It's not good with him.

Michal closed his eyes, then passed a hand over them. The women sitting by the teletypes stared curiously.

—They had to amputate his leg, the General said. There was nothing else to do. He had been on the road a long time and gangrene had set in.

—But he came through all right?

—Yes. They quieted him with morphine. The next few days should decide how he'll do. But the operation went all right and he was resting when I left. Tadzio thought that he had a chance. That's all we can ask for.

—His leg. He won't like that, an active man like that. Was he bitter? Was he in much pain? I mean inside.

—He was delirious. He didn't make much sense. And they found morphine for the pain.

—I mean the other pain.

—It's too soon for that, the General said. That will come later.

—Yes. I suppose it will. I wish I could do something to help him. But there isn't anything I can do. He wouldn't want anything from me. He and I, you know, lost each other many years ago. I don't know how. We were good friends for a while and then, somehow, we didn't know each other anymore. We didn't understand each other's language. There were too many bitter barriers separating us. I wish it could be otherwise. I had so many wishes where he was concerned, so many hopes. If hopes and wishes were horses and men I'd have a cavalry division. I think he lost faith in me too soon. I think he gave up on me, being young. And once you lose faith in someone nothing will ever make things as they were before.

—He called for you.

—Did he? Was he bitter?

—No, he just called your name.

Michal smiled. His eyes closed again and when he opened them he kept them on the ground. —Thank you. But you don't have to lie. I'm the official liar and promisemaker here. I know how Pawel called me. He must have been in great pain. Do you think he was in pain?

—I don't know. I don't think so. I don't think he felt anything by that time. It is like that, you know, with that kind of wound. The amputation brings relief.

—You should know. Isn't it strange that you and he were about the same age for this kind of thing? How old were you? Thirty-six? You were a year older. I didn't really know how you felt then but I do now.

—I mended. These things mend. No pain is forever. He'll mend too. He has enough strength to make himself complete.

—You had help, though. Oh, I know you think I never approved of you and Lala. And, in a way, you're right. It's not in my nature to approve a violation of any principle. But I know what you had with her and I was glad for you. She gave you that necessary patience to survive the waiting, the hurting time. It isn't a time that any man can face alone, not if he ever was a man. I hope Pawel will have your luck. Do you think he will? He has your loss and he should have the luck.

Janusz Prus nodded. —Yes, he said. I think he'll have the luck when he needs it.

—I hope so. He means a lot to me even though he thinks I don't understand him. There were misunderstandings, yes, of course. Too many angry disagreements, too little kindness, too much bitterness. You can't have love when there is bitterness. I hoped so much for him. . . . Well I hope he'll have your luck.

And now the teletypes clattered in battery.

—That will be Kolomyia, Michal said. They're the only people still in touch with us. You know, I feel like a caretaker here. Or an archivist. I feel I'm only collecting scraps of paper for future historians. I wish you'd go now. I don't want you to see me as I am now, the way things are for us.

—I'll leave you then.

The General went back to the street and his car and driver. The driver put the car in gear. —Where to, sir? To the barricades?

—Yes. Take the long way round to the south perimeter. Drive to the Vistula.

—The Germans shell the banks a lot, sir, the driver offered. We wouldn't get another car if they potted this one.

—It'll be dark soon.

They drove through the gutted streets among collapsing buildings, past parks and once-green squares. Now nothing was green. The parks were yellow with hastily dug graves. The streets were hollow chambers of destruction. But there were still unblasted patches of green by the Vistula where the silvergrey sand of the beaches tumbled between small trees.

The General stopped the car when he saw the grey sand. He saw a flash of it through the pines that leaned crazily towards the Vistula. The pines were splintered and partially burned. The shelling had been heavy in the grove earlier in the day.

He got out of the car and walked into the pinegrove. The grove stank of cordite. An overturned fieldgun melted in silhouette into the blackness of the river. The orange sun of late afternoon splashed brass shellcasings with its light. It made them look like the smashed teeth of a dead mastodon. The General walked through the grove into the sand. It made this riverbeach much like another he remembered. This one was narrower and steeper than the other and it had no pebbles. The other had been a broad, joyous stretch of incredibly clean sand and white pebbles where the sun was warm and the cool smell of the surf coming in from the Baltic was like a pungent perfume. Here the smell was the acrid reek of highexplosives. It was only the color of the sand that made him think this beach was like the other.

He had been to the other beach with Lala in the very old days. It had been a brief vacation for them: a refuge from the avid interest of her former friends and her husband's friends and the assaults of his own enemies, whose numbers grew as his influence declined after the coup d'état. Later they did not need the grey sand of the Hel and the Baltic surf and the sweetscented jasmine clearings of Jastarnia. Later there was the house on the Wiselka. But at first, when she had first come to him (before she came to live with him in the old house), there had been these two refuges: the inn at Zakopane (with the waiter who kept looking at them, the one with yellow teeth) and the grey beach.

The General sat down on a treestump. He took a handful of the sand and let it run out through his fingers. He didn't bother wiping off his hand when the sand was gone. He saw the fires leaping among the villas by the Yacht Club (a name he always thought preposterous: an affectation to copy the English) and in the Praga on the other side. There was a little breeze, but not much, and the river was low.

Then suddenly he thought about his wife. He had not thought about her since before the war (the day he waited for the messenger and war and thought about Adam and didn't think enough about Lala); he wondered if she had failed him when he needed her because of some lack, a form of cowardice or other weakness, some vengeful pettiness. Or because he himself had taken more from her than he had bothered to return. He thought that he had given as much as he took. Certainly, at the start, there had been much giving. But one day (long before the coup and her disappointment in his part in it, the siege and loss of arm and stature) it was all over, long before his fall from prominence, which was no more than an excuse for her to do what she would not have had the courage to attempt without some sign from heaven.

It was long gone; he did not miss it or the woman.

Because he did not love her. And he supposed, trying thought for size as he would a helmet, he never had.

But he had loved Lala. She had asked, softly (then), if he was hungry, and he, feeling rested and content and not really hearing what she said, said: —*Yes. For you.* Then she laughed, sounding happy. She said that it could be arranged.

They lay on the sand together to rest and catch their breath after swimming. He had not wanted to go into the water, conscious of his amputated elbow, but she convinced him to try it, arm or no arm. —*Look,* she said, *turn on your side like so, and put your good arm here, and put your bad arm out like the prow of a ship and push the water with the good arm. It will be easy when you're used to it. You will enjoy it. It will make all the difference to me if you come with me. I would not like to swim alone and leave you here.* He said then, laughing, that he could not disappoint a lady. She said: —*A woman, please. I never wished to be a lady.* He said he was glad, and that he would join her in the water, and afterwards he forgot that he had not wanted to go in. She relaxed and breathed easily after swimming. Small drops of water formed on her legs and shoulders. He didn't think that anything could disturb him again.

He wondered if she also felt his odd tranquillity, and then she said, as if guessing the thought, —*How quiet and peaceful it is. It's like a church in the morning with the organ getting pumped up and everybody waiting for something to happen.*

He was aware of every sound around them. He heard the waves breaking close, and the occasional humming of the insects, and the lost, sad note of the ships calling to each other out of sight in darkness. He heard her easy breathing. Below them the Baltic muttered in darkness; lights shined along the beach. A dog barked somewhere and suddenly another answered, and another, and a great barking rolled down from Jastarnia. They listened to this conversation until it died. She stirred and took her hand away from his. She shivered. The night was warm. He asked if she was cold and if he should get her clothes out of the *britchka*. She said she wasn't cold and that they should not disturb the horses at the *britchka*. —*Let them think, for a moment, that there are no people and that they are free.* They drew together, then, as though there was nothing else that they could do, and held each other, held onto each other, much, he supposed, as children might do, and he felt that desperate longing, then, to be out of the night and in warm daylight and he felt the quick pumpings of her heart. He tried to give her some idea of how he felt but somehow couldn't do it. And it was she who supplied the words.

—*I am so tired of ungentle love.*

—*Has it been so bad then?* he wanted to know.

—*It was a sickness, I suppose,* she said. *What I loved didn't love me in return and so I turned to the unimportant and gave it my love. Painting was a refuge. But when you want to love truly, you cannot for long give yourself to an inanimate object or a pastime.*

—*And in the end?*

—*No woman can survive indifference. In the end she must return to what she knows best how to do: love and its giving. If she can't do it she is not a woman.*

—*And you are, of course.*

—*Yes. Thank you for reminding me so often. If I had to go through loneliness again I think I would rather be dead. So be careful,* she said, smiling. *Be careful what you do to me.*

He said he would be. Very careful.

They went to swim again. They swam together, walking to the water side by side, his body dark and wide beside hers. She raised her hand as they walked and touched his elbow. It was a tiny gesture—he did not expect it. It startled him, feeling her cool hand on his puckered elbow. Her palm slipped under it as though to support it. Her fingers were gentle on his arm. He felt strangely quiet. She shifted her grip then and took his arm, holding it high above the elbow. It was a moment of remarkable calm.

They went together as the waves came up the beach one after the other. Almost at once he lost her and was alone, swimming the way she said he should: on his side with the naked elbow out. Most of the time he was underwater and swallowed lots of it and didn't see her until he was past the line of rocks and waves and in calm water. He lay on his back there, bounced up and down by the waves that galloped landward. And suddenly there she was, swimming carefully around him, a guardian angel of a kind.

He had a mental picture of her as a slim corvette, handy in the water, circling some crippled battleship, and he dedicated the picture to her and decided to tell her this as soon as they were back on shore. But when they got to the beach, and came (laughing and sputtering) ashore, he had forgotten it and didn't tell her.

They stayed all night on the beach, it being their first night in this particular refuge. It was a warm July night and they made love in the grey sand. Later they woke and slept and woke again. Later the morning chill came from the sea and they went back to town.

And suddenly he thought: It can't end like this. Not this time. Not with her. Not after having been as good as it was.

He got up and climbed the steep bank to the pines and mounted a small eruption of earth—a ruined battery. It was quiet there and cool, as he thought it would be.

He looked at the glimmering red coal that was Warsaw.

Under the glow it was as he remembered it. Nothing had changed, nor would it change, despite the devastation. It was exactly as she said it would be: too big to live in, too small to enjoy. Coming there had been a mistake.

He heard the German trucks supplying the artillery across the river. There seemed to be an unusual number of trucks. He heard them also in the south, beyond the woods. The woods were a dark blue and getting darker. A wind came from the river and blew the mild fog apart.

His thoughts returned to her and he wondered what she was doing. He thought that she would probably be in her apartment. He wondered if a man was with her or if she had gone out, and if so whether she would come back to the apartment soon, and if so whether she would remain alone in it.

Because suddenly he wanted very much to say something to her, anything—about how she had reminded him of a corvette that time they had been swimming off the grey beach and the dogs had barked and all the other things he had meant to say but had not remembered. This was the time to say it, the best time, and there would never be another or a better time.

The spangled, noncommittal sky, the cool wind on the blasted casemate in the pinegrove, the hum of the trucks and the clang of armored treads across the river that suddenly got loud all pointed to how little time remained for anything. He thought that if he didn't talk to her now, tell her now, at this time, he never would.

She had been cruelly disappointed, but he didn't think it mattered now. He thought that now he and she together could live with anything. And if he gave enough it would replace what he had taken.

He climbed off the battery and moved quickly through the pines towards the car and woke the driver (who insisted that he had not been asleep at all) and told him to head back for Warsaw.

Go thus and thus, he said, giving the address. The streets were blocked in that part of town, the driver said. There had been heavy shelling. And as he spoke the German guns fired from across the river.

Some thirty batteries at least, the General thought. The shells ignored them, passing overhead to burst in town.

They had their dinner in a cellar restaurant, a place she said she knew and liked well enough; a hollow imitation of French establishments of the kind, a wartime expedient. They finished the wine that had been part of the dinner, part of the atmosphere so clumsily provided with the checkered tablecloths and the candles and the inevitable Parisian prints on the walls. The dinner made the atmosphere a lie: coffee and bread and thin vegetable soup and meat that, no matter what the menu called it, had the consistency and sweet rubbery stringiness of horseflesh. They sat there, after eating, smoking the last of Loomis' cigarettes, not saying much.

She seemed disturbed and ill at ease and kept glancing nervously around them as if expecting someone to walk in on them. He wondered why she was upset; the dinner hadn't been as bad as all that.

She wore the black dress he remembered from the party. He told her she looked very good in it, that it was pretty on her; she should be sure to wear it again, the same way, whenever they had dinner. He didn't think they would have dinner again, at least not soon, and he said what he did about the dress partly because the dress was becoming and the compliment was expected from him and partly so that she wouldn't be upset.

—That dress gives you a certain fragility, he said. That's what I thought the first time that I saw you. At the party. You were in the garden and I was up on a balcony. I didn't want you to think I was spying on you, so I didn't say anything when you looked up. Do you remember that part of it?

She smiled, coming back quickly from wherever her thoughts had taken her. He thought she was relieved.

—I didn't know that it was you up on the balcony.

—If you had known would you have said something?

She shook her head, surprised.

—I wondered who you were and what you were doing, he went on. I didn't think you were particularly happy.

—Oh, I was happy enough then, I suppose. At least not unhappy.

—You had already made your decision then.

—Yes, in a way.

Then Loomis leaned towards her and took her chin in his hand and turned her face to his and kissed her. The kiss was small and unexpectedly delivered.

He waited for her to say something, wondering what it would be. He thought there would be something. Usually they said: Why did you do that? Or something equally idiotic, some silly comment to cover confusion while they went through their female multiplicationtables to find expected answers. But she said nothing. She sat very still.

He leaned close to her as she sat with her chin in her hands, elbows on the table, looking at him calmly and no longer tense. The wine seemed to relax her and, he thought, perhaps the kiss had helped. It had not been much of a kiss at best.

He laughed. —You taste like vegetable soup.

—You taste like bread and coffee and red wine.

—Yours is a better taste.

Then an explosion came.

The sound was like a thunderclap infinitely extended, a huge rush of air, and everything shook a little and a glass fell off the table without breaking.

His first thought was to run out to see what had happened. But then he thought: Why? I can't do anything about it anyway. There is no office and no deadline and no telephone and no way to report anything and who would care if there was. He thought it odd that there had been an explosion the first time that he kissed her.

Three or four men and some women hurried past the halfdrawn curtains of the private dining room, an alcove in a cellar that had never been much of a restaurant in peacetime but which, through fact of war, was fashionable because it was a cellar. Here you could eat vegetable soup and drink red wine and artificial coffee and momentarily forget about the war. War was outside. Inside were dim lights. Between the lights and war were thick walls and several ruined floors.

There was the sound of distant sirens shrilling their too late warning of disaster, and a diminishing hum of air rushing between tall buildings, and the brief cries of passersby surprised in the street.

—Shouldn't you go out there? she said.

—No. There is no way to get news out of Warsaw and there is nothing new about another raid even if there was a way to tell about it.

—Perhaps you'll need it for a book. Don't journalists always write books about their experiences?

—Not while there is anyone left to call them a liar.

—You can wait then, she said. And your customers can wait. I don't think I ever want to go outside this cellar. Do you suppose that people feel like this in every war? Sitting in cellars and not wanting to go outside again?

—I wouldn't know, he said. In Madrid, in the Spanish Civil War, nobody sat in cellars because the houses were not very strong in the workmen's quarter and would as likely as not fall on the people in the cellars. In the rich section there was no need for cellars. The Germans didn't shell the homes of the rich. The only siege with cellars that I might know about is Liège, in Belgium. But that was in the other war; I managed to miss it. Do you know what I was thinking?

—What?

—That now I'll think about you every time I eat vegetable soup.

—Or eat a horse?

—Or eat a horse, he agreed. Or hear an explosion.

—It was a very little kiss for such a big explosion.

—Let's hope it didn't do much damage.

There were no more explosions after that and no more kisses. That was not so good. Soon afterwards the sirens wailed their disbelieving note of reprieve and the old waiters moved among the tables lighting the candles and several men and women came into the cellar. They talked excitedly. There were young officers among them and one or two of them glanced at the girl and one or two looked at Loomis in a speculative way and one said something in a low voice to the others and the others laughed. She sat as though frozen; the white look came over her face and closed it up again.

—What is it? Loomis asked. Do you know those people?

—Not very well, she said.

—What are they saying?

—Not much. Something about the war. I wish they wouldn't talk about the war in here.

—Only about the war?

—That's what they are saying. About General Kutrzeba and what he is doing. About the siege . . .

He listened. He couldn't understand what the young officers and women and the two or three older civilians who were with the party were saying, but he thought it was probably true enough: They would talk about Kutrzeba and the war. His Polish was poor but his Russian was adequate enough to understand key words. And then there were words like *atak* and *ofenzywa* which belonged to every language more or less. They were the lingua franca of mankind. The newcomers were talking about Kutrzeba and his great offensive. Eventually the Polish general would bring his battered divisions to the relief of Warsaw (or at least *to* Warsaw). His regiments were the last Polish formations west of Warsaw, unless you counted the futile defense of the Hel peninsula and the garrison of Modlin. With them in Warsaw a new stand could be made. Where? No one knew. But something could be done with these troops, everybody said. It made no sense, of course, but then nothing did.

She was quiet then; her ebullience had evaporated and the harassed, uncertain look came into her eyes and for one quick, uncontrolled moment he thought she would cry.

Suddenly she said: —You're still married, of course. She said it in an offhand manner, as though it didn't matter and wasn't important; as though it didn't give the evening a special quality, defining her and him.

Usually (he thought) they said Are you married? Or Were you ever married? And then he'd say something like Sort of, or In a way, or Not particularly, or Only a little. That was the formula for the healthylooking girls. Sometimes he said Not any more, or I used to be, if that was expected.

And obviously, he thought, she expected something of that kind. For a moment he wondered which of the stock phrases to dust off, and wondered what all her other men had told her. Because, of course, she would have other men. Or would have had. He wondered if she knew anything about him and that he *was* still married, whether there was some sign on him that she could read. And then, because after all it wasn't important (being a time of war), and he didn't think it would ever matter because she was not important to him, and he wouldn't see her for much longer, and, somehow, because he didn't want to lie for once, he said:

—Twenty-one years.

She looked incredulous.

—Then how old are you?

—Forty-five.

She said she wouldn't have believed it. He did not look it.

—Thanks a lot, he said.

—I was thirteen-years old, she said, and you were already married to somebody.

—I couldn't exactly be your father.

Obviously time to her was weightier than it was to him. He felt the years then and suddenly saw them as she must have seen them: as the thousands of days and nights that they had been.

—Twenty-one years, she said, disbelieving.

He could see her adding up her last twenty-one years, summing up the grand total of experience to see if she could match his twenty-one. She couldn't do it. The weight of the days and nights settled about them and everything crumpled just a bit.

—I thought you were still married, she said. But I wasn't sure. I thought you might be or maybe may have been, but maybe for five years or six or maybe even ten. But not for twenty-one.

—What difference does it make?

—You are so thoroughly married. I hadn't thought that you'd belong so much to anyone.

—I don't belong to anyone, he said.

—Twenty-one years . . .

—Ten, six, or twenty-one. What difference does it make?

—It's a generation.

He moved impatiently. Because, of course, it was a generation.

—Don't be offended. I thought that I could talk to you about anything. I thought it would be all right.

—What made you think that?

—I just thought it. I didn't want to make you angry.

—Years, he said. They are only years. They make no difference. Once you accept the first of them the others are completely unimportant.

Except, of course, that this was not true and he knew it. And suddenly he became aware of the dark, candlelit and blacked-out cellar as a frame. They made the picture: she looking young and delicate and brave and so intense, and he a little worn, played out and hollow.

He became aware of the no longer young enough, slightly splotched surface of his hand, with the skin no longer as tight or as firm as it had been, and sagged inside and shrunk, and he whisked the offending hand out of sight and reached a little wildly for some thought that would reduce the weight of all those years. Were they good? Were they bad? He thought they were incredibly bad in their total and could find nothing there to hang on to.

But then she started talking in an animated way, a conscious effort to repair the evening.

This place, she said. It had a strange effect on her, most unusual. It made her talkative.

He thought he would go along with the conversation. —What's the name of it?

—Syrena. The siren with the sword. That's the crest of Warsaw.

—Well, that's appropriate, he said, listening. The other sirens blew their warning of renewed attack.

—I had another name for this place, she said. I was about to call it my Club Confessional. I don't seem to be able to stop myself from talking. You must be tired of it.

—Good God, no. Besides, you don't talk much.

—I talk here.

—This is our first time here, he said. That's not much talking.

Still, she said, in her Club Confessional she talked more than anywhere else and to him more than to anybody else. She hoped that he would put up with her weakness. It was something about the atmosphere of it: impermanent and therefore safe for secrets. You didn't think the place would last long enough to haunt you with what you might have said. Each time she passed the place, she said, she was surprised to find the cellar still intact. Each time she thought that *next* time she would find it filled with rubble, caved in and destroyed.

—I'll miss it when that happens, she said.

—Will you? I will too. This is the place where I first kissed you.

She smiled without committing herself one way or another.

And so for that, if for no other reason, it ought to be preserved, he said.

—But not, she said (smiling a little), as a national monument. Because those have less permanence than anything else.

—We'll do it by private subscription, he suggested. We ought to be able to raise the money in America. In fact, why don't you and I go to America and start working on it? We could make an appeal to the Conscience of the World.

She laughed. But she had doubts, she said. Because did such appeals ever work?

—Not very well. Unless, of course, there are rich oil fields or a tungsten mine underneath this cellar. You don't suppose there are any, do you?

She said she did not think so.

—Well, that takes care of that particular appeal. But maybe we can think of something else.

She agreed that nothing had the appeal of a tungsten mine. —But how about the people? Couldn't we interest anyone on the basis of people and what is happening here?

—Sorry, he said. That has no bearing on practical economics.

Later, walking through the silent and deserted streets-after-midnight to her apartment, she thanked him for the evening. It was good of him to ask her to dinner, she said. It was kind of him to be so patient and forbearing about her talking. He must have been a little bored, she supposed. If that was so she was very sorry. He had not been bored, he said, and really she talked very little.

—I didn't mean to offend you with that talk about years, she said. I think that you are kind, and that is important. I don't think you'd ever hurt anyone intentionally. I think that you need to be told how kind you are.

—Well, he said (to keep it light, because, suddenly, he was glad that she was being serious), no one has ever accused me of being kind.

—Perhaps they didn't know you very well.

—What? After twenty-one years of marriage?

—I was wrong about that, I can see. I was thinking about my marriage and my life after it when I talked about yours. I don't think one should ever do that.

Then she was silent, walking quietly. Her face was a little sad, he thought, but he couldn't see her well in the lightless streets. She tightened her hand on his arm. After a while he saw that she was crying.

—What's the matter? he said.

Nothing. It was nothing. She was just tired, she supposed, and a little nervous. There was the daily tension of the war. It was . . . well . . . she was really sorry.

He understood. She was to think nothing of it. But had he done something? Said something?

No. Really, he was to believe her. It was nothing that he had said or done. There was no triggerword to set off the crying. She supposed that she had just felt like doing it, and . . . well, there it was. It had been so long since she had had as pleasant an evening; she had forgotten, in a way, how pleasant evenings could be.

He said the evening had been pleasant. And that he knew how she felt about pleasant evenings; he also had forgotten how they felt.

Walking, she started talking about her father and about her husband, who resembled her father on the surface and whom she had married to replace her father as much as for any other reason.

—Was that your father? he said as soon as she had named him, because, of course, he had heard about him, as had so many other Americans. It was a household word for music no matter what it lost in ruptured pronunciation.

She said she didn't think her father could be called a great man away from his music but he was a good one. He had ideals. It was important that one had ideals, didn't Loomis think so?

—Of course, he said, wondering as he said it what his ideals were.

—I thought my husband had them. He was much like Father, except that Father was tall and thin and my husband was stout and less than average in height. But he talked as though he had ideals and he seemed much like Father. My father liked him. Zbigniew was a historian and advised my father about politics. But he did nothing to resist Pilsudski, despite his protestations about ideals and democracy. I am afraid he had a set of ideals for every occasion.

—Is that why you turned to the General? he asked. It suddenly seemed important to him to know why she had.

—Oh no, she said. That may have been a part of it but only inasmuch as they, that is the ideals, made up the whole man.

—Then why did you? He was a soldier, after all, and your father was opposed to war.

—At first I thought it was because Janusz was the only one to oppose Pilsudski. But of course that wasn't it at all.

—What was it then?

—I loved him.

—Don't you anymore?

—You don't know much about a woman, do you?

—Enough.

Indeed (he thought), I know enough. And I could tell her better than she could tell me why she fell in love (if that was a good name for it) with the one-armed soldier who could no longer be a soldier and who needed her. And that (he thought) is quite enough from Dr. Willard Loomis, amateur phychologist and thinker extraordinary about the mental processes of women.

—Tell me one thing, he said. What did you do after the General left you? I assume that it was he who did the leaving. I don't mean to make that sound as badly as it does. You seem too loyal and too sensitive to leave anybody. It takes a selfish, careless kind of person to give anybody so much unnecessary pain. So, when he left, what did you do?

She smiled and shook her head. She said: —I scrubbed the apartment. I took a boiler out into the courtyard and lit a fire and got the water very hot and got a lot of soap and I scrubbed everything. I took down all the pictures and washed the walls. I scrubbed the ceiling and washed all the windows. But I couldn't get the water hot enough.

—Why did you do that?

—I don't know. I was tired afterwards. But everything looked clean. It didn't seem so bad after that.

They came into Aleja Szucha, and then walked through Parkowa along the white wall of Lazienki Park. The sky was brilliant. The street was white and red with moonlight and reflected fires.

She said she would like to go into the park to see the swans. It would be good, she said, to see the white birds sailing unconcerned on the lagoon as if there were no war . . . no fire . . . peace and peacefulness. She liked to look at them, she said. They were beautiful to see.

—All right, he said. It will be good to see the swans.

But then the street darkened. It filled with a harsh drumming sound. A mass of men swung into the head of the street and moved like a black wave towards them between the houses and the white park wall. They marched in groups. Their feet struck concrete with a measured beat. The rhythm of their boots showed that they were soldiers.

—How tired they look, she said.

The beat of marching feet seemed steady enough. Sparks still flew off the cobblestones and concrete under the soldiers' ironstudded boots. But the spark of life seemed to have left them. This was an army in defeat, he thought. There was no doubt about it, no matter what anyone would say about it afterwards, what apologies were made for the defeat and how historians would retell the story. Perhaps it was true that these men had not been beaten in the field, that they had won victories and, had they been properly equipped and led and not betrayed by the Allies, would have won some more, but they had been beaten down and worn down and crushed and crumpled and had marched too much with their backs to a pursuing enemy.

He held tightly to Lala's hand. She had sought his when the first ranks of returning soldiers came into the street out of the Street of the Ensigns and the Park and now the pressure of her nails in his palm was painful.

—They are exhausted, she said. They look . . . like shadows.

He agreed with a pressure of his hand. He said something about brave men and endurance and faith and courage and devotion. Also about spirit. And about their pride. He did not quite believe it but he wanted to say something to ease her obvious pain.

And now he saw that the long street was not deserted by civilians as it had seemed to be at first. There were innumerable men and women standing by the wall and against the houses and filling the doors and windows. More came out of sidestreets and lined the avenue. This was a grey, sadeyed crowd of old men and women, who watched, dryeyed or weeping, as the ragged western regiments marched past. Many civilians walked beside the soldiers. They offered shoulders for soldiers to lean on. Women and children carried rifles for them. No one in the great crowd said one word to anyone. He thought that Lala was the only person who had spoken.

—Let's leave, he said. Let's go into the park. The swans . . .

She shook her head and gripped his hand.

—You must see this, she said. Please look at it and see it. I wish everyone everywhere could see it. There is so little time for us. It's almost gone.

—For us?

—For everyone. Oh, can't you see?

—Yes, he said.

They watched the soldiers.

First came the holloweyed infantry. Then came the cannon and the ammunition carts and the strawladen carts with their moaning load of wounded. The cavalry came last. Not much of it was mounted. The lancers and the mounted riflemen and the light horse soldiers walked beside their horses and there were no lances to be seen among them and not many sabers. The troopers carried rifles and infantry bayonets, bags of handgrenades and shining German light machineguns on their shoulders and their horses trod uneasily among this functional panoply of a new war.

Lala moved against Loomis as the horsemen passed. She pressed his hand. She was dryeyed now, unlike many other women in the crowd. It was a huge, silent, weeping crowd oblivious of the late bombers wheeling overhead on their way home to Germany.

It pleased him that she was not weeping like the other women. He moved his hand a little to shift the sharp points of her nails out of his palm.

—I'm sorry, she said. Did I hurt you?

—No. Don't take your hand away.

She watched the passing men. Her hair had sprung free from under her small hat. It was more a beret than a hat but not quite like the flat, innocent headgear of the convent schoolgirl. Still, he thought, with her hair unruly and her small face intent on the passing soldiers, she looked incredibly young.

Her hand was dry and cool in his and he was pleased to hold it and glad that she did not take it away and he thought suddenly that he would like to bend down towards her the necessary foot or so and kiss her cheek where the orange-yellow hair escaped the beret. A chaste kiss. Innocence? Miller would rumble his enormous gut into a rupture if he saw him at it.

He thought about her without any great sexual desire. Oh, it was there, of course; it had to be there. It's there when a man tips his hat to a woman. But there was no particular excess of it. Nothing overwhelming. Nothing to put into project form.

She had been an unusually pretty girl, you could see that, and was now all the more desirable, he thought, for being a woman (with the small lines at the corners of her mouth and eyes, almost invisible), and for the way she moved her hands when she talked—little jumps from the wrists up, quickly restrained, suggesting some uncertainty, some doubt, perhaps a disappointment; but she was not the kind of woman he used to want. Lately he hadn't been particularly interested. And when he was, his tastes seemed to run to tall, healthylooking girls who laughed a lot and had an easy manner and were assured (too frequently, perhaps) of their desirability: the kind who were invariably brown in white bathingsuits in summer and said the right things and drank their cocktails well and were amused without unusual effort. She seemed too intense, too self-contained. Too difficult. It was the war, of course (he thought), and her special problems. He did not want to become involved in her problems (God knows I've got enough!) and did not think that he could interest her without a special effort. But it was possible. He wondered if she had given any thought to the possibilities and, if so, what had she decided. They watched the last of the soldiers move past them, shadowlike and silent. He wondered what she thought.

When the long march was over and the crowd dispersed (becoming suddenly aware of the bombers overhead and the nearby explosions as though the sight of the soldiers had hypnotized them and had made them think themselves immune to death), he took Lala home. She asked him in. This time the cat came forward cautiously and rubbed himself against his trouserlegs. The dog yelped. He made himself a drink (without ice) from the bottle she had bought at the Europejski. He could not get the picture of the beaten soldiers out of his head. Somewhere in that infinitely weary, silent march lay the answer to the questions that had troubled him since that first evening, at the party, before the war began.

But I am tired, he thought. The day has been long.

Answers eluded him.

She was huddled on the quilt, feet drawn up under her. The cat slid towards her on its foggy legs. The surreptitious night went on.

—Talk to me, she said finally.

—What about?

—Anything.

Anything would do. Just so the stealthy silence would be broken, so that there would be sound. Nights were so terribly quiet even with the bombardments, did he know that? That was what made them hard to live through: the silence and the emptiness of it.

He said that quiet was good. He, for one, could never get enough of it. She shrugged. She said that silence made one think . . . and remember. And that brought about regret and there was nothing good about that.

—Well, I don't know, he said. What shall I say? Shall I tell you about my All-American Dream?

—What's that?

—That's something we all have in America. My dream makes a good story. Would you like to hear it?

—Yes. I would like to hear about your dream.

He warned her that it was nothing profound. Nothing ideological. It was just a dream.

—What was it? She was interested.

He supposed that it was rather stupid in a way; most things were, viewed through the curtain of time.

It was in New York, which is a strange place unless you're accustomed to it and it no longer disillusions you. It was in Sammy's Bar and Grill on Madison Avenue, he said; a marvelous place for dreams.

—My father didn't like New York, she broke in. But I would like to see it.

Ah yes. Her father. He would not find it comfortable in Sammy's Bar and Grill. —But his dreams were no more real than mine, Loomis said. As she would see.

He lived in New York then, he said. He worked at home during the day and in the afternoon he'd go to Columbia, the university there, to hear some lectures, or to the library.

—What were you working on?

—A book, he confessed.

—What about?

—People. People and love. The love of man for woman and man for humanity and the love of duty. The love of country and self-love. And the love of life. I really thought I knew a bit about them and could do a book. But, of course, I didn't know enough. And in the evening I would walk past this place to the East Sixties, where I lived, and every night I went in for a beer and a cornedbeef sandwich.

—It sounds like a very lonely life.

—It was good enough.

—Was that before you married?

—Oh no, during it. It was that kind of marriage, you see. It didn't interfere with that kind of life.

She nodded and he went on with the story of the dream.

—It was at Sammy's. One night the dream came in. She was, I remember, quite small and trim and beautifully proportioned, with a small heartshaped face and long straight hair to frame it. A full, attractive mouth. Enormous eyes and cheekbones. It was as though they had finally done the impossible and crossed the cover of Vogue with the girl next door.

—It was, he said, the American Dream.

—Sammy had caught it too, I could see that. He stopped tormenting the cornedbeef. This was the dream, you see, the promised land. This was the milk and the honey. The girl sat down near the bar and didn't say anything to anyone or look at anyone and it was then as if a curtain of some transparent but unbreakable material dropped calmly around her. Every man in the place stopped talking at the same time and looked at her and smiled a little to himself. She was so fine to look at. Then the door opened. And in came something straight out of a cave. Low. Squat. A thick black line making his eyebrows one Pleistocene bar. A wet mouth, like a carp. He, or it, sat down beside her. Right beside her. It spoke into her ear, confidentially. She didn't move or say anything or pay any attention, as though nothing like this could possibly affect her, as though she could not possibly be touched by anything like that. I moved then, ready to stand up and go to her and take that thing beside her by the head and pull the head off it at one word from her. Other men stood up. We take our dreams seriously in America, you see.

Old Sammy felt it too, I could see. He stood still with that carving knife as though he was about to lunge with it. The gross ape whispered on. I could see the fat mouth grinning. The ape took some money from its pocket. It didn't seem to be much money. He—it—laid the money on the bar, beside her hand, as though it was a lot. She picked it up without looking at it and put it in her pocketbook and left the place with him.

Lala looked at him, waiting for more. Only there was no more.

—That's all, he said. That's the end of it.

—What did you do then?

—I laughed. I laughed at Sammy and myself and the other men, but mostly at Sammy. He was a fine old man and he had been around, but that girl caught him off his guard and made him feel warm and sentimental. She made him remember his dream. All his dreams. And there he stood, like a biblical prophet with the forecast gone wrong, a knife in one hand, a dill pickle in the other. His mouth was open. Because the manna was polluted, don't you see? The Red Sea had not opened after all.

He laughed.

She also laughed. —Your American Dream. People shouldn't have dreams.

—You must have had some at some time.

—Yes, but not lately.

—But you had some. There was your art, and then (he said deliberately) there was the General.

—Yes, there was that.

—Why did you stay with him so long?

—I loved him.

—You thought he needed you. You have too much compassion.

—The need is part of it.

—Is it always a part of it with you? Do they have to need you?

—I must need as well, she said.

—And what do you need?

—I don't know, she said. Do you know? Does anybody know?

—I need you, he said, surprised to hear it.

—Do you? She looked at him carefully and a little sadly. —Do you really?

—Yes.

—I don't think you do. I don't think that you need anything, unless it is perhaps a kind of assurance. In many ways you and Janusz are very much alike. That is, perhaps, the first thing about you that I noticed.

—I don't know about your General or what he wants, he said. I know what I need.

—Do you? Then you're very lucky. Somehow it always seems much easier for a man.

—Oh come now, he said. Come now. What's easy about it? It's very difficult sometimes. Much more so for a man than for a woman.

—Is that why you relied so much on your wife?

—Who relied on her?

—You did. I could see from the first time that we talked about her in the cellar that you wanted her to give you something, some kind of reassurance. She could no longer give you what you had expected and you were disappointed. Is this what you need? An assurance that *something* is important?

—Maybe that's what it is, he said. I don't know.

It was then late. He felt tired. He didn't want to talk about Nimi and what he wanted from her.

The two-faced clock on the cathedraltower struck some late hour.

He thought that if he didn't go now, didn't leave now, he would be committed. No matter what happened from this point on he would be committed, finally, to something. If he left now he would never have to come back unless he wanted to. There was an ultimatum of a kind.

He said he had to go.

—You can stay here, she said. I'll make up a bed for you on the couch. You can go later when the sun is up and the streets have more people in them and it is safer.

—I have to be up early, he lied.

—The bombardment will wake you.

Then he was left alone with the cat she had found one night in a bombed-out house (and taken home because it was so very much alone) and the dog she had collected somewhere else and kept because it needed her, never letting them outside for long, afraid that they would be hurt somehow or leave her.

He got up while she brought the sheet and the pillow and made up the bed. Normally she wouldn't let him stay, he thought. But there was the war, after all.

Then she went off somewhere inside the apartment and he was left alone. He was aware of eyes, yellow and faintly luminous, across the room. Light came in under the door. There was the sound of water splashing somewhere and the muffled, feminine click of bottles with glass stoppers.

He got up and walked about the room. He picked up books on her book-shelves and put them down. Untired, he lay down. He did not sleep.

A month before he had left New York he had not come home but stayed out at a party without Nimi (who was, if anywhere, at another party not missing him at all), and he knew then that he was through with coming home. It was finished then, the whole sorry business. He had been impotent the last ten months of living with his wife.

The resolution to be free of her matured at that party, where he drank too much and said too many funny things and finally walked home with the girl from the advertising agency, whom he kissed in the elevator and who un-hooked her clothes before they came to her apartment. She cried and finally beat him with her silly fists, but it was no good. She said: —I had to pick you, you bastard. There were so many there. Do something, will you? Do something. You have to do something now. Then she was quiet and smoked cigarettes and he could not look at her, afraid that he would meet her eyes if he did. He left while she fell into an uneasy sleep and went to Sammy's (which was closed) and waited till it opened and had whiskey. Then, despite his resolutions, he went home and went to bed and slept. Later that day they had a civilized discussion, Nimi and he.

He thought about Nimi. She was a beautiful, nonangular woman with a flawless body and a face that should have been painted many centuries ago on some chapel ceiling; there was a wealth of warmth in that face, and under-standing and depth and dimension. Only . . . not for him. For him she had the same quick smile that she gave everybody else, only not as often. She wore her glossy black hair long and hung without much care (oh but so tenderly and so carefully arranged into disorder), and she was wonderful at many things. But that was part of the matter with her: If Nimi couldn't ride it or drive it or hit it with a racket or drink it, she didn't care about it.

God, women. He thought about the women he had had. One he remembered in particular: a Jewish girl intense about the Arabs and the Balfour Declaration who talked about the dreams of Herzl in bed and was terribly disappointed to see that he was not circumcised. There was a girl in Spain, one of many, but the only one who stuck in memory, although he could no longer remember her name. A strong, exultant girl without a name. It was with her that he had coined the best of Loomis' Golden Thoughts: Love is not the gentle sighing of a violin but the exultant twang of a bedspring. But she would hardly count, that being time of war. One was a reporter. She was a good reporter and, perhaps, that was why she was hopelessly inadequate in bed. There was the advertising girl who cried. One was a dancer. She had a mirror on the ceiling and parallel bars in the living room and all her furniture was black. There were some others.

Practically from the beginning there had been Nimi. She was the girl he was going to marry; everybody said it. She was the Golden Girl of Drubal County, spirited (yes) and spoiled (certainly), willful (of course, being Nimi Otis), brilliant, intractable . . . all those words applied. And as long as there were parties they could go to and new dances to learn and highschool and college friends to visit and be visited by, and the daily drinking, and as long as there was no time to think and certainly no time to talk about anything important, it was all right. But then it was over. So that when the wars came, and this war in particular, they were like so many doors marked EXIT for him. He couldn't wait to go. Wars were wonderful. In war you got to think only military thoughts: trajectories, points of departure, lines of main resistance, that sort of thing. It was wonderful to think only military thoughts.

Particularly if you didn't take them (the wars) seriously and could laugh about them and feel superior to them (the men in the wars), because the wars were, after all, not your wars and the men who were being killed had a different color or language or set of ideas that did not concern you, and it was only accidental—a matter of chance—that you were on their side and not on the other.

He supposed that his coming back to this country, this war, was not so much a journey by ship, train and road as a trip through the years He had been here before, not only physically but in attitude. The repetition was a retreat of a kind. Somehow each of my days has become a retreat, he thought, lying on the makeshift bed, watching the yellow eyes that were watching him, while outside the night shook with artillery fire.

He became aware of the apartment's stillness and the silence. There were no small womansounds coming now from the bathroom. There was a breathlessness and a lack of air and too much warmth and too much expectation.

Then Lala came into the room: very white in the no longer curtained and familiar dark, the warm impersonal darkness which was safe. She knelt beside the couch. Her face was enormously enlarged before him. He lay quite still and looked at her and wanted to say, Look, go away, this is difficult enough, this is too difficult, but her face was smooth and cool when he reached up and took it in his hands and she didn't say anything after he kissed her.

—It won't be any good, he said.

She said, barely audible: —You see? It was all right.

—I love you, he said, or thought he said and hoped that he had not (or, if he had, that she had not heard him or would not remember or would ascribe it to the things men said).

She didn't seem to hear him.

Her eyes were closed and her chest was still and then he remembered (with pride and a sort of shamefaced mental shrug that was full of pride) that it *had* been all right; that it had, in fact, been astonishingly right, and he remembered the long minutes of it . . . astonishingly long despite his early fears and the numbing uncertainty in the beginning and, later, the urgency that had made him fumble and slip, and her determined submissiveness at the start, her wondering, and then her gentle but encouraging touch and small words coming quickly and then *her* animated seeking, her reaching out and enfolding and grasping; and finally the lock-kneed clasp about his body, the female response to his own male ferocity, and, at the end, that madness of all mating women, of all time and of all people: her knees thrown high towards his shoulderblades and hard heels drumming him into oblivion.

There had been nothing like it, ever. Not for him. Not with anybody else. And it was nothing to do with the time and place, he thought, or the artillery bombardment—that other drumming in the torn, red night.

He moved a bit to look at her below him, remembering the hard-drumming heels, still in the sliding clasp. She kept her eyes closed. And then she made a curious gesture with her hands, as though gathering something out of herself and offering it, bringing her hands forward and down towards her hips. She passed them slowly up over his sides and waist and let them lie there.

—Don't move, she said.

—I'll have to move sometime.

—Yes, but not now. Stay like that for now.

—All right.

—It was all right, you see.

But now he saw it was not all right. Nothing would ever be all right again —not the way it was. There was a shadow of a kind with them in the room, as though someone beside them had been there, watching and waiting, outside them in the dark, looking on.

He smoked a cigarette while she was momentarily gone, hearing the clicking feminine sounds again, and saw the yellow eyes unblinking in the dark.

What do you see, damn cat?

Whom do you see?

Too late now to talk about involvements.

She came back quickly and stopped a little uncertainly (he thought) inside the door. It was as though she had expected him to be up and dressing and climbing frantically into his clothes and groping for his hat and an excuse to leave.

He lay very still. He smiled at her but doubted if she saw the smile in the halfdark room. He asked if she was tired.

—Yes. But not the sleeping kind of tired.

—What kind then?

—The way you become tired after walking a long way.

—And coming home?

She waited, looked at him.

—Yes.

He said that he knew what she meant. That he too was tired. But that he and she, they together, could sleep late tomorrow because there was nothing they could do tomorrow that they had not been able to do today.

—Except that I won't believe any of this tomorrow, he went on.

—Oh yes you will, she said, suddenly sad, and turned awkwardly and waited for him near the door.

He followed her into the other room, her bedroom, where in the shaking light of fire and explosion on the quivering horizon she was alternately red and coolly white.

Friday, September the fifteenth

I THE CORRESPONDENT

Gradually the shadows shifted in the room, and the sound of the bombardment changed, and it became colder. She rested. And he, having so much more to rest after than she did, also rested, watching the shadows shorten in the room, thinking that it had always been like that: the brightest moments seemed to come in shadow. He didn't know what it was about her that suddenly made him feel solicitous. Perhaps it was her smallness when asleep, the fragility of her neck and shoulders. She did not seem sturdy enough to hold up any burdens, the sinews not quite adequate, insufficient muscle. Yet she was generously made, he knew now, perhaps too generously. Her shoulders were broad enough for burdens. But she had a smallgirl quality about her when asleep that brought to mind the picture of the pirouette she had made the night before the war. That and the smallgirl sleeping face, the smooth skin of sleep, made him feel protective and thoughtful and a little kind. He wanted to be kind to her, a woman who had so much, so much more than other women, but who thought she had so little. She had said things about herself that showed how unsure she was, how hard she looked for solid ground to walk on, and how determined she was that none of it would show. He wanted to do something about that; to haul out his male confidence, this male assurance that she thought he had, and give her some direction. But (he thought) I have none to give. It is a rare commodity if it is genuine.

And possibly because of the shadows in the room that gave them both an aura of mystery and romance and warmth, he drew her to him and kissed her cheekbones and her eyes. He told her that she shouldn't be afraid of anything, present or future, or be sad about things past, or be uncertain, because she was so beautiful. Beauty was a currency of a kind. It was something you had that you could be sure of. You could trade it for success and for amusement and you could use it to get love. If you had love you weren't really destitute.

Then, through the intervening space, the distance between then and now, the odd new tenderness and the compassion took shape in the forbidden word. And then it was gone.

He was cold. Love. To whom had he dared to say it? He had been so careful. So careful all the other times. In all the places. He wanted to make it all light and amusing.

He was aware of his watching her and of her eyes on him. He couldn't quite determine her look in the shadow. He thought it was a wary, questioning look with a touch of sadness. But also a commitment, as though she had made up her mind about him and about herself during the night.

—How long have you been looking at me? Were you awake long?

—Not very long, he said.

—Why didn't you wake me?

—You slept so well. You needed sleep, I think. Did you get up at night? I think I woke up and you were gone.

—Yes, I got up for a little while.

—Couldn't you sleep?

—No. Not for a while. It was too hot. I went to get some water. But you slept well. I watched you for a while before I fell asleep.

—I usually snore. Did I snore?

—No. You slept very quietly. You looked like a small boy.

—You shouldn't have let me sleep, he said. You should have awakened me. Lo, I hear the trumpets call and the armed tramp of marching men. To arms. The regiment rides at dawn.

She smiled, then laughed a little. Relieved and grateful (and ashamed a little), he thought that this was good: her laughter. That was the way it was supposed to be. He told himself he didn't want her to be serious because seriousness was sadness and he didn't want her to be sad. But seriousness was danger to himself.

So perhaps it was bright again and cheerful and amusing. He felt a fleeting panic at the thought that it had come so close to being serious. Somehow, with the room grey and the darkness gone, and the artillery momentarily quiet and the bombers still on their way and not yet overhead, and the mirror reflecting him and her darkly on the opposite wall (so that it seemed as though there were many others in the room), it was no longer personal. He didn't want to stay any longer in the room, where he could see her reflected everywhere he looked and, more important, where he could see himself. The face that looked at him out of the mirror was disagreeable.

She said she would make breakfast. There wasn't much to make. But she had bread and acorn coffee and some fruit. She had brought apples with her from the country and they were still good.

—I suppose you're used to English breakfasts, she said. We don't eat that much here.

—How much is that much? A cup of coffee is all I ever want for breakfast.

—You would be easy to feed in the morning.

—No trouble at all. But I'm difficult about dinner.

—You weren't difficult about last night's dinner.

—It was the horse, he said. I have great sympathy for horses.

—How about people? Do you feel sympathy for them too?

—Sometimes, he said.

—I don't think you like people very much. But then perhaps you do. Perhaps you're shy about them. Is that it?

—Shy? With the way I make a living? You have to have as much gall as a brush salesman in my business.

—But shouldn't you like people too? Doesn't it help if you're interested in them? You can't retain complete objectivity about everything. Sooner or later everyone must take a stand, pick a side, find a path to follow. Something to believe. Sooner or later everyone has to become involved with everybody else.

—Perhaps, he said, but you can get hurt that way. You can take a beating.

—It is a risk, she said. But isn't that what being human is about?

—What? Being hurt? Taking beatings?

—Taking the risk and, if necessary, being hurt. Yes. That is what I mean.

—Isn't that a bit unrealistic? Impractical?

—Perhaps.

She said that she became easily attached to things—people and, yes, ideas too—even though she knew from experience that this was unrealistic and impractical. But you had to start somewhere, she said. You had to live outside yourself to be a human being. There were no practical guarantees of safety for any human being. No country's constitution had that guarantee.

—Mine guarantees pursuit of happiness, he said.

—And attainment of it? Does it also guarantee anything like that?

—No. No attainment, only the pursuit.

She went away and presently came back carrying a robe. It was heavy silk, black and green, and had at one time been expensive. Now it was old. The right sleeve was pinned up. She flushed, taking the safetypins out of the sleeve. She did not look at him; her face had a determined look as she smoothed out the sleeve, and there was something else (in the way she held her head and shoulders, the set of her head), another quality he could not identify.

—You can wear this, she said carefully, while we have breakfast.

He felt a tightness in his chest and stomach, a sudden anger: at himself, at her and at the General, at the grey morning and at what he thought. He was so angry that his voice climbed.

—No, he said. I'll dress.

—You don't have to. Don't you see that? It isn't necessary anymore. Wear the robe; it's the only man's robe I have. There isn't any other.

—I can't wear that. How can you give it to me?

—There isn't any other I can offer you. And really, it's only a robe. Wear it. Please put it on.

—I can't wear that.

He dressed and she, having so much more to put on, held her back to him for help with the hooks and eyes and small buttons and the snaps. Her shoulders rounded away from him and made her back narrow. He found his hands were trembling and his sight was blurred as if he were looking out of a dark room into a bright outside through a windowpane on which water ran. He struggled with his face before the mirror, and with his shaking hands.

Breakfast was less than a success. They sat in the dining room lit by yellow candles, separated by the length of the table and by their silence. Outside, the sound of the dawn artillery bombardment; it shook the walls. The sound was muffled by the blackout curtains. It was a bad setting for a breakfast; there was an impossible formality about it (the long table reflecting candlelight and glassware) suggesting dinner and the afterdinner things. There was their silence and the brutal sounds outside. Finally he got up and looked through the curtains and saw that the day had come and there was light and he blew out the candles and opened the curtains.

He said he was sorry about the fuss he had made about the robe. It was just a robe, after all. It meant no more than a robe could mean, yes, he knew that. But it was so obviously the General's robe and this had been so obviously the General's apartment and she had been, so obviously, the General's woman that all together he had been upset.

—It is the only man's robe I have here, she said. It is the only robe belonging to a man, fit for a man, that I have ever had. I don't want to collect symbols. I didn't want to attach meanings to inanimate objects. I wanted to treat this robe as another object. I hoped that if you wore it, it would make it just another robe.

—Thanks very much, he said.

—No, you don't understand. I don't mean that you would degrade it. No. That's the last thing I thought. I wanted everything to be fine between us, with nothing intruding. Nothing carried over from any other time. I didn't want to seem callous or to shock you.

—You didn't shock me, he said. You didn't seem callous.

—Of course I did, she said.

Loomis shook his head. Not because she hadn't shocked him; he had been shocked, thoroughly shaken by her gesture, which was, perhaps, too simple to understand, too unexpected. It made him think, now, that it had been a long time since he had accepted anything he didn't fully understand. It made him wonder if what he believed was true, if he could judge the right or wrong of anything, if he could justify the judgments and the condemnations. But he didn't want to talk about it anymore.

A robe; good God, a robe. What difference did it make who had worn it or if anyone had worn it and why did it upset him because someone had? What right did he have to expect anything, question anything? A robe. Sweet Christ, a robe. It was a hell of a thing to get upset about.

—All right, he said. I understand. I'm sorry about the fuss; it was stupid. The robe is just a robe, after all. I'll be glad to wear it.

She nodded, saying nothing. She seemed surprised and disappointed and she tried to show neither in her face. He went on: The word robe itself had something to do with it.

—It's something the General said to me a long time ago. I talked to him in 1926, in the hospital, after he lost his arm. I don't think you knew that. Did you know it?

—No. Either he or you said something about that at the party. But I didn't pay much attention then to what anyone said. No, I didn't know it.

—We talked about a lot of things, mostly what he believed in. He talked about the difference between a soldier and a man of the robe. It's an unfortunate expression. The word robe reminded me of it. Somehow it seemed to me that I was joining something. The men of the robe. His robe. A stupid thought. Do you know what I mean?

She nodded. She listened very carefully. She had an intent look of absolute attention carefully controlled.

—So, all in all, with everything considered, it just struck me wrong.

They went on with their breakfast, hearing the bombers come. The thin drone of motors pulsed against the windows. She got up and opened all the windows and secured them so that they would not break when the concussion came. The dull pounding of bombs bursting in some other quarter began to shake the windows.

And then she said, looking across the long, polished surface of the table, with the dust stirred by the trembling air coming down on it, across the debris of the unsuccessful breakfast: —I think he was here.

—Who? When?

—Janusz Prus. I think he came here last night.

—What? How do you know?

—I don't know, but I have a feeling that he came here last night.

—Did you see anything? Hear anything?

—No. Nothing. But I know he was here. I knew when I got up last night that he had been here.

—Perhaps you just imagined it. Perhaps you had a dream.

She agreed that it was possible, but she didn't think so. It was only a feeling she had but she was certain that the General had come to the apartment.

—I wish I knew why he came, she said. I wish I had been awake when he came.

—Does he still have a key?

—I suppose he does. I never thought about it. But that's not the point, whether or not he has a key. I wish I could have spoken to him before he left. This way it's so . . .

—Shabby? he said quickly. Conventionally shabby?

She said that wasn't what she meant.

—Oh, but it is. He could have rung the bell or telephoned before he came. Any considerate man would have telephoned. If there's anything shabby it's his fault.

The telephonelines were down and the bell was an electric bell, she reminded him. The General couldn't have used either.

—He could have knocked. He still has one hand, doesn't he? Instead he comes around like a spying husband!

She looked puzzled and disturbed and shook her head, looking at him with a measure of disappointment. She made a troubled gesture, as if to say: No, that's not what I meant; you know what I meant. Why are you being so obtuse about this? It's not so hard to understand; you seem to understand everything else so well.

Ah, but (he thought) don't you see? This is the way it's done: I'm making standard derogatory comments because I'm trying to make him appear less than he is. This is the standard operational procedure, a part of the morning. It's nothing I invented. It's part of the system, don't you see? Soon now I'll talk about infatuations and explain that there was really no love between the General and you, that it was a good facsimile, perhaps, that you were impressed by this or the other. But love? No. Something less than love. Because this other man (I'll say) was really not good enough, not sensitive enough, for you and could not have loved you. If he loved you (I'll say), would he have done this? Or that? Oh (I'll say), it's clear. He is incapable of loving you, but I, on the other hand, have the necessary understanding. That is the way: to lift *me* up by pulling him down and making us (me and him) equal on another level and justify what can't be justified. This is the way to overcome obstacles like men whose love is in the way: never head-on, directly; that is dangerous. Always the backdoor or the kitchenwindow. You undermine foundations, make things seem less fine, darken the brightness of the best and make it commonplace, reduce it to your own size, where you can handle it. And be available, oh, so available, with that understanding.

She said: —Why would he come now?

—Maybe he didn't come. It could have been a dream.

—There was no water when I got up, she said. I went down to the lodge to ask Grzes to bring some from the well. Grzes is gone. All his things are gone. He would go only if Janusz wanted him.

—The General could have sent for him, Loomis said. He'd hardly come in person for his orderly.

Yes. But she said she thought that if he had been sent for, Grzes would have come to say goodbye. He was an old soldier, after all. He wouldn't leave a post of any kind without telling someone he was moving on.

Loomis shrugged. He wanted to restore the earlier warmth and to reassure her. Look, he wished to say: Don't worry, I know how it is. This is not how you want him to remember you. But it's done now and you can't undo it and nothing can be said by anyone to erase it and that's just as well. Because he won't come back now if he is a man. No man could come back now, at least not any kind of man I know about. Now it is really done and you are free with all the bridges burned. Now you can make your pirouette with arms extended.

He didn't say it because suddenly he didn't think the General had been there. He thought: I am alive; that's proof enough. If he had come here I would now be dead. If it had been I coming here to speak to her again (perhaps to try again to bridge the gap, to explain, to reach for her again) and found her so (with the intruding man's clothes so domestically scattered and the picture so undeniable and the ruin of final hope collapsing about me and the sickness soaring and the black rage becoming red and choking me), I would have looked for something blunt and heavy. I would have erased the man and the sight, blotted it from life and memory. Because that too is part of the procedure: the happy sapper hoisted with his own petard. The yellow sickness. I remember it. You feel it rising when you telephone longdistance and she says: —*Hello, dear, how are you . . . everything is fine . . . no, I'm not doing anything . . . David is at Mother's* (or at school or playing in the garden or with some friends somewhere) *. . . yes I'm alone, just taking a nap, resting just a bit, this awful weather gets me down . . . no, nothing interesting happening . . . nothing to report.* And then, with her hand insufficiently shielding the mouthpiece of the telephone, the whisper: —*What? See who's at the door.* Oh yes, I remember it. Words fail then. You can't ask who is there because you might be told. You'd rather not be told. Inside is chaos, turmoil. There you know. Outside you don't believe, and this and all the similar events, the half-forgotten, half-explained times when you would not believe, crowd up and bring the rage. You could kill then.

And it is one thing to overhear a whisper on the telephone but quite another to walk in and see. You kill then! No man can love so much that he can swallow what he sees together with his pride. No man leaves then. There is no such man. I would have murdered both the man and woman, he thought.

—Impossible, Loomis said. He couldn't have been here.

But she no longer listened to him. She stood by the window, looking out. She listened to the drone of bombers overhead. The sound of distant bombs exploding was a continuous roar.

He said: —Don't worry. I'm sure he wasn't here. And if he was, what of it? At least now he knows that he can't come back here anymore.

—I know, she said. She stayed beside the window with her back to him.

—It's best like that, he said. If something has to end it's best if it ends without any chance for turning back clocks. When things die, they're dead. It's just as well he knows it now. It's the best way.

—I know.

—But you're sorry now? You wish it weren't over with him? Is that it?

—No, she said. I'm not sorry. I wish it weren't over but I'm not sorry that it is. Is that too complicated?

—No. I understand it.

He came up beside her and put his arm around her shoulders. He bent and kissed the edge of her cheek where the yellow hair curved away from it. She smiled at him, then pointed to the street.

—There is a soldier standing in the gate across the street. He's been there a long time.

—A soldier? Loomis looked to where she pointed. He saw a lancer half-hidden in a dark doorway. The lancer was looking up at them. He stamped his boots and beat his arms against his sides. His breath hung like a cloud about his head in the morning chill. Loomis felt cold. He watched the lancer.

—I wonder what he wants there, Lala said.

—I don't know.

Suddenly he pulled the curtains across the windows and shut out the light. He put his back against the windows. She took his hands in hers to stop their trembling. The sounds of the bombardment grew.

I ANTOS

Antos was cold. He watched the day come and felt the morning chill and he felt hungry and he thought about Pan Szef. He looked at the paper in his hand and at the house across the street, and he thought Pan Szef would be angry because he had come here and he wondered what Pan Szef would do when he found out. Because he would find out; you could bet on that. Pan Szef found out everything sooner or later. This time he might go looking for a priest.

Once in a while Pan Szef would look at him like he was saying: Well? You do that one more time and I'll get the priest. It made him worried all the time, thinking about Pan Szef and when he'd go after the priest. It made him wish, sometimes, that Pan Szef was dead.

Hooo-ha! God but it was cold.

Antos wished the sun would hurry up and the warm day would start and everybody in the house across the street would get up so that he could go there and tell the lady about the Pan Kapitan and get back to the squadron before Pan Szef missed him.

Antos' regiment had come into town during the night. They had had a big battle out towards Palmiry and Antos and a lot of other soldiers went down to the barricades closest to Palmiry to watch the regiments come in. Antos' regiment was the last to arrive. It didn't look much like a regiment, more like a squadron. The squadron (with Pan Szef riding at the head of it and Stas Guz holding to the tail of Pan Szef's horse and walking beside him and Bartek carrying another soldier on his back) was so little he couldn't believe it. There were only ten men in the squadron and everyone was sick. Their eyes were small and red. Their mouths were black. Only Pan Szef had a horse to ride. Antos came up to Pan Szef and walked beside his horse and Pan Szef looked at him in a funny way. Antos wondered if Pan Szef remembered how he, Antos, had talked to him in the field after the big battle by the river. That wasn't a good way to talk to Pan Szef. He hoped Pan Szef had forgotten, but he didn't think so. He didn't think Pan Szef ever forgot anything. Antos looked at Pan Szef and at Stas Guz. Neither said anything to him. He walked with them until the column stopped. Then Pan Szef looked at him. —*Well, sir, here I am,* Antos said. *I got the Pan Kapitan to the hospital.* Pan Szef said nothing. He jerked his head back towards the waiting column. Soldiers fell out of the column and went in among the burned-out houses. —*They cut his leg off,* Antos said. *He's not doing so good.* Pan Szef smiled then. He went *Humph-humph* deep inside his throat. He spat into the street.

He got off his horse and threw the reins to Antos and Antos caught them and Pan Szef laughed. —*From now on you take care of him,* Pan Szef said.

—*Yes sir,* Antos said. *But I already got the captain's horse.*

Pan Szef looked at him with his priest-finding look —*Forget the captain. I'm the captain now. You do what I tell you, understand?*

—*Yes sir.*

Pan Szef thought a little.

—*How is that horse of yours? You got him in shape?*

—*Yes sir.*

—*Well, get him over here. I'll take him now. There's no more officers in
the squadron now so I'll take that horse.*

—*What'll I do with your horse, sir.*

Pan Szef laughed. —*Eat him for all I care.*

Pan Szef's horse stood with head down, shaking as if ill. His sides were
bloody. Pan Szef stamped his boots. The ornamental rowels jingled on his
spurs. Antos thought about the sharp steel and about Zloto and about the
blood on this horse's sides. No sir, he thought: Nobody's going to cut up Zloto
like that. I'm keeping Zloto for the Pan Kapitan.

—*Yes sir,* he said. *I'm going to see Pan Kapitan today. I'll tell him you
want his horse.*

The sergeant-major spat. He stared. —*You're going to what?*

—*Going to see the captain at the hospital. Got to see if he's all right, sir.
Got to take a message from a general to a lady, too.*

Pan Szef laughed. His eyes bulged. He clenched his fist and raised it and
pulled it back. Then he dropped his fist. He said: —*What?*

—*Yes sir,* Antos said.

Pan Szef's eyes were red. —*Listen,* he said. *Are you mad? Were you in the
sun? Are you talking to me or am I asleep?*

—*Sir,* Antos said, feeling cold.

Pan Szef said: —*What? You got a message from a general? You got a
date to see a lady, eh? And then you're going visiting in hospitals, eh? What
the bloodyhell do you think you are and what d'you think is going on here?
You come tell me that? Eh? I'll tell you what you got a date with: It's a
riflepit. And if you're not digging one before I'm done talking you'll have a
date with a firingsquad before sunup. You dare come tell me about captains
and generals and ladies? I ought to throw you down that well! One more word
about captains or ladies or hospitals and I'll forget I'm a merciful man! I
ought to have you up against that wall right now, you horseprick! You horrible
little abortion of a footsoldier, you! There is no captain anymore. I'm your
captain now. You do what I say. Understand?*

Antos said: —*Yes sir.*

—*Listen,* Pan Szef said, *and listen good, cause next time I got to talk to
you like this you'll have your back against a wall. I'm commander of the
squadron now, you gallowsbird. There is no more captain. There's just me.
And I'd as soon splash you against a wall as look at you. You got no gentlemen and officers to suck up to now. You got me. And now get out of here
and take care of my horse.*

—*Yes sir.* Antos led the sergeant-major's horse into the courtyard and unsaddled him and washed down his bloody sides and watered him. He thought:
All right. So that's how it is. Nothing will ever be all right again until the
captain comes back to the squadron. He's got to come back. The lady's going
to help him and he'll be all right. Hadn't the General said so? Yes. He'll
come back here and Pan Szef won't get to cut up Zloto like he did this horse,
and I'll take care of Zloto and the Pan Kapitan like it should have been if he
hadn't got hurt.

After he watered the sergeant-major's horse, Antos tied him to a dead
tree in the courtyard. He thought that if he left right away he'd find the

lady's house and give her the message and come back before anybody missed him. The soldiers slept against the courtyard walls and Pan Szef was gone. Antos thought he'd get back in plenty of time. And if he didn't? Well, he wouldn't think about that. As long as Pan Kapitan was alive he would get him off. Antos left the courtyard. He walked a long time. He asked policemen about the lady's house and showed them the General's card. He found the lady's house before the sun came up. Waiting for her to be up he thought about Pan Szef.

Maybe Pan Szef was looking for him now. Asking about him. Saying: So! He's gone, is he? Is he? So . . .

The sun was well up but Antos felt the chill. He bent his arms against his sides. He stamped his feet. He looked at the lady's house and saw a curtain move. Someone pulled the black cloth across the windows.

Antos brushed down his uniform with his hands and wiped the toes of his boots on the backs of his trousered legs and looked at the card the General had given him and went across the street. He waited at the closed gate, looking up. He beat on the gate. When no one came to open it he pushed it and it opened for him. He went up the long staircase. At the top of the staircase he paused, looking at the door. He raised his hand and lowered it. He didn't know if he should beat on that door or not. He touched the door. Then he drew a deep breath and knocked.

At once the door opened. The lady stood in the door, looking at him. She looked troubled. She passed a hand over her face. She said: —Yes?

Antos looked at her. His mouth fell open. He didn't know what to do. He brought his heels together and stood at attention. Then he took off his cap. Then he couldn't stand at attention anymore so he put his cap back on again, but that wasn't right. A man didn't wear a cap inside a house.

Antos felt his mouth dry up like a summer puddle. He looked at the lady.

The lady smiled. She said: —Well, soldier. Aren't you going to say anything?

He shook his head and choked. He cleared his throat: —Hrrumph. He looked for someplace to spit. He didn't think he ought to spit on the floor. He gulped back the spit. The lady laughed.

—Well now, you really ought to tell me what this is about. Do you have a message for me? Is that why you came?

—Yes, Antos said. He had a message for the lady. It was about the Pan Kapitan.

And then a man came into the corridor. He spoke to the lady. It was a language Antos didn't understand. It sounded like geese honking in the rushes. He looked at the man the way he had looked at the old German general on the road. The look said: What's the matter with you? Can't you talk like everybody else? The lady spoke to the man in the same language and the man said: —Ah. Then he spoke quickly to the lady and nodded at Antos.

—Why did you come here? she said. Did anybody send you?

Antos thought a while. He remembered what the General said.

—A man told me, he said.

—A man?

—Yes, ma'am, if it pleases the lady. The man said the lady would mend the Pan Kapitan. He said the lady would know what to do.

—Of course, she said. Of course.

Antos nodded. —Yes, right away. Because he's not doing good with his leg gone.

And then the man spoke again and the lady looked at Antos for a long time without saying anything and then she asked him: Had he seen the General? Yes, he had, he said. Where and when? He told her when. Around the hospital. The day they took the captain's leg away from him. How did the General seem to him? Had he been hurt, being in a hospital? Was he injured? Had he been in any kind of fighting that Antos knew about? Antos didn't know about that but he said he thought, yes, there'd been a lot of fighting of different kinds. He didn't want the lady thinking that he didn't know about different kinds of fighting.

The lady spoke to the man every time Antos told her anything. The man listened carefully. He looked at Antos as if he didn't believe what Antos was saying. It was the way Pan Szef looked at him sometimes. Antos got a hard look to come over his own face.

—Well, tell me, how did the captain get hurt? Where was that? When?

Antos told the lady about the barbedwire and the charge and the trumpets playing and about Underensign Gzyms and Bartek's nose and himself (a little) and about Jozio Prosty and Stas Guz and about how he had looked for the captain in the field and couldn't find him and then about how he found him on the road and brought him to Warsaw and about how the man said she would help the captain.

—Can't you tell me who he was?

Antos shook his head.

—I know who he was, the lady said. It was the General, wasn't it? He sent you to me?

Antos sighed and looked this way and that. He didn't want to lie to the lady. It would be like lying to a priest or in the church. Or to the Pan Kapitan. But the General said not to tell her . . .

—He was a man, he said.

She nodded and said something softly to the foreignman. The foreignman nodded. He raised his hand and touched the lady's shoulder as if to say: It's all right, it doesn't matter.

But the lady shook her head and looked away from him. Then she turned and went into the apartment. The man followed her. He waved to Antos to come in and Antos went in. The lady stood by the window, looking out. He tried to see what there was outside to make her so sad. But there was nothing outside except another house.

—Well, thank you, lancer, she said. She called him Pan Ulan. Nobody had ever called him that before. Ah, but (she said) was he hungry? Could he eat a little?

—Yes, thank you, lady, he said.

—Of course you are; a soldier can always eat and sleep. I should know something about that.

And then there was bread like no bread Antos had ever seen: white and clean and smelling the way it looked. He thought the bread was like the lady, a part of her. And there was cheese and some cold meat and tea. Antos didn't care for the tea but she made it herself so Antos was careful to drink all of it out of the saucer and to smack his lips and belch to show he liked it.

The lady sat down at the kitchen table and watched him eat. The foreignman sat down beside her. The lady put her elbows on the table and her face in her hands and looked at Antos, smiling. He looked at her and the cold meat went down the wrong way. He choked and thought his eyes would fall out of his head. Nobody had ever smiled at him like that; he didn't think anybody could.

—Well, she said (when he had finished eating and had wiped his mouth on the back of his hand and had wiped his hand, carefully, on his trousers), you must have been hungry.

—Yes ma'am, he said. If it pleases the lady.

It pleased her, she said. She was very pleased. And was he quite sure the General had not been hurt when he saw him at the hospital? In any way?

—Well, ma'am, he said. He didn't have an arm.

—But other than that?

—No ma'am. Not as I could see.

She smiled. She asked if, perhaps, the General had given Antos a message for her. —Something you were to tell me and forgot?

—No ma'am, Antos said. He shook his head hard. This was a thing he didn't have to lie about. —I didn't forget anything. There was no message. Why, Pan General even said how I wasn't to tell your ladyship about him sending me to you. So if he said *that* he wouldn't send a message. If he gave me a message I would've remembered.

The lady shook her head again and got up and looked out of the window and the foreignman got up and went to stand beside her. He said something in a low voice. It was a kind voice. Antos didn't want the lady to be sad. He thought the lady liked it when he told her the General wasn't hurt, so he told her, again, in a loud voice, about the General being fine. He was very well. Sure, he had only one arm but he was better with one arm than any other man with two. He was just fine. And perhaps there wouldn't be much fighting anymore. Maybe the war would be over soon and everybody could go home and it would be just like before the war for everybody. Sure, he said (wanting to see the lady smile), that's how it would be. The war would soon be over and the General would come home like everybody else. She would see then, with no more fighting anywhere, how fine the General was feeling. Antos said this and more of the same but it didn't seem to work this time. The lady didn't smile. She said nothing. The foreignman looked at Antos and asked the lady something and she said something to him in a tired, slow voice. The foreignman said one sharp, short word and looked at Antos as if he didn't like him much.

—You watch out, foreignman, Antos said.

Then the lady went out of the kitchen and the foreignman followed her. Antos was left alone. He waited for the lady to come back so that he could tell her more about how fine the General was feeling. She didn't come back. Antos picked up the crumbs off the table and ate them. He wiped off the table. He looked at the door where the lady and the foreignman had gone but they didn't come back. Antos got up and put on his cap and scratched his ear. He felt dirty. His fingernails were black. He had never noticed his fingernails before but now he hid them in his palms. He sniffed and thought about how bad he smelled. How good the bread smelled. And the lady. He left the apartment. The stairwell was cold. He went down the stairs. Outside, he stopped and thought: What went wrong and why was the lady sad? Maybe it was about the Pan Kapitan, but he didn't think so. He couldn't think of anything he'd done to upset the lady. He shrugged. It did no good to think about that; it was like trying to figure out why Pan Porucznik made a face when he ate Army soup. It was fine soup for you but not for him. It wasn't any good trying to figure out what fine people were thinking. Don't you worry about them, lancer. No. You worry about yourself and your horse. You worry about Pan Szef and what *he* is thinking.

Antos looked at the sun. It had moved up and the day was warm. Later it will be hot. Antos wished he hadn't done anything new to make Pan Szef angry. He wondered if Pan Szef had got the priest already. He couldn't think of anyplace to go if he didn't go back to the squadron. He looked at the lady's house. That would be a good place to stay in.

And then the lady and the foreignman came out of the house. She took the man's arm. He said something to her. They looked troubled. They walked down the street, away from Antos. It was the way to the hospital. Antos blew his nose in his fingers. He wiped his hand on the back of his pants. He looked up the street, the way he had come from Pan Szef and the squadron. He followed the lady and the foreignman.

I THE CORRESPONDENT

The cracked walls trembled. I can see them tremble, Loomis thought with his back to one. The floor is swaying like a deck at sea. Plaster falls; it makes a covering like white sand. It covers broken shapes piled in the corridor. They moan and cry and shout and try to shield themselves from the collapsing mortar, and try to crawl like huge red crabs over each other or lie still and say nothing and look without interest at the crumbling walls or mumble words that no one understands while the unending crash of near explosions piles more rubble down on them.

No end to broken shapes in the white dust. They lie on stairways, in corridors and doorways, on beds and under them, in the courtyard and the street outside. Shrapnel and masonry fall on them and crush them but there is no end of them because more are immediately brought from the barricades and lie like a vast, twitching blanket of brown from which, now and again, this or that shape is plucked and taken away and vanishes in the upper floors of the hospital where the surgeons work. Up there the floor is red with blood, and the corridors are slippery and red streams are beginning to flow down the stairs and soon the orderlies no longer carry out the bloody cartons of amputated limbs but throw them directly from the windows on the great mound of grey meat spilled against the back wall of the hospital, where small carts are busy.

—Sweet God, he said. What is this place?

—This is the hospital, she said. This is where I work.

—It's a slaughterhouse. I can't think of Pawel in a place like this.

She put a large, coarse armband on her arm: white with a crude redcross stitched on. She gave him another. —Put this on.

—What does that make us? Doctors? Undertakers?

—Aides. No one will wonder why we're here if we're wearing them.

—Can you see him yet?

—Not yet. Perhaps he's on another floor. We'll have to look for him. I'll ask for him if I see anyone I know.

The wounded shouted in the plasterdust.

—Good Sweet God, he said.

It was impossible to think of Pawel in this place: with caved-in face and fat eyes and self-motivated fingers crawling in the dust, like these wounded. Perhaps finally concerned and unrecognizable. It had always been Pawel's example which had kept his, Loomis', involvements on the good, sane basis of indifference and unconcern: sardonic eyes contemptuous of intangibles.

How will I know him with the eyes of the wounded?

He held to Lala's hand. Sometimes he led her across the mounds of wounded piled on the stairs. Sometimes she went ahead between the tight-pressed ranks leaning against the wall.

Pardon . . . pardon . . .

Huge eyes reflect infinite indifference.

Grey faces.

Silent, moving mouths and wide eyes underfoot.

Black fingers without fingernails.

A question for a staggering orderly. There is, of course, no answer. There are three words, slow and enormously tired. A gesture. Then the man is gone down the red stairs. Ah, but there is another, an elderly colonel who blinks. He listens intently. His face is worn and his hands are trembling and he is scattering cigarette ashes on the red face of a wounded man underfoot. He smells of nicotine and carbolic acid and he listens and Lala is talking. She asks, explains. He nods. He points up the stairs. He turns and leads.

—Does he know anything?

She pressed his hand and smiled. —It's all right now.

—You found him? You know where he is?

—The colonel knows.

—Is he a doctor?

—He's the hospital commandant.

—You travel in good circles.

—His name is Laskowski. You probably met him, you know.

—I don't think so.

—He was the surgeon who operated on Janusz after he lost his arm. You said you were here then.

—Yes. I was. I don't remember him.

—He is an old friend.

—Whose? Yours or the General's?

—Mostly the General's.

—I should have known. Good God, isn't everybody?

She looked at him quickly. —Hush. You're making sounds like a jealous boy.

—So I am.

They found Pawel in a long room packed with cots pressed tight against each other. There was no room between the cots. Men lay on bare mattresses or straw. The moaning sound was there and the stench was there and the everpresent humming of the flies. They stood at the foot of the cot to talk to Pawel. His face had collapsed. Brown rings spread from his eyebrows to the highedge of his cheeks. His eyes were feverish and intent, and he was earnest and purposeful and he did not laugh. He talked rapidly in an extraordinary high voice, not looking at Loomis. He talked to Lala, not to Loomis, as though he and Loomis had suddenly nothing more to say to each other.

—Yes, he said (earnest as though anxious to convince when she asked if he was in much pain), it feels red. Do you know that kind of pain? Everything is red with it. It's almost a liquid. It fills you up with this one bleeding color and you think there aren't any other colors anymore except this one.

—But it will pass, she said.

He did not agree. He said the pain would not ever end but always be there the way the lack of leg would always be there whether he was alive or dead and this too, this thought of being dead, had its own color, did she know? But then he supposed that she would know about it.

Hers was a different pain, if indeed, she said, it could be called a pain at all without melodrama. What color was it? he wished earnestly to know. Dark, she said: Some dark tones which blotted out all colors.

He agreed that this was possibly the worst of all the pains because it was empty of color. It is the one of nothing left, of utter desolation, of being suddenly nothing-in-nothing having been everything. But it would pass, she said, because sooner or later they all did, didn't they? Yes, if you had a purpose, he insisted, or found another reason for not having purpose or learned to welcome it (the pain) because of what it bought: a release from purpose. Then all pains and even death, yes, and the rest of it, were quite acceptable and could be met with pleasure and a man could whistle through his teeth in their face and laugh at them. Laughter was empty if one had no purpose; did she agree or not? She said she did. Because (he went on) it was important to do it well, always, everything; it had to be done well. And if one found his reason for dying (which was always there just as there always was a reason for living) one could do both well. One could do neither well enough without doing it completely; otherwise there was no point to it. That was when life, death, everything was foolish and you could laugh at them emptily, stupidly. One could not compromise with either life or death, could not pinch pennies, so to speak, but had to throw everything on the counter, give everything one had and expect no change: Then one had Life or Death in capitals, complete, did she agree? Yes, she said, she did. He thought it more important now to die well than to live. Because it was more reasonable to expect death than life, he said. It was the likely prospect nowadays; certainly for him.

Death could be marvelous if it was met head-on with head up and hands in pockets, whistling, if possible, an indelicate song. Or with prayer. He knew a priest in Spain who chose to die with prayer, he said (as though Loomis had not fired the bullet that killed the priest). It did not matter how you met death, or life for that matter, if you had *something* with which to face it down: song, prayers, anything. Any kind of purpose. Also love, she said. Love gave this strength sometimes. Especially to a woman. A love of man or country or self-love (he said) or love of duty and honor or a woman's love or any of the other loves which were so important. Because they were important, did she know? Yes. They were terribly important. The old men knew this when they invented their intangibles. These made the difference between animal and man in the true sense. And the true woman, she said. Because it took as much dedication to be a woman.

They smiled at each other.

Listening to them Loomis had the feeling that he had heard it all before somewhere, sometime, or at least a part of it, but this time, unlike the other time that he couldn't quite remember, he seemed outside it: an invisible observer.

Thirteen years before (Loomis thought, looking into the far corners of the room, hearing the heavy breathing of drugged men and their small whimpers and the hoarseness which seemed so much like anticipation, and Pawel's urgency and Lala's gentle quietness; wondering who he was and why he suddenly seemed invisible) I talked to the Boy General, Former Hero of the Nation. Briefly, of course. You do not talk at length to the Fallen Great. He was in bed in the Jerozolimski Hospital. He had just lost his arm.

—*Yes, I will talk to you. No, I am not afraid to talk. Most military men say little and if they speak at all they use the quick, crisp monosyllables of command, and that, of course, is their privilege, and that is why there is no communication between men of the robe, who vomit words as if they didn't like their taste, and men of the sword, who are cryptic. And so the men of the robe (who have only words) say of the others, those who are cryptic and use words sparingly: They are cryptic because they have nothing to say; wise silence hides unfathomable ignorance. I am not ignorant. Test me. Granted I am in some pain and possibly delirious and I am not a doctor of philosophy. But not ignorant. Neither am I the genius my countrymen think, or rather thought, I was. I am a soldier. War is my element. I am a carefully constructed precision instrument of destruction. What the men of the robe call military genius is the result of generations of painstaking cultivation. I am designed and built for waging war. War is a human activity. Wars are waged by men. Is this too blunt? Is this too harsh for you to digest without discomfort? I think it must be hard for a man of the robe to understand a soldier.*

He breathed with difficulty as Pawel now breathed. His eyes were enormous. His slanted cheekbones gleamed like yellow candlewax.

—*I am a soldier. You think of soldiers as something temporary, something that has at best a temporary use and no permanence and is too expensive. Morally you cannot accept a soldier as a useful man: He does not toil, after all, neither does he reap; he does not build great buildings or start commercial enterprises. He is, you say, a man who would have failed at anything but his immoral trade. War is* not *immoral. It is a tragedy, yes, but there is nothing*

397

immoral about it. War is an explosion of concentrated human effort. It is a province of human activity and it has its laws as every science and its freedoms as every art and the risks of any business enterprise but it is neither science nor an art nor a commercial business. The business of a soldier is to study all the complexities of war. It is the most demanding of all the professions, calling for an enormous skill, a profound knowledge. A soldier must be a complete master of his trade: success or failure in his business are spelled Victory or Death, not merely to the soldier but to his nation. Possibly to his way of life. It is a study spanning generations. I am the tenth generation of soldiers in my family. My son or nephew will be the eleventh. I am a general. My son will be a general if he survives the stages of brave young lieutenant and courageous captain. This is not guaranteed, of course, as it would be if he was entering his father's business in another field. It is enough for me to hope that he will survive.

A thread of pink appeared then on the enormous mummy of bandage and gauze and lint and white wrappings lying across the General's chest where his arm should have been. Soon other pink threads joined it.

The General had gone on: —*Is this also immoral? That a man should wish that kind of life for his son? There are eighty-nine military families in Europe. Their names read like the honor roll of every battlefield since the Thirty Years War. These names would probably mean nothing to you. Look at the names of young men killed throughout the world in the last fifty years. Do not count war years. Take fifty years of peace and several hundred names of young men killed in them will be the names of eighty-nine families and their branches. These young men die in most unlikely places. One of my ancestors is buried in San Domingo. Another in your own America. But that is ancient history and we are not historians: We make the history but we do not write it. Whether or not there is war our young men die, because that is the nature of their business. Death is a part of the profession. It is a relative, you might say, a member of the family. It is something you live with and are familiar with and something for which you are completely prepared. The only thing for which a soldier is not ready is dishonor. If your luck is good, and your soldier's star is true, you survive and you become a general and live with honor and you have a son and he will live with death and this is good. You hope that his star will be true and that he survives. I could wish nothing better for my son, or for my nephew who is like a son, than that they should be soldiers. Honor and purpose and devotion and love and duty are intangibles. We cannot lean on them; that's not how we use them. It is we who support them, not they us: They are our rationale, our reason for being.*

The pink threads, and now there were many of them seeping through the bandage, became red and shining and the General looked at them with contempt. His face was closed. It was as though the redness was expected and needed no comment.

Loomis had thought then, being young, that he understood what the General was saying. Now, being older, he thought: I do not understand anything; I am outside. And is it so right, after all, to avoid commitment? There is no flesh on an invisible observer.

And then, because he felt himself invisible and suddenly unnecessary, and

398

because he felt a touch of terror at the thought that he would never be necessary to anything or anyone, he turned and walked out of the ward.

He didn't want to see Pawel anymore; not like this, soon to be dead but now intent and purposeful, very much concerned.

He walked as rapidly as he could among the waiting wounded in the hall and made his way carefully down the stairs among the upturned faces of other broken men with their immense commitment and out into the street where, in the reddish dust of a city under siege, the shells still fell but not frequently.

He waited for her until she came out, then fell in step beside her. Neither of them said anything. They walked to the park. After the hospital, the air in the park was remarkably clean.

They passed new graves: yellow earth piled at the foot of upended rifles, flowers around a helmet. They seemed to be the only people walking in the park.

After a while she said: —What do you suppose happened to the swans?

—I don't know. They should be here somewhere. Don't they live on that artificial island?

—In the warm months. They take them somewhere else for winter.

—That's where they are, then. On their artificial island in their artificial lake like everybody else I know.

—Is that how it is?

—Everywhere, he said.

—It can't be like that everywhere.

—That's just how it is. We go to school to learn how to live on artificial islands and then we find our artificial mate and make a little artificial love and then we all lay eggs.

—The mates lay the eggs, I should think, she said, watching him.

—Don't be too sure. It's a sweet system until something happens.

—What kind of thing?

—Somebody eats the swans because of a siege.

—Poor swans, she said.

—Oh, you can always get a new lot once a siege is over. Can't let the islands go to waste.

—It sounds terrible.

—You shouldn't be laughing. There's something very un-American about that kind of laughing.

—It's not too European either, she said. Where do you think your first island came from?

—It was carved by blind dwarfs with old razorblades and sold to tourists on the pier at Smyrna.

—Those dwarfs, she said, laughing. They're a shiftless lot.

—Ah, but they're good with razorblades, you know. Nobody's all that shiftless if they're good at something. I say three cheers for the dwarfs at Smyrna.

—Must it be Smyrna? Couldn't it be Warsaw?

—Nothing American ever came from Warsaw. You weren't marketing anything when we were shopping for our artificial islands. That's why we don't like you people very much; you never gave us anything constructive.

—Perhaps it's not too late for us to offer something. There must be something here you could use.

—No room for love of country on an artificial island. It's too *passé*. And there's no spot for honor and integrity and all that on an expense account. You must do better than that for our export trade.

—There is love here, she said. Too much of it, for too many things. But I suppose you have enough of that.

—Not on my island.

—We could export that?

—If you could bottle it or powder it and package it discreetly you'd have a billion-dollar market. I'll buy the first consignment.

She said she'd try to find some, somewhere, that wasn't being used. No guarantees, of course, on delivery. She didn't know much about production schedules and all that. They weren't very mechanized as yet.

—Please do, he said. Please try hard to find some. I don't know if I can pay for it but I must have some sometime. Do that, he said, and I'll feed you swans. We'll ask for Royal Swan in that cellar restaurant tonight.

—And we'll have horse and cabbage and Siege Soup.

—And wine. That, at least, will carry the illusion.

—And perhaps there will be another explosion.

—I think we can count on that; the Germans will arrange one for us.

They went into the Belvedere Gardens, past the ivorywhite palace with its ornamental urns and symmetrical small trees and regimented boxhedge and the brutal Roman portraitbusts, and among the poplars and the lindens on the gravelwalk out into the avenue and then north. Up the long yellowtinted stretch of the Ujazdowskie Allee with the calm, neoclassical facades looking down at them, contemptuous of time. Then, without hurry, towards the center of the town. The sun dipped and the shadows lengthened. They walked to the Nowy Swiat and crossed the Jerozolimskie, then past the intersection to the Staszic Palace. There, in the shadow of a stone Copernicus, stood a horse-drawn cab.

—I don't believe it, Loomis said. There couldn't be one left.

—The horse is very old, she pointed out.

—That must be why.

Laughing, they climbed into the cab and Lala told the driver where to take them. Shells fell infrequently; it was one of those unnatural Warsaw moments between bombardments. The shells fell as if only out of force of habit, not meaning to explode.

—Tell him to take the long way round, Loomis said.

—Why?

—I want to see the streets. All of a sudden it's as if I hadn't seen this town before. It's a fine old town.

—It's such a terribly old town, she said, pleased.

—And it's a fine old horse and a fine old cab. And I feel fine about everything. I think you must be some kind of a witch.

—I am the only daughter of an only daughter. Does that mean anything?

—It could, he agreed. I'll have to look into that.

They drove past the university into Krakowskie Przedmiescie and on down the old street and suddenly the weight of all the centuries was with them, but not oppressively. This was a noisy street: inhabited history. He took her hand without thinking. Oh love (he thought), if only it was possible somewhere. Here we sit on smoothworn leather in a horsedrawn cab in the soft light of afternoon with the sun going; cool leather polished by five thousand buttocks, men's and women's. You quiet and womanlike in the belted raincoat and the ridiculous small beret-cap with the yellow hair, honeylike blend of orange-yellow and a little brown, coming straight down and out a little at the ends like the tails of ducks, your national legs, unlong and un-American, straight out against the worn carpet, relaxed in unreasonable heels; eyes calm on the bolting sun ahead of us. And I, staring at the broad back of the driver in the black alpaca, thinking about swans. We talk of inconsequential matters like longmarried people.

—When I was young (she said) I used to love to come here, to the university museum, and watch the artists paint.

—Young? You're young now. Beautiful and young.

—Well, younger then. I used to love to watch them copying from old statues. The *Dying Gaul*. The *Laocoon*. All those magnificent fat snakes.

—Freud would say . . .

—A fig for Freud, she said, laughing. And all those unrelaxed, artificial Romans. I used to love to see them come alive on the drawing pads.

—Is that when you began to paint?

—Oh, that was later. I never loved it as much as I did watching the copyists.

—Didn't you ever feel sorry for the statues? The Romans didn't dress them for a Polish winter.

She (laughing): —I never thought of that.

Then, on the safe and welcome subject of something mutually foreign, making a critical bond: —They (the barebreasted statues) must miss their Italy in winter. Do you know Italy?

—I love it, he said. There is no place like it. I think I want to go to Italy when I die.

—I'd like to go there sometime. Before then, she said.

—Well, why not? Why don't you come with me when it is over here?

—It would be wonderful, she said. It sounds like such a warm land.

—Then come with me.

—It would be wonderful if I could.

—Why can't you? And, suddenly he meant it: Of course you can.

And thinking five years forward, an impossible thought: she and I and children (possibly three children, it having been five years) sitting in a circle at this time of evening, eating. No. After eating now and ready for bed and then (after the stories and the washing up and the tucking in) our turn. She, widemouthed and generous and smiling with a woman's soft assurance, mine with the children put away. Happily mine. Knowing me and known by me; always self-renewing and renewing me; blueveined, white, welcoming, pleased to welcome me; with woman-wisdom. Sensing. Always sensing: she and I back and forth from one to the other, no need for words, instant communication. Yes. What shall we talk about before you go upstairs to turn down the bed and I spread the ashes safely apart in the fireplace and walk from one electric-switch to another, turning out the lights? Let it be Japanese art or the strange population of my novel or the courses that our five-in-one lives will take in the future: dream of far countries. Quick, bright words spoken slowly because there is no hurry. All our own time. And then the running out of time for that one night and no more talk and night descending and the inside of your broad white thigh laid bare. Shall we have champagne breakfasts on a Sunday morning and flowers on payday? Well, why not. There's nothing in the way and what seems in the way can be pushed aside. Man, woman, children; one, two, three.

—Why not, he said.

—Why not what?

—Why don't we go away from here.

—You and I?

—Yes. You and I. Why don't we simply go?

She laughed, looking at the huge sun sinking over Wola. —There are the barricades, she said.

—Fly over them. I have an eagle on my passport. He'll take us across.

—To Italy and the warm lands, she said reflectively.

—Italy, Spain, the islands in the sun.

—And afterwards?

—I have a sort of vision of a town that you don't know about. And of some children round a dinner table and of you and me. And of warm floor-boards on a Saturday evening in a living room because there is a fire in the fireplace, and us with books, listening to music, saying very little. I see myself paternal, kind and good and pompus, being older, and glad to go to work on Monday morning and glad to come home on a Monday night. And you a little fatter, do you mind?

—Well, with the children and all that . . .

—Exactly. With the children. Glad to see me home on Monday night. And great quiet when we want it so and sound when we need sound. I think this is the peacefulness you told me about.

—A lovely vision, she said.

—Would you like that?

—Yes. Sometime.

—Not now?

—It's too soon for me. I need a little time. You understand?

—Time. Time. There is so little of it left.

—I don't need lots of time, she said. But just a little more. It is a matter of cleaning house, of setting things in order. I lost a certain skill a woman must have. You understand? There are some things I have to learn about again.

—Will you come with me when you've found it all again?

—Ask me then. Don't ask me to go anywhere unless you mean it, but please ask me then.

—But, he said, there's no harm in planning journeys, making plans, looking for the islands in the sun? In the meantime.

—No. It's pleasant to do that.

—Well then, I'll plan on it.

402

And then the shells returned. A flock of heavy shells flew towards them and landed in the next street, in the Marszalkowska, and the cabdriver said whoa and pulled his horse back hard so that the animal sat down stupidly like a dog and the cabdriver got off his seat and unhitched the horse.

—What is he doing? It looks like we've run out of transportation.

The cabdriver led the horse inside a gateway and slammed the heavy gates. Loomis laughed. He looked at the girl, laughing. She also laughed. They sat in the horseless cab for some minutes while the shells fell in the next street and glass spilled from windows.

—Well, do we walk from here? I'm hungry for our swan.

She said it wasn't far. They walked through several streets to the Syrena, but when they got there the restaurant was gone. The street was blocked with rubble. Houses burned.

Suddenly he felt both rage and fear. This was a personal affront. It was *their* restaurant, the place of the explosion and the first kiss unexpectedly delivered and of the beginning. It was where they talked and where they might have been this time and where they would never go again. Hence the rage. It was now dangerous, no longer someone else's war, impersonal and without involvement, and that thought brought fear. He was afraid for himself, of course, but primarily for her, he realized, surprised. Because without her (because of what might happen to her, *would* happen if their indestructible luck was finally destroyed and she was lost somehow in these or other ruins) there would be no firewarmed floor in a living room on a Saturday evening and no five persons round the table, finishing their dinner, and no champagne for breakfast before church (if, indeed, there was need for church); and all these would have to be sought again—for how many years? He didn't want the shelling and the bombing and the killing to go on, because they might take her from him. It was immensely important, suddenly, that she should be safe. Nothing must happen to her. Nothing. Ever. The crumpled shapes in hospital corridors . . . Pawel . . . everybody . . . could never have anything to do with her. Because there was this matter of exporting love and the warm evenings. She held the only key he knew about and she must be safe.

—We've got to stop this, he said (thinking: We?). It simply has to stop; it's gone on long enough.

She shook her head, saying nothing. She watched the rescueteams, her fingers tight on his hand.

—Can't any of you see how senseless this is? What do you stand to gain? Must you all be destroyed before it's over? Why don't you accept the German terms, whatever they are? I don't understand you. There is no reason to go on with it. There is no logic in resistance.

She shook her head. —Is that what you would do?

—I don't know. We've never faced anything like this at home. But we, at least, would think. We would use our heads. Why don't you people ever listen to reason? Why do you always make emotional decisions? Look, this can't go on any longer; everybody knows it. There's no more food, no water or electricity, your hospitals are hopeless, your soldiers are running out of ammunition, there are five thousand casualties a day among civilians, you are surrounded and there is no hope of any help. Listen, if your people are too proud to talk to the Germans I'll do it. I'll go across the lines and carry a message. I'll be an intermediary, if that's what you want.

—Would you do that?

—Listen, I don't know. I don't want to be presumptuous; if this is some sort of Passion play for you people I don't want to interrupt. If this is an expiation or some kind of fulfillment I don't want to interfere with it. But I want you safe; at least you'll be safe out of Warsaw. Will you come with me?

She shook her head.

—Why, for God's sake? What do you have to prove? There isn't anything left for you in Warsaw. There's nothing here that you could possibly want.

—I can't leave now, she said. You must understand.

—I don't understand anything. I want to see you out of here. Safe.

—But I can't leave now. No one else can leave. I can't go anywhere until it's all finished. You do understand?

—No, he said. Is it the General? Is that what you want? Are you still thinking about him?

She shook her head, astonished.

—I think you do. I think that you still love him and wait for him to come back. Well? Do you? Do you think he'll come back now, after last night?

She looked at him as if she didn't understand a word he was saying, as though she had not met him before and they were strangers. He swore.

—All right. I'm sorry. I shouldn't have said that.

—I wish you hadn't, she said, suddenly withdrawn. She didn't say it bitterly or angrily or in any other pointed way to demonstrate a hurt. —If anyone knows about that it's you.

—I said I'm sorry. It's just that I want you safe and out of here, don't you see?

She said nothing then. They walked away from the bombed Syrena and the rescueteams, and the pathetic murdered crop the rescueteams were taking from the ruins, and took the streets leading towards her house, passing the landmarks of the other nights made unfamiliar by destruction. Everything was twisted, knocked about, scattered without reason. It seemed as if the dark Warsaw streets were malevolent wild rivers changing their courses overnight to confuse and entrap. He thought he would be lost without her.

In her gateway, he hesitated for a moment, thinking that he should not go up without an invitation or a sign, because there had been a disagreement of a kind, a misunderstanding. He waited for her to sense his need for this forgiving invitation. But she was deep in thought. She went in, leaving the gate casually open. He went up the long stairs after her, angry with himself for having shouted and for having brought up the General again (and, a little, with her for not having sensed his need for invitations), but mostly with himself for having lost control. She knew the height of steps and length of stairway and the required length of stride better than he and so walked faster, and he fell behind her in the dark. When she opened the door to the flat and went in he was still many steps down and away. Alone on the dark stairs, he felt a lack of trust in the cold, dark building and the black stairwell that seemed to reach up to him out of the center of the earth. He hurried after her, suddenly afraid that she would close the door before he was inside. He took the last four steps at a run and jumped into the hallway as if the threshhold of her flat was the deck of a steamer pulling away from the dock with the gangplank gone.

But she had turned to wait for him inside the dark doorway. He fell against her. And then he put both arms around her, clumsily in the dark, as if this was the first time for him with her and for her with him, and they were new to each other, and each of them were new to love, and he kissed her. She stood quite still against him, not moving, leaning against him just a little with her face raised. And then she reached up to her face, where his hands had come to rest under her hair, and took hold of his thumbs with both her hands and held them tight. She moved his thumbs this way and that, as if steering him, and he felt an immense, relieved joy to be so directed.

She left him almost at once and went inside the flat to, as she put it, attend to womanmatters.

Outside the sound of the night's shelling grew progressively less. It resolved itself into a disgruntled muttering of heavy guns out towards Palmiry, where the returning soldiers of the western armies made their nightly assault. The city glowed like a gigantic coal. Loomis drew the curtains to blot out the town.

The cat studied him with indifferent eyes as he built a fire in the fireplace. He thought about warm floorboards and islands in the sun. He lit the fire and the candles. Warmth: soft glow of fire. Distant grumbling guns that could be summerthunder.

When she came back, with hair brushed down and makeup gone and face scrubbed and smile restored, she carried two small glasses filled with wine. They caught the yellow firelight and became coals: a deep red warmed by yellow.

He said: —What are we celebrating?

—The end of the coffee, she said. She laughed. —It's all gone now.

—So like a sort of twentieth-century Marie Antoinette you're serving wine.

—Something like that, she agreed and gave him his glass.

—Sit on the floor, he said. Let's both sit on the floor.

—Why? It's drafty on the floor.

—The fire will warm the floorboards in a while.

—All right. Would you like the rug?

—No, he said. No rug. Just the floorboards.

—Is that how you like to sit at home?

—I'd like to, yes. But there are too many chairs and couches and carpets and rugs. Too much of everything. Nobody to sit with on warm floorboards, looking like this at a fire, talking. No time for talking, anyway, and nothing much to say. Do you feel the fire? You see, it wasn't drafty after all.

—I like your fire.

—It's your fire. This is your apartment.

—You built the fire.

—Anybody can do that.

—No, not anybody.

—Well, thank you, he said. Thank you very much. I'm glad I have a role in your life. I'll be your firemaker-in-chief.

—I've always wanted a firemaker.

—It's not as good as a butler. Have you ever had one of those?

—No. We had old Grzes, of course, but butlering was not his strongest point.

—I can't claim much success with it myself.

—You're very good at pouring wine.

—That depends on who I'm pouring it for. For some people I don't go to much trouble.

—You did it very well at the Syrena.

—Poor Syrena, he said. I'll have to practice somewhere else now. And I'll have to get you some more coffee.

—Where could you get it? No one is selling it anymore.

—I know where I can get coffee and all kinds of foods. I think I'm an idiot because I didn't think of it before. Would you like Danish bacon or Westphalian ham for breakfast? Or how about a mushroom omelet with a dozen eggs. And how do you feel about caviar, anyway? I think I'd better find out these important things.

She said she felt positive about caviar; in fact, very friendly.

—Strasbourg paté?

—Yes. Positively. She looked at Loomis with a certain wonder and laughed and shook her head.

—Caviar it is then, he said. Genuine Beluga. And champagne, of course. We'll have champagne for Sunday breakfast after all. Some kind of Épernay? And how do you feel about asparagus tips?

She said she held strong views in favor of asparagus. —But you're quite mad, of course.

—I'm absolutely sane. Never felt less mad. A little slow, perhaps: I should have thought of this before. We should have had our dinner there tonight. I'm sure we would have found a can of Royal Swan if we'd looked for it.

She laughed and asked if he had paradise in mind. Because nothing except Siege Soup (dry vegetable and horse marrowbone) and Emergency Bread (coarse flour and assorted fibers) and Theoretical Veal (horse) could be found in Warsaw. He agreed that he was, indeed, talking about a certain paradise: America. —A heaven and a haven for the hungry. And I'm awfully hungry.

—Oh, America, she said.

—Don't sound so disappointed. You sound as if we couldn't go there anytime we wanted.

—It's far to go for dinner.

—It's not far at all. I don't remember the exact address but the cabdriver would have known.

—To America for dinner, she said, laughing. What a pleasant thought. But how shall we get across the sea?

—We'll walk, of course.

—You're mad, of course, but it's a lovely thought.

—The Embassy, he said, laughing. It's within walking distance. That is America. And it has larders and refrigerators and I'm sure they are full of food. And I can vouch for our ambassadorial cellars. We make a great fuss over wines when we have to deal with Europeans.

—And do you think the ambassador will have us to dinner?

—He'll never know about it. The ambassador and the staff are out of the city. All the embassies are closed. But they have cellar windows that can be kicked in. So, will you come with me for dinner in America?

—You're mad. You're wonderfully mad.

—Never more unmad. Will you come?

—I'd love to. But I'm afraid we'd have our afterdinner drinks in jail.

—Who would arrest us on American soil? They'd have to send for American policemen. Can you imagine them doing anything like that? And anyway, I'm the only American in Warsaw. Who has a better right to break into the U. S. Embassy? It's my own country, after all. I am a sort of ambassador: the only American in Warsaw.

—I think you are a wonderful ambassador. But look, the fire needs stirring.

Ah, love (he thought). We say small things. They sound small, they are easily said, but they mean a lot. They are better than the weighted big things that mean little. You sit (thus) looking at the dying fire with your chin (so) on your hands and these, in turn, on your raised knees and the dim lights throw shadows up around your eyes and darken your hair. The murderous sounds are muffled by the curtains and the miles of barricade and trench and no man's land. You keep your eyes on the blackening wood in the fireplace, your chin buried between twin round globes of knee, polished like apples, and pressed together to support a wickerfence of fingers, and the quick flicker of brief sparks (in their own miniature explosion) brushes light across the other shadows. Smooth white columns no longer a surmise. I know your beautiful geography no longer as a discovering explorer but as an inhabitant of long duration. I treasure it. And I accept the flaws and value each imperfection separately, considering them together. In their conjunction, all the elements are you. You're thinking, looking at the dying fire; you do not show your thoughts. Your eyes are open but it is too dark to read anything in them, if, indeed, there is anything to be read that I would understand. Because there is so much that I don't understand, but I do not question. Not this, like this, at this time.

Later that night, although by that time it was close to morning (red and grey in the west as well as the east because of the fires), he got up and dressed quietly so as not to wake her and went back to the other room, where the fire was dead and the ashes cold.

He was unable to sleep. He thought about the night and the many nights of that kind that would follow, and he felt a remarkable contentment. He watched the ending of the red night for a moment, then closed the windows and drew the heavy curtains and lit a stub of candle (thinking about the peacefulness of the moment) and thought of other moments, many miles away, that had never been peaceful, and he felt a lightness and a youthfulness and a sense of being. He wanted her to know who he was and how he felt about everything; it was important that she should know him and believe in him so that everything that he would do from then on would have that necessary measure of importance. If he could live for her and plan for her and get from her that necessary stimulus (all part of that warmth projected five years forward) there would be reason in everything he did.

He felt like drinking wine but they had finished the last of it before the night ended. He thought that he would bring new supplies of wine from the Embassy later in the day.

He found a pencil, wrote:

Gunfire is sporadic and without conviction. It's like an afterthought. Like two small boys tired of throwing snowballs pitching away the last of their store and already thinking about something else to do. We think in terms of hours.

Today, tomorrow, it will all be over. Today the guns sound bored with all of us and with themselves. They mock us and themselves. Their sound is meaningless. This is the fifteenth of September (although now it is close to morning of the sixteenth). The siege is nine days old. Three days ago the Germans began an all-out attack with tanks and troops and it lasted all day and all night and it ended with the Poles and Germans lying next to each other a hand's reach away, killing each other with stakes and knives and bayonets through the openings in the barricades. I saw a trolleycar full of them. The Germans came in from one end and the Poles from the other so that, afterwards, one half of the car was grey with Germans and the other green-brown with Poles and in the middle of the car was a blend of colors piled to the roof. They killed each other with shovels and with pavingstones. They strangled each other and pulled at each other with fingernails. They used teeth.

Note: A man split open with a shovel does not resemble anything.

The Germans did not fire their siegeguns during the attack, so the shouts and calls and the hurrahs were clear. Sound carries well at night.

The night before was a continuous bombardment, an elongated roar lasting ten hours. No other sound but that one. Note: You cannot hear the crackling of flames across the street and the clatter of collapsing buildings in a prolonged bombardment.

I went down into the street on another night, dutybound to see it during this bombardment. I went into Lazienki Park, where the cavalry was waiting. I wondered what had happened to the swans. I wanted to see them sailing on the smooth black water unconcerned by the bombardment. I wanted to see something that was uninvolved. But there were no swans. They had been eaten by the cavalry.

Horses stood still. They looked red in the flames across the street. Horses, or rather skeletons of horses, stood quietly along the park wall. Several were lying down. They were dead. Others bled, standing. When they had bled enough they fell down and died.

Note: The spilled entrails of a horse look like the contents of a gutted switchboard. Yellow, red and blue.

A colonel of cavalry sat near the gutted horse. He looked embarrassed. He offered me a drink out of a silver flask. The horse was still alive despite the multicolored cables falling out of him.

—His name is Cenzor, the colonel said. Three months ago he won the regimental trophy. Will you shoot him for me?

The assaults began shortly before dawn. Five were beaten off in the morning. Seven in the afternoon. The Germans captured Fort Dabrowski at noon and the counterattacks bogged down and dissipated in the rubble.

—Poor horses, the colonel said. I am so sorry for the horses.

Suddenly there was a hurricane of small-arms fire across the wall. Rifles, machineguns. Whoever was at hand caught up a weapon and ran towards the sound. I ran too, looking unbelieving at the rifle and the bayonet I carried, but there were no Germans behind the park wall. An incendiary shell had set the ammunition carts on fire. Some of the soldiers laughed. I couldn't understand why they were laughing. They looked like skeletons and they were laughing. I said this and the colonel looked embarassed. —Well, you see, that's how it is with us, he said. We never know when everything is over. We haven't learned much in two thousand years.

—But that's admirable, I said, and I meant it. —But not wise, you see? I said I didn't. He did not pursue the subject. I put down the rifle and the bayonet with which I had run into the park with the others. Then I went home. Now there is silence, the silent interval between bombardments. The silence of a city under siege not under attack, not shelled or bombed, the morning silence that is now familiar. Soon the planes will come. The siege will soon be over, everybody knows it; no victory, no relief. An end and therefore a beginning. It was always so.

But (he thought) it was different this time, yes, not like the other times, because he was no longer uninvolved. And it wasn't just because he had caught up a rifle and a bayonet when ammunition carts exploded in Lazienki (that was reflex action) and it was not entirely what Pawel had said in the hospital and, he supposed, it wasn't even entirely Lala and the new discovery. It was all of these. Each added substance to him; he was no longer an invisible man, an outside observer.

He wrote, and the familiar multiengined drone of aircraft motors drifted unnoticed and surreptitious like a fog into his consciousness so that he was not quite aware of its coming until it was there. Then he looked up, smiling.

So they were back. Late and probably ill at ease about it (such a lamentable lapse in orderly routine, in neat Germanic scheduling), but back to make the day like any other. Unnecessarily back, in view of the portents. Perhaps back out of force of habit. Or to underline some obscure German point. Or because a certain number of highexplosive bombs had been issued, signed for, earmarked for use that morning and had to be expended for the sake of orderly bookkeeping. Or possibly for the sake of sheer Teutonic frightfulness or because this was one of their last chances to kill anybody here.

But the planes didn't matter anymore, late or not. He had them in perspective and it was all right. Today, what would be left of it after he had finished writing and had gone home to the escarpment to gather up the rest of his siege manuscript, his story of the war, now given substance and meant for her, who would understand, who would see in it the cause of his commitment, and after he had robbed the embassy of hams and champagnes and had made his way again to Lala's apartment (where neither Nimi nor the General nor anything else now cast a shadow), he and Lala would listen to the spreading silence. Today, tomorrow; it might be quite complete tomorrow: the end of one thing and the beginning of another.

He thought that he must have always known that he would be committed sooner or later to something. Without a total commitment to something—anything, a person, an idea—a man was no better than an animal. This is what made the difference and this is what they had, these people who had mystified him: Lala and Pawel and the rest of them. This is the source of everything good and evil and therefore everything human: the ability to be emotionally involved. Love of a person or idea or country or God or a mathematical equation . . . a thousand years of human progress was due to it. Has been due to it. To hell with grammar, this is what I *feel*. Man needs irrational commitment to take him out of his own narrow bounds and turn his spirit outward.

He wrote his notes for Lala, smiling.

When you're a writer of any kind, it's only written words that can commit you. When she reads this she will know the extent of my commitment and see that I will never again be able to stand outside something that I do not understand. There will be questions, yes, but never indifference. Because when you're committed to one thing—totally involved—you must respect the emotional involvement of others in their rationale. Because the human spirit is a collective noun. It is the sum total of innumerable emotional involvements, an infinite variety of commitments, and in the ultimate meaning of man on earth there are no replaceable ideas; nothing is spurious, nothing can be scorned, nothing is trivial and everything has a measure of importance. Each man's love adds to humanity; evil along with good.

So there it was. And it was all so simple. If you believe this nothing can be lost.

Saturday, September the sixteenth

I THE GENERAL

From where he stood in the doorway of the hospital, waiting for the orderlies to find where Pawel had been taken and to guide him there, he could see up the red stairs and into the hall. Upstairs there was a lot of shouting. The wounded paid no attention to the shouting. They were no longer concerned with anything but themselves. If they said anything it was about the fighting in the west; most of them had been wounded in it. They were bewildered about the offensive. It had begun so well and now it went badly. The wounded didn't understand what had happened there. No one knew what was happening at the front or if there was still a front of any kind. But it was far worse for the wounded; they had been there and it was their offensive.

This was the eighth day of the offensive that was still going on somewhere on the red horizon. You heard the rolling sounds of its bombardments early in the morning or in late evening when the nearer guns quieted down a bit (before the bombers came), and you learned about it in the littered wards and corridors of hospitals, schools and churches, where the evacuated wounded told about its first days, the hopeful start of it and the early successes, the Germans in retreat, mountains of war equipment taken, prisoners in thousands, and then the gradual slowing of the impetus as the Germans hurried armor to the Bzura River. They had diverted their entire bombing force to the bloody plains. And now both sides had fought to a standstill: a stationary slaughtering competition. Elsewhere the war went on as if this bloody effort had no bearing on it. Men died. The country burned. News was uncertain and unreliable, with communications wrecked throughout the country. Still, Radio Stockholm broadcast German news and if you cut the German claims in half (and all our hopes and suppositions by three-quarters, he thought, shrugging) and if you listened carefully to the wounded and watched maps, you had a fair enough picture of the world outside Warsaw. Westerplatte had fallen on the eighth and Krakow on the sixth. Between the ninth and the fourteenth the fighting had grown fiercer, as though both sides knew that it would not go on much longer and that only a little time remained for killing men. Great battles (murderous enough to have the names of towns bestowed on them) and innumerable smaller bitter fights without any names raged along the shrinking arc spread on the forefront of the Vistula, the River Narew in the north, the Bug and the Roz in the northeast and the San in the south. But one by one these barriers were falling.

Men died. So many of them. Friends died, familiar faces vanished. Boltuc was dead: a good friend, not political enough to be more than a brigadier. He saved Bortnowski on the Ossa River, holding up two army corps for three days with his one division until the rest of Torun Army managed to escape. Dabek, another friend, commanding at Oksywie on the coast, saved his last bullet for himself at Babi Jar. Kowalski, last reported headed for Modlin (a lost cause) had held up Kuchler's East Prussian Army for three days with fourteen battalions. . . .

Prus shrugged. He watched the wounded, seeing friends. Ah, if I had a regiment for every bottle that I've drunk with Boltuc . . .

But there were no regiments to spare after the offensive, and no one's sacrifice had done any good. The French had not moved. The British had not dropped a single bomb on Germany. In the south the Germans were across the San; Szylling's Krakow Army was surrounded. The north front was now east of Warsaw, holding with only God knew what; certainly no material equipment. As for the rest, what wasn't on the barricades in Warsaw, Lwow, Lublin, Hel, the trenches on the River Bug, the Narew marsh, was falling back into Volhynia and Podole, where in the marshy woods along the Hungarian and Roumanian borders a lastditch stronghold would be built.

The wounded did not care about lastditch strongholds. Few of them knew about these things and, if told, they turned uncomprehending eyes away and said, Yes, but what is happening on the Bzura? What happened at Kutno? Are we regrouping at Sochaczew for another try? Surely it's not all over with our offensive. It just can't be over. I mean, look at me, sir, how can it be over?

The battle of the Bzura River had gone on, and was still going on, as though the men involved in it had lost all contact with reality and did not know that they were alone, far to the west of plans and battlelines. The Germans brought fourteen divisions, five of them armored, to slow down the drive.

Now it was almost over. The wounded couldn't understand the end of it. They talked about the start of it. They had attacked west for four days and the attacks went well. They marched past burned-out German armor and quiet artillery parks and long grey columns of bewildered prisoners and the shells that flew over them were *their* shells, and this made a difference, and it felt fine, then, to be winning battles. Fifty kilometers in one day, then thirty, then forty-five. One enemy division was surrounded. Another, caught drawn-out and unsuspecting in marching order on the roads, was totally wiped out. Parts of three others were dispersed. But then four panzers came up from Piotrkow, said a legless colonel, and another came fresh out of the east, and the Germans massed artillery in the center and called in their bombers and eight new infantry divisions hit the offensive in the rear out of Suchedniow. That ended the attacks aimed west and turned the charging men to the east. The wounded didn't understand why they had been turned about like that. It had gone so well, hadn't it? They sat in tight groups against the walls and wouldn't let the orderlies strip them of their weapons.

The General listened to the talking wounded.

He had expected the offensive to come to its end, but not so soon. He had thought it might last two or three days longer. But it was over now, done now, and now the regiments had turned about and started driving towards Warsaw through the German army that had hit them out of Suchedniow.

Perhaps if I had held out longer there, he thought. Perhaps if I had moved this here, that there, if I had not used up my reserve the first day, if I had had artillery . . . But nothing that he could have done with what he had had would have been good enough, he knew. There had been no way to hold Suchedniow against three divisions to save the back of the offensive. Now, at least, there was no back to it. No matter which way the men turned they would find the Germans.

—Our orders came the day we made a marvelous attack, said a blinded captain. The losses were heavy. We took what we were supposed to take and then came the orders for everyone to go back where they had started from, if those positions were still free of Germans. It's hard to take that kind of order at such a time.

—The worst of it was that it followed victories, a young lieutenant said.
—Attacks . . . Lowicz taken . . . the storming of Lodz . . . the Germans showing their backs everyday.
—Was that the worst of it?
—That's what broke our spine. That was too much to take.

The lieutenant had nicotinestained fingers and chaotic eyes. He was a medicalcorps lieutenant. He had come into Warsaw without any troops. He was anxious to explain why he had come alone.

—It was the river, he said. —I just couldn't take that after all our victories.
—The river?

412

—The river with the red bridge. It didn't seem fair, don't you see? After all that effort . . .

—Of course, the General said. The others looked at each other and smiled at the doctor. —But that's all done now. Don't think about that anymore.

—I mean, it's possible to smell victory in the air, isn't it?

—Yes, the General said.

—It was enough for us that we were moving forward and went past those long columns of prisoners and went into towns where people wept to see us and kissed our hands and cheered. That was enough.

Just two . . . three days ago (he said) the troops that he was with charged Walewice. Cut up a whole battalion. Imagine that! In less than an hour. There was no way to stop them now, it seemed . . . next stop: Berlin! and then: About face. Go back. That was the worst of it.

—I am a doctor of medicine, he said. —I am a surgeon. I used to work in this hospital before the war. When the war started I was with the field-hospital of the Ninth Division but that's been gone a long time. You can't imagine what I saw there. Horrors. No equipment. And they kept sending us more cases. Finally we stacked them outside and waited for them to die. There wasn't anything we could do. And they kept sending more and more of them and I simply left. I walked a long time. I hid from the Germans. Then the offensive started and I fell in with it. There wasn't any hospital to join so they gave me a platoon of engineers to command. What do I know about engineers? Nothing. But that's what they gave me. They said: You are an educated man, you should know something about building bridges. Medicine and mathematics are both sciences and if you know a lot about one you should know a little about the other. So there I was, a bridgebuilder. I couldn't build a plank across a ditch but what could I do? I went along with these engineers. They were all construction men from Wielkopolska, though, and I didn't have to tell them anything. And we built no bridges.

But then the attacks stopped and the army turned and there was need for bridges to recross the Bzura and he was sent to find a crossing and local peasants led him to a ford. His engineers marked the crossing, and other sappers put a logbridge up for the artillery further along the river and at about two hours after midnight the army started back across the Bzura. First came the infantry, waistdeep in water, then regiments of cavalry rode into the forest on the other side and a new battle started with the Germans who crossed the river elsewhere and got to the forest before the Poles.

—As usual, the legless colonel said. —I think we've all learned that men in tanks and trucks move faster than men on foot and horseback.

—Troops crossed all night, the doctor said.

—I know it, the blind captain said. —We were the first across.

—Then you were fortunate. Very fortunate.

The captain blinked and laughed. —Were we really?

—Yes. Please believe me.

—We had to clear the Germans out of those woods.

—Ah, but you had the night, don't you see? Not the morning. You weren't there in the morning.

The doctor put his head in his hands like a small boy. He wouldn't look any longer at the others. At dawn, he said, he saw a sight that was . . . incredible. The whole vast plain that sloped towards the river was filled with carts and wagons and cannon and ammunitiontenders . . . a boiling mass of men, animals and machines. It roared with talk. A sea of dust hung above it. The world, it seemed, waited its turn to cross the river through the single ford. The hospital train moved first. There were about a thousand wagons with the wounded. Eight hundred other wagons carried wounded Germans. Strawfilled carts with six men in each. Slowly . . . slowly. Snail's pace. So slowly. The sun rose higher and everybody knew what that meant, what that promised. But slowly . . . slowly. Very slowly with the shouting wounded.

—I wanted to hurry them along, the doctor said. —I knew what would happen. We all knew. But everytime a cartwheel bounced a bit there was a howl out of the carts; howls that had nothing human in them: terror, pain, all of that, but nothing else. I couldn't listen. There was so much of it. Can you imagine? One thousand and eight hundred carts with six men in each. That is a lot of terror, a lot of pain. You don't have to be a doctor to know what that means. But it helps to be one, yes, it helps. Then you really know.

He said he sat in a flatbottomed boat poled up and down the crossing and tried not to listen to the shouting of the wounded. About a hundred wagons got across the river when he heard the motors.

—It was about five o'clock in the morning, he said slowly. His voice was flat now, and no longer high. It was the matter-of-fact voice of the surgeon acknowledging defeat. —I think we all heard them at the same time or perhaps the horses heard them first. The horses went wild. They reared and tore their leather harness and leaped on each other. I saw a stallion trying to mount a mare. In all that this animal was trying to mount her, can you imagine? Perhaps there's some natural significance in that, some message, but I don't understand it at the moment. And then the whole field moved. Everything galloped forward, headfirst into the river: men, animals, carts, cannon, everything. They filled the river and the water spilled far out on the dry banks. It made a lake in the field. It turned the field into a swamp and the carts sank in it. Everything that was in the river tried to climb out on the steep opposite bank and couldn't do it and fell back on the mass that was pushing it and crushed it and drowned it and itself and more piled on top of it and then the bombers came. First the dive-bombers, of course . . . headdown in formation . . . up and away. Then the fighters came low over the field and the river . . . wingtip to wingtip fifty or sixty at a time . . . machineguns . . . then the heavy bombers. You couldn't count the bombs but they blacked out the sun when they passed across its face. . . .

And it was Judgement Day, he said. When he shook off the torpor of terror, and understanding made its way slowly back into his mind, he began to vomit. High banks of dust hung suspended like a buckling ceiling above the earth and the water. In this choking greyness rolled a sound. A pulsing howl. Men moaned and screamed. Incendiary bullets had set the straw on fire in the carts and the wounded were burning. Horses neighed. In the field: great craters, stacks of massacred dead, smashed carts and wagons spilled like chaff. The river bridged with carts, corpses, broken men and horses. . . .

—Across this bridge ran masses of soldiers. When they fell, in dozens, cut down by machineguns, they became themselves part of the bridge. Red planking. Don't you see? Red planking. Soon the bridge was higher than the river-banks.

And then, he said, the logs came floating down. This was the bridge the sappers had put up for the artillery. Big logs with sharpened ends rode down the river and rammed into this living bridge.

—Now, understand, these were still living men, he said. —Many were still living inside the bridge. But I had to clear it. The planes went away after an hour and I had ten antitank mines planted in the bridge and blew it up. Meat rained on us. Red meat. Red planking. But it cleared the river. You might say that this was a surgical decision. You might say that there was nothing else that I could do. I don't care what you might or might not say. It was red meat. It rained on me. But of course in half an hour there was another raid and the same thing happened and there was a new bridge and this time there were no mines and we went into the river and took the bridge apart by hand and threw the red planking into the water and pushed it off with poles. This too, you might say, was the only thing to do. But you didn't do it. I had to do it. Well, it went on like that all day.

At one point (he said) the river was full of pink cigarettes. The army's cigarette ration had spilled into it out of some ruptured wagons. Blood turned them pink.

—And that was funny, do you know? he said. —Everybody laughed. You just didn't expect pink cigarettes in that place and time. It didn't make any sense and it made everything ridiculous. It was a fitting end for all our attacks.

He only knew one thing, he said. He had to leave that place. Quickly. As quickly as he could. Because this was the place of death. He knew that no one would survive there. After each raid he ran forward with his engineers. Their uniforms were black and slippery with blood. They had blood everywhere . . . in hair and nostrils and eyes and under fingernails. Their mouths were full of blood. Blood dripped off them like sweat. Each time they had to clear the river anew: logs, broken bits of wagons, wheels, peasant baskets. . . . At midnight the raids ceased. He crossed the river by himself and walked off into the forest. Everything was red. He found a small pool in the forest and bathed himself in it but the red smell remained, all of it remained, and he did not know what to do to rid himself of it.

—The rear of the offensive is quite gone, the legless colonel said. For three days now we've been attacking towards Warsaw. We thought that here, in Warsaw, we would refit and try again. We didn't know that you were under siege. Nobody even told us at the front that Warsaw was threatened.

Such great hopes had been placed in the great offensive, and now it was over, and its end marked something more important: It had used up the last field army that was more or less intact, swallowed the last reserves of men and equipment and accomplished . . . nothing. Now there was nothing left with which to defend anything for any length of time. Two, three months at most. The Army had been thrown away in one great, gallant gesture to shame the somnolent Allies. The Allies had not stirred. The Germans were defeated on the Bzura River and would not move there for many days, but there were other Germans elsewhere, moving fast and hard (von Reichenau, Guderian, Kuchler, List, von Kluge, each of them not one man but three hundred thousand), and what was there left to throw across their path? Nothing that had not been bled white, damaged or destroyed.

—What are we going to do now, General? The legless colonel wished to know.

—We are defending Warsaw.

—But elsewhere?

—We are moving everything we have into the southeastern corner of the country. We've put our back against the Russian border and our flanks on Hungary and Roumania and on our own good forests and we've stopped the Germans in the south. The Marshal's plan is to hold there until the Allies come.

—Well then, the colonel laughed. There is hope.

—Yes, the General said.

—Then the offensive was not in vain? It was not all wasted?

—No. You bought us precious days.

The legless colonel closed his eyes and leaned back against the wall. He smiled.

—Thank you, sir, he said. Thank you. If I didn't know *that* it would be . . . difficult.

The General turned away so that the colonel would not see his face. And then he knew how Michal must have felt, day after day, telling his lies and making promises and watching the inexorable arrows streaking across his map.

And now the shouting in the corridor upstairs grew loud. The narrow space where the stairs ended filled with uniforms which were not stained or torn or splashed with the black and brown moistures of the wounded but which were clean and pressed. A squad of field police pushed downstairs through the wounded. The troopers wore the intense, dedicated faces of men who dispense death but who are not in danger. They pushed and pulled a lancer down the stairs. Behind them walked a bowlegged lancer sergeant-major who chewed on his mustache.

—Come on, you, said the senior fieldpoliceman. He pushed the young lancer. —Move out smartly, now. Move. Get going. Move.

The lancer said nothing. He looked up at the sergeant-major, who would not look at him. The lancer sighed and hung his head and went on down the stairs. The fieldpolice corporal gave him a hard push.

—Move out, you bastard. You deserting bastard. (And to the cavalry sergeant-major:) You got a lot of slowfooted bastards, don't you? Can't you teach them to move out like soldiers?

—Shut up, canary, the sergeant-major said. I don't need you to teach me my business.

—So keep your scum on the barricades, the fieldpoliceman said. Move out there, you. Keep moving.

He pushed the lancer. The lancer slipped on the bloody stairs and fell. The sergeant-major swore. The fieldpolicemen laughed and slung their carbines across their backs and picked up the lancer by his arms and elbows. When he got up his uniform was red.

—Get up. Keep moving. (And to the sergeant-major:) You got a clumsy lot of bastards, don't you? Can't you even teach them how to walk?

The sergeant-major moved his mustache up and down. His face was deep red. He motioned down the stairs. The lancer shrugged off the fieldpolicemen's hands and walked carefully down the stairs among the wounded. The General saw that it was the young lancer who had brought Pawel into Warsaw.

—Wait, he said. A moment, Sergeant-major.

The sergeant-major and the fieldpolicemen sprung to attention. The sergeant-major and the corporal saluted. The sergeant-major stood very straight, at rigid attention. The lancer slumped a little and swayed on his feet. He wiped blood off his nose. Someone had hit him in the face and his nose had bled. He looked at the fieldpolice corporal and spat on the floor.

—Stand at attention, scum! the corporal shouted.

—Shut up, the General said softly.

It was then very quiet in the hall and on the stairs and the wounded pushed forward to look down, to see, and only the blinded captain went on talking. The legless colonel chuckled to himself.

—How is your captain, lancer? the General said.

—I don't know, sir, the young lancer said.

—Didn't you go to see him?

—I can't find him, sir. They moved him somewhere. And before I could find him they . . . the *kanarki* . . . came for me.

The fieldpolice corporal's eyes bulged and his face swelled and became scarlet and then bloodred like the sergeant-major's. The sergeant-major bit down on his mustache. He made a rumbling sound. The wounded hooted on the stairs.

—Ah, the policeman's lot, the legless colonel said. He laughed a little.

—You musn't talk like that about our fieldpolice, the General said, and the lancer stared.

—Yes sir. Well . . . them *headhunters,* then.

The sergeant-major choked and the wounded howled and the fieldpolice stared hard at the wall and the blinded captain asked what was happening, please, would somebody tell him? And the General shook his head a little, keeping down his smile, and the young lancer looked surprised. The General asked the sergeant-major what this was all about. Because he knew the lancer. The sergeant-major's eyes became small and careful. He looked quickly at the lancer in a speculative way.

—This man is a deserter, sir, he said finally.

—Is he? That's a serious charge. The punishment is death.

—Yes sir, the sergeant-major said.

—You can prove desertion?

—Yes sir. He left the barricades against orders.

—I ordered him to come here, Sergeant-major, the General said.

And now the sergeant-major's eyes bulged and his face swelled and he glanced quickly at the lancer (who was careful to keep his head high and stare at the wall above the General's head) and he opened and closed his mouth several times, saying nothing. Then he reported that the lancer was also a convicted murderer. He had been sentenced by court-martial to be shot.

—When? Where? (And when the sergeant-major gave the date and the place:) Who deferred the sentence? (And when the sergeant-major said that it was Pan Kapitan Prus, squadron commander:) Has your commander changed his mind? Do you have new orders?

—No sir, the sergeant-major said. But, he reported, he was now commander of the squadron.

The General looked long and carefully at the young lancer, who now stood very straight but whose eyes were closed. He didn't think the lancer was older than Adam. His eyes had been clear and still believing; they were not the eyes of a man who could murder anyone.

—Whom did he kill?

—A woman, sir, the sergeant-major said.

And then the thought of Lala and the correspondent was there at once. He saw the dark-red room with the flash of fire outside the open window lighting up their faces. The curtains billowing, reaching out to them. His hand moving to the holstered pistol. The General felt the nausea and the shock again and the beginning of the empty darkness.

—You killed a woman?

The lancer stared at him with enormous eyes. He shook his head. He sweated. And now the sergeant-major also started sweating and his chest rose and fell like that of an exhausted horse.

—Tell me the whole story, the General said.

And the lancer told it, about the train and horses and the girl who laughed and shared her food, and about what was done to her and who had done it and how he had hit the girl because of her screaming and because she bit him and how the girl was thrown out of the train.

—You threw her from a train?

—No sir, the lancer said. He wouldn't do that then. He didn't know then about killing people. That was before the Germans came, before he killed the German on the road and the other Germans, before he knew anything. But nobody had asked him then if he had done the killing and he didn't understand what they wanted from him or what could happen to him until they put him up against this wall. Then he knew, but it was too late then and it was too late to tell anybody anything, to explain anything; nobody would listen. And it was only when the Pan Kapitan came that it was made all right. And that was why he had to look after the Pan Kapitan, why he had brought him all that way to Warsaw so that the doctors would make him well and everything would be all right again and nothing bad would happen. He was sorry that he had lost the captain in the big battle by the river. And he was sorry that it had taken so long to get him to Warsaw. But he *had* got him here and had got the lady and now, maybe, the captain would get well. Pan Szef said not to leave the barricades and he had left. Well, that was bad all right. He knew that. But it was either him, and not making Pan Szef mad at him, or getting somebody to get the captain well. Well, when that's how it was (the lancer said) that's how you had to do it.

The General listened and the wounded listened. The young lancer spoke in a low voice, looking for the words. When the lancer said that Pan Szef threatened to look for priests, that he could always find one if he wanted to and that he'd find one now, the wounded made a sound like one vast breath expelled, like a sea. Someone began to curse in a highpitched voice.

The General said: —Enough.

The lancer stood quietly. The sergeant-major seemed unable to move. He looked at the young lancer and at the General and opened his mouth and said nothing and shut his mouth tight on his mustache ends.

—You'll save everyone much embarrassment if you forget you ever came here for this man, the General said.

—Sir! said the sergeant-major.

—And it doesn't matter if he told the truth about what happened in that train. I think he did, but he could be lying. That's something a new court-martial can find out. We can have a new trial when trials and firingsquads and executions with or without priests make sense again. At any rate, you are no longer to concern yourself with finding priests. Is that understood?

—Sir . . .

—There will be time for that. For now, forget about it.

—Sir . . .

—As for desertion, there was no desertion. You will agree that my orders take precedence over yours?

—Yes sir, the sergeant-major said. His eyes were narrowed. He would not look at anyone. His fists were clenched. He'll make the boy wish he *had* been shot, the General thought. But that was the Army, all armies, any army, and it would be up to the young lancer to find his own solution.

—That's all, Sergeant-major. You can go.

The sergeant-major clashed his heels and saluted, and the fieldpolicemen clashed their heels and all of them turned about and marched out of the hospital down the steep marble steps. The sergeant-major marched carefully around the young lancer and looked at him slow and hard and the young lancer's hands began to shake. He followed the sergeant-major with his eyes long after he and the fieldpolice were gone.

—You've caused a lot of trouble, the General said.

—Yes sir. The lancer hung his head.

—Keep out of trouble from now on. And stay out of that sergeant-major's way. An old soldier like that, with his experience, can find a thousand ways to make you wish you'd never seen daylight.

—Yes sir, the lancer said.

—So watch your step.

The lancer stared with huge eyes.

A portrait of old Grzes when young, Prus thought. Trust and infinite devotion: rare commodities in the new world being born outside.

—But you did well to bring your captain here, the General said. I'll see to it that your colonel knows it. Now come with me and we'll find your captain.

They went up the stairs, where the wounded grinned. The wounded did their best to make room for them. The wounded moved their spilled limbs out of their way whenever they could. One of the wounded reached out and touched the young lancer. —That's for luck.

They walked a long time through the corridors, peering and asking and lifting overcoats off dead faces and moving on. No one could tell them anything. Finally a doctor pointed to a hall behind him. It was a long hall, with no windows and with one wall down and with dead leaves and dust blowing in with each new explosion. There was surprisingly little sound from among the men lying on their greatcoats and on straw. The hum of flies was murderously loud; all human sounds were soft and insignificant.

—Why here? the General asked.

The doctor looked away.

—It's more convenient for the stretcherbearers.

These moved among the wounded men like carrion crows peering into faces and pointing now and then at one or another and lifting and carrying out (frequently dropping and picking up again) and at once replacing one body with another. This was the waiting room, the last step before the carts outside and the filled-in trench in the Saxon Gardens or in Kilinski or Lazienki Park or in any one of those innumerable grassy enclosures that had made Warsaw like a flowergarden with structures put up absentmindedly among the flowerbeds: yellow mounds headed by a lone upended rifle, steelhelmet or cap; the last conclusive argument of war, pathetic exclamation.

The airraid sirens sounded before he reached the shelter of the General Staff building, and deep waves of silver and black bombers floated across the town like a thinhumming cloud, and bombs fell and there was fire, and dust filled the streets. Act Two of the day's tragedy, he thought; the morning intermission between shells and bombing was over. Inside was the coolness of tall rooms, and long boots clicked across parquet floors. Heads were bowed confidentially one toward another, and comments were weightily exchanged and lips were pursed and brows furrowed profoundly and briefcases and portfolios traveled this way and that, up and down stairs and corridors and halls, cradled under arms. Smiles were exchanged and opinions offered and confidence maintained and suppositions made. and messages went back and forth between desks and pins were moved on maps and a meteorologist predicted rain for the last week of the month.

The General passed through the bustling lanes of staffofficers with their look of knowledge, past sentries frozen like brown statues beside doors, and on through the immense downstairs hall where stained and tattered and bandaged officers were standing.

They looked less knowing than the glittering others but probably knew more. Two or three hundred, maybe more, waited, saying nothing. More came in from the street. Each time the huge door swung to admit another, a cloud of dust rolled in before him and another followed, so that it seemed as if each of them walked in the billowing smoke of a personal hell. Their faces bore the stamp of it. A General Staff captain took their names.

Name, rank and branch of service. Unit number. Where and when destroyed . . .

Prus went on until a man stepped from the waiting ranks.

—Sir . . . General?

It was the redfaced major, his skin now burned brown by the sun.

—Tarski, isn't it?

—Yes sir! I didn't think the General would remember . . .

—Of course. What are you doing here?

—Well sir (the major looked embarrassed), I need an assignment.

—Of course. I meant, Where did you spring from?

—We broke out of the Kampinos Forest yesterday, came in this morning. Ah, but I'm glad to see you, sir! Last time was at Suchedniow. It seems long ago.

—Yes, it does. What happened to you?

—Well, there was Suchedniow. You know how that was, sir. Then we went on to Modlin and joined up with one of General Kutrzeba's groups and went on to Kutno.

—So! You were also in our marvelous offensive.

—Yes sir. We were among the last to get there so we were about the first to turn east when they hit our rear. We joined up with General Abraam's cavalry below Kampinos and cut our way through the German lines this morning. And now we're back.

—I'm really glad to see you.

—Can you use me, sir?

—Use?

—I would be happy, sir, if you could find me a place in your command. I have seventy men fit for duty . . . after they've slept a bit and had something to eat. Can you take us, sir?

The General laughed. —The question is, can you take me?

—Sir?

—I have no command, the General said quietly.

The major stared. —But that's impossible.

—So maybe you can find a place for me, eh? And then we'll find ourselves a quarry and some Germans. Well, what about it, Tarski? Will you give me one of your platoons?

He thought the redfaced major would laugh. He looked as though he needed laughter of some kind. But the major stared, and shook his head, and blinked his dustencrusted eyes. —Well, if you have no field command, sir, you must be with the staff. Of course, that's it. I'm not much good with pushing papers. Still . . .

—Wrong again, Major. I am unemployed. This is a skeleton staff at best. Everyone who still has a real job to do has gone to Kolomyia with the Marshal. These shining gentlemen are only caretakers.

—But who commands here, then?

—Warsaw is now an outpost under siege. It has a line command like any other outpost. You don't need staffs and planners to direct troops on the barricades.

—But the field armies, sir? Who directs the war?

—God, I suppose. (Then, seeing the lack of understanding and the shock, the immense pain and fear and disappointment:) The Marshal is in Kolomyia. We are still directed.

The major looked from him to the others as if somewhere in the still ranks of waiting officers whose troops had been destroyed, with their grey bandages and stains and hastily dusted leather and dull eyes, and in the glittering confidence of the staffmen, there was an answer to be found. He shook his head. He said he didn't understand . . . anything.

—What's there to understand?

—The war, the major said. This war. It is incomprehensible.

—Only the rules, the General said. The new rules are different. Otherwise this war is like any other. Give yourself time and accept the new rules and you'll understand.

The major passed a hand across his face. He swayed a little. The General said: —When did you eat last? Did you eat today?

—No sir . . .

—Come with me to the War Room. My brother has food brought there every day. And who knows, perhaps he might have news. He is touch with Kolomyia and the Marshal's people. If anyone here knows anything it's Michal. He hears everything first.

They went down the long stairs to the cellar and the deepvaulted chamber where teletypes clattered and men with palegrey convict faces sat at batteries of silent radiotelephones and the white glare of carbide battlelanterns threw shadows on the situation map.

The huge map seemed to move in and out of shadows as the shadows moved, so that it looked as if the map had a pulsing life of its own. Its outlines stretched and shrank in turn as if convulsed. The shadows were uneven: deep in the west and north, where no more flags or lines or arrows of any color marred the orderly, calm surface. The fallen towns and battlefields were dark. Light did not touch them. Light struck the eastern borders, and at first the General thought that this artificial pall, spread over the dark half of the map, was a coincidence or a melodramatic trick of lighting. But then he saw that the arrangement of the battlelanterns was intentional and that dramatic symbolism had nothing to do with where the shadows fell. New flags grew like a malevolent red forest in the white glare on the eastern border and seemed to spread and snap impatiently as their own shadows moved in the hissing glare of the carbide lamps. As he watched, an officer moved from the teletypes and placed a scarlet arrow among the new flags. The arrow pointed west: to the border.

The General felt his heart beat up and his pulse quickened and suddenly there didn't seem to be enough air to breathe. This was the ancient enemy, now not yet a declared enemy or friend. The hammer raised. The sickle was a questionmark.

If to be a friend, never more welcome, but if to be an enemy, doubly dangerous. Because despite the crumbling riverbarriers and the deep withdrawals and defeats and victories more costly than defeats, a front had been successfully set up against the Germans. Volhynia held: There the blue lines were firm. The Army flowed south and east towards the River Stryj and new fortifications. Great battles went on among the woods and yellowpainted swamps of Bilgoraj and Krasnystaw and blue lines held and scarlet arrows slowed and turned away and now blue lines thrust through scarlet lines and became arrows in the darkgreen woods above Lwow, and the inexorable scarlet sea (slowed by the siege of Warsaw and Modlin and by Kutrzeba's charges) halted and hung suspended and began to ebb. Nothing had been decided yet. The huge perimeter held firm for its second day. Thus there was hope. Not of victory or anything else that could be conclusive but of defending the southern third of the country until the allies came. The new red flags and arrows flowing west in Russia brought a chill.

—What is happening there?

Michal stared quietly at the map. His fingers moved in small circles among pink messageslips and communicationspaper spread without order on his desk. His eyes were dull and without expression but he had shaved during the morning and wore a fresh uniform. Someone, Janusz Prus noted with surprise, had shaved Michal's head.

—What are the Soviets doing?

—Nothing. I don't know.

—They're massing troops. Is that aimed at us?

—No, Michal said. That's quite impossible.

—Thank God. Because if they also throw themselves on us . . . But how do you know what they're going to do?

—I don't know, Michal said.

—Then this could be aimed at us?

—Oh no, impossible.

Michal looked calmly at the map and smiled a little. He nodded at the major in a friendly way. He brushed dust off the corners of his desk.

—But you don't know. You don't know their intentions.

—No, we don't. They haven't told us yet. But I'm sure they couldn't mean us any harm. After all, would it be logical? Why would they want to do it?

—In other words, you hope they won't attack us. But you don't *know*.

—Yes, that's true, Michal said. I don't know what they're going to do. But I would rather not believe they want to attack. It simply wouldn't make sense anymore. Not at this time. It would be quite impossible for us. I couldn't believe it. There must be some excellent explanation of what they are doing.

—Yes, the General said. Yes, I think there is.

He looked at his brother's calm face and fixed smile and at the hands wandering hopelessly among the messageslips and at the redrimmed situation map that mocked them in the white glare of the lamps.

—Listen, he said.

But Michal interrupted him with a quick gesture and the fixed smile slipped and the eyelids trembled. —They won't do anything, he said. It's a preventive move.

Preventing what? Do they think we could attack them?

—It could be just a demonstration for the Germans.

But the mocking map said it wasn't so, and each looked at the other as though one of them could come up with a reassuring answer that could be believed, that proved the map lied. There were too many grand units for any kind of reasonable demonstration: corps and divisions and army groups massed in depth, and supporting lines stretched too far back into Great Russia and the Ukraine and beyond. All Asia seemed on the move westward out of the edges of the map.

So there it was again, the General thought: Asia on the move. And who would stop this human sea this time if it spilled on Europe? There would be no battle of the Vistula this time to turn back the flood. Once spilled and unchecked, it would drown continents.

He asked how many Red divisions waited on the border and when they had begun to concentrate. The time and numbers had significance. Fifty divisions, Michal said, and more on the way. As for the start of concentration, the giant massing of men and vehicles and horses, no one was sure. No one could swear to any date. Although it looked as if most of the Red divisions had begun to march before the war began.

—They couldn't get that much together in less than a month, Michal said. They're even worse off mechanically than we are.

—Ribbentrop flew to Moscow a month ago, the General said. Don't you suppose that has some bearing?

—Absolutely not. They simply can't do that to us now. I will not believe it.

—Oh, Michal, you know better than that.

But Michal said no, he didn't know better. He didn't know anything. And he would not believe that Hitler and the Communists could ever climb into bed together. And there was more. A thing like that, at this time, when the front held . . . well, it was just impossible to believe.

—It would be just too much, don't you see?

Still, the General said, shouldn't one be prepared for anything? And why didn't Intelligence report those troop movements?

—The Bolsheviks sealed the border, Michal said. They're good at that. Our people couldn't get the word out until yesterday.

—What does Intelligence think the Russians are planning?

—We've asked Moscow for an explanation, Michal said, evasive. We're waiting to hear. Also we've told the French and the British.

—I can imagine their reaction.

—They said we were not to antagonize the Soviets. No matter what they do.

—What do they think is going to happen here?

—They said they didn't know. But they supposed the Soviets were friendly. They said that if we fight the Soviets, we'll lose their support.

The General laughed. —What support? Their valiant *Sitzkrieg* in the west? Their leaflet bombing of Berlin? Is this to be a repetition of September first? Listen, if the Soviets come they'll never leave again. We'll be finished here.

—They won't come, Michal said.

—I envy you your confidence.

—I don't have confidence in anything, can't you understand? But I must believe in something. There could still be another explanation.

—No, the General said.

—I will not listen to you. I tell you, the Soviets can't attack us now. I don't know what they're going to do. All I know is that we've finally stopped the Germans. We are holding them. There are decisive battles now in progress and we are not losing. Not winning, true, but not losing either. The scales are even. It could still go either way. The crisispoint is here. And I think we finally did the impossible and the Marshal's plan will work and that we'll hold until the Allies move. I tell you, we've come too close to victory for our whole house to fall about our ears. Granted, it's a negative victory, victory because it isn't a complete defeat. Holding them, having stopped them after all this time, is victory. It's victory because we haven't let them overwhelm us. Building and holding our perimeter, the way the Belgians did it in the other war, making it impossible for the Allies to ignore us here, that's victory. We've stopped the Germans, do you understand? They are no longer running over us. We've lost a quarter of a million men! It cost too much to stop them to have it all made suddenly meaningless by somebody else! I can't believe the Soviets will attack us. I won't even consider the possibility.

—Wishes, the General said. Hopes and suppositions.

—I won't listen to you.

—Be calm, the General said quietly. And think. Aren't you the man who always found the rational solutions?

—There are none now.

—Of course there are. Listen, it's time for us to think about the country. Not our own honor or our reputations or about what the Allies think or about what some politicians will decide in the next ten years. When the Soviets come it'll be finished here. We'll have to stop what we are doing here. I think we've made a sufficient sound for the frontiermakers of tomorrow. It's time we started thinking about the people. It won't matter what the frontiermakers paint on the map after the war unless we have saved enough people to live in the country. We have to stop this thing, here, in Warsaw, and all the other beautiful, senseless sacrificial gestures. No one will understand it anyway. We have to save what's left of the Army for another fight, and we must let the people live, help them survive until this whole nightmare is over.

The others stared at him as though they didn't understand a word he was saying, as though he spoke a foreign language, one they had no desire to learn. Wide eyes and puzzled stares. Confused small gestures of hands across tired faces.

—The war goes on, don't misunderstand me. But we must take it to another battlefield. We can no longer afford to fight on our own land.

—That's treason, Michal said.

—Treason? You've never called me a traitor before. Not even when everyone else was so free with that word. Treason to what? Blindness, stubbornness, the inability to understand that we've destroyed our country for a gesture? The Germans and the Soviets aren't our greatest enemies anymore. Our own stubbornness now, when there is nothing left but death for the whole nation, that is the enemy. We must stop the destruction of our country.

—Treason, Michal said.

—What are you saying, sir? the major said.

—Surrender, Michal said. He is proposing a capitulation.

—Of course we can't surrender, the major said.

—We go on, Michal said. This is our country and this is where we fight. No one will dare to order us to surrender Warsaw. We wouldn't obey such an order if it came. It simply isn't possible. Everybody knows that.

—The garrison has enough rifle ammunition for another week, the General said slowly. The artillery will shoot itself out of shells today or tomorrow. Eventually we will have to lay down our arms here. There can be no relief. When the Bolsheviks attack it will be all over in the south. No allies will come. I tell you that we, here in Warsaw, must attack the Germans now, while we still have men and ammunition, while there is still a perimeter and an army to fight our way to, so that we can take as much of the Army as we can out of the country. The war must go on but not here. It's gone on long enough on our own land.

—And give the capital of the country to the Germans?

The major suddenly sat down. He began to laugh. —Surrender now, he said. After all this?

—General, Michal said formally. He stood at attention. —We have other orders. The Marshal's orders were specific for the defense of Warsaw: to the last man and to the last bullet. No one can countermand the Marshal's order.

—Events can countermand them and events will manage. We must take orders from events when the Soviets come.

—I do not recognize the authority of events!

—Ah, look, the General said gently. There is nothing you can do. When the order comes to surrender Warsaw you will obey it as you always have.

—No, Michal said. I have the Marshal's order. I have my soldier's honor. There can be no discussion of that. Whether or not the Soviets come, it doesn't matter, do you understand? I have my orders and I will obey. Everything else is treason.

The major said: —I can't believe this. You, sir, saying this? It's quite impossible that you're saying this. One just does not end something like this because of events. There has to be a constant of some kind, an absolute, something in which a man can always believe. To fight here to the last man is an absolute. That is a part of everything for which we've lived.

—The time has changed, Tarski. Absolutes must change.

—Sir, with respect, a man can only live in his own time. Or die in it.

—And this country, Tarski, must it also die? Were we also ordered to destroy this town? Would you turn something that has been a symbol for eight hundred years into rubble for the sake of constants? Are we also to fight here to our last monument, our last museum, school, library, and our last link with a thousand years of human progress?

—I was born here, sir; but without hesitation . . .

—No! Eleven thousand buildings have been destroyed here and winter is coming. The civilians are dying like rats in the sewers. Soldiers eat when food is found for them but the civilians live on crusts and household animals. There are no medical supplies and most of the hospitals are gone and yesterday they reported typhus in the city. What is your last man and your last bullet when opposed to that?

—There must be some way out, the major said. It can't all end like this.

—You think you face a terrible new discovery. Listen, I know what you feel. Your blood boils, eh? This is something you think you can't live with. This is, you think, beyond endurance: a negation of your entire life. It makes your life a lie, eh? It makes our thousands of dead look ridiculous, eh? You say there must be some way out, and what you see is fire and smoke and fixed bayonets and then a comfortable oblivion. It can't just end like this, you say, after so much, and so you won't consider an order to surrender Warsaw. You think that you will fix your bayonets and mount your regiments and charge and be destroyed so that historians, if they're so inclined, may say that you at any rate never surrendered. You can do this quite naturally, without a pose. It would be fitting to us all, in keeping with everything we've believed. This has been our way, I don't deny it. But it's too late for that sort of heroism:

No one understands it. We can no longer afford the luxury of charging into history books.

—I can't believe . . . The major's voice was slow.

—Then don't believe. But think. It is your duty as a soldier to remain alive. You must think of this war as nothing more than a lost battle, a campaign, only the first of many. The next one starts as soon as this one ends. We go on, yes; as Michal says, we do not stop. But we take our war with us, away from our own land. France and wherever the war spreads. We don't destroy our country.

—Surrender, Michal said. And here we surrender.

—If we must, yes. If we're not strong enough to surmount disaster we don't deserve a victory. If we accept disaster, learn to live with this catastrophe, we'll win eventually.

But Michal didn't listen anymore. He turned his back on Janusz Prus and walked carefully to the situation map and studied it and moved a small flag here and an arrow there, calm and unconcerned. He did not look at them. The map moved in the shadows: huge and bland and orderly and defined.

Outside, the sky and sun hung hidden behind smoke. The day was grey. And in the red twilight of a city under siege the sound was enormous. Sirens, explosions and the roar of collapsing buildings. Grey faces in dark doorways. Time to end it soon.

—Sir, Tarski said. I think now I understand what you were saying.

Prus nodded. He felt empty. He didn't want to talk.

—It's just that it's so difficult to believe.

—Yes.

—When the time comes to give Warsaw to the Germans I hope you'll let me know. France . . . hmm. I've never been to France. Not much of a traveler, never was. But when you're ready, sir, I'll go along. Seventy men isn't much, but they're good men and maybe we'll get a few of them to France. Just let me know when you're ready, sir.

—I will.

—And there are others. I'll talk to others. We ought to let everybody know what you plan to do and talk to them so they'll understand. It takes some time to understand something like that.

—Yes. Thank you.

—Goodbye, sir. The major went back inside the General Staff building.

Nothing moved in the street in front of him, in the huge sound under the grey, redtinted lid of smoke. The pavement shuddered like a dying animal. The General felt remarkably alone. Suddenly he knew he had to leave this place and find a refuge. From his thoughts. Peace and a peacefulness and lack of thought, and rest and no doubt about anything: They seemed as distant as the invisible white sun. Were there still such things? Peace and the gentle certainties of a day?

He knew where he would go: There was no other place, and what had happened there in the red light of nightfires (coming like a nightmare through the windows) was not important except to a man's pride, and that was not important out of context. That was a small part of a man, not his whole being; it could be struck down, but the man went on if he had something else. Love, yes (of self or country or a woman), that was enough. That is what stopped the hand rising of its own volition with a weightless pistol pointed like an accusing finger, judge and executioner in one, avenging blow to pride. That and the thought of what had been; these were imperishable and surmounted pride. And if the daily taking and giving of a love could not go on because of what had taken place, what had been said, let her know that there was no bitterness.

And then, in a rare flash of intuition, he saw her in danger. The wild-striking bombs crushing the town were falling close to her. He could almost see the smoke and new fires and collapsing buildings and lampposts twisted lovingly about each other and fallen trees and gutted shells of houses with the dust and smoke rolling lazily out of ruptured walls and the innumerable avalanches of mortar, brick and wood raining in the dust. And she in the midst of it all.

—That's where they're falling now, isn't it?

—Sir?

Grzes had come from the ruin across the street where he had been hiding.

—Isn't that where they're bombing now?

—By madam's house . . .

—Yes.

The sound of the explosions died down a little then and the smoke rose fatly, hung heavy over the unfashionable quarter where it had been so difficult to find an apartment. (—*Of course we can find something for the General . . . but under the circumstances . . .*) Their house: the windows tall and conventlike and now swept clean of glass, the heavy gates unhinged.

—Call the car.

Grzes whistled and the driver brought the staffcar out from under a half-demolished gateway. The General got in. Grzes got in. The driver spun the car among the shellholes.

—Left here, the General said. Now right. Now right again.

Direct routes were blocked. The driver wove a wild course among shell-holes. When they could drive no farther because the rubble filled the street and the collapsing buildings slid about them, the driver stopped the car and the General got out. He walked around the corner. He didn't recognize the street.

—Grzes, where was the house? Where that tree is lying?

—Yes sir.

—Are you sure?

Because it didn't seem possible that this was the place where the house had been. Now it had spilled itself into the street. All of its contents lay abandoned in the street.

Where is she?

He asked some men who were busily pulling at the rags and flesh buried in the rubble. Had they found a woman, young, who was so tall and with such coloring and hair? Yes, he knew there were a lot of women they had found and many of them had been one thing and were now another. But had they found that one? Because it was important.

No? What about the wounded? Were there any wounded and, if so, where had they been put? In the church square?

There, under trees, he found her.

She was flat on her stomach in the grass and gravel with one shoe off, with the small things that could be anything, and the jagged things—metal and glass—all twisted. She made some sound, some gesture. As though to brush him and the sounds and devastation and all of it away. As though it could be done like that, with a small gesture.

He said: —Are you all right? She seemed all right, lying there.

—What? She was angry. That was good. She would be all right being angry.

Her dress was crumpled, partly torn. It was the black dress that had always made her seem more delicate than she was. Because really she was not all delicate. She was finely built, true, but she was strong. Her weakness was that she was a woman. Her skirt hung in long strips. He had liked the dress. It was her favorite, she said, and she wore it only when she expected something good to happen. Her legs showed through, strangely twisted. A gummy brownness spread away from her. Suddenly she retched.

—Lie still, he said. Don't move.

—Oh God, she said. God.

She vomited.

—That's right, he said. That's it.

—Oh for Godsake. Oh sweet God.

—Keep still until you're sure that nothing's broken.

But suddenly she turned on her side, sat up and started to brush her dress with both hands. Grass, gravel, specks of mud and vomit spotted it. Her hair was wildly down. One stocking wilted in torn spirals of silk. Her hands moved with a certain helplessness from this to that: from her dress to her face and hair, back to the dress, the stocking.

—Hold on, he said. Till you're sure. I'll get a doctor.

She pushed the torn skirt up over her knees to strip the stocking. And then she paused and looked down at herself and, oddly, at him, and made a small shaking motion with her head, as though not quite able to believe what was happening, and carefully covered up her knees and drew them together. She closed her eyes and sighed into his shoulder.

He watched his hand. It was around her body, under her breast, which fell towards it as though by force of habit, like a nuzzling puppy confident of welcome. It was as though this woman part of her instinctively sought his protection, the male hardness of his fingers which could stave off the inevitable.

He felt empty. His hand was motionless.

No help from it for that confiding breast.

Nothing to give.

He had been on familiar terms with death and laughed at it and scorned it and showed his contempt for it and finally it had defeated him and mocked him now with this quiet body.

Why now?

There was no point to this. What was its significance in the total framework of the war? Couldn't the war have passed her by and gone on? It was all over, after all, between them, and no more hurting needed to be done. And there was no more need for death in this town, where now the war was almost done and the guns would be silent soon and the next sound would be the cobblecracking cadence of the conquerors.

Evening came and it was quiet. The bombers flew away with their day's work done, and the artillery began its desultory shelling in the suburbs. Dull bumping sounds of shells, like a closed fist beating on a punctured kettledrum, replaced the huge sound of the day. The smoke lifted. There were white stars in the darkening sky and presently a crooked moon came out, and then he heard the sounds of children and a bird.

The bird made April-morning sounds in the September evening. The children cried rat-tat-tat in the rubble. They were playing war.

The sounds of the bird and the children fooled him. It seemed that he had not heard either for such a long time. He thought that he must be hearing them elsewhere. He thought that he had been asleep and was now awakening, and soon he would get up and walk carefully to his desk, making no noise so as not to wake her. She slept so soundly when she slept, so thoroughly. He envied her intense dedication to the slightest act. But she was not asleep, was she? And he was not asleep and would not wake from this nightmare as he had from others. It would go on and so would he, and she would not. If she would only awake; but she could not.

His eyes were open but he saw practically nothing. The darkening night blotted out the sights and threw a curtain on the debris and sheeted the ruins. Somewhere a dog barked and another answered, but there was nothing after that, no great wave of sound as there had been elsewhere when he and she had slept in each other's arms. Now only she slept. And she would not awaken.

He felt that he must do something, make some gesture. He lifted her gently and carried her into the church and sat beside her lifeless body in the roofless nave, which glittered with spilled glass. He felt the nightchill come. Quiet nave with stars on ceiling cheerfully remote. Small sound of mortar trickling in the ruin of decapitated arches. The white light of the crooked moon sliding on stainedglass crystals in the rubble.

Sleep. The day will soon come; we will all awake.

Soon the small click of metal on stone and the scraping of a shovel. He saw Grzes outside digging the black grave. When did she die? Was it when the sigh came or was it all those days ago when the messenger brought the answer to his secret letters? Or when?

It had been when he left, he knew well enough. Still, he had to ask. Because a punishment was due and he would be the president of this court-martial and the judge advocate, the firing squad, and also the condemned. No pistols this time in the Napoleonic tent. The so-slight weight of the familiar body underneath his hands would be the punishment.

He had not wanted anything like this. He had not wanted to believe that it was over for them when he left. She said it would be but he would not believe it.

And suddenly he felt an overwhelming anger at the loss: the useless, purposeless senselessness of it. Why does a day end, why does brightness dim, why can't the good go one better than the bad and beat it and survive?

It was impossible to believe that she would not awake. After all, what was the point—now—of not awaking? She was merely sleeping, tired as after love. She often slept like this, with her mouth just a bit open and the rest of her slightly crumpled, slightly crushed . . . and the blood was just an error, a part of a dream of his that had intruded on them in their weariness.

Soon Grzes came. He waited, bowed and heavy in the shadows.

The General got up and picked up the dead woman. She slipped from his clasp but he caught her and held her, supporting her head with his wooden arm, and moved his feet experimentally in the rubble. Grzes came to help.

—No, Prus said. I will carry her.

—This way, sir.

And suddenly he couldn't remember his name or his purpose or what he was and had been or what he wished to be, or who she was, this woman who had sighed into his shoulder. Who was she to die as though she had invented dying? And who was he to ask twice, for he was alive? He had to go on with it, the whole bloody business, and that was more important than inventions and names and identities, which were accidental anyway.

A man walks upright.

Honor i Ojczyzna.

Life goes on, green things grow eventually. Nothing ever stops until it is ready. The hurt that is forever grows less. It becomes the ordinary pain that a man can live with. Grief fades. Directions change. Love finds new forms. Purpose transcends defeat. Day follows day in sameness.

Tomorrow will come soon. It is another day. Live through this day and wait for the other. Nobody will be dead tomorrow; nobody will be dying then.

At first he didn't see the man with the packages and papers sitting in the rubble. The man sat at the point where the gates had been; one of the huge ironstudded doors lay there halfburied. The iron fence had stopped there to make room for the dark entryway to the house and courtyard. But now the entryway was gone, as was the courtyard and the house, and the bent spearpoints of the fence protruded from the rubble like masts of sunken ships. The General saw the man without really seeing him at all: a dark mound vaguely piled on crumpled stone. Immobile. Broken glass and papers and the blurred form there. He went on.

—General, the man said softly.

The voice was blurred like the man: thick and undefined and dark.

—A moment of your time, the man said. Your valuable time. Surely you have a spare moment or two at this kind of time.

The General stopped and looked at the man, who now got up and moved uncertainly, reaching out for balance, and started down towards him. It was the correspondent. He was drunk. The thick, dark voice and the uncertain steps said he was drunk. The General watched him, waiting for the man to come down off the mound of rubble. He felt no anger. He supposed that he should have felt something; this was the target of the weightless pistol, after all, last seen through scarlet rage. This face, now glazed with drink and moonlight and streaked with dust, was *that* face; the face you can't forget because it lay on *that* pillow with that other face, in your place on your pillow. He watched the man and he felt nothing and his thoughts were slow, as if the simple process of thinking was just too difficult and all thought unimportant anyway.

—There's something that I want to know, the man said. Won't take much time. In fact very little time. Just a thing or two. Is she dead? They told me here everyone was dead but that's impossible. I'm not dead and you're not dead so that's two right there. But is she dead?

—Yes.

—I see, the man said. You're sure, of course?

—Yes.

The blurred, duststreaked face came into partial focus: a shocking mask with the bland lines gone, greying and unfirm. The correspondent's mouth was loose. His eyes were wet and pouched. The long, wellbred face had collapsed like sodden grey-and-yellow cardboard.

—They didn't know her. They could've thought I was talking about some other woman. But you know her. Yes. Oh, you know her. You wouldn't make a mistake about her.

The General said nothing. He looked down the street towards the square. Black ruins leaped in firelight. Thin shell of walls and gothic arch and stone filigree with the stainedglass gone. The tower clock still worked. The bell struck one, even as he watched it. But the rest was gone. Dead shell.

—Well, so it's over, the correspondent said. I might have known it. Nothing like that could last. When it's so close to being what you've wanted, you can bet somebody'll take it away from you. That's part of the system. (The correspondent laughed.) Where are you going? Wait. I want to know why you let it go on. What are you getting out of it? Some more deathless glory? Ah, but it isn't deathless, don't you see?

—Be quiet, the General said.

—Oh sure, of course, the correspondent said. There has been a death.

He came down the mound, swaying in the darkness, his face streaked with reflected fire and dirty tears. He had a bottle of champagne open in one hand and carried crumpled sheets of paper in the other. Bluegreen glass halfway down the mound showed where other bottles had been thrown. Loomis tripped and dropped the sheets of paper and a quick wind caught them and flung them up into the rubble. Loomis reached for them as they flew around him, staggering in the rubble, but he couldn't catch them.

—There's the whole bloody war. He began to laugh.

His knees bent outward and his feet slid forward in the broken glass and he fell heavily back on the mound and lay there, laughing, then sat up and put his back against the ironstudded door and closed his eyes.

—Go on, he said. Shoot. I know you'd like to do it.

—Get up and go home and go to sleep, the General said.

Loomis went on laughing. —Didn't you tell me once you were an instrument of destruction? Well, start destroying. Or don't you think I'm worth a bullet?

—No. I don't.

432

—Too easy, eh? Or is the craftsman just a little weary of his trade? Well, I don't practice my trade either, General. We are two of a kind.

He went on laughing. The wetness spread across his face so that all of it shone in the harsh light of moonlight and the fires. He shook the bottle and the light exploded on the boiling bubbles.

—Champagne for Sunday breakfast. Well, it's Sunday now. Warm floors by firelight. What nonsense to believe. There aren't any islands in the sun. And even if there were it's too late to look for them. A man would be a fool to waste his time.

He wiped his face with his hand, in wide circles, and studied his palm in the poor light.

—Damnedest thing. Haven't done that since I was a boy. Didn't think I could do it anymore. A grown man crying. Well, that's part of it: the looking and the hoping and the dreaming. It isn't practical. A man ought to put that kind of thing behind him. Well, I'm done with it now. Listen, I'll tell you how it was. It was just two people meeting in the middle of a war.

He drank and held the bottle up to the moon to check its contents and then extended it towards the General.

—Have a drink, General. No? Well, maybe you're right. So you're leaving. Well, I am too. It's time for me to get out of here (he shouted at the General's back). I leave you your war. Tomorrow morning I'll be with the Germans. Tomorrow night I'll be in the Adlon Bar. I'll do the rest of your war from there. It was nice meeting you again, General. Nice little war you've got here. Sorry I can't stay to see the end of it.

But the General was already outside the range of his voice.

He drove back to the General Staff building through streets where great dark crowds suddenly appeared, running softfooted and burdened like thieves from shadow to shadow, never a hand's breadth away from the walls. The wailing klaxonhorns kept them at the walls. No one said anything in this enormous mass, there were no signals or explanations, but each black gateway added people to it. The huge, lumpy river flowed between the houses, lit up by the red and orange of the fires, slowing down as it spilled into the wide enclosures around public buildings. Something had happened, after all. The dark crowd flowed around the General Staff building and the National Bank and the Municipal Hall and stopped there, growing, compressed and motionless and silent.

No one paid attention to the staffcar or its klaxonhorn, and the policemen (there were policemen in the crowd, carried along like unresisting driftwood) made not attempt to guide it. They too became a part of the crowd.

The crowd was still. What sound there was was beaten down by the roar of fires and distant explosions and the howl of firesirens and the bells. The crowd swayed slightly, growing tighter. The windows of the buildings they besieged were blind.

The General left the car at the edge of the crowd and pushed his way through on foot. He was strangely unaffected by the press of people. It seemed unimportant why they had come and why they waited and what had brought a part of them to the General Staff building.

The gaunt facade of the building was unchanged, cold and aloof. The heavy doors still hung on their polished ornamental hinges, and the striped sentryboxes still contained their frozen occupants. Only the white scars of new shrapnel splashed across the stone made it different.

Inside was chaos. Officers stoop in groups, shouting at each other. They moved aimlessly around the pillars and asked questions that no one stopped to answer and argued and waved paper to prove some point, or sat silent and weteyed at their desks or moved about vacanteyed, saying nothing. Complete strangers buttonholed each other and began animated conversations, but when someone interrupted them they stared at each other as if each thought the other was out of his mind.

An elderly Provost Marshal colonel with a yellow mustache went from group to group offering cigarettes from a chased-gold case saying: —Egyptian on the right, Virginia on the left, and asking: —Well? Well? What do you think?

A police general said: —Well, now, listen, I always tried to do the right thing, always the best thing. There were some painful decisions, to be sure, but it was always for the best.

A flock of corpulent civilians in expensive clothes pressed around a brigadier, asking questions. Their arms moved like windmillsails. Their voices were uncertain. The brigadier's face was grey. His mouth had collapsed. He looked worn, General Prus· thought, passing him and the terrified civilians.

—What now? somebody said.

And someone else said: —Well, what do you think?

The Provost Marshal colonel offered his cigarettecase to the General. Prus moved the case and hand aside and went on.

He felt coldly calm. It was as if a part of his brain had declined to function and the reports, so dutifully forwarded by his eyes and ears, were carelessly put aside. Referred for later study. He moved quite unaffected through the gesticulating crowd. No one stopped him on the stairs leading to the War Room, and he went on down, feeling nothing. He passed a captain who was weeping and a major who sat as if asleep in the door to the teletype room, with the machines clattering unattended behind him. The major nodded as if they were old friends and the General stopped and put out his hand and wondered why it was so brown. It was the blood, of course. He studied it as if it were something extraordinary: the hand no part of him and the blood unidentifiable. But it had identity, this blood. So he said nothing to the major and put his hand carefully behind him and went into the War Room.

The vault was hot. The battlelanterns hissed. The huge sweep of the situation map moved in and out of shadow. Michal sat there, his back to the door, bowed before the map. His head was down and cradled in his arms as though he was infinitely weary, and dust, revolving in the glare of the lamps, settled on his head and made it soft and vulnerable and grey. The pistol and the message were under his hand.

Touching his face and hand, reading the message flattened by the weight of the hand and the pistol, the General saw the lost years of childhood and youth and the innumerable differences between them. Suddenly aware of the quarrels and the disagreements and misunderstandings, the small betrayals of boyhood and the adult conflicts, he wanted to erase them all. He regretted nothing. But feeling sympathy and sorrow and pity, the General thought that his brother had not been dead long.

He had shot himself neatly through the chest and had not bled much.

The day, the coded dateline on the message told him, was the seventeenth of September. And while the outside world still slept, and here men died and women died and a country burned and hopes went up in showers of brick and mortar and regret, and while the men of Anders and Czuma and Przedrzymirski and Piskor and Szylling and Prugar and Langner and Sosnkowski and Kleeberg and Podchorski and Kutrzeba and Unrug (alone with his back to the Baltic to keep the shrinking coastline open for help that didn't come) beat off and stopped the Germans at Brzesc, Wlodawa and Parczew, successfully defended Lublin and won at Krasnystaw, recaptured Zamosc and Tomaszow and Bilgoraj, relieved the siege of Lwow and defended Warsaw and (in the far north, in the white sands of the Baltic) the Hel Peninsula that hung like a bent antenna from the roof of Poland, won a pitched battle at Palmiry and began the last drive of the great offensive out of Sochaczew, one million Russians, Ukrainians, Mongols, Turkomans and Uzbeks, Georgians and Chinese and Tartars, Kirghizes and Circassians and Letts and Lithuanians rolled into Poland from the east and northeast like a great colorless sea of pointed Asiatic hats and conical furs and mudbrown anklelong overcoats and moved, formless and alldevouring, like a plague, into the west. Behind them, towns and villages and fields and woods and manorhouses threw pillars of black smoke into the sky; dark hordes of Ukrainians rose to cut throats, pillage, rape and loot and burn and murder and destroy. Again, as for so many bloody centuries, the eastern borders were a funeral pyre and Asia fell on Europe.

The Hour of the Hawk

The stars in their courses fought against Sisera . . .

Sunday, September the seventeenth

I THE CONQUEROR

Headlights were pale spots crawling behind them. The forms of the men were clear. There was a ripple of light, very pale, along the helmet rims.

In the uniform greyness, no longer the deep darkness of night, color was beginning to return. The greengrey of the uniforms, the lighter, sandygrey of helmets, the maroon, brown and yellow of rifle stocks and the black and the silver of machineguns grew brighter.

—It will be hot today, Schindlecker said.

He had to shout above the roar of the motors and the grinding of the troopcarrier's tracks.

—Hot, hot. Keep your eye on the road, said Rottenführer Bar.

He had been stabbed in the thigh during the battle in the quarry and winced each time the carrier struck a stone.

—Watch out! Here is another bump! *Heilige Sakrament!*

One of the others laughed.

Then they were quiet again, watching the flat country north of them, to their left, and the wild mountains south of them, and the naked monster the Poles called Lysagora, Bald Mountain, in its bed of black trees that turned a dark grey, flecked with green as the sun rose higher.

Erich felt hunger, the hunger of the morningtime in the first chill, and at once nausea made him dizzy. He did not think he would ever eat again. Sooner or later everything he ate came up in vomit. The smell of diesel fuel and oil and gasoline and sweat and the bitter smell of dust and burned soil combined invariably into the everpresent smell of death that had been in his nostrils for nine days. It was nerves, of course. It was seeing what he saw every day. It was the orchard with Libesis weeping in it and blaspheming in it while the firingsquads came back with their dark work done. It was the nightlight beckoning through the blackout blankets in Dietrich's quarters, and Kuno Saal's white devilmask pointed at him, and it was Libesis with his head removed. It was the black field with the barbedwire and the pits and the horror of what had been done afterwards to avenge it. All of this floated suddenly before him in the swaying troopcarrier and he leaned over the side and retched. The others did not laugh or comment or even keep their dutiful embarrassed silence. They were used to it. They had had time enough to get used to it. Bar cursed when the carrier lurched. Nickel ate apples. He had an inexhaustible supply of apples. Each time they came to a new village Nickel stripped it of fruit. It was something to do with his being a Berlin gutterrat as a child; never enough fruit, Erich supposed. Schindlecker drove. He liked driving. He had been a chauffeur for Ernst Lieverman, the Jew deputy to the Reichstag in the days when there still were such things, and Erich wondered if Schindlecker had driven more carefully for the Jew than he did now. Lieverman had been killed in 1933. His own car had backed over him accidentally. Schuppanzigh slept. Schreiber slept. Mataushek also slept, Erich thought, but not in the troopcarrier. The same grenade that had torn off the head of Libesis had also blown out the insides of Mataushek. Dietzel was also gone. They never found him after the night between the woods, there beyond the mountains. He was still there somewhere, in the bloody quarry or in the *Totenwald,* the woods of death, or in those living pits. The new men Erich did not know and did not want to know. They were newly come from Bavaria. There were ten of them. They sat very stiff in the troopcarrier and tried not to look at their vomiting lieutenant.

They came off the mountains into the valley of the river that slanted across this flat, inhospitable land to Sandomierz and Rozwadow, and then to Jaroslaw and up, in a twist, almost as far as Lwow. All these places had German names, but Erich did not use them. It was better to use the Polish names; then what happened here would have no relation to anything that resembled home. The valley was a famous one, a bed of invasions. The Walking Castles of Gustavus Adolphus, the Hungarians, the Austrians, Mongols, Tartars, Cossacks, Russians and Turks had, at one time or another, flowed lavalike into it. And now, Germans. Columns moved ahead and behind them, each under its own canopy of dust. Tanks squatted under netting that crewmen were taking off to join the flow through the dried riverbed, among the yellowing meadows and waterless creeks and the hard highgrass swamps. As the sun rose, slumped figures appeared at the sides of the road. They sat in the ditches. Mostly these were Slovaks in ill-fitting boots. When they crossed rivers, now shrunken to the size of creeks with green, foulsmelling water thick with village refuse, men leaned down the sides of the carriers and dipped their helmets in the cooler pools among the stepping stones and poured the water over head and shoulders.

Soon the sun was high and white and it was hot. The columns pressed harder. The carriers swayed. Dust billowed. Dispatchriders weaved their machines between the swaying carriers and tanks and guncarriages. Overhead endless columns of Luftwaffe bombers droned east. It seemed as though the whole world was driving eastward.

Hurry!

And the motors roared and the gears clashed and the mechanical river rolled. The dull hammering of artillery and the rolling thunder of distant bombing pulsed through the dustclouds. Somewhere northeast of them another battle was beginning. Each day a new battle began somewhere. But this was not their battle. They flowed southeast away from the sound of it. Erich hoped that they would always continue to move away from the battles. Fighting, yes, perhaps; that could not be avoided. But he did not want to see another quarry or another dark field fill with bloody corpses between two strips of bloody woods. He did not want to see another Kielce with burning and butchered men and women drowning in their own blood in the gutters, and certainly, please, no more necks suddenly uncorked and human fountains twitching and spiderfingers clutching and no more slashing, sabering, bayoneting madmen pouring down the slope like an avalanche of trees. Then, perhaps, he would be able to close his eyes at night and not see a scarlet glare, and his nostrils would not fill with the nauseating smell, and food would not turn into horror on his tongue and he would be safe.

They passed through Bodzentyn. Schindlecker threw the carrier into a tight turn and the metal box ground over a dog. The animal vanished, howling under the tracks. The air filled with the roar of tracks on cobblestones. North of them, the roar of artillery grew louder. It seemed to pulse and tremble with life of its own. But the town was quiet. Only the cables swayed drunkenly overhead. Nothing else moved. The sun shone down, white and pitiless. It lighted up the ruins and filled each recess and corner so that the full horror of its contents was exposed. At one corner a corpse dangled stupidly from a truck. The truck was flattened and propped up against a wall like a board. Its tires were still burning. The face of the dead man was charred. His teeth stuck out like the tusks of a grinning animal. It was a Pole; he still wore the soft, square cap with the silver eagle.

Then the column ground out of the dead town into the countryside, which was also dead: scorched fields of wheat and corn, hollow farms, black telegraph poles pointing at the sky. It was a pale sky, nearly colorless. It had the washed, cold blue of Kuno's eyes. At the thought of Kuno Saal, Erich threw himself against the side of the carrier to vomit, but he had nothing left inside.

The column rolled through the dead country. A general's dispatchrider rode with screaming siren between the vehicles and vanished in the dust. Then came another. Then others rode by with their scarlet lights twinkling. And then the column stopped, and the dustcloud spread over the fields and the dried beds of ponds and the powdery blackened hayricks, and the tanks and the carriers and trucks and all that sea of metal left the road and drove into the fields.

—All right! *Raus!* Everybody out! Bar shouted.

Then he remembered that Erich was there and looked at him, confused. Good, Erich thought. Forget me. I wish to be forgotten. Since the red night of Kielce many men forgot to wait for Erich's orders. It really did not matter. He was no longer interested in giving orders. Or taking them. Or executing them. Particularly not in executing them. He turned away from Bar's confusion and climbed out of the carrier.

The earth heaved under his feet. He would have fallen, but the hot plates of the metal box behind him propped him up. That is what I need. A prop. Something solid that I can lean against. Something that will not die uncorked in a black field. He slid down the hot sides of the carrier and sat down.

Dust settled while he sat. The others stood and sat and lay about in ditches and under the protecting walls of the tanks and carriers. He could see the lines of huts, brown against the yellow hills, with the bright skirts and the shining white shirts of the village women moving among the huts at the edge of the valley.

They had stopped along a dried-out tributary creek that paid no tribute that September to the Kamienna River. The Kamienna was dry. Erich wondered if the Vistula would also be dry. They would cross that sometime in the morning.

He looked up and down the broad, dusty arena of the valley that stretched out of sight to the northwest and the southeast, straight as a warrior's spear. He didn't know exactly where he was and didn't much care. The Order of the Day had mentioned Opatow, south of Ostrowiec. So that could be the area. What he saw was a yellowbrown sea of burned grass and dust. The tanks were small ships on it. Men lay, relaxing, in the shadow of the resting steel, under the greater, fleeting shadows of the bombers that flew between them and the sun. There were many bombers. There were, he told himself, two air armies supporting the tanks. And this was good. Four thousand planes and a sea of armor. This was as it should be. The war would not be lost. It *could* not be lost. One could not bear to think about losing this war. Loss brings about facing of consequences. Only the losers pay after the game is over. Dead men would extract payment. And then towns with familiar, pronounceable names would be burning, and men and women with pronounceable names and well-remembered features would drown in their own blood in the burning streets.

Breakfast was coffee and bread and monkey-ass paste. There were also herring in tins. There was the smell of gasoline and urine. It was not a successful breakfast for Erich, who could not keep it down. He thought he could probably keep down one of Nickel's apples but the SS *Sturmmann* did not offer to share his fruit. He kept his back to Erich and ate apples and blew loud farts. He threw apple cores at Rottenführer Bar when Bar wasn't looking. Bar nursed the stab wound in his leg. Schindlecker slept. Schreiber was looking for lice in his underwear. Before them the gaunt massif of Bald Mountain and the *Totenwald* hid the stench of corpses. Erich deposited his breakfast in the bushes and sat down. But the new SS from Bavaria kept their hurt eyes on him. He got up to move away from these accusing eyes and walked into Huneker. The eyes of Huneker were not accusing. They were without expression. The red scar on the sergeant's jaw was black in the morning light. It stretched and moved as Huneker worked his jaws. He has jaws like a wolf, Erich thought, and listened to what Huneker was saying. The Standartenführer wished to see the Fahnrich, was what Huneker was saying. No, he did not know what for.

Perhaps he had a medal for the Fahnrich. It was possible, *nicht wahr?* A big one with a yellow ribbon to match the underwear of the Fahnrich, ha ha.

It was quite possible about the medal, but perhaps not this morning. There was to be a meeting of the officers this morning, and the Fahnrich was an officer, wasn't he? Huneker did not know what the Fahnrich was an officer of —perhaps the BDM? The Bund Deutscher Mädel could use such a Fahnrich; certainly better than the SS could use him. Perhaps the Standartenführer wished to arrange the transfer.

—All right, Huneker, Erich said.

But was it all right? There was a matter of a score that had to be settled. A matter of a scar and a humiliation. That was not all right. Surely the Herr Fahnrich, Puffenbundführer of the BDM, understood that much? That was not all right.

Huneker kept his voice low but the others heard. They kept their backs and faces rigid but they listened carefully. Nickel stopped eating apples. Schreiber stopped scratching. They were careful not to look at Erich. They had been equally careful not to look at Libesis the time that Libesis was drunk in the orchard. Erich shouldered his MP Feuer and went towards the commandtruck of the Standartenführer. Behind him someone laughed and someone else swore.

He knew as soon as he entered the halfcircle of officers by the squat commandtruck that he had been one of the last to hear about the meeting. It was as though he had been told to come only as an afterthought. The meeting had been going on for some time and it took him several minutes to understand its purpose. The meeting was addressed by a Hauptsturmführer Schroeder, a piglike man with pale-blue eyes scrunched down in layers of diseased fat. Erich knew Schroeder slightly. The Hauptsturmführer was a member of Brandt's special staff. He was the regimental chief of propaganda, whitewasher of errors and smiler of secret smiles. Before the revolution he had been a lawyer. He was a pastyfaced replica of Huneker but without the scar. There were no scars on a Schroeder, Erich thought. Such men do not wear their scars on their bodies.

—This, then, will be our task, Schroeder was saying as Erich joined the officers around the commandtruck. We shall be issued the newest and latest equipment. It will all be new. We shall drive into captured cities spotless and undamaged, without a hair out of place, without a touch of dust on our boots, and we shall sit, clean and erect in our shining vehicles, our oiled tanks and carriers and polished trucks and motorcycles and armoredcars, stern, proud and confident, and, of course, assured. We will not win victories but we shall be a victory. We shall be the personification of German victory. This is the task that the Führer has selected for us. Our Führer, that man of genius, that great military mind, knows that it is not enough to win victories. It is more important to impress the world with the completeness and enormousness of victory. And so when the line troops have won their bloody victories we will implant the banners on the ruins. We shall march into captured cities as though on parade. And they will look at us, in those towns and throughout the world, and they will say: Look. Look how clean they are. They are untouched. Look how easy it was for them to capture this city, to defeat their enemies. Are they immortal? Are they irresistible? How can anyone resist the irresistible? Surely they cannot be touched by bullets, these shining Germans. Who and what can harm them? Nothing can harm them. Let us not resist. And the photographers will be there to greet us. And the world's correspondents will be brought to see us. And the world will see in us the inevitable German victory.

With upraised eyes, the Hauptsturmführer consulted the sky. The pale eyes of Kuno Saal stared at the Hauptsturmführer and Kuno was smiling. Dietrich was smiling. Krasberg was also smiling. But Krasberg had been smiling constantly, like a sleepy child, since the massacre in Kielce; his expression meant nothing.

Still, Erich had to ask someone what was happening and he didn't think he'd get an answer from anyone else. So, softly: —What is happening, Krasberg? What is he saying?

—That the war is over.

—How's that? Have the Poles surrendered?

A distant rumble like thunder came as if in answer. Heavy artillery or perhaps a bombing. Krasberg looked troubled. He made a vague gesture with his hands, smiling his gentle smile.

—No . . . but I think we have.

—What?

—There will be no new battles, not for us, Krasberg said. The SS Panzerkorps Germania, newest and soon to be the cleanest in the finest of all armies of all time, handpicked by special orders of the Führer, has a brave new mission.

—What mission?

—The construction of a myth. You have an opportunity to see how history is made. And do you know something? People will actually believe it! We are to enter corpsefilled ruins with buttons polished like the breastplates of the classic heroes. With leather gleaming to reflect the disappointed sun.

—But what is this about?

—Germania! The new corps of paper heroes. Oh yes, white gloves are going to be issued to the officers.

They had reached the far edge of the group, where nobody knew them. A sergeant with a papercarton passed among the officers handing out black armbands embroidered in silver. Erich put his on as the others were doing. He looked at the tortured Gothic script and it made no sense.

—Germania, Krasberg said. Read it there. We have now formed the Panzerkorps Germania. It's a historic day. You don't understand, do you? It's a historic day for anyone who had illusions about the idealism of war. Libesis would have understood, all right. What happened to him anyway?

—What? He is dead.

—Oh yes. I had forgotten. He would have been glad to miss this day anyway, our idealistic friend. You see, he had ideals. Did you know that? He really believed.

—We all believe in something.

—False. You see how myths are made. There is no truth in history. Only fear. And falsehood. You have heard Dietrich on the necessity for fear. You have heard Hauptsturmführer Schroeder on the subject of constructing history. What would you like to believe after that?

—But what is this about?

—The sweet smell of war. The odor of victory.

Several of the other officers looked closely at them and Erich pulled the muttering artilleryman away. —Be careful, Krasberg. They can hear you.

—Can they? Well, what of that? I'm a German hero. I am a member of the newformed Panzerkorps Germania. I make the world tremble.

(—*Sieg Heil!* called Hauptsturmführer Schroeder.

The officers responded, Erich's *Sieg Heil* as loud as the others'.)

—Each one of us must go his own way from now on, Krasberg said. There is no truth in massformations anyway. I have a bottle of cognac in my kit. Would you like a drink?

—Yes, I suppose.

—Good. It will wash away the sweet smell of war. My nose is full of it. Then we can practice our lines for the correspondents. Listen to this. From the River Warta to the San and from the Baltic to the Tatra Highlands lies the corrupt carpet of the dead, softly sinking under its own weight into dust, tens of thousands of corpses. They have fallen on the hillsides and in the woods, on the banks of rivers, on both sides of bridges, in the open country, around the summit rims of hillocks, in ditches, before and behind fences. They have been scythed down as they fought: in battalions.

—I have seen them.

—Yes you have, haven't you? But I am practicing my lines for the correspondents. Often the piles of interlaced bodies are a meter high, as though a plague had thrown them down. Ask me about this war. If anyone asks me I will say it is a monstrous mass of decomposing corpses.

—Well, but there is a reason . . .

—Oh, there is? You must mean German destiny and the Righting of Intolerable Wrongs. You must be talking about our duty to history. We have just seen how history is made. Well, I will look irresistible and untouched enough for the correspondents. They will not be shown the carpet of corpses.

They had come past the stafftrains then and into the artillery bivouac. No one challenged them. The soldiers slept under the few roadside trees and along the ditches. The distant rolling of artillery fire had a hollow sound.

—I heard a marvelous sound the day after the battle in the quarry, Krasberg said. It seemed to come out of the earth itself; I thought it was the earth speaking to me. But it was the corpses.

—What?

—Yes. At certain times of day when the sun is hot, gases distend cracked cages of ribs and seep from bellies and then an unbelievable murmur sweeps over the fields.

—Good God, Krasberg!

—Ask me about the glorious sounds of victory, Herr Foreign Correspondent. It is the muttering of the ballooning dead. What do they talk about? How should I know? Perhaps they are discussing glory and its many facets. Perhaps they are merely laughing at the living. Everyone laughs at the great joke of history, so why not the dead?

—Enough, Krasberg.

—But I digress, Herr Foreign Correspondent. How was it? Why, the easiest of all things. No casualties to speak of. A mere joyride through an odd, inhospitable land; a matter of a week or so riding through the country. Yes, there are certain inconveniences. When we camp in the fields and in the woods and beside the picturesque streams and hillocks, we must first spray the carrion with gasoline or quicklime. Benzine is quickest but far too expensive. Quicklime is cheap and more efficient but it takes too long. We move with such irresistible impetus, you see; our bivouacs don't last long. I mention quicklime only for future reference. Still, you can see that we think of the land; we fertilize it as we occupy it. That is organization, don't you see. That is forward thinking. We are the modern men the Führer talks about: the Heralds of Tomorrow.

Erich began to laugh.

—Good. You are laughing? That means that you are getting history in perspective. You now have the proper reverence for corpses.

—You sound like Libesis, Erich said.

—Libesis is dead. He died because he was ineffectual and fat and thought too much. He did too much thinking. He was a rhetor. Rhetors make good corpses.

—You too have that sound about you. Are you an idealist?

—*Jawohl*, Herr Foreign Correspondent. I believe. I believe in Dietrich. He is the new God and I pray to him. I also pray to the Hauptsturmführer Schroeder.

—Be serious.

—How? That is the quickest way to become a corpse. Look at your fat intellectual friend.

—You confuse me.

—Well, don't admit it. It doesn't fit your image of uncompromising sternness; you have to be irresistible and untouched now, you know. You are a German hero. But go away now and be heroic somewhere else. I've changed my mind about the cognac, and besides, I don't know where I put it. I'm going to sleep. You should try that too. Or, better yet, get something to eat. You look as if you've lost some weight. Then go and kick some of your SS and make them respect you. That's the way it is done; nothing else is true.

Erich left the bivouac then. He took a wandering yellow path to the main road, then walked along that for a while. He was aware of hunger, the first time in ten days. He thought about Krasberg's insane talk and about Libesis. There didn't seem to be much difference between them. There was an air of uncertainty and doubt about them, a lack of direction; there was their futile struggle against reality, as if they thought they could change natural orders with their words. Dietrich and Kuno Saal trod a firmer path.

He went on like that for several minutes, feeling the hot sun on his back and, inside, the hunger. He felt remarkably restless; he had to do something and he didn't want to go back to his own bivouac, where the old troopers would ignore him and the new ones stare. Well, he would have to do something about that.

But hunger came first and so he turned towards a group of Polish huts squatting silent by the roadside, an abandoned village. There was a larger village at the other end of the valley but it was too far to walk there in the hot sun. He went by an appleorchard where a small stream ran with difficulty along the bottom of a dry ditch and there was Nickel stalking head down with the cranelike pace of a ragpicker among the fallen apples.

—Nickel, hey Nickel, Erich said, wanting an apple. The soldier looked up, saw him, and went on. Erich felt sweat breaking out on his forehead. His heart beat up suddenly. He wanted to run after the applesearcher and strike him in the face. Instead he turned off abruptly at the first hut and walked up to the shuttered window and beat it with his fist.

—Open it, he shouted. Open it!

But the shutter remained closed and the door was closed and he hammered on each of them in turn with the butt of his Erstalt.

—Open it, damn you, open it!

There was no sound inside the house, but he thought he could detect

446

heavy breathing. He beat upon the door with his fist and the pistolbutt, shouting the order, which was not obeyed, which, he realized furiously, would not be obeyed, and found himself short of breath and kicking with his ironshod boots against the frame of the door.

—Open it!

Sweat and anger blinded him. It was no longer a matter of finding food. He did not think about his hunger. It was the barrier of the shuttered window, the closed door which would not open when he told it to.

—Open up!

A ring of men had formed behind him and, turning rapidly, he saw some thirty SS watching him curiously. More came up the road from the orchard. Some grinned. Others stared vacantly. A tall, incredibly thin sergeant asked if anything was wrong.

—Wrong? Wrong? (At first he did not know what the soldiers wanted.) What do you want?

—Perhaps we could assist the standard-bearer, the sergeant said. If the Herr Fahnrich wishes . . .

What?

Yes.

Break down this door, kick it down.

Drag out those animals who resist and butcher them.

Ah-h-h, but he did not say it. Instead he said: —Nothing. There is nothing wrong.

—Because it is the house of the priest, the sergeant said.

—So? Are you religious?

—No. But the priest is locked up in the cellar under the commandpost. He is a hostage and the house is empty.

This could not be, but then he saw it was. The smiles of the soldiers told him so. The sergeant who was thin did not smile. He looked at Erich as though Erich was an interesting animal in a zoo. Adrianne had looked at him like that when he had told her about the impossibility of their marrying. She had looked like that before she laughed.

—It can't be empty, he said, feeling foolish. I hear a man in there.

—It is empty. (The sergeant stared at Erich with cold eyes.) I took the priest myself to the commandpost.

Erich felt the familiar nausea starting up in the pit of his stomach. Good God, that's all I need: to vomit now in front of all these men. I must look terrible, he thought. What are they thinking? Is this the way I've been for the last ten days?

And suddenly his anger spilled over. He could not control it.

—What are you up to, Sergeant?

His voice was high and weak.

—Nothing, the sergeant said. Just thought you might need assistance. These Poles put thick doors on their pigsties.

—Who sent you here? Was it Huneker? Do you know Huneker?

—Sure. Everybody knows him. But nobody sent me here or anywhere. I just came along to see who was trying to kick down the priest's house. You want some help with it, all right, here we are. You don't want help, that is all right too. But what the hell, Fahnrich.

All the SS were laughing then. The group broke up slowly. Erich watched the men walking away with, here and there, a backward glance at him, a gesture, a laugh, a comment that preceded laughter, an imitation of a man kicking. One soldier made the gesture with the finger circling about his temple.

Erich left the hut. He walked unsteadily up the road towards his own bivouac. After a while he began to laugh. He knew what he had to do. He laughed, anticipating the surprise of the young SS. The soldiers in the bivouac looked up at him and quickly away. The new replacements were bewildered, yes, he could see that. This was not the way they thought an SS Fahnrich, officercadet, should behave. The older *grenadieren* kept their backs to him.

He couldn't stop laughing and fought to control himself. It had to be kept stern, this demonstration, as fitted an SS officercadet. He would laugh later but no one else would laugh.

He walked up behind Bar (feeling light and bodiless) and kicked him carefully in the spine. It was a light kick, no more than a nudge, but Bar leaped to his feet. Bar stared. Schindlecker stared. Nickel watched with an apple halfway to his mouth. His mouth was open. Erich thought that he would not be able to stop himself from laughing. But he could not allow himself to laugh. Not yet.

A demonstration of my dignity and rank, my power, if you please. That must come first. He smiled. He was pleased.

Bar also smiled, although with some uncertainty, and rubbed his back. Nickel grinned and Schreiber made a sound between his teeth. The sound was . . . what? Surprise? Admiration? Well, well. How little it takes to be respected by my brave SS. Kick them and they respect you. The young SS stare with such enormous eyes. Now they have reassurance. Their world is right and orderly and perfectly *korrekt*.

Still with a smile. —Well, Rottenführer? Don't you know your manners? (Softly, the way Dietrich said it to the tall Pole in Kielce.)

Bar snapped erect. You could almost hear the inner spring uncoiling in his spine. Click-snap. Erect. *Korrekt*. Erect is *korrekt*. Up came the arm in the stiff salute. —Heil Hitler, Fahnrich!

—Bar, Erich said. Rottenführer Bar. You gave an order, I believe, when we stopped here?

Bar stared.

—Oh, come now, Rottenführer. Someone gave an order to make the men dismount. They got off the carrier. You gave the order, did you not?

—*Jawohl,* Herr Fahn—

Yes yes. *Jawohl.*

—Are you, perhaps, my senior officer? Is that your impression? Do you believe me incompetent to give such simple orders as *Raus?* Is this your belief?

Bar's eyes blinked rapidly. (Ah, but this was an excellent demonstration!)

—I don't believe you are my superior, Erich said. I must correct your false impression on the subject, Bar. You really must try to wait until I give an order; you must really try. And I am going to make it easy for you to try, my dear Bar. I am going to arrange a loss of your stripes so that you will not fall into the temptation to give orders. Do you understand?

(Oh, but you could hear the grassblades falling and the dust settling yellowly and the breathing of the young SS was like the rolling of a distant sea.)

—That is all, Bar. At ease.

—*Jawohl,* Herr Fahnrich!

Erich wondered how much longer he could keep from laughing.

He wondered how long it would take the SS to spread the word about the demonstration. How soon Dietrich and Huneker would hear about it. He did not think it would be long. He nodded amiably at the young SS, whose eyes were huge. He took the apple out of Nickel's hand and bit into it. Sweet juices ran down the corners of his mouth. These were no longer tight when he smiled. His mouth was moist and cool. He licked his lips to reach the last of the sweet juices.

He lay down in the hot shadow of the scratched and bulletpitted and grenadescarred battlewagon, whose many reeks and stains and smears could no longer nauseate him, and wondered when it would be exchanged for one fresh from the Skoda works. He wondered if white gloves would indeed be issued to the officers.

I THE JEW

They had been hiding in the woods for several days, avoiding the Germans, and they would still be there (Berg thought, tired beyond thought) if the Walnut wasn't so close to dying. It took them all night and most of the morning to get the wounded soldier off the mountain. Berg did not know where they were going. He thought he was beyond hunger and beyond fatigue as he and the tracker carried the fat soldier. He hoped the tracker knew where he was going.

They made no stops. There was no time to rest. The Walnut did not have long to live, they both knew that. Berg wondered if the Walnut knew how soon he would be dead. But if the fat soldier knew anything he gave no sign of it.

The small tracker led the way into a village. It was not his village, he explained. His home was far to the east in Malopolska. But he had come to this place with a hunter shortly before the war and there the war had detained him.

They came into the village in midmorning and took the dying man to the priest's house but the priest refused to take them in. The Germans would come soon, the priest said. Where would he be then? They had to think of the priest's position.

—Nevertheless, Father, he is a soldier and we must take him somewhere, the tracker said.

—Why did you bring him here? The Army has hospitals and ambulances for wounded soldiers. That is the place for him.

—Up there the dogs have been eating the wounded, Berg said. He did not look at the priest. He stared past his shoulder at a calendar on the wall. It read 17 September.

—I cannot help that, said the priest. I did not make this war.

—He will die soon, I think, the tracker said. He will not be any trouble to you, Father. When he dies we will bury him but until then he should be in a bed. It is not too much to ask, I think.

—Ask someone else, then, the priest said. Why don't you go to the house of Gosin? That devil has nothing to lose; he has no respect for anything.

—I do not know Gosin well, the tracker said.

—And do you know me? How many times have you been to Mass? When did you last make a confession? Have you ever seen the inside of the church? Well, then, why do you come to me now? A Godless man and a Jew. And what shall I tell the Germans when they find this man in my house? They will shoot us all when they find him here. Take him out to the woods, if you want. You should never have brought him.

It was hot and high clouds of dust boiled above the far fields in the valley where the Germans were coming off the mountains. They had cut off Berg's troop after the battle in the woods. You could see the tanks and the trucks in the dust. You could hear the motors. The priest stepped back into his house and shut the door quickly.

They put the Walnut down near the *zagroda* next to the house of the priest and Bogacz went away to look for another hiding place. Berg sat down to brush flies off the Walnut and keep the dogs away. Peasants came and looked and, after a while, brought apples and bread and buttermilk. The peasants stood around watching Berg eat and drink. They had heard about what had happened at the priest's house. They looked guiltily towards the priest's house when they brought the food. Clearly they did not wish to offend the priest, who must have had good reason to send the soldiers away, but they wished to do something for the soldiers. You could see the way their minds were working. The peasants stood around the soldiers in a loose half-circle and did not say anything.

What am I? Berg thought. Who am I? And what am I doing here?

Last week I was one thing and the week before I was something else and now I am something else again and what will I be next week? One thing was certain: He would never be again what he had been before the war began; he could never again live in a Quarter and agree and smile and be polite and not offend anyone who needed offending and stand when he wished to sit and sit in silence when he wished to speak. If this meant that he could no longer be a Jew then he would not be one. But he did not think that Jewishness had anything to do with it. It was the Quarter that imposed such rules upon a man, and it did not matter what kind of men lived in it; Jews, Poles, Germans, anyone would be emasculated by the egoism of a Quarter. If you turn your back upon the world for a thousand years how can you expect the world to remember your face? Or that you have a face? Go out and it will know you.

Only three weeks ago the two policemen had come for him in Mendeltort's room on Solna and had made the joke about the Devil and the alternatives and the unheroic qualities of Jews. They were the first policemen that Berg had ever had anything to do with, having been, as he had been taught to be, inconspicuous, inoffensive, humble, in short the little Jew that Mendeltort had talked about, and they had surprised him. They did not beat him as the innumerable tales about policemen warned that they would. They did not shout or inflict any physical pain. They made a joke. It was a bad joke and he had heard it before anyway, but as he listened to the elderly policemen he became suddenly aware of himself. He saw himself. He saw arms and legs and hands and feet and part of a body. He saw Mendeltort enormous on his bed and his own small body and knew, then, that one was as the other except for the size. He looked at his arms and thought: Why have I not used them? He saw the legs and thought: There is another way to walk, one does not have to shuffle timidly. And suddenly he became tired of jokes applied to himself and of depending on things and persons other than himself, outside himself, for his protection, his precious survival. *Gowno,* he said to himself long before he said it to the elderly policemen. The Quarter was *gowno,* and the men and women in it were even greater *gowno,* and he himself was *gowno* unless he himself did something about it. It was his decision to make. No Quarter or any Mendeltort could make it for him. What are you if you never leave a womb? A *Mensch,* perhaps, if that was what they wished to call it. He had another name.

He heard the laughter of Mendeltort as he went down the stairs between the policemen and he felt gratitude. He did not think that Mendeltort was laughing at him. He was no longer the subject of a joke, and it was he himself who had done it. Certainly the policemen went along with it: this transformation. Of course, they were elderly policemen. Had they been younger they might have been brutal. But neither the policemen nor the military policemen who took charge of him made any further jokes. He was quickly armed and quickly uniformed and the soft square fieldcap with the silver eagle felt light on his head.

It seemed to him (sitting on the hot ground outside the enclosure of the priest with the wounded Walnut breathing heavily and the peasants staring, with the flies exploring the Walnut's chest and his own encrusted eyes, hungry and incredibly dirty and equally tired) that this was the first of his several transformations.

First he had been the little Jew hiding for no reason except that little Jews always hid from everything. Then he had left the Quarter. When he said *gowno* to himself and later to the elderly policemen, he had left the Quarter. Without the Quarter and without his *mycka,* his black *kaftan* and sidelocks he did not feel himself a Jew. He was not quite a Pole but no longer a Jew, if those things were what made Jewishness.

The second transformation, the third of his identities, came in the cabbage-field. He had come there with the others, not knowing what to do, where else to go, wondering with the others about going home. He was as the others: equally hot in the field and equally thirsty. He was equally bewildered. And then the Walnut had weighed his own set of alternatives and had made a choice and in that moment Berg knew that he too had his choice to make. He had watched the Walnut getting ready and had thought: What should I do? If I go with him I will probably die. If I stay or go home I will not be killed. But if I do go home I will be dead as surely as if the Germans had killed me. It is the sort of thing the Quarter would expect, and I am done with it. I am no part of any Quarter either inside or outside a man. What am I, then? The clothes I wear and the little cap tell me that I am a Pole. Small, perhaps ridiculous to some of the others, and certainly not warlike, but a Pole.

Still, he had been surprised and excited when he found himself erect and getting ready to go into the woods. And when the others followed him and Walnut, and Kublarz shared his pipe, it was confirmation of his identity and acceptance. His heart beat quickly then. And sometime in those woods, during the battle, prone behind logs with his riflebarrel hot (and then cold without ammunition), on his feet with the bayonet extended, shouting at the others, killing, sliding down the slope on the dead pine needles, falling, getting up and shouting, seeing Ryms shot and Ulanko crushed under a tank that came from nowhere along the slope, killing the screaming German who had shot Ryms (repeatedly and coldly using the bayonet, watching the wounds open up like mouths in the German's chest, feeling nothing) and coming back when the red sun went down, clothed in the uniform butcher-red with blood from head to foot, he knew that he was *not* small, and never would be ridiculous to anyone again.

He did not fall asleep on the red field as the others did but went to look for the Walnut. He thought the Walnut dead: the iron shards of the shell that exploded in the clearing had torn into the soldier's chest. But the man was not dead. The Walnut moved his lips to whisper and Berg heard him begging for a priest. No man, the wounded man urged, should die without a priest. —*Who is this?* The wounded man did not recognize him. —*Is it the Jew? God, why is it the Jew, why, God? He cannot even pray for me. Why you, why you?* —*Quiet now, quiet,* Berg said. But the wounded man went on: —*Get me a priest.* —*I will,* Berg said. —*Will you?* —*Yes* (thinking of Mendeltort's scorn as he talked about the promise of a Jew), *I will get you a priest or I'll get you to a priest.* But even as he said it he knew he would not, because where was a priest to be found on a battlefield? Thus, he said to himself, you have it, Berg: The promise of the Jew. And suddenly the little square cap with the silver eagle did not mean anything, and the uniform was just a dirty suit of clothes no different from the black *kaftan* and *mycka* he had worn in Warsaw.

It did not matter that he stayed with the Walnut, cut off by the Germans, until Bogacz found him and the others. And that he kept the promise and brought the wounded man off the mountain (helped by the tracker, truly a great help in the darkness that bewildered him). A low branch had knocked off his cap somewhere in the woods and he did not bother to pick it up again. It was just a cap. It did not mean anything. It did not make him anything.

He sat now in the dust, himself dusty and smeared with the hard varnish of other men's blood, his eyes halfclosed and his sight blurred. Beside him the Walnut moaned quietly and breathed with difficulty. Some peasant woman broke sticks to make a small roof with her apron over the wounded man. Another woman brought an earthenware jar of water with which to wash his face. The wounded man drifted in unconsciousness. He wept. Perhaps he knew that he would not be brought before a priest. Berg thought he knew.

Why not? It was the promise of a Jew.

He laughed then, or rather made a fishlike motion with his mouth, because although he opened it no sound came out. The silent nothing, he thought. But even a dog must know he is a dog before he can bark. What will you do, Berg, giggle like Rosenblatt?

Surprised, he heard the thin giggle come from him.

—Hey Mr. Soldier, someone said. Hey Mr. Soldier.

It was an old peasant with hands like burned hams. He looked at Berg sadly but uncertainly. I know what he is thinking, Berg thought. I was a Pole long enough to know what peasants think. He wants to do something for me but he does not know what to do without offending me. He does not want to make me angry by offering help. When you accept help you confess to weakness.

—Yes, he croaked.

—Is the Pan Zolnierz well?

—Well? Who is well?

This was so much like a line from the Yiddish theater in the Quarter that Berg laughed. This time the sound was there.

—I am well, Mr. Peasant, he said.

The peasant nodded at the sun and at Berg's bare head.

—You have no cap, he said. The sun is hot.

Berg agreed that the sun was hot upon his head. But he was used to it, he said. The peasant nodded.

—Where is the Pan Zolnierz from? The peasant wished to know.

—Warsaw. From Nalewki.

That must be far away, the peasant said, and Berg agreed. Too far away and yet not far enough.

He felt the peasant's shy friendliness, his desire to help. He could not do much with the priest's position made so clear, but he did what he could, in his shy peasant way. He was a man who knew what he was. He probably did not even think of himself as a Pole. Poland . . . he would not see how he fitted into it. Such a vast concept. All those towns, those people. But he had some land of his own. And maybe he had been to Kielce at some time or to Bodzentyn, and certainly he had gone to market at Opatow. This gave him a horizon, his own frontiers. But what were the frontiers of a Jew? The land he lived in? He could never be a part of it, that much was clear. Berg wondered what the peasant would do if he knew that he, Berg, the Pan Zolnierz, was a Jew. Probably nothing. He would not believe it. Or he would cross himself and spit three times and go away. But why make him do it? It would prove nothing new, show no new guideposts, blaze no trails, and would make the man look stupid in his neighbors' eyes. Besides, there was the bread and buttermilk to consider. And the red apples. He looked at them and at once the peasant took some from a woman and gave them to Berg.

—Let the Pan Zolnierz eat, he said. In good health.

The old voice was shaking.

—I thank you *gospodarzu*. I am grateful.

The fruit was good. He was indeed grateful. The peasant shook his head slowly from side to side. His eyes were sad and he made stricken gestures with his hands. Only the fingers moved, grasping nothing, in the small gestures.

—Ah, what they did to you, poor ones. Ah, if I could . . .

The peasant's hands hung limp but his fingers moved. He looked at the priest's house, where the curtains moved, and at Berg and at the motionless Walnut and at the flies assaulting the bloodybrown swathing of shirt and underwear and puttee pushed into the Walnut's chest, and back at the priest's house. Most of the peasants were looking at the priest's house, and some of them muttered. I would not like to be that priest, Berg thought. No matter what good he may do from now on, he is finished here. The peasants moved their feet in the dust and looked first at the soldiers and then at the priest's house. Berg's peasant, the one who had spoken to him, struck one fist against another. —Marylka! he shouted. Come here, girl! And then he shouted: —*Kaska!* and then spat twice in the direction of the priest's house. Soon the two women came. They looked uncertainly at the peasant. Their hands moved in the folds of identical aprons. Both wore white kerchiefs on their heads and white shirts and their skirts were dusty. But where the older woman was brown and bowed and wrinkled and moved cautiously, the younger was all white and pink and golden where the pigtail slipped out of the kerchief, and her blue eyes twinkled and skirts flew with a sound of birds' wings when she moved.

—Pick him up now, the peasant shouted. Get him in the house. Get water from the well and bread for his wound. Move, girl! Move, mother! This is not a dog.

And cursing horribly the man marched off towards the house.

At once the halfcircle of worried faces and sad faces and faces marked with pity and faces on which no emotion showed broke and the peasants moved. Four huge men lifted the Walnut like a log.

—Hey . . . ooop!

They took him to the house.

Arms grasped Berg's elbows, lifted him gently. Hands brushed at his uniform, the tattered coat with the eaglebuttons. Small boys behind him screamed in competition to see who would carry the rifle. Six picked it up and carried it into the house bayonetfirst like a battering ram. The house was cool, dark and comforting. There was no sun! No heat! The eyes could see and the skin could breathe!

Berg's body shook and his teeth cracked against each other in the cool dark and his knees slid out to the sides and he would have fallen if the strong arms at his elbows had not held him up.

He moved to the corner by the stove and sat in the dark shadow. He didn't want to think. He was afraid that if he fell asleep the Germans would come for him and pick him up like a sack of fish, without resistance. But he had not reckoned with the extent of his exhaustion. The darkness of the room and all the other darknesses, of woods and quarries and jasminescented clearings and dark slopes where men ran and dark fields and pits and vacant eyeholes and open mouths that bled and Quarters where no light could live, moved over him and massed above him and came down and swallowed him and he spun round and round in the black sea of sleep.

Monday, September the eighteenth

I THE CONQUEROR

They had left the valley and driven into the village shortly before midnight, when the heat of the day was no longer with them. The valley was no longer a quiet, restful place when they began to leave it.

The valley was a smoldering junkpile of torn metal and flesh, and angry Germans who were horrified and wondered why, by what right, the three lumbering Karas bombers had come at them. The Poles had come out of the low evening sun but seemingly from nowhere. All eyes (even the sentries') had been kept carefully from the sun, meticulously shielded from the rays, and the first attack had had a measure of success.

Erich had seen the bombers coming with incredible slowness no more than a hundred meters above the fields. They were like great aerial freightcars, driving with hopeless dignity through the cloud of shellbursts and crosscrossed latticework of machinegunfire as though held on invisible rails. He had seen the small square opening under the leader suddenly fill with glittering fireflies as multiple lines of incendiary bullets hit the bomb bay, and then the ponderous, slow machine shuddered and vanished in a ball of fire and some of this fire and jagged lumps of steel the size of soup plates fell on his armoredcarrier. The carrier exploded. He rolled away from it, across a headless corpse (colliding face to face with the head some meters away: the foolish face of Bar). The two remaining bombers came solemnly through the smoke, making their painfully slow suicidal run, and rose straight up into the sky, opening out left and right at the top of their climb. It was a beautiful maneuver precisely executed and the bombers seemed to hang motionless on the spinning arcs of their propellers and then with a sweeping wingover they came down again. Both were on fire before they leveled out above the fields and went on, gravely smoking, to unload their bombs. These fell in clusters on the tanks and carriers. A gasoline tanktruck blew up in a yellow ball, and then the smoke obscured the sky, in which the shadows of the bombers still moved with somnambulistic slowness. The last remaining bomber made a lone attack, looking much like a comet: a shapeless mass of flame out of which tracer bullets still emerged. The bomber fell across the ammunition trucks of Krasberg's battery and the explosion threw nearby men, tanks, trucks and carriers about like broken toys. In time the smoke dispersed and the dusty debris of metal, earth and flesh settled in the craters, and then the regiments were assembled and sent out to neighboring villages where there were woods and orchards and barns and huts to take cover in.

The men were dazed and silent in the carriers. Their eyes were bewildered. Of his ten SS from Bavaria three were dead in the valley. Nickel had lost his teeth. Someone's boot, with the foot still in it, had come flying and kicked him in the mouth. Erich was immensely angry. There were supposed to be no more battles. No more killing of Germans. He felt a hungry hatred. He felt betrayed and cheated.

The village where the Ostland Regiment was to be quartered lay less than a half hour's drive away across the fields. It was a small place with about fifty men and women, mostly old. The people hid when the SS arrived and the children ran away. Later the children returned and one or two of the smaller boys (smaller and therefore blessed with fewer tears, unmarked by the terror of their parents, still trusting in the goodness of adults and—above all—curious) came close. They stared in awe at the scarred machines. Their bare feet scratched marks in the dust. Bright eyes stared from their dirty faces at the resting soldiers.

—Animals, Kuno Saal said. Filthy animals.

They were, indeed, filthy. Their small peaked faces had not been washed of tears and their bare legs were yellowgrey with dust and fuzzy like the legs of does, and they did have the wondering, liquid eyes of small animals. But Erich thought, you cannot hate a child. No matter what or whose it is, or what its countrymen did or would do, you cannot hate it.

He said so and Kuno turned on him. —Now you are the regimental philosopher? Have you inherited the mantle of Libesis, perhaps? I can hate children. I can hate the world. I would rather feed one mangy dog in Graz than save all of this vermin from starvation.

It was a long speech for Kuno Saal to make with his crushed throat. He choked on the last words of it.

Saal had been groping for a stone to throw at the children when he began to choke. Erich picked it up and tossed it carelessly at the human animals, who scattered with small frightened squeaks. A woman ran into the street after one of them, her face grey with terror.

Night passed and a new day came. The children came back warily with sunrise. They stared as before. Erich stared back at them without really seeing them in the hot haze. An old man came out into the street at the end of the plum orchard and looked at him and quickly disappeared. The wounded men had their cuts and burns treated and bandaged, and the unwounded slept under the trees or played cards or lay with their faces to the ground. The only near sound was the soft hum of countless flies about the sleeping men. Erich no longer felt the heat, but he felt morning hunger. He was to be the company duty officer that night, replacing Kuno Saal, and so he tried to sleep in the hot sun. He closed his eyes but could not keep them closed. There were too many bloody sights behind his eyelids. His empty stomach churned. He felt uncommonly hungry, thinking that soon he would resemble a skeleton, surely, not having kept food down for days. He felt the hunger and was glad of it: At least he would be able to eat from now on. Sleeping would come back later. He sat stiffly against the trunk of a plumtree and ate some of the fruit, but it was dry. He looked for Nickel, who would have some apples, but Nickel was gone. Where was he? He shouted for him. Schindlecker said that Nickel had gone after apples as he always did.

—He eats more apples, that one. I have never known a man to eat so much fruit. What is he, a hog? But he can't eat those apples now with his teeth gone.

—Maybe he'll have you chew them for him, Erich said.

Hunger brought anger. Erich got up and walked down to the kitchens but the cooks had nothing ready for him except coffee.

456

—All right, then, give me coffee, damn you, he said and sipped the thick, hot liquid and scalded his tongue and threw the cup angrily into the cauldron, where it sank.

Damn it to hell and heaven! If not here then elsewhere. The peasants would have food.

He walked back to the village at an unnaturally quick pace that pulled at the muscles of his calves in the short boots, past rows of cars and trucks and motorcycles under netting, stepping over booted feet in the narrow street, past the four antiaircraft guns hastily emplaced in a garden (fine time for it, he thought, now that the bombers are burned up), along a row of blind, windowless huts with doors barred and a silence born of terror huddled behind the doors. Krasberg was seated in his shirtsleeves on a doorstep (with the whitewash powdery on his trousers like a baker's apron), holding a vacant, smiling face up to the sun, feeling the pull of the sun on his uncovered head.

—Go in out of the sun, he said to Krasberg, but the artilleryman paid no attention to him.

Well, that was his business. It was his head, his face and his idiotic smile. Let it be his sunstroke.

He followed the line of the crooked fence to the next *zagroda,* the small enclosure that the peasants built about their houses, and pushed open the gate in the fence and walked into a garden. This house was bigger than the others. It was of stone. It was roofed with straw, as were all the others, but here the thatch was firmer and tidily clipped, and evened out, and laid more carefully, and well secured with neatly stitched ropes of plaited straw and grass, and there were windowpanes of glass under the half-open shutters in carved frames and the shutters were painted, and the door, also painted, had the freshscrubbed look of care lavished on a well-liked object. I used to keep my skis like that, he thought. Somebody likes this house.

Around the front of the house was the garden. It had cucumber vines in it. It had tomato plants tied to little sticks. Small patches of autumn flowers and the withered stalks of earlier plants clung to the border between fence and furrows, and tall sunflowers nodded heavy with late black seed, and there were bees belligerent about a conical hive and on a bed of moss stood a threelegged tower like a gallows on which enormous cheeses had dried. *The SS had eaten the cheeses.* Behind the house rose a cartwheel nailed flat on top of a wagontongue. Straw still clung to it but the storks were gone.

There was an unreal quality about the house. It stood in a kind of stubborn peace against the back fence of the *zagroda* as though it had retreated there step by step and now, having nowhere to go, waited for the inevitable in its garden, patiently and with dignity.

Erich went to beat upon the door.

When he awoke a new day had come. He felt clamps on his arms and shoulders and on his legs and a coolness on his face and then a wetness. Someone was washing him with a wet cloth, and the touch was gentle.

He lay perfectly still and felt the clamps relax and knew them to be fingers. Why did they have to hold him down? He had been dreaming of the battle-field. He breathed quietly under the cloth. They must have brought wellwater in a bucket; it was so cool.

The clean, milksmelling, shining girl who bathed his face with water turned away to moisten the cloth when he opened his eyes so that he had time to look up at the beams in the ceiling where the onions and ears of seedcorn and storage pouches were hung without order, and to feel the smooth coldness of the tabletop where they had put him down. Someone had taken off his rotten shirt.

Then the girl's pink face (the eyes blue and enormous and dilated at the sight of him, mouth trembling a little) was back between him and the ceiling and she hesitated with the cold wet cloth in her hands. I must look terrible, he thought.

He tried to smile.

—It's good, this, he said about the cool wet cloth.

His voice surprised him. She nodded, saying nothing, and stood still.

—Did I frighten you?

Again she nodded. —You were shouting, sir.

—I had a bad dream, he said, feeling inadequate.

She nodded, her eyes wide open and believing, as though she understood about bad dreams.

—It's something that happened to me. It is very foolish.

—It was so loud, she said.

She did not look as though she could believe that he could be afraid. A soldier and afraid? Oh, you could see her thinking. Fear was for the ordinary man. He smiled at her and she shook her head, also smiling.

—You laugh at me, Sir Soldier?

—No, I am not laughing.

But you are right: It is no good to be afraid of dreams. There are so many better things to fear every day.

She smiled, shaking her head. The yellow pigtails flew. You could see that she had laughed before at jokes made by a soldier. It was a bright girl-laugh that admitted nothing, consented to nothing, but did not forbid anything either. The laugh brought the older woman to the table where Berg lay grinning. The older woman was not laughing. She said something sharply to the girl in dialect and took the wet cloth from her.

—It's all right, Mother, Berg said, sitting up.

He did not want the attentions of the old woman, in whose hands the grey cloth was just a grey cloth and not comfort. Also he did not want her to worry about the girl and himself.

He got off the table and looked about the room.

The room took up all of the house. It was whitewashed up to the beams. A small back door led to a leanto addition, where, he supposed, the great bed would be. The floor was wooden but the boards had been laid directly on the clay. The boards, like the additional backroom, looked like an afterthought. They had been added as the peasants' wealth increased over the years. The furniture was simple. The long plain table stood on trestles flanked by benches. There were several chests that might be used for sitting, there were embroidered pillows and several handwoven tapestries on the walls. The hearth was deepset in the wall, blackened with smoke. All this was solidlooking and secure and permanent and Berg thought about the littered, crammed impermanence of his room in Nalewki where no one was ever at ease.

He asked about Bogacz. Where had he gone? The peasant said the Bogacz had gone to watch the Germans. Because there were now Germans in the fields. They had stopped in the village.

—He wants to know where they are and where they are going and what roads are still free. He wants to take you up to the mountain.

—I can't carry my poor friend up any mountain.

—You won't have to. He will soon be dead.

—Can we get him a priest?

—Our priest won't come, the peasant said, ashamed. There are such priests.

—I promised him a priest.

—He won't come. But you can pray for him.

—Oh no, Berg said. No. I can't do that. Are you sure my friend is still alive?

—Look for yourself.

The Walnut lay on some bedding near one of the chests. He appeared asleep. He did not seem to breathe, and at first Berg though that the soldier was dead. He looked at the old peasant, who shook his head and shrugged. There was not much the peasants could do for the wounded soldier. He had no right to be alive with such a wound. He would have died much sooner, Berg thought, if it had not been for the mass of fat which closed over the wound to stop the bleeding. The old man had kneaded bread into the wound and this had also helped. But the Walnut was unconscious and it was only after he put his ear against the slack mouth that Berg could hear a breath. The wound had a sharp rancid smell.

—It is the fat of a bear, the peasant said. It will bring the iron out of him. If he could drink it, it would be best. Then all the iron would come out and he would live, perhaps.

—I've heard about putting bread on a wound, but not bear fat, Berg said.

—We have always done so, the peasant said. The fat of a bear draws out the iron from the body. That is why you cannot kill a bear with iron but must use wood. Everyone knows this.

Berg nodded. It did not seem to matter and the Walnut would soon be dead no matter what was put upon his wound. Perhaps when all is hopeless a jar of bear fat is as good as anything else . . .

—How do you kill a bear with wood?

The peasant pointed to a set of objects in a corner: long spearlike poles with sharpened ends hardened in a fire. Berg had a sudden vision of the old man with his wooden spear and a German tank. Iron did not seem to touch those either.

—Do you have many bears here?

—There is still one.

—Have you hunted him with your spears?

—I am too old, but there are those who did.

—And did they kill him?

—Not yet. He is very cunning. But they will. And when he dies it will not be by any of these guns and bullets. It will be in the old way.

Berg became suddenly aware of chill on his naked chest and back among the many small hot islands of cuts and scratches and the purpling bruises. He looked for his uniform blouse but could not find it.

—Where is my coat? he said.

—We would not steal your coat, the peasant said. It must be washed and mended. And you must eat. You are very thin.

The peasant touched Berg's ribs with a finger like a root of a tree. Berg felt hunger then.

—Tell me, the peasant said. Did you kill a German?

—Yes.

The peasant nodded with grave satisfaction. He looked towards the big rifle with its brownstained bayonet propped against the hearth.

—They can be touched by iron?

—Yes, Berg said.

—Many have died in the woods. The crows have been flying there for ten days and last night we heard wolves. Are there many Germans?

—Yes.

—Why do they come?

—I don't know, Berg said. They come because they're Germans.

—Well, then they'll come here. What do you think?

—Your priest thought they would.

—Ah . . .

The peasant thought about the priest. He looked through the halfopen shutters to the priest's house. The old woman said something in dialect from beside the hearth and the peasant shrugged.

—Well, if they come, they come. (He looked at the black spears in the corner.) Others have come before. Many others, many times. But the only ones who stayed have been the dead. So it will be this time. It is always so. Still, you must go before the Germans come. Bogacz will take you safely to the mountain.

—Why to the mountain?

—That is where we go, the peasant said. In the last war we went there and in every war. Always a few go first, like Bogacz and you, and then others come and they grow strong and nobody can touch them and when they're strong enough they come back and then it is over. The mountain keeps them safe.

—Bogacz said nothing to me about any mountains.

—He said it to me. Where would you go if not to the mountain? The mountain keeps you safe until more men come.

—I cannot go there, Berg said. There would be nothing for him on the mountain. —The others can go if they want to, but not me.

—What others? This man who will soon be dead?

—Three others wait for us in the woods. They are soldiers. They were

460

with us in the battle in the quarry. Bogacz was going to take us through the forest towards Warsaw, as soon as we could find a way to get past the Germans.

—Ah, Warsaw, that is far away, the peasant said.

—That's where I want to go.

—Well, Bogacz will soon be back. He and another, a man called Gosin, who also wants to go up on the mountain. If you don't go maybe they'll carry the wounded one tonight. But it is strange that you don't wish to go up on the mountain.

—It's not my mountain, Berg said. That's all there is to it.

—It seems strange to me.

—Not to me, Berg said.

Then the old woman brought food to the table. There was a meal paste made of corn and flour and water, and a piece of thick pork sausage cased in the thin entrail of a pig, and a pitcher of sour milk and thick black bread and cheese, and radishes and sunflowerseeds in honey, and hard wheatcakes, and apples, and cold *pierogi* filled with cabbage; all piled on the same platter. Berg thought of his parents' horror if they could know what he ate and how. It did not matter, though. Eating according to a ritual could not make a man what he was not. The old woman motioned at his boots and trousers to show that he should take them off so that they also could be cleaned and mended. He stripped and dressed in clean white sun-and-water-smelling homespun the old woman brought. He ate the peasant's food.

While he ate, Bogacz and a young man came in. The tracker looked tired. His huntingcoat was held together by rough thongs with thorns thrust through them. He bobbed his head, politely, coming in.

—The Lord be praised.

—For centuries of centuries, the peasant replied gravely.

He motioned Bogacz towards the bench, where he sat down beside Berg. The tracker looked at Berg's peasant clothes and smiled a little. Berg pushed the meal bowl towards him and Bogacz helped himself after first looking at the peasant, who nodded consent.

The young man did not sit down. He was squat and broad and browned by the wind. He wore a town shirt without a collar and rough pants thrust into the tops of boots and a town suitcoat and a cap twisted over his right eye. He stood by the door, watchfully. The peasant couple did not look at him. The young girl looked once quickly, and as quickly away.

—How is the wounded man? the tracker asked. We have to leave before the Germans come.

—As you see.

The peasant nodded towards the Walnut. No sound of breathing came from the dark corner by the chest, but everyone knew that the dying soldier was still alive. The cold feeling that comes with death had not yet come into the room.

—Not good, eh?

—No. Not good.

—I think he will be dead soon, the young peasant said.

—Yes. Well, we must stay here until night, anyway. There are now Germans all around the village. Several have come in at the other end of the street. And one is coming this way.

—*Jezus Maria!* the old woman cried.

—Well, he might not come here.

—But what if he does?

—We will just have to wait and see. Wait and see.

They were quiet then, all of them, listening to the sounds outside: the clatter and roar of German trucks, calls and laughter. And then they heard the rapid steps of short hobnailed boots on the gravelstonepath. A German came up to the door and beat upon it with a pistolbutt.

The old woman gave one cry (—*Jezus-Maria!*) and dropped the bowl of meal and the girl rose with both her hands about her mouth and the old man said: —All Spirits Praise the Lord (in awe), and all these sounds were one.

The peasants sat as though frozen. Strange wooden figures painted white by the fallen whitewash: the old man with limp hands like hams beside his thighs, the woman with her eyes wide on her husband and lips moving. Gosin, the young man who had come in with Bogacz, stood with his back flat against the door, as though to bar it, Bogacz was strangely shrunken with narrowed eyes and teeth bared; the girl was motionless and with head cocked as though listening to a voice somewhere in the ceiling. And himself. How do I look? Berg felt his broken nails in his palms.

The girl moved first. She picked up Berg's uniformcoat and boots and threw them quickly in the chest. Gosin woke next. He picked up the rifle and the bayonet and looked for a place for them. The peasant took them from him and pushed them up the chimney. Bogacz went to the shutters. Berg did nothing. He did not know what he should do. Death was behind the door, in the loud street.

Soon now there will be boots on gravel on the path outside. Hobnailed, loud. Then fists on doors. A riflebutt perhaps.

Raus!

What is *raus?*

It means *outside:* a command.

Outside what? And why?

And *who* outside?

Me?

Why me? I have done nothing!

None of this has anything to do with me. What has this war of *goyim* got to do with me? Let them kill each other. Let the Ulankos and the Malys and the Walnuts die. Maybe they have a reason. I do not want to die. I did not make the war. Whoever heard of Jews making war on anyone? And why should a German wish to hurt a Jew? Didn't the Jewry of the German Empire strip themselves for the Other War? A Jew invented poison gas, synthetic benzine. Ask anybody. I ask you. Whoever heard of such a thing?

Ah, but (Berg thought) this time it will not be two elderly policemen.

It is one thing to say *gowno* to two elderly policemen.

It is one thing to stand up in a cabbagefield with someone else.

It is one thing to ask What am I? and What will I be? when I think that I will have a chance to be anything.

It is one thing to speculate about this and that, to say that I am this and not the other or perhaps something else, and throw off the *mycka* and lose the cap with the silver eagle when it seems convenient, and eat meat and milk off the same plate, and have dreams about a battlefield, and turn my back first on this and then on the other, while walking on the yellowsafe path between two choices.

It is one thing! A rejection of one thing is not the choosing of another. But this *is* another.

I have run out of yellowsafe. I cannot turn back.

I had no choice about what I *lived* as. No real choice. You live as what seems best; identities can be convenient to the moment.

But you must *die* as some particular thing.

I THE CONQUEROR

The room was shadowed with the shutters closed, but Erich thought there were several people in the room. He heard the silence of multiple breaths held in anticipation. White eyes were turned towards him from the shadows. There was a sound that was half sigh and half sob, a curious creaking mutter as of something dying, and this sound did not seem to come from anyone in the room but from the house itself.

Ghosts now? Old rafters, Erich thought, reversing the pistol.

—Open the shutters, he said. Get light, *macht schnell!*

But they did not move. Someone spoke in a low voice, a cascade of Polish that Erich did not understand.

—Silence! Speak German!

He thought that very shortly he would start to laugh. He did not think that he would manage to control himself. It was so easy! This was what was needed. A loud voice and a pistol and a man was God. But it would hardly do to laugh.

—Open the shutters, he shouted, and when no one moved he turned and smashed the glass of the nearest window with his pistolbutt.

At once a young peasant began to push the shutters open.

That is the way!

They understand the sound of breaking glass, these animals.

Light came into the room. It was like a blow with a fist. It flooded the dark corners. Now he could see them. Several men and two women frozen like white statues in their fear. The man who opened the shutters was young. He had swung the door open so quickly that the last of Erich's pistolblows had struck him on the shoulder. Now he stood beside the shutters with one hand curled about his collarbone, his eyes low. He might be in his early twenties; you could not tell with these Polish peasants. Of the three other men in the room, one was old and gnarled. His hands hung like red meat beside his thighs. One was still older and drier and more wrinkled, and browner than the others; a little man dressed in a shabby huntingcoat with the elbows out. He had the hard look of a woodsman, but his eyes were bland. He smiled and looked relaxed and infinitely dangerous. The third man was not a peasant, despite his homespun clothes. He was thin-faced. His hands were delicate and long despite their dirt. There was something not quite right about his face. It was like a composite of two faces: The upper portion was lighter than the lower, as though a line had been drawn across his eyebrows, above the black eyes. His head was shaven.

Of course! Erich pointed the Erstalt at the shaven man.

A soldier! Only a soldier wears the double face where the peak of the military cap holds off the sun. Erich stared at the thin face of his enemy. Now in civilian clothes, he could be shot.

But there was something else about this face that stirred curiosity. It was . . . too thin. Too sensitive. The eyes too black and the lips too full and the lids curving . . .

A Jew! Erich laughed, relaxing. No one else in the room laughed with him, but the thin man in the huntingcoat chuckled a little. The young man with the injured collarbone sucked air through his teeth.

—You! *Jude!* Erich said. You understand German?

—Yes, the Jew said.

—*Bist du Soldat?*

—*Jawohl,* Herr Offizier . . .

—Where is your uniform?

The Jew did not say anything. He looked at the ground. He would know that he could be shot as a spy, and that he probably would be. The peasants in the room could also be shot; first because they hid an enemy soldier, then because they hid a spy, and then because they hid a Jew. They could be shot three times for hiding one man.

The moral of this lesson is care in the selection of the man you hide.

—What are you doing here?

The Jew said nothing. His thin hands hung straight down. He looked sideways at the floor. Following his gaze, Erich saw a large mound of bedding on the floor. It was halfhidden by a chest with wooden platters on it. The mound moved. Erich walked up to it and pulled back the bedding and saw a huge man dying under it. His chest was stained red and strangely caved-in under twisted linen. The face was bloodless. The eyes glazed over as Erich looked into them.

—You brought this thing here?

The Jew nodded. He looked sadly at the corpse of the fat man. Erich threw the bedding over the dead man's head.

—You should have saved yourself the trouble, Jew. He is dead.

—He was not dead when I brought him here, the Jew said quietly.

—What did you bring him here for?

—I could not leave him in the woods.

The Jew nodded towards the west, where the mountain was. The mountain and the dark woods where men had run screaming.

—You were there?

—Yes.

—And this?

—He was also there.

Erich felt the rise of familiar nausea. He pointed the Erstalt at the thin Jew. But he did not fire.

Something about the stillness of the men inside the room stopped him from shooting. No one moved, but it seemed as though everyone had taken a step forward. They were suddenly close. Erich backed to the door. He moved his pistol from side to side. Still no one moved. The Jew stood at attention with his back straight. Erich was surprised to see the posture of the Jew. He stood as though a general was about to pin a medal on that thin concave chest. The thought of Jews and medals made him laugh. The laugh was loud in the still room, but no one else laughed. The bearing of the thin Jew angered Erich. Who was this Jew to stand erect?

—Down on your knees, Jew. Pray.

The Jew shrugged then: a burlesque imitation of the Shrug, the Gesture of the Jew, as though he wished his Jewishness underlined and remembered.

—I do not kneel to pray, he said quietly.

Erich looked at him carefully.

—Pray for your friend, he said.

—He does not need my prayers, the Jew said. He is dead.

—Pray for yourself, then. You will soon be dead.

—So will you, the Jew said, his eyes closed.

—I can kill you now.

—If not you now then another like you later on. —You know that much, do you?

The Jew nodded. He opened his eyes. He looked at Erich without an expression. —Yes, he said. You must kill all the Jews and all the Poles and burn all the bodies and scatter all the ashes in the wind. Because if there is one Jew or one Pole left alive he will kill you someday. If there is one arm that has fingers with which to strangle you, it will strangle you. There is no end to what you have begun.

—Long speech, Jew, Erich said. It may be your last. Kneel and pray and I will not kill you. Yes. This is not what I thought war would be like, but I am learning about war. You and your carrion friend taught me about it. I am learning well. We Germans learn by our mistakes, you see. We learn remarkably well. I do not think that I would hesitate to kill you now.

The Jew shrugged.

—I *must* kill you, Jew.

Again the shrug. Erich began to sweat.

—Don't you see that? I must now. Aren't you afraid of me?

—Yes, the Jew said with dignity. I am afraid.

—But not afraid enough to kneel and pray?

—Perhaps enough even for that. I do not know. But it does not seem worth the trouble to find out. Besides, it will be prayer enough for him when you are killed.

Erich stared at the thin Jew and the Jew stared calmly at the longbarreled Erstalt. Erich lowered the pistol, looking at the Jew.

—I do not understand you, Jew, he said. Then a suspicion touched him. Are you a Communist?

—No, the Jew said.

—You have the dedication.

—I am a Jew.

—What is that? That is nothing. No one can believe in being a Jew.

—I don't know about that. I have only begun to discover what I am.

—No man can die as a Jew, Erich said. You must be something else. No one has fought as a Jew or died as a Jew for two thousand years. You can die as a Pole. You can die as a Communist. But you cannot be willing to die simply as a Jew.

—I do not wish to die at all.

—Then will you kneel? Kneel, Jew!

—If I knelt I would not die as anything.

Erich looked at him carefully, as though to remember each feature of this man whose features were not extraordinary, not unusual, marked by neither zeal or madness.

—What is your name?

—Million, the Jew said.

—Million what? What Million?

—Million nothing. It is from a Polish poem. I understand now what this poem is about.

But this was contrary to the laws of nature, Erich thought in the shadowed room. There are no such Jews. Europe is standing on her head. What can a German do in such a Europe? Suddenly he knew he would not kill the Jew. He was sick of all of them and wanted to get out. He heard the woodsman chuckle and turned on him.

—You are amused?

The woodsman did not understand and spread his hands, grinning. The Jew spoke to him in Polish and the small man answered. The small man talked for a long time, smiling pleasantly at Erich.

—Talk German, Erich said. Tell him to talk in German!

—He can't, the Jew said.

—Then tell him not to talk at all.

The Jew said something to the woodsman and the man stopped talking. But somehow the atmosphere in the room had changed. The woodsman and the Jew watched Erich carefully. The young man who had opened doors and shutters began to whistle through his teeth. Erich wondered what the woodsman had said to the others. He looked at the bland, deceptive eyes of the small man. The old peasant sighed and sat down heavily on the wooden chest beside the corpse. Now the older of the women began to mutter.

—What is she saying?

—Prayers, the Jew said.

Now the young peasant leaned against the wall. Something had been decided in the room. Erich knew. He felt as though he stood alone in a cage of tigers. He backed towards the door until he was outside. There the sun had dipped. Soon night would come: the time for cool rest after the day's white sun. Erich walked slowly towards the plum orchard. He thought about the Jews and Poles who would have to be killed. An enormous task. He thought about the dangerous bland smile of the woodsman and the strangling hands the Jew had talked about.

I should have killed them, he thought. He could still order a detail to take them in. It would reflect well on him. They were harboring a spy, a soldier who was out of uniform. But he was confused. Somehow it did not seem right to do the thing that way. Not with the kind of Jew he had suddenly come upon. He would bide his time, and when the moment arrived for the right move he would see it clearly. Meanwhile, there was nothing they could do to him, nowhere they could go that he could not find them.

He lay down in the orchard to get some sleep before he went on duty. The night would be cold. He felt hunger returning and remembered why he had gone into the village in the first place.

—Nickel! he shouted. Bring me an apple!

But Nickel had not come back from the apple orchard, Schindlecker said.

—What is he up to? Is he burying that fruit for the winter?

A young SS giggled dutifully. Schindlecker grinned.

—He wants to load up for the future, Herr Fahnrich. We told him that where we are going there will be no apples.

—And where are we going?

Schindlecker laughed.

—To hell eventually, Ensign. Anyway, that Nickel is so stupid. He will believe anything, I think.

—Do you have food? I am hungry.

—I have the M-A paste.

Erich told him to find a monkey and put the meat paste where the Army's lore said it had come from. The SS laughed. This laughter was a quiet, respectful sound. Erich stretched out and closed his eyes. But sleep eluded him.

Day ended and night began, and with the passing of the day the chill of night returned. It was a gradual transformation, this progress from heat to the night chill: a series of even steps leading in measured cadence from light into darkness.

In the village the laughter of the children ceased.

You would not think that they would have anything to laugh about. The sound of laughter in this burned, gutted, devastated land was an obscenity. But these were peasant children, he supposed, and they had never seen machines of such size and in such quantities, and this sight was a wondrous thing, and the smells were new, and the children, who at first had watched their arrival with small whimpers and then ran away, had returned, afraid but curious, and by evening their laughter was a constant, curious chirping across the wide fields.

As the day ended, this sound also ended as though stepped upon.

There were quick calls of women: a singsong cadence.

Tallow candles began to flicker in the windows and then the patrols shouted and a pane of glass broke somewhere up the street and a fist hammered distantly upon a door and there was a shot.

Soon all the lights were out.

Erich looked towards a house where a young woman suddenly appeared on the porch holding a lamp in one hand, the other hand held overhead against the carved upswing of the beams. Erich moved towards her. He felt a great desire to talk to a woman, to sit down behind a table spread for him alone. He was aware of the night and of himself in it. He wanted to tell her not to be afraid, that he was a soldier and an officer and made no war on women. In war everyone is innocent, he wanted to say. And then he recognized the house behind the woman. It was the house where he had gone, where the Jew and the woodsman and the silent peasants had defied him. He could smell the rancid grease of animal fat smeared on the hinges of the door and saw again the woodsman and the Jew and the sullen youth and the old peasant man and the old woman. He did not want to see them again. This was not the moment. Later, perhaps, when he went on duty, he would bring a patrol and arrest the Jew. Arresting the old people would make the girl agreeable to conversation. She'd be a lot less reserved with the old man and the woman in the guardhouse. It was a pleasing thought. He thought of Adrianne's parents in a guardhouse with, say, Kuno Saal in charge of them. Adrianne would not laugh then. Not at all. Adrianne would be agreeable again. And when he was done with her he would give her to Huneker to play with. Who knows, perhaps Huneker would be grateful.

He looked at the woman on the porch and grinned, thinking he would be back with the patrol. She lifted the lamp a little and saw him. She backed away and closed the door between them. He heard the rattle of the bolt and he was alone.

Ha! Erich smiled.

They learn, all right, if you teach them well. The course has just begun. We have been here only half a day, a couple of weeks in the country, and already the Poles know the difference between the *Brustvogel* of the Wehrmacht and the *Armvogel* of the SS. The bird on the shoulder made a man alone. So be it.

He walked down the darkened village street wrapped in his greatcoat, the weight of his helmet a comfort to his head, the machinepistol bumping lightly against his back and hip. Sentries stood silent. Some stamped their feet.

He was halfway between the house and the appleorchard when the first thin cry came from the night ahead.

It was the wail of a young man's horror. He listened to it, then went on. He checked the sentryposts in the artillery park and the men outside the small wood where the tanks were hidden and the machinegun posts dug around the village. Reports had warned that the Poles had taken to fighting at night, when the German planes and tanks could do them no harm. Most of the sentries were awake. Some were not. Schindlecker was sleeping. He made the most jokes about the sleepiness of Bar, and now that Bar was dead Schindlecker was the champion sleeper. Erich kicked Schindlecker and wrote his name in the discipline book. Sooner or later there would be discipline. There would be clean vehicles and spotless uniforms with which to impress the foreign correspondents.

And then the shout came from the appleorchard.

There had been several calls during the night. Some laughter. Sound was not unusual. But this shout had a quality of terror.

Erich began to run towards the apple orchard. He knew, as he ran, that this shout and what prompted it had something to do with him and the woodsman and the Jew. He thought that perhaps nothing had happened after all: a young replacement scared by a cow. But he did not believe it. He was sure that now the right moment had come.

The young replacement stared with enormous eyes. Nickel's corpse lay half in and half out of the dry creekbed. A ruptured bag spilled apples. The

468

dead man's fingers were buried in the apples. Out of his head protruded something like a wooden lance.

The young replacement said: —Oh my good God. My sweet God. He trembled. He opened his mouth to scream again and Erich hit him quickly across the face: a sharp slap expertly delivered.

—Calm yourself, SSmann, he said. Did you see them? Which way did they go?

The soldier shook his head.

—You saw nothing?

Again the negative motion.

—What are you doing here?

—Apples, the soldier said. I came . . . for some.

Another apple-eater! Erich grinned and knelt beside the corpse. He felt great excitement. He touched the white face of the corpse. It was still warm and flexible. The upturned eyes were incredibly surprised.

The wooden spear had been driven into Nickel's mouth as though to muzzle him. Its point passed through the soldier's head into the ground. The shaft stuck out like an enormous tongue pointed derisively at the sky. Greedy old Nickel looked as though he had been trying to swallow the spear. So much for apple-eater Nickel, Erich thought. His last meal proved indigestible. But there were questions to be asked and not much time for them if a pursuit was to be launched for the murderers.

—You, SSmann, what is your name? When did you find him? When did you come here? Quick, man. Stop mewling and report!

The young man said his name was Bauer and that he was a *Waffengrenadier* of the 2d Company and that he was eighteen years old and that he liked apples and that he had come into the orchard only two or three minutes earlier and that shortly after his arrival he had seen the wooden spear against the light of the moon. He had not seen the dead man underneath the spear until he was almost on top of him. That was what had startled him. He had not expected anything like that. He was not in the habit of losing his nerve (he wished the Ensign to believe) but he had not expected to find what he did.

—And then I gave the alarm, he said. I shouted to give the alarm.

Erich laughed.

—I heard your shout, Bauer, he said. The Poles in the next village probably heard it. And you did not see anyone else here? For example, did you see three men? One small and dressed like a woodsman. One a Jew. One a young peasant. Nobody like that?

SSmann Bauer said that he had seen no such men. Nobody at all . . . except him. He had met no one on his way into the appleorchard.

—All right, Bauer. Very good. Erich was thinking swiftly. —Do you know Lieutenant Saal?

Kuno Saal had been made acting Unterstumführer to replace Libesis. Bauer nodded and put his hand instinctively to his throat. Oh, they would know about Saal, Erich thought. He had already managed to become a legend.

—Well, Bauer, go into the village and find the lieutenant. Tell him about this and tell him to come here. Tell him that if he comes quickly there is a chance to catch the murderers. They can't have gone far, and since they must

469

move quietly they will have to move slowly and carefully. A strong patrol could catch them before daybreak. Tell him I know the way they've gone. Can you do that, Bauer?

The soldier nodded. He was much impressed.

—Tell Saal to hurry. And then go to the tank squadron of Scholtz and find Sergeant Huneker. Tell him to come here, but do not tell him that I sent you for him. Do you understand?

—*Jawohl*, Herr Fähnrich.

Bauer stood erect.

—Then execute the order.

—*Zum Befehl!*

The young soldier set off for the village at a run. How much of this haste was zeal for his orders and how much a desire to get away from the corpse of Nickel, Erich did not know.

He sat down beside Nickel and made himself comfortable. He picked up an apple. The fruit was ripe and cold.

From where he sat, looking across the corpse with its stiff wooden tongue stuck out at the stars, he saw the valley with its black hulls of abandoned vehicles and burned-out bombers and, farther west, the blackness of the woods and the Bald Mountain. In moonlight the mountain was white, streaked with black where the pine struggled upwards.

He thought the killers must have gone towards the mountain. If they came from the village to the appleorchard and then continued in the same direction they would be heading for the mountain. Poor stupid Nickel must have come across them while they were creeping through the appleorchard. He could imagine what happened then: a startled cry, black forms leaping up from the ground, the swift club descending, and then the wooden stake driven expertly into the crying mouth. Poor stupid Nickel.

He looked in the creekbed for Nickel's machinepistol and did not find it. The killers must have taken it. He tried to imagine which of them had the machinepistol now and thought that the Jew was the likely one. He had been a soldier. He would know more about the operation of an MP Feuer. Erich had no doubt about the identity of the killers.

They would be moving now into the valley on their way to the safety of the mountain. Quick halftracks could go after them into the valley and bring them back dead. If Kuno Saal led the pursuit the killers would die quickly. They would not live to speak about Erich's failure to arrest them, even if anyone gave them the chance to do so. With Kuno Saal they would have no chance, but to make sure they kept their silence he would go along. This would leave only their accomplices: the old peasant couple and the girl. Huneker could be trusted to take care of them. Erich thought about the girl with a touch of pity. She had looked pretty. Ah, but you cannot make an omelet without breaking eggs.

But the best part of this would come afterwards. It would be walking into Dietrich's quarters and quietly reporting and calmly telling him about the murder of poor stupid Nickel, the dispatch of a pursuing party and the destruction of the terrorists and the arrest of the accomplices, all in one quick, efficient movement. Dietrich would ask no questions. He had not spoken to Erich since the afternoon in Kielce and had promoted Kuno Saal into the vacancy left by Libesis, and what would he say now, faced by this marvelous efficiency? Particularly if something should also chance to happen to Kuno? Erich laughed. He looked at Nickel fondly. Nickel had made all this possible. Poor Nickel. A good man. He should be properly avenged.

Ah, Libesis, Erich thought, laughing, if you could only see me. He too had meditated in an appleorchard and was dead: uncorked and thoroughly deflated. So farewell, Nickel. Farewell, Libesis. You are dead and I am alive. This means that you were wrong and I am right. It is the only proof.

Erich got up, toying with the apple. He walked a few paces away from the corpse, looking down the valley. He looked at his watch. It was ten-fifteen. There would be time enough that night for everything.

Now from the village came the sound of voices, orders shouted, and the beat of many feet running towards the orchard. Clearly the young replacement had told his story not only to Saal. Soon there would be many men in the orchard. This was all the better.

Erich took his machinepistol off his shoulder and pointed it towards the valley. He fired three quick bursts. The MP Feuer shuddered like a thing alive. There was a pleasant reek of cordite. The footsteps of the running men were close. Then Kuno Saal was with him. His white face was strained with anxiety; his whisper gurgled with excitement.

—Are they dead? Did you kill them?

—No. I thought I saw some men running in the valley, but they were too far.

—I can't see anything, Saal said. (He stared suspiciously into the moonlit valley.) Are you sure you saw three men there? I cannot see them.

—Oh, I saw more than that, Erich said, controlling his laughter. There were at least a dozen.

—That soldier said there were three. Two peasants and a Jew. He was positive about that.

—He saw two peasants and a Jew?

—That's what he said. How do I know what the fool saw or didn't see? He said two peasants and a Jew. And you say a dozen?

—Perhaps they had more men waiting in the valley, Herr Untersturmführer, Erich said gravely. Perhaps they have a reinforcement.

—Do you think so? Good. If you saw a dozen, there may be two dozen or three. I ordered a squad in a carrier to chase two peasants and a Jew, but if there is a platoon of them I must take more men. I shall take two platoons in four carriers and three armoredcars. Put your platoon on firstdegree alert, Sonnerling. We leave in ten minutes.

Kuno Saal had become most formal since his promotion, even though it was only to an acting rank. He did not use first names anymore. Erich had to turn away to hide his smile.

—I regret, Herr Untersturmführer, but I cannot come.

—What? What is this?

—Duty, Herr Untersturmführer. I am the company duty officer tonight. Kuno's voice broke. He coughed, grimacing.

—Ah, but I need you. You know what they look like. You saw them. This time you'll go along all right, and you'll do your duty. I'll see to it that when we catch those bastards you will get to kill them. Personally, do you understand?

—*Jawohl,* Herr Untersturmführer.

—What are you twisting your face away for, Sonnerling? Are you going to puke?

—Oh no sir. No sir.

—Well then. Control yourself. And take care of that! Kuno pointed to the corpse with the toe of his boot. I'll alert your men.

—*Zum Befehl!*

There were now several dozen men in the orchard and more were coming. They looked at Nickel with the wooden spear protruding from his mouth. The stake was thick. It made Nickel's mouth enormous. It looked as though the dead man's mouth stretched from his nose to his throat. Ants mounted the sides of the dead man's face and walked hopelessly around the stake, trying to find a way in.

—Fahnrich . . .

It was the tall thin sergeant who had led the men outside the priest's house.

—What do you want?

—Maybe we ought to take that thing out of him. We ought to get him to the village and bury him. What do you think?

—No, Erich said.

—We ought to take that wooden thing out of his mouth.

—No. Leave him as he is. I know what I am doing.

—Yes sir, the sergeant said, looking at Erich curiously. Erich hid his smile.

So sorry, Nickel, but we need you yet. You have to keep your mouth plugged up until Dietrich can see you. The gallant Obersturmführer must be made so furious that he does not take the time to ask any questions. Later we shall unplug you, Nickel. We shall bury you. But for now keep your mouth tight around your last meal.

He waited for Huneker while the crowd of soldiers shifted uneasily around Nickel's corpse. Soon the Scharführer came through the crowd. Erich beckoned to him. Huneker's eyes were flat and his mouth tight but he came readily enough. He squatted beside Erich away from the others. He looked from Erich to the corpse and inspected the spear. He did not say anything. Erich grinned.

—Well, Huneker, what do you think of it?

The sergeant spat and looked at Erich with contempt.

—Is it pretty enough for you, Huneker? How do you like it?

The sergeant picked at the long pistol scar across his cheek. He stared sideways at Erich. He spat again and Erich laughed a little.

—You'd better be careful where you spit. And how about a little respect for an officer?

—Shit, Huneker said. What are you up to, Sonnerling?

—Nothing, Huneker. Here is a German soldier dead and mutilated. He has to be avenged. All these men have seen him and they will expect some kind of vengeance. We must not disappoint them. We must not fail them, Huneker. Isn't that right?

—Why ask me? Tomorrow Dietrich will burn down the village and hang everybody in it. And nothing you can do, little Christ, will change that.

—But will he, Huneker? Since that little affair in Kielce the Wehrmacht is keeping a sharp eye on things like that. There isn't going to be anything like that happening while we are attached to the Wehrmacht. Dietrich will scream, but he will not do anything as long as we are under Army operational control. So think about that, Huneker. Use your bird brains for a moment, will you?

—Come to the point, Huneker said.

—Be patient, Huneker. And a little careful about how you talk to me. Things have changed, Huneker. I now understand what Dietrich was talking about in Kielce. I speak your language, you damn animal. So take care, Huneker, because the next time I draw a pistol on you it won't be to break your ugly face.

Huneker laughed abruptly.

—You're getting handy with that pistol, aren't you? It's you who should be careful, *bubi*. I might just take that Erstalt from you and stick it up your ass.

—Well, well, still angry, Huneker? I might have to preach a sermon after all.

—Well, you are good at that, the sergeant said. Now what do you want?

—Your respect, Huneker, Erich said. The respect of a bloody animal. You are my comrade, Huneker. I love you like a brother.

—I will spit into your coffin, Huneker said. (His voice had lost conviction.) I will kiss a Jew before I shake your hand.

—You are a bitter man, Huneker, Erich said.

This is how it must be in a Spanish bullring, Erich thought: The animal is goaded into futile charges, its strength expended, vitality wasted, the flickering cape as elusive as ever and the matador unpierced. I must ask Dietrich about the Spanish bullrings. I have never seen them. There is no climbing worth the journey into Spain, and so I never went there. Who knows, I may go there yet, with our SS Panzerkorps Germania. Untouched and irresistible as a matador. The darts have sunk deep into Huneker's bullneck and the lances have opened up his sides and with each snort his fury is less. He is bewildered and no longer sure. Oh, he still charges, but soon he will stand as peaceful as a milk cow.

—I have work for you, Huneker.

—I will not work for you.

Still snorting? Still pawing the ground? Huneker's replies now have the automatic anger of a gramophone. He does not know what is happening to him and no longer charges. If there were time, I could bring him to his knees. But there is no time.

The sound of Saal's small army burst over the village. The carriers and the armoredcars and the running men. The clash of riflebutts on steelplate. Motors. Nailstudded boots climbing over metal. It would be time to join them soon. Erich had to hurry. His watch showed seven minutes before midnight.

—Listen to me, you pig, you Huneker, he said quietly. There is a house in the village next to the house of the priest. It is the second house from the end of the street as you come from the orchard. Is this clear so far?

The sergeant nodded. He said nothing.

—In this house there is an old peasant, a woman and a girl. The girl is young, Huneker. Are you interested? I understand you like young girls. But more important than that, Huneker, is a certain corpse you'll find in the house. It is the corpse of a Polish soldier. And if you search the house you may find his rifle. So now what have you, Huneker? Not an old peasant and a woman and a girl but three spies hiding an enemy soldier. It is true that the enemy is dead, but we do not have to say that you found him dead. He has not been dead long and he may still be fresh enough for this deception. So there you have it, Huneker. The brave Scharführer Huneker, alerted by the most efficient Fähnrich Sonnerling, searches the house of suspected terrorists following the brutal murder of a German soldier. In the course of the search he discovers a sharpshooter left by the Poles to assassinate the German commander. The brave Scharführer kills the sharpshooter. Preferably with a handgrenade. You will see the reason for the handgrenade when you see the corpse. He arrests a man and woman and, possibly, the girl, although that is left to his discretion. In due time he brings the prisoner or prisoners to company headquarters. He brings the corpse and other evidence. I suggest that you collect some of the Polish rifles the men picked up as souvenirs. They will make excellent evidence. And so what do we have now, Huneker? We have poor stupid Nickel who must be avenged because the men have seen him. We have the Wehrmacht insisting on court-martial and other legalistic nonsense. We have Dietrich screaming for a victim and we have two authentic spies and terrorists caught by you personally within an hour of their crime. There is also the matter of the girl, but there may be no girl in the house if the brave Scharführer does not say there was. What do you say now, Huneker? Come, come, you were quick enough to speak before. Speak up, you animal!

Huneker did not say anything. He stared at Erich with dull eyes.

—Well, Huneker?

—*Jawohl*, Herr Fähnrich.

He got to his feet.

—Very well. Execute the order.

Huneker saluted and marched off through the orchard. Erich laughed.

Lights were still showing in the windows of the house where Dietrich was quartered. A peasant featherbed had been pushed into the windows, but it was too short and lamplight glowed in the unprotected spaces. Erich turned in there. Behind him four men struggled with the corpse of Nickel. The spear kept tripping up the men. Nobody wanted to hold the dead man's head with the spear in it.

—Well, Sonnerling, what is it? Dietrich said.

Erich told him.

—Take a platoon! Take two! They must be caught.

They will be, Erich said and told what he had done: the orders and arrangements for Saal's expedition. The search for other terrorists in the village, certain to succeed. But now he had to go, if he was permitted. Because it was his man, after all, who had been murdered. One of his own SS. A brother from his own platoon. He had to be avenged and Erich would do it.

He left the hut and Nickel's corpse and Dietrich and ran to the roaring carriers. He smiled broadly. Later, he thought, I will laugh. But not yet. There will be time for laughing when it is all done. He smiled all the way through the valley and hummed a little and was immensely pleased when he finally followed his men into the cool, calm green of the forest.

Tuesday, September the nineteenth

I THE WOODSMAN

The hill that Bogacz chose to fight on was shaped a little like a burial mound, and from the beginning Gosin did not like the look of it. It was, he said, too much like a grave.

—It will not bring us luck, he said now.

The Germans had been close behind them since the killing of the apple-eating German, and although this hill was not the best possible hill, it was the only one that they could reach in time. At that, it had been close, what with the weight of the machinegun and the ammunition and the handgrenades that the three soldiers brought. Bogacz was very pleased about the machinegun. He had a great respect for mechanical things.

—Luck or no luck, it will have to serve, Bogacz said. There is nowhere else that we can go with the German so close. Perhaps after we fight him here a little he will go away and we can go to another part of the mountain.

—We will not go anywhere from here except headfirst, said the soldier who had the machinegun.

—How do you know this? said the little soldier. If we hold out until night we could get away.

—And if your auntie had four wheels she would be a tramcar, the oldest soldier said. They've got us here all right, on this shitty hill, and nobody is coming off it until the Germans carry us all down.

The big soldier, the one who had not been in the battle but who had joined them later, laughed. He shook his head.

—It might not be so bad, the little soldier said. Berg is down there somewhere with the German rifle.

He said he thought Berg could attack the Germans' rear.

—Berg is halfway to Warsaw now, said the oldest soldier. Don't count on Berg to do anything. We are here, I tell you, and we are staying here. Tell them about that, old man. Am I wrong?

475

—We have your machine, Bogacz said, looking at the machinegun. There are plenty of bullets for it and for all the rifles. We have the little bombs to throw. Perhaps the German will not want to come up here when we have all that.

—And perhaps the English will bring a battleship to help us, the machinegunner said. And perhaps I will grow two wings and be an airplane.

—One must believe in the best, the little soldier said.

Bogacz sighed and moved closer to Gosin so that both could look down between the rocks into the clearing and the path that led into the clearing from the other side. The Germans would use that path to get to the clearing. They could hear the Germans on the lower path.

—What do you think, *Bogaczu?* Gosin said. Do you think that it will be as they say?

—I don't know, Bogacz said. The soldier Berg is down there somewhere. He has the German *maszynka* and knows how to use it.

Gosin thought a moment. —Is it true that he is a Jew? Do you know anything about that?

—I don't know, Bogacz said.

—If he is, then we cannot trust him. But perhaps he isn't?

—I don't know. He did well enough at the battle in the woods.

—You also did well, *Bogaczu.* The others told me.

—I do not think I killed anybody, though. I shot too quickly.

—I think you killed the apple-eating German when you hit him. He fell on his face, and that is a sign.

—No, I wounded him. I heard him moan before you struck him with the spear.

—I wish I knew about the other soldier, Gosin said. I wish I knew if he is a Jew.

—I do not think he is, Bogacz lied. He liked Gosin and did not want to worry the younger man. —And he did well in the battle and in the village when the German came. If there is something that can be done he will do it.

—I hope so, Gosin said. This will not be easy.

—It is an ambush, that is all. They are not difficult if you know the mountain.

—I hope so.

—You will see.

But he did not believe it.

If there had been hope of help from anywhere it had vanished with the disappearance of the Jew. The Jew had told him in the orchard that he would not go with the others to the mountain. They had just started for the woods, where they were to meet the other three soldiers who had come with the Fat Soldier and the Jew after the battle in the quarry, and Gosin, who had been wounded by the apple-eating German, was tired and fell back a little. Then the Jew told Bogacz that he would not go with them.

—*I am not one of you,* he said. *I cannot go with you.*

At first Bogacz did not understand what the soldier meant. He thought

476

that, as a townsman, the soldier would not feel safe on the mountain, and he tried to tell the soldier that the mountain would protect them all. Had it not done that for the animals? But the soldier said that he would not go with him and the others.

—*Down in the village . . . you know?* the soldier said. *I thought the German officer was going to kill me.*

—*I thought so too,* Bogacz said, waiting for the rest.

—*I wanted him to kill me. I did not want to live. I have lived as many things, and it was convenient. But when it comes to dying, I have to decide what I am so that I can die as some one thing and not one of many. Is this too difficult for you to understand?*

—*No,* Bogacz said.

It was not difficult. Each animal died in a different way according to what it was. It would not do for a bear to die like an eagle.

—*Where can you do it, then? Is there a place where Jews fight?* he asked.

—*We will make a place.*

—*What will you tell the others? They will be angry. They might want to kill you.*

—*I will say nothing. And you will say nothing. But I want you to know why I will not go with you to the mountain.*

Bogacz said nothing then, and he said nothing when they met the others. Their names were Kublarz and Maly and Kula, and they were very tired. They had brought a machinegun and a sack of small bombs like iron eggs. They had not eaten anything but roots and berries since the battle in the quarry. They ate all the food Bogacz, the Jew and Gosin had brought from the village, and it was as they ate that the Germans found them. The German officer fired his small machine too soon and gave them warning. It was enough time to send the three soldiers up the path to the hill in the clearing where they were to set up the big machine and to make the ambush. Bogacz said this to them, then shot quickly at the German who was closest, and aimed at one of the others but, before he could shoot him too, the Jew fired with the small machine they had taken from the German they had killed in the orchard. The German fell. The remaining Germans hid behind the trees. Another ran back down the path calling to his people.

—*Perhaps this is the place where Jews fight?* Bogacz said then. He grinned at the other.

The Jew laughed. —*No. But we will find a place.*

—*Go then. Before other Germans come.*

—*Goodbye, tracker. Good luck.*

—*And to you, Jew.*

Then the Jew was gone. . . .

Bogacz wished that the Jew had not left them in the pitchmaker's hut. The Jew was very good with the German *maszynka.* He could do damage to the Germans, especially in the dark. But the Jew spoke as though he meant everything he said, and Bogacz did not think there would be any help from him. Now he lay on top of the tombshaped hill in the clearing and waited for the

Germans to come and listened to the soldiers talk about the Germans and about the chance they had or did not have of coming down the hill alive.

At first it will be easy, Bogacz thought. It will be just another ambush in the forest. The German will come and we will shoot him well. If luck is with us, we will manage to kill several Germans before they know what is killing them. Then the Germans will lie down around the hill and wait for help. They will send for one of the big machines, perhaps, the grey boxlike things that crawl across the ground.

Bogacz did not know if these machines could climb up the mountain. The Germans will get one of those to get up the hill, he thought. Or they will call for one of their airplanes. They have so many of them that surely they can get one to come to the clearing. Or they will send to the village in the valley for one of their mortars.

Bogacz had been at the quarry long enough to know about mortars. He had been very much impressed by them in the Zagnanski Pass. Also, they frightened him. There was no way to hide from one of those. If the Germans got one of those into the clearing it would not be long before they killed everyone on the hill. Of course if they did not get anything like that and attacked with rifles, they could be killed quite easily. Bogacz hoped that the Germans were stupid enough to attack with rifles. Perhaps if he and Gosin and the soldiers could live through the day there would be a chance to come off the hill in darkness and to escape across the mountain to the other side. Bogacz thought that there might be a path somewhere here to lead across the mountain. He did not know such a path at this point of the mountain, but he hoped there was one. As the small soldier said, the one whom they called Maly, one must believe in the best. So perhaps there was one. He had a bad feeling about the place, as though this was a place where he had been unlucky once before, and this had nothing to do with the tomblike shape of the hill. There was something familiar about the way the sandstone cliff hung over the small clump of trees north of them on the side of Lysagora. He thought he had been there before, but it was not until Gosin chuckled and said what it was that he knew this clearing.

—Do you remember this clearing? Gosin said.

—I think so. It is familiar, Bogacz said. But I do not know when I was here.

—This is where we came that time with the hunter. The time when the sound of the machine frightened off the Old One.

—Is this the place? he asked. It could be but he was not sure.

—It is the same place, Gosin said. I remember it.

He would have reason to remember, Bogacz thought. And, as he looked at the thick clump of trees where he had tracked the Old One, he recognized it for the place that Gosin talked about.

He knew then that there was no way here through the mountain. He had gone up above the bear that day to make sure. They were, then, trapped as the bear had been. The motorcycle of the messenger had warned and saved the Old One. What would save them? He did not think that anything could, if the Germans came. They had the motorcycles and the mortars.

—That is where the hunter sat, Gosin said. Down there, do you see it? You brought him his card and he did not go after the Old One.

—I see it, Bogacz said. The Pan Kapitan had said that there would be other bears in the forest. He gave me this rifle. It is a good rifle. I have seen none better. I can use it for these other bears when they come. But they have bigger rifles, and they have the mortars.

—I was angry then, Gosin said. I am not angry now.

—Why were you angry?

—I wanted him to go after the Old One. I did not think the message was important. I thought that he was afraid. I wanted him to kill the Old One for what the Old One had done to that girl. She was a good girl and I liked her. Her father liked me well enough until that time. After that he wanted to kill me. Did you know about that?

—No, Bogacz said.

—It was after you went away to be with the soldiers.

—He was not angry with you yesterday.

—He was, but there were other things for him to do. Perhaps he will forgive me, eh? Someday, perhaps. When we come off the mountain and kill all the Germans. Perhaps some day I will find the Old One.

—His other girl was not angry with you, Bogacz said. He grinned at the other and chuckled a little. —I could see that.

The young man turned his head away. —Someday they will forget about Hanka and the Old One. Maybe Marylka will forget it too. What do you think?

—I think so, Bogacz said.

The young man sighed and scratched his ear and stared into the clearing. He had the long rifle of the Jew outthrust before him. Bogacz looked at him, liking him, and looked at the mountain. There was no way to cross it. He knew that none of them would leave this hill when the Germans came.

He looked at the others: the three soldiers who spread themselves out behind the rocks and boulders on top of the hill. They had the machinegun in the middle, aimed down the path and across the clearing. The soldier Kublarz sat behind the handles of the gun. The soldier Maly lay beside him with a shining belt of bullets ready to push into the gun when it was emptied. The big soldier, the one they called Kula, lay some distance off. He appeared to sleep. He had been sleeping as much as he could and said very little. Behind each soldier lay a little mound of bombs. Bogacz wished that he knew how to throw them. It would be good to throw one before the end came. It would be good, just once, to shoot with the machinegun.

And then he heard the twigs breaking, and the rustle of the brush, and the dry snap of rotten wood carelessly trodden on, and then the first of the Germans came into the clearing.

The sun was then clear of the trees. It hung behind the German who came out of the dark tunnel of the path and stepped on the border of shadow and light and looked up at the hill.

It was perhaps the oblique angle of the light, or the uncertain morning air that still carried a shred of nightmist, or perhaps it was eyestrain due to watching in the dark, but Bogacz thought the German immensely tall, almost as tall as the trees behind him, a nonhuman apparition. A spirit. The German's face was nearly white in the strange light. Bogacz aimed his rifle at the pale German's face. But before he could fire the rifle, the machinegun roared and the German jumped into the air and rolled over backwards. He rolled down the path out of the clearing. He had come like a spirit and now disappeared like one, and Bogacz whispered the old incantation against spirits and quickly made the sign that was so much older than the sign of the Cross, and then, to make sure that no one was offended, he also crossed himself.

In the name of the Father and the Son and the Holy Ghost.

Go, Spirit. All spirits praise Lord God.

All spirits praise . . .

The slapping roar of the machinegun and the tinkle of bulletcases falling on the stones and the splattering sound of bullets hitting rocks around him and a thin cry somewhere to the side of him . . .

—Look out there, Kublarz . . . left a bit . . . there! In that yellow patch. Down under that pine. They are coming around. More lead, you son of . . . there! Watch it, Kula! Watch it! They are on your side now.

And the explosions of grenades rolled down the slope into the running Germans, who now came from the path and into the clearing and ran for the first of the boulders at the bottom of the slope.

There!

The Germans came up the slope in a grey bobbing wave, an undulating carpet that rolled out of the woods like morning mist and began to mount the sides of the small hill. On they came among the boulders, with broad leaps and great bounds like frogs or with heads down and running fast like boars or pounding heavily upward bellowing like bulls or harelike with little cunning dashes to left and right. Grey shapes hurtling upward. Perhaps a hundred. Bogacz could not tell. He saw the grey shapes run in front of him and heard the shouts and shots and the cra-ack-boom of the little bombs to his left and right, and out of the corner of his eye he saw a grey mass leaping over boulders, and then there was the flash of a bayonet and the mass fell off the hilltop and rolled back with legs and arms thrashing. A red face, twisted in a shout, wavered in front of him and he shot into it. A broad chest blocked out the green of the woods and he shot into it. A shoulder flickered at the edge of vision. Another face, more grey. He shot into it.

Cra-ack-boom!

The roar of the machinegun.

In front of Bogacz, under the edge of the smoke but above the boulders, a German made his way painfully up the slope. He was on his knees. His face was pale. The front of his grey uniform was black and red and his face was streaked with red lines as though a bucket of paint had been thrown at him. He put his hands carefully before him on the ground, seeking stones, some handhold, and hauled himself steadily up the slope. Hand over hand like a mountainclimber on a rope. His legs were no help to him. The German's white face was pointed up the slope like the muzzle of a gun. In front of him the ground was brown and yellow. Behind him it was red. Grey shapes tumbled around him. Men fell and flew past him down the slope. Some man fell on his knees beside him shouting, pointing down the slope. The white-faced German officer shook his head and pointed up the slope. Bogacz aimed carefully, fired and shot them both.

Cra-ack-boom! The little bombs.

The rattle of the big machinegun.

—Aa-a-ah . . . *Hilfe!*

Smoke.

A German moves towards the hill. He is small. In his grey uniform against the yellowgrey of sandstone and chipped stone, he looks strangely flat, not human. He crawls carefully around a boulder and works his way between stone obstacles towards the hill. In each hand he holds wooden sticks with round cans on them. These are little bombs. Bogacz has seen those in the pass. He aims at the German. He wonders why no one has hit the German, why no one shoots at him. Perhaps they cannot see him through the smoke, but Bogacz can see him. He follows the flat German with his rifle sights, but each time he is ready to fire the rifle the German crawls behind another boulder. It is a game of hide-and-seek. Each time Bogacz thinks that the German will come around the left side of the boulder and aims at the spot, the German comes out on the other side. This is a clever German, Bogacz thinks. He must be a woodsman. He works well with the boulders and the fallen treetrunks.

Cra-ack-boom!

Duh-duh-duh-duh!

—Left! Watch your left! Kula . . .

—From below!

Cra-ack-boom!

But now the German has run out of boulders. There are no more between the clearing and the hilltop. There is just one big boulder and he is behind it. He is very still. He must be getting ready to jump up and throw the grenades. Where will he jump up? It is important to know where he will appear; there will be no time for more than one shot and the German must be shot before he swings the handgrenade over his head. The last two times he went to the right. Then he should now go to the left. It has been like that, has it not? Twice to the right and then once to the left. But this is not a stupid German. He *must* be a woodsman. Will he do what he should do now, when it really matters, or will he do the other? What would I do? I would go to the right again. I would do what no one would think I would do. Therefore I will shoot to the right of the boulder. There. About a foot above the boulder and to the right. That is the way I would go, the way a cunning animal or a good woodsman *will* go. Lord God I pray he is a woodsman.

Come, German, I am ready now. Come.

The tracker held his breath so as not to disturb the lay of the rifle or jog the sights.

He looked through the sights of the Mannlicher and suddenly saw the grey chest of the German solid behind the sights and pressed the trigger gently and the rifle bucked only a fraction of a centimeter and the German vanished. Two loud explosions flashed yellow-white behind the boulder.

So, German. So you were a woodsman.

Bogacz worked the bolt of the Mannlicher to slide another bullet ready for firing. He looked between the stones for something else to shoot at. But there were no more Germans showing anywhere. They all lay down among the boulders at the bottom of the slope.

The killing of the grenadier was a sort of signal. No more Germans appeared in the boulders and no more tried to rush the slope as they had before. They were down and still behind the boulders and the trees around the clearing. There were some shouts among them. Bogacz wished that the Jew had not left them so that they would know what the Germans were saying. But Bogacz thought he knew what the commands had been without a translator. He wondered how long it would be before the Germans sent for their machines.

He looked at the sun and judged by its position that a quarter of the morning had gone by. It would take the Germans the rest of the morning to send to the valley for one of their mortars. And to get one back here. And then it would not take long. It would be over quickly. Bogacz wondered if the Germans would try to attack again with handgrenades and rifles. They might become impatient if it took too long to bring up the mortar, and then he and Gosin and the soldiers could kill a few more of them. But it made no difference in the long run, Bogacz knew. Sooner or later they would have a mortar, or perhaps an airplane would come, or one of the crawling machines.

Ha, if only there were no machines like that. If only it were men and men and not men and machines.

He looked down into the clearing from between the stones. There was a German dead halfway up the slope. Another was half in the bushes and half out, and another lay between the boulders. He looked for the woodsman-grenadier but he could not find him. He noticed with surprise that a large piece of rock had split off from the boulder. Where the rock had been attached, the boulder was clean and white. The outside was dark. There was much power in the little cans to break a boulder like that. You couldn't do it with a rifle. Beside him, Gosin moved a little and Bogacz looked at him.

—How is it with you?

—Well.

The young man's shoulder wound was open and blood had turned his white shirt brown about his back. The apple-eating German had struggled. He had stabbed Gosin with a bayonet before Bogacz managed to knock off his helmet and hit him with a stone. The German fell down then. He tried to get up, but could not. He crawled among the apples. The blow on the head must have done something to him, because he kept on crawling into the trunk of the appletree. He would crawl headfirst into the tree, then back away and crawl into it again. Bogacz and Gosin watched him butting the tree like a goat. Finally Gosin pulled him away from the tree and turned him over and drove the bear stake into his mouth. This is what started the Germans after them, Bogacz thought. If we had not killed the German in the orchard they would not have gone after us and caught us on this hill. But the German had seen them in the orchard and had to be killed. So one thing starts what another thing ends. It is always so. Bogacz wished they had not killed the apple-eating German.

—If we had bread and cobwebs we could stop the bleeding, Gosin said.

—Use clay, Bogacz said. This is good earth here.

He scooped up a handful and applied it to the wound.

—I do not want to bleed, Gosin said. I will be too weak to move when night comes. Do you think the bleeding will stop?

—I think so.

—What do you think will happen now?

—Who knows what will come?

—I know what will come, the soldier Kublarz said. The Germans will come.

—They have already come, said the soldier Maly. And where are they? Down there on the slope.

The soldier Kula laughed and repeated: —Down there on the slope. He said it several times and laughed each time he said it.

—When do you think the planes will come? asked the soldier Maly.

—They should have come already. But maybe the pilots want their breakfast first. They will come after breakfast and eat you for dessert.

—They will eat you too, the soldier Maly said.

—I am old meat, said the soldier Kublarz, but they will gobble you up and smack their lips, little one.

—They will not eat me, the soldier Kula said suddenly. He began to laugh.

—Oh? And why not?

—Because I'm full of shit, the soldier Kula said. Didn't you always say so?

—That you are, said the soldier Kublarz.

Everybody laughed.

—But the one that's a real shit is that dirty Berg, Maly said. That one is *gowno* of prime category.

—What do you want him to do? Fight all those Germans down there by himself?

—He could attack them in the rear and we could come down.

—There must be a hundred Germans all around the hill. What do you want him to do? He did well enough in the pass and in the cabbage field. If he has a chance to make it out of here, all the better for him.

—I wish I could make it out of here, Maly said. It would be good for me too. And what about old Kula? After he got his ass out of the cabbagefield and came after us?

—Oh, we all will when the planes come.

—What kind of plane will they bring here? Maly wished to know.

The soldier Kublarz lit his pipe. He grinned and said that the German plane would be a hillock-in-a-clearing-bombing plane. —They have a plane for every kind of job. Remember what Kleinert said?

—That Kleinert, Maly said. That son of a whore. Do you think he is down there now?

—They've probably made him a general by now.

—That son of a whore.

—I wish I had a fat whore right now, said the soldier Kula. I had one once, painted up like a townwoman, but you know something? She was from the next village to mine. It made me feel bad. My sister went to town too, you know?

—Maybe it was your sister, said the soldier Maly.

Kula thought carefully. —No, he said, it wasn't. Nobody ever got that fat in our village.

Bogacz listened to the talking soldiers and looked down the slope. Somewhere in the woods at the bottom of the slope the new Germans would be coming with the mortar machines. The soldiers talked about planes but they did not say anything about mortar machines. He did not mention these machines to the others, only thought about them. They would find out about the mortars soon enough.

The sun was then well into the first half of the morning. That is the first quarter of the sun. There was a number for this hour of morning, but Bogacz did not tell time by numbers. He told time by the trees and the sun and the length of shadows and by a feeling he had inside him, and by the way the ground gave or did not give under his boots, and by the sound the twigs made when they broke and by whether or not there was water on leaves and on blades of grass. He told time by the actions of the animals. Animals did a certain thing at certain times of day. Thus there was an hour of the sleeping fox and an hour of the waterhole and an hour of the lynx and an hour of the feeding of the bears. Animals were the most correctly ordered creatures in the world and never did anything without the right conjunction of light, temperature and shadow. Each function had its time, so why look at numbers under the glass face of a clock? There all the hours were the same and you could do anything during each of them and this was, clearly, not the way that Nature meant.

Now is the best of all hours: the hour of the hawk. It is the time, and the only time, that the great grey hawks of Lysagora wheel over the burrows and the meadows and the clearings and fall out of the sky without sound or mercy and strangle their prey before they reach the sky again. It is an hour of warmth, but there is no heat. In that time there is a promise of a golden day, of splendid hunting. The soil may be dry but it is not parched, and there is dew enough upon the clay to show track and there is sap enough in broken twigs to show how long ago an animal has passed. Later the day may dry out and become a red day. But sometimes it continues all of gold.

Bogacz looked out over the forest, which sloped towards the south, cut by the creek where he had tracked the Old One, dotted by yellow clearings and patches of brown where rotten trees piled over a morass. There were many such patches among the dark-green canopies of trees. Some of them wound like brown snakes dotted with the yellowgreen of swampgrass that pushed its sharp blades into coils of mist. It was a land both beautiful and deadly; brilliant and rotten; peaceful and in turmoil; where large and small things died by violence, having killed some other thing to live.

In the hour of the hawk the forest seemed asleep but Bogacz knew better. It was still but convulsed, motionless but reaching, the home of green peace and sudden death unexpectedly encountered.

It is my home, he thought. Once there was another, a village somewhere in the east, in the Malopolska, where villages grew one on top of another and there was no room for a man to breathe. What was that home? Bare feet and cotton pants and one shirt; women working in the fields for sixty copper coins a day and stopping their work long enough to give birth (cutting the cord with the sickle, wrapping the newmade man in a kerchief and laying the bundle in a furrow for shade) and dying of old age at thirty with a grateful prayer; a father beaten flat in a tavern quarrel; a sister gone to town; a boy of four taking sheep and goats to the grass, one meal of maize a day; drink, prayers, priests and tavern-keepers, more prayers, more drink, a hat in hand when the master passed, work, drink, a quarrel, a blow struck and a man killed in the quarrel and then escape over the border. The border was his second home, a place of caves and mountains and a pack into which flints for automatic lighters could be packed, or fountain pens could be loaded by the Hungarian Jew, or small square packages or watches or tins of English-cut tobacco, all to be taken to the Polish Jew across the hills where the sharpshooters of the Border Corps asked questions with a bullet. A rifle soon became the mainstay of the border home. How long ago was that? Bogacz did not know. He did not know how old he was or when he first came to the forest. There had been two wars, he remembered, and several women and several animals that had been difficult to take, and for a time he named his years after them. He still remembered the year he ran from home. The man had cheated him. Bogacz had a pig for sale, an old sow no longer good for anything. The man showed him a coin which was big and brown and bigger than the smaller silver coins, and the man said that this coin was better. Was it not bigger? Bogacz took the coin and brought it home. There his mother shouted and his father beat him and threw him and the coin out of the house, and Bogacz took the sickle from the wall when the others slept and went back to the market to look for the man. He found him in the tavern and followed him into the country and hit him in the back with the sickle that he was hardly strong enough to swing. Then he hit him several more times and took a silver coin. He ran most of that night, he remembered. Other years he remembered similarly, by events. He thought that he had married once, in Hungary, but he was not sure. Certainly he had awakened beside many women and some said that he married them, and it was possible that he had married some, but in those years, the years of the border and the pack, there had been much to drink and many songs to sing, and who could keep track of the women? But his best years, he thought, were those of the forest. There had been many hunters that he had guided, some good, some bad. It was not often that a good hunter came to look for a memorable animal. Mostly they were rich men and rich men only want a trophy for a wall, and sometimes they will pay you to take a good trophy while they stay in the camp with the women. Still, there were some good hunters. There were good days with those. It was good, Bogacz thought, that his last hunter had been good. There will be no more hunters now. It is well to go with a picture of a good one. It is well to go in the best of all the hours, when the forest is clean and still and only the grey hawks of Bald Mountain move above it.

Bogacz squinted his eyes against the sun to look into the clearing. The clearing was empty. No one moved behind the boulders. But the occasional crack of a rifle shot, the soft splattering of a bullet against the stones around him, the singing sigh of a ricochet showed that the Germans were still there. They would be too sure of their quarry to leave now that the mortars were coming.

Bogacz again measured the distance traveled by the sun. It now stood high. The hour had changed. What was the hour now? It was the hour of the mortar, Bogacz thought, and he cackled a little. At once Gosin stirred beside him and the others looked around.

—Why are you laughing, old man? asked the soldier Maly. But there was no way to explain to them, and so he shrugged and made an old man's face and they too shrugged. Just an old man. Who knows why they do anything? That is what young men think.

Bogacz smiled.

He heard the hum of motors long before the others, and he looked towards the valley, but it was too far to see the German machines. They were behind trees and many meters down into the valley.

But the Germans also heard the motors and began to call out to each other, and some of them laughed and they began to fire their rifles at the hill. And then one of them started shouting up the hill. He shouted in a terrible, harsh Polish that made Bogacz laugh.

—To heaven! the German shouted. All Poles fly to heaven soon! Like the nightingale!

The soldiers on the hill looked at each other. They did not say anything.

—Boom! Boom! To heaven!

And the Germans laughed.

—Laugh, swine, the soldier Maly said. No one else said anything.

—Do you have wings, Poles? Do you have your halos?

—What are they going to do? Gosin wished to know.

—Boom boom boom! the German shouted at the bottom of the hill. Now all the other Germans began to shout among the boulders and behind the trees and in the dark tunnel of the path beyond the clearing.

—Are they going to attack again?

Bogacz said nothing. He looked into the forest, where above the lower path that led into the valley a flock of crows beat upwards, cawing, in their threatening spirals. The soldier Kublarz sat back from his gun. He lowered the barrel of the big machinegun. His pipe had long gone out and now another light seemed to leave his face. An old soldier like that; he would know, Bogacz thought. The soldier met the tracker's eyes and looked away.

—It will not be the planes, he said. His voice held regret. He stroked the walnut handles behind the machinegun. —They have brought up a mortar.

And at once the Germans started their shouting again.

—Boom boom! the Germans laughed and shouted. They fired rifles and machineguns straight into the sky. —Boom boom boom! Fly like the nightingale!

Boom boom boom!

On the hill no one said anything and everyone was careful not to look at anybody else and, soon enough, the first of the white clouds burst on the yellow slopes of Lysagora.

I THE JEW

Berg lay under a tinderdry dead log for several hours, not daring to breathe. A single breath could have betrayed him to the Germans. Once a small animal brushed against his leg and stopped, and came a little nearer with questing nose outthrust, and Berg thought: Do you bite? Bite, I won't move. The animal stared at him and suddenly threw itself out of his line of vision into the underbrush. Once a long mountain adder glided past his face and raised its ugly triangular head to his and flicked its forked tongue at him and, he thought: Strike, I won't move. He closed his eyes and waited for the hissing strike. When he opened his eyes the adder was gone.

Ants bit him. His nose filled with the dry dust of the powdery dead log. His eyes itched with the dust and congealed sweat. The coarse wool of his tunic combed the cuts and sores and irritations on his back. He did not move. He watched the Germans working with their mortars. They had two mortars. The tubes were long and black. The shells flew from them faster than he could work his rifle. The German mortarmen worked hard.

It had been several hours since he'd heard a rifleshot from the men on the hillock. Berg didn't think the men were still alive up there. Thinking that they were dead, and that there was nothing he could do for them now, made him feel less ill.

After what seemed like hours of cramped pain, he thought that he himself had stopped breathing and that his body and its many cuts and bruises and irritations did not hurt at all. He felt bodiless and light, and grateful to his body for helping him so. The German mortarmen were so near that they woud hear him if he breathed; he was sure of that. They would see him if they looked at him hard, the way the small animal had done. But their attention was all on their mortars and the shells which flew with such astonishing rapidity to burst on the hillock.

The other Germans were not busy. They rested in the bushes and among trees back of the yellow clearing. They pointed at the hill where the shells exploded. Some laughed. One shouted: —All good Poles fly to heaven.

More than once Berg had asked himself if he should help the others, if he should take the Germans in the rear and attack them with the machinepistol he had taken from the apple-eating German. He thought he had considered all the alternatives and that he had decided that he *could* not help them, being so outnumbered, that they could not *be* helped, that they knew it and would not expect help from him or blame him for not helping. Later he thought about all that again, on the long road north, hiding from the Germans, sleeping in hedgerows and haystacks. But that was later. Now he waited to be found and killed.

But the Germans were too busy. They mortarbombed the small hill for another hour and then went up it cautiously. Some of them carried small torn objects when they came down again. The objects could have been pieces of uniform, caps, helmets. The Germans sat around the dead log and ate their field rations and rested and some slept. Their officer sat at a distance, smiling to himself. This was the German who had come into the hut. Berg recognized him. The German sat so near that Berg could have hit him with a stone. Several times he thought that the German saw him. Their eyes met. Berg thought: Now he has seen me. Now it is all over. But the German made no sign of having noticed the crumpled brown form under the dead dry log. The German smiled a lot. He closed his eyes from time to time and laughed to himself. He had the body of another German officer brought down from the hillside and placed beside him and he looked a long time at the body, smiling, and said something to it (while the other Germans stared at him and each other) and he laughed a long time. The other Germans whispered among themselves. Clearly they couldn't make out what to think of the laughing officer. They sat like that for close to an hour; certainly the sun was well on its way after noon before the German officer got up and stretched and buttoned up his uniform and brushed off his trousers and told some other Germans to go up the hill. They looked startled when he told them what he wanted done. But they went up. They came back with the heads. They had five heads. They said they couldn't find the sixth one. They packed the heads in a small canvas sack. Then they went downhill through the forest to their carriers and then the sound of motors came and then the sound ebbed and Berg came out from under the log.

He sat down on the log and put his head down in his hands and breathed deeply. His heartbeat was extraordinarily slow. He looked up at the hillock and at the woods around him as if not understanding what either they or himself were doing there. After a while he went up the slope among the boulders.

They were all dead behind the barricade of boulders and piled-up earth. The mortarbombs had torn them into pieces so that at first he could not tell one of them from another, particularly since each had been beheaded. But he found Bogacz and knew him by his old jacket with the hornbuttons. The tracker seemed shrunken. He was no bigger than a child, a headless doll. Berg knelt beside him for a while, touching the withered hands, gnarled, rootlike, without life. Then he was unconscious.

Wednesday, September the twentieth

I THE JEW

Berg awoke among the headless men at first light. Walking downhill and out of the forest, he became aware of his fatigue and of a strange thirst. It was not for water. He wanted spirits. Vodka. Berg had never tasted vodka but he had drunk wine and he could imagine how the stronger drink would taste in the broken corners of his mouth: harsh in the throat and burning, and bursting in his stomach with hot tendrils spreading out into his arms and feet. He became aware of a pulsing pain. His boots had split and the thin soles had holes in them: Some manufacturer had made a profit.

He felt inside the torn pockets of his peasant coat, among the balls of rolled-up thread and shredded tobacco (remembering Kublarz who had given it to him) and the residue of things that had been in the pockets at other times. His fingers touched a box of matches as they probed inquiringly into the holes that led inside the lining and found a coin.

He watched the scattered columns of smoke and the distant fires, and the long strings of bombers droning overhead, and listened to the bombers and rolling explosions, and his hand fell beside him and he dropped the coin. The coin rolled on the ironhard packed clay of the highway and into the blackness of a ditch. Go coin. I don't need vodka. I don't need anything. I am me, Berg. I am a man and I am a soldier.

And as a soldier Berg knew that the death of Walnut (being a death by choice, a death for an idea) was a hero's death, in the sense that a Hindu priest would know the right of a widow to destroy herself on the funeral pyre of her husband and thus, ascending to Sati through the fire, become a saint. It was a matter of belief which saved those who believed; a constant: it observed a code of honor in a world where any measure of devotion to a rationale brought scorn.

A Jew, too, could have honor and belief and could choose death for an intangible but it was still too early for the Rosenblatts to seek intangibles.

He made his way carefully to the outskirts of the village that he and Bogacz and Gosin had left the night before, the place where Walnut died. He didn't want to think about how Bogacz died and could think of nothing else. The thought made him ill. He hurried to the village but he remembered to be careful. It was the way the Tracker Bogacz would have done it. So I have learned this much from Tracker Bogacz. Berg did not think the tracker blamed him for not giving help. But this (what he had come to do in that village, what he would do) would help to make amends. So he was careful. He waited patiently outside the village, near some trees, where he saw that the Germans had been going to defecate. Neat people, the Germans: everything had to have its proper place. An hour passed before the right German came and, even then, Berg did not think he was the right German. Berg hoped the German would be an officer but the German who came was not an officer. Berg hoped that, perhaps, the German officer who had been in the hut and who had the heads taken from the hill would come along. But perhaps German officers used some other place for their natural needs. None of the Germans who squatted in the trees were officers and so any German whom Berg finally selected would have to be the right one. There were no Germans near the trees when this German came. He was a sergeant with bowed legs and deep black scratches on both cheeks and a blistered mouth. He smelled of liquor. The German stopped close to Berg and opened his trousers. He took his penis out and grunted as though he was sore. The sound of water hit the dead leaves and the German sighed. There was steam. The German grunted and hissed between his teeth. Berg rose behind him and came close to him before the German heard him. The German didn't look around.

—*Christ, am I sore,* he said over his shoulder. *She was a virgin. Can you beat that? Who'd have thought it here.*

Berg drove his bayonet into the German's ear. The German gave another grunt and knelt on the ground (with his hand still clasped around his penis and his other hand reaching up to his ear as though to scratch it) and then he fell face down into his urine and there Berg left him to be found. He thought about the German each time he thought about the mortarbombs bursting above the round hill at the foot of Lysagora. It helped. But gradually he lost the detail in the picture. Soon he could not remember into which ear he had thrust the bayonet.

Berg supposed there were at least two hundred kilometers to cover before he got to Warsaw. He wondered how long it would take him to get there. He knew he would have to look for transportation of some kind; his feet wouldn't get him that far. In his disintegrating boots. He threw away the boots and found another pair on a corpse.

But despite his pain and fatigue, and the hunger that began to gnaw at him along with the thirst, he went rapidly enough. An hour's march took him to a ruined village: black skeletons of chimneys pointing upward, and the sweet stench of burning. Nothing moved there. He stopped, unsure which way to go, feeling weakness stealing up his legs, the pain in his feet, and then he heard the bellowing of a cow beyond the ruins. The sound was so unexpected in this devastation that he sat down and laughed. All this destruction and the only sound of indignation came from an unmilked cow. He looked for the animal and found her in a caved-in byre, a small shed halfburied under bigger timbers. The cow was badly burned but her udders were full. He sucked milk from her while she went on bellowing, and then crawled under the warm, polluted straw and covered himself up with it, hoping to sleep. But sleep refused to come. He found a bucket and milked the cow as well as he could and drank more milk and, going through the ruins, found some burned potatoes. These he wrapped in his shirt. He wished there was some way to carry off the leftover milk. With the potatoes, it would make a fair meal when he needed one.

He left the village and headed northeast, along the highway. At intervals the sound of trucks chased him into ditches and then he watched long columns of German transports, watertrucks, assaultguns and armoredcars flowing in the yellow dust. Aboard the troopcarriers the Germans were singing.

Once a truckload of German infantry swung close to him before he could hide and a laughing soldier reached out and snatched up his cap and another threw something towards him and Berg threw himself facedown in the ditch thinking: Grenade! But there was no explosion and Berg, opening his eyes, found a halfeaten can of German rationmeat lying beside his head. His hands shook as he ate it.

He knew that he could not go on like this. He had to find a quicker and safer way of getting to Warsaw. At any rate, he thought, he had better make himself less conspicuous.

He buried the German submachinegun under a roadside shrine, thinking in an offhand, hardly conscious manner that he had better remember where he put it because sooner or later he would want it again. Now, unarmed, in his peasant shirt and pants, he looked like any young peasant. He didn't think the Germans would bother about him. He went on thus for some hours. In early afternoon he found an old grey horse grazing sadly on a yellow hill and got up on him, grinning, thinking that now his disguise was surely quite perfect. He rode the horse for another hour beside the road, past halted German vehicles and resting troops, past brokendown peasantcarts and discarded household goods (babybuggies, handcarts, featherbeds, pots and small furniture, clothing) and a black-and-white-checkered Warsaw taxicab tilted foolishly on its side a long way from home. The road was full of people flowing like a soundless river. No one paid any attention to him or his horse.

But eventually the horse stopped and groaned and sat down and refused to move. —Come on, horse, Berg said. We have a long way to go. The horse groaned and lay down. Berg kicked it a little. The horse looked at him reproachfully. —Come on, horse, Berg said. He couldn't kick the horse hard, his feet hurt too much, and Berg continued on foot. He kept to the high embankment beside the road where the walking was easier. He could see far up the road from his small elevation. The road was straight, unshaded. But he thought he saw grey movement far ahead where the road curved away towards a river; men and armored cars blocked off the bridge. The human stream halted at the roadblock. He saw small groups of people led off into the woods and other groups pushed back to the road. Some shots came from the woods. The human river spilled about the bridge, drifting north and south on the near bank. Only the trucks could cross the bridge.

Berg came off the embankment, keeping the mound of earth between himself and the road. He found another pair of boots beside some shredded greybrown rags in a drainage ditch and put them on. They did not make the walking any easier but they would protect his feet from the dust and small sharp stones. He would be well hidden from the people on the road until he came to the flat area, beaten down by many feet and bodies, where the trucks waited to be cleared for crossing.

He crawled up on the embankment, holding his head well down. The road and bridge and river were straight ahead now. It was as he had thought: The drifting mob of hopeless walking people was not allowed to cross.

There were two bridges, one a small stone ruin halfsunk in the river, with twisted steelbeams making a skeletal arcade over the water, and the other a ribbon of fresh yellow planks laid across pontoons. The Germans stood in two ranks before the pontoonbridge. They had set up a light machinegun in the ruins and a small conical tent at the side of the road. There was a field-desk in front of the tent. An officer in a flat peaked cap sat there among papers. He had rolled up his sleeves. The Germans herded the grey crowd together like a huge bellowing mass of cattle and pushed it off the road into a level enclosure ringed by armoredcars. They went into the crowd in small groups and picked out men in uniforms or parts of uniforms and pulled them out of the crowd, beating them and pushing. Some of these fought and were clubbed down with riflebutts. Others went unresisting to the officer behind the fielddesk, who shouted questions at them. Then they were led under trees where open trucks waited. Whitefaced men stood tightpacked in the trucks with more guards around them. Armoredcars closed the bridge on the other side of the river and more of them stood in a small copse between the ruined bridge and the pontoon crossing. When the crowd broke and began to run the armoredcars moved out from under the trees.

Berg took a long look at the Germans in front of the bridge and around the trucks and at the blackcapped armoredcar commanders standing in their turrets. He saw the spreadout eagles on the sleeves and the metal gorgets; these were SS and fieldpolice. Clearly this was no place to try to cross the river. Berg hid behind a clump of grass on the embankment. Down on the road a long column of German Army trucks halted before the bridge. The fieldpolice made room for the trucks. Berg saw that they did not look into the trucks. They checked the drivers' papers and waved the trucks across in groups of five. The SS beat the crowd away from the trucks. Their shouts drowned out the great massed wailing of the crowd. The crowd boiled like angry water and squads of SS and fieldpolice fished there for men in uniform.

From time to time they dragged some man in civilian clothes to the shirt-sleeved officer behind the fielddesk and the officer looked the man up and down, inspected his hands and his forehead, and then the SS men took the man to the ruined bridge and led him down the riverbank under the stone arch and shot him at once.

And all this time the long line of Army trucks moved up to the bridge and halted and moved again. Once across the bridge the trucks vanished in huge clouds of dust as if the drivers couldn't wait to put distance between themselves and the fieldpolice.

Berg watched a moment longer to make sure tht the SS did not inspect the truckbeds. Then he backed down the embankment to the field and made his way back among the small bushes there, a matter of half a kilometer or so. The shouts and shots and roar of motors were behind him then. He crawled up on the mound of earth again and looked down at the line of trucks parked in the road. The drivers had all grouped beside the leading truck. They watched the show by the pontoonbridge whistling and laughing each time the fieldpolice caught another soldier in the crowd. Berg slid on his belly down the embankment to the roadside ditch and crawled along the ditch to the last group of trucks. Then he jumped up and ran to the last truck in line and quickly climbed into the back of it. He couldn't control his trembling body and chattering teeth. The truck was open to the sky. It was loaded with grey sacks: oatmeal and potatoes. Berg sweated and shook, shifting the sacks. He cleared an area big enough to hide in. He crawled into it and pulled some sacks on top of him. The dusty smell of sacking and earth pressed down on his face. He could not stop shaking. He pushed the corner of a sack aside so that he could see the blue sky and feel the hot sun.

He waited a small eternity, feeling his heartbeat gradually slowing to normal. He heard truckmotors starting up the line and eventually there were footsteps and somebody yawned and somebody said: —I hope nobody looks under my potatoes. I've got a case of vodka hidden there. And someone else said: —Well, all they can do is send you up for looting. And someone else laughed. —Well, see you later, boys. —Right, let's get going. And then a cabdoor slammed shut and the motor started and eventually the truck moved forward. Berg lay still under the shifting sacks. Then the truck stopped again and a quick, harsh voice asked for the driver's papers and there was rustling and a quick curse and a disinterested —All right move out. Berg listened to the whine of the engine in lowgear and the hollow rattle of the planks across the pontoon bridge and then the shouts of the crowd on the riverbank and the shots fell away behind him and the driver pushed the truck into highgear and the motor roared. Berg lay back then and closed his eyes and found that he had held his breath all the way across the bridge. He expelled his breath. I'm getting good at this, he thought. He shifted himself around in the small hole among the sacks. He watched the sky. Tops of trees flew past, telephonepoles moved by regularly. The truck swayed on the uneven pavement of the clay road.

The sun was well along towards evening when Berg came awake (wondering where he was and what he was doing, thinking himself a prisoner of some kind) and pushed the sacks aside and looked about. This was dead country, totally destroyed. Nothing grew here.

Berg felt hungry. His bones ached. He wondered how long he had been sleeping in the truck and how far the truck had come from his rivercrossing. He wondered if the truck would go all the way to Warsaw. It would be good to get a ride all the way home. But he knew that he couldn't risk being caught by the Germans and, sooner or later, the truck would stop for fuel or the driver would want a drink of vodka. Berg didn't care to force his good luck any further. He moved out from under the potatosack and crawled to the far edge of the truckbed. He could see nothing in the dustcloud behind the truck but, he remembered, this had been the last truck in the line. He waited until the truck slowed down at a sharp bend in the road, then jumped clear, landing on his feet.

The pain was enormous. Berg shouted out with the shock of it. He fell into the ditch and lay there for some minutes until the waves of pain died down. Then he got back on the road and went on.

He walked as though mesmerized, feeling nothing except his tormented feet, unaware of time and its passage, ignoring the hours and the falling sun. Later he recalled having had a long conversation with an invisible Rosenblatt, a ghostly Mendeltort. He begged several other rides aboard a variety of vehicles (small peasant ponycarts, laddertrucks piled with hay) and eventually he entered what had once been a town. Ruin bordered ruin. The streets were gouged with shellholes. Trenches. Whoever had fought here held onto every inch of ground. Now nothing moved. There was no living sound. It was like landing on the moon, Berg thought, walking into it.

Night fell and a white moon came up. The hard, cold light of the moon made the craters huge.

Still, for all the silence and emptiness and blank windows, Berg thought that a thousand eyes watched him: hidden generations.

He stood still for several moments, peering into the shadows, hearing the soft trickle of mortar in the rubble, the whisper of curtains. Nothing living moved in the shadows. He went on.

He felt lightheaded, almost religiously elated, as though he had made a discovery of some kind. He was the first man on this moon, and it was his. Somewhere, eventually, he would find a place to sleep and eat. He had the feeling he was following many other people, vast crowds lost in the darkness of the ages, submissive and mild, although he knew there couldn't be a real, flesh-and-blood crowd ahead of him. No one preceded him in the hollow streets, he was the first of his kind. He went on, shaking with the cold and wondering where the chill had come from. Why should it be so chilly in September?

The gutted shell of an overturned streetcar told him where he was and he thought: No, it couldn't be, I must be sleeping and will soon awake. But the white nameplate on the car wouldn't disappear no matter how hard he rubbed his eyes. He had spent many holidays in this town, one of the favorite Sunday-picnic places of the city, no farther than forty kilometers from home. He couldn't believe it. The shellplowed streets confused him. He lost his footing in the dark and fell into a shellhole. He swore, tripping over rubble. This had been a perimeter of defense and the destruction had been thoroughly accomplished.

He almost fell into a wrecked trench that cut across the street. It stopped him. He didn't think the invisible vast crowds he was following could have come that way. They would not have been able to get across the trench with their mild, shuffling walk. But then he no longer wanted to follow the others. After a moment he turned right and followed the trench into a sidestreet, not caring where it took him. The world seemed extraordinarily empty of men, although he knew that the houses and the cellars and the yards were graveyards for hundreds. He had trouble breathing. Dryness seemed to have sealed his mouth and throat. His heart beat so slowly that it seemed to him that the pumping muscle had collapsed and wouldn't serve him anymore. Coming to a bunker he groped his way into it on his hands and knees. A piece of canvas scraped his face and then his head pushed through the folds of a musty blanket hung in the entrance. The blanket wrapped itself around him and he pulled it down.

The bunker was empty. He sat there on the floor for a moment, near collapse. He was indifferent to everything: the pain in his feet, the dryness and the hunger and the lightheaded feeling. With shaking hands he found the box of matches. By matchlight he saw a candlewick protruding from its small pool of grease on the flat oval lid of a tobacco can, and he lit the wick, thinking that there was nothing quite so black as the unlit wick of a used candle. With the light came warmth. He thought that he would lie here for a while and then go on.

Ah, but where and what for? Wouldn't it be easier to lie down? To give it up? To surrender?

His stomach shuddered, expanding and contracting.

Where? *Into Israel* . . . Why?

And the impassioned voice of a longago-heard lecturer rattled among the fantasies of exhaustion, fear and hope in his brain. For the Jew Israel is a biological and cultural necessity. . . .

Hunger tormented him.

He thought in turn of everything that he had ever eaten: rich dishes so skillfully prepared by his mother, rivers of juices and fats and creams and oils, an endless march of black and white platters staggering under their many-colored loads: tarts, strudels, nuts, fish chopped and fish unchopped, Army food and black bread of peasants, fruit bought and fruit stolen and sweets stolen from the candyseller on the corner of Solna.

Enough. He shut off this stream of thoughts and rose. His legs trembled under him, and he almost fell looking down at his swollen feet.

Legs, attention! He laughed or thought he laughed. Hold me up a bit.

We've come a long way. A long walk. And there's far to go. Not as far as when we started. But still far. How far? He didn't know precisely. But it was far for such swollen feet and such tired legs.

This was the edge of the Kampinos Forest; not a big forest like the black woods around Lysagora but big enough. It ran to Warsaw in two strips that were perhaps twenty kilometers wide but thickgrown and difficult to cross.

He would go through them to avoid the Germans. Germans could surely be expected anywhere between that point and Warsaw.

There was a time, maybe a century or two before, when he would not have thought of going through the forest alone or with anybody else. Forests were black and dangerous and awesome and enormous. But that was long ago. He knew about forests, their darknesses, their loneliness, and he knew about determination.

I have, he thought, all the meanings of determination in me: purpose and conclusion and fixed resolution and a delimitation and determining of bounds and a fixing of the extent, position and character of anything, of anybody, and therefore also of me.

He sat down because he could no longer stand. He slit his boots open with a bayonet he found on the bunker floor. They were German boots, he noted without curiosity. They burst open before he was done with the slitting as though they wished to spring away from any contact with his feet. His feet were beginning to bloat. They hurt so much when the boots split open that he screamed.

The candle sputtered in its grease. He saw a flash of light vague on the right in the far corner of his eye. There was a ledge or a seat of a kind hollowed out of the dirt sides of the bunker, propped up and reinforced clumsily with concrete and broken flagstones and small pieces of uprooted asphalt to fill in the cracks. There was a remnant of an Army blouse wadded up in the corner of the seat and from its brown, malodorous folds a small light blinked at him.

His first thought was: a rat. The reflection of his pathetic candle in a rat's eye. He moved to kill it, but then he thought: Why? He has more right in this rubble than I. He was here first.

Then, looking carefully at the small gleam flickering in the candlelight, he saw that it was not a rat, not an animal, but a piece of metal, a small disk beaming back the candlelight: the cap on a waterbottle. He reached out for it, grasped it and felt that it was full. He got off the cap and smelled the hot strong smell of spirits. With trembling hands he brought the bottle to his mouth and hit himself several times in the teeth with it and finally got his teeth around the bottleneck and the liquid gushed into his throat. He took six chaotic gulps, then choked and retched. The sweat was icy cold about his head. The spirits burned hot in his empty belly. He thought he would faint. But the heat felt good. The discovery, the luck, might be an omen.

He tore some strips of blanket and wrapped them around his feet, then went outside again. He saw two giant bonfires in the distance. The nearer one was Warsaw. The farther was Modlin. He began to hear the cannonfire clearly in the still night.

He walked a long time without keeping track of hours, blindly, through tangled undergrowth. Several times he lost his way, but the red fires set him on his course again. These are the new constellations of the twentieth century, he thought, the new guiding lights: the fire of burning towns.

The woods were full of shadows, men moving towards Warsaw. Most of them were in uniform. Some wore civilian clothes. But all were soldiers, armed with rifles and bayonets and sabers, with belts and bandoliers stuffed with ammunition. Berg kept away from them. He passed small groups of them forming under trees and larger groups drawing up in clearings. He didn't want to be stopped or questioned or formed up with the others. He had no wish to fight his way to Warsaw; there was a better way that one man, alone, could try with some assurance of success.

He turned east when the sound of gunfire became enormous and he could see the distant glow pulse under the explosions. The woods thinned out as he approached the Vistula. In two cautious hours he was on the steep banks of the river and followed the brightlit ribbon of water until he found a rowboat hidden under overhanging roots. He pushed the boat away from the bank and climbed into it and paddled quietly into midstream and felt the slow current catch and hold the boat. He lay down on the wet floorboards and let the water carry him towards the glowing town.

Somewhere ahead were home and friends and family and his own bed and comfort and time to decide what he would do and where he would go. He would see Mendeltort and find out what Mendeltort was planning. He would rest.

The water lapped against the boat. It lulled him. He slept, dreaming nothing. The river carried him gently to the center of the town.

The house was three black walls reeling against the sky. It spilled its gutted contents into the street. He saw his parent's brass bed buried in the rubble: the scarred and squeaky symbol of Family and Virtue and Respectability and Safety and Order and Orderliness and Place-in-Life and his own inexorable submissiveness to it.

The bed waved at him mockingly with a ruptured spring. Why are you mocking me? How have I offended? Be still, you symbol of the Dead Impossible. Still (he thought), some small respect is due this symbol of my parents. I was born in that bed.

He made his way among the fallen masonry and timbers. His feet no longer hurt so much. He had stripped a pair of hobnailed boots off a dead policeman and replaced the blanket strips with them.

Behind him Rosenblatt had long since sat down. Rosenblatt did not want to go into the rubble. The floors swayed drunkenly and he was afraid. Berg was unconcerned about the dipping planks above his head. They were black, as the walls were black, as the high granite slopes of Lysagora had been in the moonlight. He went on until he found the bottom of the staircase. It hung crazily out of the wall and twisted upward in an unsupported spiral beside the exposed, sagging floors and out through the emptiness where the roof had been, high into the yellowstudded sky. Berg put his hand on the railing and his feet on the first corroded step.

—Please, Morys, it is dangerous.

—Then stay where you are.

But why go up there?

—Be quiet, Berg said. I don't want to hear you.

—Ah, what they did to you, Rosenblatt said. What they did to you. (His voice was plaintive like the waving bedspring.) I am older than you. I could be your father. Is that a way to speak?

—Could you be anybody's father?

—I am a man. I am older than you.

—To be a father you need to have balls, do you understand? Where are your precious eggs?

—Ah, what they did to you.

Berg climbed the stairs. They swayed and great iron nails creaked their way slowly out of the wall and there was more plaster falling and more dust and little crumbs of mortar spun off into the blackness under them. Up the first flight. A black hole of a doorway. Yellow wallpaper waving. A brown chair with the springs and horsehair spilling out of it. Old Schulmann used to sit in it at night reading the Zionist papers and dreaming of sand and palm-trees and cold waters tumbling out of the rocky springs of Galilee. The second floor. The Rubins had had ten children, noisy brats. Then up the third floor, the last, where the massed smells of the stairway hung under the ceiling. Home.

It was as though a giant with an axe had cut his home in two. One half of each room still hung in the night, almost undisturbed. There was Father's chair and the stove. There were newspapers piled beside the chair. The stove had a dish on it. Fish stank in the dish. A chamberpot. An umbrella stand. The other half of his home was down below.

Here, as you stand, the carpet starts and runs to there, where on the wall Papa had hung the pictures of Herzl and Pilsudski, uneasy partners now gone with the wall. The bed had stood there. The carpet spills into nothing like a waterfall. The door to his small room, its narrow window and his own bed neat and undisturbed on the edge of nothing. Berg stood beside his bed. He did not touch it. He felt cold and empty. He did not feel anger or sorrow or pity. It was cool up here in his room in the night with the roof gone and the wall gone.

—Morys, come down, eh?

It was Rosenblatt. His voice was more than frightened. It was terrified. I terrify him, Berg thought. He does not know me anymore. I do not want to terrify the Rosenblatts: They do not matter.

—Morys, eh? (Again the pleading note.) It is dangerous. It will not support you. Come down. Morys?

—Shut up! he shouted. Rosenblatt was quiet.

Berg stepped towards his window and put both elbows on the windowsill and leaned on them the way he used to do when he was little, when there was the grey of a narrow alley to see outside (and, if you twisted your neck and stretched it and looked up, blue sky), but nothing was there now. He saw the Vistula across the grey acreage of rubble that stretched between the Quarter and the river. The water was silver, striped with black and yellow where the shallows were, and the black shapes of the Praga bridges sagged into the river. The riverboats lay immobile on their sides like drowned reptiles.

(*Hoooo*. The sound of the steam whistles. *Hoo-h-h-h-h-hoo* . . . I remember them. The moon on the river. Where the dead white light could not reach, the water was black.)

Berg heard the sound of water lapping against the sunken hulls. He heard the sound of motors (Germans transporting new artillery for the next day's shooting) and saw the suburbs downstream with their scarlet mushroomheads of light. Black outlines of spires and steeples and latticework of tall walls with light coming through the windows. Moonlight was all around him and he felt suddenly small again and safe in the good yellow light of it and for one moment he wondered (stupidly, catching himself immediately in his stupidity) why one side of his room should be so very dark, why the light ran out and disappeared in blackness.

—Morys? (Rosenblatt, below.)

—Yes?

—Are you coming down?

—Yes.

Then, later: —Why did you go up? It was so dangerous.

—I had forgotten something up there.

—What?

—It's all right. I found it.

—What was it? What could you forget up there?

—Never mind.

But he said it calmly and kindly and respectfully enough.

—Well, I was worried, Rosenblatt said. It is dangerous. What good would it do to fall down from there? Eh? You could break a leg.

Berg laughed.

Rosenblatt looked at him a moment and sighed and shook his head and led the way among the ruined buildings.

They walked for several minutes without speaking. There was no sound of anything alive in the street, or in the alleys that fell emptily away from the moonlight like thick black strips of funeral cloth rolled into nothing, or in the caverns made by hollow houses. The ruins were delicate in the cold, pale light.

Two thousand yesterdays turned overnight into today, Berg thought.

He asked about his street.·

—When was it smashed up?

(Only to ask; I don't want to know. After I've thought about it and it starts to mean something again and is important and the darkness is all on the outside and the coldness is gone from the inside and I can feel pain again in feet and mind and heart, then I will ask about my father and my mother and my brother and when they died and how.)

—Two . . . three days ago. It was a raid . . . bombers . . . or perhaps the shelling. No one knew what it was. There was so much shelling and so many raids that no one, nobody could tell. You didn't know when one was over and the other started.

—That was no shell, Berg said. He nodded at the house behind them: skeletal in the dead white light reflected in the river, white eyes of a dead horse spread across the pavement. —Not even Germans have shells like that.

—Well, Morys . . . you should know.

—I know.

Rosenblatt sighed. He looked sideways at Berg and sniffed and wiped his nose with the back of his hand.

—Morys, aren't you afraid?

—Of what?

—Of what is coming. Everybody is afraid of that.

—Even Mendeltort?

—That madman! That anarchist! What has he got to lose? But am I Mendeltort? Are you? It's different for us.

—You used to be like *that* with Mendeltort, Berg said. He held crossed

498

fingers under Rosenblatt's nose. —Isn't that what you used to tell me?

—That was before. But now it's like this! Rosenblatt crossed his thumbs, then threw his arms wide. —We made him go away, do you know that?

Berg laughed. —You? You made Mendeltort do something? What army did you get to back you up?

—No army, that's it. No army. There will be no army. We told Mendeltort to go, to take himself somewhere else to make his army. We told him we didn't want him here.

Berg felt the night close in around him. He felt as if a cold, restraining hand had pushed against his head. Rosenblatt talked on, waving hands, but he didn't listen. He saw that they had come to the Untenbaum's on Solna. He had not meant to go there. It was the house where Mendeltort had lived, the impermanent apartment where two policemen had beaten on the door, how many days ago? How many years? A telescoped eternity. The shadow of the ruined gate blotted the moonlight.

—Army? Berg said.

—An army, yet. Can you imagine that? That Mendeltort is mad, I tell you, crazy in the head! He wanted to make an army here in the Quarter. He wanted us to fight the Germans when they come. Does that make sense? I ask you. Fight? With what? Who ever heard of such a thing? An army, yet. Who would be in that army? Can you see old Rabbi Feldmann on a horse? God would laugh at him! And what would such an army do? It would bring trouble!

—An army, Berg said. An army in the Quarter.

—Well, I tell you, we didn't want him here with ideas like that. We had a meeting and we told him. Go away, we said. You want an army? Make an army. But don't make it here. We don't want any trouble here. We don't want to give anybody something they can kick. You go away and make your army and fight Germans. Fight anybody. But don't do it here. No offense, Mendeltort, we said, just go away and don't bring us trouble.

—You fool, Berg said. You blind fool.

—What? What?

But Berg no longer heard him, and the darkness came thick about him, inside as outside, and he was with Bogacz on the knoll by Lysagora and waiting in the jasminescented clearing with the Walnut, but all of this was dark and vague and reminiscent of the streets where no such things had ever taken place and Bogacz was not Bogacz but Untenbaum and the hot wolfeyes of the peasant Gosin burned in the face of Melnick and the fat soldier rising in the cabbagefield was Rosenblatt.

Berg went up the narrow stairs hearing the fall of his hobnailed boots echoing in the stairwell like cannon. He struck the door of Mendeltort's room with his fist. The door swung in. The room was empty. Moonlight made shadows black.

—Rosenblatt! Rosenblatt, you dunghill, he is gone!

—What? What?

—Where did he go? Where is he?

—I don't know.

—He wanted to make you fight, Berg said. So you drove him out.

—Drove? Drove? We didn't drive anybody out. We just said, Go away please, Mendeltort, and he went away. We just said we didn't want trouble. He would have brought such trouble, such terrible days. . . .

Berg sat down on the stairs. The stone was cold. His feet bothered him again and his arms felt weak. An army in the Quarter . . . a place where Jews fight . . . it was too much to hope for.

—Morys, are you all right? Are you sick?

—It was for you, Berg said.

—What?

—He didn't need it for himself, don't you see? He knows who he is. It was for you. To make *you* big.

—Listen, you'll be all right. You are tired, eh? You come home with me now. I got food. You can eat. You can sleep a bit. It'll be better after you sleep, eh? Tomorrow we'll look for some place to stay. You'll be all right. The Germans won't do much when they come. They are civilized. It'll be all right after all, you'll see. There'll be no trouble; it'll be all right.

Berg said: —Tell me about this army.

—What's there to say? Nobody ever heard of such a thing. We wouldn't allow it. We had a meeting. Everybody was there who is anybody. Even the Socialists were there. Even the Communists. Nobody except the Communists wanted to listen to Mendeltort's ideas. Such ideas!

—Tell me what happened.

—Well, Mendeltort called the meeting. He had everybody come. Malik from the Zionists, Mayer, Untenbaum, the Jewish League, the Self-help Society, Schmul from the Communists, Piatek, everybody. Nobody listened to him except the Communists, but you know how they are; they're for trouble anywhere. Well, we said, you want an army you should wait till you got a country to defend. You get a rich country first, a fine country, and then you have something—land, property. That's something to defend. But what're you going to fight about here?

—What did he tell you?

—He said we had people here. That our country was where the people were. He said we had to earn a country, not just dream about it, and that we could start earning it here. You never heard such a thing!

—And what did you say?

—What was there to say? People are people and countries are countries. Nothing will happen to the people here. We have no quarrel with the Germans. They don't want anything from us. We got nothing they could want, do we? We don't have a country. And look how much our people gave the Germans. We've always been on their side, no matter how bad it was for us. The Germans will respect that. That is what we said. We will survive if there's no trouble to annoy the Germans.

—Survive. Survive no matter what . . .

—That's it. It won't be so bad with the Germans. A little trouble. Insults, certainly. Has anyone ever died because of an insult?

—That's what you said to Mendeltort?

—That's right. But you know what that madman said? Eh? He said the Germans will cut our throats to music. Can you imagine such a stupid thing? A civilized nation like that. He's crazy, that Mendeltort. We laughed at him. Ah, Morys, I tell you, he's gone crazy. Such an alarmist, such stupid talk. We always come out all right in the end because we don't make trouble. You make an army and they have something to fight. What are they going to fight if we don't show them anything? At worst they'll make us work for them, and what's so bad about that? They won't last forever. Somebody will beat them. And then we'll go on as before.

—So you think that in memory of Heine and Mendelssohn and Fritz Haber and Hermann Cohen they won't cut our throats?

—Cut throats, cut throats. Right away cut throats.

—To music, Berg said. To the *Blue Danube Waltz.*

—What's this? What kind of talk is this? Why should the Germans do us any harm?

—The Nazis. Don't you know about them?

—Propaganda! Polish propaganda. And what's it matter what they call themselves? They want to be Nazis? All right, let them be Nazis. But they are Germans first. They will answer for what they do as Germans. Ah, Morys, you are tired. That's why you talk like that. Come home with me now and rest.

Berg said: —I can't go anywhere with you.

—What? What? Then where will you go?

—There is a place . . . there is a place somewhere . . .

—You're tired. You need sleep.

—Go away, Rosenblatt, Berg said, infinitely weary.

He sat a moment longer in Mendeltort's doorway. He watched the dust drifting in the white moonlight. Then he went down the stairs and into the street. The darkness lightened rapidly. The sky blurred with the red reflection of the burning city. The shelling was desultory; the explosions came as if in afterthought.

I am not Mendeltort and that is just as well. I am Berg and Schmul is Schmul and Unterbaum is Unterbaum and Rosenblatt, God keep him, is Rosenblatt. And if we stand upon each other's shoulders we can reach the clouds.

I know, Berg thought.

He moved down the grey street looking for soldiers. The new day came slowly. Cannon pounded the new day.

Thursday, September the twenty-first

I THE CORRESPONDENT

He awoke in a cool, cleansmelling bed that he didn't like, in the magnificent hotel that he didn't care for, watching the columns of dust move in the sunlight. They swung from the ceiling like glittering snakes. They had kept him close company for a few days and now the snakes were friendly.

The evening bottles put the snakes away but in the morning the bottles were empty. The bottles were most effective at night (which was unbearable without them) and that was the time when the snakes were down. When the snakes were up and aware and looking at him curiously, the bottles were empty.

Loomis looked past (and through) the snakes at the careless blue sky. The room was one of two, each equally ornate, and roomservice was swift and inexhaustible. The water was hot, and porters and chambermaids made their eyes blank while cleaning up the debris of the night, and no one questioned arrivals or departures or difficult requests. This was the almost-best suite in the best hotel in the soon-to-be capital of the world and he a favored guest. There was no smoke in the magnificent blue sky. Smoke in the sky belonged to Warsaw and this was Berlin.

The two facts of (a) no smoke and (b) Berlin were still as unbelievable in the morning as were the facts of (c) himself being a guest of a not quite specified government department, (d) the affable nature of his hosts, (e) the almost diffident friend-and-ally treatment accorded him from the moment of his arrival (via Luftwaffe Storch) in Berlin, and (f) the envious eyes of the other foreign correspondents. With morning gone and the affability advanced towards evening the facts were more believable. By nightfall they were quite unquestionable. At night they were welcome.

He got up, feeling his mouth close on a dungheap of stale tobacco, vodka, bourbon (courtesy of the information section of the foreign department of the unspecified ministry whose guest he was) and lipstick savagely ground in between his teeth, and tried to remember the girl who had worn the lipstick (recalling only that she had asked to be allowed to sleep in her stockings)° and the particular party where he had found her and who had said what to him and what he had said, but it was all too difficult to remember before noon and so he gave it up. In due time (he knew) he would call Miller or Miller would call him and then he'd find out, more or less, what had happened. Later, one or another of his affable hosts would confirm it.

In the meantime there was the matter of getting up and calling for coffee and showering in hot water and shaving and having a reinforced eyeopener sent up from the bar and reading letters from the accumulated pile Miller had collected at the bureau office and sending a messenger to the ministry for the morning communiqué and dressing and being visited by one of his hosts. Later he would meet other correspondents and would compare Impressions About the Situation, and he would talk to this or another German spokesman, this or another neutral visitor (for the Overall European Attitude), this or another propagandaministry official, and write the story of the distant war (with all the names spelled correctly, all *vons* and middle initials properly documented and effortless miles of conquest dutifully noted) and he would meet another affable representative to discuss the story and he would agree to this or that helpful suggestion, inserting this or that and deleting the other, and he would type in his byline and a Warsaw dateline or a SOMEWHERE ON THE EASTERN FRONT explanation of his whereabouts, and he would *not* read his story (remembering that somewhere, in another time, he had had a stomach that would spill over in such a situation) and he would give the story to the helpful German, who would clear it before lunch with the censors and the ministry and dispatch it to New York in time for morning deadlines.

Then it would be time for lunch and Miller and the Ku'damm and the Adlon Bar and various introductions and the afternoon briefing at the propagandaministry or pressconference (depending on who in the hierarchy was back from a visit to the front and who was going there) and then the cocktailhour while a messenger brought over the afternoon communiqué and the official version of the briefing and pressconference and other correspondents pumped him for his magnificent localcolor (page one success at home, according to cables) and then dinner and an early nightclub and the night's new party and then the waking and the wondering about what had been said and perhaps a girl.

It had been so yesterday and the night before and would be so today and, presumably, tomorrow and so on while the war went on distantly somewhere, and the authoritative bylines would accumulate and the reputation grow and his position would become impregnable and if it proved a little hard to look into a mirror and other dreams mocked and memories came calling, there were always dry martinis to keep down the snakes. Dead voices don't have much of a carrying range.

But none of that was really part of this morning with the magnificent smokefree sky and hot water waiting. He stayed a long time under the hot shower. He thought about the night's party: the canapés and liqueurs and chandeliers and music and jolity and friendliness and the sound of people and the batteries of smiles. He had forgotten what it was to be lonely, to be by himself. The Polish girl had made him forget about a lot of things. Now that it was all over, so thoroughly finished, the girl and he, he remembered all the terribly important things that he had forgotten.

He thought about Nimi and how that had been and also, suddenly, about his son and about the last time that he had gone to see them, in New York. It had not been a happy occasion despite his plans for it.

He had gone to see them on an impulse, having made an appointment on the telephone like any other salesman pleading to be allowed to show off his line, hearing polite reserve as the appeal was granted; no promises, no commitment. It was to be in the afternoon. For tea. He dressed carefully and a little hopelessly. The wrinkles and folds in the long face would not disappear, would not smooth out, and the conciliating smiles he tried before a mirror did not convince, and the bland wellbred face would not stay bland and unaffected, and it frightened him. The street was the same and the trees with the little fences were unchanged and the doorman was just as carefully polite, and at first it seemed that Loomis had not been away at all and still lived in that marblefaced filingcabinet where each morning he had taken himself outside to go and read the books and listen to the lectures and at night come back to file himself away. It seemed impossible that he had not been there for several months. Upstairs, in the apartment that Nimi had picked out and decorated and paid for, nothing was out of place to show that he had been away. The school diplomas that Nimi had framed and hung in the washroom off the hall (taking everyone in to wash their hands as soon as they came into the apartment) were still there, and the inevitable towels marked HIS and HERS and YOURS (a wedding gift from her demented maiden aunt), and in the living room the flowers seemed to be the same rich, tired yellow tulips that were the last thing Loomis remembered closing the door on after that final civilized discussion.

And there was Nimi. He felt a moment of unaccountable panic seeing her so unchanged, unsuffering, as though she and he had had their lunch together and earlier a breakfast and, still earlier, had slept in the same bed (she insisting that twin beds or two bedrooms were an admission of failure) and had inspected David to see that he was properly dressed and combed before the stationwagon came to take him to school. Her arms were just as round and tanned and braceleted as he remembered them and her shirt, socks and walking shorts were just as well matched and her thick black hair was as neat. He said: —*Have I been gone somewhere?* (To keep it light.) *It seems as though I slept here last night and we had breakfast. Are you sure we didn't?*

—*If we did I didn't notice it. How have you been?*

—*Fine. You?*

—*All right. We're getting along splendidly, David and I.*

—*Where is he?*

—*Playing with some friends; he'll be here in a while.*

—*How has he been?*

Under his arm he held the stuffed animals, the great lion and the grinning elephant he had stopped to buy; both bigger than David. He did not want to put them down. He wanted to give them to David and he didn't want David just to walk in and find them lying there.

—*Sit down,* she said. *I sent David out to play so we could talk.*

—*I'd like to see him. Does he ever ask about me? What do you tell him when he does?*

—*He never asks. And since the subject never comes up I tell him nothing.*

—*But he must have asked where I was? Why I wasn't home?*

—*No,* she said. *He hasn't.*

She was lying, of course; he knew that David asked about him. He hated her enormously then because she was lying.

—*We've had a little trouble lately,* she said. *David was ill—no, nothing serious—chickenpox. He really looked pitiful with all those filthy spots and he would scratch them.*

She didn't write about it, no, she said because it wasn't serious.

—*You can't do that,* he said. *You can't shut me out like that. I want to know about it every time he has the sniffles or scrapes his knee.*

Oh, he wasn't likely to scrape anything, she said. He was really quite the gentleman and careful.

—*A careful gentleman,* Loomis said.

—*That's right.*

That wasn't much like David. Loomis heard him in the hallway then, or hoped that it was he, and presently the boy came in and said hello. He was no longer anyone whom Loomis knew. He didn't ask who the strange man was but he might as well have asked, the way he looked at Loomis. He was beautifully dressed in a smart woolen suit with short pants, black shoes, white kneesocks, neat white shirt and a striped tie. He was dressed as he would be for a visitor.

He called Loomis sir with the painful seriousness of a child speaking to a stranger. He stayed close to Nimi all the time and called her *Mummy.*

—*How have you been, David?* Loomis said. (My God, can't I say anything else to him? he thought.)

And he said: —*Very well, sir, thank you,* and Loomis felt dull and angry and suddenly tired but, still, he smiled and held out the lion and the elephant and said: —*This is for you.*

The boy took them and looked at Nimi. She took the stuffed monstrosities from him, saying that he could open the packages later. Now they would have tea.

Loomis said: —*I'd like him to open them now, if you don't mind.*

—*Oh, he'll be grateful later. Tea might get cold.*

They had the tea. There were little cakes. It was a distressing meal. David ate quickly and excused himself, wanting to go out to play. Loomis asked if he would like to stay at the table longer and talk to him perhaps. —*If you wish, sir.*

Loomis said he could go. Before he went the boy looked at his mother. She told him he could go and then he went. —*He has beautiful manners, don't you think?*

Loomis looked at his wife as though seeing her for the first time, the rich hair a novelty, the rounded arms unkissed, the long thighs unstroked, hearing her talk about the beautiful manners of his son who had been at the table, whom he, Loomis, had not imagined because the crumbs from the little cakes were there on the plate and the glass had milk on it. Loomis looked at the unopened packages with the lion and the elephant—the two pathetic bribes he had bought—and said: —*Yes, he has manners. Beautiful manners. You've taught him well.*

How proud she was then (he thought afterwards), how satisfied; her eyes were somehow new—just as innocent in that angelic face that always, even then, took his breath away a little and made it difficult for him to speak—but also cold and watchful and ever so politely interested. He asked if he could have David stay with him now and then. From time to time. She flushed and looked incredibly beautiful and said no. She was sorry. —*You know that I am not vindictive.* But it was really out of the question. Couldn't Loomis see it? —*I hadn't meant to bring it up,* she said. *Not at all. These things are up to you and I presume you know what you are doing, what you want. But since you were the one to bring up the question, tell me, do you have any right to ask?*

—*What do you mean? Of course I have a right.*

—*Do you really? What would you do with him while you were at work? Hire a babysitter? Your girlfriend, perhaps? I can see how that would be convenient.*

She said that she had no objections if he had his women. That's fine, he said, he had no interest in her tennisbuddies. She supposed that there were many girls who would accommodate him, although, for the life of her, she couldn't see what good it did them. It was none of her business now, of course. A separation was a separation. But she objected to David and Loomis and Loomis' mistresses eating together and playing house; surely he could see that? And she said, across the remnants of the little cakes, that she didn't think it would quite do for David to sleep in Loomis' apartment. It was, after all, such a small apartment. Two rooms? There would hardly be room for Loomis, David and some girl in Loomis' bed. Hardly. Of course, there was a way he could have David. Possibly (she said) they could come to some agreement, if Loomis became a little more aware of his responsibilities. But that was up to him. He had to make that particular decision. She remembered how bad Loomis had been about making decisions; how he faced up to his responsibilities: squarely, by avoiding them.

—You've made your bed, Will. Now you must lie in it.

He wanted then to tell her something about her bed, about how glad he was not to be in it. About how it was when a man couldn't bear to touch his wife anymore without feeling a hundred unknown fingers under his, and couldn't look at her for fear of the faces he would see reflected in her eyes, and how this made flesh rubbery and cold, and the short nylon nightgowns no longer did the trick, and he closed his eyes every time he was with her so that he could imagine it was someone else, and the act of love was the most insignificant act of all. Instead, he smoothed down the muscles of his face and shrugged and tried to look unconcerned and was offhand about everything. He caught sight of his face in a mirror and saw to it that it was unconcerned. David did not come back. Having done so much asking, Loomis didn't want to ask when he would come back. As he was leaving he thought the least she could have done was to let David open up the lion and the elephant. Outside the sun was going down. The salesman had had his appointment and there had been no sale.

He dressed and after a drink had his breakfast. He went through his mail. There was a letter from a small South American republic which had recently run through its semiannual revolution. It was from Charles Robert Hartbeck, a not so distant cousin of Nimi Loomis, the always-there friend quick with sympathy and quiet understanding, a favorite tennis and martini partner and (in the days when Loomis still thought bitterly about it) a partner in the associated social arts. In Hartbeck's measured heartiness and constant presence Loomis had found everyone who had ever come between himself and Nimi. Even when Loomis himself came between himself and Nimi it was easier to have a Hartbeck to shoulder the blame. Hartbeck had never been known to think or say anything unusual, and this had been a restful thing for Nimi. She would take anything from Hartbeck, believing anything. Hartbeck never angered Nimi, who resented anything she didn't understand, and he could look deep and sound witty while telling a salesman's joke. He never disagreed with her. He was simultaneously simple and complex, physical and philosophic, sensitive and animal, false and honest. He could never be accused directly of anything, and Loomis hated his guts. And Hartbeck, knowing Nimi, repaid the hate with bland and honest friendship. He had the widest eyes and firmest handshake in Russett, New York, and everybody liked him, and everyone was happy to conspire on his behalf with Nimi and to make sure that Loomis, as tradition had it, was the last to know. To Loomis,

Hartbeck seemed to be as changeable as a chameleon, as slippery as an eel, and he could never understand why Nimi could not see this.

Now Charles had written that he and Loomis had something in common. He, Hartbeck, had become a writer. He had decided to Enter Journalism and to Write a Book and it was just as he had always thought it would be: no trouble at all. He had been writing about the revolution for the Otis chain and Mr. Otis was extremely pleased. Nimi was also pleased, but then he and Nimi had been good friends for such a long time. He really wished that he and Loomis could be better friends. Perhaps he had read Loomis wrong but he had a feeling that Loomis didn't really like him. *I mean, not really.*

It was too bad that two regular fellows like himself and Loomis shouldn't get along. He got along so well with Nimi, after all. *So how about looking me up next time you're in Russett* (Hartbeck wrote). *Just rattle my cage. Or better yet, why not call the old sweatshop?* He was to become Mr. Otis' special and personal assistant when he came back from the revolutionary wars.

Reading the letter, Loomis felt dull emptiness settle in his stomach. He could imagine Hartbeck as he had seen him on infrequent visits, sitting at ease in Nimi's Russett home as if the place and woman and boy were already his. Already so proprietary and patronizing, sure, blandly calm. He damned him to hell.

There were two other letters. One was a note from his father-in-law, who was on holiday in the Bavarian Alps and would eventually come to Berlin and wanted Loomis to come and see him there. He was in Germany on business as well as for pleasure; he had many friends in German industry and banking and the pressmonopoly to see and would be in Berlin throughout October. The war in Poland should be over by then. Would Loomis have lunch with him? There were some things (he thought) they ought to talk about. The Otis chain had grown bigger and would grow even more and what he, Mr. Otis, had in mind might interest Loomis.

It must have been hard for Otis to write that kind of letter, Loomis thought, opening the third letter. It was from Nimi. It had been mailed, he noted, the day after he had gone to see her and David in New York, the day he had left for Europe.

Nimi wrote to apologize for David, for his manners that day: the day of the stuffed lion and the elephant and the tea. David had acted badly, as though he wasn't glad to see his father, and, she supposed, she had also acted badly, *being nervous,* but she didn't want Loomis to imagine that she had staged anything like that. That would have geen gratuitous and vindictive. She wanted Loomis to remember that she was not vindictive. She knew how much Loomis wanted to see David, how important that was, but David had not wanted to see *him.* She was sorry if the visit had given Loomis the wrong impression about anything. Now she had talked to David, there had been a long talk, and she had explained to him as much as one could explain to a little boy, and he understood and was sorry too; next time it would be better for everyone.

She wrote that she had been in touch with her father, who thought that their marriage could still be repaired, that it was all a matter of maturing and growing up and facing up to one's responsibilities, and that their separation had not been inevitable and could be ended and things could be patched up, and he had offered to mediate. She thought that he would write to Will inviting him for a little talk. She hoped that he would be courteous enough to hear what her father had to say. She didn't think that much could be done without a lot of trying (so much had been tried, after all, without any effort), but who knew? *Daddy has a way of amalgamating things, making several corporations into one.*

So would Will go to see Daddy when he wrote? Because she was sure that Daddy would write. Would he make it a point, please, to go to that small trouble?

Would he?

He didn't know.

But suddenly the emptiness and nausea and the anger were gone and forgotten. He read the three letters for a second time, and this time Hartbeck's letter made him laugh. Rattle my cage indeed. He crumpled Hartbeck's letter and threw it contemptuously on the floor. He tossed Mr. Otis' note up and down in a speculative way, read it for a third time and put it away. He let Nimi's letter lie where it was on the breakfast table.

Later, he telephoned Miller in Charlottenburg.

—Good morning, Fat One.

Miller laughed. Loomis could hear other laughter in the background: the sounds of friendliness and possibly friendship.

—You have a fat laugh, do you know that?

—You wouldn't know it was fat if you didn't know what I looked like. Friend, you're a fraud. A laugh is a laugh.

—It sounds fat.

—Only because you know I'm fat. I wish I had your secret for staying thin.

—I go to places like Warsaw and lose weight. You should have come with me.

—I could lose some weight. But then I wouldn't be me anymore, would I? I don't think I want to lose anything. It's too hard finding it without losing it too.

—You could eat and drink a lot and get it all back.

—Especially drink a lot?

—Fat Friend, are you about to preach about my drinking?

—Heaven forbid, friend. Everybody drinks.

—Besides, how do you know about my drinking? I've only been here a few days. How many has it been?

—You got here Monday afternoon. Deluxe Luftwaffe service direct from trenches to Berlin. Topdrawer treatment all the way. They had a lovely party for you Monday night, remember? And yesterday was work, if you'll pardon the expression, and last night we had another lovely party. And there's another lovely party tonight at the Adlon and a magnificent one tomorrow at your own hotel. Is it all clear now?

—Enough, enough. Our hosts are certainly bending over for us.

—Not for all of us, friend. Some of us don't get your kind of treatment.

Oh, it's a lovely war here in Berlin, but not as lovely as the one you're fighting. But then, not all of us are in your privileged position. Have you wondered why your hosts are so accommodating?

—Haven't had time to wonder about anything. Too busy reenlisting in the human race. But I suppose they've discovered what a fine fellow I am. D'you think that's it?

—No, friend. I think they have more practical ideas in mind. I think they'll want to talk to you about your loss of weight and about everything else you might have lost in Warsaw. They're really very much interested in that. They even wondered if I knew anything.

Loomis swore. —Why should they care about what I lost?

—Oh, it's not *caring*, friend. Nobody really *cares*. But they're *interested* in very many things. They'll talk to you about it when they're ready. In the meantime they're talking to everybody else who knows you. And, friend, I suggest you give a lot of thought to what you're going to tell them. When they're *that* interested they're really anxious and when *they're* anxious it's best to be careful. Understand me, friend? There's still a thing or two you could lose.

—I don't know what you're talking about, Loomis said. All I lost in Warsaw was a little weight.

—Really? Then it's all right. You won't have any trouble with our friends.

—Trouble? I don't want any trouble. I've had all the trouble I ever want to see. From now on I'm staying strictly out of anything that even looks like trouble. I'm going to be a very good boy indeed.

—Well, that's just fine, friend. But our hosts are really anxious about what you had there.

—I didn't have a goddam thing there. There was nothing worth having. I didn't get involved in anything. Why don't you tell them that?

Miller laughed. —Oh I did, friend. Really I did. I told them that you never get involved. It's against your policy to get involved. But I don't think they really believed me. They've got a lot of people over there to check with and they're really interested. They're even interested in what you drink and who you've been drinking with lately. Like, for example, champagne for breakfast and walks in the park and what all that might mean to you. There hasn't been anything like that, has there?

—No. Nothing important.

—They made some pointed comments about that champagne. Oh, they are very friendly and very polite but obviously this is important to them. I told them all Americans like champagne. I like champagne. Makes me think I'm young again, restokes old fires. I used to be able to get laid anytime I wanted with champagne. Now I can't get laid with a case of it, but that's the way it goes. Who wants to get laid, anyway? It's an overrated pastime. How've you been doing, by the way? There must have been something doing there, wasn't there?

—No, there wasn't.

—No? Well, maybe our friends don't know as much as they think. But they're really interested in that subject.

—Maybe I'm not the only one who's been drinking, Fat One.

—If you drink you don't think. Is that the policy?

—They ought to make a law to forbid thinking.

—Our new friends are making lots of interesting laws. That's one of the things they want to talk to you about.

—I don't know anything about laws. And I don't care, so long as nobody brings back Prohibition.

—Oh, they wouldn't do that. But they like to have things looking legal even if they're not. A very middleclass bunch, our new friends. Appearances are terribly important. They like figureheads to run things for them. That way they don't have to take all the responsibility. They're really not at all fond of responsibility. They like to pull the strings and have the natives make and execute the laws. And now they're looking for a figurehead to run things for them over there.

—What's that got to do with me?

—Maybe they think you can help them get the man they want. They'd like to find somebody who is, perhaps, a former friend of somebody else. Then they can say to that somebody else: How about helping out? You do this and we won't do the other. It would have to be somebody who was pretty big and who got a raw deal and might want to get his own back. They're really stuck for somebody to run things for them there.

—Nobody I know would do a thing to help them.

And suddenly Loomis realized what Miller was saying. He laughed.

—Yes, that's a thin laugh, Miller said. You must have lost a whole lot more weight than you show. It must be quite a joke, though, whatever it is.

—It's a joke all right. I just got the point of all your little hints. Fat One, you don't know how funny it is.

—Well, let's hope everybody thinks it's funny. Some of these people here don't have much of a sense of humor when they're anxious.

—So they want her, Loomis said. They want to find her.

—Careful, friend, no names. Him, her, it doesn't matter. I didn't say anything about anybody's sex. And maybe you shouldn't say much about it either till I see you tonight at the party. Or tomorrow's party. The way things are these days, what with all the technological advances, there's no way to know who's listening where to what.

—The stupid bastards. They don't know it but nobody could help them.

—Maybe. But it's your attitude that counts. I wouldn't be interested except that I want to see how you'll handle it. That thin laugh of yours worries me, do you know it? It sounds like a lot of other laughs I hear every day. You ought to look around and do a little thinking before you make up your mind what you're going to say. It's easy to lose weight and all that but it's not so easy to stay what you were.

—No thinking, friend. I'm up to here with thinking. What counts is living, from now on. I'll go with what I've got.

—Well, think this one time and then do your living. Look around real good at tonight's party, see the happy people. Then maybe you can try a big fat laugh. Okay?

—Okay. But you sound too profound. I guess it's your weight. It pins you down so you can't move too fast. Is that it?

—When you support three hundred pounds of lard and disillusion, friend, you tread mighty softly and carry a big gut.

—You're a good friend, you know that?

—I'm nobody's friend. There's no such thing as friendship. I never bust my balls for anybody. Except that once in a while I come across somebody who has a fat laugh. I hate to hear it go thin. I got a thing about thin laughs. They make me think about Mr. Otis and Presbyterian publishers and pendulous purses and all that. There're just too many people with thin laughs. So, think one more time, friend. Okay?

—All right.

—You're coming to the party, aren't you? I have a strong suspicion that our hosts have a surprise for us.

—They're good with surprises.

—This one will be interesting, I'm told. You coming?

—What else is there to do?

Miller laughed. —That's the spirit. Lunch soon?

—All right.

He looked for cigarettes (his hands suddenly shaking and his mirrored face slipping out of focus) and found he had none and reached for the roomservice bell to summon a waiter and let his hand drop. He didn't want their service now; perhaps later. Somehow he didn't want the Germans to do anything for him for a while. He wondered why he hadn't guessed why they had made themselves so accommodating, so abnormally friendly. They'd want the General if they could get hold of him. Obviously they thought that Loomis could lead them to the best possible hostage. It was equally obvious that they didn't know that the girl was dead.

He himself had not allowed himself to think that she was dead. Or, if she was, that she was anyone who had been important. He did not think of her by name; he had made that effort. But suddenly now he saw her as she was the last time he had seen her: sleeping in the dark room with her particular female lack of order, that disarming trust that made her at once vulnerable and exposed and very much protected, with the strength you remembered so well concealed under fragility. She had slept and he had picked up his notes and left the house quietly to go back to the Vogel flat on the escarpment for the rest of his manuscript and then to burglarize the Embassy of hams and champagne. He hadn't thought then that anything would ever erase that picture: her sleep and complete peace, as if she had finally decided to shift all possible impediments to peace onto his shoulders. He had felt immense pride in himself and in his commitment and he had hurried back despite the bombardment, feeling invulnerable.

He had not seen her again. He was glad he hadn't seen her dead. When he had come back (happily burdened with manuscript and bottles and the best of the ambassadorial larder in a paperbag) the house and street were gone; everything was gone. He had felt overwhelming terror. He could not wait to leave Warsaw then. The blackened streets and fire and uprooted cobblestones and the ubiquitous yellow mounds of graves and the enormous pall of smoke pressing down from the invisible sky had filled him with senseless horror. He had broken out a bottle to drown the horror. He remembered talking with the General in the destroyed street but he could not recall anything he had said. The General, more than anything or anyone else, brought his unreasoning terror into focus.

He supposed he must have run all the way to the Polish outposts (shouting at the men who reached out to him out of the trenches, beating off their hands, his passport held in both hands overhead like a battleflag) and then crossed the gaunt no man's land to the German side. There he received an immediate welcome, then rest and an airflight to Berlin and the excellent hotel. He remembered answering many questions, although he could not recall what the questions were about. He supposed he would be just as happy if he never remembered.

It was, in fact, better to forget everything connected with Warsaw; everything but the sights and sounds that could make his copy. He had done well, forgetting. He had thought that he would never have to remember. Now Miller's words brought it all back.

He went down to the hotel lobby to buy cigarettes. The lobby looked cool. The light was diffused among the exhibits. It slipped along the edges of the displaycases and ran confidently up and down the trophies. There were the captured battleflags, weapons, regimental standards. The huge goldtasseled crimson of the Lodz Municipal Fire Department. Caps. Dented helmets. Maps with the black greasepencil hieroglyphics of the priests of Mars. The gold and scarlet banner of the Association of Patriotic Volunteers of the Eastern Lands for the War of Liberation (1919–1922). A ten-by-ten-meter supermontage showing a captured mass of bearded, holloweyed Poles side by side with the victors marching into Krakow, into Lodz, into Sandomierz, lighthearted men, glittering in white gloves and untouched by war.

There were huge photographs of hair-raising Polish atrocities committed against German children and smaller renderings of brutal-looking Poles led to their just deserts by handsome SS men. Shysmiling small girls presenting flowers to laughing Wehrmacht motorcycletroops. Laughing *Panzergrenadieren* shaking hands with laughing Russian tankcommanders on the bridge at Brzesc nad Bugiem. Laughing young Luftwaffe pilots straining to hold their chests up under the weight of decorations. Goering shaking hands. Adolf Hitler peering through binoculars. General Bach-Zaleski's 400-millimeter mortar (with laughing gunners) across the Vistula from Warsaw. Adolf Hitler peering into General Bach-Zaleski's 400-millimeter mortar. Rudolf Hess shaking hands with Molotov (with Ribbentrop peering furiously over his shoulder). Laughing Danzig SS on the broken roof of the commandbunker on Westerplatte. An incredibly handsome and delicatelooking officer of the Waffen SS embraced by Adolf Hitler (both peering in emotion at the camera).

There was a lot of laughter. The lobby was crowded. It was like a salesman's convention in Detroit, Loomis thought. He supposed it would be thought an excellent convention: Everyone liked the product and exhibits and the entertainment committee had done a fine job.

He was aware of an emptiness inside him, a hollowness. He felt that none of this was happening to him, that he was an observer and that at any moment he would wake safely among the glittering snakes and bottles.

Someone bumped into him, stepped back and apologized. He saw a slim, distinguishedlooking SS officer; fine features, calm smile and remarkably clear, penetrating eyes made a firm impression. This was no party bullyboy. Still, the black uniform made its own impression.

The German's smile was interested, friendly, somewhat conspiratorial.

—I hope I didn't hurt you, Mr. Loomis.

—It's all right, Major. Do we know each other?

—Everyone knows you, Mr. Loomis.

—No, I don't think they do.

—Well then, let us just say that *we* all do. I thought your article on Warsaw was particularly fine. I was struck by your description of the siege. A wealth of detail there. You are a very skilled observer, Mr. Loomis, excellent with words.

—You do all right yourself, Major.

—Thank you. But I'm an amateur. I don't have the trained eye of the correspondent. I lack the editorial judgment that focuses at once on the essentials. You seem to go immediately to the significant and ignore the spurious. I envy you your ability to choose among events.

—Well, thank you, Major . . .

—Reinhardt.

The major introduced himself as an officer of the Special Detachment. Had Loomis heard of it? Yes, of course. Brandt's office of the SS/SD, political division. Not much in the headlines, perhaps, but well enough known in Germany.

—I've heard of you, Loomis said. He found himself impressed. He looked with frank curiosity at this man whose shadowy power was immense even in a country of great secret powers. Brandt's men were said to be responsible to no one. He was annoyed to find himself impressed.

The major was in Berlin for a conference, he explained. His current station was Vienna but he imagined that he would go to Warsaw in due time.

—I specialize in eastern affairs. That is why I'm particularly interested in your experiences in Warsaw. Perhaps we might have a talk sometime. In the meantime, I hope your quarters are comfortable. If there is anything you need simply let us know.

Loomis laughed a little. —I had wanted to ask, Major. When do I get the bill? It's as you say: I like to get to the essentials.

—Yes? Well, I appreciate your frankness. There are a few small matters we'd like to discuss. There is a little project on which you could advise us. But, if I may return your frankness, we are not yet ready to discuss that project. At any rate, if there is anything you need simply ask for it. I am returning to Vienna but the management in this hotel has clear instructions about you.

—Thank you, Loomis said. He felt uneasy and at a disadvantage, as though the German could read his thoughts, as if those candid eyes had seen deep into him, inspected everything inside him and tabulated it. —I don't think I'll need anything.

—Then you are fortunate. But one makes one's own fortune, Mr. Loomis, wouldn't you say?

—Yes. I suppose that's true.

—A matter of sound judgment. I call it perspective. A matter of making the right decision at the right time. Decisions should be made only in the

513

context of their time and place. Don't you agree? You, Mr. Loomis, merely for example, might make a good decision in one situation only to find it quite disastrous in another. One must remember the overall situation, the changed perspectives.

—Is that the secret, Major?

—That is the key to a pleasant life. It makes for orderly living. It's quite amazing how unpleasant life can be if decisions are made emotionally. So often men are hurt.

Now Loomis laughed, because this was a challenge of a kind.

—Hurting, he said. Yes. It's easy if you know something about someone that might do him harm. But there's a chain reaction about doing harm. Injury is like a row of dominoes. One falling piece upsets another and in the end it doesn't really matter who knocked the first piece over. They're all down, Major.

Now it was the German's turn to laugh. —Touché. I see I've taken on a master. If I must fall in an argument let it be before a master. You are an astute man, the kind of man who makes decisions in perspective. I'm sure that I can learn a lot from you.

—I doubt it, Major. You don't seem like a man who has anything to learn.

—Ah, but there is so much to learn for all of us. So much to consider. The present and the future and the past. What can be gained in the future without risk of being spoiled by the past. How the present can be bent to serve the future. It's the future that counts. The past may be unsavory, the present is seldom bearable, but the future is bright and clean. The problem is to keep it in good condition.

—And how do you do that?

—By something we might call a rational investment. As an American you know the value of investments. You have so many forms of prepaid insurance in America. Some you buy with money and others with services and through your wonderful American sense of realism. You are judicious in your choice of friends, the causes you embrace, the groups you join. You measure all their merits in advance, weigh their respective worth. You calculate the value of everything in realistic terms. This foolish Europe has so much to learn from you Americans. It's such a sentimental old continent, so emotional. I wonder how it managed to survive these two thousand years. Of course, we're trying to change all that; you might say that we're Americanizing Europe, improving old methods, streamlining operations, carefully removing all the inefficient ways that have made Europe such a ridiculously muddled continent. Europe has been mismanaged by humanitarians who never understood the truth of realism. They looked into the past for guideposts to the future, they sentimentalized a hazy dreamworld present while looking at the past. They were idealists of the heart. We, just as you Americans, Mr. Loomis, are idealists of reason. While these sad, foolish old Europeans said, We think, therefore we are, we say, We are, therefore we act. And this is rational. This is the making of decisions in the present to influence the future. This is emotional uninvolvement with both past and present. Nothing is quite as wasteful as emotion. One should make only rational investments. To think emotionally is not to think at all. In fact, I sometimes wonder whether thought is at all important. To act is everything.

—I'd say it took a little thought before they put up the Empire State Building or tossed the Hoover Dam into a gorge.

—Planning, Mr. Loomis, not thought. Planning has clear goals. It's a constructive, rational use of the brain. Pure thought is theoretical and has no end product. Planning is applied thought, if you must use the word, or harnessed thought. It is exploitable and it brings tangible results. Unharnessed thought produces nothing tangible, and the best that can be said for it is that it serves to exercise the brain, like mental gymnastics. Up, down, arms in, arms out, and now touch your toes. Useless by itself. Add an emotional content and you are actually doing yourself harm. Feelings, or any other emotional extravagance, are no more than weakness. When you feel, you indulge in weakness. Daydreaming is no more than a chronic inability to act.

—And to act is everything, of course, Loomis said.

—Of course.

—Never considering anyone except yourself? That doesn't seem like much for two thousand years of human growth.

—Oh, come now, Mr. Loomis. Of course there must be feelings of a kind. A father trains his children, a teacher teaches them. There is a certain emotional relationship between them. But it is disciplined, controlled, and it has a purpose. We Germans are known for our affection for our children and for small animals. You Americans are known for the same sentiments. We can both afford to sentimentalize over anything small enough not to present us with a real problem. It takes no thought at all to be a good parent or to be kind to a dog. It calls for no particular emotional investment.

—I suppose you mean like love or honor. Pride.

—Exactly. Have you ever seen love, Mr. Loomis? Can you describe its length and width and height? How much does it weigh? Do you know its shape and general dimensions? Is it square or round? Can you lift it with one hand or does it take two?

—If you had ever known it . . .

—But I never have. And, if I may suggest, neither have you nor anyone else whom I respect. If it existed, someone would have seen it. You think of love in terms of its object, not in its own terms. But would you describe water as the jug that holds it? The jug is one thing, water is another. Water has its own characteristics; it has definition. Love is intangible and it has no recognizable physical characteristics or mechanical properties or form or definition. It is a word used to describe an irrational commitment, a sort of temporary mental aberration. I think poets used it because they didn't know about mental aberrations. And it's a prettier word. And if you know that love and all the other products of abstract thought do not exist, it makes you wonder a little about thought itself. Have you ever seen a machine, Mr. Loomis, whose end product is nothing? Only one thing produces nothing. Nothing produces nothing, Mr. Loomis.

—And if intangibles don't exist, then the emotions that produce them don't exist either. Is that your point, Major?

—You understand me perfectly.

—There is no love, you say, no honor, pride, respect, compassion, sympathy or hope. There is, in fact, only human machinery.

—Rational machinery. Beautiful sentient mechanisms which can plan and act and be emotionally uninvolved, which are motivated exclusively by reason, and which pursue a preset course towards a logical conclusion.

—I understand now how National Socialism could develop here.

—Ah, Mr. Loomis. We are the Americans of Europe. Nothing I've said is new in your country. Our values are the same. Our routes may differ but we both agree on the ultimate goals. Germany has merely accelerated the application of your philosophy. The development, the genius behind the philosophy, is yours.

—Thank you, Loomis said. He felt himself trembling. —I can't tell you what this makes me feel.

—We are the first to admit how much we owe America. Your country is the first capital of reason.

—Yes. Thank you. I would be proud, if pride existed. . . .

—Ah, Mr. Loomis. A little trap for me?

—No. No more traps.

—I am delighted to hear it. But, of course, you are American and that makes the difference.

Loomis clenched his fists to control the trembling. —Does it make any difference? Does it really alter a single fact?

The major smiled. —Oh, I would say so. Good-day, Mr. Loomis.

Loomis went up to his room and poured himself a drink.

Drink and you don't remember.

When you drink, the faces blend one into another and truths can be forgotten and halftruths expanded and twisted to suit what you want to believe, and you can find that necessary righteousness, that invaluable sense of injury that lets you feed on another's sense of guilt, and you can hurt viciously without feeling anything and you can find a rationale for everything you do. Everything you want to do. Everything that makes it hard for you to look into a mirror. I mean, without the drink. Without your precious sense of injury you'd avoid the mirrors. Because of what might wait for you in one. Or might not wait. Because it isn't really a matter of what you might see. It is a matter of what you might *not* see if you looked hard enough into a mirror. Because, perhaps, you'd find it empty when you looked hard enough into it and then, perhaps, you'd never want to find yourself in it . . .

So drink. And do not think. And then you don't remember.

He stood by his window looking out, thinking that the view was not nearly as pleasant as the view from his apartment in Warsaw had been. Tomorrow I will write to Nimi, he thought, and to Mr. Otis. He did not think that, being an American and a neutral, he would be troubled further about Lala, especially in view of his father-in-law's German connections. He decided that after lunch he would look for souvenirs for David.

Friday, September the twenty-second

I THE CONQUEROR

Coming into Vienna on the noon train from Krakow, Erich was conscious of his lack of pleasure. It wasn't anything as definite as anger or as undefined as apprehension, but a combination of the two: a vague, displaced irritation and a lack of ease. Certainly there was no reason for irritation of any kind; everything had gone remarkably well for him and if anything he should have been pleased. He was alive and well and not in danger of any kind, and no one else in the Panzerkorps Germania could claim that distinction. There was, in fact, no more Panzerkorps Germania. What was left of it was wandering about in woods northwest of Lwow, drowning in quicksand, hunted by peasants with pitchforks, lost and no longer soldierly, while here he was, comfortable on red plush in this firstclass (officers only) compartment of an excellent fast train, smoking a delicate cigar with a long white ash. The train rolled through peaceful countryside where nothing was damaged, nothing was displaced or injured or on fire, and the neat towns and townships and checkered fields and somnolent blue woods slipped past the moving windows of the train as if they were part of another planet. Nothing suggested war or a thought of war; it was as if this soaring, mountainous, clean land (with air bright and sparkling as if after rain) had never known destruction and never would, and the combination of Austria, Germany, and any kind of devastation was impossible.

—Have a drink, Lieutenant, said the Wehrmacht major sitting across the aisle. He held out a bottle of Zubrowka. —I recommend it.

—I don't drink, Erich said, feeling the irritation.

—No? Pity. It's excellent stuff. Wonderful cure for combat fatigue. But then perhaps you gentlemen of the SS aren't very tired.

—No reason to be tired, Erich said softly.

—Ah.

The major laughed and poured himself another drink and looked at it with pleasure, and the Luftwaffe fighterpilot looked bored (being young), and the staff colonel in redstriped trousers looked at the major with measured annoyance. Careful, the quick look said. Don't involve us all. He was a thin colonel with a withered face and a *Pour le Mérite* from the other war shining at his throat. He made a point of staring through the window while the major laughed. Erich watched the major, tasting the man's enmity and contempt and feeling the beginning of that other feeling that came at such times. He felt a slow excitement and a warmth. It was like that time in the fields before the bombers came and he was walking up to Bar with secret laughter, and like the time he sat over Nickel's corpse in the appleorchard, waiting for Kuno Saal and Huneker, watching the huge wooden tongue of Nickel nodding at the sky.

He waited for the major to go on but the Wehrmacht officer said nothing more. The slow warmth ebbed and there was only that curious irritation. There was no reason for the irritation. Certainly the major had nothing to do with it; it had been there before the not quite sober officer had first got on the train.

Erich thought that he could crush the major and the withered colonel and the Luftwaffe pilot any time he wished. He could erase them, make them vanish. The small green card so carefully buttoned down in his left breast-pocket made possible the quick destruction of almost anyone. The green card and the contents of the scarlet envelope in the new flat briefcase on the baggagerack. They made him a modern magician. He thought he could turn the major into an animal anytime he wanted and the thought of the laughing major (no longer laughing) jumping through hoops or sitting up to beg and (if pressed to do so) howling at the moon made him want to laugh. But he did not laugh. He hoped the major would continue to show his contempt so that the slow excitement would come back. He watched the major. He smoked the excellent cigar.

He had come into Krakow two days earlier, miraculously plucked from his regiment in the Janow Woods. The regiment had come into the woods with the other regiments of the Panzerkorps Germania and had spread itself among the sand dunes and yellowclay mounds of a Tartar battlefield, between the highgrass swamps and belts of quicksand there, and waited for the fall of Lwow so that the grand triumphal entry could be made. This was to be the corps' first triumphal entry, and everything was new. Guns of unheard-of caliber (self-propelled 155-millimeter pieces), Czech Mark IV tanks, armored halftracks and troopcarriers, a huge motorpool, beautiful lightweight motorcycles with chrome handlebars, lacquered steelhelmets and (for officers) patentleather boots, belts, crossbelts and pistolholsters, highpolished leather mapcases (complete with maps and acetate and multicolored mechanical pencils) and binocularcases, soft woolfiber uniforms with permanent creases in the sleeves and trousers, ribbons and decorations and ceremonial daggers and silverlooped cords and badges and chromed insignia and silverembroidered armbands, tall hills of crates and bales and freshsmelling cloth, woodstocks deepstained with protective oils, and new men. The old men rested and renewed themselves. Replacements sang songs in the clearings. The corps waited in the cool woods listening to Fieldmarshal List's siegeartillery and to the airbombs bombarding Lwow, all distant. No trees ran and no one died. It was a Sunday outing, a *Wanderjahre* day with scat, volleyball and accordionmusic. A picturebook war.

It had the campaign smells and the faroff battlesounds and the soil was foreign and the hard warmth of comradeship was near and no one was being hurt who mattered. It couldn't be better. And then the Fiesler Storch touched down in a clearing and presently the pilot handed Erich the scarlet envelope, and war, peace, hopes, career, in fact everything connected with his previous life became unimportant. Everything lost significance in comparison to this. And then (as the Sturmbannführer made fond fatherly noises and Dietrich stared at Erich with immense respect and officers who had turned their backs after Kielce now tried to catch his eye with congratulatory smiles) Erich knew that no one would ever turn away from him again and no more demonstrations would be necessary. The scarlet envelope contained orders calling him home to Vienna and also the green card of membership in the most exclusive club in the world: Brandt's special office of the SS/SD, the modern magicians who could make anybody vanish with a pointed finger. The green card was a passport to everything and payment in advance for everything and it was a key to every door and a weapon against every threat. Its bearers were answerable only to the Club.

Reading the contents of the scarlet envelope, Erich thought that there was a mistake. His father had insufficient influence for this kind of appointment. His father was a loyal party member, one of the pre-Putsch old guard whose partycard bore only two numbers. He was a Doctor and Professor without benefit of formal education, and a luminary in the department of education in Vienna, and he had a ten-room apartment not far from the Hotel Metropole, and knew everyone. But not even the lownumbered card could secure for Erich his particular appointment.

Only luck remained, and he had learned that luck was never to be wholly trusted. Luck needed skillful hands to help it along. But he knew better than to spit at luck. He flew to Krakow, where he found that his luck had been even better than he thought. While he was finishing an expertly prepared dinner in the Wawel, with the old, legendweary city spread like a blurred mosaic pavement under Castle Hill and the messboys were advancing with dessert and coffee and the first of his delicate cigars, two regiments of Polish infantry came off the road somewhere northwest of Lwow and began to run silently through the Janow Woods. They went in lines of companies abreast, each soldier holding his bayoneted rifle with his right hand and his neighbor's elbow with his left, and they fell on the unsuspecting Panzerkorps Germania and in the eight hours between Erich's dinner and the morning's breakfast the corps ceased to exist. Four thousand men died in the Janow Woods and the surrounding swamps and quicksand and morass, and another thousand vanished during the pursuit, and what remained was scattered over eighty square kilometers of hostile land where pitchforkbearing peasants hunted for survivors, and the beautiful new guns and tanks and motorcycles and the hills of crates and bales first drowned in gasoline and then burned in blue and yellow fire. There was enough equipment to motorize half the remaining Polish regiments, but (the reporting SS officer said, laughing) wouldn't you know it? There weren't enough Poles who knew how to drive; they took no more than a dozen cars and motorcycles. They burned the rest. (—*Well, I suppose that's small consolation,* the officer said. *You must have had friends there, lieutenant.* —*Yes.* Erich said, trying not to laugh. *I had friends there.*)

He thought of Dietrich and the incredibly thin sergeant who had made a fool of him in the Polish village, and he thought of the SS men who had laughed and those who had turned their backs and those who had seen his weakness in Kielce and those who might have suspected his weakness in the village where he had let the Jew and the peasants live. They were most likely dead and he was free.

Erich laughed, watching the countryside pass through the train window. The major stared at him. The withered colonel looked into some papers. The Luftwaffe fighterpilot stroked the broad ribbons on his chest.

—Well, you can laugh, Lieutenant, the major said. That is at least something. It's proof that you're a human being, I suppose.

Erich smiled at him and the major frowned.

—Well, what about that drink? Changed your mind?

—No.

The window blurred then with industrial smoke and the trainwhistle blew. Small homes of factoryworkers slid past. Erich watched them falling away from the train. Ahead was Vienna. He wondered what his job would be and who had wanted him in the Club and why. He wondered what the drinking major would do if he knew that he, Erich, the inconsequential lieutenant of SS whom the major baited, carried a green card. Well, he thought, looking at the major, feeling the warmth returning, you just never know about that sort of thing. Not until the men in leathercoats come knocking in the night.

Warmth, yes; he felt it: It was good.

With the slow warmth returning and excitement rising, the irritation died. He felt it but it didn't bother him. He smiled and settled himself deeper in the red plush cushions and crossed his legs and yawned. He moved his booted foot up and down as he watched the major. The patentleather boots glittered like black jewels. The major's boots were scarred and not particularly clean. Erich smiled at the major, feeling the slow excitement. The major did not smile.

Erich got up and stretched, observing the annoyance of the major. The long white ash broke off his cigar. Flecks of ash settled on the major's trousers.

—What in hell do you think you're doing? the major exploded.

—Sorry. It was an accident.

—So you're sorry, are you, you imitation soldier?

—Yes. Your leg was in the way.

—What?

—Gentlemen, said the withered colonel. Please. Remember who you are.

—Who we are, sir? I know who I am. I am an officer of the Wehrmacht. An insolent puppy is spilling ashes on me. Damn it, Lieutenant, if you can't handle a cigar don't smoke! And, incidentally, do you mind addressing me by my rank, Lieutenant?

—No sir, Erich said. He smiled. —Not at all, sir.

—Well, do it, damn your impudence!

—*Jawohl,* Herr Major.

—That's better. If you people want to play at soldiers, then act like soldiers. You need discipline. You need to learn how to drink and handle a cigar. Or did you take some sort of vow of abstinence?

—No vows, sir, Erich said.

—That, at least, is something. You SS gentlemen take the damnedest oaths about all kinds of things. Abstinence until victory. You might get pretty thirsty before you have your victory.

—Indeed, sir? I thought the Polish war was almost over.

—Nothing is over till it's done. And you won't hurry it along with vows. You SS gentlemen with your vows. Those are monastic habits. Don't you think there can be too much dedication? Next you'll be buggering each other.

—Now really, major, the thin colonel said. He cleared his throat and the decoration jumped. The fighter pilot laughed.

—Sorry, the major said. Hard to remember that a man must watch his tongue among his brother officers. It's quite a testimonial for our times. Well, dammit, Lieutenant, what are you grinning at?

—Nothing at all.

The soft warmth was all around him then, the excitement soared. He closed his eyes. He thought his eyes would betray him. He folded his arms across his chest to keep his breathing even. He felt the card in his breastpocket move with each breath he took.

When the train stopped and the doors were opened and the other officers stepped down on the platform, Erich took his time about getting out. He gathered his bags and his shining briefcase and lit another of his excellent cigars and sent a porter in search of a taxi. Then, comfortably seated, totally content, he had himself taken to the Metropole.

Smooth plateglass storefronts slid past the carwindows. They flowed like molten glass speckled with brilliant colors.

It seemed then as if a shadow of some kind passed before the windows. Was it only the excitement of the train gone now? But even the street darkened for a moment. Clouds? There were no clouds that autumn in the magnificent clear sky, here or in Poland. Clouds . . . rain . . . snow . . . a blue wall of ice rising out of mist at sixteen thousand feet . . . snow hissing under skis . . . These belonged to impossible, innocent yesterdays, days of the long schuss and the arrowlike dive down the difficult skiruns, the multicolored crowd gasping like a distant thunderclap, wind singing, body light and heart full and singing, boards whistling on the crisp snow. Everything magnificent and fresh and now not quite believable, as though years had passed between that time and this. He had mastered the slopes but never the mountains. Not the true mountains, the blue giants that drained into the moon. Adam had done that and he had not, and he knew he never would, and he envied Adam and hated him for his familiarity with the world of giants, dazzling with rock and ice.

—*What do you see there?* he had said once.

—*A sea of gold clouds and blue wind and other summits and there is no end to the horizon.*

—*You mean infinity?* (Purposely derisive.)

—*It's like infinity, only you know it isn't. Up there you're only given what you bring up with you.*

—*A means of self-expression, then? Man overcomes himself, affirms himself in danger?*

—*I think it is the struggle more than the danger. The reaching for the absolute. You see, up there the universe disappears. Space, time, dimensions, fear, suffering no longer exist. Everything becomes very simple; there is a calmness. Not an empty calmness but the essence of activity . . . like on the crest of a wave.*

—*But what do you feel there? About yourself, I mean.*

—*You'll laugh.*

—*Not I. What is it?*

—*I am absolutely sure that there is something indestructible in me and that the summit I have reached is only a beginning; I know that I can go on forever, you see, against anything.*

Immortality? He wanted to kindle such a flame in himself. He made the seasons' rounds of Chamonix and Cortina d'Ampezzo and Zermatt and other climbs but never to the top. He knew the splitting headaches that attack at sixteenhundred feet, but not the great calmness.

He didn't want to think about Adam, and so, of course, he did. He couldn't get away from Adam. His heart raced and he felt the start of nausea deep inside his stomach. Envy and gratitude and hate and the old liking too.

There had been liking, certainly. A pleasant friendship. And there was that dramatic rescue on the Gerlachowka. He recalled black night and blueblack icewall in the crevice, thin calls like the baying of lost hounds, distant pin-pointlights of torches like so many fireflies on another slope, and the immense, ironic sleepiness that meant death by freezing. No amount of shrugs and smiles and humorous detractions could reduce Adam's act.

Adam (he thought) worked his way down the blueblack icewall in the night. Click of piton and hammer, chink of axe. Roping and hauling, rubbing and massaging, slapping and wakening and bringing back to life. Adrianne had been so quiet that night, looking at the boy.

Erich rummaged in his kitbag and found the cognacbottle. The drink was tasteless and he didn't feel it. He massaged his hands and wondered why they hurt. He drank again and saw his face blurring in the sheetglass between the taxidriver's back and himself, and he turned away from it. Outside the sun had fallen behind tall buildings and made them grey and the trees skeletal and set the roofs on fire.

The great warmth, the good feeling of excitement and total assurance, was beginning to dissipate. He felt cold sweat forming on his forehead.

He tried to freshen the good feeling, whip up the hot excitement and call back that inestimably bright picture of a certain future (all possibility of humiliation gone, all roadblocks demolished), but he knew that the warm feeling had crested for him and in a moment or two would be quite gone. Cognac didn't bolster the crumbling good feeling; he could no longer bow ironically to the redstreaked, pale face in the sheetglass mirror, because there *were* uncertainties ahead and there were humiliations and the future was studded with pitfalls like an untried mountain sheeted in fog. He felt an immense pity for himself. It was like what he had felt one day as a child (hating it and longing for it at the same time) when a teacher had humiliated him in front of his class. He had prepared the wrong lesson for the day and heard the questions asked of him in bewildered disbelief that changed to nightmarelike awareness and then the bittersweet self-pity as his ignorance was exposed and his classmates hooted. Home from school and still engulfed in his luxurious sorrow, he had suddenly, in an icecold, calculated fury, snatched his goldfish Theobald from its ornamental bowl and scalded it to death in the washwater boiling on the kitchenstove. He had watched the glittering small creature leap crazily in the steaming water, spinning in the thin blue bubbles, then die at once.

He felt the cold sweat bursting from his temples. What made me do it? Who forced me to do it? Who humiliated me and jeered and laughed at me and made me do it?

I don't want to hurt anybody, he told the plateglass mirror, but they don't give me any choice.

Later, as he waited to be interviewed by the Major Reinhardt his orders had brought him to, he grew calmer, and then he had an illumination that would always stay with him, that would always afterwards be confirmed. He saw himself at this moment of his best good luck as destroyed beyond repair, and it came to him that he would never possess anything good in life because he was not whole enough to hold it. There would be the moments of sudden warmth and excitement, but they would pass and the darkness would come and the good things would slip from his grasp. He wanted to protest out loud, but the SS sergeant-receptionist was watching him, and besides, what could he protest about, whom could he blame? His parents? Hitler? His own commitment to the cause? Libesis had said something and he was trying to recall it when the buzzer on the sergeant's desk made a noise of a bee. Erich roused himself.

—The major will see you now, Fahnrich. Sorry to keep you waiting, but he has just returned from Berlin.

Erich got up blinking away the tears he had tried to shed for the loss, the waste, the everlasting destruction.

1 ADAM

He lay on his cot, unblinking like a cat in the new dark, to which he had not yet become accustomed, waiting for the Germans to come with his dinner. He wondered if Reinhardt would be along tonight. He had not seen Reinhardt for some time. He thought he had seen him a day or two before, watching from an upstairs window while he walked around the garden with the orderly, Werner, along the rectangle of glasstopped wall. He had felt a great urge to do something silly, like standing on his head or thumbing his nose. But whoever it was had not watched long. He stepped away from the window. And Adam's urge to show how well he was feeling, how unharmed and untouched by his imprisonment, passed just as quickly. Adam went one more turn along the wall. Then it was time to go back to his room (complete with window, and time's daily passage marked beyond doubt by the changing light) and, eventually, sleep.

Sleep meant dreams and dreams still meant the chessboard. He dreaded sleep. He didn't know when Erich had first appeared on the chessboard and then stayed on after the dreams had ended. It was some time during those not quite clear days when the dream of chessboard never really ended but went on, interrupted for the chessgames and then resumed, and each time it began, the conclusion drew inexorably closer. It was the only logical conclusion: The falling wall of time, the mad uprushing of the tilted earth, could not be avoided. Each time the dream resumed, the chase across the chessboard grew more frantic, the white pawn was harassed with greater cunning, and the final moment between the cornering of the white pawn and Adam's merciful awakening was longer, more uncertain. Soon that crouching moment in the corner of the chessboard would be long enough; there would be time for his invisible opponent to point to the white pawn. Adam could not hope to keep the white pawn permanently running.

His friend the Communist had no longer screamed for him and time had slipped back into uncertainty, although he had known one thing: Whatever measure of time the Germans were providing was a fraud. He had clung to that one piece of certain knowledge, the one shred of reality his tortured friend-clock-calendar had provided.

Time had brought no solution, after all; time was not his friend.

He supposed that, in the end, he must have won the secret game the Germans were playing, because he had been taken out of the whitetiled room and restored to time and, certainly, no one treated him unkindly or paid particular attention to him, which was a mercy in its own right. But he had a vague recollection of words, his and another man's, which were more like impressions of words than anything recognizable but in which he had either agreed to something or had not agreed; he could not be sure. The voices were a threatening background to the game of chess; what they said was quite unintelligible and therefore could not be important. They had brought Erich to the shadowed edges of the giant board and then to the board. The words were threatening and confusing because the threat was undefined and it was quite impossible to detach them from words that came later.

He had a clear impression of his father sometime along then, swept up and off the giant chessboard, disappearing without sound; and this too had something to do with the words that Reinhardt was saying. Adam was then awake, or thought he was. He could not quite remember if there had been any interval between these words of Reinhardt's and those that had come earlier as impressions. Time had compressed into a solid unit and was no longer fluid; the words came slowly enough but still too fast for him: grey blur of words falling away like birds violent in the slipstream, yellowgrey whorls of fog. Everything then called for enormous effort; the fine prismatic edges of his mind were sheeted with lead.

But Reinhardt smiles and so the words appear to smile and now some have color. There is a flash of this in the thickrolling fog. There are the moonlight-yellow words of night: peace, rest, lack of motion, lack of need for effort. These close the eyes. And the purpling blueblack of the flat earth-before-sunrise falling away from mountains and, now and again, a calm seagreen word: low valleys in the afternoon. No longer grey. And then the rushing fall towards the time wallslows and the wind is no longer hurried and deafening in his ears and the mad checkerboard of the spinning earth no longer roars upward but recedes, steadying.

—*Well, that is excellent,* Reinhardt says. *But I had no doubts. Logic is always irresistible. You've come through handsomely and I have a reward for you. Listen, how would you like to see your good friend Erich? We've sent for him. The two of you can take a little holiday, perhaps climb some mountains.*

Can't say anything.

—*Too much all at once? Well, don't say anything. There'll be enough time for all the talking in the world; all that can wait. We are going to move you to a pleasant house where you and Erich can enjoy yourselves.*

—Thank you, Adam says.

—Well now, you see? From now on there will be nothing for you but the best.

Adam thinks of the best things. They mean life. He has a clear enough conception of death, having climbed mountains and made his bid, time and again, in the no man's land between life and death, the border zone of infinite strain and danger, and so he knows what life means, what the best things are. The taste of clean air after rain. Hot coffee in a metal cup drunk on a bittercold morning three miles in the sky. The smell of clean clothes freshwashed in a river and dried in the sun. Climbing up on a small hill, looking down. Houselights in a valley. The sound of rain on slateroofs and the taste of rain. The smell of new rope. The smell of linseed oil on aged wood. Wet stones, round and palmable. A red stove in a lodge with snow piled outside. Blue peaks coming up through cloud. A marmoset whistle.

He knows them well enough; he remembers them. But the words are still too fast to be caught and spoken.

So, Reinhardt says, *I have to leave you for a day or two. I must arrange a few things. But you'll be well looked after. Just go along with the men who are taking you and they'll look after you. I'll come to see you soon enough, and Erich is coming.*

—Yes. Thank you.

But no other words come to him although he can hear them in his head. He wonders why there is no chessgame. There is a strong arm around his shoulders, and then a long white corridor blinding with light and tile and reflectedlight where men in black move with hard assurance. Cool elevator falling. Stairs and corridors and stonesteps out into the street. Outside, a great revolving sun in a paleblue sky. Harsh sounds of traffic like broken pavingblocks. Heat. Glowing concrete. But a small wind comes down the avenue through the lindenbranches and it smells of trees.

—Gently now. Open the door, soldier.

Small car with open door. Dark interior. Someone helps him in. Huge weight of heat descends from the metal roof. The leather is immediately wet as he touches it, and then as quickly dry. The air is hot but sweet and it tastes dangerous without disinfectants; he can't breathe enough of it fast enough. He fills himself with it and it makes him dizzy and everything revolves and he lets go; everything lets go. Everything collapses and the tears come.

—Well, Reinhardt says and Reinhardt is laughing. *Does it taste good to you? Smell good? Fill yourself with it, breathe all you want. Goodbye for now.*

Then the car moves. The ride is long and unsmooth and the small car lurches. Adam can't hold himself erect on the seat. His rubber legs don't brace against the floor. He rolls about the seat like a soft balloon but he doesn't feel anything. His arms are also made of rubber; they won't brace against the slippery hot seat. But someone holds him steady. He smells the coarsewoolfiber of uniformcloth, sees black. Someone spills capsules from a small brown bottle. Faint sound of water poured out of a flask into a metal cup. *—So . . . Eins, Zwei, now relax.* And soon enough coolness comes and there is ease and the mad spinning of the car roof stops and a faint drumming starts low in his stomach and this pulse spreads into his arms and legs and soon enough this tappingbeat numbs everything. Breathing is quick and shallow. Difficult. Like after climbing up to sixteen thousand feet. The mind slows then and the body takes command from the icewind, and men deteriorate and falter and their resolve dissipates in the tempting wisps of cloud and strange fantasies leap out of the thin air into the oxygenstarved brain. So easy then to listen to the voices in the wind. But the quick breaths find length, after all, and gradually the arms and legs regain solidity and substance and the quivering rubber face is still and a man's will is everything.

Blackness comes to him out of the upper right corner of his field of vision; ease; lightness of a kind.

He had awakened refreshed as they slanted down the serpentine into a small town made familiar by recent memory: Baden. Erich had a summer home there, he remembered. He had spent part of a summer there; one of his best anywhere. The little town was beautiful. There were tall hills to climb—not even practice for a mountaineer but a way to enjoy golden afternoons. And woods to walk in. And there was young goose to be eaten and May wine to be drunk, and there were cool pools to sleep in, halfsubmerged at noon when the sun was hottest. At night the antiaircraft regiment turned searchlights on the ruined schloss above the town.

He sat up, looking for familiar sights: landmarks of that summer. And soon they drove up to the villa at the blind end of a dull, somnolent avenue of chestnuts and lindentrees. Blank walls with narrow doorways cut in the center with uncompromising sternness like sentryboxes, greenshuttered windows and slate roofs. The villa was one of two dozen, possibly more; the repetitious sameness of the walls confused the count. Each wall was four meters tall, Adam recalled; white, yellowing white and grey paint or a whitewashed brightness. Each enclosed a picturebook frontlawn and backgarden with summerhouse, whitepainted rustic bench, shrubs, two or three trees for hammocks and afternoon shade, the rope-and-canvas hammocks, deckchairs in white and red or green and yellow stripes. And the house. Each house was an exact replica of the others: whitepainted rectangles, Italianate stucco, two stories with six windows orderly as if for inspection on the upper floor, the groundfloor hidden from the street by the wall. The green shutters were either closed or open—the only difference. And greenglass rosettes in cloverleaf pattern above every door.

The roar of city traffic was a distant hum here, like the massed droning of an airfleet of bees. Broken green bottles on the walls speared the flat beams of the afternoon sun.

The car stopped at the villa, at the last wall. The wall was like a dam. Adam looked at the villa in astonishment. He could make no mistake about it, he was sure. (Downstairs: a hall with mirror splashed with the green light from the cloverleaf rosette, umbrellastand and elephantfoot wastebasket; kitchen in the rear; up front a dining room and a combination receptionroom-study-library. Upstairs: four bedrooms and a bathroom. Behind the house: a garage with quarters for the servants.)

—That's Erich's home.

—That's right. (This from his smiling escort.)

526

—Is this where we're going?
—Yes.
—Is Erich here?
—Not yet.
—But who said we could use it if he isn't here?
The escortofficer laughs; genuine amusement. *—Don't worry about it.*

It seemed like excellent advice since nothing made sense. What counted was that he was out of the whitetiled room where time was either fraud or sounds of pain, and that he was in this house which was so pleasantly remembered. He had an uncomfortable thought now and again that he had forgotten something important, an idea that he had done something he should not have done (why else this reprieve from the chessgames?), but he couldn't remember what it was. It seemed more likely that he had won the timegame the Germans had played, he with his friend the Communist; he had outlasted them. It was a lot more pleasant to think that. As for the other (the house, the garden, Erich's coming), why waste time guessing? The Germans had some plan, that was enough to know. He would wait to see what they wanted this time. And, in the meantime, there was a comfortable room with a window and days that had a morning, noon and nightfall, that were above suspicion, and Erich was coming.

He heard the cars drive up on the streetside of the villa and, later, the voices: Werner (reporting) and Reinhardt and one or two others. Then footsteps up the stairs, doors opening, the dull thud of baggage. Dull drone of voices indistinct through walls. He got up and put his ear to his keyhole but it was no better. He went back to his cot, careful about the creaking floor.

An hour went by, perhaps more. He heard them coming down the corridor, two men taking care to walk quietly. He rolled his face at once into his pillow and pretended sleep. They would expect him to be sleeping; his midday meal had included tablets, which he had kept under his tongue until Werner had left him.

The key turned. The door opened. Voices.

—Adam?

Keep the breath shallow, quick. The mouth open.

Reinhardt: *—Well, what do you think?*

Erich: *—I wouldn't have known him.*

Reinhardt: *—Yes. He's changed a bit. So would you. Anyway, he's got to look better than that.*

—He looks like a corpse.

—Makeup and a retouching brush will do for the pictures. But he won't fool the journalists, not even my tame stable of foreign and domestic scribblers. He must be absolutely right before we show him.

—Fresh air would help.

—We had to nail up the windows. Security precautions. You can charge the repairs to the state.

—I didn't mean that I objected . . .

*—Never mind that now. Get him presentable as quickly as you can. I want

to show him to the correspondents before we take Warsaw. Prus is in Warsaw. I want the boy in the foreign papers before we march into that town. I want Prus to know we have his boy before he tries to get away from Warsaw. We'd have a devil of a time finding him then. All clear?

—One question, sir. Isn't it enough for Prus to know that we hold a hostage? Why do we have to make Adam cooperate with us?

—So that he will look pretty for the correspondents. Would you want to show them a martyr? There will be quite unsympathetic neutrals among the correspondents.

—Ah, I didn't think . . .

—That's clear. (Then, with the more familiar ring of kindness, the firm benevolence:) You're still new to this and it's a big job for a starter. We can run Poland with Prus or without him. But what counts is to get him in our hands. He is a symbol to too many people. Symbols can cause trouble. And we can't let our Russian allies get their hands on him; they know too well how to exploit symbols. We're lucky to have Adam. Now you know why we must have a smiling Adam for the correspondents. Your former friendship makes everything simple.

Erich laughed.

Reinhardt: —What's that about?

—An irony. I owe him my appointment to the special branch. I should be grateful to him.

—Feel anything you want if it helps your job. What do you think of it?

—The job, sir?

—Yes. The job.

—It's easy, I think.

—Perhaps it is. But you must be careful. Suddenly Reinhardt's voice changed. —Do you know what would happen to you if you lost him? What has happened to him would be like a moment of bliss by comparison.

—I understand, sir, Erich seemed to whisper.

He must have made some movement then, or perhaps a sound, some small sign that betrayed him. He wondered how he could have managed to control himself as long as he had. His chest felt as if it would explode at any moment. His mouth was dry and his eyes were burning. He smelled Reinhardt's cologne and the sharp smell of their leather as they bent over him.

—Adam?

The voice was still kind and authoritative. Still benevolent. But it held no reassurance of any kind. The slap was sharp and expertly delivered and he had waited for it and let his head roll. He felt their fingers pulling up his eyelids and he rolled his eyes upward.

There was a sound that could be anything: a cleared throat, a grunt of satisfaction.

—Still out.

They left him then. The door opened, closed. The footsteps receded. The footsteps went downstairs. Soon a car started up on the streetside. The car drove away.

Adam lay a long time on his cot, watching night come on. He felt weak, used up.

What were his weapons now? Where was the advantage? No help here from a screaming Communist. None from Erich. He was, himself, a German weapon, aimed at his father and his country.

He cursed himself for his stupid hopes. He felt the tears come and fought to keep them back. There was no one to see them, so what did it matter? But he didn't want the comfort of tears, not yet. He wanted to keep his thoughts calm and orderly, and worked to piece them together, to slow them down. Poland . . . his father . . . pain and disappointment . . . bluetipped pine and the charges of small boys . . . war (suddenly vivid, suddenly personal) . . . his thoughts chaotically enmeshed and intertwined like twisting rolls of fog reaching out of night.

He stared down the long tunnel of the window, falling away in darkness. The moon, a small crooked slice of light, splashed at the bottom like the reflection of a distant sun in an abandoned well.

He thought about the longago once-upon-a-time when he had lived, successfully hidden from the world, disguised as a child. They had been magic years in which he had been the small and secret center of a universe that moved about him with great roars and creaks and heavy thumps, taking infinite care not to tread on him, pressing hardstubbled and softsmelling cheeks against him, mussing up his hair and, for all its heaviness and hugeness, making him warm with infinite supplies of lovingkindness.

The planets of this universe were his father and mother and old Grzes and a succession of maids and an uncle and an aunt (who was not a particularly happy planet) and his cousin Pawel. These revolved above him, looking down at him in a puzzled but friendly way as though unable to believe that this small human sun would someday revolve as they did. The spaces occupied by this universe varied from time to time but each had its own battery of wonders. There was the town space, which was an apartment of seven rooms, and one of these was a salon with marvelous overstuffed armchairs that one could hide in, and many albums and photographs of fierce faces and frockcoats and soft faces and enormous sleeves that one could inspect, and a silky antimacassar that one could blow on to make it move, and a carpet splashed with blues and reds and golds to walk on carefully, and darktoned paintings in huge golden frames and an infinity of objects that you couldn't touch but that you fingered in imagination to see what they would feel like. Another room was the *gabinet* with hardleather chairs (which could be pressed into service as battlechargers like the hard brown battlechargers in the paintings) and with the huge glass pool of his father's desktop which caught the red light of the sun in the afternoon and was like fire but cold, and the rows of books in cases, and rolls of maps. There was the small, pipesmelling room of Grzes and his fantastic leather trunk in which lay an assortment of amazing treasures (brown bits of paper tied with ribbon, greenish medals, old coins and paper banknotes with bearded men and delicatelooking women peering from the corners, soft and hard books with grey paper in them, dry flowers in them, bits of grass and powdery blue petals) and which itself looked like the treasure chest of pirates. There was the kitchen where the peasantwomen brought jars of milk and cream and sourcream in the morning, with its delicate smell of baking bread that you could taste at the roof of your mouth as soon as you smelled it, and the slaughtered fowl and fish and bulbous potatoes and feathery green tops of vegetables heaped on the wooden table, and the start of the dinnersoup bubbling on the great black stove, and the small pieces of magnificence sneaked to him by the cook. There was his parents' room where you had to knock on the door before you went in but where you hurried every Sunday morning to scramble up on the huge bed, much bigger than your own bed, to bury yourself between Her softness and sweetsmellingness and His hardstubbled, gentlehanded roughness. Everything was enormous, huge; those were the words. Everything was new and if not new it could renew itself at will and everything delighted. His mother's face was soft and like the antimacassar in the salon (fringed with brown gossamer tendrils) and her eyes looked at him calmly and her hand was gentle and reassuring although firm enough but you had to be gentle with your mother (father said) because she was a woman. You did not have to be gentle with your father, who tossed you up in the air with your nightshirt husked off your rump if you flew rumpfirst and who had a knee on which you could ride or which you could use as a slide and whose face scratched and smelled of leather and tobacco. This was the Sunday-morning room, the best of all the rooms next to your own. Your room was a familiar place where everything was yours and you could do what you wished with everything and *you* were the biggest, the strongest and the most important, but the best thing about being the strongest and the biggest in that room was that whenever you wanted you could go into another room and be small. And waking up in your room every morning was a marvelous experience because each day was good and would be better (you knew) than the one before no matter how good that day had been. You watched the sun come through the scalloped edges of the curtains, between the curtains and through the fluted muslin columns that were then pink and shining like the brilliant moist grooves of the gills of fish. You woke in silence and waited for the day to start with the first sounds from the kitchen: the thump of wood laid in the stove and the lowered voices of Grzes and the cook grunting in early-hour brevity. Eventually, he would hear the ringing of the little clock beside father's bed, the quick stopping of this sound and then the thud of his father's feet striking the floor and then his footsteps. That was the signal for leaping out of bed into the middle of the cold floor and a quick gallop on the cold parquet to watch Father shave.

Father with white beard of foam before the mirror, long squarecut razor flashing, slicing into foam, flicking foam into the basin: —*Good morning, son. Had your shave yet?* —*No, sir. Waiting for you to finish.* —*We can share the mirror. Your little face doesn't take much room.* Then the happy scramble up on a stool and his round face pushed into the mirror between his father's arms. —*Hmm. Little rough today. Had a big night?* —*Pretty big, father.* —*Watch that stubble, son. Don't want you to scratch up my chest. What would your mother say?* —*Ha ha.*

And then the heavy finger scoops up foam from the marvelous jar and spreads it on the smooth, round face. —*Don't cut your nose off, now.* —*I'll be careful, sir.* And the unbladed safetyrazor slides softly on his cheeks. —*A little cologne, son?* —*If I may, father.* —*Of course you may. We men don't smell as pretty as your mother, but that's no reason why we can't try, is it*

—*I expect it isn't, sir. Why don't we smell as pretty?* —*We have to work, son, we have things to do. There's little time for prettiness of any kind for you and me.* —*But I don't work, father. I have time.* —*Of course you work, son. When I'm gone you're the head of the household, aren't you? You look after your mother. That's man's work.* —*But doesn't Grzes look after us when you are gone, sir?* —*I hope so. He looked after me at one time. But he is a servant and not part of our family no matter how much we may like him. No, when I am gone you are the man here. You missed a part under your chin.*

And then the toweling with the icecold towels Grzes brought from the refrigerator in the boxroom, a large towel for his father and a smaller one for him, cold and stiff and rough. It made him gasp and laugh and brought tears to his eyes at the same time and made his face red. His father's laugh: —*Ha ha ha. Rub that sleep away, son, chase it away. The battle of the day begins.* His father's body under the cold towel was as smooth as his and as red, but huge and hard and knotted, and his hands were long with thin blue lines on them. These were veins. There was blood in them. If one cut through a vein the blood would come out. His father's arms, above the hands, were corded, with thick ropes of muscle bulging out at the shoulder. —*Well, all ready now? Get dressed and go and kiss your mother. I'll see you at breakfast.*

This was a quiet meal with rustling newspapers and small things said. —*Will you be late tonight?* —*I don't believe so.* —*I'll plan a small dinner, then. Michal and Zofia may come by this evening. I hope they'll leave that impossible young man at home.* —*He's just young.* —*He's a Cossack.* —*More like a Tartar. We have Tartar blood, you know. He's a spirited fellow.* —*I would like to despirit him a little when he is here. I wish you'd tell Michal to make him behave when he comes here.* —*I'll be damned if I will.* —*Must you swear with Adam at the table?* —*Sorry. But I'm not going to tell Michal how to bring up his son. Mine keeps my hands full, don't you, little one?* (A laugh and then a disapproving look from mother.) —*So you don't think you will be late today?* —*No. There is nothing special scheduled for today. There is the usual trouble with the politicians.* —*Someone should do something about them.* —*I expect so. But it'll probably be another politician.* —*You haven't been to the palace lately?* —*No. Why do you ask?* —*It would be good for us to go there more often..* —*Hmm. I'm told I make the politicians nervous. Soldiers make them nervous.* —*You don't make the President nervous.* —*He is too busy to make himself nervous over anybody.* —*Aren't the others busy? I would have thought they'd have enough to do.* —*They have enough to do but they don't do it.* —*Someone should make them do it. And if the President can't do it it should be someone new.* —*Meaning me?* —*Why not? You are a national hero, aren't you? You have an immense following. I'm sure that if you don't do it somebody else will.* —*Not while I command this military district.* —*More coffee, dear?* —*Thank you. And I won't be late.* —*It will be a small dinner, as I said.*

Each morning darkened just a bit when the man rose from the breakfast table and tugged his short uniformtunic abruptly into place (thrusting his chin fiercely up and out, the jaws tightening, the skin gleaming tightstretched on his cheekbones and on his chin, and the high, silverbraided collar glittering below it) and Grzes came in with the beautifulshining belt (catching the new light on brass stud and buckle and the golden saberloops sewn into the leather) and Grzes held the belt around the man's waist from behind and the man fastened it with one quick, unsmiling swing of snakelike pointed end, over and under the buckle, impaling it, and his face hardened and his mouth thinned out as though with this act of fastening the broad band of gleaming leather around his waist something went out of him and something else entered, and Grzes slipped the forward end of the Sam Browne belt under the backedge of the silverstudded shoulderstrap and the man reached up and grasped the beltend and pulled it down across his chest and snapped it into the first of the loops and his chest arched out and he stood in the coldmorning sun above the wreckage of the breakfast table banded in brass and leather like a god. Then Grzes handed the man the hardcornered, squaretopped cap with the silver eagle and silverbraid wriggling across the crown, and the gloves, and the short, leathercovered stick, and the man smiled once, abruptly, but he was no longer smiling at anyone in the breakfastroom but at something inside himself and outside the room. When his heels struck the parquet after that they had the sound of thunder.

The universe shrank and held immensely still when the frontdoor slammed behind the man. When it stirred again, each movement was hesitant and each sound was harsh; each click of coffeecup on saucer, spoon on plate, clattered unbearably, and it was only afterwards, when the universe expanded into the yard and the small park across the street, that movement resumed its several degrees of speed and there was gentle sound and color and acceptance of the truncated day and the sun had warmth again and the grass and tree bark had texture.

Trees, park, grass. Crickets roared in the grass. His mother: —*Crickets chirp. They do not roar.* But he knew better. Crickets chirped to people but to other crickets and things smaller than themselves they roared. Across the street from the small park and grassplots (and the roaring crickets) were the houses. It was a town of narrow houses that leaned upon each other as if in mutual support of their old age, infirmity and disappointment; they were pressed together so closely that they seemed to spill upwards to escape. Their chimneys showed a sagging lack of spirit. Still, they had grandeur of a kind and a longsuffering sort of patience and tolerance toward small heavenly bodies. Their cornices supported gaping gargoyle mouths (avid and fishlike) and carved granite filigrees with heads, faces, moons, suns and intricate designs which moved this way and that as the light changed. Thick ironstudded gates hung by enormous hinges, and behind them were the dry and damp smells of the halls, stairways and (beyond the halls) yards. There laundrylines slapped into each other with their windanimated cargos, and the peddler cried the virtues of his fish and chestnuts and vegetables, and knives and scissors could be sharpened on a whetstone trundled in by a Jew in black *kaftan,* and old clothes and newspapers and rags and bones and assorted discards could be lowered in a basket from the kitchen windows. This was the world commanded by the kitchen windows, a wildly different portion of the total universe where voices were shrill and the smells made up their own cacophony, and where one could not go to play. Park, grass, trees, roaring crickets: That was where one played. You said: Who will be the Marshal, and you said: I will be the Marshal. You be the Bolshevik (or the German or the Swede or the Tartar or the

Cossack or the *Moskal*) and this bench will be the fortress of Zbararz and this stump will be the cloister of Jasnogora, the Mountain of Light. And if you didn't get to be the Marshal or Hetman Czarnecki or King John Sobieski—in which case you needed some additional equipment like (a) a Vienna to relieve from Turks and (b) CHRIS-TI-ANI-TY to save and (c) Turks and (d) a girl to play the role of CHRIS-TI-ANI-TY so that she could be saved—and got to be, instead, Ulrich von Lichtenstein or some other Grand Master of the Teutonic Knights or Bismarck or Karol Gustaf Adolf or Tuhaj-bey or Bohdan Chmielnicki or (most unfortunate) Catherine the Great, you struggled and protested and sometimes wept because the outcome was inevitable: Your side would lose and you would be tied up with laundryline and led in a triumphal procession past the parkbenches where the mothers and the governesses sat. If you were the smallest there was no doubt what your fate was going to be. If you had to be something that you didn't want to be it was best to be Ivan the Terrible. He did a lot of shouting and rolled his eyes a lot and had, in fact, a chance to hold his audience for a while before the inevitable caught up with him and he was bound and forced to march. But there was nothing to be said for being Catherine the Great, who was tied up extra tight and usually pummeled before it was her turn to be somebody else because she was not only a *Moskal* (which was bad enough) and a German (which was just as bad) but she was also the Great Whore (whatever that meant). You tried your best not to be Catherine the Great. But if the bigger boys felt particularly mean they might insist on being Kosciuszko or Prince Jozef Poniatowski, and that called for a Catherine. Not necessarily from the point of view of historical accuracy, but from the point of view of bigger boys' meanness. And then the day, which had lost much of its brightness early in the morning, would lose more. You would say that no, you wouldn't be Catherine the Great, that you couldn't be, because you were who you were and nobody like *you* (who was the son of the man whose son you were, who listened to Grzes talking about Budyenny and the Mongols and the Savage Cavalry, who watched the morningsun congeal on glittering leather and brass and silverbraid and heard the thundering footsteps) could ever possibly be anything but the Polish Hero.

Boys, choosing sides: —*Is that so?* —*Yes. That's so.* —*Who says so?* —(Grzes . . . my mother.) *I say so.* —*Well, it's not so.* It was and yet it wasn't. Because a game begun like that was over before it properly began, because there would be the inevitable final argument, the unforgivable one, and Adam tried not to use this most terrible of all weapons, but sooner or later he was forced to use it because no other argument would be left to save him from Great Whoredom. Adam, desperate, knowing that with this argument the game would be over: —*What does* your *father know about it? He works in an office.* —*Doesn't!* —*Does!* My *father is a soldier!*

(Oh, small friends and bitter enemies of those fierce sunny battlefields where the crickets roared and the battlecries came in treble voices and the fate of Europe and CI-VI-LI-ZA-TION and CHRIS-TI-ANI-TY hung upon the position of the sun and a mother's boredom with *Madame Bovary,* don't turn your backs on me. . . .)

Boys, silent little suns with their own particular planets shown to be no brighter than a waxedpaper moon, hurt unforgivably and walking away:

—Aw well . . . come on. Let's go to the fountain. They got some new goldfish in the fountain. . . . What are we going to do?

His mother, removing sunglasses, patting a stray brown hair into place, turning her calmsmiling face to him, not touching him: *—Are you tired? Is that why you're not playing anymore? —Yes Mother. —Wasn't that a short game? —Yes. I just got tired. —What did you play? The usual game? —Yes Mother. —Well, it's time-to-go-home-tea-is-almost-ready. Will you carry my book?*

Dinner was served at eight; a warm time with the biggest of all planets back in the center of the universe and the universe restored. The brass and the leather were put away and with them that cold inward smile that froze the universe and shattered the morning. The long English ridingboots shivered under the polishingcloths in the kitchen and the spurs waited their turn with silverpolish powdering on the cruel rowels, and in their place was the glitter of white shirtfront and silk lapel blue in the candlelight, and there was banter and warmsmile and lovingkindness and the day which had begun so brightly and had dimmed was returned to brightness despite the soft blackness pressing in from the outside. He was allowed a sip of sherrywine before the dinner and watered port afterwards and his milk or *Owomaltyna* was served to him in a glass like his parents' wineglasses with the soup and the fish and the meat and the afterdinner confection, and his knives, forks and spoons were the same in number as those of his parents (only smaller, and he knew better than to use a knife to cut his fish), and he said nothing unless spoken to and then listened intently and answered carefully and he was happy because this was his universe and he knew exactly where he belonged in it and this was comforting. Little was said during dinner, anyway. The talk began after the last of the *petits fours* were cleared away and the port was served (his mother preferring a Madeira sherry) and then he would tell about his day, omitting nothing. *—You say they walked away from you? —Yes father. —But you know why they did. —Yes sir. They always do when I say that about you and about their fathers. —Do you think they were wrong to walk away? —No sir. I would walk away. —Would you? —No sir. I probably would not. —What would you do if one of them said something uncomplimentary about me? —Uncomplimentary, sir? —Yes. Something that wasn't very nice. —I would try to hit them. —Would that change what they said? —I don't know, sir. —Yes you do. It would change nothing, would it? —I would hit them, sir . . . because I wanted to. Because they were wrong . . . because they don't know you. —But they don't hit you? —No sir . . . Well, some of them do but not much. They didn't today. —Why not? —Because they know that I am right, sir. —You were wrong to say what you did about their fathers. Don't you think that they feel about their fathers the way you feel about me? —But how could they, sir? Their fathers are different. —They do different things, yes. But to them their fathers are just as important as I am to you. I don't think you should use me to decide your roles for you, do you? —No sir. I'll be Catherine the Great tomorrow, if you like. —No, I don't like. But if you don't want to be Catherine then refuse because you, yourself, can be something else. Not because of what I am. Do you understand what I mean? —I think so, sir. (His father, laughing:) —Thank you for sticking up for me, though. I'm glad you are my friend. —Oh sir . . .* And the warm evening

534

turns into the night and that too is warm and the darkness of his room is not frightening and the corners contain no shadows which twist into nightmares because the man is talking in the other room and his voice comes clearly through the thin wall.

This is the best time, or the secondbest time, and you can't really tell whether or not this time is better than the early morning but you think it might be. Because there is the warmth and the protecting darkness of which you can never be afraid and every shadow in your room is cast by a familiar object and in the room behind the wall is the strong voice of your strong laughing father and your calmsmiling mother and (often) of your thoughtful, softspoken uncle and of your aunt, whom, perhaps, you do not love as much as you love the others. The voices rise and fall and these are voices of people who are fond of each other, and you can never overhear bitterness or recrimination and with this thought, which promises to extend warmth and the orderly beauty of your universe indefinitely, you are lulled to sleep. You have no doubts of any kind about the permanence of lovingkindness, and when small doubts come (such as the hard-to-understand coolness you sometimes hear in your mother's voice, or the wry smile and watchfulness you sometimes see on your father's face) you can resist the doubts.

That was the spring and winter place, the town space. The other space that contained his unshakeable universe was the country with the white house crouched on its shelf, the woods and orchards, and marmots whistling in the broad fields that sloped into the Wiselka where fat wildgeese built their complicated nests and beavers went about their own fortifications and the huge trees roofed them all with green. This space was sun and being brown in summer and bobbing up and down in the slowflowing stream among the treeroots that boiled up out of the oily brown banks and fell into the water. It was an all-day-out-in-the-sunshine space where there was no question about who was going to be King John and later, after school began, it was the holiday space. And later, after *that* spring (with thunderlike drumming rattling the windows in the town apartment and his mother's closed, very white face and her angry words, and the quick packing and abrupt departure and the journey in the rented carriage to the shuttered white house) it was a place where shadows were no longer recognizable and his mother looked at him in a troubled way and there were DIF-FI-CUL-TIES. These were his mother's troubled silence and her anger. He did not understand them and thought that they were somehow connected with the hasty journey out of town and thought that all these DIF-FI-CUL-TIES would be resolved once his father came but they were not. It was a long time before the shiningest of all the planets swam back into the universe and he was greyfaced and silent and seldom smiling and there were no more Sunday-morning scuffles and there was no more shaving in the morning. Grzes shaved his father in his bed. And there was no more glittering braid and leather and his father's walk did not sound like thunder and, with his sleeve pinned up and his grey face, he did not look like a god. Childhood was over then, despite the games that still went on among the trees. At night he heard words spoken in bitter voices. And there was coldness instead of the warmth he had thought would go on forever, and his small mercenary armies (which he paid with buttons cut from his father's uniforms, no longer worn) grew smaller and, one day, turned on him. He fought them terribly and later asked his father: —*Is this true?* (Knowing that it couldn't be true, what they said about his father.) But it was true; his father said it was. And then his indestructible universe exploded and the best of all the spaces became the worst without a universe to fill it. Nothing could be trusted to remain as you thought it would. The days came brightly as before but their warmth was false and their promises were a lie. And when, one day, Grzes packed his mother's cases and Adam's things, and crated many other things, and Adam and his mother left the countryhouse, he felt nothing. He never saw the countryhouse or his father again and didn't want to see them and tried not to think about them but, of course, he did. He was never allowed to forget his father. —*Your father is a traitor.* —*No he isn't!* —*He is. He fought against the marshal.* —*He is not a traitor!* And then the small fists and feet and fingernails, the blood and bruises and the lonely vigil in the classroom corner and later, after school, his mother's troubled look. —*Why do you fight them? Just walk away from them.* —*I can't.* —*Why not. It isn't difficult.* —*I don't know why not, Mother. I can't walk away.* —*Then find other friends.*

What were friends? Days had no magic; he was not a child. He was a naked exposed center of a depopulated universe. Everything sooner or later became hostile. Everyone knew what had happened in 1926. But Erich had not known; even if he had found out he could not care less about the politics of Poland. And Adrianne had shown her own affinity for treason. And so he had built a new, an ersatz, universe in which the planets were not so near, were not so bright or warm, but comforted him, and now that they had fallen away, out of orbit, he was not so terribly alone. Adrianne had disappointed him, Erich had betrayed his hopes. But he was still whole, still able to think, still able to do what he had to do.

He got up. His legs were unsteady but his mind was clear. He thought that he could weep now, but he didn't want to. It was no longer necessary to be comforted. He remembered everything that Reinhardt had said and it didn't matter.

He had thought of himself as without resources, a weapon without a will, and that was what they thought too. But they were wrong. There was something he could do. And Erich would be paid back the debt that he owed him: He would have the mountainclimbing trip that had been called off in Mariazell.

—*The charge, Father. Did you see my charge?*

And he heard the man's laughter and the universe was filled with laughter like the peal of trumpets.

Rain

The stars are dead; the
animals will not look . . .

Monday, September the twenty-fifth

I THE HUNTER

The hospital was the one in which he had had his appendix removed when he was ten years old. Even though he couldn't get his eyes open, he could smell it sometimes, and he thought he was in the whitepainted room with the tile and the hard bed he remembered from his childhood. Sometimes when he was close to getting his eyes open he smelled the other smell: the sourcoffee smell of soldiers, the stalebread smell of clothes washed in a river and dried in the sun. It was then that his visitors came in quickly and did not stay long. They stayed longer when the soldiersmell was not there (he thought) and he assumed the soldiersmell offended them and he wondered about that a little because so many of his visitors were soldiers of one kind or another. His mother came once. She was as he remembered her the year before she died, when he was eleven: small, grey, silent, authoritative, saying, as she did when he was ten: —*Find Pawel and see what he is doing and tell him to stop it.* She had been quick to scold and always impatient, as much with Pawel as with his father, and she resented more than anything the existence of her brother-in-law, the Boy General, Hero of the Nation, who would not live the way tradition and goodusage and politesociety wanted him to live and who overshadowed her husband completely and made her smaller than she wished to be. Her hair had turned white quickly within her twelve-year marriage, as though to witness the variety of crosses a good woman had to bear. There seemed to be no end of them: a wild son, an uncertain husband, a brother-in-law doing the unexpected. Not to mention an insane father-in-law. Not to mention a certain lack of assurance about the solidity of her socialposition (despite the title of Pani Pulkownikowa—Madame Colonel—and the *britchka* driven by an orderly and the soldier who carried her shoppingbag three steps behind her and the regulation respect she extracted from Madame Major and the Mesdames Captain and the awed flock of assorted wives of sublieutenants). Had it not been for luck and a lack of ambition and other shortcomings of her husband, she might have been Pani Generalowa. Not being what she wished to be was unforgivable. The combined weight of all her crosses augmented by cholera proved too much for her, and she died the way she had lived: resentful, angry at her inability to awe the cholera, which didn't know its place and had no care for her position. Cholera wasn't a respectable disease. It was the killer of the poor. It was quick and brutal and came from dirty drains. It was the final unbearable cross.

Pawel's father came once. His face was disappointed and closed, his eyes cold. With him came the smell of cologne and soap and fresh linen and always the smell of leather. His back was straight but not stiff (somehow not erect enough to match the smell of leather), the way it was when he left the overdecorated apartment each morning to walk to the office, measuring the distance with the sharp clack of his heels. When Pawel was six years old, he

539

liked to greet his father when he came home in the evenings, bringing the bootjack his father used to pull off his boots. The jack looked like the claw of a giant lobster. The boy liked to polish the long English boots of rich maroon leather that yellowed in the creases and under the straps of the spur. He also liked to polish the brass knob on the belt and the beltbuckle. The long curved tongue of the beltbuckle was like a little golden saber. But mostly, Pawel saw his father's disapproving face, and the cold eyes and the disappointment. He supposed that his father must have had many disappointments. They came with his kind of life; like the straight but not quite erect enough back and the polished skull and the thin wrinkles, and he wondered how many disappointments had been caused by himself, by his inability to fit prescribed patterns.

Colonel Kern came once, his round, amused face marked with the generous wrinkles that came with *his* sort of life, and the colonel quickly became Uncle Janusz, which was impossible but welcome. With the General came recollection of pain: a terrible white ache sawing at his hip and crowding up into his throat like the howl of a dismembered animal. Why should the thought of the General bring such a pain? There had been other pains connected with his uncle: sorrow, regret and sympathy. But this pain was sharp and brilliant like a knife and entirely physical. There must be something which combined physical pain and Uncle Janusz for him and Pawel thought he would remember it in time. He had plenty of time. He no longer had to hurry. Whatever he was expecting was coming for him and all he had to do was wait for it. Bogacz came once, staggering slightly in the underbrush the way he did after rum (but never enough to miss tracks), and Loomis came often, and many men and women he remembered from ballrooms, bedrooms, racingfields, gymkhanas, darkened rooms, clubrooms, fields, woods, towns, villages, camps, roadside halts on marches, clearings and barricades, cafés and barrackyards, and places he could not remember made quick appearances. It was strange to see all those people. He didn't care about seeing some of them. They came anyway. Once his grandfather came: the terrible old man who drilled invisible regiments in his bedroom and howled like a wolf when his bullet moved.

His father's second wife came once to the hospital but did not stay long. She and Pawel never had much to say to each other. Gomez, the Spanish colonel-motorman, came once, and once his cousin Adam looked in briefly with a frightened face, and one day he heard this conversation:

—*Tadziu, a moment of your time.*

—*Of course.*

—*How is he?*

A pause; then laughter without humor. —*As you see.*

—*From the beginning?*

—*No. At first he was conscious enough. It was the pain, I suppose. He was quite rational. Did you know that Lala came to see him? They had a long talk. She brought an American along with her. Pawel was a popular young man for a while. Oh, we had hopes for him at first.*

—*But not any more? What are his chances of coming out of here?*

Again the pause and laughter. —*Alive or dead?*

—*Alive.* (The General's voice was flat.)

—Not good.

—Why not? The amputation was neat enough under the circumstances. He is young and strong. Why should he die?

—Oh, come now, dear friend. Really. That is for you to say. Why should any die? But from a medical viewpoint, consider his wound, a shattered hip, gangrene, a journey in a peasant cart in the dust of the road, consider this crowded hospital with brick and plaster falling and every fly in the world coming through the shellholes, think about a total lack of drugs and disinfectant, lack of instruments, no electricity or water, and, yes, if you'll excuse me, think about the man's lack of will to live. There is that too.

—He must live.

—Why? Why he more than another? Ah (the pause again but this time without laughter; with a touch of sadness, this time) *well, perhaps he will. I don't know much about anything anymore.*

—Can I do anything?

—I doubt it. Oh, you could get them to stop bombing the hospital perhaps, and you could get water and electricity restored and you could get us sixty more surgeons and about three hundred orderlies and you could get us several hundred tons of drugs and about thirty more operating theaters and possibly you could make the walls stand still long enough for one operation. But if you can't do that, then no, there is nothing you can do.

—Perhaps we can do something for him.

—Yes? Is there anything you would care to try?

—I wouldn't give up on him if I were a doctor.

—No? I suppose you wouldn't. But we have. Because there is nothing more that we can do. We've cut as much as we could but now there isn't any more to cut. This man is poisoned up to his ears. (Then, gently:) *We did all we could.*

A pause.

—I suppose you did.

—We really did.

—It's just that he should live, the flat voice said, the well-remembered voice. *Because such times are coming as to make such men as Pawel very necessary. Hard men who do their killing well. We'll need his kind of man in the coming years.*

—Haven't we always? Isn't that our story? But don't we always find them when we need them? If he dies there will be others. Now, if you'll excuse me, I must go.

Everyone expected him to die: his uncle (if the voice he heard was, indeed, his uncle's) and his father and the doctors and, certainly, the orderlies, who saw the most of him. He waited to be dead, not caring about it one way or the other. He watched a darkness shape itself into a form, familiar at the foot of his bed, an indistinct black shape moving up the ridge made by the legs under the blanket while the white faces of his visitors grew perceptibly dimmer. That was the thing about his visitors: They, like the hospital smell and the soldier smell, vanished as the darkness grew. Night was coming. It was time for sleep.

And then one day he woke and it was bright in the corridor where he lay on straw, and shadows moved about on the wall in front of him: back and forth, leaping without music. The light came through the wall that wasn't there at the other end of the corridor and it was red and yellow. It was fire-light. A building was burning across the street. He smelled smoke and dust and indescribable smells and he heard the sounds: human and animal in the corridor, explosive outside. These were the first sounds and smells of the new day.

He saw a face, dulleyed and incurious: a soldier's face. The soldier peered into his face.

—*This one's come around.*

—*The worse for him,* said another soldier. *He'd be better off if he crapped out.*

—*Well, he's come around, poor sonofabitch.*

—*That's his hard luck.*

The soldiers moved away up the corridor and presently came back carrying something rolled up in a blanket. A grey arm hung from it. When they came back they had a stretcher and on that there was another man under a brown blanket. They put the man where they had got the other. They stood above Pawel, looking down.

—*His mouth is open,* said the soldier who leaned on the stretcher. *Maybe he's going to crap out.*

—*Maybe he's trying to talk.*

—*I don't hear anything.*

—*Jesus Christ, listen to that shelling.*

—*Come on, there's another one crapped out down the hall.*

—*I think this one wants something. Hey, friend, you want a cigarette? Water?*

—*Come on, come on. He's going to crap out anyway sooner or later.*

—*Maybe he won't.*

—*And maybe you will grow horns and give milk* Psia krew! Idzierz czy nie? *Are you coming?*

—*All right. Where's the carcass?*

They picked up the stretcher and left the corridor.

Pawel watched them go. He felt pain. He was thirsty. He closed his mouth and opened it and moved his hands and he tried closing and opening his eyes and it was all right. He tried to move his legs and it was not all right. He could not sit up. He tried and the pain which seemed to lie like a hot belt about his hips pinned him to the straw. Night came again and left him and he lay quite still. He watched the red and yellow lights and the shadows on the wall. He made an effort to lift up his arm so that he could look at it. He got it high enough to see it before it fell down. It was grey. Like the arm hanging from the blanket that the soldiers carried. But the hanging arm was dead and his was alive. He didn't care one way or the other.

Later (after a time that might have been anything between an hour and a day) the soldiers came back. They looked at him again.

—*He's moved his arm,* said the soldier who had asked about the cigarette and water. *See? It was here and now he's got it across his chest.*

—*So he's moved his arm.*

—*Well, if he can move he'll be all right.*

—*What do you know about it? You a Pan Doktor, maybe? Maybe you*

*played doctor as a kid, but that's the closest you ever got to it. If he wasn't
a crapout candidate, what,* do cholery, *would he be doing here?*

—*Maybe I know and maybe I don't know. Maybe you don't know everything. Maybe I know a little about doctoring.*

—*And maybe I'm the King of England. Come on, for Christ's sake.*

—*Water,* Pawel said.

—*See? He's trying to say something. What did I tell you? I know a thing
or two you don't know about. I didn't used to be a doctor's assistant for
nothing, let me tell you.*

—*A horsedoctor. A* weterynarz *at the Iron Gate who used to prick the
blisters on the carters' horses. And you swept out his stable.*

—*All right, but I was right about this one, wasn't I? I can tell when a
man's a crapout candidate and when he isn't.*

—*Oh, you know about crap, all right. You swept enough of it.*

The soldier who had been the stableboy for the veterinarian at the Iron
Gate shrugged and wiped his nose on his bloodencrusted sleeve and knelt
by Pawel and asked what Pawel wanted.

—*Water? Sure, comrade. I'll get you some water. Want a cigarette? Here's
a storebought one I got off an officer that crapped out down the hall. Makes
you cough, eh? That's good for you. Coughing throws all the bad air out of
you. Here, take another pull. There. No coughing now, eh? You'll be all right.*

—*All right,* the second soldier said, *don't choke the poor bastard. Get him
some water if you're going to.*

—*Look who's talking,* said the soldier with the cigarette. *Look who knows
all about doctoring.*

—*The poor sonofabitch said he wanted water, didn't he?*

—*So go get him some. I got to be here, see? I got to get him comfortable.*

—*Gowno,* the second soldier said. *Now I got to carry water for crapout
candidates.*

But he got the water.

It was warm and dusty. Pawel thought he would never get enough of it.
He spilled most of it trying to get it down, with the soldier holding the cup
for him and pushing too hard against his chin. But some of it went down. He
choked and coughed. The coughing jerked his body and awoke the pain. He
closed his eyes and tried to stop it. Stop it, he told the pain.

—*Here now, watch out,* the first soldier said. *You're choking him.*

—*You just said a cough is good, it gets the bad air out.*

—*But you're shaking all the good air out of him too.*

—*Maybe I never pricked a blister on a horse's ass but I know when a man
is thirsty.*

—*Horses don't get blisters on their ass. That shows what you know.*

—*So it was up his ass. What do I care where it was? The only horse's ass
I ever had to look at is you, so watch what you're doing. There. He'll be all
right. See? He's drinking good now.*

Later (after a doctor came and looked at him and shrugged and shook
his head and smiled as though nothing would ever surprise him again) the
soldiers put him on a stretcher and carried him out of the corridor and into a
ward. They put him on a cot, grunting and muttering and swearing because
it was difficult. The ward was full of wounded men. It was nothing like the

hospital room which Pawel remembered from the time his appendix was removed. Pawel lay between something that was burned and smelled like scorched rubber and an armless man. The armless man moved his head from side to side and made small sounds. Pawel looked at him and thought about his uncle, which was ridiculous because there was no similarity between this human metronome and the General. He thought the General had come to see him; certainly he remembered a conversation between his uncle and another, and thought that the General had been among the other visitors in the hospital room that he remembered. But then he realized that there had been no room this time in this hospital. There had been a ward and then nothing and then the corridor and now the ward again. And the pain again. Pawel waited for the pain to dissolve and to leave him. No imaginary visitors came when the pain was there. He didn't care so much about the visitors as he cared about the pain. The pain and the lack of visitors and other fantasies meant that he was mending, he thought. And that meant . . . what? No end to the brightly painful journey between the black horizons. He had been injured before and knew about pain. Once he had broken his leg, the same leg that was hurting now. Arab had slipped on wet grass in the morning and a cinch-strap broke, and a red-eyed morning after champagne had been no preparation for a steeplechase, and after a puzzled flight through the air had come a dull sound of an object landing in the grass and then a pain. But it was not this kind of pain: pressing outward from the inside, gnawing to get out as if imprisoned in his leg. Other pains were clean and bright and of short duration. This one went on and on like regret. What do I regret? It came in waves like the roll of detonations outside where the shells were falling. It came in broken cadence. It kept time to the irrational beat of the bombardment.

And then one day (and it was a definite, real day and not one of those dreamdays in imagined rooms), he got ready to leave the hospital.

The doctor-colonel, hospital commandant and family friend, a lean man smelling of tobacco and brandy and carbolic acid (a yellow-tinted man with nicotine-stained fingers and mustache), wished him good luck. He winked. He said that Pawel was a fortunate young man.

—You're lucky to be going, he said. There's something terribly wrong here.

—Why?

—How, not why. People always say why when they mean how. And anyway I couldn't tell you. I wish I could go too.

He sat down on the side of Pawel's bed. The side of his face closest to Pawel had a twitch in it. The smell of brandy was particularly sour.

—I have not been opposed to war on principle. I am a doctor but also a military man. War is in some ways good. It dissolves old ties and forges fresh worthwhile bonds. It teaches some men bestiality but others nobility, and it throws up great leaders while ruining other men who profess greatness but do not have the essential qualities. It breaks hearts and bodies, true, but it also breaks up systems which need destroying, and while it poisons the meaning of existing words it kindles new languages to express new thoughts

544

and new ideas. It accelerates the process of change from old to new and revolutionizes science and brings new art and literature and gives such wonderful new ways for killing off whole groups of humans, masses of them in the millions, but somewhere in the process it produces a vaccine to cure a fever in a child. So much for human turmoil. Well. But this war is not quite right. Something is terribly wrong. I am not learning anything from it. In my time it was a lot easier to understand.

—How?

—Ah, you see? You do mean how, not why. Why, in the other war I learned that human butchery, through ignorance and helplessness and military ineptitude, is still possible, and with that died some marvelous assumptions about progress. But in this war of yours I am not learning anything! I see no meaning to two thousand years of belief in the human spirit! I shake in the cold stench of mania dredged up from some Pleistocene cave by this insane Germanic butchery, which is not hot and emotionally driven (something a mind can understand) but coldly premeditated down to the last medicalchart and graph and fraction of a heartbeat. And so I say that you are fortunate to be out of it and going home. I envy you your ability to resign. Ah, shall I tell you something else?

He bent down and put his yellow mustache against Pawel's ear.

—You are a very special person, my dear fellow. Quite remarkable, you know. You are the last one who will leave here. *The last one!* Nobody else will leave ever again. We shall all remain, for the rest of an eternity, looking at each other and wondering what it was we did on earth that was so very bad, and which of the others here we offended. That is what makes this place unbearable; the black eternity of thought. It was not like that in my time. Tell me, though: How did you get your dispensation? My dear fellow, you really ought to tell me.

Pawel looked at the doctor carefully. The huge eyes, yellow and malevolent, peered at him with curiously diffused intensity.

—Come on. Be a good fellow. The doctor smiled.

—Madness, Pawel said. He felt cold. He began to shake and he closed his teeth around the words but they seeped through the cracks.

—Ah, so that's it!

The doctor nodded and began to chuckle to himself.

—Of course, I should have known. It's obviously the only explanation. Yes. You know you really are a find, my dear fellow. You are the first who understands the real meaning of all this. Remarkable.

He sat up briskly on the bed and looked around and nodded to himself and studied the ceiling, where the enormous, glutted flies hung in somnolent stupor.

—Well now, look here, since you understand and since you're leaving anyway, I'll tell you something. Have you ever seen dogs fighting with each other?

—What?

—Out there. (The doctor waved his arms like brownstained windmillsails towards the door.) They fight like human beings.

—What?

—Like men. Animals now have the insane ferocity of men.

He repeated the statement, winked and raised a yellow finger.

—Well, what of it? Pawel began to sweat. His throat was suddenly tight.

The doctor smiled and dropped his voice confidentially. —Why, that's it.

—You're mad, doctor.

—No more than you. No more than you. Not for at least another generation will anyone be able to say who is mad here and who is not.

He put the fingertips of both his hands together and rested his elbows on his knees and balanced his chin carefully on his fingertips.

—Not until everyone can fasten in their proper place all the small beads of experience, bright and bloody, glittering and corrupt, that memories will have hoarded in the vault of time. Time is the essence of it, don't you see? It's the perspective which will narrow the whole panorama of men and minds in motion through these fantastic days; and the crushing impact, the total weight of it should leave these future arbiters dazed with the sheer enormity of the madness they will discover, the monumental scale of man's vileness. It should, but I suppose it won't. Ha. Well. God, nature or whatever you will call it limits man's imagination in a war for his own protection. The nerve ends, you see, cannot remember pain or its accumulation, otherwise the total weight of it would be beyond endurance. The other day I cried when some woman out there in the street died in my arms. One woman, nobody I knew. But the groans of the seven or eight or nine or however many there are thousand men in here leave me unmoved.

My leg, Pawel thought. I have lost a leg. Why, no, it's quite impossible. It is just that I cannot see it.

—If man could add pain and multiply it and see the total size and shape of it, there would be no wards like this. There would be no wars.

—What? Doctor . . .

Cold.

But I can feel my leg perfectly well and, certainly, I wouldn't if it wasn't there!

—Exactly, my dear boy, exactly. Men will not scream and run at the thought of war because the *idea* of their own death is unthinkable to them and also because death cannot be multiplied in the human spirit. How many empty places do you think are left by one million deaths? Eh? Tell me. Eh?

—I . . .

—One at each dinnertable!

—Leave me alone, you madman!

—And it's not only that the world will glut itself with horror before this war is over, that it will be possible for us to look at the death of millions with a wry face, with the sort of distaste you might feel stepping into dogshit. We feel our *own* pain, we are not callous about our *own* suffering. It's not the numbers of the dead that make us tolerant of death. We, men, are incapable of digesting more than our small, primitive minds can contain; we cannot physically accept more than we can digest in safety! And this is wonderful, old man, quite wonderful! This is why we can hurt each other so beautifully each day in little ways and still sleep well at night. Pain must be personal. Another's pain is quite incomprehensible. And so we say: Are you in pain? Don't be ridiculous. Don't be a child. I don't feel anything, how can you? That's the crux of it. I don't know what this means in terms of humanitarian progress, but I tell you that we condition ourselves every day to the acceptance of monstrosities because we cannot feel outside ourselves.

He sat up straight and looked with affable curiosity about the room: a vast expanse of beds and cots and strawfilled mattresses pressed close together, a waxfaced, blanketbrown sea of pain and misery. Outside: the scream of falling shells and the explosions. Inside: the constant ululating moaning of the wounded and the soft tapping of brick and plaster in their own innumerable explosions.

The doctor pressed his knees together. He chuckled pleasantly and tried to cross his legs in the narrow space between Pawel's bed and that of his neighbor, the human metronome. The armless man groaned. The doctor nodded at him, then looked at Pawel. He seemed immensely pleased, like a lecturer whose demonstration models haven't let him down.

—That's clear enough, isn't it?

Cold. Only my head is hot. It is on fire. But everything below it, from the feet, both feet, two feet, up is cold and getting colder and I can feel the cold solidify my legs.

—I say, it's all clear now?

—What?

—The dogs, you fool!

—Dogs? You mean . . . outside?

—Yes! And this.

—That man? You mean . . . that man?

—And this!

Winking, the doctor stroked the blanket where one of Pawel's legs should be. Pawel did not feel the gesture.

My leg. Have I lost my leg? How do you lose a leg? My leg!

The doctor took his hand away and there was an obscene flatness beside the mound of the remaining leg.

—Now it's clear to you, eh? You no longer have trouble understanding.

—For God's sake go away!

—You should see those dogs. Be sure to look at them when you leave here. They are excellent. They tear each other to pieces, just like men, you know. And they don't even stop when you throw stones at them, and they scream so, and there is so much hate and the violence is so enormous that you can stand over them and beat them with a club and they will go on tearing each other apart. You really can't get them to stop.

—Go away!

—Even while you are kicking them. They just go on. Senseless. Like human beings.

Cold.

Jezu.

Cold.

—My leg! What did you do with it?

But the doctor went on inexorably.

—They are invincible. They will outtear and outdevour man and own the world. Ha. Listen here. Do you know that an African hyena, a wounded hyena, will devour itself? It will actually tear itself to pieces and eat itself until there are no guts left in it to contain whatever the guts it has eaten. I have it on the best authority. Well, *you* can explain that if you're so good at it.

—In Heaven's name, explain what!

—This, you stupid fool! (Pointing to the blanket where it was flat.) That human timepiece! This slaughteryard! If you can explain everything else why can't you explain this? Why can't you see your own face staring up out of these beds? Your leg? Well, what about it, eh? The dogs have eaten it, I think. But you can explain everything. It's all clear to you. Explain this if you can!

And the mad doctor jumped off Pawel's bed into the narrow space between it and the iron bed supporting the human metronome and he grasped the sides of this other cot shouting: —*But he can explain!* (while the armless man stared at him in terror) and he threw the cot over and its occupant fell out like a macabre white sack with a head on it and struck the floor face down. The armless man shouted in a peculiarly high voice and tried to inch away like an enormous worm before the sharp sides of the cot came down on his back, but his knees collapsed and his face would not slide fast enough on the dust-and-plaster-covered floor and the cot came down and pinned him to the floor screaming. The blind man in the bed beyond sat up and turned his bandagewhite mask towards the shouts, himself shouting, and the doctor fell on his knees in the cleared space and raised his arms and prayed loudly, and the wounded shouted. Everyone shouted and cursed and wept and they threw themselves about and beat upon their blankets and their shouts and curses and terror and obscenities superimposed themselves upon the name of God.

All this time Pawel shouted for the orderlies who, eventually, came.

The blind man in the bed beyond the bed in which the armless man had been (and from which he had been thrown out so unceremoniously, and which eventually killed him by smashing his spine) shouted the longest. Everyone else had given up but the blind man continued shouting. His shouts raged on as the orderlies (who also shouted) pursued the mad doctor (who climbed on chairs and over bunks seeking higher objects, shouting: —*Altiora Peto!* as though safety and reason awaited him somewhere on the ceiling and teetering on his grotesque pulpits above the howled obscenities) and threw him down and sat on him and twisted his arms behind him and tied him up with an electrical extension cord (as he called upon St. Joseph and St. Anthony and the patron saints of medicine and on the Holy Mary Ever Virgin Queen of the Crown of Poland to witness that what he was saying was true and it *was* the dogs and not the humans and he himself had nothing to do with any of it, nothing at all!). The blind man's shouts accompanied the wounded as they came howling out of their brown lairs of pain to tear at the doctor. They crawled and skipped and hobbled, supporting each other, and waved their metal cups and spoons and broken bedslats and tried to kill the doctor. They tried to trample him with their stumps. They tore at his face with fingerless knucklebones. The orderlies hit them and kicked them out of the way and pushed them down, and eventually more orderlies ran in and the angry wounded were driven back into their corners. They lay on and under their beds and on the floor under the falling plaster. Their screams and blasphemies became a murmur, like a sob, an afterthought of sound. The orderlies paid the blind man no attention. They were too busy protecting the doctor. The blind man's face was a shapeless mass of bandage with a black hole in it. The shout came from the hole. The blind man sat perfectly still in bed and pointed the hole in the direction of the doctor and the orderlies and shouted: —No-o-o-o-o-o! Finally he stopped, possibly for breath, and in that interval he heard the silence of the others and the wild conversation of the dogs outside. Then he lay down again. He did not move or make a sound again, listening to the dogs.

The blind man's name was Schwartzkopff, and this, he had thought at one time, was unfortunate enough. It marked him as a relative of his father. But it had been a long time since he had given his father any thought other than relishing the fact that his father was dead and that his death had been extremely painful. He did not mind his blindness in the least. In fact, after the phosphorus had splashed his face and had glued itself to his eyeballs and shriveled them up (and after the initial pains and shocks), he welcomed the darkness. It was comforting and warm. It protected him. He felt at home in it. He was sure that the darkness was general and that the sun itself had exploded and was gone and that everyone everywhere shared his inability to see. If that was so, then he, through a set of circumstances that had nothing to do with war or phosphorus, had a particular advantage in the dark new world. His eyes had never been good and had always caused him trouble, as had his name and his father and his father's occupation (he was a policeman) and swarms of gross little boys who liked to torment animals. His father had been murdered by convicts in the Pawiak prison who had broken out after a bombing early in the siege, and with him had gone his occupation and also the infernal power of his name, and the small boys were either dead themselves or dying or soon to be dead. The only thing that Schwartzkopff regretted was the death of the animals in the zoological gardens. This, he felt, was a horror he could not live with.

First had come the bombs and the explosions and the iron gratings flying about like grassblades and the concrete crumbling and then the rain of phosphorus setting the animals on fire, and then the other keepers and policemen had begun shooting at the animals, the poor, beautiful animals, tumbling about and leaping and falling, shot down and breaking free and running through their murderers into the streets and being pursued there, trapped and slaughtered. The smaller they were the harder they tried to get away, but the keepers and policemen got most of them eventually. The bombs got the others.

Schwartzkopff shot at as many policemen as he could. He didn't think he had hit anyone and didn't really expect to hit anyone, but it was the idea that counted. He stood in front of his elephant house, shooting at policemen and wondering if any of them had been his father's friends and doubting it because his father could not possibly have any friends, even among policemen. They had given him the rifle and the bullets and told him to exterminate the elephants and so he tried to shoot as many of the policemen as he could. He didn't think that anyone noticed what he was shooting at. There was too much noise and everyone was running this way and that and, anyway, it did not last long. Soon after Schwartzkopff started shooting, the phosphorus bomb exploded at his feet. And then the elephant house began to burn and white phosphorus spotted the grey beasts like a blistering disease and they threw themselves against the walls and the enormous bars screamed like children. He knew that if he could hold off the murderers long enough the elephants would manage to crash through the bars and concrete and be free. He couldn't see the other keepers and policemen well enough to hit them even before the phosphorus bomb exploded but still he could hear the sounds of their running and their distant breathing and their calls and he fired the rifle at the sounds. Then he himself was burning and he could not shoot. Later, in bed, in the hospital, he remembered that the elephants had not gotten out. He screamed a long time in the hospital, thinking about the murdered elephants.

He had not always been a keeper, a defender, of elephants. At one time, although it seemed unlikely to him at his age, he had been a small boy with weak eyes. Someone had said that he had had smallpox as a baby and once someone had made reference to a disease his father had had. He thought it might have been his mother. She had said things like that when his father beat her. His father beat his mother with a piece of wood, but he used his leather belt to beat Schwartzkopff. Then, briefly, Schwartzkopff was a schoolboy, but he could not learn to write because he could not see to read. He had a habit of marching stolidly into the blackboard when called out in front of the class. It amused his classmates. His classmates liked to point him toward the windows instead of the door when it was time to go out for recess. He became quite accustomed to falling out of windows. His teacher asked his parents to buy him some glasses, but these were expensive. His father took the first pair of glasses he could from a student arrested in a demonstration and hung them on Schwartzkopff's ears. But they did no good. They were enormous and kept falling off his head, and they did nothing about helping him distinguish doors from windows, and they gave him thundering headaches and most of the time he tried keeping his eyes shut when he wore them. He stopped using his eyes at all, after a time. Instead, he listened. He developed an ability to hear the objects he was walking into. He could distinguish the rustle of a textbook page of (say) *The General Elementary Arithmetic* from (say) *The General Elementary History,* and he could actually hear the fall of snow and he was always the first to hear the first fat fly that awoke in spring behind the porcelain stove and he could tell by their scamperings how many mice there were in the kitchen at one time at night and what they were after. Eventually he learned to distinguish the sounds of various wheels heard in the street outside his house, and he could tell, without seeing the vehicle at all, whether it was Pan Kublarz with the watercart or Pan Purpura with the coal or an unfamiliar garbagecart and where they were stopping. It became easy for him to sort out the sounds, so that while hearing them in a total mass he could also hear them individually and could tell what made up the total. His eyesight, or the lack of it, made little difference after that, except that it made his father angry and he beat him often. Schwartzkopff's father was a corporal of mounted police (and later a turnkey at the Pawiak prison, after he fell off his horse during a pacification of railroad workers and shattered his hip) and his mother did a great deal of laundering and he, Schwartzkopff, became a deliverer of box lunches to the *komisariat* and the jail and a carrier of laundrybaskets after the end of his career as a schoolboy. In neither case did he ever make a wrong delivery or get lost or get hurt in traffic. His ears guided him between the cars and trucks and horses and horsedrawn cabs and through a variety of differentsounding hallways. The echoes of one hallway were different from those of another. He got to know them all. He made no mistakes. Unless one knew that he saw only a grey, shifting mass in front of him, one could think that he was normally equipped. His former classmates knew, of course, and so did the neighbors. And so he was generally excluded from the courtyard games: football and *palant* (a game involving the hitting of a ball with a stick); and no boy in his right mind would take the son of a policeman to steal apples or paint mustaches on political posters or write uncomplimentary messages about the teachers on the *gimnazjum* walls.

Deprived of human company, Schwartzkopff turned to animals. Stray dogs and cats, the carters' horses, the enormous rats that lived among his mother's laundryline in the attic—these were more interesting than people anyway. He knew their special shapes because he touched every part of them. He could describe them perfectly, although he never saw more than a denser grey in a general greyness rubbing itself along his legs and biting his fingers softly. If they were injured he would treat them with unerring skill. His fingers, like his ears, acquired all the sensitivity that his eyes lacked. With pins and needles (stolen from his mother's workbasket) and string and wire (found) and with a variety of ingenious splints and bandages and small rags unraveled to make thread, he performed minor miracles of veterinary surgery in the attic. But the animals proved to be his undoing. They came to love him as he loved them and then he learned how terrible love could be. He learned that no one should give or accept love unless he was equipped for the responsibility, unless he was big and strong enough to defend it. Otherwise one exposed oneself and it to horror.

The animals came to him from every quarter of the city. Regiments of dogs camped in the courtyard of his house. Gaunt cats patrolled the stairways by platoons. When he set off with his deliveries of laundry he marched surrounded by a plunging, barking, spitting, yowling mass which halted traffic, snapped at heels (other than his), sniffed, bit, ate, defecated, pushed over garbagecans and trailed fishheads into hallways, frequently copulated (and distressed the housewives) and created chaos. Enraged women found other laundresses. Infuriated janitors beat on the Schwartzkopff door demanding action. Schwartzkopff was beaten with his father's belt. His father brought his saber from the barracks and charged the dogs in the courtyard and was bitten. Schwartzkopff was beaten with a chairleg. Enormous quantities of old shoes, broomhandles and other hard objects were hurled at the cats. Poisoned meat was scattered in the courtyard by the kilogram. The cats dodged the missiles and the dogs urinated on the poisoned meat. Schwartzkopff was beaten with a rolling pin, a lampstand (iron) and a laundryline. And then, one day, Pan Kapral brought eleven guests for dinner. They were his policemen. They were tall and had red faces and mustaches and said very little. They ate cutlets provided by the neighbors and drank beer. Each one had brought a carbine with him from the barracks. After they ate, they closed the courtyard gates. They sat down at the windows and at the neighbors' windows and began to shoot. They shot each dog and each cat and went on shooting long after every howl and scream and trace of movement had died down.

They walked up and down the stairs shooting at the cats. They counted ninety-seven different animals in the courtyard, excluding several which were household pets and had been locked up in the courtyard by mistake. Pan Kapral then took his son by the ear and led him out into the courtyard. He twisted the ear. He pushed him into the yard among the piled-up animals. He made the boy carry each one to the garbagecart waiting in the street. Some of the animals were still alive in Schwartzkopff's arms; he could feel them breathing, and through the red pain of his twisted ear he could hear the feeble beating of hearts. His feet slid in the blood. He vomited and wept. As he walked to the garbagecart other boys shouted at him and threw things. They threw the things that had been thrown by their parents at the animals. When all the animals had been removed, the yard was hosed down and scrubbed by the women and every trace of slaughter was carried off.

For many years after that Schwartzkopff did not say one word to another human. From that time on he spoke exclusively to animals, but he was careful first to chase them away from his house and went far into the wooded suburbs every day to meet them. Eventually, when he became a junior keeper at the zoological gardens (first in the birdhouse, then, gradually, working his way through the cats and the monkeys to the elephants), Schwartzkopff resumed speaking to one or two humans. He acknowledged orders from the headkeeper and the Pan Dyrektor. This did not involve extensive conversation; nods and grunts sufficed. He also shouted at small boys who thrust things at the elephants and teased them. Other than these he made no sound directed at a human being. He spoke often, long and passionately to the elephants, whose grey bulk he saw only dimly but whose every sigh, groan, gurgle, snort, and bellow had significance to him. He could hear the creak of their skin as they moved. He had gone over each of them with his hands and knew their dimensions. He moved among them, and often slept among them, with complete confidence, and they took care not to tread or roll or sit on him. For all their size or because of it, they were gentle and considerate and not at all like people. They wouldn't think of hurting anybody the way people did: just to see what the one you were hurting would do or say.

War, when it came, had no meaning for him. True, it woke him violently with the first bombardment. True, the monstrous sound of it beat on his ears harder than on other people's: Its roar and crash and sirenwailing and explosion threatened to blow his finelytuned eardrums out of his head. But it did not otherwise concern him any more than it concerned his animals. It made the animals nervous and upset their feeding. The elephants stood very still and would not eat, listening to the bombings. Schwartzkopff tried to soothe them and make them eat. He tried to tell them that nothing would happen, that this was nothing to do with them or with him and that it would soon be over and their lives would go on. But they were nervous and wouldn't listen to their keeper. They listened to the bombings. And then came the day when the zoological gardens were attacked and the animals were burned and then destroyed and Schwartzkopff tried to defend his elephants against the policemen, and that was something Schwartzkopff couldn't think about without screaming. He screamed and tried to get out of the bed and away from people and back to his animals, which had to be fed. Who would feed them if he, Schwartzkopff, was tied down in bed? Only of course the animals were dead.

And it was not their fault. They had done nothing to be dead for. It was the people's fault. And when the mad doctor said it was the fault of dogs, Schwartzkopff shouted: —No-o-o-o-o-o! (long after all the others had given up shouting). And it was only the good sound of the dogs at feeding that reassured him, and he lay down again.

Because, of course, it wasn't their fault. It was the fault of people.

They were whispering, but, of course, he heard them. They could put pillows on their heads and whisper but he would hear them. Even through the bandages and the massed sound of moaning and the hysteria of the dogs outside the windows.

There were two voices, two men whispering on the bed beyond the bed on which the other man had been, the one who had fallen or been thrown out and on whom the bed had fallen.

One voice was young. It was flat. The other was older. There was a similarity of timbre the way there is a similarity between two statues cast in the same mold. But you could tell, listening to them, that one had been cast many years before the other. That's if you had the ears for the job, and (Schwartzkopff thought, laughing to himself) he had them, all right. There was a mixture of authority and sadness in the older voice.

—How is it with thee? said the older voice.

—With me it is in order.

This was a formula, a way such things were said, and Schwartzkopff knew that the men were soldiers.

—And the pain? Is it very bad?

—Yes.

—It will pass.

—Will it?

—As I said. We are taking you away with us and you will soon be well.

—Not quite well enough, Uncle. One can't grow a leg.

—You have another. And you have two arms. Think of that and don't regret that which you can't have back. What is gone is gone, so don't think about it. Soon it will be as if you hadn't lost anything at all.

—You should know, Uncle.

—Yes. All the pains pass in time. Everything heals in time and is all right again and you can live with it.

—When you say that you don't sound like yourself, Uncle. You sound like your brother.

—Is that how he sounded to you?

—That's how he sounds. He has a way of saying things like that. Like God dictating to a secretary. As if he had invented pain and life and death and knew all about them. As if nobody else could know about them. As if only he knew and nobody else could possibly know.

—He's had his share of disappointments.

—Oh, of course. And I'm the biggest one, is that it? Well, he won't be disappointed now. You see, I've made a contribution to mankind. I have been of service. He should be quite delighted now, I think.

—You are a fool, boy. He won't be delighted.

—Well, pleased then. Proud. Imagine, I have finally made my father proud. Do you think he'll find the time to come and see me here?

—You're leaving here. We're taking you away with us.

—Where are we going?

—East first, then southeast to where the Army is gathering. There is still work for us to do. We have a cart outside for you, and when we go you will come along. You will be comfortable enough and you'll heal up quickly once you're away from this butchershop.

The young voice laughed. A quick, brutal sound like the rattle of a riflebolt.

—And so all the wounds heal and all scars fade and time is stopped and everything flows smoothly and nothing changes and no one ever learns. I think this must be that Polish miracle my father believes in. I don't believe in it, Uncle. I believe in reason. So save your cart for men who can still fight and who still believe in the impossible.

—Do you think I don't know what you believe in? Do you think that you've invented something new?

—I don't know, Uncle. But I have resigned. I have paid the initiation fee into the Mystic Order of the Missing Limb, the international brotherhood of the unfit. There are no wars for us, no gallant charges, no lastditch fights, nor any other participation in the course of history. It's in the bylaws of the club. Why won't you learn it? Besides, I'm comfortable here.

Now it was the older man's turn to laugh brutally.

—I am sorry, boy. I can't feel desolate about your missing leg. I am not moved by your great loss and I can't join you in your enormous pity for yourself. I am not taking you with me because your are my nephew or because I think that you deserve to be taken out rather than go into a prison cage. But I have several hundred men to take into the forests and to lead through the forests to the Army, and there is no man in this country who knows the eastern forests as well as you. So I'm afraid you have no choice. You'll go by my order.

—By your order, sir, the young man said in the prescribed way.

Then they were quiet and Schwartzkopff strained to hear them because he didn't understand much of it and it was different from any talk from any men that he had ever heard. The younger man began to laugh. It was laughter only by the staccato sound of it. There was no humor, joy or pleasure in it. There was pain in it, carefully controlled. And there was something else which Schwartzkopff didn't recognize, not knowing men.

—So it goes on, said the younger man. The hunt is not over and I might yet keep my unavoidable appointment.

—Would you have it any other way?

—I thought the time had come to try another way. I thought I could do it. Do you know the proverb about the egg and the ox? It sounded good to me today.

—I know it. It is not a good one.

—*Better an egg in peace than an ox in war.* I thought it was time for men to start believing that.

—It is not good for us. That is the philosophy of the moral bankrupt, of the coward who does not dare to reach for the impossible and then complains because he doesn't have the fruits of another's daring. You must have met people like that in the West. That's where they make cults out of the negative.

—But if the object is impossible to reach, why bother to reach out for it?

The older man laughed abruptly. Then the young man laughed. He made a small gesture: Schwartzkopff could tell by the whisper of the man's naked arm on blankets.

The young man said: —Well, since it's to be the ox and not the egg, tell me about the war. Have we lost it yet? I have a right to know, as a participant in the course of history.

—No, and we won't lose it in the long run.

—Ah, but it is the short run that concerns me, Uncle. I don't expect to be present at the conclusion of the long run. There is, you see, my unavoidable appointment.

—We still hold Warsaw and Modlin and the Hel. The Army is collecting in the south. We have made a front of sorts in the eastern marshes. We are to hold out until the Allies come.

—Are they showing any interest in coming to see us?

—Not the slightest.

—Then why are we going on with this? Who is it for?

—Ourselves. Your father thought that it was for the Allies, to show them that the Germans could be fought, to encourage them and ultimately to shame them into action. Of course, you can't shame Englishmen into anything, and the French threw away their courage in the other war. So now I think that it is for ourselves. I think we need to end it as we have begun. We'll go to France and take the war with us.

—And my gallant father? Is he to go with us into the forests? I warn you, Uncle, he won't care for it. He won't like it at all—it isn't civilized enough and not at all orderly.

—Your father is dead, the older man said brutally.

The young man said nothing. Then he said: —Dead? But how can he be dead? He wasn't the kind that gets killed in wars.

—Oh? There is a special kind of man for that? You are a fool, *Pawelku*.

The young man was silent again. Then he asked: —How did he die?

—He killed himself.

—I don't understand. Why should he kill himself? Why in God's name should anybody kill himself in war, when there are so many opportunities for dying? Oh my poor, pompous father, always so correct and ending life a suicide. The way out of a weakling. What a wasted gesture.

—He didn't do it for a gesture. Try to understand. I know there were differences between Michal and you which prevented you from understanding one another. But he was not a weak man. He was a man who believed in something and he loved you and he was disappointed by everything he loved and believed in. He had built his world around one idea, leaving himself nothing in reserve. He was strong enough to commit himself totally to you and the idea, and when both you and the idea proved to be false and rejected him he had nothing left. A man lives by his symbols. His symbols failed him. Don't sneer at him unless you understand it. It is much harder to be strong than to be weak. A weak man has no feeling except for himself. Your father had compassion. He had the courage to commit himself; his mistake was in his choice

555

of you and of the idea and his inability to see you both for what you were. The day he killed himself—it was the morning of the seventeenth—you were considered lost. I had gone down to the suburbs the night before to watch Kutrzeba's men coming in. I had been here earlier but you were unconscious. The doctors told me you wouldn't last much longer. I had told Michal that your case was serious. Michal didn't say anything. He felt guilt about you. I won't explain that now; you wouldn't understand unless you knew what he knew about the war before it began. He went to his skeleton headquarters thinking that you would die that day. He had already lost his faith in honor, the idea that motivated him, our allies saw to that. And then he got the message about the Bolsheviks and knew that he had also lost his country, that his world had ended, and he killed himself. There is nothing to despise in that.

—What is this about the Bolsheviks?

—I forgot that you don't know about them. We are at war with them. They attacked us on the seventeenth.

—*Kanalia . . .*

—The Lithuanians attacked us on the eighteenth. All our neighbors are hurrying to throw themselves on us before their own turn comes.

—Even the Roumanians?

The older man laughed.

—No. Not the Roumanians. We have been spared that indignity. Besides, they are our allies in this war, motionless like the others. We really have an unfortunate collection of allies. Your father thought we didn't need an enemy with allies like that. Would you have another proverb for this situation?

—*In peace, lions; in war, hares.* And what about Hungarians?

—They side with Hitler but they have refused to attack us. Michal would have been pleased. There is, it seems, one honorable nation left. As for all the others, the Slovaks invaded us with Hitler. The Ukrainians have begun to turn our eastern lands into a slaughterhouse. They burn and pillage and murder everything Polish. The Jews have greeted the Bolsheviks with open arms and act as guides for them. Our own Jews and our own Ukrainians. My only consolation is that their turn will come. Germans pay their debt in peculiar coin, and even the Jews should know about Russians by this time. But I am glad Michal didn't live to see how thoroughly his world will be erased, although none of this was important once the Bolsheviks attacked. Because, you see, we had finally managed to stop the Germans. Oh, not permanently— I have no illusions—but long enough to catch a breath, to form a line and hold it. They even brought reserves out of the west. And then in one morning hour on the seventeenth the Bolsheviks came in and then all hope of holding out was over. Now we must take the war out of this country, fight elsewhere and for others, for those same people who betrayed us here. But that is not the way that Michal saw it. For him this was not just a campaign, as it is for me. Nothing is lost for me, although we're beaten here. We'll win elsewhere. For Michal this was the entire war. When we lost here we lost everything forever, the way he thought of it. He got the message about the Bolsheviks and he had been told that you had little chance of living and thought that he had helped to condemn you to a useless death, and he saw no goodness anywhere, no honor, no nobility of spirit, and without you and his country and his faith in honor he couldn't live.

Then there was silence. In the silence, the snarling of the dogs was unnaturally loud. The young man said nothing. Then he said: —If only he had let me live my own life . . .

—What makes you think you have a right to one?

The older voice was no longer whispering.

—Everyone has the right.

—Does he? Is it guaranteed? Is there a charter guaranteeing everyone the right to do as he pleases? You earn the right, boy. You pay for the right. But you weren't paying anything; you were taking, always taking, and giving nothing in return, and that is common fraud. What have you done to claim the right to live the way you want to live? Are you an artist? Are you a philosopher? Has your genius given the world something of value? Have you paid the price of nonconformity? Personal freedom is a privilege; it is a reward. Why did you deserve it? You chose the easy path of self-indulgence. That's the coward's way. To turn your back on the world isn't to face it and to conquer it. Stealing the rights of a conqueror doesn't make you one; it only makes you contemptible. Your father saw where you were going: selfishness, overwhelming egotism, escape into trivia—all cloaked under the veneer of personal freedom to which you had no right. Friendships as empty as the circumstances under which you made them. Your self-destroying, self-loving gallop into nothing: That's real cowardice. Perhaps you didn't pull the trigger for your father, but you helped to load and aim the pistol. Perhaps a weaker man would not have killed himself. Perhaps he would have turned that pistol on you. But he loved you and he had compassion and you tore at him every day, like those dogs outside, and you destroyed a piece of him at a time, and he hoped that what he saw in you wasn't really there; he thought it couldn't be there because he loved you, and he thought that you, in time, would realize what you were doing and would stop, that you would be ashamed to go on with what you were doing—as a man would be ashamed, a true man, not a shell of one—and that you would start to earn the right to your own life, which he wanted you to have. Do you want to hear more?

—No.

The voice was flat.

—Then rest. We will come for you in an hour.

Then there were footsteps. And a jingling spur. Then there was nothing. Schwartzkopff went to sleep.

Tuesday, September the twenty-sixth

I THE GENERAL

He had become used to the empty streets after nightfall, the curfew of the siege, although at first it had been hard to reconcile the gaunt quiet of the shattered avenues with the careless, carefree, cynical old town that he remembered.

Boots echo so in streets where you've known laughter. The ghosts of all the yesterdays fill the depopulated boulevards, no longer gay but silently mocking.

If only I could weep, he thought. Perhaps the tears would unfreeze his mind, thaw his numbed brain and let thought flow again. But no tears came or would come, he knew well enough. And anyway it was too late for them.

First Lala, then Michal and now this: Adam was dead. Earlier in the day someone had come to tell him how sorry they were and he had listened without understanding (too busy planning what had to be done next morning, impatient with so little time left before the breakout) and he had said: —*What? Oh yes. Thank you very much.*

The man had stared at him with astonished eyes. He had said: —*Terribly sorry, General . . . a tragedy . . . my condolences.* And Prus had said: —*What?* Because tragedies were so common and he had work to do. But the man's words came home to him:

—*Radio Stockholm . . . your son . . . no possible mistake . . . several broadcasts . . . tragedy . . . so terribly sorry.*

He had listened then, unbelieving, and the man had told him what he had heard from Stockholm. It had apparently been on all the broadcasts; a dramatic story. Adam had been well known among mountainclimbers, and the way he had died ruled out the possibility of an accident, according to Stockholm. It had been murder. There was some reaction. A shocking thing. German authorities declining comment, but. . . . A brutal incident, a senseless appendage to war.

He had gone with the man to his home, to listen to the radio. There were not many radiosets left in the town, but the news must have traveled its own mysterious way, because several other men he knew stopped him on the way with their condolences. By midday he had heard the story in several broadcasts: from Stockholm, from Geneva (with a statement from a famous Swiss mountainclimber who had apparently known Adam), from the BBC in London. He could not bring himself to listen to a German station, but via shortwave from America he learned the German news.

Adam (according to the Germans) had been interned in Austria at the start of the war, had had a nervous breakdown, had been under medical care and was recuperating at the home of an old friend, also a mountainclimber. His internment had been nominal; he had been sympathetic to the German cause. He had climbed a hill, near Baden, alone and at night and had apparently become ill or disoriented or otherwise confused and had been unable to descend. He fell four hundred feet and was killed instantly. He was a friend of Germany. He had been scheduled to appear at a pressconference later in the month.

But the non-German versions carried other details. Adam had not died unseen in the dark. He had fallen down a granite cliff-face that he had apparently climbed without difficulty in the night in the broad light of midday, with a hundred persons watching, with policecordons and firelines and men climbing to him. It was, the Swiss report said, as if a Channel swimmer had drowned in his bathtub.

He listened to the broadcasts, feeling little beyond the unbelieving horror, unable to puzzle out the truth. It didn't matter how Adam had died (he thought) or why he had died. He was dead and that was enough. It was senseless; however, it had happened. But later (on his way to the General Staff building and at the Staff conference) he grew certain it had not been a murder. The Nazis did not kill before an audience with floodlights and policelines. But if not murder, what? Not the accident the Germans claimed. He had followed Adam on many difficult climbing expeditions through infrequent newspaper accounts and, more reliably, Michal's letters. He knew that Adam had been a firstrate climber. Already his death had brought statements from presidents of mountainclimbing societies in several countries. These removed the possibility of an accidental fall. Adam had simply been too good. So if not murder and not accident, it must be suicide. The boy had killed himself. It was not difficult to imagine why.

He tried to picture Adam, alone on the cliff-face, waiting for day, for the pursuit, for the witnesses, so that his death would not be meaningless. What had he thought about? What had he remembered? Had he forgiven what he had been too young to understand so many years ago? Had he been calm, at peace? It was the sort of thing that he himself might have done under the circumstances. He felt proud. He felt enormous sorrow. He wished he could tell Adam how proud he was, and how responsible.

He supposed that it would be impossible to explain to a man who was not a soldier how he could feel anything but horror: horror, regret, pain, profound loss. Certainly he had felt all these things when Lala had died. And he felt them in Adam's death. But Adam's death was also a death for an ideal, and as a soldier Prus knew that there was beauty in it.

Men spoke to him throughout the day. Condolences. Regrets. A tragedy. It was a tragedy, he knew, but not in their sense. The tragedy lay in empty years never to be filled, in lost years. He shook the hands they offered him, said nothing. He would say nothing to them, would not share his pride. They took it for grief and respected his silence. He went about his work saying nothing. And it is possible that his grey silence, his abrupt demands, his fierce, shortclipped expletives and orders did more than persuasion would have done. The men whom he told what he wanted, what he needed in order to do what he would do, did not put up many obstacles. They saw that they could not stop him from leading a breakout without arresting him. They said they could not help him. They would not approve. He knew why they could not approve and it didn't matter. What counted was that they would not hinder the attempt. They would not order men not to follow him.

He worked as if in fever all night and all morning, because this too was an act of faith and had to be performed with total dedication. At noon he walked through the streets to clear his head, to think. Grzes cooked a meal for him, later, on a Primus stove.

At nightfall he went to the barricades. During the night, lit up as if in mocking celebration by innumerable fires, the last troops of the armies of the west, the field armies of the great offensive, came into Warsaw. He wanted to see them. They came like seamen who, after a month of storms, make port at last. They were worn and tired, in rags, and often barefooted, but their weapons gleamed. They didn't know what to expect in Warsaw, but, he thought (watching them, listening to them), they believed there would be no more retreats; on this battleline of a thousand years, they would stay. Prus thought they would be cruelly disappointed. He hoped they would continue to be soldiers with their disappointment.

During the night, while these men had fought their way into the capital through the German lines, the commanders of the city had decided to surrender Warsaw. It would be cruel pay for a month of battles. But what was left of Warsaw had to be preserved. The generals knew better than the optimistic soldiers the extent of the catastrophe elsewhere in the country. There was no hope of relief for Warsaw and none for the country. The Allies had not moved, in their bombproof shelters. Still, the German terms were generous enough, and that was compensation of a kind. It was to be an honorable capitulation. The troops would not lay down their arms while the Germans watched. They would march out as soldiers.

Tomorrow, he thought, watching the optimistic soldiers, would be the last day of the fighting siege. The siege would lose its angry voice on the twenty-eighth: There would be silence, the ceasefire. The regiments would be assembled for the last time. They would be shown their standards. The standards would be hidden or cut from their shafts and wrapped around the bodies of the standard-bearers, who would take them to France, where, the commanders hoped, the regiments would reassemble if they could. And then the soldiers would draw pay. The regimental funds would be shared among them. There would be decorations and promotions and goodbyes, and on the twenty-ninth the troops would march to parks and citysquares and lay down their arms, and on the thirtieth, in the morning, they would leave the city. The next morning the Germans would march in.

One day of fighting left.

He thought he had prepared well enough for it, covering every possibility (including rain), but in war it was impossible to tell. War is a province of chance. He would attack out of the northeast sector and drive east through the woods there and cross the Vistula high above the city and then march through Volhynia, south, to the Hungarian border. Men would come to him on the way.

He hoped that the men on whom he depended (Kern, Tarski, other friends who knew war when it was simple) were still with him. He thought they were.

They were that kind of men. They would not disappoint him. And he hoped that he would not lead them to disaster.

Well, he thought, I'll know tomorrow night. Tonight there was more work: troops to move and prepare, orders to issue, and the assault to ready for the morning.

He went to Kern's perimeter, where his officers waited. Kern's men and Tarski's infantry and the troops brought in by his old friends would be the backbone of his force. He had arranged for their replacement on the sector so that he could move them. There even was a promise of artillery support. A wagonload of rifle ammunition would come from the arsenal. The commanders at the Staff had known that there was no way to prevent a breakout without disarming troops, an indignity that would come soon enough. So they had done nothing to prevent the breakout.

(—*Look,* they had said: *We think it futile. You'll have a thousand kilometers of hostile country to cross. We think it better if the regiments disband and the men make their way south individually, on their own. But if you're going to do such a thing, do it well. Fight your way out and become a focal point for the disbanded men after our capitulation. We cannot help you, but we won't hinder you. Gather as many as you can on your way south.*)

There were innumerable small breakouts planned in the various sectors.

He made his way carefully through the gutted streets lighted by German starshells and the fires, remembering landmarks, and suddenly he was sure that he would never see Warsaw again. This was the last time he would see the city which had been so many things in his life, good and evil; so much had been his here and so much lost.

What lay ahead? He would not think beyond the morning. Soon he saw the glint of a bayonet ahead and a sentry stopped him and then he went down narrow stone stairs to a cellar where the others waited.

The officers rose when he came into the cellar: worn men covered with dust, but cheerful enough. They watched him with the grave eyes of children. The only one who did not get up (who could not get up) was Pawel. He lay on straw on the cellar floor. He was quite still. His face was bloodless, and only his black, fevered eyes, made huge by the deep bruises under them, burned in the white mask to show that he was still alive. A horseblanket had been thrown across his lower body.

The cellar was the middle one of three cool vaulted chambers linked by a tunnel built by the engineers. The walls were thick, lined with red and yellow brick now uniformly black with age and the dusty accumulations of a hundred years. In the first cellar men stood on benches under narrow windows and fired carbines at the Germans. More men sat on the floor, priming handgrenades and wrapping their small wounds and waiting for their turn to get up on benches. Each time a man fell off a bench another would get up and take his place and two others would pick him up and take him to the last of the three cellars. The wounded lay there quietly in neat rows like equipment laid out for fieldinspection, staring at the ceiling. The ceiling moved each time a bomb or shell or mortarbomb fell into the house. Nothing was left of the house above the cellar (as there was nothing left of any house along the street) except the greyblack walls, gutted and scorched and pocked with holes like open dead mouths. The walls were like great boxes without lids, and shells and bombs and mortarbombs fell into the boxes. Between the boxes, running crazily across the street, with sharp bends and wild loops and gaps torn by craters, were trenches, with other trenches leading to them out of other boxes; and ragged mounds of pipes and rails and cobblestones and concrete slabs uprooted from the pavement and furniture and objects that were no longer recognizable as anything were piled in front of the trenches between the overturned streetcars and skeletal cabs. A thick grey haze of dust hung over all of it. Men lay in the trenches and stood under the cellar-windows of the vaulted strongpoints and fired at the Germans in similar trenches and boxlike ruins fifty meters away. The Germans had the church at the end of the street, and they had hauled machineguns up into the steeple, and a small cannon shot long tongues of fire out of the church door. The Germans wheeled the cannon to the door, fired, and pulled it back. The shells fell in the stone boxes and blew up the rubble.

—Here it comes, shouted the men under the narrow windows. —A cigarette for the man who gets the gunner, shouted the sergeant-major. And the flat crack of the cannonshot and the thump of shell exploding overhead were lost in the sharp crash of riflefire. —Missed him, you horrible abortions you, the sergeant-major said. But in the street someone gave a long, agonized shout and went on screaming for several minutes.

Colonel Kern saluted and reported.

How many men and horses were there? What and who could be used for the attack?

Kern gave the headcount of the men and horses. Then others reported. The General listened to the quiet voices, the flat figures that had no relation to the dead and living, the cold professional tabulations of men in terms of bayonets and sabers. So many hundred sabers and bayonets for the morning breakout, so many rounds of ammunition for each rifle (carefully hoarded out of each day's ration), so many kilograms of bread and hardtack divided among so many of these impersonal bayonets and sabers.

Few, he thought, listening to the voices. Damn few. But always enough no matter how few there were.

—Show me the map.

They brought one.

They stood around the map as if it had its own malevolent life and could injure them. The General's pencil moved across the map with quick, angry strokes.

—And so (he said, watching their grave faces) we shall go here and here and then through here. Out of these woods. Then that way to the river. Past this small hill and that ridge and through that small town. And then the next objective.

He didn't want to think about the next objective.

—The ridge is number fifty-two on your maps. We will begin from there. There is a German battery somewhere behind that ridge and we have to take it. As far as I can tell there is nothing else behind that battery. The battery must be taken quickly. The cavalry will do it. That way the infantry will have a shorter time under the battery's guns. From then on it will be as I've outlined to you. I hope that's how it will be. I hope that I am right about everything. Now, I suppose, I should tell you some fine, inspiring words. Do you want to hear some?

He felt no enthusiasm of any kind. He thought it must show. He looked into the eyes of the officers and tried to hear what the men were saying in the other cellars. (They did not talk about war. They said they were hungry. They wondered when they would have a chance to sleep.) The officers looked at him with dusty eyes. They stared unblinking as though to say: Don't pretend with us. You feel as we feel, so why the masquerade? We'll go on because we have to, because there's nothing else to do. But for what?

He couldn't find the words for them.

Poland?

That he didn't have to say: That they understood.

Honor? You either have it or you don't, and no fine words can give it to you, and anyway it's not a thing that one man can tell another. Not at any time.

Comradeship? Duty? It was more than duty. Because there are limits to a man's duty, after all. As for comradeship, they all had shown more than enough of it. What then?

High strategy?

Political commitments?

No man can be asked to die for his country's political commitments. That is neither *dolce* nor *decorum*.

He said nothing more. He turned to the map (thinking suddenly of Michal) and its delineated order. After a moment he asked if there were any questions. There would be none, of course; these were professionals and they knew their work. Still, that was the immemorial ritual.

There were no questions. Colonel Kern said something about horses: Everyone should try to spare the horses until the last possible moment or until they themselves were shot out of their saddles.

Tarski wished to know if there was hope of artillery support. —Not that it would do any good. But it would make the men feel better. They like to hear the sound of their own guns.

—A battery will fire ten rounds before we move, Prus said.

Tarski sighed. —I would feel better with a little more. The men would feel better.

—There isn't any more. Those are the last ten shells in Warsaw.

—Perhaps we can have the men sing marching songs, Pawel said. That might make them feel better about not having artillery support.

—We might do that, the General agreed. When you have no artillery you might as well sing songs.

The others smiled gravely.

—We have time, Prus said. We can't do anything until we are relieved here. There will be some policemen coming here today. You can start moving to the attack position as soon as they come. No one is going to ask why you are off your sector. Headquarters knows that there will be breakouts before the surrender. They will do nothing to prevent them, although they have to honor the spirit of the capitulation and so won't help either. So rest the men, if you can, during the day. They'll have a busy night and morning. And, as somebody once told me, sleep is as good as food if there is no food.

So, if there was nothing else, would the gentlemen see to their dispositions? Advance and quartering parties, rations issues, lines of approach and assembly areas: the mechanics of moving large bodies of men, old when Caesar was an officercadet.

The others left at once. And soon junior officers and old noncommissioned officers and small patrolgroups set out from the strongpoints and a redfaced, mustached sergeant-major (whom the General remembered from somewhere) walked carefully past with several lancers and the youngest of the lancers looked quickly back at Pawel and the General as if to reassure himself that they were really there.

He had two brandnew silver stripes sewn on each shoulderstrap.

—Take care, Corporal, Pawel said.

—Yes sir!

When the forward parties had departed the officers returned. Colonel Kern wished to know if the General had had breakfast. Prus laughed. —Have you? Has anyone?

—The morning ration came an hour ago but I'm afraid it's horseflesh.

—Won't the men eat it?

—The young men eat it. The old men couldn't eat that any more than they could eat their own hearts. We've all been cavalrymen too long. But, if the General doesn't mind, it's the best the regimental mess can offer these days.

—I remember your mess from other days, Prus said. You've always had a reputation for excellent cooking. I'd rather keep on thinking of you as gourmets. One could dine better in your mess than at the George in Lwow.

—Well now, I wouldn't quite say that, Kern said, pleased. But it's nice to be remembered at one's best. And just to show you, General, that our hospitality does not depend on the quartermaster, I have something that will take our minds off our unfortunate rations.

—A surprise, Kern? Have you been trading with the Germans?

—Not exactly, sir. Merely anticipating the capitulation. We are a drinking regiment, General, if you remember. We do not marry but we certainly drink. I don't see why we should lose our reputation because of a war. A gentleman remains a gentleman no matter what the circumstances, don't you agree, sir?

—Certainly. Prus laughed. —Despite all circumstances. What is your surprise?

—I sent a wagon to the presidential palace yesterday and some good, understanding friends of mine put something for us in the wagon. I had just happened to hear, you see, that there were some national treasures in the presidential cellar. I couldn't think of giving up our treasures to the Germans.

—Most patriotic, Colonel. Most commendable.

—So, with the General's permission? It's not a treasure that we can carry with us when we go.

Prus laughed, and now the others also laughed.

—Of course.

Kern bowed and nodded to the soldier peering from the last of the three cellars and the soldier grinned and his red face vanished and then he and three others reappeared in more or less clean messjackets carrying a fielddesk (which they placed with some ceremony on the floor) and a grey sheet with which they covered the fielddesk and marched out again. They came back with glasses and a silver tray.

—Canapés, General?

It was hardtack and ration sardines.

—Just like the buffet at the George, Prus said, laughing. And then the soldiers came in with the colonel's presidential treasures: old, mosscovered bottles, ancient Burgundies, Tokay wrapped in straw with hundred-year-old seals stamped across the wrappings, Madeira that could be cut with a knife.

—You are a genius, Kern, the General said. You should be quartermaster general.

—I should be retired and growing cabbages in Podole. But I'm too much of a patriot to let these wines fall into German hands. They are too fine to surrender.

Kern filled the first glass and raised it and the others looked at the rich gleam like a giant ruby. The colonel handed the glass to the General. Then he filled the others.

—I don't believe in scorched-earth policies, but I don't think we should make the Germans comfortable, either. This was laid down by the Grand Duke Constantine in 1840 before we chased him out of Warsaw a few years later. So let's drink to the Russian duke and hope for better times. I started service in the Tsar's dragoons and, for all I know, I'll end it in the Ethiopian lancers, but I'll drink to anything in between.

—A toast, sir. Tarski said.

The General shook his head. —I am too old for toasts. Toasts should be drunk by men who have a lot of time.

—I have a toast, Pawel said. (He was laughing softly.) To victory and the laughing gods of war.

—To victory.

—To the regiment, said a young lieutenant. His face was red with wine and emotion and he swayed a little.

—All right, the colonel said. To the regiment. There's little of it left, but even so it's worth drinking to. I'll never have another regiment like it, and so it's doubly worth drinking to.

—To the Ethiopian lancers, Pawel said, laughing. I hope they accept cripples for enlistment.

No one else laughed. And so the General said: —To us.

—Us, Uncle?

—Why not? We are unique, you know. We are the dinosaurs, passing into history. That is worth drinking to, I think.

—To us, the major said.

—But how can it all end like this? the young lieutenant said. We could have won here, couldn't we?

The colonel smiled. Pawel laughed. The General poured a glass of wine for Pawel and sat down beside him.

—That's a mistake a lot of people are going to make. There will be many claims about how close we came to winning here. There'll be innumerable historians and apologists talking about rain, the perfidy of our allies, poverty, lack of equipment, this and that, and none of it will be entirely true. The truth is that we had no chance of winning; not the slightest hope, no matter what future apologists will decide to say. And it's no use blaming anybody for losing the war, just as it's useless to blame anyone for starting it. Our glory lies in the fact that there was no hope of winning. That's worth remembering; it's better than debating causes and effects and looking for somebody or some event to blame. There will be people who will blame specific men and particular events for starting the war. They'll say it was the animal greed of the Germans or the incapacity of the English or, for that matter, that it was part of an international conspiracy of bankers. The truth is that there can be no blame in war. For true guilt to exist there must be perfect innocence on the other side, and no one comes into a war with clean hands, and, certainly, no one comes out without touching dirt. I think it's only the unborn who can talk about moral rights and innocence and lack of guilt. For the rest of us, the difference is the amount of dirt, the degree of culpability, and that's an issue decided by winners. I don't think we should ever get involved in that kind of haggling. Let the others do it. Let them say: You did this, and failed to do that, and are responsible for so many milligrams of tragedy, so many English pounds of horror. Why make our effort and ourselves cheap with that kind of haggling? We should never do it. We are the luckiest men who will fight in this long war, I think. We are the last who will know without any doubt why this war was fought. The issues are still bright for us because they are new. No one else, no matter what slogans they invent or whom they accuse or what righteousness they manage to wrap around themselves, is ever really going to be sure what this is all about. It will be a long and difficult war and innumerable new issues will enter it from now on and everything will become just a bit confused, a little grey, a little uncertain, and then the bright absolutes will disappear and then we shall all be killing each other just so that we can stop killing each other, fighting to end a war that no one can quite justify anymore. And so I say that we should regret nothing, because we are truly fortunate. And now if someone will share some more of this regimental hospitality . . .

They drank more wine. The morning passed slowly. The German rifle and machinegun fire gradually slackened and then ceased altogether. Shells still fell occasionally, as if the gunners fired out of force of habit, no longer interested. Before noon the Germans withdrew from their positions, and they did not make any new attacks for the rest of the day.

I ANTOS

They came into the woods late in the afternoon with the sun well on its way past the tallest trees, going in a long line of watchful men and indifferent horses past the old fort where the fighting had been heavy early in the siege. Now the gun galleries were quiet. The fort had changed hands several times a day in the early days, but now it was deserted. The glacis slope was pitted like a cheese and the parapet had come down on the flat parade and the inner way and the earthworks had erupted in spilled slate and concrete. There was no fighting here anymore. The Poles had drawn back closer to the city and the Germans had moved themselves out of these woods and up to the ridges in the north and northeast, and the dead fort and shattered woods and demolished gardens were left to small animals and insects. The animals scrambled off when the men and horses came singlefile up the track, but the insects flew to them in a cloud.

The men cursed the insects.

—So many of them, Stas said. You'd think a rain was coming.

They halted and grouped in a clearing. And, after hobbling their horses (which immediately lay down) and marking with quick saberstrokes and bandages the track that the regiment would follow in the night, and after finding the several clearings which (Pan Szef said) would serve the regiment as troop assemblypoints and marking them with cards Pan Szef pinned to trees, they sat down or lay down to sleep or went in among the small skeletons of villas and the ploughed-up gardens to look for food. The day was hot and there was time before the others came, the regiment and infantrymen who would make the attack. No shells flew behind them to the grey mass that was Warsaw, indefinite shapes of stone halfhidden by smoke. The insects made the only sound.

—It's like back home, Stas said. D'you think we'll ever see it?

Antos shrugged. —We'll see it when it's over.

—It's over now, Stas said. I mean, after we leave here it'll all be over. Maybe we should go home from here. What do you think?

—Nobody said we could go. So it can't be over.

—Well, I don't know. Seems to me we could just go. What difference would it make to anybody?

—No. It's not over yet. Besides (Antos stopped and looked back among the trees), Pan Szef would be angry. He'd send the *kanarki* after you and then *trach-trach* against the wall. You better stop talking like that when he's around. Listen, that's no man to fool with, I can tell you.

—He's only a man.

—What?

But Stas said nothing more. He turned into a small patch of shellpitted garden and tumbled appletrees and among the trees he found a ruin. His hunched, slowmoving body moved towards the ruin. He did not look at Antos and Antos went on to find a garden for himself where he could search for food. They had passed one earlier where the trees were upright and the house still had a roof and glass in the windows and (Antos thought) maybe there'd be something there he could find. But he saw a squad of infantry already in the garden digging for vegetables with their bayonets.

—Any luck, comrades?

—*Gowno,* said one of the infantrymen. The bastards cleaned it out.

Antos nodded. He was not surprised. The Northern Army had passed that way five days before and patrols had gone that way for several days before both sides abandoned this small corner of the war, and now even the bark was gone from the trees. The infantrymen dug and cursed and presently went away. They sat among the trees, saying nothing. One of them, a small, thin-faced soldier with bad feet, went into the house. When he came out he had his boots off and sacking wrapped around his feet. He sat against the fence. He began to eat. He moved his feet carefully as if they hurt a lot. He had a grey (once white) cotton shirt, the kind peasants weave, under his open jacket. He bent low over both his hands, eating like a dog.

—What do you have there, comrade? Antos said. Is there more somewhere?

—Cheese, Corporal, the thin soldier said. He showed a small cheese, the size of a fist. He looked doubtfully at Antos and then at the cheese. After a moment he broke the cheese in half and held it out to Antos.

—It's your cheese, Antos said. You found it so you eat it. I'll look around for my own.

—There isn't any, the thin soldier said. I brought this with me from a long way off. Besides, I've had enough. Here, take it.

Antos took the cheese. It was old and dry. He ate it carefully. He picked up each small crumb that fell on the ground and ate it. When he was done he sucked all his fingers. He licked his hands but his tongue was dry.

—Good cheese, he said.

The thin soldier shrugged.

—I got some water, Antos said. You want some?

The thin soldier licked his lips. He looked carefully at Antos. —All right. (And then, as if ashamed of accepting favors:) My canteen's empty and there's a dead horse in the well.

Antos nodded. He knew what troubled the thin soldier. In war it's bad to owe anybody favors. You never knew when you'd be called on to settle the debt.

—Drink up. I've got another canteen on my saddlebow, he lied. That's how it is in the cavalry, see? We got to carry water for the horses.

The thin soldier drank a little. Then a little more. Clearly this was the first water he had drunk that day. —Ah, he said.

—Is it good?

—It's good.

The thin soldier leaned back against the fence and closed his eyes. He spread his legs wide like a machinegun tripod. He was careful how he moved his bundles of foot. Antos sat with his back to the wall of the house. They faced each other. They looked at each other, unsmiling, as if they had known each other a long time.

—You going to be in the attack? Antos said.

—That's what I'm here for.

—How're you going to make it with those feet?

—I walked a long way with them. I can walk some more.

—Well, they're your feet. Where did you come from?

The infantryman waved towards the south. —Down by the mountains. It's a long way off.

—Maybe you ought to ride in one of the wagons.

—They aren't taking anybody who can't walk. They aren't taking any sick and wounded. Anybody who can't make it by himself has to stay back and go to the Germans. Don't you know that, Corporal?

Antos felt anger. What the hell was that? No private soldier talks like that to a Pan Kapral. No. Especially a footsoldier. But then, he thought, I haven't been a corporal long and the man has sore feet. So he said nothing for a while. Then he said: —You must want to go awful bad to try it with those feet.

The soldier nodded. —They're not as bad as they look. I can make it.

—Well, we got a good general for it, anyway, Antos said. I know him. He'll get us through, all right. The way I hear it, we're going to go through first and take some battery and then you footsoldiers will come after us. I don't like that kind of fighting, you know? Too many horses get killed that way. But that's what the General wants. He knows what he's doing. Listen, it's good to know you got a general who knows what he's doing. That way you don't have to worry about anything.

—I wouldn't know, the thin soldier said. I don't know that many generals.

—I just know this one, Antos said. He's good, all right.

The thin soldier laughed. He stared at his feet. He watched a troop of ants spread at the base of the brown hills of sacking. Then he looked up at a column of infantry that suddenly came out from under the trees along the track. The men were weighed down under their equipment. Some of the officers rode horses. It was very hot. The smell of sweat came from the column on the track. Dust came from the column. It was difficult to talk in the dust. The thin soldier and Antos said nothing while dust settled on them.

Then a whistle blew.

Then other whistles blew inside the column and the men stopped walking and the officers' horses also stopped and the soldiers sat down and lay down among the trees and the horses lay down and only officers moved in their small groups, talking.

—Is that your outfit? Antos said.

The thin soldier shrugged.

—Where are you from?

—I was born here. Back there in Warsaw.

—It must be something to be born in town, to live in a town. It was good, eh?

The thin soldier laughed. —No, I can't say that.

—Not good? Antos was astonished. He looked at the thin soldier with suspicion. —But you eat meat every day, don't you? You got water in the house and there's glass in the windows and you wear clothes like a lord and there's more food to eat in the restaurants than I see in my village all year. That isn't good?

—A man needs more.

—Ha! (Antos stared at the thin soldier.) What more?

—It's got to be yours, the thin soldier said. You have to know it's yours. You have to have that feeling. (Then he shrugged and looked at Antos and smiled a little.) Tell me about your home.

—Ah. What's there to say about a village?

Home's far away, Antos thought. And the Bolshevik is in it. He shrugged and watched Stas Guz and Bartek coming across the garden.

—A village is a village, he said. It's all the same there. You work and you got nothing. Some villages are poor and others are rich but you still got nothing. My village is poor. The village of Stas Guz, there, is a rich village. It's got an inn and it's got a Jew. We don't have a Jew. Maybe we'll get one after it's all over. Maybe I'll get one and bring him along. That would be something, to get one of those. But I don't know; either way it's no good in a village.

—So you want a Jew, the thin soldier said. He started laughing. —What do you want him for?

—I don't know. They make a rich village. Every rich village I know has a Jew in it.

The soldier went on laughing. —Believe me, you're better off without them if they're little. And big ones are hard to find. But maybe it'll be different when the war is over.

Antos nodded.

—A lot's got to be different when the war is over. It's got to be better for everybody, not just some, you know? It's not much good the way it is now.

—Yes sir, Corporal, the thin soldier said, laughing.

—What are you laughing at, soldier?

The thin soldier shook his head. —Oh, just a thought I had. I'm learning something new every day. And there's so much more to learn. That's why I was laughing.

Antos nodded again, looking at the soldier.

—I'm learning too, he said. When you think about things you see how bad they are. And you think how you're not going to live that way anymore. And the more you think the more you see and pretty soon, I think, you know what to do. That's what I think.

The thin soldier nodded gravely. He smiled at Antos.

—That's a lot more than glass in the windows and meat every day.

Antos also nodded. Then Stas and Bartek came up and sat down. They had found no food. They sat against the fence, feeling the hot sun, saying nothing. Soon Pan Szef came along the track. His red skin hung about his neck in folds like a turkey's. He sat away from the other men and looked at Antos with red-and-yellow eyes and his mouth moved up and down as though he were eating. He chewed the ends of his mustache.

—Well, what d'you think, Antos? Bartek said.

—About what?

—I don't know. About what's happening. We'll be going home soon, eh?

—The Bolshevik is there.

Bartek scratched his head. —Hmm. Yes. So we can't go home?

—Not till it's over.

Bartek sighed. Stas looked up at the others and quickly away. —I think we ought to go home now, he said. He kept his voice low. It was the kind of voice that seems to come out of a man without his knowing it. Antos had heard men speak like that on the barricades. When they were tired or hungry or hurt or when nothing mattered to them anymore.

—But what about the Bolshevik? (And when Stas shrugged and looked away, careful not to look at Pan Szef or at Antos, Bartek said:) Hey, Antos, is that what you think?

—I don't know, Antos said. I don't know what's over and what isn't over. When it's all over somebody will tell us.

—But what if it's over and nobody tells us?

—Somebody got to tell us. If you're a soldier somebody tells you what to do.

Then Stas Guz sighed and scratched himself and got up again and went away among the houses, looking at the ground. Then he went into a house. The thin soldier laughed.

—That's a good question, he said. What if everything is over and nobody bothers to tell us about it?

—I'll tell you, Pan Szef said suddenly. He had been listening to them. —I'll tell you everything you have to know. So cut out that stupid talk and get some sleep. Maybe you won't get a chance like this after today. And you, Mocny, watch your step. You don't have your generals and your captains here.

—Yes sir, Antos said.

He closed his eyes but he was too tired to sleep. The sun was hot. It had moved down closer to the trees but not close enough for the nightchill to come. Antos could see it red through his eyelids. He wished Pan Szef would go away. But the sergeant-major sat in the corner of the garden looking at the others. He looked particularly hard at Antos. He had looked like that ever since that day in the hospital when the General told him to forget about the priests. He looked like that was the last thing he'd forget.

—Uh, ha, Antos sighed.

The thin soldier sat back and stretched his ragwrapped feet in front of him.

—What's wrong with your feet? Bartek said.

—I walked a long way from the south.

—Is that where you were fighting? (And when the thin soldier nodded:) How was it there?

—It was . . . bad.

—Bad!

Pan Szef was suddenly up, and Antos, who knew every look that Pan Szef had, saw that the sergeant-major was very angry. He wished that he could go away. Bartek got up and scratched himself and yawned and quickly went away. Pan Szef came at them rolling like a bear.

—So it was bad for you, footsoldier, eh? So you got beaten?

—No, the thin soldier said.

—So you beat them?

—No. Nobody beat anybody but they won.

—That's stupid, Pan Szef said. This is a war and in a war two things happen. Either you beat or you get beaten and if you didn't beat them then they kicked the piss out of you. So don't give us any of that *maybe* horseshit. We are old horses here and we know oats from corn.

The thin soldier shrugged and looked away. Antos thought that no matter what Pan Szef said the thin soldier would go on thinking that he wasn't beaten.

Then Stas Guz came back and sat down at the corner of the fence and house and tried to make himself invisible. He kept his back carefully to the others.

—You shrug at me? Pan Szef said to the thinfaced soldier. At me, you abortion?

Antos got up, but Pan Szef looked at him, grinning terribly, and Antos slowly sat back down again.

—Is there something you don't care for, Corporal? Something disturbs you? Well, keep your officerloving ass on the ground till I'm ready for you. And you, footsoldier, where're you from? Are you a deserter?

—He is from Warsaw, Antos said.

—Who asked you, you officers' favorite? Shut your stupid mouth. They give you stripes but that don't mean anything to me. To me you're still gallowsbait, still waiting for a rope,' understand? And believe me, I'll get you rigged up for a dancing collar before I'm done with you. So keep your muzzle shut. This bird can sing his own songs. Where are you from, footsoldier, did you hear me?

—Nalewki, the thin soldier said.

Pan Szef spat. He laughed. —That's where the Jews live, right?

—That's right, the thin soldier said.

—And that's you, right?

—That's right.

—Ha, Pan Szef said, looking at the others. And he wasn't beaten? And I don't suppose he ran all the way to Warsaw? Where did you run from, *Zydku?*

—I didn't run from anywhere. I walked.

—Ha, so he walked. Look at him. I bet he walked. At eighty kilometers an hour!

The thin soldier shrugged. Some flies came and settled on his feet. The thin soldier didn't bother chasing the flies off.

—Down south, he said, where I've come from, we beat and got beaten too. Nobody won and nobody lost and nobody got anything out of it except maybe the dead. A lot of Poles and Germans got killed there. But there were always more Germans. Always more. They were like these flies. They'd come and you wouldn't be able to hit out at them because to hit them would be to hit yourself on a part that hurts. It would hurt worse and the flies would come back anyway. So soon you learned to leave them alone and hit them only when they settled on something that was not a part of you.

—*Gowno,* Pan Szef said. If you got guts you hit them no matter where they are. War is war. There's got to be pain.

—Maybe, the soldier said. I am not talking about war.

—Why not? What else is there to talk about? What's there to talk about at all? You do your bloody duty, soldier, and keep your mouth shut. That's all you got to do. Don't give me any of that talk, that Jew talk, that deserter talk. I'll have you up before a firingsquad so fast you won't know where you've deserted from! Shit on that talk, I say, and do your duty.

—I didn't desert from anything, the thin soldier said.

—So how come you're all alone? Where's your regiment?

—It's everywhere. Some of them are dead. But I didn't desert anything that I believe in. I'm not a deserter.

—Talk, talk, talk, Pan Szef said.

The soldier shrugged. —Call it what you want.

—It's all over anyway, Stas Guz said. His eyes were closed and he was speaking in that hollow voice.

—Shut up! the sergeant-major shouted. He swayed above the others like a drunken tree. —Shut your dog's mouth! You pig! You sniveling bastard! So you think it's over?

—Yes sir, Stas Guz whispered.

—I'll show you if it's over! It won't be over till I tell you, understand? You horse's prick, you! Nothing's over! We'll take the German and we'll take the Bolshevik and then we'll take care of the likes of you! It hasn't even started, you mother's mistake.

—Don't talk like that, sir, Antos said.

—You too, you gallowsbird? You dare to go against me? You don't have your bloody Pan Kapitan with you now, you little shit. You got me! Me! You got me to deal with! I am in charge. It's my squadron now and there's no officers, no fine cardplaying, bearhunting gentlemen for you to run to, nobody to hide behind, no finetalk people to worry about if there's a priest or not before they shoot you. No! There's just me! I am the regulations here! All I worry about is if there's a tree tall enough and a rope strong enough and a sonofabitch traitor to hang from the rope.

He looked huge and angry and dangerous and (Antos thought) like a bear. He was hunched over like an angry bear with his head pulled down into his shoulders and his eyes, red and halfclosed, sunken deep inside his head. Something was going to happen.

Antos hoped it wouldn't be anything terrible.

He thought that he had had enough terrible things and he didn't want any more to happen.

He looked towards the woods, where, with the sun going down, sinking in the treecrowns, the other men and horses were coming in from Warsaw. He looked at Stas Guz. Stas sat with his mouth and eyes wide as if he wanted to shout with both and couldn't with either. He looked at the thin soldier. The thin soldier had closed his eyes and was touching his feet with his fingertips. He looked at Pan Szef. Pan Szef's face was shaking.

—Listen, he said. Are you listening to me? Well, listen. Don't try to pull anything on me. I am one of you. I was a boy in a village just like you and I took the geese to the goose hill like you did, and I milked our cow and when our cow was dead I pulled the plow in spring and my mother looked two hundred years old before she was thirty just like your mothers did. (He talked so quickly now that they could hardly hear him. Antos couldn't remember any time when he had heard Pan Szef talk so much so fast. His red face was wet with sweat and Antos wondered where the sweat had come from. It was so hot, so dry, the sun was so fierce, you would've thought all the sweat would've boiled out of them long ago. Still, Pan Szef was wet with it.) There's no difference between you and me except that I'm a soldier. That's something you can never be. You don't have it in you. So things are bad, eh? So you seen men killed, did you? So you got nothing to eat and it don't look like you're going to get anything soon, eh? That's war, you puking bastards. You know what war is? You think because you seen some dead men you know what war is? Listen, when war comes the Devil makes hell bigger and he don't do it to pass the time away. War is for killing. You'll see a lot more of it, I promise you. What do I care about the German and the Bolshevik? It don't matter how many of them there are or where they are, not if you're a soldier. You'll kill them and you'll go on killing till there *is* no more. You don't give up, you understand? Nothing is over till I tell you, understand? Over, he says. Over, nothing. Nothing is over!

—Nothing is over, Stas Guz said in his new voice.

—Humph, Antos said. He didn't know what to say and he felt as if someone had reached a hot hand inside him and pulled everything out.

But the thin soldier laughed.

Don't laugh, Antos wished to say. This is no time for it. Something terrible will happen.

—You laugh? This was Pan Szef in a terrible loud voice.

The thin soldier hugged himself and rocked up and down laughing without a sound.

—Laugh? Laugh? I'll show you laughter, you bloody deserter you, you foul nothing! Here! Brush this off!

And in one short jump the sergeant-major was before the soldier and in another he had brought both of his ironshod heels on the thin soldier's wrapped-up feet with a sound that was like air coming quickly out of a burst balloon.

The soldier screamed. Antos jumped erect. But it didn't seem to Antos that he had moved at all. He thought that he was still seated on the log with his back against the hot, sunsoaked fence (feeling the dryness of the heat spreading inside him, entering his bones, filling him with fire, lapping inside his head against the back of his burning eyeballs) and watching this other soldier whom he didn't know, who looked like himself but couldn't be, rise and pick up the carbine by the barrel and swing the barrel high above his head the way he had been taught to do by Pan Szef and bring it down applying pressure and he saw the brass-and-walnut carbinebutt descend in the proper manner and hit and bury itself in the short grey hairs.

Grey hair surprisingly streaked with red.

He hit again and again and the grey head sank and he hit it while it spilled itself along the ground, and finally he was exhausted. He dropped the carbine. It was red. The head was red. He did not see the rest of the man on the ground.

—Oh my God, oh my God, oh my God, Stas Guz said.

Antos didn't say anything. He looked at the thin soldier. The soldier had stopped screaming. He had dropped the feet he had been hugging.

—Antos, Antos, Stas Guz said. His voice was the old voice that Antos remembered. —Oh my God.

—Quiet, be quiet now, Antos said. What's the matter with you?

—Oh my God, *Boze moj!* Stas Guz started shaking. First his head shook, then his shoulders, and then his body. His legs were the last to shake but they shook the hardest.

—Oh my God, he said.

—What's the matter with you?

I didn't do anything, Antos thought. Nothing has happened. I didn't do anything. Nothing. I was just sitting on a log. And then I was up. Yes. And I had the carbine. But I didn't hit Pan Szef, no sir. I wouldn't do that.

—I didn't do anything, he said.

Now Stas was weeping. He shook and he was very much afraid.

—Stop crying, Antos said. Stop shaking. It's like Pan Szef said, be a soldier.

—It's all over, Stas Guz said. Now it's all over for sure.

—Nothing is over.

—You better go away, soldier, the thin soldier said. Somebody'll be along any minute.

Antos looked at him. The thin soldier was pale. Patches of yellow-white stood out between the streaks of dirt on his hollow face.

—Why should I go away, and where? I didn't do anything.

—Well, I'm going.

The thin soldier got up. —You'd better get out of here quick, he said. You don't have much time. There is a bunch of officers sitting behind those trees and somebody will be here to find out what all the shouting was about.

—We'll tell them, then, Antos said.

—Not me. You killed a sergeant-major, friend, and they'll give you about five seconds to explain before they put a bullet in your head. I'm going and you'd better go along. I am not staying to make any five-second explanations.

The soldier picked up his rifle and reversed it and put the butt under his arm to use for a crutch. He started walking towards the trees, going across the garden and past the pitchmaker's hut. Antos watched him go. He looked at Stas Guz, who had stopped weeping. Stas Guz stared at him with wide eyes the way he had stared at the sergeant-major. Antos looked at the sergeant-major. He saw the man was dead.

—Did I really kill him? he asked.

Stas Guz said nothing.

—What d'you think we ought to do?

Stas Guz shook his head.

Antos took off the cap and scratched his head a little. He didn't scratch hard. His scalp was burned badly with the sun (cap or no cap the sun got through to it) and hair and skin came out under his fingernails. He looked at the cap with the silver eagle on it and at the trees where the thin soldier had gone. He put his cap back on his head and buttoned his buttons. He didn't know what to do.

—Maybe we better go, Stas Guz said.

—Where?

—Home.

—That's far away.

—Well, if we go far enough and long enough we'll get there.

—I don't know, Antos said. It don't seem right to go away like that. Nobody said we could, and it's like Pan Szef said: It's not over yet.

—Well, Stas Guz said. He sighed. He looked at the dead man. —Maybe we better put him away somewhere. We ought to put him down before we do anything.

—Well, yes, Antos said.

—Where'll we put him?

Antos looked around.

—In the house? There's a bed in there.

Stas sighed and came closer to where the sergeant-major was lying. He bent down and picked up the dead man's feet. Antos picked up his hands. They were hard and worn and like his own but older. They were like his father's. He remembered his father's hands on his head before he went away to be a soldier. His father had put both his hard hands on his head and had kissed him. He had never kissed him before. He had hit him often, sure, all the time, but he had never kissed him. Antos didn't think his father liked him much until then. His father had a hard red face and a long grey mustache. He bit his mustache after he kissed him and went into the house. He did not look back. Antos looked after him, but not very long. All the other young men were forming in the street and he had to go. Women wept and boys shouted and girls laughed and waved and once in a while one of them would run up and kiss one of the young men. Then all the others would laugh and she would giggle. All the young men were grinning. Pan Szef was grinning too. He stood apart with the *Wojt* and the elders grinning at the young men. The elders spoke to him respectfully. He said short things to them. He looked about ten meters tall in his boots and in his braided jacket and with his spurs and saber. He stood with feet wide apart and his hands behind his back and the brassbound peak of his square lancer's cap pulled over his eyes. He looked like a god. I'll be like that too, someday, Antos thought, looking at Pan Szef. And now he picked up the hard, dry hands and pulled the dead man off the ground. Stas lifted the feet. The head hung down. It was red and broken and the face was turned towards the ground. The face brushed the stones and the dust on the track and left red marks on them.

—Lift him a little higher, Stas Guz said.

—He gave me sugar for Zloto, you know? Antos said.

—Ah, sugar . . .

Stas Guz stumbled and dropped the sergeant-major's feet. They fell like wood with a hard, wooden sound, and the cracked toes of the boots buried themselves in the dust. Stas started to shake again as he picked up the feet.

They carried Pan Szef into the house. The door was broken open. Some soldiers had knocked it down to search for food. They put Pan Szef on the bed and covered him up. There were some floursacks and some potatobags. They spread the sacking and the bags over the dead man.

Outside a whistle blew.

—Well? Stas looked at Antos and towards the window, at the dark-green screen of trees where other whistles were blowing.

—Well, Antos said. We better go. They're blowing the whistles.

—Where will we go? Home, or what?

—Outside, Antos said. We'll go with everybody.

—Not home then?

—We'll get home someday. But it's got to be over first, see? It's like Pan Szef said. When it's all over somebody will tell us and then we'll go home.

Stas nodded and said nothing. They went outside. Men were coming out from under the trees and forming on the track. Some of the horses wouldn't stand up and the men pulled at them and hit them.

—They oughtn't to do that, Antos said. Pan Szef would really give it to them if he saw it.

—Listen, Stas said. I got to go back in there a minute, see? (He nodded at the hut.) I forgot something.

—What?

—My cap, see? I don't have my cap.

Stas pointed to his dusty, sore-encrusted head and his mouth moved and he licked his lips a little and he wouldn't look at Antos.

—All right. I'll see you on the track. (And then as thought occurred:) You're coming back, aren't you?

—I'll be back.

—All right.

Stas went back to the house. He was almost running. Antos walked to the fence and the log where he had been sitting before the others came. He picked up his cartridgebelt and grenadebag and his haversack. He put them on. He picked up his carbine. The blood had dried brown on the brass-and-walnut butt. He tried to brush it off. He brushed the carbine carefully against his trouserlegs.

None of this made any sense to him. He couldn't understand what he was doing. He knew that he should be doing something to show how sorry he was. Because he was sorry. He wished nothing had happened. He felt bad. This wasn't like any of the other times: the German in the road and the German who was hanged and the other Germans and the horses.

This was different.

Was it?

He didn't know.

The blood had begun to dry on the track and on the grass where the dead man had been. Dust was sifting over it. Soon it would not show.

If only Pan Kapitan was here to tell him what to do. *He* would know what a man should feel. But there was no more Pan Kapitan, just like Pan Szef said; the captain was sick and Pan Szef was dead and now there was nobody except, maybe, the Pan General.

He put on his equipment and picked up the carbine but there was still blood on it, or he thought there was. It made him feel bad. He couldn't clean it off no matter how much rubbing he did. And so he turned and threw it as far as he could among the trees. He waited for Stas Guz on the track, feeling his hands empty and not knowing what to do with them. No one said anything to him and he didn't see anyone he knew.

Then the column moved. Stas had not come back. Antos supposed he had known all along that Stas wouldn't come back. So he marched on with the column, leading Zloto, and he didn't think about anything, and no one said anything, and there was only the dull thudding of the boots and hooves and the dry crack of branches. Trees closed over the column and then it was difficult to breathe. Woods had fine smells, Antos remembered, and he tried to smell them, but the smells weren't in the woods that day. There was a dryness and a lack of air. The sun was still hot, still burning. And then the sun fell into the woods behind the column and then it was dark.

Antos smelled the black night.

You can smell a night. You can smell it better than you can smell day. Day has dust in it. The dust and the heat spread themselves over everything that makes the smells sharp and clear and then you can't smell them. You can't smell the good, clean smell of rifleoil or leather, or the way Zloto smelled when you rubbed him down with new grass. All the good smells. They run one into the other in the dust and heat and you can't tell the good from the bad.

But night is clean. It is dark and you don't see the dust. And if you don't see it, it's as if it wasn't there at all and everything is clear. Sights as well as smells. And sounds. You think about what's coming, not what's gone. And if you look down on your empty hands you don't see them empty. You know you can find something for them somewhere.

Antos looked at his hands. They were good hands. They were empty but that was all right. They wouldn't be empty for long. He would fill them. Then he would go on being what he was, what he wanted to be, and nothing would be over. It was up to you to be what you wanted to be. Nobody would fill your hands for you with anything. You had to do the filling.

Ha. There it was, all right.

—Hey, Bartek.

Bartek looked at him.

—What?

—How come you're so stupid?

—I always been like that, the big soldier said. He grinned. —Hey, Antos, you know something?

—What?

—You sound like Pan Szef. He used to say I was stupid. All the time.

—I'm not Pan Szef. I'm me. If you think I'm like him you're stupid, all right.

—Sure, Bartek said. He laughed.

—What are you laughing at?

—I don't know.

—That's what the stupid do. They laugh at nothing all the time.

—Sure. I'm stupid all right.

—You sure are.

They marched a long time. The men led their horses. They passed through woods and across moonlit clearings and into other woods and eventually night ended and the red horizon came alive again. At five o'clock a flight of shells passed them overhead, flying out of the grey, waking town behind them, like a last gift, a message of good wishes. The shelling ended and the columns formed. Form in the woods, mount, regiment in line, no reserve, forward!

The remnants of the regiments rode out of the wood and spread across a red-and-black panorama of crumbling earth and shrubs and country fence: grey land under a bruised crimson sky and black shadows moving without a sound between them.

As the sun rose above the trees German shrapnel began to whisper in the treetops.

The ground is hard.

It is parched and dry.

They ride like bobbing wooden animals on a merry-go-round.

Each man locked alone within himself.

Through rows of trees.

Shallow pools.

Over fences.

Shells fly towards them: Find them.

Red fountains of animals and men and earth and shredded stone.

Trees fly again and blood races and fear and fatigue ebb.

Horses groan, climbing a height of land.

Smoke.

They run through the smoke.

Before them is a battery.

It is an ordinary battery: ten howitzers, about two hundred men and horses.

They ride towards the battery and the smoke comes with them as though unwilling to be left behind on the crest of the hill and so it looks as though each of them wears a ragged cloak of grey which falls apart a little more with each step that the horses take.

Two guns fire together.

Some German gunners run into the woods and there are pistolshots.

And then there is silence.

Men fall off horses.

Horses roll over on their sides and moan.

No one says anything.

The battery is taken.

Wednesday, September the twenty-seventh

I THE GENERAL

They did not shoot or saber anyone or hurt anyone in any way. They simply arrived.

The lancers sat down on the ground. Some lay down. The Germans stood among them immensely surprised. No one told the Germans to do anything and so they did nothing.

It occurred to Prus that if the Germans wanted to change the situation, to capture their captors, they could get on with doing it without any trouble. No one had disarmed the Germans and it was at first impossible to determine who had captured whom, and no one seemed to care about that. The Poles and the Germans stood and sat and lay together in the field and tried hard to pay no attention to each other, to ignore each other, and looked every-whichway but at each other as though wishing that the other side would take advantage of being ignored and disappear. Some Germans walked away, but not very many. Most of them sat in the field and kept their backs carefully turned to the Poles.

The sun rose quickly.

The General leaned across the breechblock of a howitzer and watched the Poles and Germans ignoring each other. The Germans had thrown their carbines away and sat down in a row behind the howitzers.

The General wondered what the time was. Because this moment was important. Because (he thought, close to laughter but not close enough to laugh) this is a historic moment: the last mounted charge made in the history of mankind. And that was something for historians to note for their memoirs.

But if anybody else in the field had feelings for history he showed no sign of them. Some of the Germans began to eat. They had hardtack and white bread and canned meat and fish. The Poles lay beside the Germans and watched them. One German looked hard at a Pole who stared at his bread and he broke a piece off the hardtack he was eating and gave it to the Pole. The lancer ate it. At once all the Germans put down their bread and hardtack and cans and stepped away from them. One of their officers got up. He was an elderly major. He wore the red-and-white ribbon of the First World War Iron Cross and the Pour le Mérite. He asked how many Poles there were. He spoke good French. Colonel Kern counted the lancers in the field. The head-count did not take long. The colonel said that there were one hundred and seventy-six lancers and nine officers in the field. The German major said he understood. He offered his compliments to the lancers. He also offered two hundred rations. Colonel Kern regretted that he was unable to accept the rations but he was grateful to accept the compliments.

—We cannot rob our prisoners, the colonel said.

The major saluted.

—These are the fortunes of war, the major said. We will be honored to share our rations with the gallant lancers. I notice that your men are not eating and our rations are more than adequate.

—We are not hungry, the colonel said. Our rations are also adequate. But I appreciate your courtesy. Is there anything that I can do for you?

—Your courtesy is quite sufficient, the major said. But then that is what one could expect from a Polish officer.

—Thank you, the colonel said. Courtesy at such times is one of the compensations of a soldier's life. It will be a sad life when all courtesy is gone.

—I am afraid that such times are coming, the German major said. I regret to see a certain lack of manners among my younger officers.

Colonel Kern agreed that lack of manners was deplorable.

Somebody laughed.

Prus saw that it was Tarski and he frowned at him. Courtesy was always to be valued. Still, there was the matter of the men and food. They had not eaten anything the day before and most of them had been living on only scraps of meals for days before that.

And so, Prus told the colonel and the German major, let us adjust our military courtesy a little. Salute all you want, my friends, but share out the food. Let's make a compromise between the centuries for the sake of history and the hungry men.

Then he sat down behind the howitzer and smoked a cigarette. It was a German cigarette and he enjoyed it and he laughed to himself a little about several things.

He was still laughing (and the men were eating the German rations, and the German soldiers stood or sat in small groups among the Poles, watching them, saying nothing, reaching now and then to give a hand with the unfamiliar cans) and Colonel Kern and the German major were still politely speaking their excellent French and sharing the contents of the colonel's flask, when a short breeze came from the southwest and it brought a sound.

Bombs and artillery: the last day of the siege of Warsaw.

There would be no sound from the town tomorrow.

The General gave the orders and the column formed.

Some men rode, others walked, holding the tails of the riders' horses. They could not walk without a prop of some kind. The tail of a horse is as good a thing as any for a man to cling to when there is nothing else.

They climbed the hill from which they had first seen the battery. The Germans followed them, walking beside them and behind them almost like a silent crowd of wellwishers seeing them off. The Germans' carbines had been broken across stones and their howitzers had been blown up with grenades and without these the Germans had nothing else to do. They sat on the top of the hill and watched the Poles march into the field. They did not seem surprised to be left behind. They knew as well as the Poles that there was no Polish rear to which they could be sent.

There were no clouds.

The sun was bright. The land was blasted and grey in the sunlight. It looked like the surface of the moon. The men and horses walked in silence across the soft grass, which morning had dampened. They marched through the lunar landscape.

They marched all day. They made no halts. By nightfall they were well across the Vistula and riding into the blacksoil country, where peasants came out of their huts to greet them with food. The slow kilometers fell behind them marked with their own milestones as the wounded died. Men fell out into ditches. Others walked away. But for each man who died or left the column, ten more came from the woods to join the march. Soon whole troops of cavalry and lost infantry platoons, and bands of men of all arms and all ages who had been part of longdemolished units, came from the woods and out of groves and fell in with the column. No one reported their arrival or questioned them. The column flowed southeast. Peasant carts joined them to carry the wounded. Later somebody said that after nightfall there was a short rain but no one else could remember it.

Sunday, October first

I THE HUNTER

That day they stormed a little town southeast of Zamosc, a place of no importance except as yet another bloody milestone on their way to the Roumanian border, and when the quick, brutal killingmatch was over, and the corpses were dragged out of the streets and hurled into the ruins to make way for the carts and horses and the cannon and the staggering soldiers, they set out through the woods towards the next small town.

Behind them the little town collapsed upon itself under the smoke of fires. A strong wind came out of the north halfway through the day and blew a veil of smoke between them and the sky and screened them from the bombers. They saw the sun red through the smoke and they heard the bombers searching for them but the wind held out until they reached the trees.

It was cool there. Safe. Safe again.

Until the next time. The next attack on the next town. Until the human ammunition was exhausted.

Pawel rode in a litter slung between two horses. He had not taken any part in the attack. The horses were exhausted and gaunt and each time the litter swung into the side of one or the other both of them groaned.

—They won't last long, Pawel said.

—When they fall they fall, Corporal Mocny said. But we'll get the Pan Kapitan to the border.

—I'll have to ride on you, Pawel said.

He laughed and the young corporal laughed and the huge soldier who pulled the horses forward also laughed.

—Bartek will carry you, sir. I'll make him do it. That one could carry you and the horses, sir.

—And when he falls?

—When he falls, sir, there won't be anybody to see it. We'll get you to the border. You'll see.

—You'll see, said the enormous soldier.

Men fell around them without saying anything. The only sounds were the cries of the wounded in the lurching carts and the splintering crash of small trees under the falling men and the highpitched groans of the artillerymen pulling their cannon on the forest path. No one stopped to rouse the exhausted men who fell into the bushes. They lay where they fell and the officers and noncommissioned officers no longer hauled them to their feet and pointed them south and pushed them into motion. There was no time to stop for them. The Bolsheviks were coming up fast east of them and behind them were the Germans, also coming fast, and more Germans waited in the next small town.

The columns staggered through the trees. Lancers pulled their horses forward by the bridles. The gunners, whose last horses had fallen dead three days before, harnessed themselves to the cannon. There were now eleven cannon in the group and thirty-seven wagons and seven hundred and seventy soldiers of all arms, and this was one of hundreds of similar columns fighting towards the border. They had been marching for five days, if this was, indeed, the first of October, and they had fought five battels in five little towns and had scarcely slept and had eaten only what they could find on dead Germans, and Pawel wondered how long they could go on and why they did.

Soon they would all fall and refuse to move. There was a limit to endurance, after all. And then the Germans and the Russians would gather them up like kindlingwood and it would all be over.

Somewhere north of them a last Polish offensive had begun. They heard the rhythmic pounding of artillery on quiet nights and thought, at first, that they would fight their way towards this sound. But each morning the General pointed them to the south and when another small town lay burning behind their column they marched away from the battle in the north.

The border was a beacon of a kind. Beyond it was the lean Roumanian plain, and green Hungary, and beyond them the Black Sea, Turkey, Africa, and eventually France, and there the Army would reform and be rearmed, and new men would come to it out of this land where nothing now remained except destruction pressing in like two walls out of east and west.

Trees shake as the cannons overturn against them.

The wounded spill, screaming, from overturned carts. Horses fall with blood streaming from their ears.

Late in the day the Ukrainian peasants set the woods on fire.

Three are caught, hanged at once on cannontraces.

The woods burn in the red glare of the sun but by evening the column has left them behind and enters new woods and here it spills to left and right and forms in troops and companies and officers go among the soldiers checking ammunition and German shells begin to fall into the woods and the attack begins.

They attacked the Germans in the woods and took them by assault. Bayonets. Grenades. Knives, teeth and boots. Night fell on shadows locked murderously in the trees. Explosions. Yellow faces lit up by the flames. Distended eyes and nostrils. Beards. Shouting mouths. Then silence.

Sleep?

March.

—Hunh . . . ha . . .

Then they began the new attack on the small town that lay beyond the woods.

When it was over, and again the corpses were pushed into the ruins and the one long street of the small town was cleared of rubble so that the carts and cannons could pass through, and fresh woods spread their green canopies between the column and the searching bombers, the men and horses turned off the track and fell among the trees and were immediately asleep.

Pawel did not sleep. Why sleep? Shortly there would be time enough for it.

He lay under the tree where the enormous soldier and the corporal carried him from the litter, and he moved his fingers in the slippery dead pineneedles and crumbled them into powder and listened to the forest. There was no sound of any kind from anything alive. No birds called and the animals were still. Nothing moved in the shadows. But trees make their own soft sound whispering to each other and he listened to them.

—It's time, the trees said. It's time.

Well, let it come.

He had thought that he would reach the border with the others and would eventually find a hospitalroom where his corrupt, evilsmelling stump could be attended to and grey flesh sawed away and crumbling bone picked out, and life extended and the dark doors kept locked up a little longer. He didn't think so anymore. He knew the signs. His body, when he looked at it (secretly, when the others couldn't see), was bloated, a dark, violent blue from hip to ribcage, and a scarlet burn like a bloody handprint reached from his abdomen towards his heart. So it would come. But not in putrefaction.

You cannot hold it off but you can pick your category: large or small. You can choose the manner in which it comes, and that tells whether you were large or small.

To wait in stink for final putrefaction is the way of maggots. But to go on to meet it, to seek it out and force it to come to you while you are still strong and large enough to laugh at it, to scorn it, is the way of the maneating bear.

I shall not wait. I am awaited on the other side of the forest. So up, but carefully. Do not wake the others. Do not fall. Carbine for a crutch. Ah . . . pain. Red mists of it swallow up the forest. The earth moves and the trees are laughing. Up. Stand. Move now. Carefully among the sleeping men and horses. A horse wakes. Its eyes are full of blood. The forest whispers. Carefully.

The pain blinds and ears fill with blood and distant roarings, and the too short crutch slips away on the dead pineneedles and the one unsure foot trembles on the end of the unexercised, wilted leg and despite huge effort the man falls and strikes the ground with the blue redstreaked barrel hung below his ribcage, and the pain is then the ultimate agony, like betrayal by something that you trust, loss of love, the final humiliation: the pain that hollows out the braincase and breaks the spine and guts the soul and sends a cold wind whistling through the entrails and plucks the heart out of a man's chest. Ah.

You scream to let it out. You eat your scream.

And a man wakes.

—Sir! *Panie Kapitanie!*

—Quiet. Keep quiet.

—Sir! Bartek, hey!

—Keep quiet.

—*O Jezu.* Bartek, look at this.

And a sound of retching.

—Help me up.

—You just stay down, sir. We'll get a doctor. Lie still, Captain.

—Get me up.

—But sir . . .

—*Psia krew!* I said to help . . .

—By your order, sir . . .

Up again. This time with the young soldier for a crutch. But the man shakes and is afraid to clutch the painfilled barrel and the ground sways and hands are wet with sweat and slide off the stinking wool of the soldier's coat and the weak, untrustworthy leg slides away and the barrel tips towards the ground again and the tight scream gathers up inside the barrel.

—Bartek!

The soldier comes through the undergrowth like a bear with arms extended. Pain. Something has burst below. Everything revolves. And then the dry pineneedles crumble under you.

Whispers:

—Phew. That's bad, Antos, huh! Phew! What a stink.

—Shut up and help me with him.

—What are you doing?

—I'm taking off his clothes. I'm going to wash him.

—Watch out! He's stuck to the rags. He's coming off with them.

—Shut up. Get water.

—I got none. Where'll I get it?

—Go get it, damn you.

—But I don't know where.

—All right. Go get the doctor.

—Where shall I go for him?

—Christ! I don't know. Go look for him. He's somewhere in the column back a ways.

—Well . . . I don't know . . . it's far . . .

—At the gallop, soldier!

—Yes sir, Sir Corporal.

A sigh, then footsteps.

—Sir. You just keep still, just lie there, see? That's good. I got to get these rags off you . . . wash it all up a bit . . . There. You'll be all right. I'll get you to the border. You'll see. You'll be all right. Another three, four days we'll be there. Everybody says so. Now just you lie still and let . . . me . . . get these . . . rags off. Ah.

The soldier's lips are moving and, yes, there is sound but the words (if they are really words and not just unintelligent sounds without meaning) are incomprehensible. Hah. But the pain abates enough, in time, for understanding to return.

—Soldier . . .

—Yes sir.

—Can you make me a pair of crutches?

—Well, yes sir. I can carve them for you quick enough. But what would you be needing crutches for? We'll get your litter padded out for you. You'll be all right in that.

—Make me two crutches. Strong ones.

—Yes sir.

—Soon.

—But sir, the soldier says (smiling down, scratching his head, looking peasant-sly), what would you want them for?

—To walk with.

—Ah? Where would the captain want to walk? Is it far?

—Maybe to the border.

—Well now, ha ha, the soldier says. Ha. Yes.

He supposes that the Pan Kapitan is making a joke. Because it is three, four days to the border and you can't walk it if you only have one leg. And why walk, anyway, when you have a litter and two good horses to carry it and the litter all padded out and good like it is going to be when he and Bartek get done with padding it? Why it is as good as an armchair the corporal found himself in Warsaw.

—Better even. Nice and soft and no springs coming out of it to ram you up the ass. That's better than crutches. Hey ha.

—You make the crutches, though.

—Sure sir. I'll make you the best crutches anybody's ever had.

585

—That's the kind I need.

But if the Pan Kapitan wants to walk somewhere that is *not* very far, like maybe oh just around a bit, to get his leg working again so it would hold up, why, all he has to do is lean on him. The corporal would be glad to be a crutch. All right, Pawel says. He will do that. But will the soldier whittle him the wooden crutches anyway? For when, perhaps, the necessary exercise is needed and the soldier is asleep.

—All right, sir.

So . . . not this time. But there will be another. My leg betrayed me and the pains reduced me. I was diminished by my weakness. I was betrayed so that I was no longer one of the privileged large and became a small thing, a morsel for maggots, and being small I had no right to seek a different end. But I will not fail another day. I will have my crutches. They will do what the traitor leg did not: hold firm in slippery pineneedles. I will go through the forest to the other side, where the Enemy is waiting. He will come erect and I will call him out and challenge him and I will be erect as he comes to me and laugh at both of them. And everything trivial that has gone before and the brieflyheld cause of the autumn will have a measure of importance.

Life, left like that, is left well.

Death, met like that, makes the life memorable. It gives truth to the life which, with the other death, would be a lie.

So to our meeting, Brother Bear!

In whatever guise you may choose to come.

I will wait for you on the other side, Mine Own Dear Enemy by Any Name.

Monday, October the second

I THE JEW

While Berg slept and the woods burned, black shadows of Ukrainian peasants darted among the trees and there were shots and the quick dry explosions of grenades and strange animal howls of murdered men, and men woke to see a sickle falling at their throats and other men never woke to see it, and horses screamed with their bellies slashed by scythestrokes, their entrails spilling about their legs like hobblingropes, and handgrenades flew out of the darkness to burst in the few screened cookingfires and then the night passed and day returned.

He woke long before the sun came up. He felt the arm on his shoulder before it touched him and he was up and crouching with his bayonet before him while the soldier stood back.

—Hey now, watch out! Hey.

Berg sighed and stretched himself and looked into the forest where the red fire flickered through the trees.

—Aa-a-huh . . .

—Bastards make a lot of noise, eh?

—Yes.

—But a man still sleeps.

—A man needs sleep so he sleeps. What do you want?

—Well, that depends, the soldier said. I may want one thing from one man and another thing from another man. It all depends on who the man is, see? Now if you was the man I'm looking for I got a message for you. I got something else too, but first I got this message.

Berg spat dust from his mouth and rubbed his face. He put his bayonet away.

—What's the message?

—Well now. Wait a bit. I got to know first if you're the man I want. Are you Berg?

—Yes.

The soldier stared at him carefully. He shrugged and scratched his head. He was a big lancer with a scarred nose. Berg remembered meeting him before, the day the lancer corporal killed the sergeant-major, and there was a look of recognition on the big man's face as he eyed Berg up and down.

—You sure? I'd sure get in a lot of trouble if I gave you the message and you wasn't the Jew.

—I'm the Jew. What's the message?

—Well, you don't look like no Jew. Haven't I seen you someplace before? I'm sure I saw you before. Well, you weren't a Jew then.

—I was a Jew then, only you couldn't tell because I had my hat on. Now I'll take off my hat and you'll see the horns.

—Horns? *Jezu.*

The soldier stepped back and crossed himself three times. He spat twice and pointed two fingers at Berg. Berg laughed. The soldier stared at him.

—Hey now, you're laughing at me, eh?

—I wouldn't laugh at you, Berg said.

—Well, everybody laughs. That's all right. I'm stupid, everybody says so. Even Antos says so and he ought to know. So you can laugh if you want to. Hey, you don't really have horns?

Berg took his cap off and pointed to his head. —Just hair, see? He tossed the cap up and down and watched the red fire of the forest gild the silver eagle. —No horns. Now what's the message?

—Uh, the major wants you, *ot tam,* in the clearing. He says it's time for you to go.

—To go?

—Yes, time to go, the big soldier said. He watched Berg curiously. He, as all the others, knew where it was that Berg had to go. He looked at Berg as if the thinfaced, slightlybuilt Jew was three meters tall, up and down and sideways, and he shook his head and sighed. They had all looked at him like that when the word got out about what he had volunteered to do. They looked as if they had never seen anybody like him and they made room for him near the cooking fires and they said very little when he was within hearing. Once in a while one or the other of them would offer him tobacco and paper to twist it in. They were polite. But they said very little until he went away from them and then they looked at each other and away and said less.

And now it was time to go. He had almost forgotten about volunteering. It had been a particularly bloody day, with the Ukrainians attacking the staggering column and no longer saving their murdering for the dark hours. They had grown bold, the Ukrainians. The Bolsheviks were less than ten kilometers away and soon now, any day, they would be in the woods instead of the Germans and with the Ukrainians to show them the way they could block all the tracks and trap the columns. Each day the Bolsheviks drew closer, the Ukrainians made bolder attacks. They lay in bushes by the forest track and scythed down the horses. They set the woods on fire. They cut down stragglers and put the wounded to death. You couldn't say that they just killed. No, Berg thought. Not if you were, or had been in some distant and impossible past life, a student of semantics. The deaths of the captured soldiers were worse than killings. They were acts of hate-deranged minds. Sharpened stakes driven through the anus. Eyelids cut away. Drownings with urine (while little sticks kept the mouth open and pegs nailed through hands and feet held the body to the ground). Skinnings alive and draggings with horses and simple castrations and disembowelings and burnings of victims hanging upside down over an open fire. And all these things were done by women as often as not.

The column marched through burning woods, firing to left and right, and the rearguards fought a continuous pitched battle. The soldiers gave no quarter to the Ukrainians. They shot them on sight, flitting through the trees, and if they came across a wounded peasant they bayoneted him at once, and if they captured one they hanged him without question. And they hanged the Jews. Most of the leaders of these Communist militias were young, pale Jews in leather coats and officers' riding boots pulled off some corpse and red armbands with the hammer and sickle and two or three pistols in belt and innumerable grenades. These were seldom caught. But one day, the day that Berg volunteered, the infantry of the rearguard caught a wounded Jew and hanged him with his own belt and Berg watched the hanging, feeling nothing. The Jew died noisily and badly and Berg did not move until the man was dead. Then he stripped off the leather coat and the bandoliers and pulled off the boots, and when he told the redfaced major what he wished to do the major looked at him the way the others did after the word got out. It was a mixture of surprise and disbelief and respect and considerable suspicion, and Berg watched the man's sunken eyes measure him carefully and he did not turn his own eyes away. —*You would do that? Yes,* Berg said, he would. —*You must be anxious to die,* the major said. *I wouldn't hurry towards death. There will be many opportunities for it for all of us. How old are you?* Berg told him. And he also said that no, he was not in the least anxious to die, and if he were he would not choose the sort of death available in the forest. —*But these are not people anymore, do you understand? They would do things to you that neither you nor I could even imagine. To die like a soldier is one thing. To be butchered like a suckling pig is something else.* —*Yes sir,* Berg said. He knew about the various deaths, but it was important to him personally to be allowed to go. —*None of our other scouts came back,* the major said. —*Yes sir,* Berg said. He knew this. Everybody knew it. But he would have a better chance than any of the others because he was a Jew. —*You are a Jew?* Berg said he was. And laughed a little to himself, without showing it, because this was the first time since he had joined the Army that being what he was proved an advantage of a kind. And then suspicion grew. Oh, he could see it. The redrimmed, sunken eyes narrowing and the mouth grown taut and the comradely smile disappearing. Of course it would be so and should be; he had had no illusions about that.

—*Oh yes,* the major said. *They would think that you had come to join them.*

—*Yes sir,* Berg said.

—*Ah, but of course you wouldn't. You would discover which tracks are still free and you would come back to report.*

—*Yes sir.*

—*Very interesting. But I would like to know why you are so anxious to do this quite heroic and important service.*

Berg wasn't sure why. The idea had not occurred to him until he had watched the execution. Then it had come over him suddenly. Perhaps it was because of the man's lack of dignity while hanging and noisy lack of courage before he was hanged and the terror in his eyes before he strangled and the eyes turned inward. Perhaps it was because the hanging man and he were of a size and bore a certain resemblance to each other in the red night. Viewed in a certain light they were much alike, he and the hanging man. Certainly their long, narrow hands were similar, although Berg's were black with dirt and the thumb was deformed by the little tumor that you got by working the bolt mechanism of the Polish rifle. And their small, narrow heads were similar and their noses and their hair and their eyes. Except, of course, that the dead Jew's hair was long and slick and Berg's was short and matted. So there it was, Berg said: a family resemblance. Perhaps it was because he, Berg, was a Jew.

—*So is he,* the major said about the hanging man.

—*No sir,* Berg said. The hanging man had been a Communist.

—*A fine distinction.*

Yes, Berg said. It was a distinction. And perhaps that was why he wanted to go among the Ukrainians. And come back.

He stood before the redfaced major at the side of the track while the grey and brown and sweat-black column flowed past. The major stared at Berg as though he wished to see the contents of his body and judge the size and weight of his heart. Berg looked at him untroubled; he was at peace. Then the major nodded and said that he would let Berg know when it was time to go and Berg said: —*By your order, sir* (in the prescribed manner) and stepped into the column, which immediately swallowed him and carried him away.

Now, glad his feet were sufficiently numb, buttoning his uniform where it still had buttons and buttonholes, he thought about his volunteering. He could think of no good reason for it, no reason based on anything approaching reason. He laughed. He had had to do it, that was all. That had seemed sufficient reason to be doing it. That and the look in the eyes of the redfaced major now reproduced in dumb caricature in the big soldier's eyes. The big soldier watched him carefully, his smile awkward as he tried to help Berg with the weights and straps of his equipment, and he looked as though he had never seen a man do anything as wonderful as what Berg was doing: arranging the greasy remnants of his uniform. Berg let the big soldier help him into his packstraps, buckled his belt (feeling the hard edge of the bayonetscabbard nestle below his hip) and picked up the rifle and felt its heaviness and comforting solidity. It was only after he fixed the soft, squarecornered cap on his head at the proper angle that he remembered he would need none of these where he was going.

—Well now, you ready?

—Yes. Let's go.

He wondered what it would be like to wear something other than a uniform. It seemed impossible to believe that he had ever worn anything else. Even this uniform: rags stained black with dust and sweat and the innumerable greases ringed with white tidalmarks of salt under the arms and like a target on the back.

—It's not much longer now, the big soldier said.

—I know.

The soldier coughed and spat into the ground.

—Listen, he said. I got to know this, see?

—What? Berg said.

—I'm stupid, see? Everybody says so. They call me Bartek the Stupid. They're right. I guess I'm pretty stupid. I wouldn't know what to do if I was smart.

—Well, what about it?

—It's like this, see? It's all right with me if they think I'm stupid. One day on maneuvers they set my sleepingstraw on fire for a joke. It didn't do me no harm. I let on like I thought it was fire from heaven for the bad dreams I had. It made them laugh, see? I didn't let on I saw them set the fire.

—All right, Berg said. He wondered what was coming, although he thought he knew.

—So there it is, see? They think I'm just about the biggest *duren* in the regiment. Well, that's all right with me. That way I know what I am and what I got to do and they know too. I got a place, see? Nobody makes me do anything they don't think I can do and nobody gives me any trouble. They just got to laugh at old Bartek the Stupid. They got nothing to worry about with him.

—So how come you're telling me about how smart you are?

—Me smart? Ha ha. I'm stupid, soldier. I got no more smartness than a horse, and he's got to be a pretty stupid horse. But then (and the soldier scrunched up his face, grinning, and winked and laughed a little and looked sly and pleased with himself and poked Berg in the ribs with a finger like a smoked *Krakowska*), with you going where you're going and all, it don't look like you'll get a chance to tell anybody what I said.

—Don't worry about it.

—Worry? Me? Hey now, I got nothing to worry about. I'm not smart enough to worry and everybody knows it.

—Maybe I'm not so smart either, Berg said.

—Oh, you're smart all right. You know a lot. So maybe there is one thing you can tell me. I been kind of wondering about that.

—For a stupid man you do a lot of wondering.

—That's just because I'm so stupid. But there's this one thing maybe you can tell me.

Berg laughed and the big soldier chuckled. For his enormous size he had the chuckle of a little boy. Berg wondered how many years it had taken the enormous soldier to cultivate that harmless, inconsequential chuckle.

—Like why I'm going? I don't know.

—Well, that's not what I had in mind, the big soldier said. I guess maybe I know why you're *going*. But what I want you to tell me is why you'd *want* to go. I mean, there you was, all set. You had yourself a place and everybody knew it. And everybody knew what you was and that was all right because when they think they got it all figured about what you are and what you're likely to do they don't worry about you. Like they don't worry about me.

—Maybe I want them to think things aren't the way they thought.

—Why? It won't do you no good. They'll think what they always thought, only now they'll worry. It'll make them feel bad. Like when you got a horse and you know what a horse will do. All of a sudden the horse says, Horseshit, I'm going to fly. It makes everybody feel bad. They don't know what's right anymore. It don't do you no good to get everybody stirred up like that.

—Is that what you think?

—Me? I don't know how to think. I'm Bartek the Stupid. But if you want to know what I *don't* think, I'll tell you. I don't think you was smart. They'll be wondering about you now, and that's no good.

—Maybe it's time for everybody to start wondering.

—Well, suit yourself. But if I was you, I mean if I was smart instead of stupid, maybe I wouldn't come back. Because it wouldn't be any good here for me no more. Not if I let everybody know how stupid they was to think I was stupid. They wouldn't forget something like that, no. Hey no. You can bet they wouldn't.

—So that's what you think.

—Hey, what's the matter with you? Didn't you hear me say I don't know how to think? I'm not smart enough. I guess we can't all be smart, and that's all right with me.

Then they walked without talking.

Later they waited in the forest clearing where the General was sitting. Berg watched him. The General's empty sleeve looked like a hanging wing. It made him look like a gigantic bird of prey resting before flight. He looked at a map at his feet and once in a while he said something to the officer lying beside the map. The officer was strangely flat beside the map. Berg looked at him and saw that it was the captain whom they had carried in a horselitter from Warsaw and he looked at once at the hip where the grey bone had protruded and saw that the hip was gone. There was a black bundle like a grenadebag where the captain's hip had been. The General would point at the map with a stick and he would say something and the captain would answer and the General would nod. The other officers sat in small groups under trees. Some slept. Others looked at maps and at the General and the captain.

Others looked at the sky and at the trees. The stars were bright, but not as bright as they had been earlier. It was cold then, the quick cold before dawn when it is the coldest. Berg felt the chill. He supposed that another assault would start before morning. The officers talked in low voices to each other, and that was a sign. He listened to the voices of the officers.

—The Bolsheviks are five, six kilometers away. . . . There's little time.

—Gorski's column ran into them yesterday. . . . Our turn tomorrow.

—Well, what trail is best? This one looks big enough for cannon.

—We aren't taking cannon. There's no more ammunition.

—We are abandoning our cannon? Unthinkable.

—Oh for God's sake, this isn't Austerlitz. It'll be easier to find trails without cannon . . . a bigger selection . . .

—And the wagons? Are we abandoning wagons and the wounded?

—The Bolsheviks gave Gorski's wounded to the Ukrainians.

—Well, which trail, then? This one looks broad enough.

—Ah, but what's on it? Yesterday's prisoners said the Second Light has come from Tomaszow. No fun, that . . .

—*Psia krew,* handgrenades and bayonets again against panzers. That's Jew's Service, not a war.

—Will that be new for you?

—Well no, but still . . .

—Well, we'll push on. The General wants to break through towards Lwow today.

—Before the Bolsheviks come up.

—We can leave the wounded with the German prisoners. They're Europeans. . . .

—Well, when they remember it.

—Maybe they'll remember with our wounded.

Low voices of officers before an attack. Berg listened to them, feeling cold. He wished that he had alcohol to drink. He thought about the spirits he had drunk in the abandoned bunker and he tasted it and wanted more. It was warm, good. He thought that he would get some vodka in the village. If there was one thing you could expect from the Ukrainians it was that they'd have vodka and a lot of it. Most of the prisoners the column caught were either drunk or on their way. Ah . . . vodka. What would Papa have said? He felt like laughing, but this was no time to laugh. He waited for the redfaced major to notice him.

—Two columns coming up on the right. —Kettling's and Ellenhardt's. Should be here by morning. —Enough men then for the attack, eh? —Yes. —Well, morning is coming soon, time to get ready. —You still have men to get ready? Mine are more like shadows. —Well, men or shadows, they will do for the attack. —Well, good luck if I don't see you before the attack. —And to you, Zbysiu. —Take care. —And you . . .

The officers getting up in small groups and alone and moving into the forest. —You know, the day the war began my brother said to me, —*But did they teach you how to fight?* —Well, we've attacked before without artillery. —And I laughed at him and he was right, you know. —If you don't bring your people in from the right, Jasiu . . . —I didn't know how then but I do

now . . . —Why, we'll be slaughtered. —Luck . . . —And to you. —*Servus.*
—See you in Krasnostaw . . .

They dispersed and soon enough the redfaced major came. He asked if Berg was ready and Berg said he was.

—Well, then it's time. Be careful.

—By your order, sir.

—We'll be attacking due south when the sun comes up. Meet us tomorrow in the next woods.

—Sir . . .

—Yes?

—Will you get through? Where will I meet you if you don't get through?

—If we don't get out of this wood before the Bolsheviks come in, we'll meet elsewhere. Your Ukrainian friends will know where to find us.

—Yes sir.

Berg clicked his heels. The major nodded and walked to where the General was sitting. He said something and pointed to Berg and the General nodded. Berg turned to leave.

—Well, so long, the big soldier said.

—So long.

The big soldier joined another lancer beside the captain who had lost his leg. They picked him up and carried him away. And then the clearing was empty and Berg was alone and suddenly the pack and rifle and the cartridge-belt no longer meant anything except weight and the uniform oppressed him and he couldn't wait to get them off and put on the pants and boots and blackleather coat of the executed Jew.

Then he was walking in the forest.

Leaves shredded light into yellow lace. The forest was remarkably still. There was a freshness and a cool promise of rest, and the sun was not yet the enormous furnace of the afternoon and light cut through the thick green canopies in tentative small streams and there was innocence of a kind in the new day.

He walked easily enough despite the undergrowth. His feet pained him only mildly. He did not hurry. There was time. The morning chill went on and passed and he began to sweat and feel his thirst and then he took rests. Lowhanging branches reached for him but he avoided them. At midmorning he sat down to rest in a little clearing.

He searched his pockets for somethig to eat but there was nothing. Well, so there it was: If you had no food in the forest there was always rest. Bogacz had said so. The forest would not give you food, you had to find your own, but sooner or later something turned up that you could kill to eat. You killed and you survived one way or the other in the forest.

Berg smiled. He was aware of eyes watching him from among the trees. Go carefully and the time will come.

He got up. He had slept little in the night but he was not tired. It was important not to become tired, and also to let the watching men become used to him. He walked slowly towards the village, some eight kilometers away now. He did not hurry and he took care to show the hidden Ukrainians that he was unconcerned and waited for them to come out to him.

Rest. Time for it again.

He found a fallen tree, sat down and took off his boots. He stretched and yawned and whistled a small song for the Ukrainians.

Come out, come out.

Somewhere ahead of him a shotgun boomed and he saw a crow spin out of the black circle overhead and fall to earth in a small cloud of feathers. Silence. He rubbed his legs. He was not winded and his legs felt hard as iron but hunger made them tremble now and then and it was necessary to show no sign of weakness. He listened to the forest but it told him nothing. Nothing moved in the dark spaces between the trees where the shadows shifted with the light.

Ha. Yes. He yawned, then whistled. He leaned against the treetrunk.

From where he sat he could see dark treetrunks and the darker shadows in between the trees and the still-blacker darknesses falling away from behind the trees deeper into the forest. He saw the ragged sky, blue through black crowns of trees. There were no pinetrees in this part of the forest. These were oaks, he supposed. He thought that only oaks could reach eminences. They owned the earth and sucked its juices and grew ever taller while less fortunate small plants rotted under them.

In the distance was a splash of yellow among the trees. Berg looked at it, pleased. That must be the forest path. He hadn't thought he'd find it this soon. He looked up at the sun. It had moved into its second quarter and hung malevolently white just out of reach. Soon it would become the furnace of the afternoon, but not for him. Because he had the path and it was safely yellow among the black shadows and it would take him quickly to the village and there he would have shade and drink and, yes, food, if his luck was good: If those who watched him out of shadows believed what he would say to them.

If they did not believe . . . ah, but he didn't want to think about anything like that.

They would believe. Because he wanted them to. Because he was Berg.

He got up and walked towards the path and soon the dead grass and the crumpled small plants and the downpounded sandy soil of the path were under his feet and the brilliant blue overhead was compressed into a continuous thin line by the parted treetops. The sun climbed there steadily. He looked at it, feeling good. This was the first time in a long time (he thought) that both he and the sun had found a firm and clearly marked-out path to follow.

He walked on. Yellow path. Soon the trees thinned out.

A bird called where the trees were thinnest.

There was a meadow of a kind behind the trees and at the end of it a smudge of thin smoke like a morning mist where a fire had been set earlier and abandoned. The grass was beaten down and flat where people had sat around the fire. There was a smell of freshly roasted meat.

It made him gag and swallow. He moved quickly towards the fire, still careful not to run, and reached the ashes and poked among them. Some of the coals were still red. They set the grass on fire when Berg kicked them out of the ashes. Then he found the potato he thought would be there: black and shriveled, itself like a burned-out coal. It burned his mouth and tasted of ashes, but he licked his fingers after eating it. He found two bones. He broke them with a stone and sucked out the marrow. It was sweet and hot and bubbles popped in it. He started chewing on the bones and some teeth moved outward in his gums and he tasted blood. He spit and threw the bones down and looked for more bones and then he found the source of the sweet roasting smell. It was spreadeagled near the fire halfhidden in grass and he went to it and saw it and felt the vomit gathering in his stomach and fought to keep it back and kept it down. This was no time to give way to weakness. The fresh coals were a sign that he couldn't miss. The murderers were near. Where? Anywhere behind him or before him beside the path. They would have heard him coming long before they saw him and the birdcall he had heard before he came out into the meadow might have been a signal. He felt their eyes, felt hot, and fought his stomach. It wouldn't do to show them anything like sympathy for the spreadeagled thing.

So he stared at it and smiled. He wondered what it was, man or woman. It had been one or the other before the axe had chopped it open at the groin, where its own little fire had been lit, but it was nothing now, all black and yellowtoothed and bald and featureless. Flies left it drowzily and flew to Berg and flew off again.

And then he heard the people in the grass behind him and out of the corner of one eye he saw a dark shadow detach itself swiftly from the deeper shadows of the trees.

Birds began to call.

He looked at the spreadeagled thing and laughed at it. He kicked it with his boot.

Ha. Ha.

Berg turned and, smiling, hands in pockets of the blackleather coat, watched them coming to him through the grass

Tuesday, October the third

I THE GENERAL

The assault started before dawn. There was no longer any ammunition for the cannon and the useless guns were tipped over and abandoned. They went in with bayonets and handgrenades and knives and engineers' entrenching tools and woodcutters' axes taken from the Ukrainians, and at first their loud hurrahs drowned out the automaticweapons fire of the Germans. They cleared the first line of woods and ran into the second and there the battle moved back and forth in front of the crossroads shrine for the first three hours of the morning.

595

The General watched them. Men died. He sent more men to die. He watched them die in the huge, green arena that spread from the corpsefilled ditches of the crossroads to the black woods. Beyond the woods was the small town they had to have. Beyond it, other black woods on a black horizon and then other towns and other woods and then the border.

Beyond the border . . . what?

Small hearts on foreign soil, yes. But also the war. And hope.

He thought of the anthem.

Jeszcze Polska . . . It lives while we live.

We do not despair.

We do not change no matter what is changing, and that is, possibly, the final Polish truth: that we go on as we have always done.

Nil desperandum . . .

There is no despair because there can be no defeat and nothing must be given up because nothing is ever permanently lost. Catastrophe, yes, there is that. And there is agony and pain and personal disaster, but these pass in time. There is no catastrophe so enormous that man cannot survive it. The sum of all the parts makes an enormous whole, and this is larger than disaster and it has permanence and it sustains the parts. Alone, a man gives way before catastrophe. As part of the whole he wins.

Disaster . . . ha. It is a classroom of a kind, he thought.

Men died and the country burned. But the sun shone and did not explode and day did not turn into everlasting night and there were no trumpets sounding in the sky. Here men died; elsewhere, in other countries, people were doing what they had always done and nothing was changed.

And then the shouts grew fainter and less frequent and the forms of men were more often still than moving and erect and soon the shouts were gone altogether and there was only the huge sound of the German shells and machineguns.

The shells fell among the trees and shrapnel whistled and small shards of it tore at the undergrowth. Leaves came down in small circles, finely shredded as if by worms: iron caterpillars.

Somewhere behind him, close inside the woods, a shell exploded and small branches flew past him into the field and the air moved behind him like an invisible whirlpool. A man sighed and the small rainlike beat of shrapnel splattered the treecrowns.

—General . . .

—Yes.

It was Tarski. He looked embarrassed. His uniform coat had split down the front and he tried to pull it together with one hand. He wiped his face with the other. His head was white with dust. He had lost his helmet. Where there was no dust on his face it was black with smoke, and blood made red spots on it like a small boy's illness.

—Are you hit, Tarski?

—No sir. It is not my blood.

He pointed to the bushes where a man lay halfhidden in the undergrowth. An old soldier can sleep anywhere and at any time, the General thought. And this was an old soldier. The bushes still shook from his fall among them. He had been with me a long time. He cut off my arm and sabered the corruption in the regulation manner and now he is resting.

Grzes moved a little then. He made a sound. His hands and feet fell out of the bush and spilled along the ground. The hands curved in the dead pine-needles and plucked at them. The feet rubbed softly one against the other as if in shame.

The major shouted for a medical orderly but no aidman came. The aidmen and the telephonists and the trumpeter and the horsehandlers and the standard-bearers and the cannonless cannoneers and the clerks and the cooks and the chaplain and the legal officer and the paymaster and the sailors from the river gunboats of the Pripet fleet were in the field with rifles and grenades and bayonets. They lay between the two black belts of woods and on the road and in the ditches and around the shrine. Earth heaved around them. They flew up with it to the sun. The sun returned them to the torn-up soil husked and flat.

The major looked at Grzes. He went on wiping the old soldier's blood from his face and hands.

—He was with me a long time, the General said.

The major said that he was truly sorry. He said he knew how it was to lose someone whom you had known a long time.

—But you never know people until it's too late. Perhaps you don't want to know them. You see them every day and you don't think about them. You are fond of them. But you also grow used to them. You do not have to think about them and then suddenly you have to.

—Yes sir, the major said. He knew how it was.

—And you don't even see them. And later you feel badly because you didn't see them. But you don't think of the good words you have to say until it isn't any good to say them.

—Still, said the major, as long as they are seen eventually . . .

—You mean *sometime,* major? Is that what you mean?

—I think it helps. I think it is important.

—What good does it do when it's too late?

—I think it does some good.

—It might do you good. It isn't any good for them. They don't know what you have really felt. That is what I mean.

—Yes sir, the major said.

—Look at his boots, the General said. He has holes in them.

—Yes sir.

—He should have mended them. An old soldier like that should have known better than to march in broken boots.

Tarski said nothing. He tried to pull the torn halves of his uniform together. He tried to wipe the old soldier's blood off his face and hands. He wanted to say something. You could see it. But, whatever it was, it was too difficult to say. The General waited for the major to say what he had come to say.

—It's been a long time for him with me, Prus said. More than twenty years. I never knew what he thought about or if he thought at all. And now all I can think about is that he has unmilitary holes in his bootsoles. There is an irony in this that I don't quite understand. I will later. God has a monstrous sense of humor, don't you think?

—Sir . . .

—Yes.

Men were dying and there was no time for thought about divine amusement. Let God laugh behind the fat shield of the sun; men had forgotten how.

—How did it go with you?

Because it was time to hear the major. Tarski looked away.

—I see. It didn't go? Why not?

—No sir. I am very sorry.

—What happened? No, don't tell me. I can guess what happened on the right. They brought the Second Panzers up from Tomaszow, is that right?

—Yes sir. They waited for us in the clearings. They blocked the tracks and the firebreaks. We didn't get through.

—They moved them fast. I didn't think they'd get the panzers here today. We could have broken through without the panzers. Well. We'll have to try it once again elsewhere.

—The men tried, General. I am very sorry. It simply didn't go this time.

The redrimmed eyes were dull with disappointment and too much awareness and the soiled face had caved in on itself.

The General observed the face and nodded. Then he looked at the black field where men still died and at the far woods where now stray men appeared among the trees and started running back across the field between the explosions. Their legs moved with a painful slowness; they seemed hunchbacked with the effort. The shells pursued them and fell among them and threw them upward.

—When can you try again?

The major stared and shook his head.

—The tanks sir, the artillery . . .

—I know. But we must try again. We have no other choice.

—We cannot do it. It simply didn't work, sir. I am very sorry.

—Yes, but we can't stop now. The Bolsheviks will be in the woods by nightfall and we must get the wounded out before they come. There isn't any time for being sorry.

—Oh . . . do not . . .

—I don't reproach you, Major. And I have no wish to humiliate you. I think you know why we can no longer reproach anyone about anything. But we must try to break out before nightfall and we must be through the Germans before morning.

—Because of the wounded . . .

—That is part of it. Also, because we can't let the Bolsheviks catch up with the rest of us. With the Ukrainian peasants to guide them through the woods they would pick us out like fish from a sack. Well, rest awhile. Sit down on that log. Wipe your face. Here, use my handkerchief. I still have handkerchiefs, thanks to my Grzes. Now then. Control yourself and tell me when you want to start the new attack. We have to get through on the right to get control of the tracks that Pawel has suggested.

The major shook his head.

—The General must understand. I am very sorry. We can't break through on the right. They have brought tanks from Tomaszow. I don't have anybody left to try again.

—I suggest we start in the late afternoon when they have the sun in their eyes.

The major stood up and sat down again. He wiped his face and looked at the blood and dirt and grease caught in the linen. He spread the handkerchief carefully on his knee. Then he folded it.

—The General suggests, he said. Of course. I understand.

—Get the men from Kern.

—There simply isn't anybody left. I am very sorry. They simply had too much of everything this time.

—Control yourself. Be calm.

—Sir, by your order. I am controlled and calm, I have the honor to report.

—If you can't carry out my orders I'll have Colonel Kern replace you on the right.

Tarski got up and stood at attention. His head was shaking as though he was ill. His hands moved up and down his sides. He saluted.

—Yes sir. By your order, sir. Colonel Kern is dead, I have the honor to report. And as a point of interest, General, I might add that I found holes in his boots. It seems to be the fashion.

—That's enough. That's quite enough.

—Yes sir. Colonel Kern also has a large hole where his chest was. He is completely dead. His men are largely in the same condition. As are mine. Those of them who are not are on their way back here at this moment. If you will look across the field you will see them coming. Sir, it is no good anymore. The General must understand that it is no longer any good. It has gone on too long and there has been too much of everything and there is just so much that anyone can do. *We can't get through anything anymore!*

The major started laughing. He sat down. He looked at the ground as if he never wanted to raise his head again. He looked at dead pineneedles. His hands shook and his head swayed from side to side.

The General watched the men coming back across the field. They moved with a terrible, unseeing concentration, their eyes fixed on an invisible point that moved steadily before them. They were careful not to look at the officers. They collapsed behind trees or crawled under bushes and pressed themselves into the shadows there. Some went on walking purposefully deeper into the woods, their necks rigid and their eyes searching the distant shadows.

The Germans shelled the woods all day. Shortly after noon the divebombers came. The woods burned and the country burned. No one would move out of the deep forest clearings for the rest of the day.

I ANTOS

—Hey, you, Bartek. Have you seen the captain?

—What you say . . .

—Where's the Pan Kapitan?

—Aa-ah . . . (Then a shrug.)

—This is where he was.

—Aa-ah . . . Pan Kapitan?

—Yes, you oxhead. Where'd he go?

—I dunno. Where is he?

—That's what I want to know, you goat's asshole!

—Well, he was here, all right. You can smell it. Well, he's not here now . . .

—*Oh Jezu moj,* Antos said. I know that, you dumb shit. Everybody knows it. (But where is he now and where is he going and can we find him before the Ukrainians get to him.) Jesus Christ!

—Hmm. I guess he went somewhere, all right. Where d'you suppose he got to?

—Come on, get up. We got to go after him. He can't get far with crutches, not the way he was. We got to get to him before them other bastards. Jesus Christ, they better not get to him!

—Hmm. It's dark in there . . .

—You want the sun to shine for you in the night? Get your ass off the ground, you horrible 'bortion you. Let's go.

—Yessir, Sir Corporal.

—If I just knew which way he went, Antos said.

Hmm. Where would I go if I was him? Hmm. I wouldn't go anywhere, and that's the truth. But I'm not him and he's not me. He's the Pan Kapitan. He wouldn't go for nothing. Maybe he's trying to find a new track for us for tomorrow.

Bartek sighed. —Maybe he's gone down to the river.

—What river? There's no river here.

—It's a small river. It's there on the left. I guess you didn't see it, huh? You was on the right. But I was down there with the colonel and I saw it all right.

The river. Yes. That could be. If there was a way to get across the river they would all be out of the woods tomorrow. So maybe the Pan Kapitan was looking for a way for them after all.

—Is there a lot of Germans on the river?

—There was a lot. Sure. Ha, such a lot of them. But they've gone away.

—Gone away, eh?

Antos swore because he had heard that the Germans would pull out when the Bolsheviks came.

—You saw them going?

—Sure. They was pulling out.

—So whyn't you get across the river?

—Well, see, the colonel got it and all and nobody said to get across the river . . . I dunno.

—Christ what a shithead. Jesus Christ.

—Hum ha. Yes. But there's a river all right.

—Come on, then. Come on. Jesus Christ.

They stumbled in the undergrowth among the low shrubs and the potholes and the rocks. Brambles tore at them. Antos walked cautiously but quickly. Bartek crashed through the bushes beside him. He was laughing a little.

—What are you laughing for? Keep quiet.

—I just thought of something.

—You think? Keep quiet and come on.

600

—Mind the hole o'er there, Antos. Ha ha ha.

—Oh the hell with it. I told you to keep quiet. You want them Ukrainians to hear us?

—Ha ha ha.

Bartek went on laughing. They stumbled through the brush to the bank of the river. Under the trees the night was black but it was bright where the river ran. The moon was on the river, yellow in the rushes. It made the river like a clean white road. Across the river, among the blacknesses of tall trees and bushes, they saw white lights moving.

They heard men shouting where the lights were moving. After a while all the lights had moved together, and they stayed grouped like that a long time.

I THE HUNTER

He moved cautiously away from the ring of torches that tightened around the knoll where he had lain in bracken, dodging into the deeper shadow where light could not reach. He had time. There was a lot of time. There was no point in making it easy for the others.

He moved well among the heavy roots of the big trees despite the pain. The crutches were strong and supported him. He swung himself over them with ease. He thought that if he wasn't careful he might even outdistance the others. But the white lights came on and soon enough he heard the voices calling in the darkness.

—O'er there to yer left, one voice shouted, and —Don' walk together like a lot o' geese, another shouted, and the lights spread out, flickering among the trees like the small candles children lit on All Saint's Day. He worked his way deeper into the undergrowth, laughing a little.

He was the hunted this time and yet still the hunter. He had the instinct and the necessary knowledge and the dark forest skills, and the clumsy peasants tripping in the undergrowth had nothing. They were the animals, although numerous. He was still the man. He knew where they would search for him before they thought of it.

They tore their black peasant hands in the undergrowth where the brambles were thickest. Huge kneelike roots tripped them by the river. They fell and hurt themselves in the tightly matted trees where it was darkest.

Hunters and trackers? Ha. He laughed at them.

They were less than the animals he had tracked. The boar and the lynx and the Indian leopard and the last, the maneating Old One, had been full professors of the murderous art. These pathetic men were nothing.

There were perhaps fifty of them, judging by the torches. They beat a wide, incredibly inept path through the forest, shouting, falling, cursing, getting up, losing their way, destroying telltale track and losing heart. The light from their torches burned whitely on the prongs of pitchforks.

Oh Old One, Brother Bear! At least we were well matched, you and I.

He moved almost soundlessly despite the crutches. Slower, true, than he would have done if he had had two legs, but still more than adequately. He was behind the men and beside them as often as in front of them. His heart beat steadily. Nothing wrong with it. He felt good, really, remarkably good. He felt so good he laughed.

—Hey, what's that there? Vasyl, is that you?

Ha. Ha.

In time, of course, they would bring out their hunters from the village, if they had hunters. Pawel thought they had them. Not much had changed in the villages of the Eastern Lands since they were border settlements planted against the Tartars. There was a savage pride in occupations, and these were carefully set apart one from another, and a man inherited his work from his father as likely as not. The hunters hunted for the village and the fishermen fished for it. The pitchmaker made the pitch and the blacksmith (if it was a big enough village to have a blacksmith) shod the animals and made iron cleats for the men's boots and sharpened the scythes and the sickles. And if there were no hunters in the village, they would find some in a neighboring village. Because this was a fine forest and game was plentiful. There would be many hunters for such a forest.

He felt a gladness and an eagerness and a fierce awareness.

Soon the hunters would come from the village. They would say: Fools. This is the best of all the game and the most dangerous. It's the shrewdest game; stalk it shrewdly. Honor your antagonist, respect him. Stalk within you head before you set one foot before the other. Where have you looked? Look here and here and not in the obvious places. Not where game would be trapped. Look in high places where no animal would hide but where a man would go if he knew the forest. Man is large. He does not have the nimbleness to run from tangled cover. He needs space in which to move, to circle fools like you. That knoll, now. Have you looked there? Ha. Then go and look, but carefully, with respect.

And they would come, cautiously with their torches, not knowing what to expect. He was unarmed but they wouldn't know it. They would come for him in fear, with respect. Then death would also come and he would face it scornfully, laughing at it and it would be reduced by his contempt and laughter and he would rise above it, being large at the last.

He rested on his crutches, listening to the shouts and curses of the searchers. He heard his breathing and the beating of his heart and waited to make sure that it was steady. He was a little winded, but he still felt strong.

Earlier in the day, while the sun still hung red above the trees, he had walked by the river. He had seen a boat with two men in it, and as he watched it go by he shouted to the men, once but insultingly. He moved into the shadows of the tall trees by the riverbank before the men could shoot. They had fired a shotgun at him then bent to their oars. But he had known that they would be back later with others.

Then a dog barked. He stopped and listened for a long while and smelled the air (himself like an animal) and nodded a little and walked around the hollow where the dog was barking. He saw a small hut and a stone shed hunched over a small stream that would, eventually, fall into the river. A redpainted boat with yellow oars lay there on its back. A crude wooden structure, like a rack, held drying nets.

He had seen nobody near the hut but had gone on cautiously, keeping the trees between himself and the dying sun. Their shadows covered him and made him a shadow; no stark silhouette betrayed him against the lighter backdrop of the sky.

The dog barked longer, then gave up. It came around the shed to look at Pawel and sniff at him and then it growled and backed away and turned and ran into the fields. Pawel followed it. He found a gardenpatch. Suddenly he realized he was hungry. He had eaten nothing for two days. Scratching in the concretehard soil with a crutch, he uprooted some carrots. Clumsily, with effort, he picked them up and stuffed them into his shirtfront. Then he backed out of the garden and eased himself down the edge of it, among the dead stalks of the corn. He watched the house. Nothing moved in it. Nothing gave the impression of anyone near, but he thought there was a human being in it.

Was there or wasn't there? Not knowing made it good: It was the element of risk. And if there was, what was it? Small child with uncurious eyes or woman with suspicion or man with shotgun? Any one of these could be the Enemy. Watchfully, he began to eat the carrots. He watched the sun fall into the river behind the woods, and the crows spiral upward, and he hugged himself in the blue coldness that rolled up the river.

When he decided to move the hut was still dark. The dog did not come back. By leaning on one crutch he was able to maneuver the redpainted boat into the water. He got into it and drifted across to the other bank and beached the boat in rushes. He walked along the riverbank where the trees were thick, treading softly, his head down, watching for traps.

He knew by the way the searchers' lights spread out and their noise abated that they had brought their hunters. A new note entered the rhythms of pursuit. He watched the lights fan out and narrow towards him and he moved deeper into the protecting darkness of the thickets. He knew it wouldn't take much longer with the hunters there. He moved carefully, then, but they must have heard him. A beam of light licked out to where he was and some of this light brushed him, passed, then swung back swiftly to where he had been. No longer there, of course. He ran from the lights but they pursued him, found him, and drove him into shadows.

And now he crouched in the shadow.

It was the time.

He began to laugh. Because it is only with contemptuous laughter that you can summon death. That is if you want to die erect on your feet as you have lived, larger than your life, giving your life truth and justification, making it memorable.

Stand up.

Now.

Stand!

But he couldn't do it.

His body moved unordered down the riverbank, bent in a crouch. A voice shouted: —I hear him! O'er there! —Where? (Another voice, shrill like a woman.) —To the left there, by the bank, i' the roots! (From the first voice again.) And then the other voices: —Come on, come on! —Quick now, hurry now, move now! —Look out! —Around the front, somebody, hey you, Vasyl! —Come on! —Spread out there, spread out! —Hey you boatmen, come in from the river! —Christ! (Followed by the splintering sounds of a body falling through the branches of a riverside bush into the water.) —Aa-a-ah! —O'er there, by the trees there, by the trees, you blind whores! —*I see him!* And the roar of a shotgun fired close behind and the pellets rattling in the undergrowth (screams, then, and shouts and curses and an idiot's laughter), and the ring of lights wavered, then steadied and came on to where he was hopping, onelegged and grotesque, among the giant treeroots that crooked like old men's knees into the water.

—Don' let him get away! Ring him, ring him! shouted a great angry voice and Pawel thought (surprised) that the voice was scarlet.

The pain was enormous. He rolled down the shallow bank into sand and struggled to get up. He had lost one crutch and he heard a longdrawnout low animal howl that was like no animal he had ever heard. As he moved on he couldn't escape the howling animal and it was only when his breath ended momentarily that he realized the sound was his.

The boat, oh Christ. And then across the river . . . But he could not remember where he had left the boat.

He must get past the ring of lights that were like animal eyes and the black shadows coming towards him. They were enormous in the darkness under trees. He stumbled on.

—There! Heading for the river!

Everything was hazy now and for long moments the pain controlled him and he knew that he had to move away from the lights and the shadows and the voices that crossed each other in bright patterns of multicolored light.

—There he is, see him? a white voice shouted, small and shrill, and —Where! Where! shouted the great red voice, and —I see him! Stop, ye fuckin rabbit! And he turned to go out of the trees into the rushes, where he saw the boat, and then he heard the new sounds.

One was the beating of oars on the river, the creak of hardworked wood against leather tholepins, and another was the sudden crackle of carbinefire on the other side, and there were shouts and a body falling into water and a clear young voice shouting: —*Panie Kapitanie!* Here, sir! Here! and puzzling him because it was familiar but out of place. He stopped, confused, and redness came at him out of the darkness in a booming sound and stunned him, hurt him and threw him up against a tree and then he fell away from the tree in terror, shouting as the others shouted, stumbling through the undergrowth. And the booming came again and the leaves rustled.

And then he broke through the last line of trees, into the rushes and out again, onto clear sand, feeling it sink beneath him. The swift blackness of the river ran before him and barred his path. The shouts behind him resolved themselves into a roar of one single manycolored voice and then he too was shouting: —Come on!

—All right! he shouted. Yes!

And life never seemed brighter, more desirable, and it had contour, shape and definition, and the shotgun boomed.

And then he moved towards the river that was no longer a river but a huge yellow shape rising in the moonlight up to the battlements of the world where a stray cloud hung at three thousand meters and promised rain. He ran towards it, shouting, and a great black shape rose on it with outspread arms and roared, and the red sound came to him and lifted him and the cloud came down.

Wednesday, October the fourth

I ANTOS

They went back to the column after they had shot out all their ammunition on the riverbank and the peasants had put out their torches and walked off in the woods. The peasants took away the man they had been hunting by the river. Antos told Major Tarski about Pan Kapitan (how he was gone and how they went after him and how the Ukrainians were hunting somebody by the river that he, Antos, thought was the Pan Kapitan) and the major told the General and the General got all the men together. The men were tired and didn't want to come. But everybody liked the Pan Kapitan. He had found good trails for them in the forests and had gotten them safe as far as they had gotten and the men became angry thinking about the peasants killing him. In spite of their being tired, here was a chance to do something to the Ukrainians who had been shooting at them and killing the wounded. And it was also the only way out of the woods: It looked like with his last action the captain had found another track for them. The men got together and after a while (after the major and the other officers checked their ammunition and handgrenades and set all the wounded on the road to where the Germans were) the column formed ranks and the companies marched south out of the woods and then they crossed the river. They didn't know exactly where the village was. They sent out a patrol on horseback and when the lancers came back from the patrol the General divided the column.

All men who still had horses rode ahead. The rest of the column marched on foot behind them. The village was not far from the river. The night was warm and clear and the stars were bright. Later the clouds came. They hid the stars and the moon so that it was as if the sky was closing up its windows to lock out the sight of what would happen. But at first, when they began the march, there were no clouds. The earth was gaunt and black under the moon and stars. Trees, skeletal bushes, sand dunes and their shadows made the land look like the setting of a nightmare. The men said little, riding cautiously. The horses were nervous and tossed their heads a lot but they were quiet. The horsemen reached the village before morning and the General sent them in a circle around the village and they hid themselves in the grass and the sand dunes and in the skeletonlike bushes. The village slept. No dogs barked and there were no lights. The horsemen waited for the rest of the column to catch up, and then all the men lined up around the village and walked into it. They were about halfway towards the village when the dogs smelled them and began to bark. Lights went on in windows and doors opened, and they could see men in the doors looking into the night. They smelled the woodsmoke from the chimneys. It was like the smoke from the chimneys at home. And the village had other good smells that Antos remembered: dry straw that made you choke a little, and dogs and animalsweat, and cabbagesoup and earth. And the men in the doors and (now) in the street had the familiar hunched-over peasant look: broad and longarmed and looking up with small eyes while their foreheads slanted towards the ground. And their white homespun shirts and peaked caps and too short jackets were the same as they were at home. So that it was as if he were riding into his own village: a soldier with his horse and saber coming home from the war and the war all over. But this was not his village (he told himself) and the war was not over. The war was here, with them; they had brought it. And then the sun came up, quick and red above the woods, scudding through the clouds. The peasants shielded their eyes to look at the soldiers. And then the peasants shouted and began to run into the houses and out again and in between the houses into the orchard and the fields and up and down the street out of the village. They tried to run into the woods but the soldiers caught them. The soldiers stood almost shoulder to shoulder around the village. They drove the peasants back into the village and penned them in the street and then went into the houses, a house at a time, and brought everybody out into the street. They searched every house and every barn while the peasants waited in the street, guarded by soldiers, and the peasants said nothing and made no sound of any kind and they stared at the ground in front of them. And then, in the yellow dust in front of one house, a soldier found a button. It was a button with a silver eagle. He showed it to Antos and Antos brought the button to Major Tarski.

—Whose house is that? the major asked the peasants.

The men answered nothing. The women hid their faces in red kerchiefs. The children were quiet. The major tried to talk to the children, patting their heads, but the children stared at him with huge eyes and backed away and hid behind the women.

Then Antos saw the General. The General walked very quickly down the street. He was almost running. He walked right into a group of peasants and he shouted at them.

—Whose house is that? The fourth one from the end of the street? (And to the major he said:) He is there. Buried in manure. They killed him with pitchforks and an axe. (To the peasants, shouting:) Well? Whose house? Answer or I'll shoot every one of you!

The peasants said nothing. They kept their eyes on the ground and one of them sighed. Then the sighing peasant said: —He is gone.

—Gone? Gone where? asked the major, who had drawn his pistol.

The other soldiers cocked their carbines and drew pistols when they saw the major.

—Gone, the peasant said. With the others. They went to bring the Russians. The Russians are coming.

Antos began to run up the street towards the fourth house from the end. As he left the peasants he heard the major tell the men to step away from the women, cross the street and line up there. Antos went into a small apple-orchard. He reached for an apple. He bit the apple and went on. Next to the wall behind the orchard was a manurepile. Soldiers were digging in it. A leg protruded from the pile and the soldiers pushed the manure and the straw and the soiled earth away from the body and brought the body gently out and placed it on the ground. The captain had been killed with pitchforks: his body was spotted with the small red bites of tines. His belly had been split open with an axe and a fire had been lit in it. But his face was untouched and calm, although the lips had drawn back from the teeth, as in some terrible grin, and the eyes were staring.

Antos began to cry. He ran out of the orchard and into the house, and didn't know what to do and ran out again. He ran down the street, wanting to leave the village, to run away from it, but he couldn't. He stopped where the major had lined up the peasants. There were some fifty men in a ragged rank on one side of the street and some one hundred and fifty women and children on the other. An old, greyhaired sergeant-major of infantry went among the women and pulled the bigger boys out of the women's rank and pushed them into the rank with the men. The redfaced major stood before the rank with a big German pistol in his hand. The General stood behind the major. The major's hands were shaking and his red face had white lines drawn thinly on it and it too was shaking, but the General looked calm. He looked like a statue, Antos thought, the kind he remembered from the park in Warsaw where the swans had been. Very white and with nothing in his eyes and his mouth so thin you could hardly see it. It was like Pan Kapitan used to look when his leg hurt him—when the pain got so bad he could hardly stand it. It was no good, then, to talk to the Pan Kapitan. He didn't hear anything you said.

—Get on with it, the General said with his thin mouth.

—Yes sir, the major said.

He pointed the big pistol at a peasant, a slight thin man with a scraggly white beard and darklined face. His eyes were red and blinked.

—Who did the killing?

The peasant closed his eyes. —Ne znaju . . .

The major shot him in the head. The peasant flew backwards against a house and slid down the wall and lay in the dust. The women and the children started shouting and wailing. They threw themselves on the ground and tried to escape. The soldiers beat the women back with riflebutts. They didn't try to stop the children. Some of the children ran away, between the houses, towards the woods.

—Who killed him? The major asked the next peasant in the rank.

The man stammered with fear. —I . . . don't . . . know.

The major shot him through the face. The man fell face down in the road. The next man in the rank fell on his knees. He wore a military greatcoat.

—It wasn't me, sir, not me . . .

The major shot him through the head. The man went over backwards and flopped like a fish and sprayed blood in the dust. The men tried to break out of the rank. They screamed and shouted. The soldiers raised their carbines and a sergeant shouted the peasants down. And then the major started shouting. He ran up and down the ragged line of peasants, who fell to their knees

607

as he neared them. The peasants wept and prayed and cried out and raised
their arms towards the sky while the major shouted: —Who? Who? Give him
here! And from the midst of this insane cacophony Antos heard the sudden
voice, then voices.

—He did it! He did it! It was him!

A peasant was pushed to the front by other peasants who hit him. The
man fell on his knees and looked blindly ahead. He had a long white face
and his eyes were dry.

The major ran towards him and stopped in front of him and drew a breath
and asked in a terrible calm voice whether he was, indeed, the butcher, the
one who had worked with the axe and the fire.

The man said nothing. —Yes yes yes, said the other peasants.

—It was him!

The man made no sound. He stared into distance at some invisible object
suspended over the major's head. His eyes were motionless.

And then the major started beating him. He struck him about the face and
head with the pistolbarrel and kicked him and reversed the pistol in his hand
and struck him with the pistolgrip and smashed his nose and split the slack
mouth and scattered yellow teeth.

The man fell down but rose to his knees again and made no sound.

Then he stood up.

The major beat him as he slowly rose to his full height. He was taller than
the major. He was a tall, gaunt man with narrow shoulders, cadaverous like
the soldiers, with workblack hands. The major scarcely reached the peasant's
chest. He beat him until the peasant's bloody head rose out of reach. Then
he threw down the pistol and caught the peasant by the waist and lifted him
as if he, the peasant, were no heavier than a child, and threw him down and
stamped on him. The man did not defend himself. He covered his broken
face with one hand and his genitals with the other. He groaned like a horse.
The other peasants were no longer making noise. Everyone was quiet. You
could hear the breathing. The crowd breathed and the man groaned as he
was kicked.

And then the major suddenly turned and reached towards Antos and
caught the carbine that Antos was holding and took the carbine and shot
the peasant three times through the chest and twice through the stomach and
threw the carbine into the corpse's face and leaned against a wall and burst
into tears.

No one said anything. Only the old sergeant-major of infantry moved. He
walked with paradeground precision down the rank of peasants and pulled
out every other man and counted off a squad of riflemen and these surrounded the selected peasants and led them to the appleorchard and shot
them at once.

When the volleys had ceased the General turned and walked away and
then the major followed and then the soldiers. The peasants stayed in their
ranks in the street with their heads down. They didn't move until the soldiers
started setting fire to the houses. Then they got up and ran between the
houses for the woods. The soldiers did not watch them running. They set

fire to each house separately. They made sure each roof was properly alight. When all the houses and all the barns were burning they formed in the street and marched out of the village.

Saturday, October the seventh

I ANTOS

After leaving the village they had marched south all that day through woods where autumn was yellow, then they had gone to earth, like hunted foxes, and marched again at night, and then they marched only during the night, resting in daytime, although there was no rest from watching, and they took special care to avoid villages and settlements. They were like animals then, hiding in the forest. The forest covered them with its hot, dry shield, and they learned to move in shadows without making sound, and to watch like wolves out of thickets surrounded by hunters. The hunters were long columns of Soviet soldiers in pointed caps with red stars on the crown and needlelike bayonets and rifles slung with string and bands of armed peasants and Communist militias. In their restingperiods between marches they did not take off clothes or wash or shave or clean anything other than their weapons and each of them who was old enough had a beard and their uniforms were torn and ragged and they did not resemble soldiers of any kind. Their uniformity lay in their sun-blackened faces, their gaunt bodies and their hollow, redrimmed eyes. They marched south in the beauty of the autumn forest, across a red-and-yellow blanket of fallen leaves spread out for winter, and past the bright greens and blues and reds and purples of the marshlands where, at dawn, the ground steamed so that it was as if they walked on clouds. But they had no time for sylvan beauties. They were pursued. The Soviets and the Communists tracked them and attacked them and each rivercrossing was a battle and each time they moved across meadowland they went in attackformation. It seemed then that this land which they had defended had turned against them. Earlier, Polish peasants had brought them food, slaughtered cattle and news and had taken away the wounded until they could mend. But now they were in Ukrainian country and news came to them from stragglers, lost soldiers walking south, hiding Polish peasants (who were as starved as they), and every man they met was an enemy. They sent spies to the villages and some of these returned. Twice Antos had seen the thin Jew come in dressed in black leather and speak to the major and then go off again.

They had marched through the difficult broken country of Lower Podole (lighted at night by burning Polish manors and churches and the tarbarrels that illuminated the singing and the drinking of the Ukrainians) and they had fought a quick battle with Soviet cavalry outside one burning manorhouse. It was a skillfully prepared ambush and they lost heavily before breaking through. But the border was near. *Granica!* Magic word. It gave them strength.

They had gone to earth again after the Soviet ambush. They hid in many-colored leaves and thought of sleep and rest and sweet lack of danger and they dressed their wounds, peering into shadows.

The General wanted two days in this camp to get the men ready for the difficult march over open country. The woods were thinning out and soon their dark protective cover would be gone. One last forced march at night would take them to the border. The ground was baked to a concrete hardness and the walking was easy and after two days' rest they could make the necessary fifty kilometers between sunset and sunrise.

They made camp in a valley where a small river ran among enormous trees.

It was quiet there.

It was the thickest and most hard-to-reach part of the forest. They saw many deer tracks and set traps for them. They thought it would be safe to rest in this place. A thin mist hung over the valley because of the river and this screened their cooking fires.

But now the night ended and their first day in this camp began, and the sun did not come up as usual but black clouds came. They boiled in like smoke and blacked out the morning and then thunder tore the clouds apart and rain fell. It fell relentlessly and soon it formed a hundred streams and several dozen rivers that poured into the valley and uprooted trees and dislodged boulders and flooded hospitable caves and the small valleyriver turned into a roaring cataract. Many men drowned and many horses and the last dozen wagons were lost. The river carried them downstream out of the forest, where the enemy would find them and then know, by this sad debris, where the former owners were. They had to leave the valley. They got up on the red ridges above the valley and marched off in the rain and the mud and fell and cursed the rain and some of them did not get up after falling and the others left them. The sky was black. There was no sun and there was the weight of rain.

—You ever see rain like that? Antos said.

He walked carefully in the yellow mud, trying to put his feet outside the worst of it, outside the puddles. But there were puddles everywhere. The mud sucked at his boots and held them and he tripped on thick roots drowned under the mud and his feet slid in the mud and on the matted wet leaves.

—Goddam this rain, he said. How come it's got to rain now, when it's all over and don't do any good? Who wants it now, goddammit?

—It's some rain, Bartek said.

—It's the Holy Father of all rain. I never seen it rain like this. First you get sun like you never seen and then you get this.

Antos slipped, fell, cursed, got up.

—Goddammit, he said. Goddammit to hell.

—Some rain, Bartek said.

610

The rain drummed on their helmets. It ate into their clothes. It was cold and made them cold.

—Who'd have thought they'd have so much of it up there? Antos said. It don't ever stop.

—No, Bartek said. How far we going tonight?

—What's the matter, you tired? I thought an ox like you'd never get tired.

—Hell no, I'm not tired.

—So what you want to know for how far we're going? They'll tell you when we get to where we're going. That's all you got to worry about, soldier, so keep your mouth shut and walk.

—I'm walking. I'm not tired. Only I'd like to kind of sit down for a while. But I'm not tired.

—It's only maybe a day's march to the border. Then you can sit down.

—Well, I'd like that. Yes. But I'm not tired.

—That's all right, Antos said. That's all right. Everybody's tired. But it don't do no good to talk about it, see? So you just keep your mouth shut, lancer, and keep walking.

—A lancer, huh? I'm a fine lancer. Where's my horse if I'm a lancer? I ain't no lancer anymore. I ain't got a horse.

—Well, there's not many of us that still got a horse. The General still got one and there's maybe thirty, forty others. A horse can't keep going like we been doing, lancer. You just feel lucky you still got your feet.

—I know it, Bartek said.

—But you're tired, huh?

—Not me. I'd just like to sit down for a bit. But hell, I'm not tired. Not me.

Well, I am, Antos thought. *Jezuniu,* but I'm tired. Never been so tired. Never. Hungry and tired. *Jezu.* Feet so heavy and big in the mud. Awful hard to get them up and out of the mud. Big yellow feet. Mud holds them. It makes smacking sounds like it was kissing your boots. It's like hands reaching up to you in the village. The hands and the pleading. The mud. It's red and yellow like blood in the dust. Like in the village the day before the rain began, when they burned the village. It was like my village: same long street and the houses with straw roofs and the orchard and the long yellow fields sloping to the river. The cows would mire in spring there. Red blood in the yellow street. Fire. Straw roofs burning. No rain then, and the straw is dry and the roofs burn well. The village burns. Ah. But there's rain now, yes. Rain. Drumming on the helmet: *I ain't no lancer anymore I ain't got a horse.* The rain says it and the night repeats it.

What kind of thing is this? I don't want to think.

The peasants killed the Pan Kapitan and we killed the peasants and we burned their village and that's the way it is when you're a soldier. You kill when you're a soldier. That is war. And you can forget about Pan Szef with his head bashed in, and about the old man who they said was a German general and about the girl in the cattlecar and about what you didn't do to keep the Pan Kapitan safe. Because that was war too, and none of the bad things you did would have happened if there had been no war and you were not a soldier.

Huh . . .

Rain.

He listened to it falling in the trees and on the track in the big yellow puddles so they wouldn't hold him and kiss his boots. Rain whispered in the trees. It said: *You ain't a lancer anymore. You're a . . . what?*

A soldier, he said to the rain.

I'm a soldier.

I am a soldier and everything's all right.

Rain.

There was no end to it. The noncommittal sky provided the final mockery. Rain, now. When it no longer mattered and could not help them and it was not important whether tanks rolled and bombers flew.

Silvergrey sheets of uninterrupted rain.

The land sagged under the weight of it.

—Goddam this rain, Antos said.

I   THE JEW

They came to a small hill pitted like a wart with ancient dugouts: an outpost of the Great War overrun by forest where strands of old barbedwire hung like a belt of thorns in the undergrowth. The hill was brown and bare between the bushes at the foot of it and the caved-in riflepits around the crown. There a copse of blasted trees thrust skeletal pleading fingers toward the sky.

Berg watched the narrow column file towards the hill out of the blackness of the forest, as he had watched it every time he came back from his mission. Each time the column was smaller.

The General stopped at the foot of the hill. You could make no mistake about who he was. The empty sleeve was tucked away, but the hardness, the separateness, the austere loneliness of rank made him distinct and identifiable even in the darkness and the rain and the small distance between the column and the crown of the hill. The General studied the hill a long time.

—This will do, he said.

Tarski nodded and motioned to the men and they in turn, passed on the signal to the men behind them and the files came out of the forest and turned towards the hill. They were all staggering, Berg observed.

One of them said: —Here?

—Sir, the corporal said. (It was the young corporal who had killed the sergeant.) Say sir, you pig.

—Sir, the soldier said.

Tarski said: —Bring them inside, Corporal, if you please.

He meant the clearing in the copse on top of the hill. Their old-young voices came clearly to Berg on the hill. He watched the soldiers climbing the brown slope and filing into the grove where the thin fingers of young saplings and new trees plaited themselves into the leaning trunks of the old burned giants and buttressed them against time and made them into walls. It was a sort of chamber, a gothic hall with vaulted ceiling and the sky a black roof resting on the branches. A place (he thought) for sacrifices at midnight and other mystic rites. Still, the walls would stop a tank if it came to that.

A ditch ran there, an old trench filled in by the forest and hidden in grasses, and there were boulders and grey planking and strips of rotted canvas and a fallen cabin in it. Walls of greybrown earth sloped downward from the caved-in roof of the cabin, where sandbags had rotted and fallen away, and now innumerable small animals moved in the trench and in the cabin walls and fled out of the clearing downhill as the men came.

Berg stepped out of the shadow of the fallen cabin and watched the men. A breeze came up and threw the slanting rain into their faces. Most of them did not see him. If they did, they paid him no attention. They had seen him come back like this before: a shadow in the shadows, unexpected and never to be welcomed, a bearer of news that was never good and meant more danger and more rapid marching and no rest. Death was never far behind him.

As at this time, he thought, listening to the wind. It came up suddenly out of the flatlands where the forest ended and the lights were moving. He could see the lights from where he was. The others couldn't see them. They would see them when the climb up the slope was over and they were all massed under the tall treewall in the grove. And they would hear the sounds carried on the wind. The lights were four kilometers away. They were paired like eyes. The conquerors had no need for blacked-out headlights or for camouflage, no need for surreptitious stalking. They were the hunters and the hunt was ending. Only the hunted still had to cling to shadows, but the perimeter of darkness and safety had now shrunk to one small wind-and-rain-swept hill. The wind was cold. It brought the sounds of motors warming up in the flat plain below the forest, and it brought the distant calls and the neighing of horses and bursts of laughter and the iron clatter of tanktreads on steel rails. The soldiers heard the sounds and stopped and looked at each other and those who saw Berg looked from him towards the humming motorsounds and then back to him accusingly as if he were responsible, as though he had brought them.

Well (he thought), perhaps I have. Sometimes the warning cannot be separated from the blow. Sometimes the warning can be more terrible than the blow.

The soldiers heard but they did not understand the full meaning of the sounds, Berg thought. This was not uneven battle. This was a trap from which there was no way out for the column. The men would have their choice, yes, their alternatives, but no way out. Rain drummed its cadence on their helmets and on their sodden packs and the rhythm was a measured beat.

Berg shrugged and squatted on his heels against the cabin wall. He waited for the officers to come up so that he could report what waited for the column.

It was just before midnight, and if down on the plains the howitzers were still waiting for the gas shells, there was perhaps another hour before the attack. The Ukrainian peasants had done their work well: They had tracked the column and harried it until there was no other place for it to go except this hill, and now the Soviet troops had come to finish the hunt. They brought the Sixty-seventh Siberian Rifles Regiment and this was now spread out along a railroad embankment with eleven tanks, and the militia occupied the nearby village, and three squadrons of Cossack cavalry covered the three trails that led from this part of the forest into the plains, and beyond them the howitzer battery had unlimbered, and twenty-one armoredcars spread out beyond the guns to stop the survivors of any breakthrough by the Poles, if a breakthrough was attempted.

The Russian colonel had been unconcerned about a breakthrough. *—We have them now,* he had said. The Jew from Jaroslaw, who led the militia, had smiled. He drank and smiled and said nothing and was unconcerned. The Russian also drank. He was an elderly man with an enormous capacity for drink. *—We will establish contact as soon as the shells come for the howitzers,* he said. *A dozen gas shells on that hill will be enough.* Berg asked when the shells were expected and the colonel shrugged. *—At dawn or thereabouts,* he said. *It really doesn't matter.* The shells were coming from the German demarcation line and the roads were bad. What mattered was a neat, quick job. The Germans insisted on the complete destruction of this and other columns making for the border. It was the price one had to pay for the alliance.

Berg drank and listened. The colonel talked about Poles, whom he did not like. He did not hate Poles the way he hated Turks and Germans, but he did not like them. He said he did not understand them; no Russian could for long. A Russian knew all the so-called Polish truths, yes, but he also knew the real from the unreal. The Russian had the necessary discipline and knew the sound of a master's whip and had obedience and this was good, according to the colonel. And this had nothing to do with politics or ideologies, the colonel said. It was a matter of tradition. It made for strength and order and success and it had been so for a thousand years and always would be. It was fortunate that the Poles had never understood that particular truth and preferred anarchy and pride and the impetuous. They had not learned, and would never learn, to accept what both the East and the West had learned in their different manners. *—All a Pole may have is one shirt with five thousand lice in it and one pair of pants with five holes to the square centimeter and he thinks he can spit anybody in the eye. Well, devil take their mothers.* Pod stienku *with the lot of them. If they won't learn, the wall will teach them. Up against a wall you learn fast enough.* Berg nodded and uncorked another bottle. The colonel drank and the militia leader drank and presently both slept and Berg went outside.

The night was cold and fresh after the heat and closeness and the sweatiness of the hut and he took deep breaths and licked at the rain on his hands. Then Berg left the village and went into the forest. No one stopped him. The Siberian riflemen on the embankment looked at him without interest and the Cossacks spat and searched themselves for lice and drank and sang and waited for the morning. Somewhere in the woods was a hill and the Poles were on it and when the gas shells came they would be finished off. So what did one small Jew matter to anyone? Cossacks know about Jews: Their time always comes. Hu-u-u ha! That also had been so for a thousand years.

Now Berg watched the soldiers. The rain obscured them. It rattled on their packs and weapons and made their greatcoats heavy.

Someone said: —Where are we? and someone else said: —*What's the difference?* and the big soldier said: —*I'm hungry* and someone else said that he had something the big soldier could eat but nobody laughed.

Berg didn't think that any of them had done much laughing lately. They had walked and hidden themselves in woods and had walked and been hunted down and had walked and not slept and had walked and eaten when their saints had sent something edible (dead birds, drowned animals, sick horses stuck in mud, the roots and berries of the forest) and had walked and fought when there was no way to avoid fighting and had walked and become mortally exhausted and now they were wet and cold as well as exhausted and many of them were ill. They were limp with fatigue and they wanted rest, sleep. Time to rest.

But they wouldn't get it.

Because the news Berg brought this time was a verdict which would set them on their feet again and topple them off the hill and push them into the forest to hide again like animals and thus, perhaps, delay the inevitable by a day.

But perhaps it wouldn't. They had their choice, after all, their alternatives. And, perhaps, they would elect to die on this wartshaped hill. Berg thought that this was the last lesson they could teach him.

Which would it be? Well, he would know it soon enough.

He watched them coming up the hill and into the trees. They fell among the trees and into the ditch and lay like dead men. When all the men were in the grove and the officers had come out from among them and had grouped themselves about the major and the General, Berg came forth and gave his report.

The General nodded and then the officers began to speak.

—We must stand and fight, said a young voice, and —If we have to die this is as good a place as any, said another young voice, and —There is surely enough time to push through the woods and to attack the village and break out for perhaps many valuable kilometers, said another. —But what after sunrise? The open road . . . the planes . . . the country swarms with Soviets, said an older voice. —Fight through . . . —Pretend a surrender and attack . . . —Send delegates . . . —Wait until nightfall in the woods, then infiltrate . . . —Then reorganize . . . —Then attack . . . Then the older voices: —No ammunition . . . —No artillery . . . —The men exhausted . . . —Only one machinegun . . .

To wait was death and to attack was death and to hide in the forest was to delay destruction only temporarily.

—We could surrender, said a quiet voice. And then there was silence and then all the voices spoke at once to break the silence and erase the words. —I don't know, said one voice, and —I don't know, said another, and —Perhaps we could negotiate something, said a third voice, and each time the silences grew longer.

Soon there was only silence. It was as though everyone had suddenly lost his mind and could no longer think. And now the soldiers had come up behind the circle of officers sitting in the clearing and the soldiers listened and the officers did not order them away. The officers and the soldiers looked at the General and made no proposals anymore. He looked from one of them to the other, at each one of them.

And then he told them what they would have to do. And with that there was no more fear or doubt of any kind. And the officers got up and looked at each other and were immensely relieved. And the soldiers nodded and looked at each other and sighed and went to form their ranks before the treewalls, and the officers took their places at the prescribed distance before the dark ranks, and the standard-bearers shook out the folds of the regimental standards, and the adjutants formed their own rank at the side and the General faced them.

Rain made a curtain between the soldiers and the General. It beat on the dark ranks massed under the trees and drowned words.

He said: —Listen, boys. And then he said: —Poland, and then he said: —Report! Rain rattled the papers the adjutants took from their pockets and straightened out. One by one they read the names penciled on the papers. There were many names. The column represented what remained of three regiments of cavalry and five of infantry and three batteries of fieldartillery and a divisional column of supply and a medical detachment and a communications company and three companies of the Border Corps and the mechanics of a fightersquadron gathered up somewhere in Volhynia and the crews of five gunboats of the Pripet Fleet and a class of pinkcheeked military-cadets, and there were men who had joined the column after walking from the forests of Tuchola and Wielkopolska, and there were men from Silesia and soldiers who had been at Modlin and at Proszkow and at Kielce and Krasnystaw and in the Janow Woods and on the River Niemen and at Kutno on the Bzura River, and others who had been in the siege of Warsaw and Lwow and Lublin and in the unnamed places where other men stayed. This was the General's army. The rollcall took a long time.

They said: —Present . . . present . . . (and more frequently) Killed . . . died of wounds . . . Killed . . . Missing . . . Wounded and a prisoner . . . Killed . . . Died . . . Died . . . Dead.

Rain and the trees muffled the reports. The ranks were still. Only the eight regimental standards and the naval pennant brought by the gunboat sailors and the huge silver flag of the cadets moved in the wind. The wind tore at them.

Then the General began to speak. His voice rose and fell in the wind. It was cold and dry. He said what everybody knew: that this was the last rollcall and that after it the regiments would be dissolved. He would dismiss the men, he said. And they could form small groups to make their way through the woods towards the border and elsewhere if they wished. They could go home. There would be no way to enforce obedience to his final order.

But none of them could dismiss his own sense of honor or duty. These things remained and did not die and could not be killed. They would enforce the order for each man who carried it away.

The wind tore at his words and carried them away.

—France (he said) . . . our next meetingplace . . . the war goes on . . . expands . . . new battlefields . . . old duty.

Each man would have to do what he had to do.

The thirty-seventh day since the beginning of the war had just ended; it was the eight hundred and eighty-ninth hour of uninterrupted slaughter. Somewhere north of them, the last grand unit of the Polish Army was making its last attack. When the day ended and the next day came and the broken regiments walked off the battlefield, the war as they had known it, with regiments and uniforms and battleflags, would be over. No one would sign an armistice to say it was over, but it would be.

The war had come like none ever before seen in Europe: in an Asiatic fireflood pressed into cold Germanic channels, and its principles were terror and extermination. Nothing like it had been tried before by civilized man.

They had fought the war on an enormous battlefield, from the Baltic Sea to the Carpathian Mountains in the south, and from the Forest of Tuchola and the fecund plains of Wielkopolska and the Silesian slagheaps (in the west) to the black soil and morass of the Pripet in the Eastern Lands. The guns were not yet silenced. They went on with their work, and the bombers with theirs, along the Baltic coast, where the defenders of the Hel peninsula refused to surrender. But this was not war any longer. It was stubbornness, a final gesture of contempt for enemies and death and the inevitable end. The war of armies, maps, strategies, and sanctified destruction was ending now.

Before the pall of smoke lifted and blew away and was forgotten by the world, many millions of men and women would be destroyed; they, in this forest, knew it. Nobody knew how many dead would follow them and it didn't matter.

The General said: —Remember . . . France, and his rainwet face dissolved in the dark.

He said: —Present arms! And the standards dipped and the men moved and the slapping of wet hands on wet wood was a huge single sound that woke the crows in the woods, who rose with a shrill cry of laughter and weeping. Then the officers cut the silk squares of the standards away from the poles and tucked them carefully away in their tunics.

The General said: —About face! Disperse!

Then he walked away into the woods.

No one else moved. The ranks stood frozen at attention. The corporals and the sergeants and the standard-bearers looked at each other and the standard-bearers looked at the naked flagpoles in their hands and opened their hands and let the poles with their silver eagles fall into the mud. Then the forward ranks moved and the officers moved. The men turned their heads carefully to look at each other and the officers walked away from the silent ranks under the treewall and then suddenly someone coughed and someone else swore terribly and a fool laughed and the ranks exploded and there were no more soldiers in the grove. There was only a mass of men.

Who would have thought it, Berg thought. He moved away from the mass.

Some of the men began to take their uniforms off and to pull peasant shirts and pants and boots and civilian coats and flowered scarves and neckties and brightcolored underclothes out of their packs, and those who had no disguises cut away buttons and regimental numerals and facings and badges of rank, and packs and grenadebags spilled everything that could identify and betray them.

617

And they said: —You can't take your horses. They're Army horses and they'll give you away. —Anybody got a shirt to sell? I got twenty zlote. —Well, you'd better get rid of that, capitalist, the cash will betray you, ha, ha. And they said: —Well, see you . . . —See you, ah, soon, eh? —Sure, sometime soon. —Take care. —Sure. —See you . . .

Some of them broke their rifles against trees and stones. Some took their rifles with them. They traded for pistols and revolvers and piled up their handgrenades and bayonets and wrapped their German machinepistols in overcoats and buried them in the fallen cabin.

They left the grove in twos and threes.

Embarrassed handshakes, quick voices:

—*Servus,* old one . . . see you.

—In France, eh?

—Sure. What do they drink in France?

—They drink wine.

—Wine. Hmm. I never got no wine. They got vodka there?

—Sure they got vodka. But mostly they got wine.

—Well, see you there.

—See you.

—Save some of that wine.

—Sure.

—See you.

—See you . . .

Some took their horses. Others shot their horses. It seemed more difficult for some of them to say goodbye to their horses than to other men. They stroked their horses and whispered in their ears.

—Here, old one, here. Got to go now, so . . .

Then the quick shot and the many echoes roll among the trees like thunder, and the crows start up, cawing, and the animal falls sighing and is quickly dead and the man breaks the carbinebarrel on a treetrunk and walks into the forest and does not look back.

—Antos, what you going to do?

—Do? You heard the General. That's what I'm going to do.

—But isn't it over?

—He said it isn't over.

—Well, it's over here.

—Well, that's here, see? That don't mean its over in that other place.

—That France, huh? That must be far to go.

—So it's far. So what? You do what the man tells you when you're a soldier.

—*Ha* ha ha.

—What are you laughing at, you big shit?

—It's this about a soldier. What kind of soldier am I? Look at me.

—You sure as hell don't look much like a soldier. You look like hell.

—Well, see?

—See what, you oxhead?

—I ain't no soldier no more. I'm going home.

—Home? That's not what the General said. You do what you're told.

618

—I don't care about what the General said. I'm doing what I want to do.
For me it's all over.

—What? What?

—So long, Antos. I'm going home.

—Well, goddam you . . .

—Sure.

And so you—Little Jew—stand here watching the others go off and you remember everything you've seen and you think of a small room at the top of an evilsmelling staircase, and of what a man with yellow eyes of tigers said about a chair, and you think of heavy feet ascending and a giggling man, and of yellow jasmine in a clearing and of men talking in a cabbagefield and getting up to go into a wood, and you also think of a chancreshaped hill under Lysagora and of what an old brown tracker said about a place and you remember the sound of mortarbombs exploding on the little hill while grey-helmeted men were laughing. You remember this and think of the other, you hear old words and newly learned expressions, and you know what you are and what you must do. You know where you will go.

Because somehow (and this is not yet comprehensible to a small semanticist and student of letters who has been pale and soft but who is now black-brown and hard, whose hands were thin and fluttery and given to trembling but are now black and crisscrossed with the welts of barbedwire and thorns and stained green with the copper of innumerable cartridgeshells, who used to smile and bob his head and be inoffensive and keep his fastblinking small eyes permanently down in some impossible past life but who has looked out of redrimmed hollow eyes across the leveled whiteblade of his bayonet, listening to the sounds of shells, their passing and explosion) two thousand years have passed in a thousand hours, and the roar of chariotwheels on sand and the battlecries are in a language which has had no roar or battlecry for twenty centuries, and your place is any place where a man has his pride.

Berg watched the clearing on the wartshaped hill empty itself of animals and men and soon he was alone in it with the abandoned uniforms and broken weapons and deal animals and naked standardpoles and he looked carefully around so as not to miss any of it, to make sure that he saw all of it and would remember it. It, and what men said, how they acted and how they died and why and what they did to survive within themselves, would be worth remembering when the time came.

Then he looked for (and quickly found, being now good at this) the westward track. He thought that if his soldier's luck held out and his star was good he would reach Warsaw by November.

619

Monday, October the ninth

I THE GENERAL

The peasant's pony neighed and looked curiously towards them and they caught their horses' nostrils in their fingers to keep them quiet. Antos pressed his cap against his horse's nostrils and the General brought a handful of oats out of his pocket and held it under the soft muzzle of his mare. She began to chew. He stroked her neck and pressed his forehead to her head and whispered: —Quiet. Be quiet now.

They watched the old peasant unharnessing his pony. He rubbed down the pony with dry straw and combed the small animal's mane and tail with his fingers and he stroked the animal with slow, patient motions and he talked to the pony and soothed him in a peasant way.

—He likes his horse, sir, Antos said. He'll be good to ours.

Prus nodded.

The old man was kind, yes. You could see that. This was a good place to leave the horses. The man would not abuse them. They had brought the horses a long way and (Prus thought) if they had to leave them it was only right that they should find them a place where they would have kindness.

He didn't know why they had brought the horses. Perhaps it was because of their inability to leave them in the forest for the gas shells and the Ukrainians and the wolves that would be on the way out of the east now that autumn was ending. Perhaps it was the equally impossible task of destroying them. Something had to be salvaged, after all. Some warmfleshed link with the recently obliterated past. They took the two animals with them out of the forest and led them carefully through woods and tallgrass fields and through riverside rushes, but they did not ride them, so that the hoofbeats would not betray them and bring the Cossack cavalry patrols. The sound of hoofbeats carried far at night. They marched the rest of the night, secretly like animals. In daylight they hid in woods and kept the horses quiet and watched the Soviet soldiers passing in long columns westward, a loosestrung mass of shapeless overcoats and pointed caps and furhats and roundcaps with the bloody star and needlelike French bayonets, and they watched Cossack cavalry and Kalmuks and Circassians and Mongol horsemen on small ponies driving small groups of Polish soldiers to the east. Both captors and captives were stained with mud and the roads were wet brown rivers running with clay, and the landscape was brown and yellow and grey and desolate and over all of it the black clouds hung malevolently spilling rain.

At first they marched west to skirt the trap laid for them at the southern edges of the forest. Then they turned south, then east. Mud slowed them and the rain washed their strength away. They ate raw vegetables dug up at night from peasantfields and stole oats for the horses out of peasantsbarns and walked and hid and walked and watched and now they had come to the outskirts of a small Ruthenian town split by a river.

One half of the town lay in Poland and the other in Roumania and beyond it was a railroad and other towns and rivers and mountains and beyond them was France. But having come so close to the border they could not bring themselves to cross it. Across the river (the General thought) the distances would be measured in years rather than in kilometers.

How many years?

Perhaps the distances would exceed the years allowed to him. Perhaps, once they had crossed to the other side, the crossing would be final. No return. It had happened before, many times.

And so they were dawdling over horses they did not need, concerned about a peasant's kindness to a pony. Which was not to say the crossing would be easy. There was, after all, no good way to get across the river. There was a wooden bridge, yes, the General had gone down to the river early in the morning, before sunrise, to look at the bridge, and he had counted the Soviet soldiers on one end of it and the Roumanians on the other, and the flat colorless faces at both ends were alike and unfamiliar.

And there was no way to swim across the river at that point. The river was narrow and swift between granite cliffs and the rains had made it turbulent and trees and the wreckage of huts and small debris spun in the flood of it. Where the bank was gentle and flat and approachable as here, in the place where they waited and the pony neighed, it was bare and towering on the other side. Below the town the river spilled fatly and became lethargic. If there was any swimming to be done it would be there, and to get there they would have to walk through the town and they couldn't walk through with cavalry horses. They had come too far with the horses to be betrayed by them.

The General felt more than heard the mare's soft muzzle working on the oats in his hand. He felt her warm breath. He stroked her long face and whispered to her so that she would be quiet and watched the old peasant. The rain splashed steadily on the water. The rushes bowed with the weight of it. The water lapped against their chests and splashed their faces when the raindrops hit it. Antos parted the rushes with his hand so that they could watch the man and pony on the riverbank. The man said something softly and the pony stepped forward from between the cartpoles and shook himself like a dog and jumped a little, straightlegged, up and down, and followed the old man. They walked to the barn. The barn stood in the bend of the river. Beyond it was the hut, where smoke lay flat about the chimney, beaten down by rain. The pony waited until the old man had unbarred the barndoors and opened one half of them and brought a pitchforkload of hay into the barn. Then the pony went inside the barn. The old man brought a wooden bucket to the river. He sat on the bucket and loaded a pipe. The pony looked out of the barn and saw the old man sitting and came back to the river, looking at the rushes. His ears moved.

Prus pulled the soldier's sleeve.

—Be careful now, he said.

The soldier nodded. He pressed his cap firmly about the mare's mouth. A frog leaped up between the men and looked at them with gloomy eyes and Antos pushed the cap into his own mouth and his shoulders shook.

—Keep quiet, the General said.

But his own shoulders shook and he closed his eyes to keep the laughter down. They stood chestdeep in water, parted by the rushes. The horses were quiet. The old man sat forty paces from them, puffing his pipe, and the frog gaped at them stupidly, and brown water splashed them and the pony came down to the river, sniffing the wet air. His ears moved like scissors. He looked towards the hidden men and horses and neighed and the mare moved uneasily and pointed her ears.

—Well, come on, Whitey, if that's the way it is, the old man said. Get your drink.

The pony came down to the riverbank. He kept his eyes on the rushes. His nostrils moved, opening and closing. Clearly he had smelled the mare and liked the smell. He turned his head curiously this way and that and looked at the rushes and dipped his head and began to drink in long slow draughts. He made loud smacking sounds and slurping sounds and his belly rumbled and quivered and he blew enormous farts and with each trumpetblast his tail flew straight out like a lance. Antos doubled over and began to laugh. He laughed into the water.

—Oh *Jezu,* Antos said. Or *Jezuniu* . . .

He could not stop laughing. He shook and quivered like the pony and tears ran down his face and he switched his cap from the horse's muzzle to his own, then put it back, then became confused and this set him on another round of laughing and the General laughed.

—Keep quiet for God's sake, soldier, the General said, but he himself was laughing.

—Oh *Jezu* . . .

—Come on. Quiet (whispering). What's the matter with you?

Antos took the cap out of his mouth but couldn't stop laughing. —It's like old times, sir, he said. Like an old soldier eating soup. An old sergeant-major.

The General felt his eyes fill with tears and he closed them and scrunched them down tight to keep from laughing but he couldn't do it. Because these were exactly the sounds of an old soldier: the smack and slurp and gurgle and rumble and the enormous trumpeting behind. Pea soup with barley and *slonina* and a little cabbage eaten with the explosive dry *suchary* in the regulation manned followed by the unprescribed noises. Only the grunt and the uprolled eye and the broad, satisfied *A-a-a-ah* and the conclusive belch were missing. And then the pony raised his head and looked contented and immensely pleased and his mouth opened and he belched and the rushes shook.

The General went underwater to drown his laughter.

When he raised his head from the water the old man was no longer sitting there. He was walking slowly up the bank towards his hut. The pony backed away from the river and watched the old man. Clearly this was a change in routine and the pony was puzzled, and the General felt a momentary danger.

—I think he knows we are here, he said. He must have heard us laughing.

—Oh *Jezu* . . . Antos was still laughing.

—The sun will set soon and then we'll be all right. I wonder if he can get the militiamen here before the sun goes down.

—It would take him an hour to get to town, sir, Antos said. Oh *Jezuniu.*

Then he grew serious and contrite. He said that he was sorry about laughing. But it was the frog first and then the pony. His face broke into a grin and he stuffed his cap into his mouth again. The General smiled, nodded.

—It's all right. It's good to laugh. When did we laugh last?

—I don't know, sir.

—I don't remember laughing in a long time.

—No sir.

—It felt good. It's almost as good as having something to eat.

—Ha, Antos said. Sir, let us not talk about eating, please.

—Why not? The General was amused. It had felt good to laugh.

—I'll laugh again, sir. It's been that long since we ate something good.

Then they were quiet because the peasant was coming back, and the peasant carried a small sack and an earthenware pitcher and the pony nodded a little at the sight of him and dipped his head again into the river. The pony drank.

The old man came up to the riverbank and put the sack and the pitcher on the ground beside the wooden bucket and picked up the bucket and filled it in the river. Then he drank from it. He stood astride a board, the kind that women use for scrubbing clothes, and drank in the same slow gulping way as the pony. He wiped his mouth with both hands and dried them on his mustache. He kept his head turned carefully away from the rushes. The pony looked at the rushes and at the old man. The old man picked up the bucket and went to the barn and when he was beside it he whistled and the pony backed away from the river and went to the man. As he walked he kept turning his head and looking at the rushes. He neighed. The General and Antos held their animals' nostrils. The mare flipped her ears forward and back and began to walk sideways in the water, but she made no sound. The pony neighed again, this time a short, sharp sound. When the pony went into the barn the General smiled.

—Relax, he said. It's all right now.

—Oh, it's some pony, sir, Antos said. The way he drank that water.

—Like an old soldier, eh?

—Like a sergeant-major.

—More like a trumpet-major, it sounded to me.

Antos laughed.

—More like an artillery sergeant-major.

He tried to imitate the various sounds that the pony made and the General laughed. Antos laughed. He made more imitations. They were not good imitations but they were close enough. Enough to make them laugh and they went on laughing. They were still laughing, weakly, foolishly, like children, waistdeep in swiftflowing rivermud, while the frog looked at them stupefied and croaked, when the sun went down. It went down almost imperceptibly. The day was grey with rain and the sky was black and suddenly the day was also black and there was no warning. They came out of the river and lay down on the bank.

The General felt chilled. Hungry, of course. And wet and now nightcold.

He thought the old man must have heard them in the rushes. There had been that certain stiffness in the peasant's neck and that careful lack of interest in the rushes.

He thought the peasant had an hour to get into town and find the Communist militia or the local Soviet *komandir* and to report the men and horses hiding in the rushes. The Communist militiamen would need an hour to get to this part of the river. Less if they had horses. A truck would be no good to them in the riverside mud. So, say, twenty minutes if the militiamen had horses. He had seen no Soviet cavalry in the town earlier in the day and thought that if anyone came from the town it would be militia.

He told the soldier not to worry and to rest. Because they had a long night's march ahead of them into and through the town.

—We have an hour to rest, he said. So rest. Relax. Try to sleep a little. Get your strength back again and dry out your bones. Then we'll go across the fields to the highway. They won't expect us to make for the highway and so they'll spend more time looking for us here. We'll be in town and out of it before they track us to the highway.

But the soldier laughed. He sneezed and laughed and scratched himself and looked pleased.

—What now? What's the matter with you?

—Ha ha ha, the soldier said. We got more than that.

—More than what? Speak up.

—More than an hour, sir. That old man didn't go to get no militia. Look at that, sir, here.

And he held out a sack to the General and it was the sack that the old man had brought from the hut after he heard them laughing and in it was a footlong length of fresh bloodsausage and a halfloaf of round blackbread and a fanshaped *pajda* of goatcheese and fat bacon.

—And milk, sir, Antos said. In the pitcher. It's still warm, sir. It's real milk.

And suddenly the General felt fatigue. With danger momentarily removed and nothing threatening him, nothing imminent, the strength slipped out of him and flowed down the riverbank and fatigue returned. While there had been danger there was no fatigue. With danger gone every cell of him filled up with a liquid weariness.

More than food he wanted sleep. But he knew that the nightchill and the rain and his wetness would not let him sleep.

Perhaps later. When?

Later, perhaps.

The rain made the night blacker then it could have been. The darkness was absolute. The rushes and the river disappeared. There were no stars, although a yellow moon hung overhead in a small rectangle of indigo which shrank each time he looked at it. His body shook with cold. Through the small window of the hut in the bend of the river he saw the red glow of a hot stove. There it would be warm and dry and, perhaps, there was a bed. . . .

He stretched and shook himself. He took the food out of the bag and divided it. The soldier sat patiently and waited. When everything was more or less halved they began to eat. They took turns gulping milk. They ate everything the old man had brought them and licked their fingers and did not save anything for another day. There was no certainty of another day, and if it came it would come after they had crossed the river.

—Ah sir, Antos said. Ah sir. Did you ever eat anything that good?

—No, Prus said, meaning it. I have not.

They led the mare and the soldier's gelding out of the river and rubbed them down with rushes and fed the rest of the oats to them and took them to the old man's barn.

—They'll be all right here, sir, Antos said.

—Of course they will.

—That old man. He's all right. He'll be good to them. And he won't tell no militiamen about you and me.

He could still betray them, of course, but the General did not think he would. The old man would be sure in the morning of what he might only have suspected at night (and, being cautious, protected himself against by calculated kindness). But in the morning it would be too late to denounce anyone. When the new sun came up they would be drying themselves on the other side of the brown river. Besides, to go to the militia would be to invite inspection, and that, in turn, would mean discovery of the horses and confiscation and a loss. The old man would not boast about good fortune if boasting meant the loss of it. No. The old man would keep his mouth shut, the General was sure.

He smiled. He said (to himself, smiling): Old man, I'm sorry. Perhaps I misjudge you and you have no thought of betrayal and you are truly kind. But men have died spreadeagled in village squares and, after that, there can be no trust between strangers. If I misjudge you, take a horse in payment for the insult.

He smiled and patted the warm flank of the mare. She looked at him, wondering, and looked at the pony. The pony looked at the mare and ignored the men and neighed a little and the mare answered. She and the gelding would be safe here and they would have kindness, and what more could a mare or a man ask for in these times. No one would hunt them down or try to destroy them. No one would shoot them. They were valuable. And it was something, these days, after all, to be valuable. It was an advantage that horses had over men.

They led the horses to the stall where the pony stood and left them. The barn was dark and warm and dry and smelled of new hay and old straw and it was quiet and nothing terrible could happen to anyone or anything in it. The General felt a momentary pang of envy, looking at the mare and the gelding. They stood remarkably still and watched the pony. The pony neighed again. It was a warm, inviting sound. The mare moved beside the pony, and the gelding followed, and they stood one on each side of him, and bent their necks over the hayrack and began to eat. The pony looked from one to the other and went on with his feeding. Outside the rain beat on the roof and on the open doors.

Warm barn.

The overwhelming peace of it.

The General felt the steelbars snap and the supports collapse and the weakness come in a flood of sorrow for the total loss, the emptiness that could never be refilled. The consciousness of what-had-been could at times be balanced by what-yet-may-be if there weren't a third factor in the impossible equation, the what-might-have-been, which made all substitutions insignificant. He felt a sense of panic as the weakness came, but he could not stop it. The unforgivable. He put his face against the mare's warm flank and wept.

He made an effort to control his tears, but they came as if of their own volition. His mouth was open and his eyes were closed and they spilled onto the mare and his lips were salty with the taste of them.

—Sir . . .

The young soldier took his empty sleeve and shook it a little.

—Come on, sir. They'll be all right here. They got enough to eat and it's warm and the old man's all right.

The soldier took the General's hand and led him outside. Rain and the night fell on them. The soldier's hand was cold and moist. They marched across the fields towards the highway and in an hour they were on the sucking brownness of the road and in another hour they were in the town.

There were perhaps a hundred houses on each side of the street in the town. A cemetery lay between the town and the river. The graves were new and running with fresh yellow mud and the crosses stood in orderly ranks. Some of these still held the deep Polish helmets and the wilted caps.

They walked down the street slowly, peering carefully out from under their greatcoats, watching for Soviets. At times they passed townspeople, who looked at them briefly.

—There, Antos said, nodding. An armoredcar and two horsedrawn wagons stood before the schoolhouse and a wet red flag hung out of the window. A sentry sat on the doorstep with a longbayoneted rifle across his knees and a cigarette drooping from his mouth. The headquarters. They passed it, unhurrying.

—We'll have to separate, the General said. We attract too much attention: two scarecrows who were obviously soldiers at one time. No one will take us in without worrying about their throats after the lights go out. And we can't go on if we don't find a place to sleep.

—Yes sir, Antos said.

—Don't call me sir.

—No sir.

—You have to remember. And don't stand at attention when you speak to me. We're just two soldiers going home. A young one and an old one. Two old friends, understand?

—By your order, sir.

—For Christ's sake, Antos!

And then they heard sounds: insane laughter, shouts, the highpitched screaming of women and wild singing. A door flew open, making the night loud, and a body tumbled out and landed heavily in the mud. Then the bright yellow rectangle disappeared as the door was shut again.

—The inn, sir, Antos said above the noise. I'll try it in there.

—Watch yourself.

—Yes . . . friend. I'll be all right. Where'll you go?

—I'll try one of the houses by the river. Behind the cemetery.

—There's not many people there.

—That's why it's good. The fewer the better, I say. I'll look for a house that stands by itself close to the river. If anything goes wrong . . . splash.

—Splash, Antos said. He sighed and shook his head. —Will you be all right sir?

—Listen, the General said, angry. He felt cold and his hand was shaking and he didn't know why he could not control it. —I'll be all right alone. If I stay with you I'll be dead.

Antos laughed as if to try the sound. —Well, so long as you're all right. Where'll we meet . . . old friend?

The General punched him in the shoulder. They both laughed a little.

—The first man across waits for the other at the first Roumanian milestone. Agreed?

—Agreed.

The General turned and walked slowly, without any sign of haste, towards the cemetery.

Outside the cemetery the mud was thick and fresh. It hugged his boots and held on to them as if to delay him until the soldiercatchers came, and yellow water moved heavily against his knees and he had the feeling that if he stopped and let his boots stand still in the persistent mud, the yellowness would begin crawling up his legs and up his body and would envelop him and devour him and suck him down. He slipped and fell face down (tasting the cloying sweetness of the mud) and it seemed as if hours passed before he could pull his face out of the water and then, in turn, raise himself, get up and move. Nothing made sense, it was all insane: the rain and the wild night and the malevolent mud and the drunken singing that followed him like a shadow of pursuit out of the inn and the new crosses beckoning.

Somewhere a dog was howling, but there was no moon. There were no stars. There was only rain. It did not seem to fall from clouds any longer, but from him, boiling coldly outward through his coat and flowing up in stubborn defiance of gravity.

Cold.

Sleep.

Rest.

There had to be a place somewhere where he could sleep.

And then the town was behind and the cemetery spread its bright-yellow mass and orderly white crosses in front of him and he saw the small house with the light dim through the waxedpaper in the rear window and he went there, aware of the vast splashing sounds he made, and beat upon the door. His fist was loud and threatening and the first of the three wooden threshold steps broke under him and exploded like a pistolshot. He listened for a sign of movement in the house but there was nothing.

He walked quickly away among the orderly wet crosses. It was still dark then, but greying in the east, and he walked faster. He went into a field and circled the town until he found the highway. He marched east for an hour, perhaps more. Then he left the highway and followed a small stream to the river and took off his boots and clothes and folded them into a bundle and waded into the broad, slowflowing brown stream. He walked as long as he could still touch the soft mudbottom of the river and then the ground fell away from him and he was swimming, holding the bundled clothes and boots in the crook of the amputated elbow and with his good arm out.

Day came before he came ashore. The sun was bright red in the east and the clouds were thin. The rain no longer fell heavily and soon enough it stopped: He came out of the river and lay on the bank, breathing steadily, resting.

He looked across the river. There was a small mist rising in the rushes. It made the brown land soft, and the land steamed after the rain and there was a haze. He looked a long time at the land under the mist and the red sun.

Then he was walking, naked, away from the river, and the sun dried him as he walked to the white clay road and then he stopped and looked back towards Poland, but he could not see through the morning mist. He dressed and buttoned up his uniform and put on his boots and marched along the highway for a time, thinking nothing, feeling the hot sun on his back.

Then he heard Antos: *Panie Generale!* and it did not seem to him, at first, that he heard anything. It was a mirage. A delusion. A part of the insanity and chaos of the thousand hours. It was behind him, he had left it under the red sun. How could it follow him across the river? It belonged there, in the fire and the smoke, and not in this dry land where no rain fell. It was the sound of trumpets and the thundering beat of horses' hooves in gallop and the dry rattle of lancepennons in a charge and it was kettledrums and spotted horses and the sun exploding on white bayonets and it was brass and steel and iron and a thousand sabers catching the light freshly sprung out of the east and it was tall grass flying under horses' hooves and it was white and scarlet battleflags and silver eagles and young mouths calling, young mouths singing, and it was the song.

—Sir. *Panie Generale!*

It was the young corporal, sitting on a milestone. He ran up, laughing, hand outstretched.

They shook hands.

—Well, here we are sir. Here we are.

—Yes.

—Yes, sir.

The sun came up high and white behind the mountains and the river and they turned towards it. They marched, swinging their arms as if to strike the sun.